PAK MIYAZAWA FARRELL KHOLINNE ANGULO

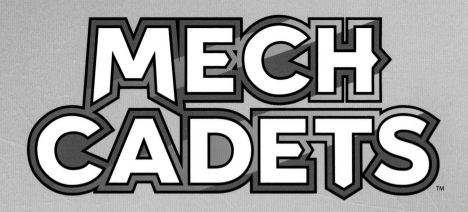

MECH CADETS™

BOOK ONE

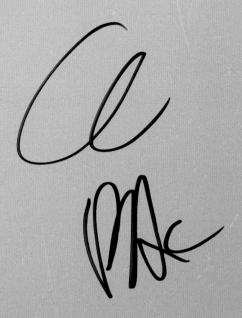

Published by

kaboom!™

Original Series Designer
MICHELLE ANKLEY

Original Series Editors
CAMERON CHITTOCK & ERIC HARBURN

Collection Designer
MARIE KRUPINA

Collection Editor
SHANTEL LaROCQUE

MECH CADETS Book One, May 2023. Published by KaBOOM!, a division of Boom Entertainment, Inc. Mech Cadets ™ & © 2023 Pak Man Productions, Ltd. & Takeshi Miyazawa. All rights reserved. Originally published in single magazine form as MECH CADET YU No. 1–12 ™ & © 2017, 2018, 2019 Pak Man Productions, Ltd. & Takeshi Miyazawa. All rights reserved. KaBOOM!™ and the KaBOOM! logo are trademarks of Boom Entertainment, Inc., registered in various countries and categories. All characters, events, and institutions depicted herein are fictional. Any similarity between any of the names, characters, persons, events, and/or institutions in this publication to actual names, characters, and persons, whether living or dead, events, and/or institutions is unintended and purely coincidental. KaBOOM! does not read or accept unsolicited submissions of ideas, stories, or artwork.

BOOM! Studios, 6920 Melrose Ave, Los Angeles, CA 90038. Printed in China. First Printing.

ISBN: 978-1-68415-917-8, eISBN: 978-1-64668-906-4

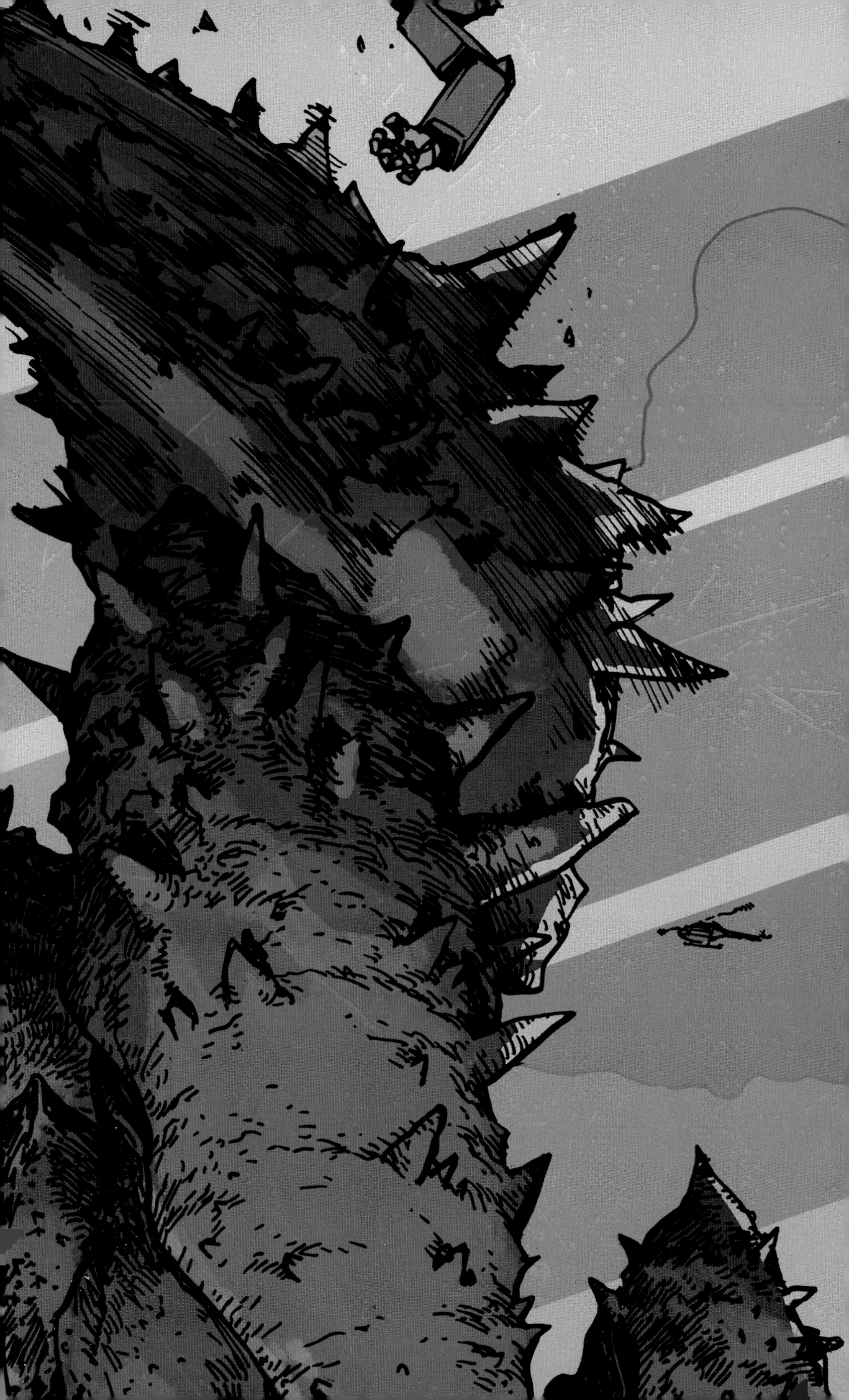

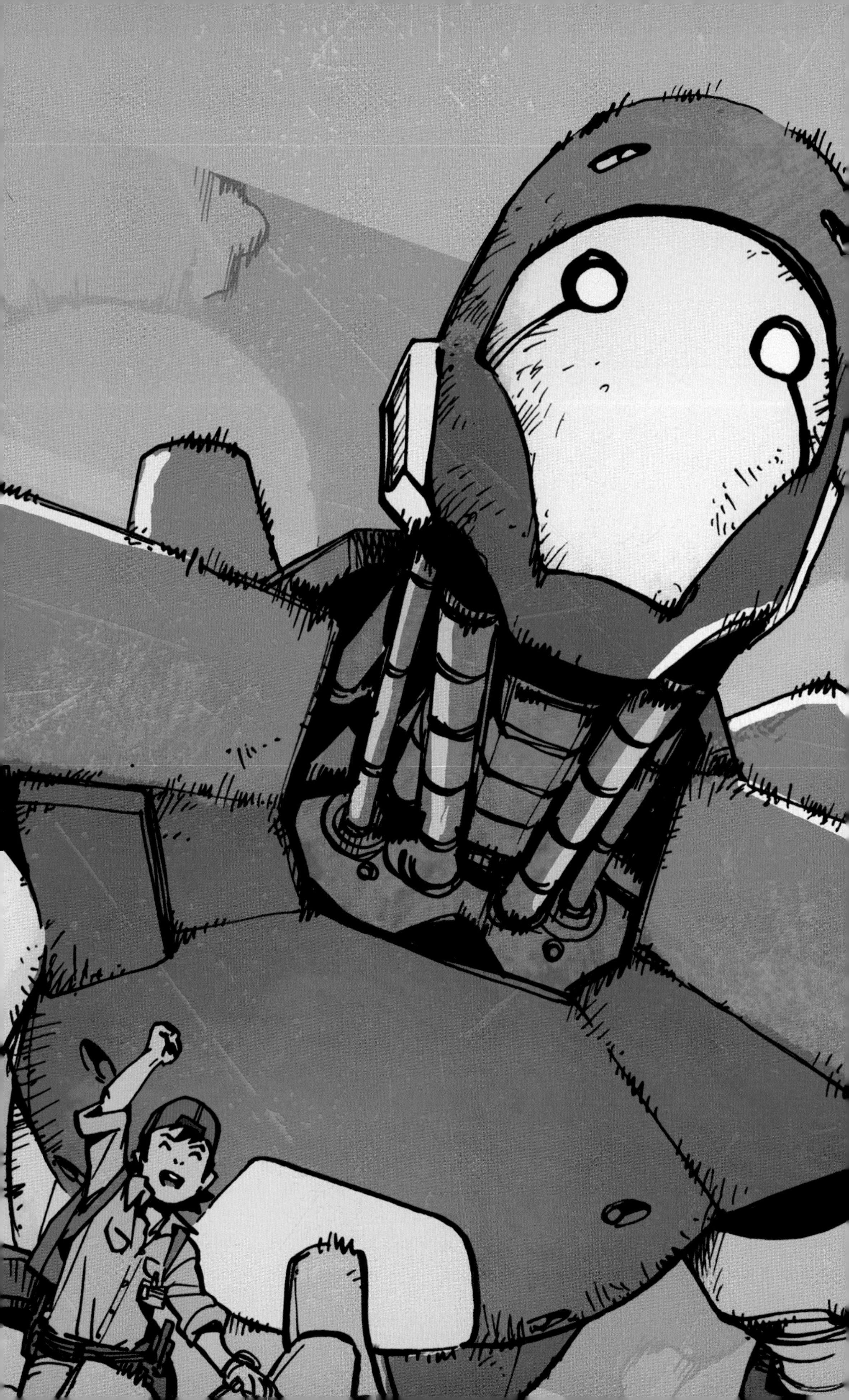

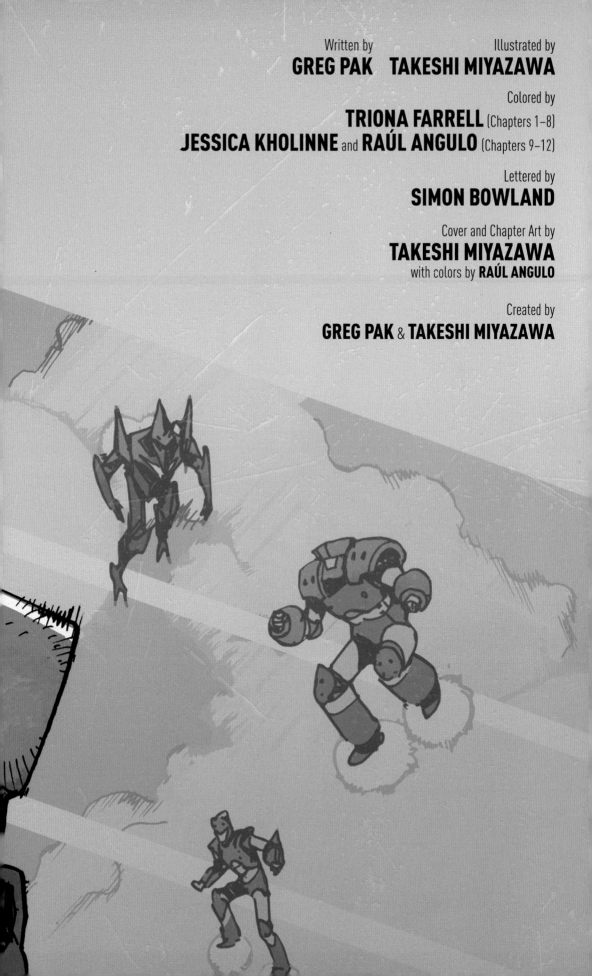

Written by
GREG PAK

Illustrated by
TAKESHI MIYAZAWA

Colored by
TRIONA FARRELL (Chapters 1–8)
JESSICA KHOLINNE and **RAÚL ANGULO** (Chapters 9–12)

Lettered by
SIMON BOWLAND

Cover and Chapter Art by
TAKESHI MIYAZAWA
with colors by **RAÚL ANGULO**

Created by
GREG PAK & **TAKESHI MIYAZAWA**

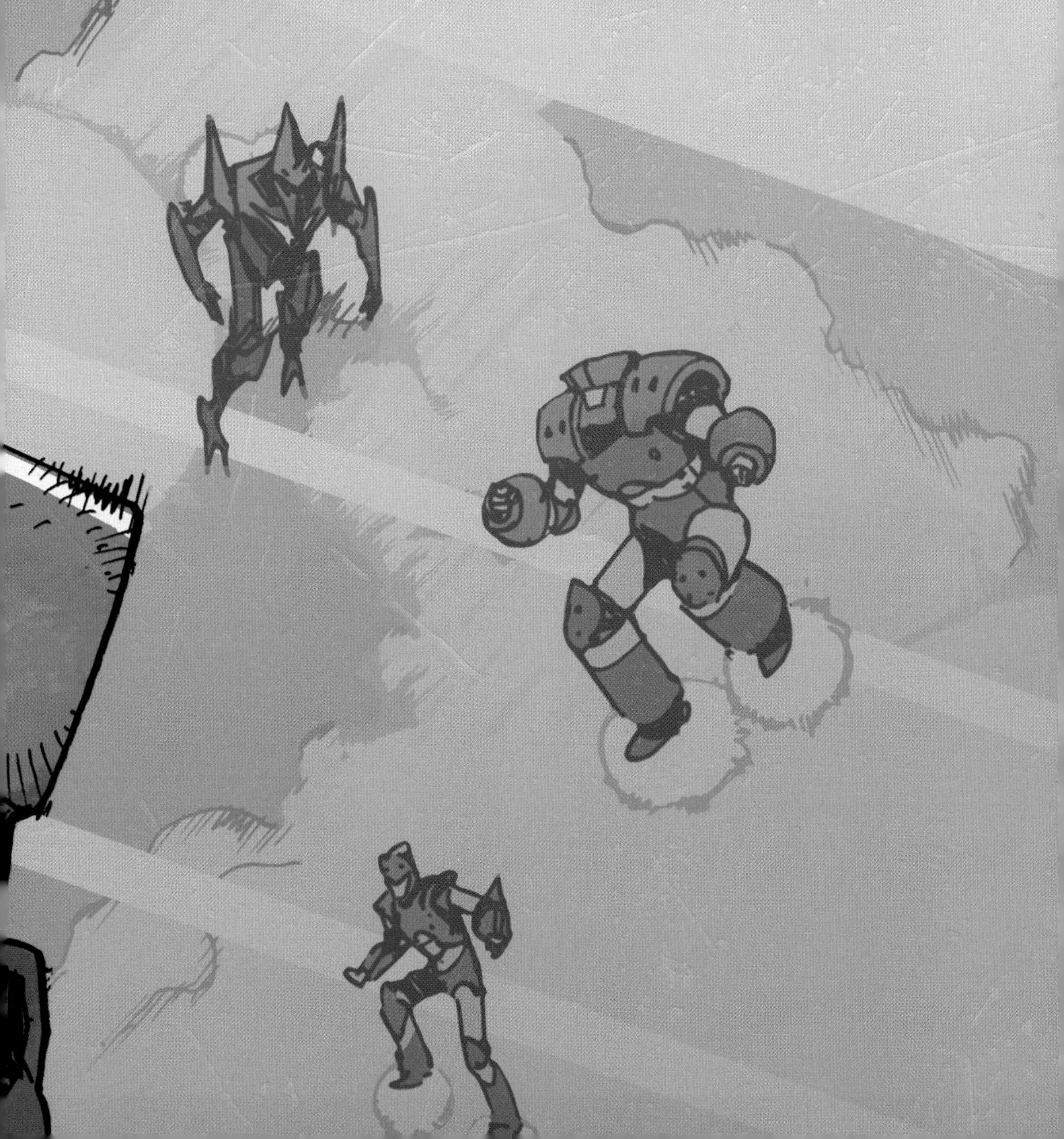

CHAPTER
ONE

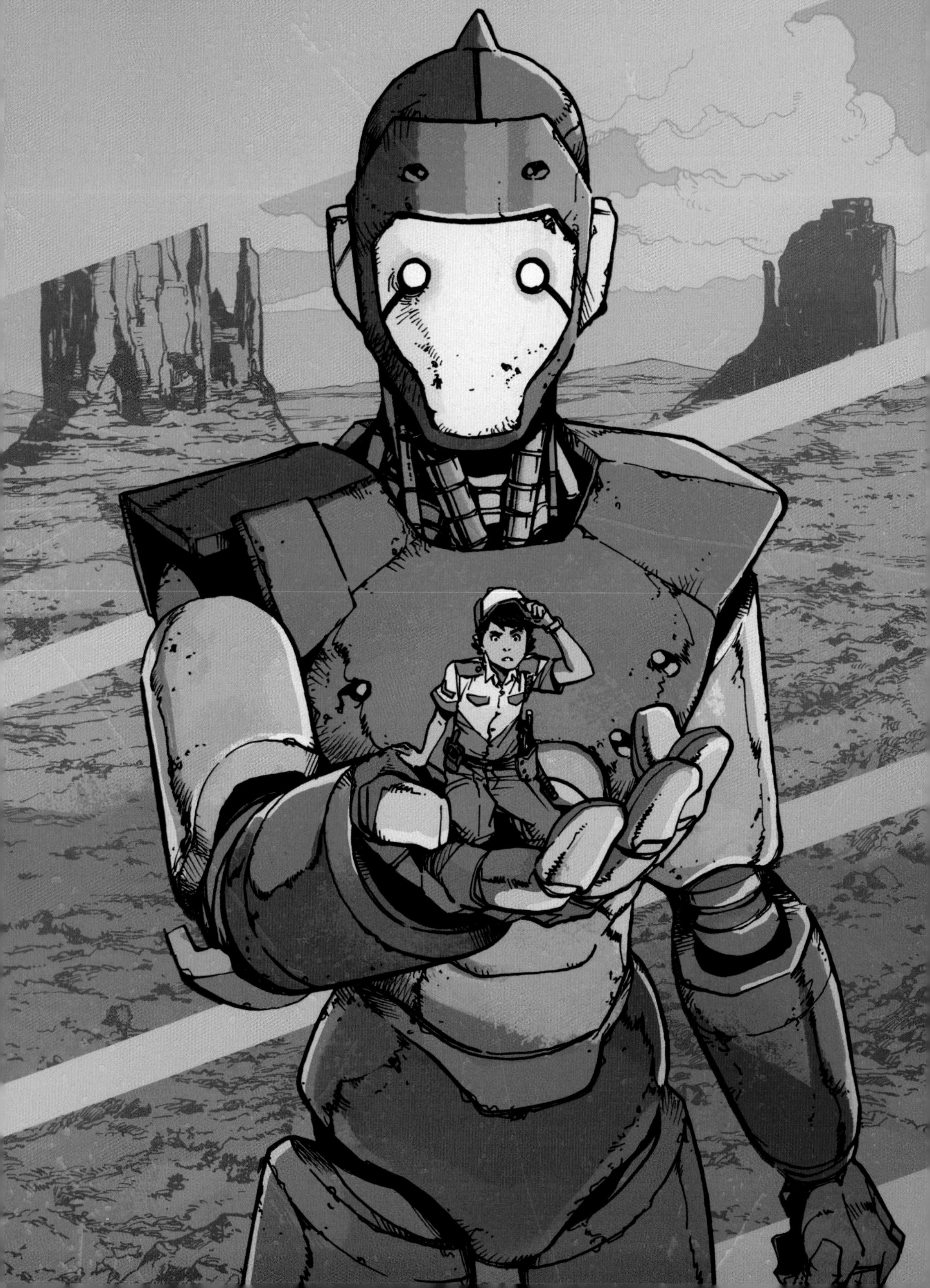

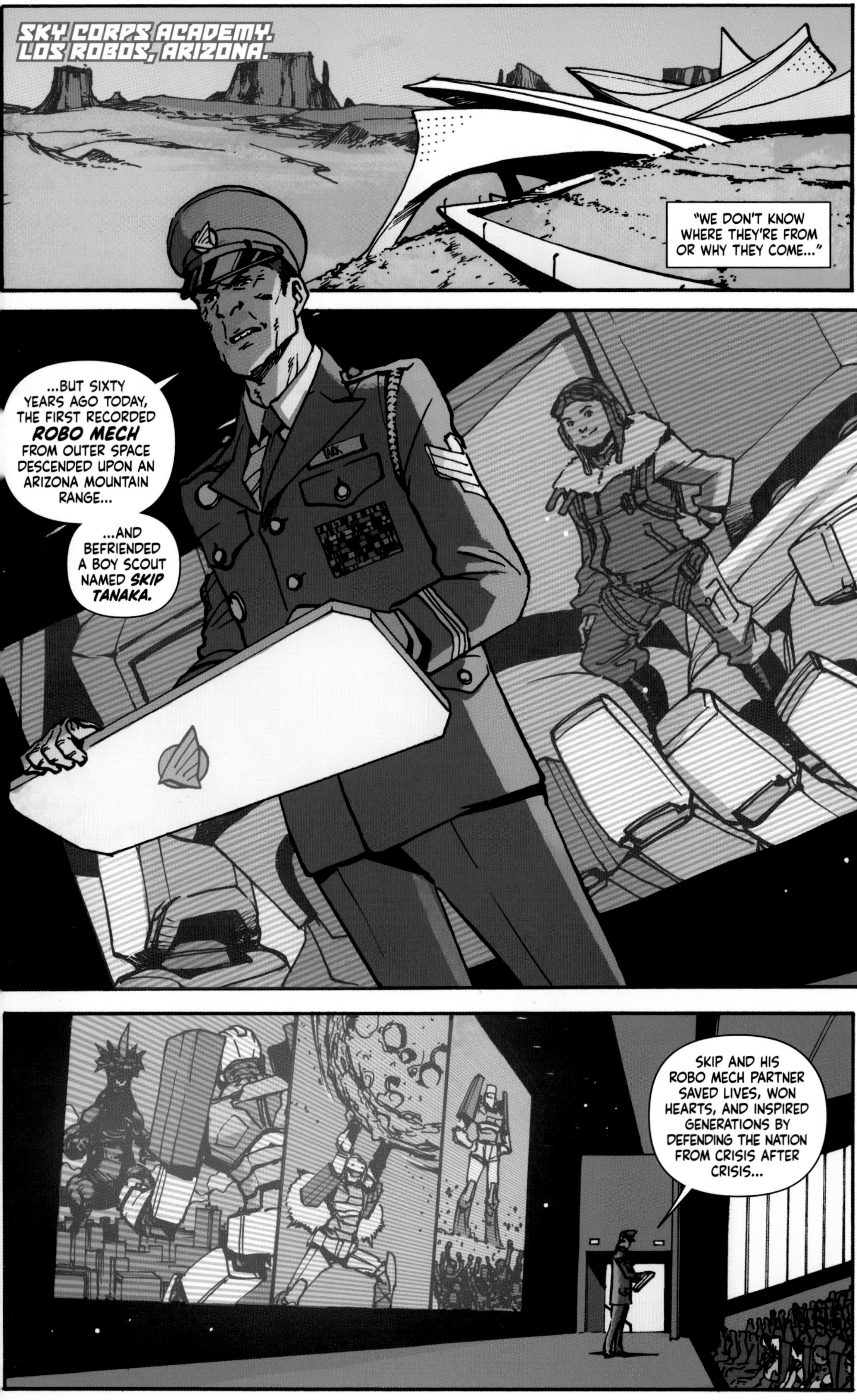
SKY CORPS ACADEMY. LOS ROBOS, ARIZONA.
"WE DON'T KNOW WHERE THEY'RE FROM OR WHY THEY COME..."
...BUT SIXTY YEARS AGO TODAY, THE FIRST RECORDED ROBO MECH FROM OUTER SPACE DESCENDED UPON AN ARIZONA MOUNTAIN RANGE...
...AND BEFRIENDED A BOY SCOUT NAMED SKIP TANAKA.
SKIP AND HIS ROBO MECH PARTNER SAVED LIVES, WON HEARTS, AND INSPIRED GENERATIONS BY DEFENDING THE NATION FROM CRISIS AFTER CRISIS...

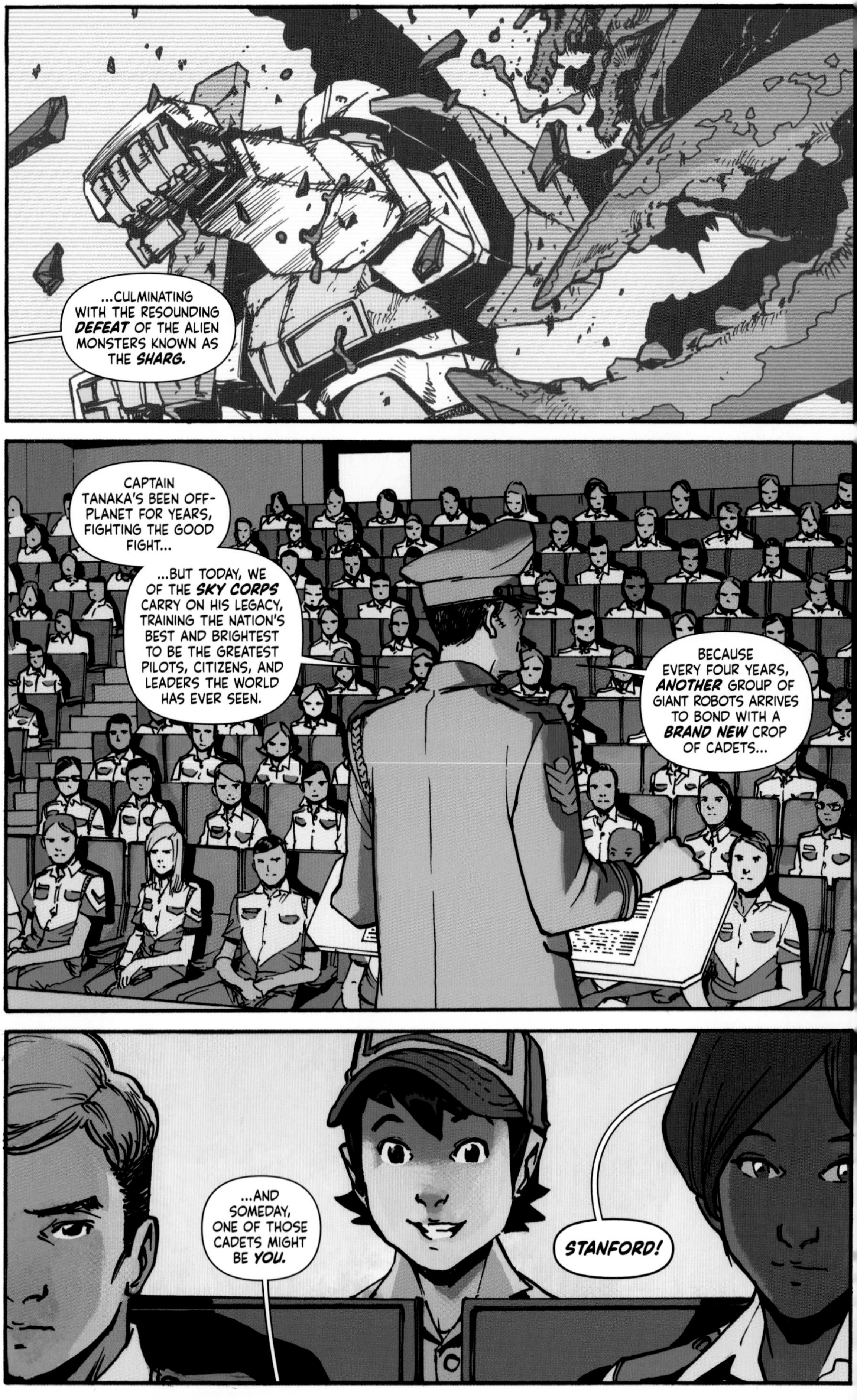
...CULMINATING WITH THE RESOUNDING DEFEAT OF THE ALIEN MONSTERS KNOWN AS THE SHARG.
CAPTAIN TANAKA'S BEEN OFF-PLANET FOR YEARS, FIGHTING THE GOOD FIGHT...
...BUT TODAY, WE OF THE SKY CORPS CARRY ON HIS LEGACY, TRAINING THE NATION'S BEST AND BRIGHTEST TO BE THE GREATEST PILOTS, CITIZENS, AND LEADERS THE WORLD HAS EVER SEEN.
BECAUSE EVERY FOUR YEARS, ANOTHER GROUP OF GIANT ROBOTS ARRIVES TO BOND WITH A BRAND NEW CROP OF CADETS...
...AND SOMEDAY, ONE OF THOSE CADETS MIGHT BE YOU.
STANFORD!

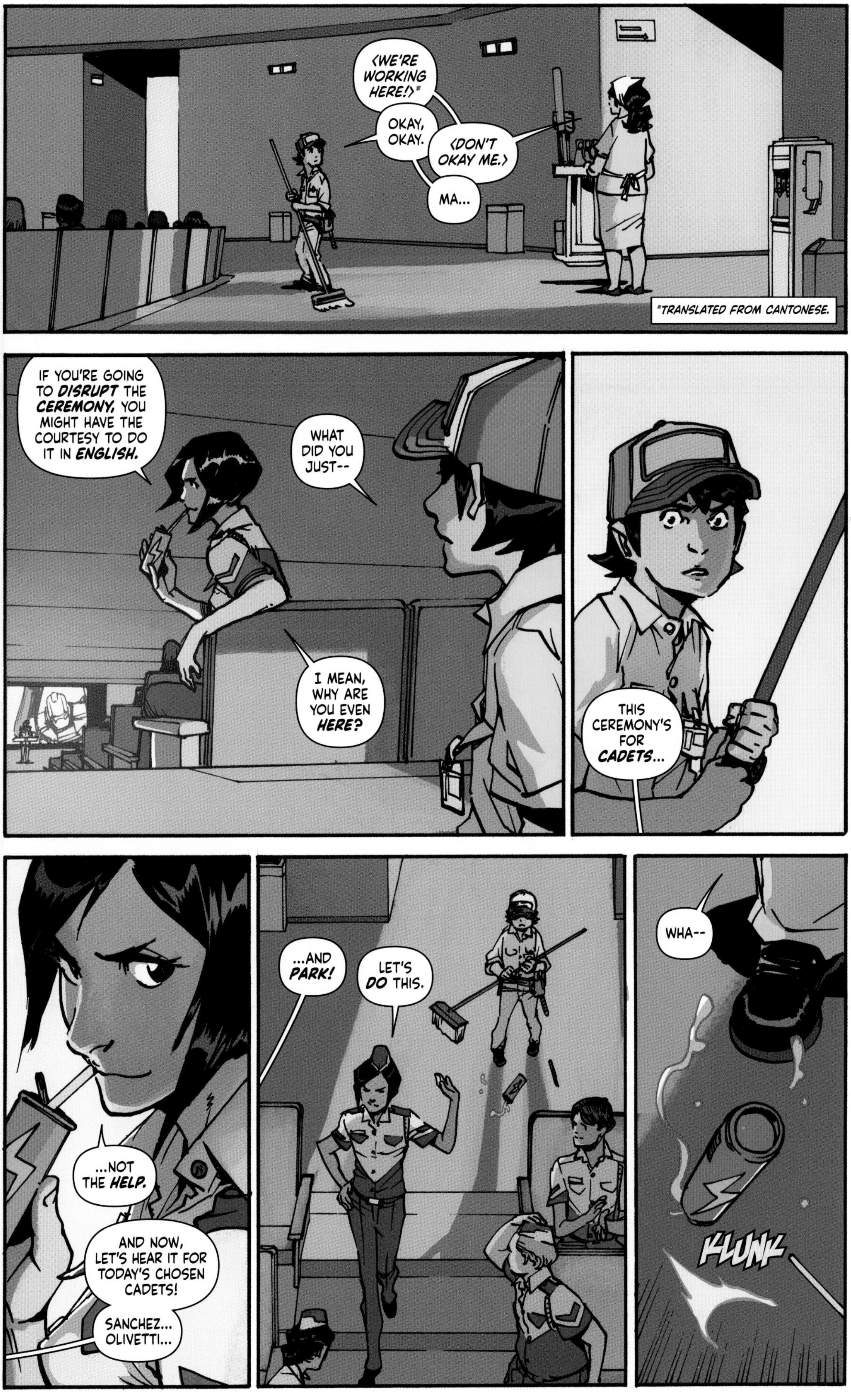

<WE'RE WORKING HERE!>*
OKAY, OKAY.
<DON'T OKAY ME.>
MA...
*TRANSLATED FROM CANTONESE.
IF YOU'RE GOING TO DISRUPT THE CEREMONY, YOU MIGHT HAVE THE COURTESY TO DO IT IN ENGLISH.
WHAT DID YOU JUST--
I MEAN, WHY ARE YOU EVEN HERE?
THIS CEREMONY'S FOR CADETS...
...NOT THE HELP.
AND NOW, LET'S HEAR IT FOR TODAY'S CHOSEN CADETS!
SANCHEZ... OLIVETTI...
...AND PARK!
LET'S DO THIS.
WHA--
KLUNK

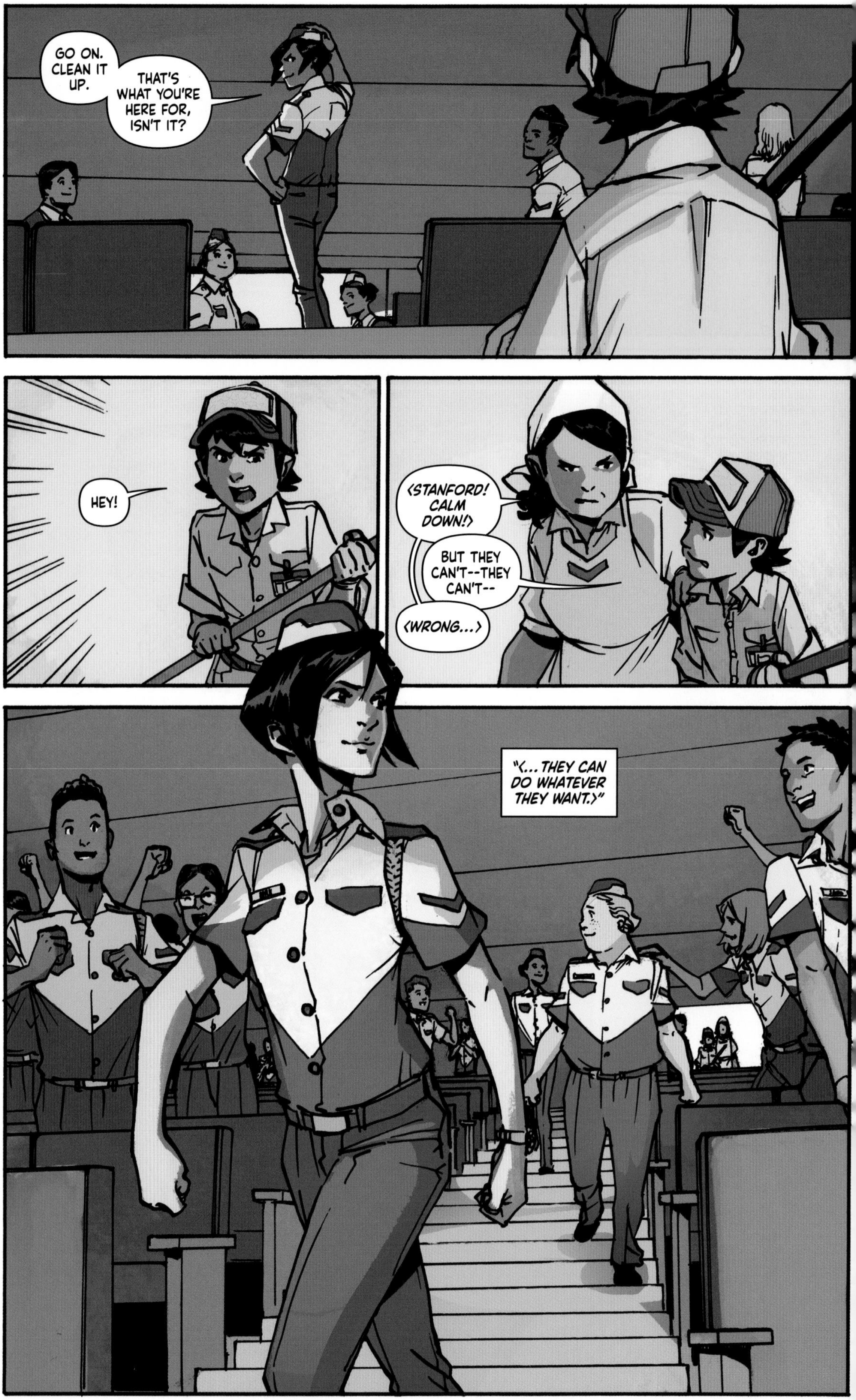
GO ON. CLEAN IT UP.
THAT'S WHAT YOU'RE HERE FOR, ISN'T IT?
HEY!
‹STANFORD! CALM DOWN!›
BUT THEY CAN'T--THEY CAN'T--
‹WRONG...›
"‹...THEY CAN DO WHATEVER THEY WANT.›"

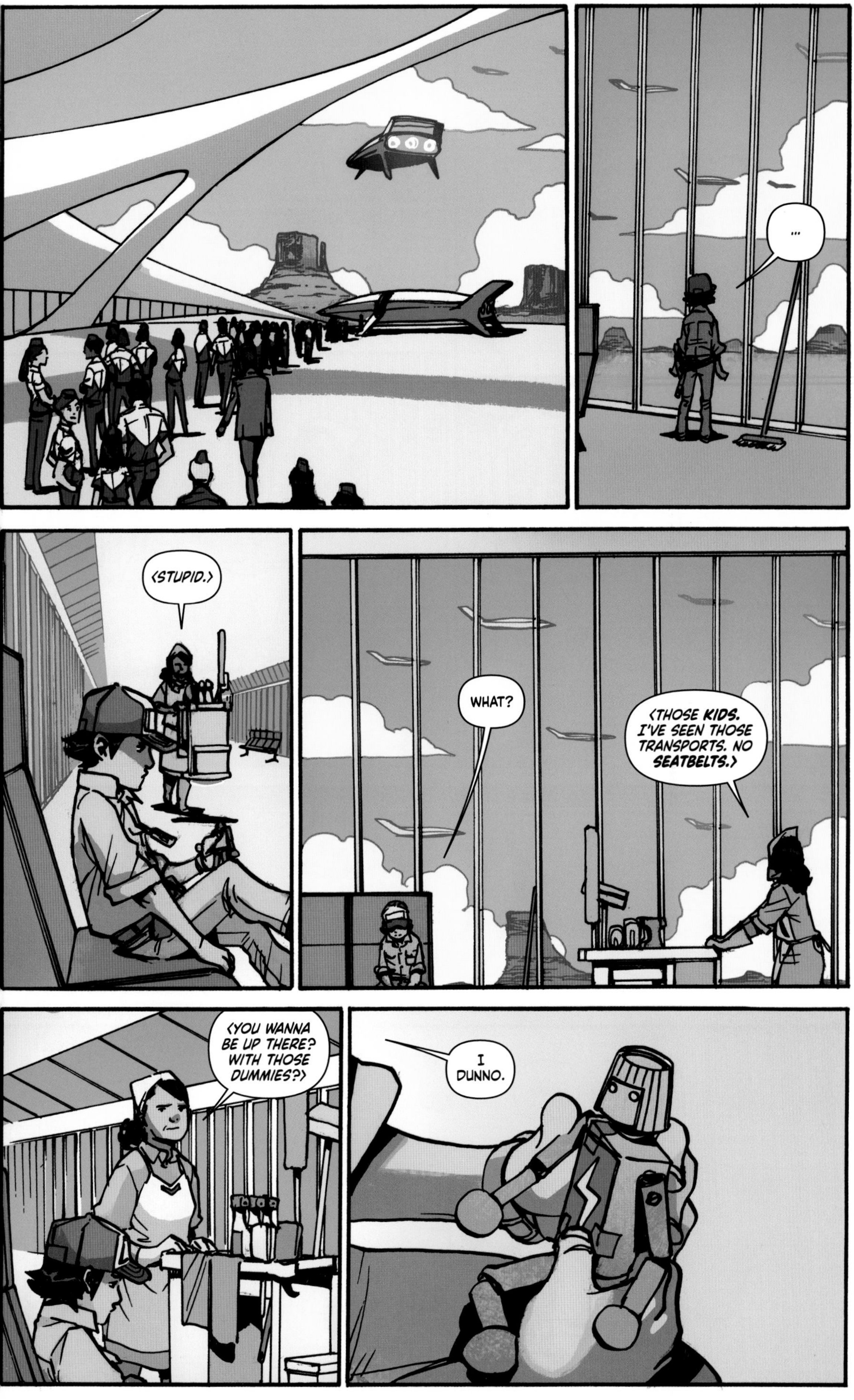
...
‹STUPID.›
WHAT?
‹THOSE KIDS. I'VE SEEN THOSE TRANSPORTS. NO SEATBELTS.›
‹YOU WANNA BE UP THERE? WITH THOSE DUMMIES?›
I DUNNO.

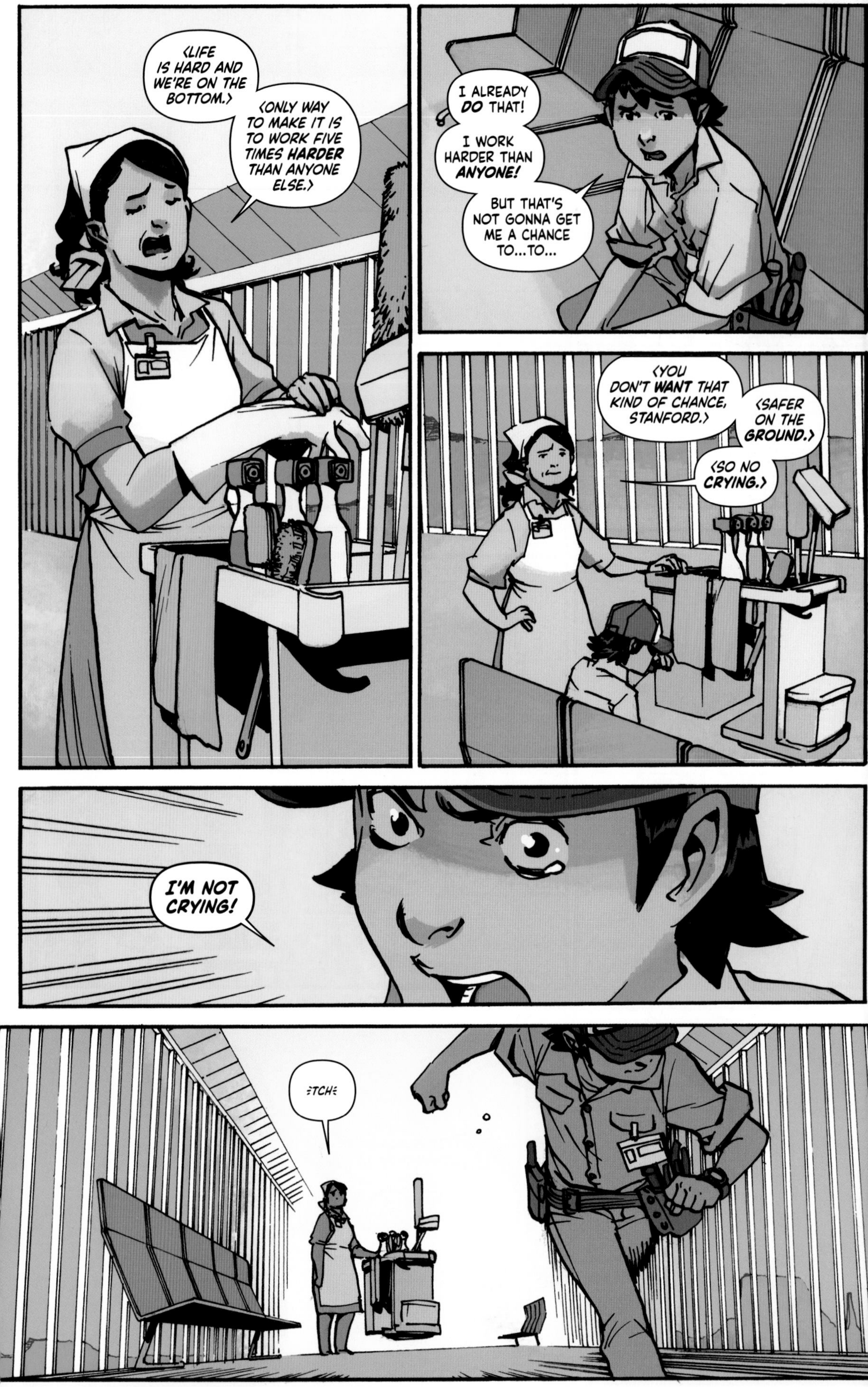
‹LIFE IS HARD AND WE'RE ON THE BOTTOM.›
‹ONLY WAY TO MAKE IT IS TO WORK FIVE TIMES **HARDER** THAN ANYONE ELSE.›
I ALREADY **DO** THAT!
I WORK HARDER THAN **ANYONE!**
BUT THAT'S NOT GONNA GET ME A CHANCE TO...TO...
‹YOU DON'T **WANT** THAT KIND OF CHANCE, STANFORD.›
‹SAFER ON THE **GROUND.**›
‹SO NO **CRYING.**›
I'M NOT CRYING!
TCH

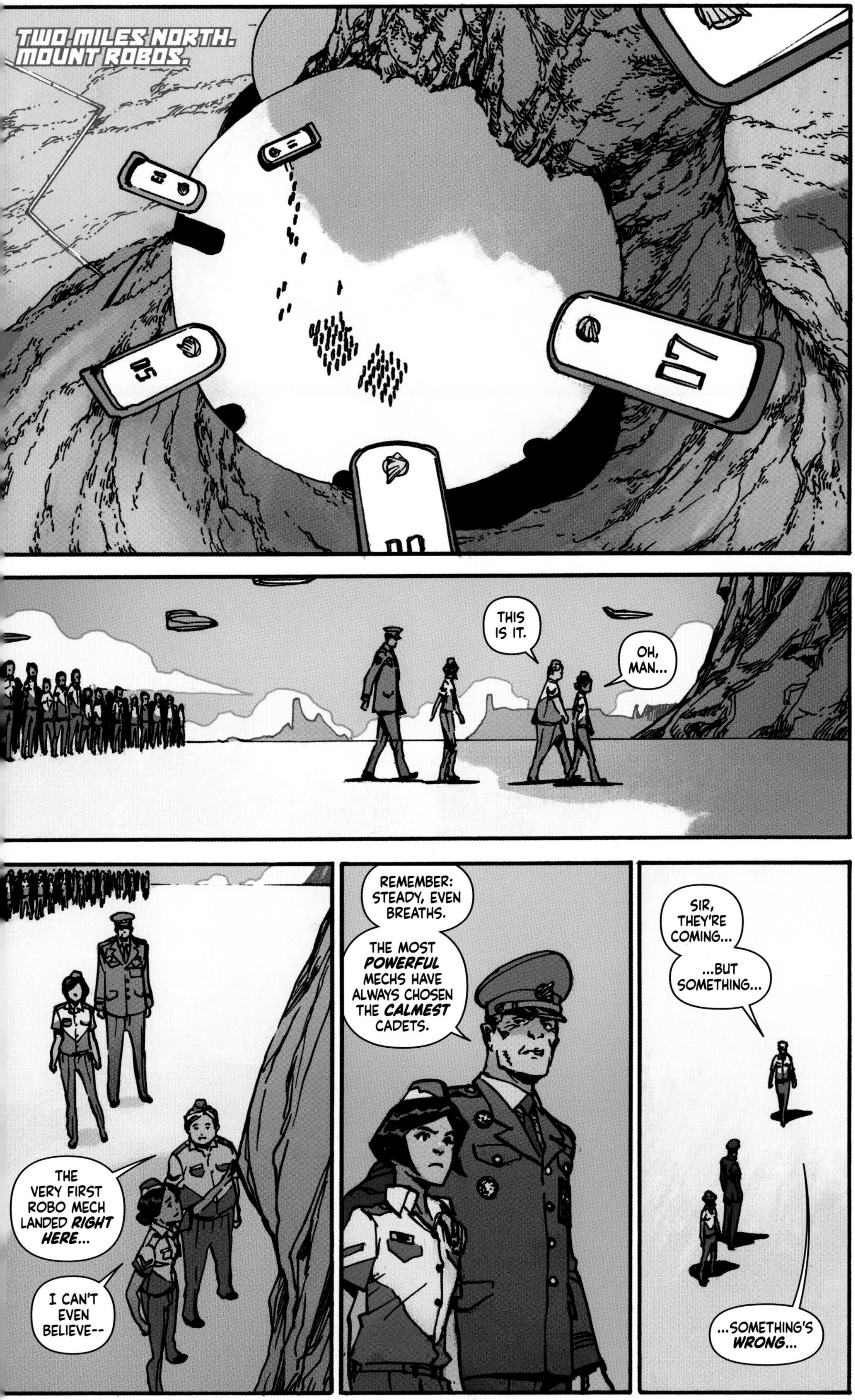
TWO MILES NORTH. MOUNT ROBOS.
THIS IS IT.
OH, MAN...
THE VERY FIRST ROBO MECH LANDED RIGHT HERE...
I CAN'T EVEN BELIEVE--
REMEMBER: STEADY, EVEN BREATHS.
THE MOST POWERFUL MECHS HAVE ALWAYS CHOSEN THE CALMEST CADETS.
SIR, THEY'RE COMING...
...BUT SOMETHING...
...SOMETHING'S WRONG...

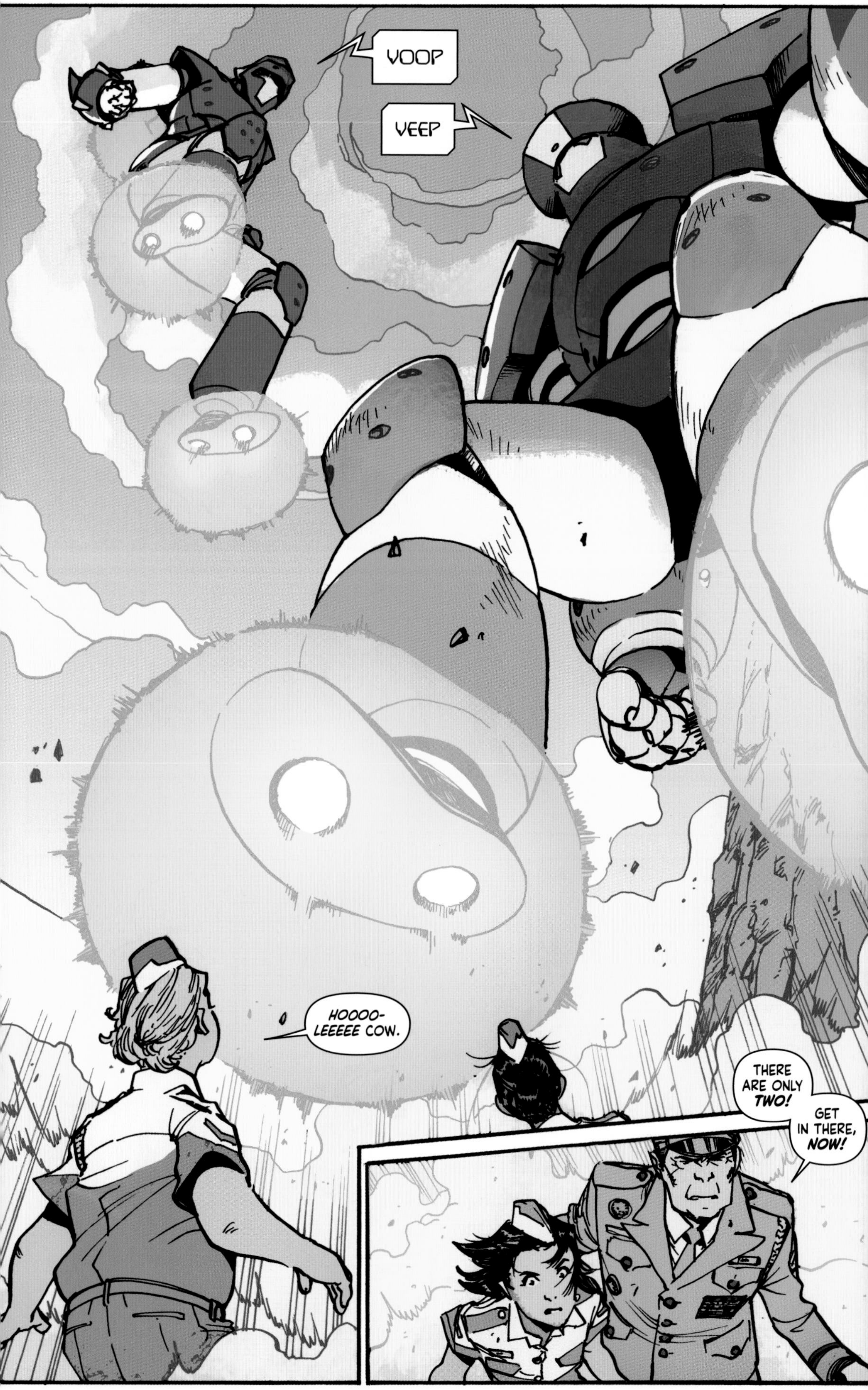
VOOP
VEEP
HOOOO-LEEEEE COW.
THERE ARE ONLY TWO!
GET IN THERE, NOW!

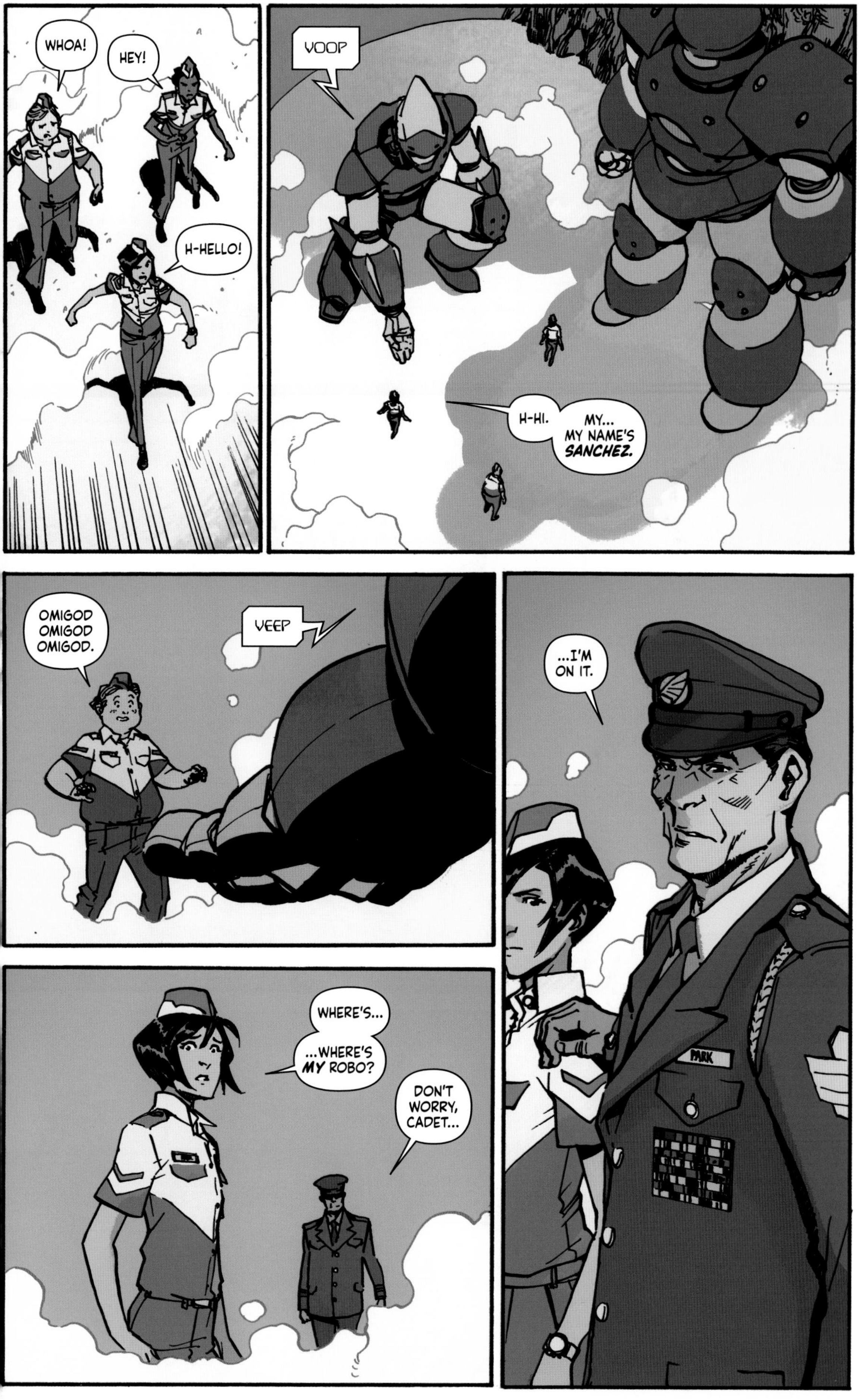
WHOA!
HEY!
H-HELLO!
VOOP
H-HI.
MY... MY NAME'S *SANCHEZ.*
OMIGOD OMIGOD OMIGOD.
VEEP
WHERE'S...
...WHERE'S *MY* ROBO?
DON'T WORRY, CADET...
...I'M ON IT.
PARK

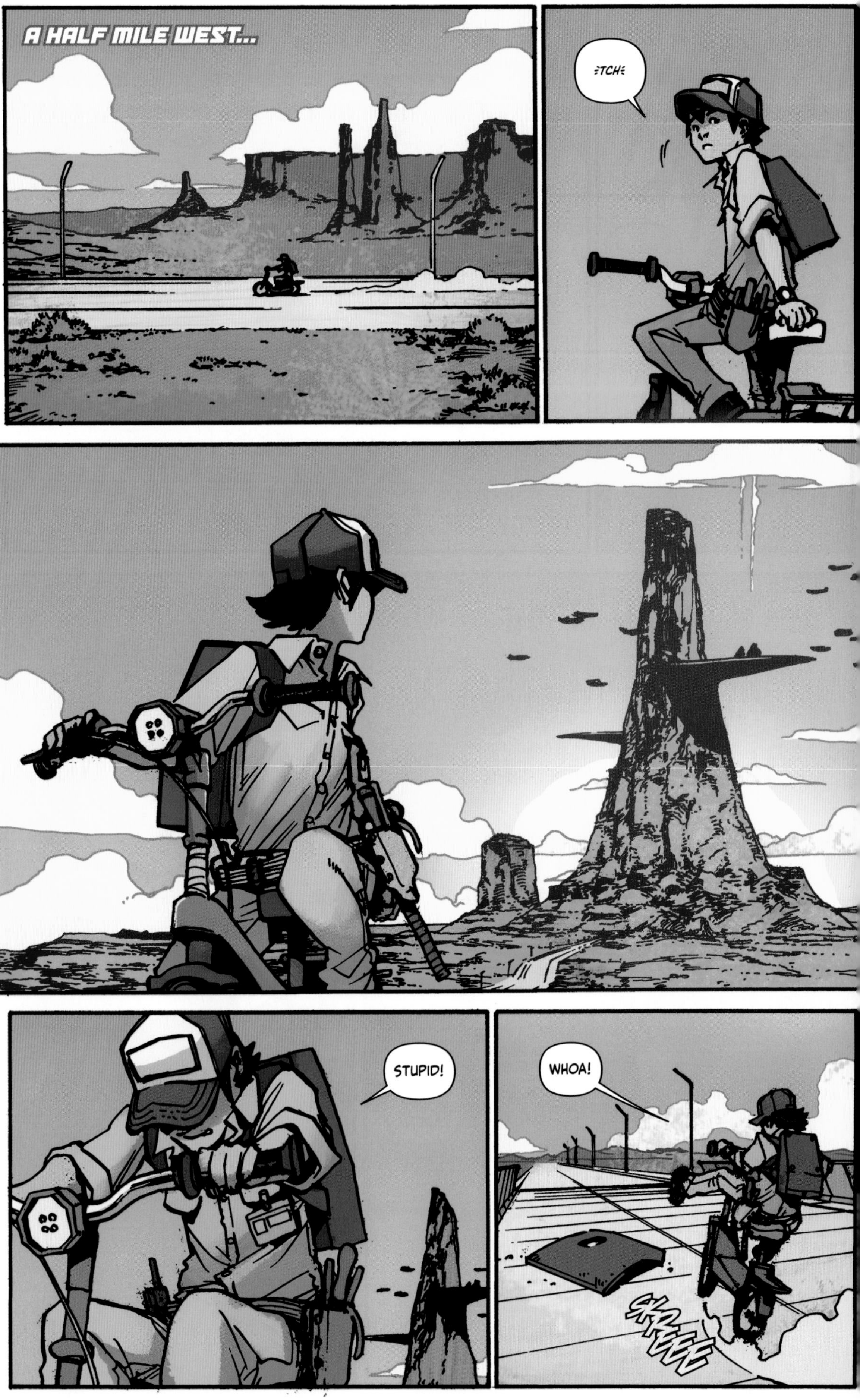
A HALF MILE WEST...
TCH
STUPID!
WHOA!
SKREEE

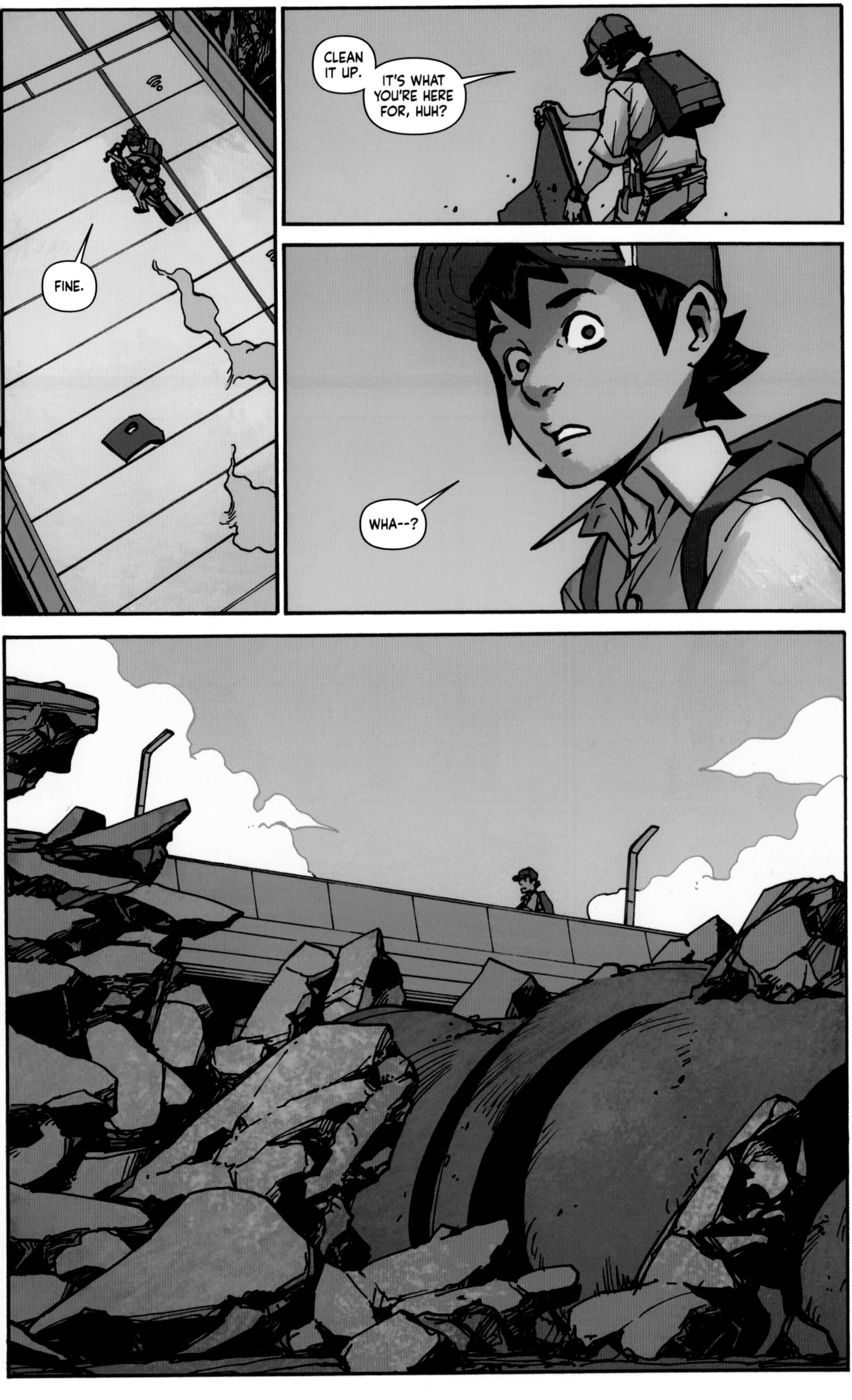
FINE.
CLEAN IT UP.
IT'S WHAT YOU'RE HERE FOR, HUH?
WHA--?

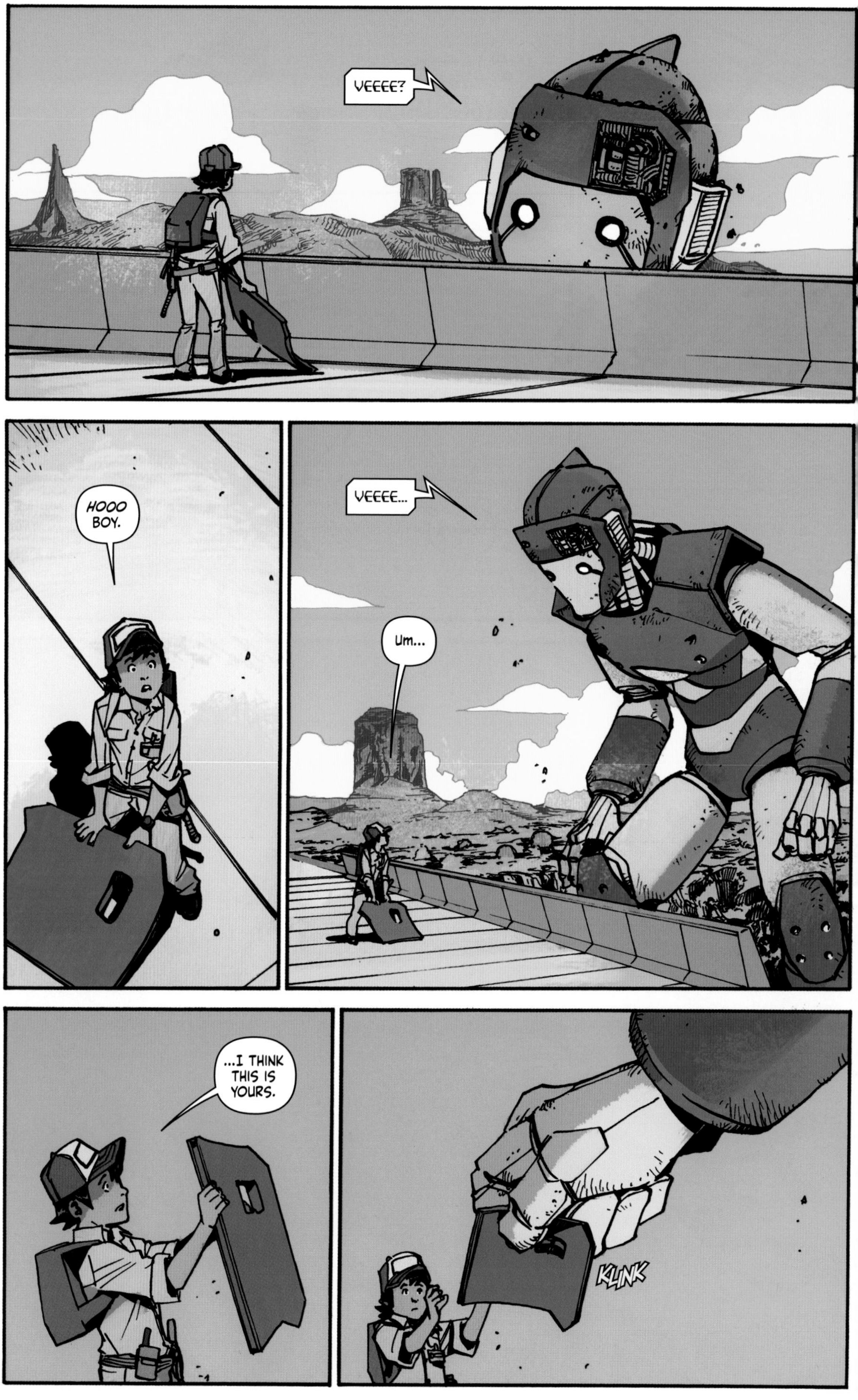
VEEEE?
HOOO BOY.
VEEEE...
Um...
...I THINK THIS IS YOURS.
KLINK

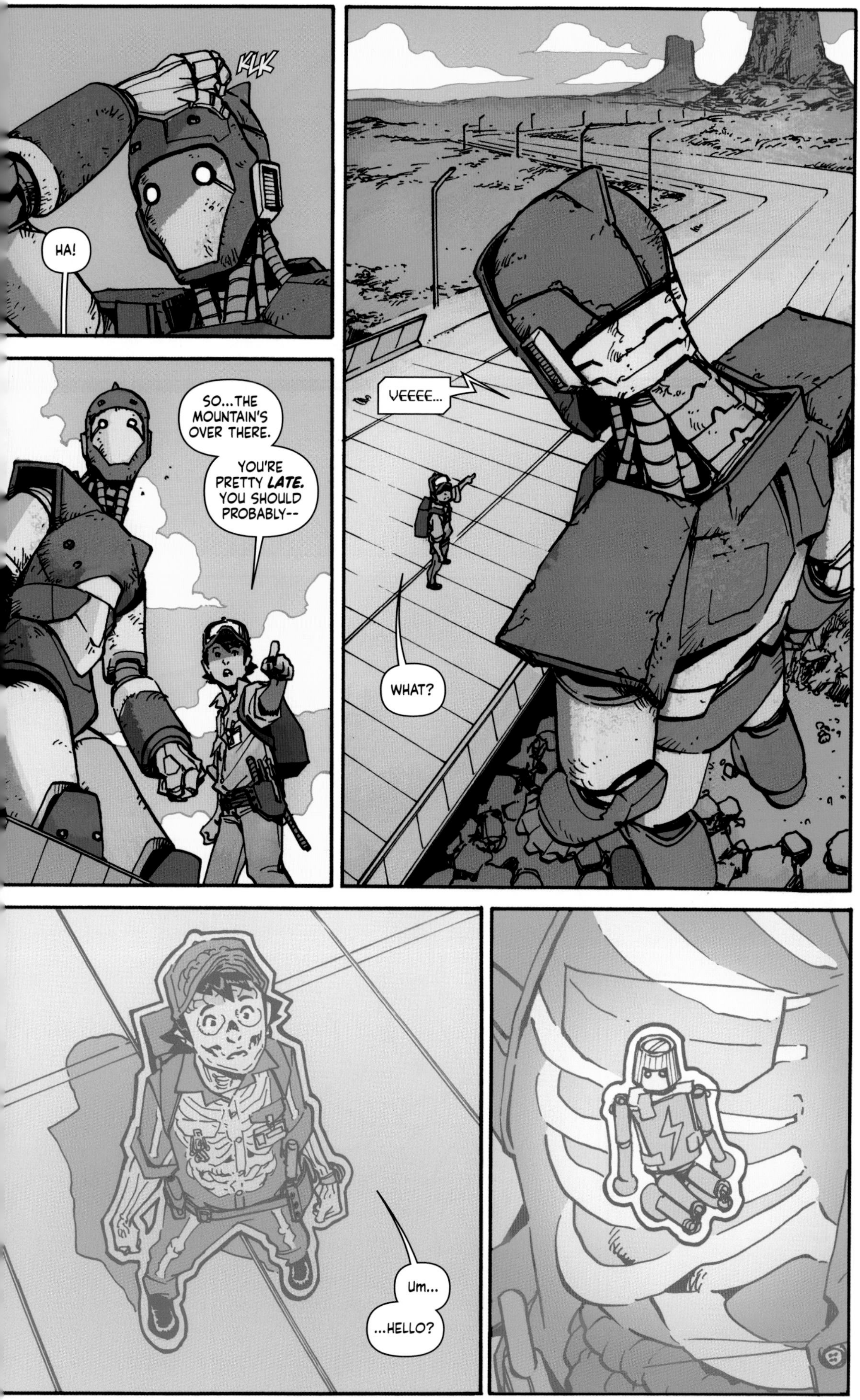
KLK
HA!
SO...THE MOUNTAIN'S OVER THERE.
YOU'RE PRETTY *LATE.* YOU SHOULD PROBABLY--
VEEEE...
WHAT?
Um...
...HELLO?

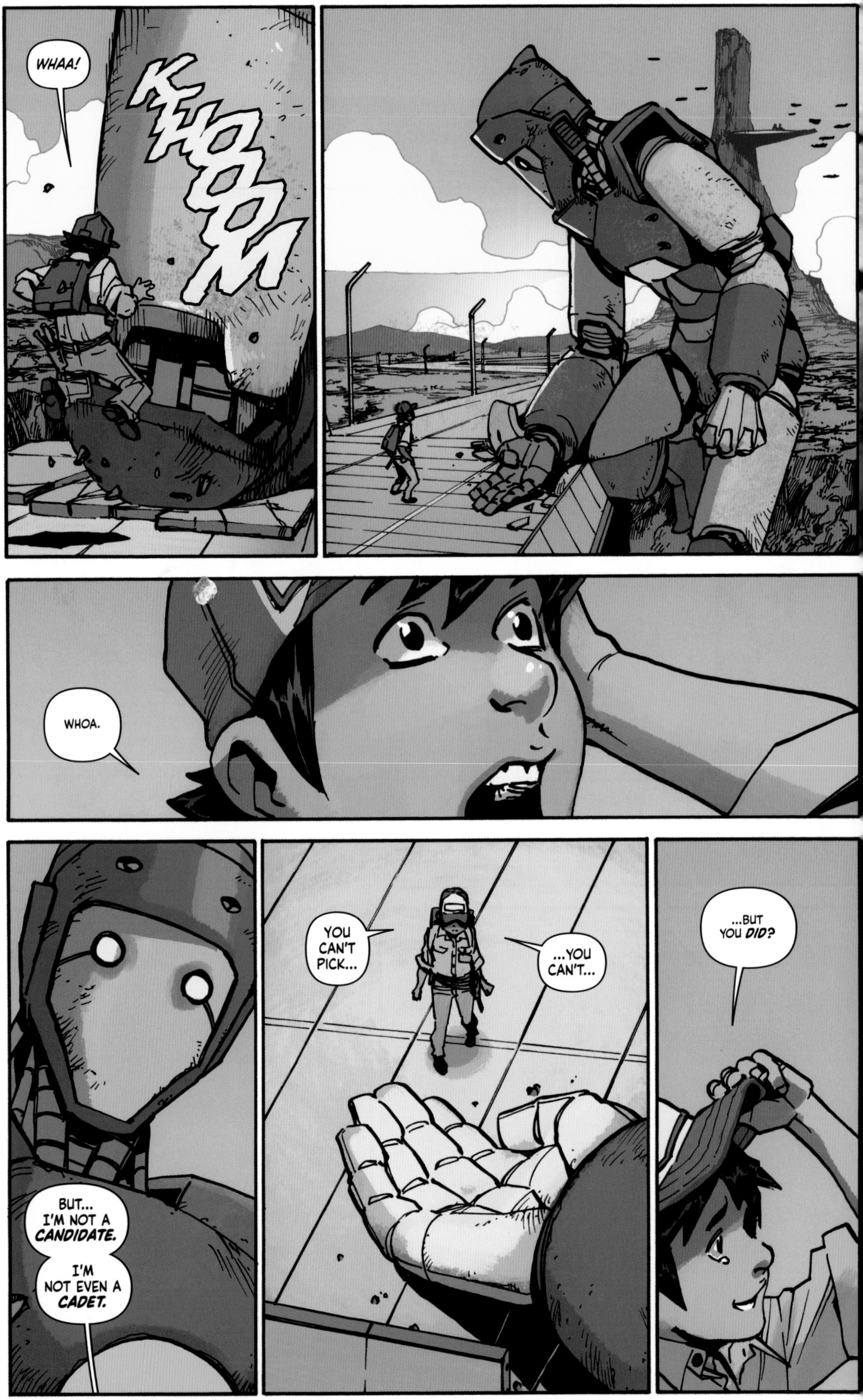
WHAA!
KHOOM
WHOA.
YOU CAN'T PICK...
...YOU CAN'T...
...BUT YOU DID?
BUT... I'M NOT A CANDIDATE.
I'M NOT EVEN A CADET.

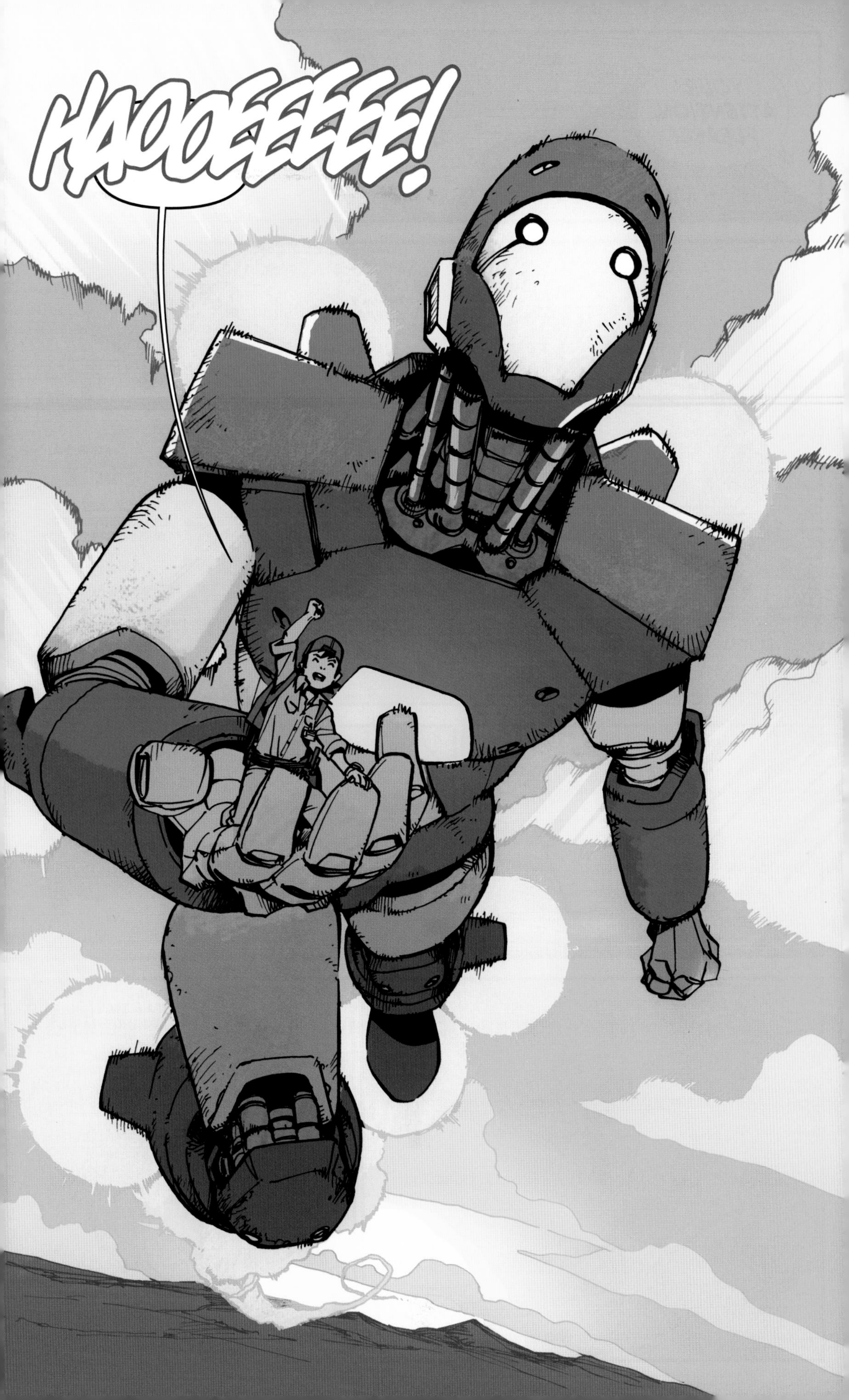
HAOOEEEEEE!

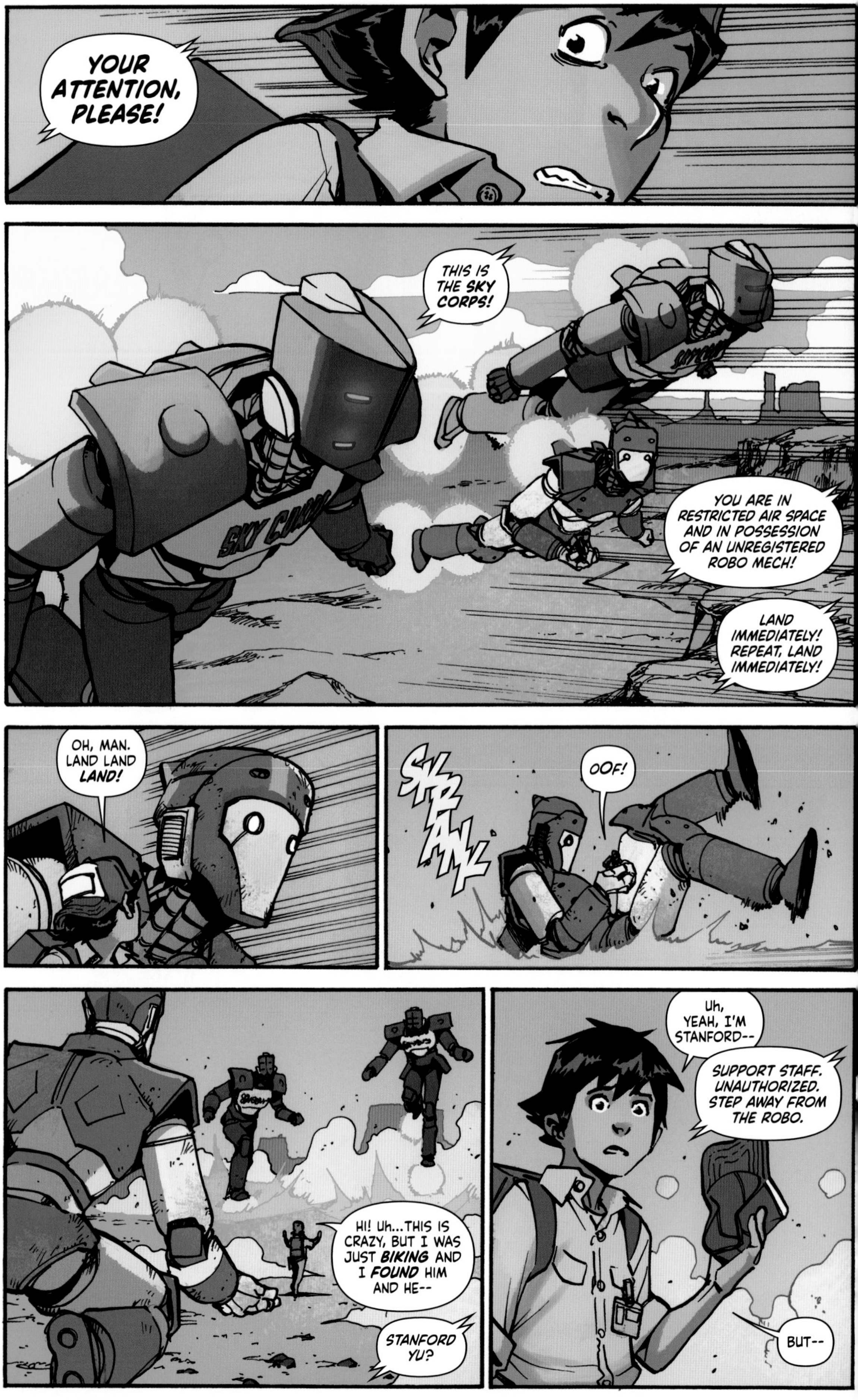
YOUR ATTENTION, PLEASE!
THIS IS THE SKY CORPS!
YOU ARE IN RESTRICTED AIR SPACE AND IN POSSESSION OF AN UNREGISTERED ROBO MECH!
LAND IMMEDIATELY! REPEAT, LAND IMMEDIATELY!
OH, MAN. LAND LAND LAND!
SKRANK
OOF!
HI! Uh...THIS IS CRAZY, BUT I WAS JUST BIKING AND I FOUND HIM AND HE--
STANFORD YU?
Uh, YEAH, I'M STANFORD--
SUPPORT STAFF. UNAUTHORIZED. STEP AWAY FROM THE ROBO.
BUT--

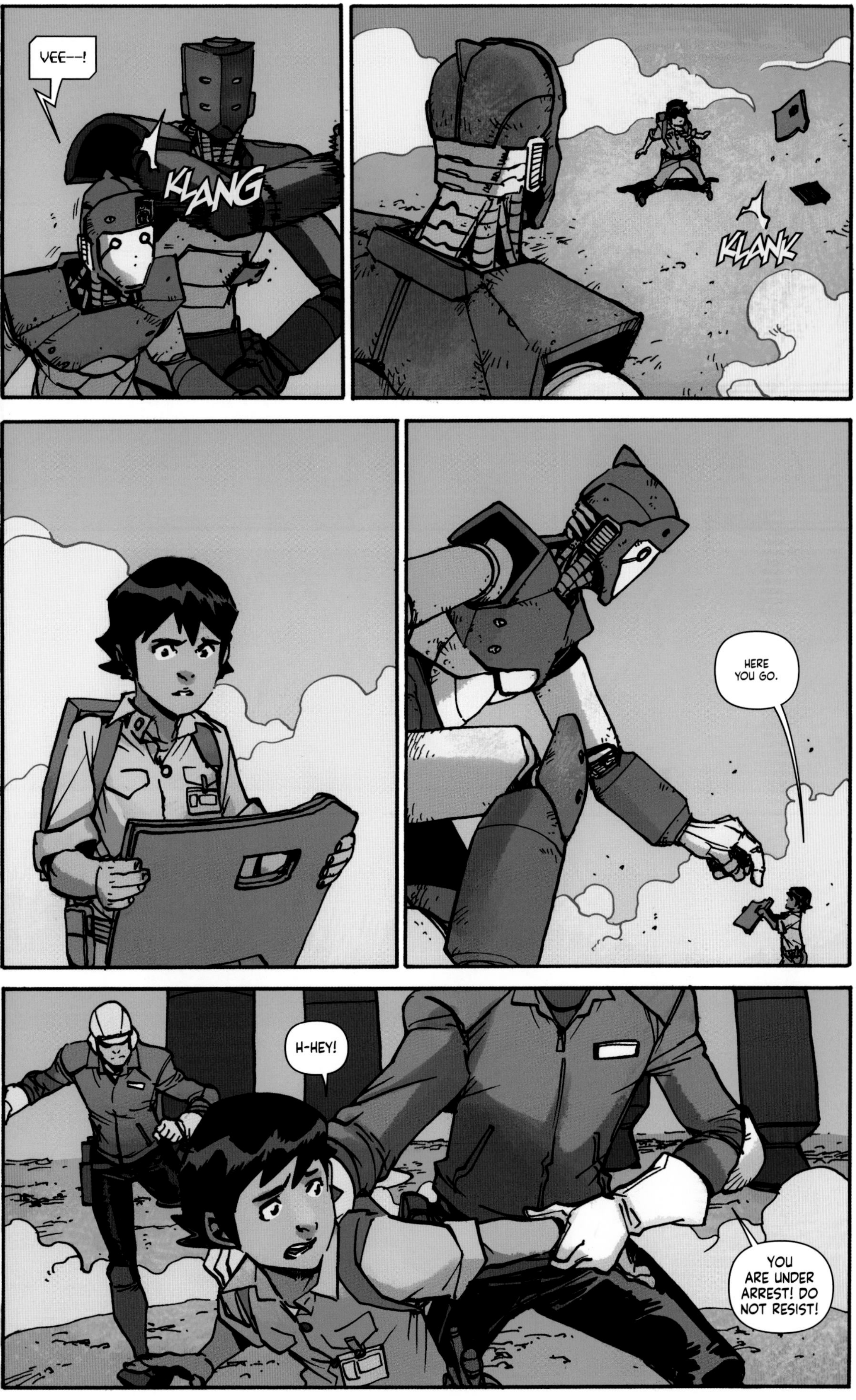
VEE--!
KLANG
KLANK
HERE YOU GO.
H-HEY!
YOU ARE UNDER ARREST! DO NOT RESIST!

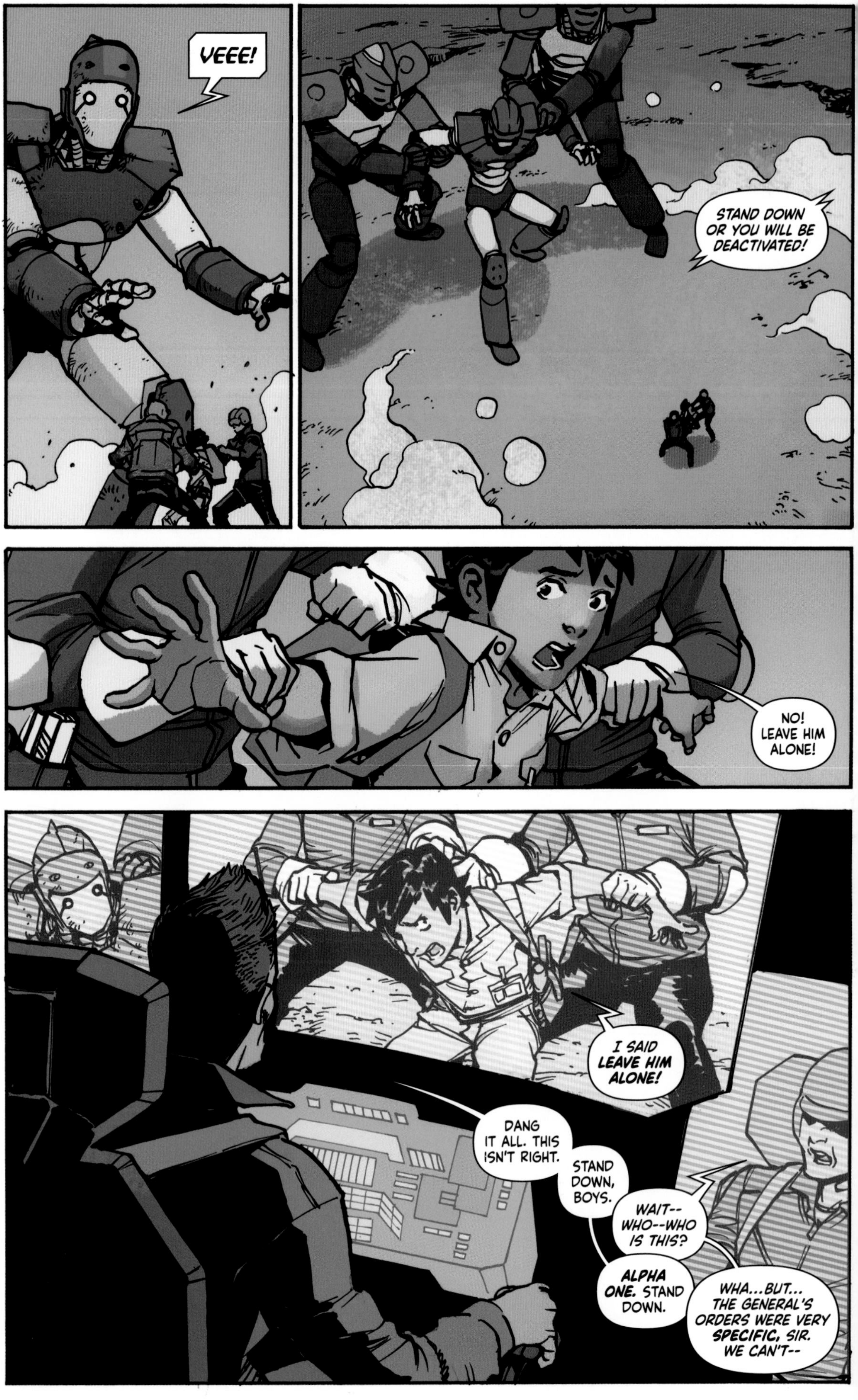
VEEE!
STAND DOWN OR YOU WILL BE DEACTIVATED!
NO! LEAVE HIM ALONE!
I SAID LEAVE HIM ALONE!
DANG IT ALL. THIS ISN'T RIGHT.
STAND DOWN, BOYS.
WAIT-- WHO--WHO IS THIS?
ALPHA ONE. STAND DOWN.
WHA...BUT... THE GENERAL'S ORDERS WERE VERY SPECIFIC, SIR. WE CAN'T--

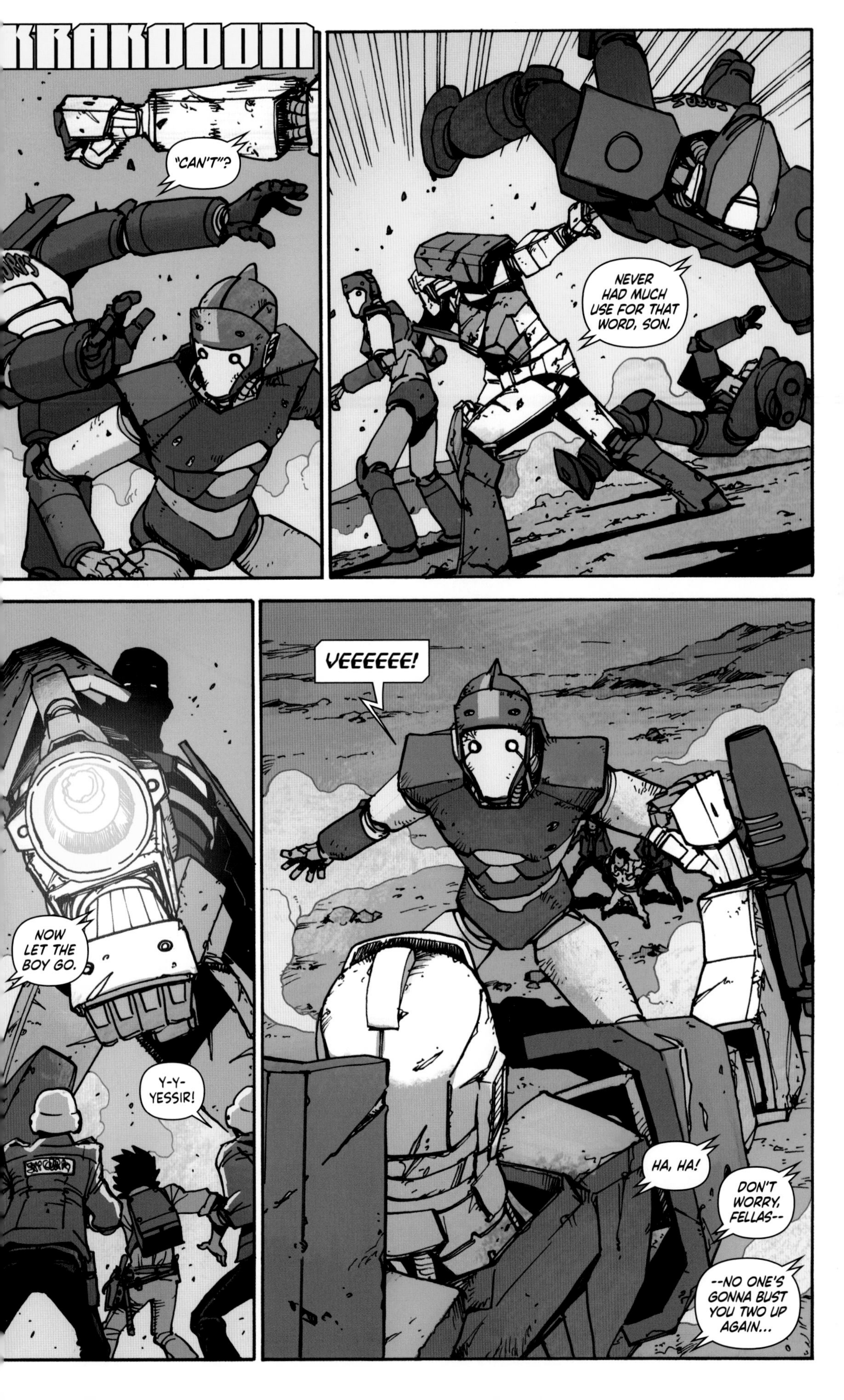
KRAKOOOM
"CAN'T"?
NEVER HAD MUCH USE FOR THAT WORD, SON.
NOW LET THE BOY GO.
Y-Y-YESSIR!
VEEEEEE!
HA, HA!
DON'T WORRY, FELLAS--
--NO ONE'S GONNA BUST YOU TWO UP AGAIN...

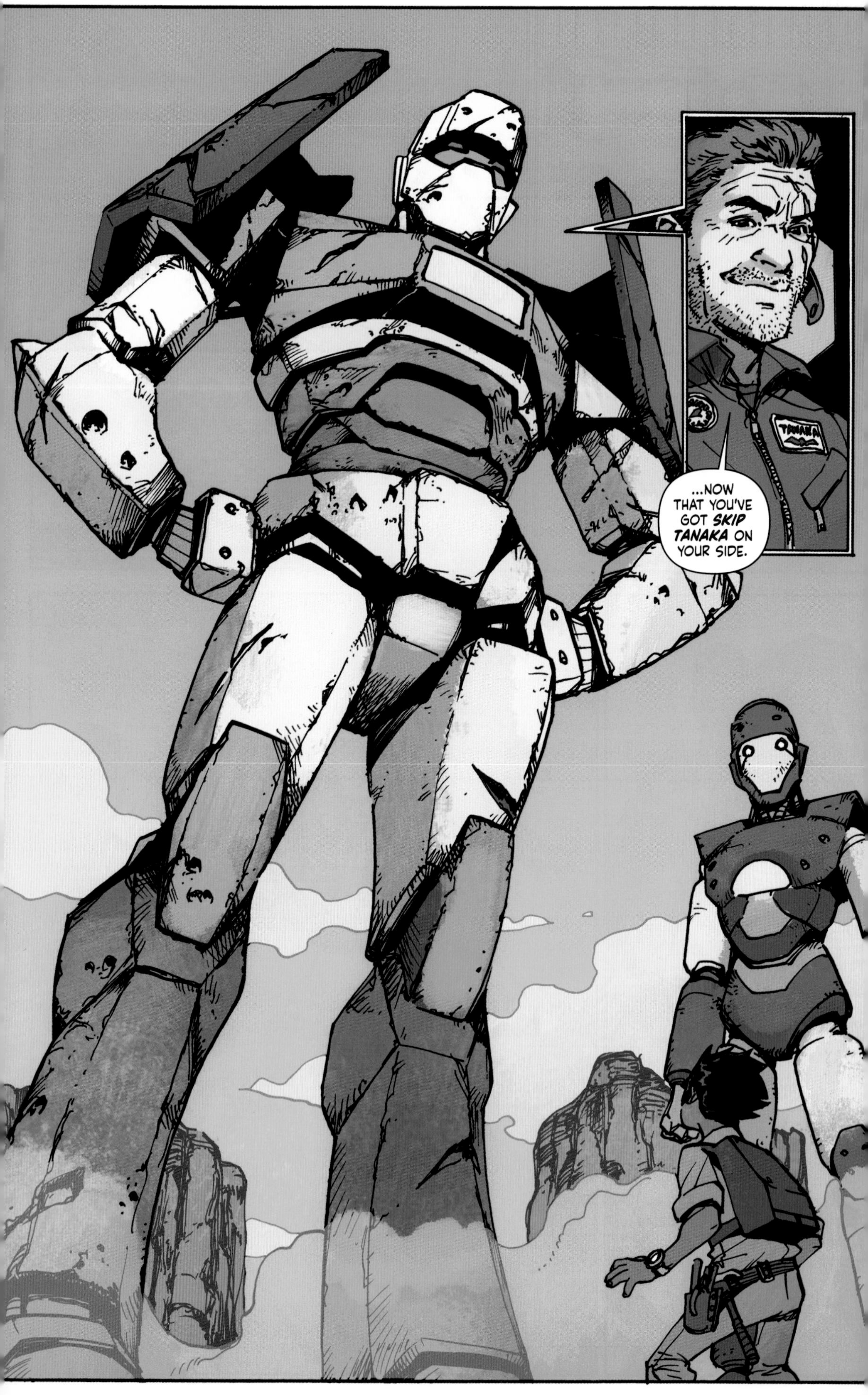

...NOW THAT YOU'VE GOT **SKIP TANAKA** ON YOUR SIDE.
TANAKA

MEANWHILE...

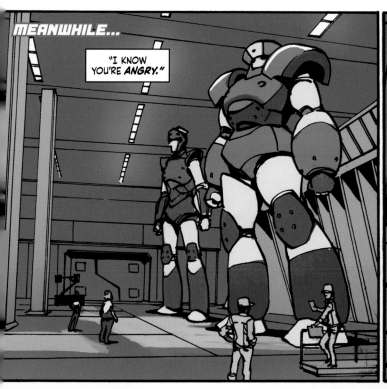

"I KNOW YOU'RE *ANGRY*."

AND YOU *SHOULD* BE.

YOU WORKED HARDER THAN *ANYONE* IN THAT SCHOOL.

BEST GRADES, BEST APTITUDE TESTS, BEST *EVERYTHING*.

10

I'M MORE PROUD OF YOU THAN YOU CAN IMAGINE.

BY *EVERY* OBJECTIVE MEASURE, *YOU* SHOULD BE PILOTING ONE OF THOSE ROBOS.

BUT I'M GLAD YOU'RE *NOT*.

WHY SHOULD YOU BE AT THE *WHIM* OF SOME ALIEN ROBO'S *FLAWED CHOICES*...

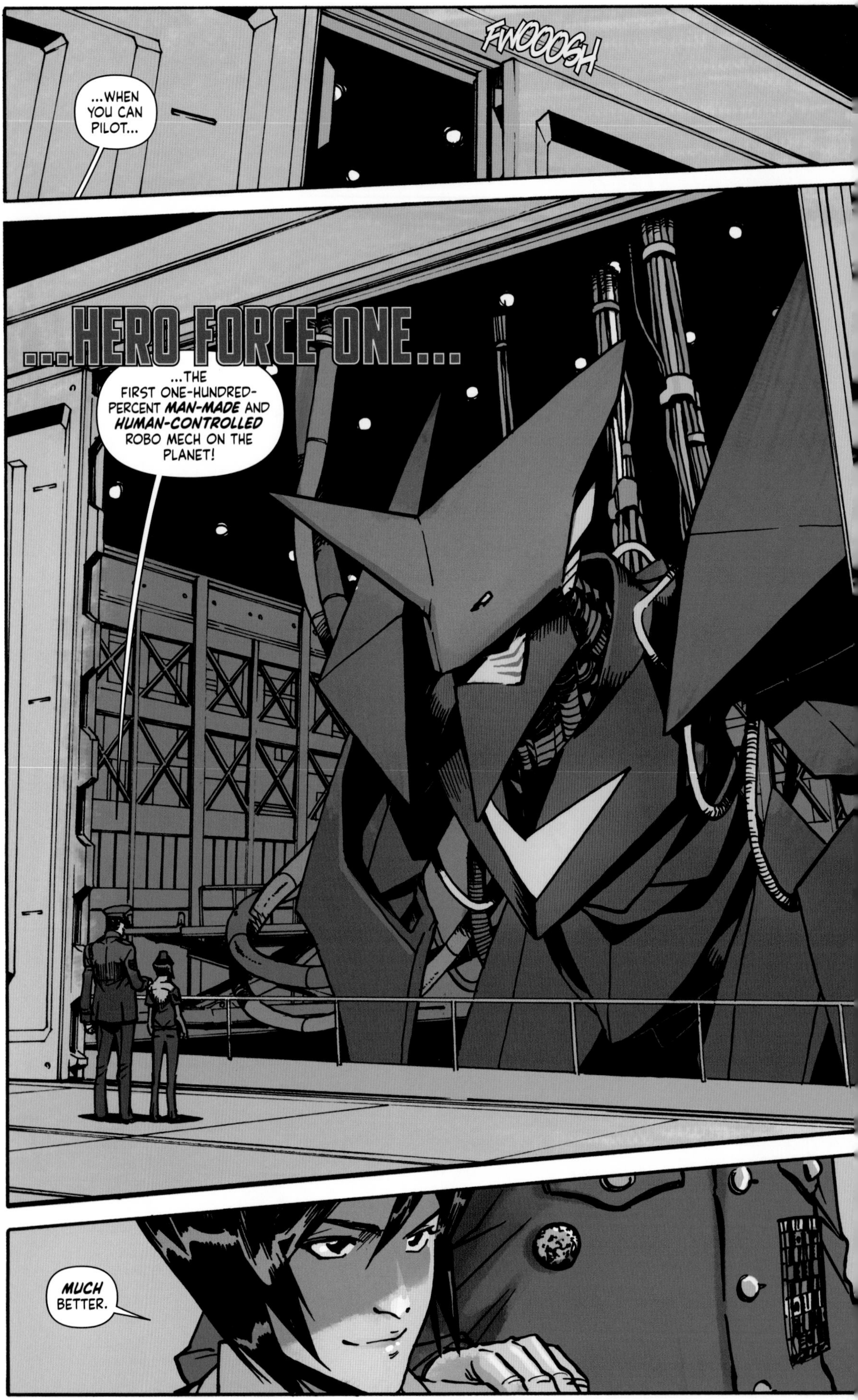

FWOOOSH
...WHEN YOU CAN PILOT...
...HERO FORCE ONE...
...THE FIRST ONE-HUNDRED-PERCENT MAN-MADE AND HUMAN-CONTROLLED ROBO MECH ON THE PLANET!
MUCH BETTER.

CHAPTER TWO

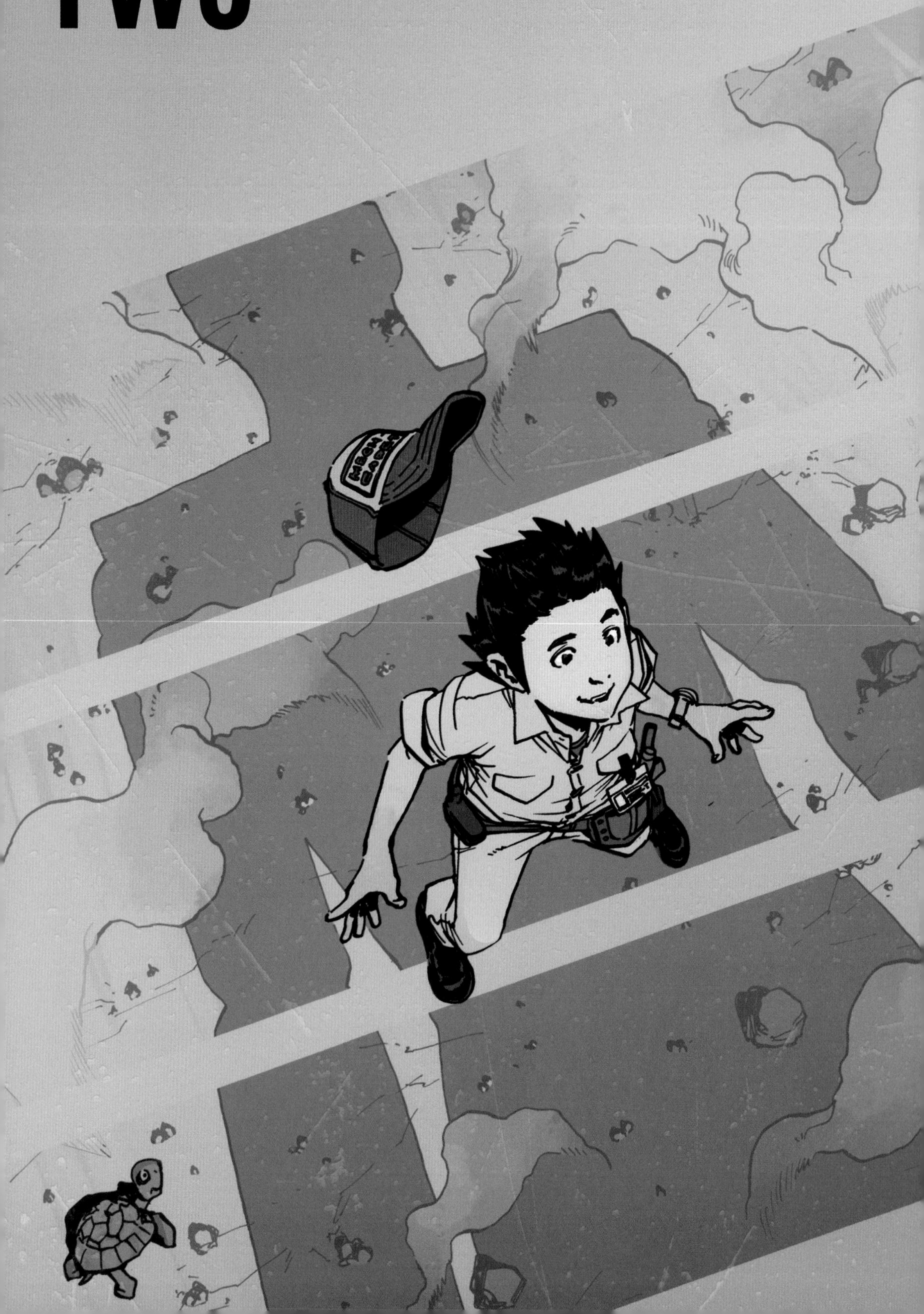

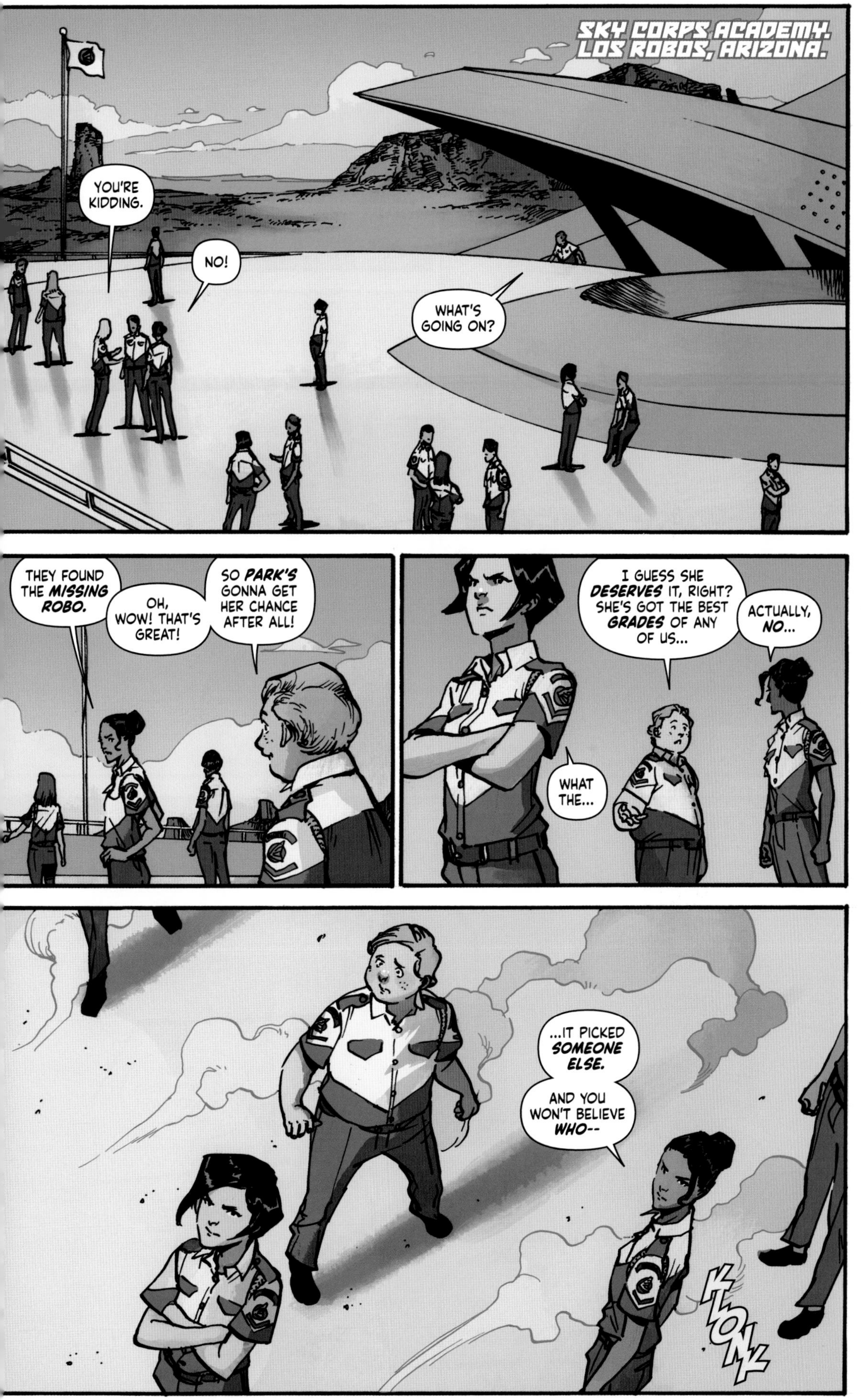
SKY CORPS ACADEMY. LOS ROBOS, ARIZONA.
YOU'RE KIDDING.
NO!
WHAT'S GOING ON?
THEY FOUND THE MISSING ROBO.
OH, WOW! THAT'S GREAT!
SO PARK'S GONNA GET HER CHANCE AFTER ALL!
I GUESS SHE DESERVES IT, RIGHT? SHE'S GOT THE BEST GRADES OF ANY OF US...
ACTUALLY, NO...
WHAT THE...
...IT PICKED SOMEONE ELSE.
AND YOU WON'T BELIEVE WHO--
KLONK

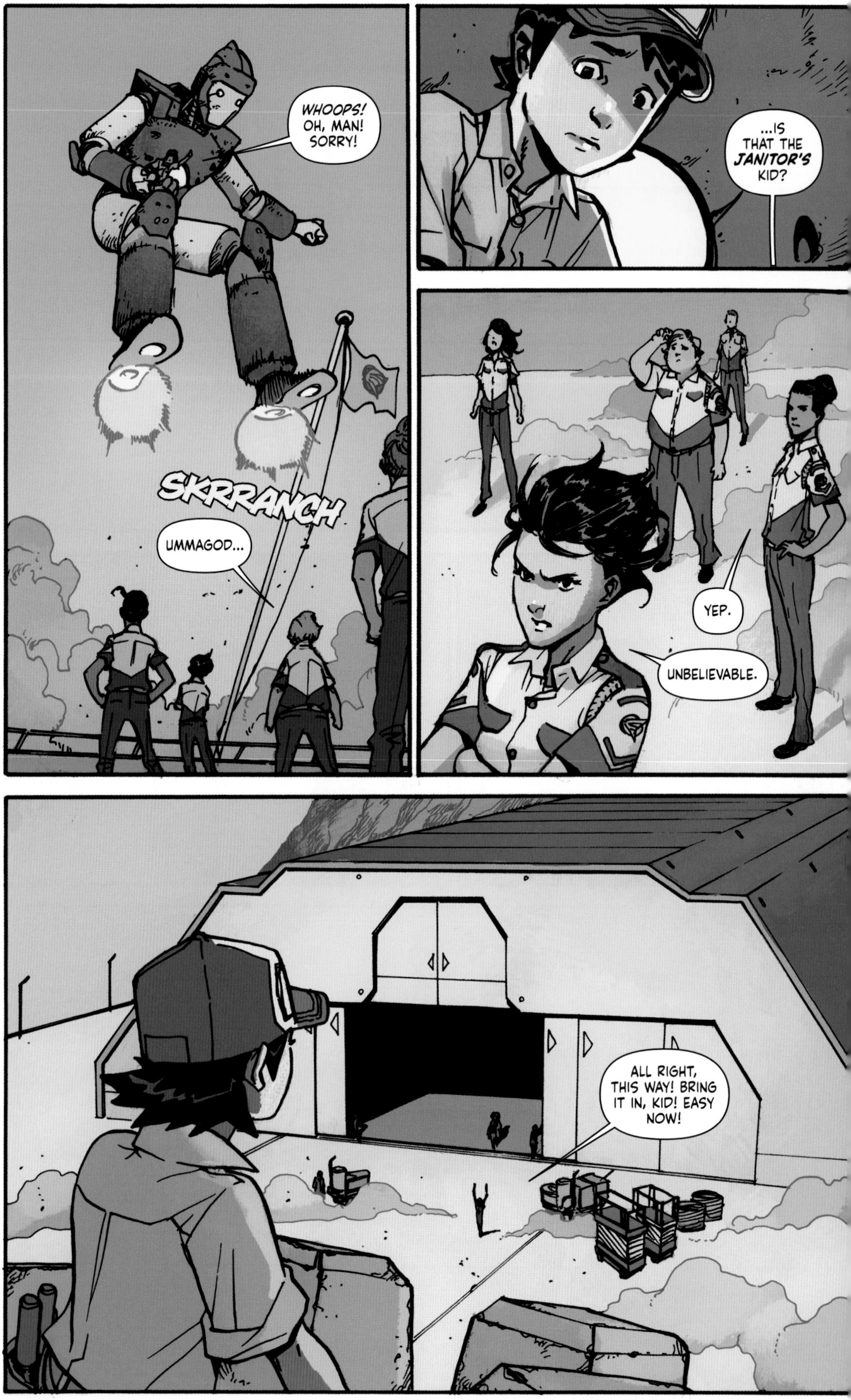
WHOOPS! OH, MAN! SORRY!
SKRRANCH
UMMAGOD...
...IS THAT THE JANITOR'S KID?
YEP.
UNBELIEVABLE.
ALL RIGHT, THIS WAY! BRING IT IN, KID! EASY NOW!

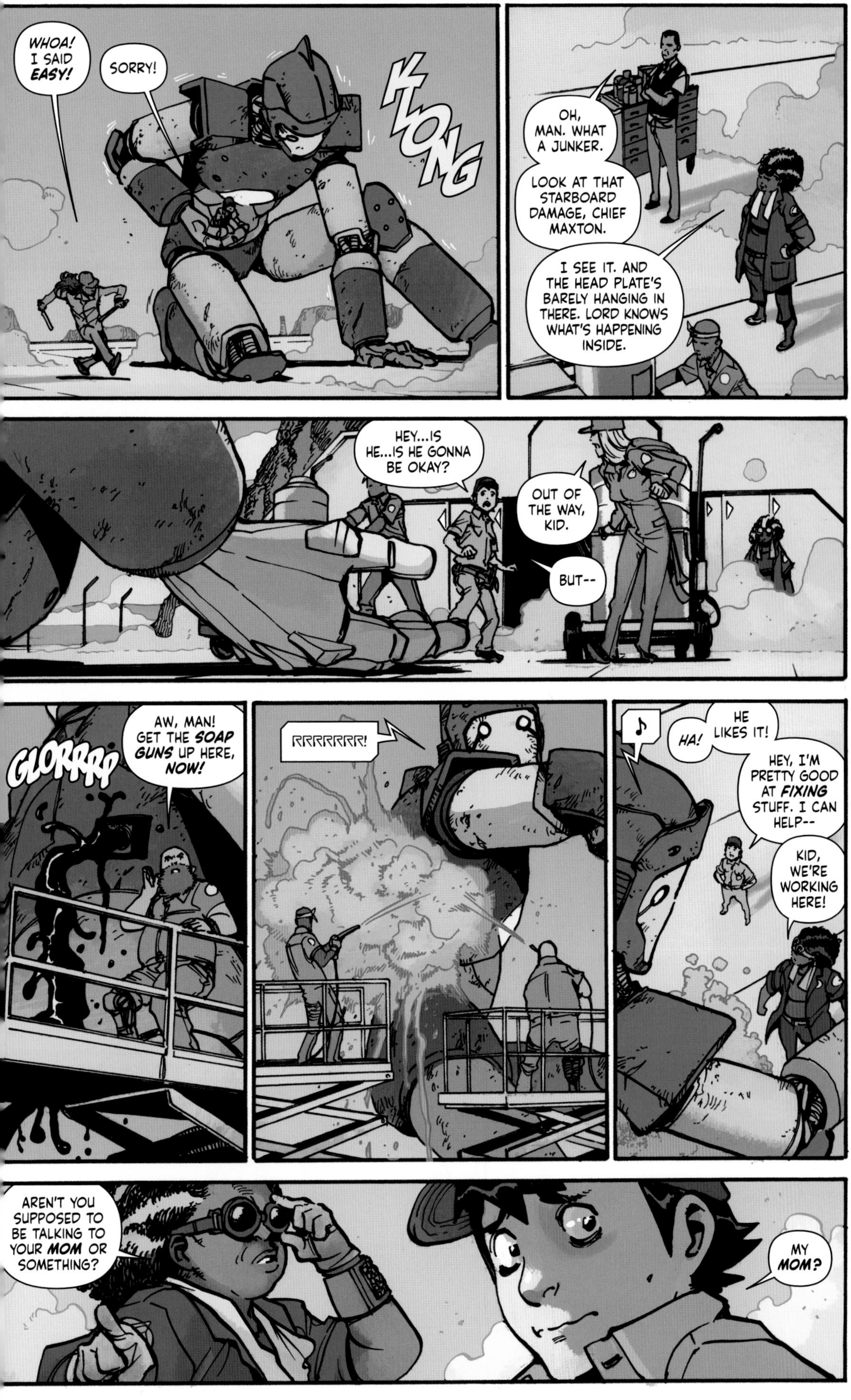

WHOA! I SAID EASY!
SORRY!
KLONG
OH, MAN. WHAT A JUNKER.
LOOK AT THAT STARBOARD DAMAGE, CHIEF MAXTON.
I SEE IT. AND THE HEAD PLATE'S BARELY HANGING IN THERE. LORD KNOWS WHAT'S HAPPENING INSIDE.
HEY...IS HE...IS HE GONNA BE OKAY?
OUT OF THE WAY, KID.
BUT--
GLORRRP
AW, MAN! GET THE SOAP GUNS UP HERE, NOW!
RRRRRRRR!
♪
HA!
HE LIKES IT!
HEY, I'M PRETTY GOOD AT FIXING STUFF. I CAN HELP--
KID, WE'RE WORKING HERE!
AREN'T YOU SUPPOSED TO BE TALKING TO YOUR MOM OR SOMETHING?
MY MOM?

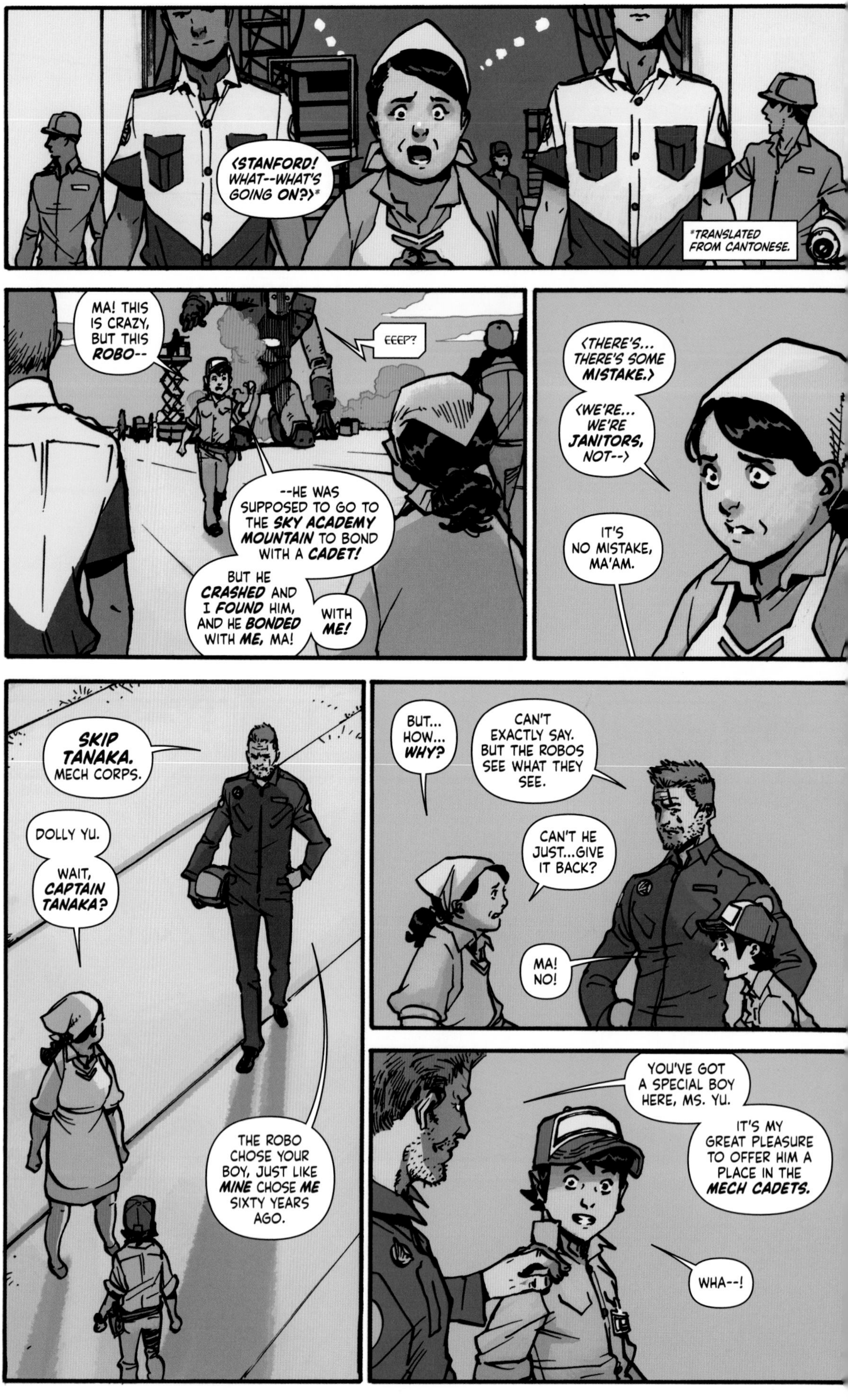

‹STANFORD! WHAT--WHAT'S GOING ON?›*
*TRANSLATED FROM CANTONESE.
MA! THIS IS CRAZY, BUT THIS ROBO--
EEEP?
--HE WAS SUPPOSED TO GO TO THE SKY ACADEMY MOUNTAIN TO BOND WITH A CADET!
BUT HE CRASHED AND I FOUND HIM, AND HE BONDED WITH ME, MA!
WITH ME!
‹THERE'S... THERE'S SOME MISTAKE.›
‹WE'RE... WE'RE JANITORS, NOT--›
IT'S NO MISTAKE, MA'AM.
SKIP TANAKA. MECH CORPS.
DOLLY YU.
WAIT, CAPTAIN TANAKA?
THE ROBO CHOSE YOUR BOY, JUST LIKE MINE CHOSE ME SIXTY YEARS AGO.
BUT... HOW... WHY?
CAN'T EXACTLY SAY. BUT THE ROBOS SEE WHAT THEY SEE.
CAN'T HE JUST...GIVE IT BACK?
MA! NO!
YOU'VE GOT A SPECIAL BOY HERE, MS. YU.
IT'S MY GREAT PLEASURE TO OFFER HIM A PLACE IN THE MECH CADETS.
WHA--!

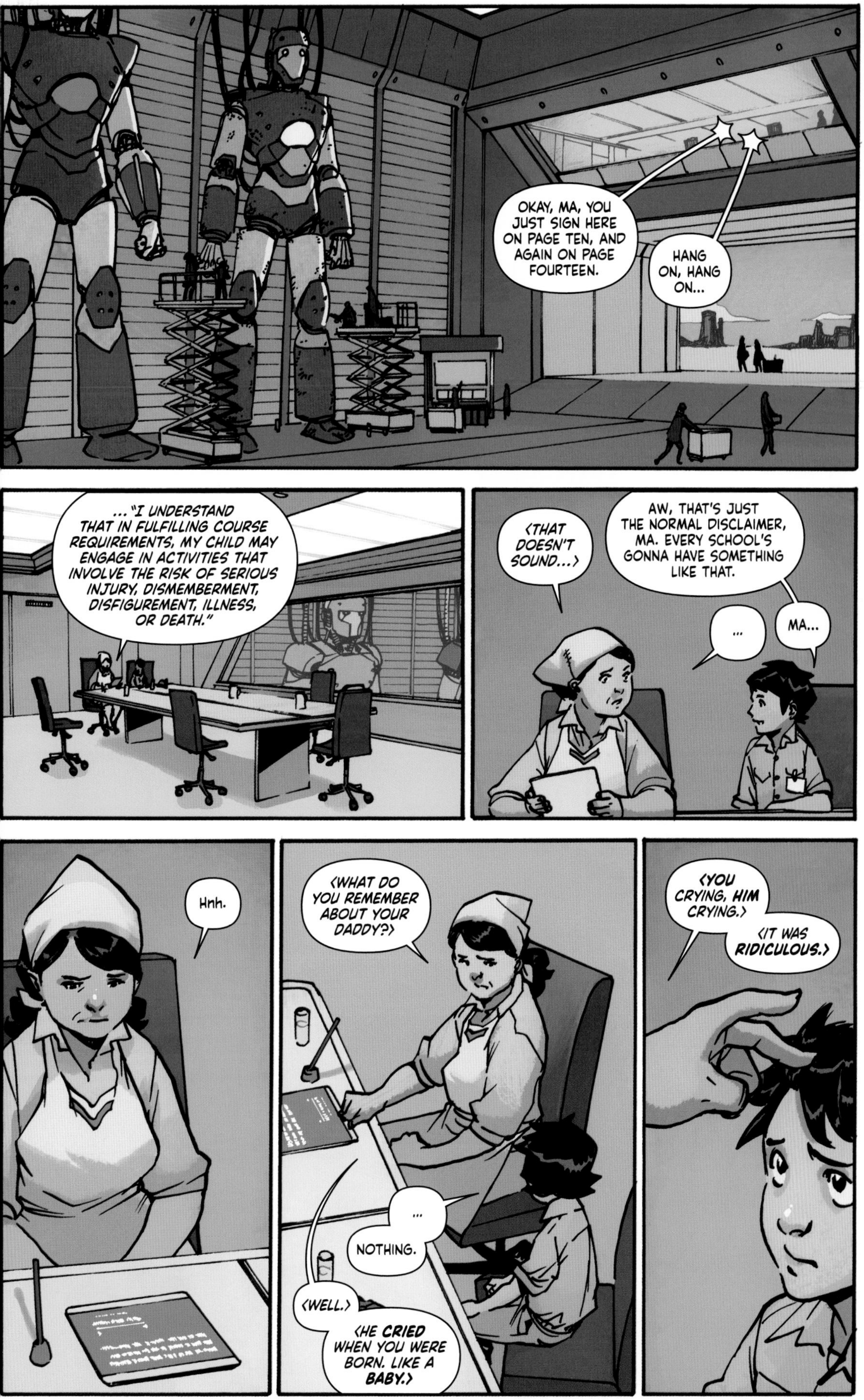
OKAY, MA, YOU JUST SIGN HERE ON PAGE TEN, AND AGAIN ON PAGE FOURTEEN.
HANG ON, HANG ON...
..."I UNDERSTAND THAT IN FULFILLING COURSE REQUIREMENTS, MY CHILD MAY ENGAGE IN ACTIVITIES THAT INVOLVE THE RISK OF SERIOUS INJURY, DISMEMBERMENT, DISFIGUREMENT, ILLNESS, OR DEATH."
‹THAT DOESN'T SOUND...›
AW, THAT'S JUST THE NORMAL DISCLAIMER, MA. EVERY SCHOOL'S GONNA HAVE SOMETHING LIKE THAT.
...
MA...
Hnh.
‹WHAT DO YOU REMEMBER ABOUT YOUR DADDY?›
...
NOTHING.
‹WELL.›
‹HE **CRIED** WHEN YOU WERE BORN. LIKE A **BABY.**›
‹YOU CRYING, **HIM** CRYING.›
‹IT WAS **RIDICULOUS.**›

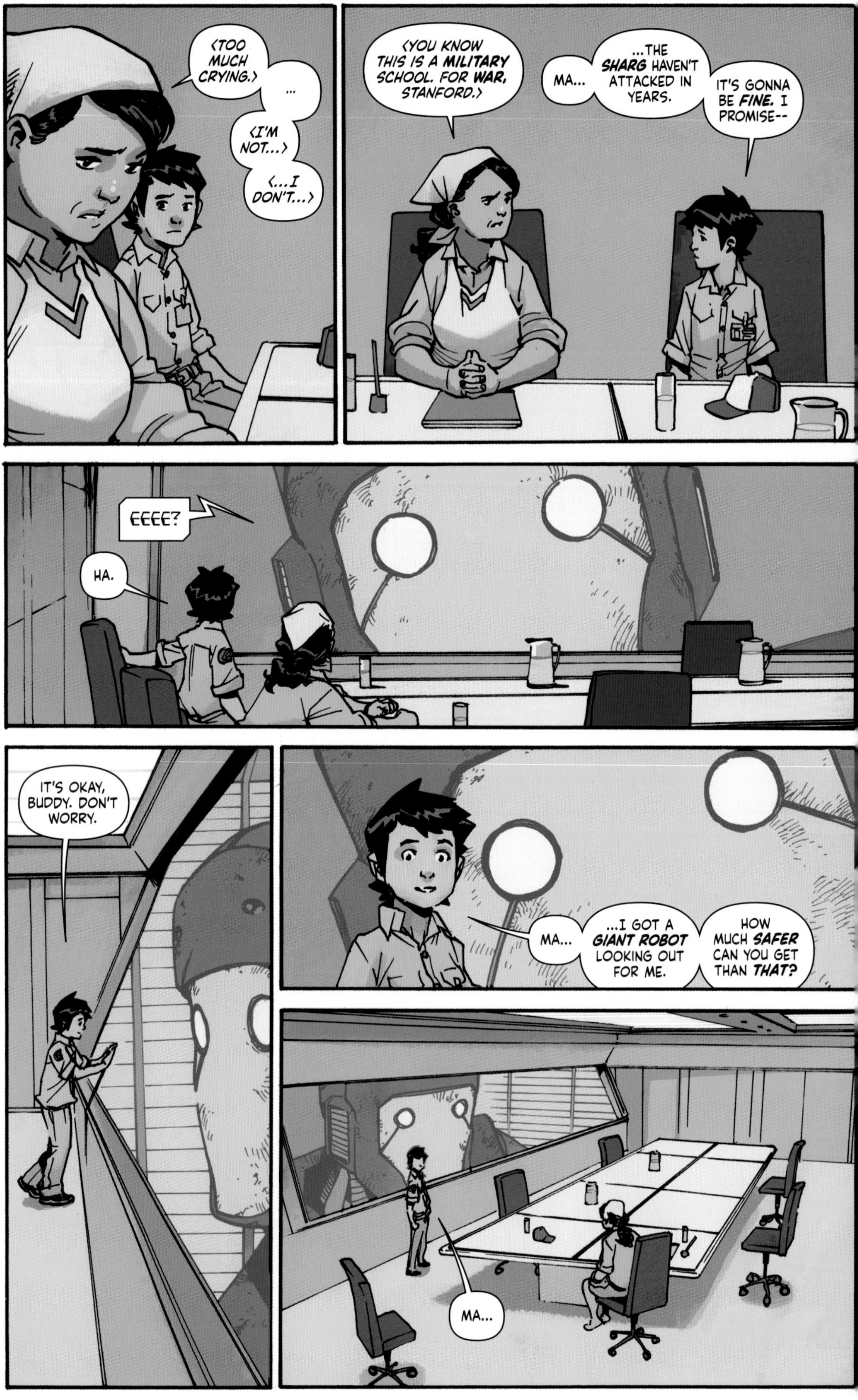
<TOO MUCH CRYING.>
...
<I'M NOT...>
<...I DON'T...>
<YOU KNOW THIS IS A MILITARY SCHOOL. FOR WAR, STANFORD.>
MA...
...THE SHARG HAVEN'T ATTACKED IN YEARS.
IT'S GONNA BE FINE. I PROMISE--
EEEE?
HA.
IT'S OKAY, BUDDY. DON'T WORRY.
MA...
...I GOT A GIANT ROBOT LOOKING OUT FOR ME.
HOW MUCH SAFER CAN YOU GET THAN THAT?
MA...

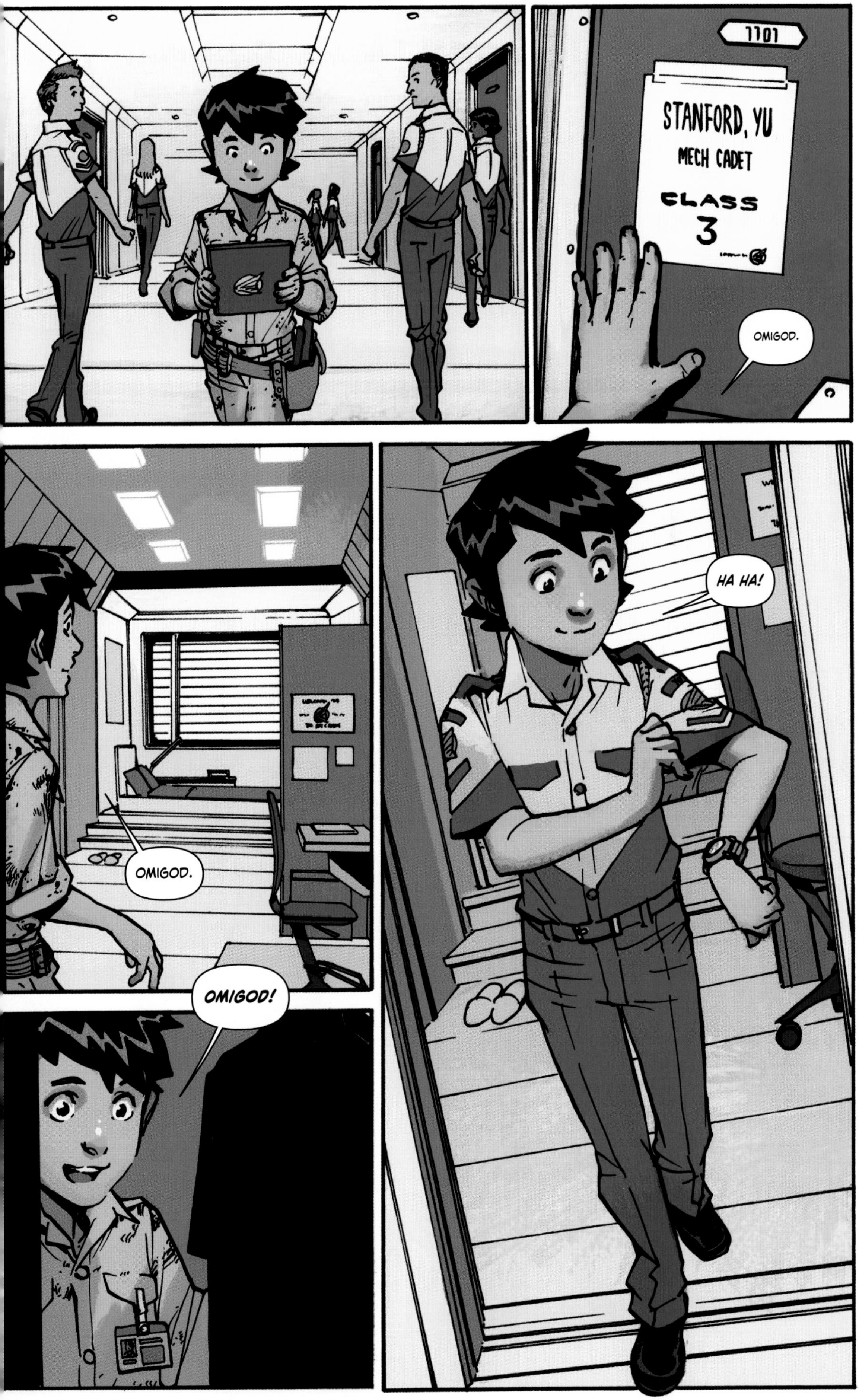
1101
STANFORD, YU
MECH CADET
CLASS
3
OMIGOD.
OMIGOD.
OMIGOD!
HA HA!

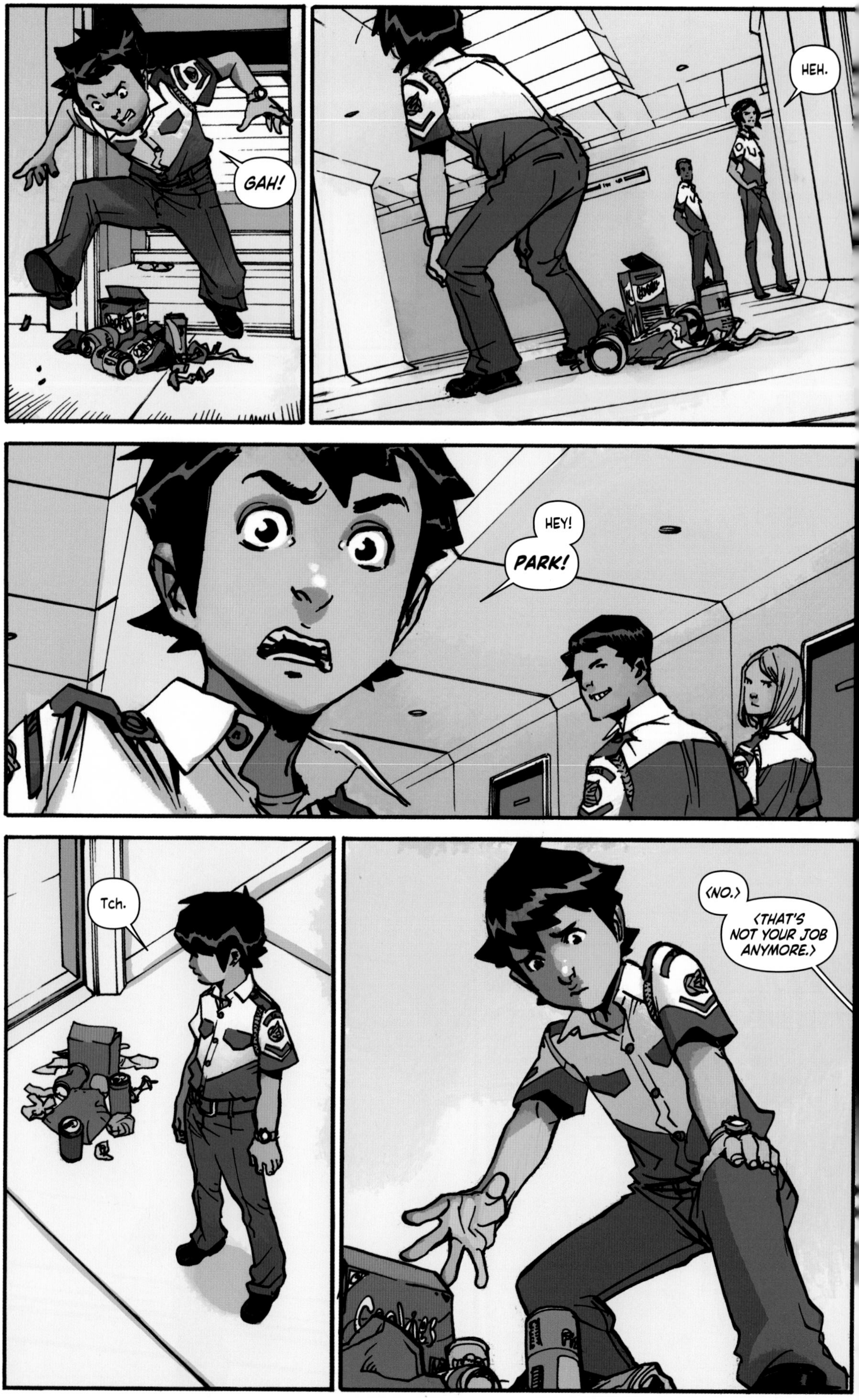
GAH!
HEH.
HEY!
PARK!
Tch.
‹NO.›
‹THAT'S NOT YOUR JOB ANYMORE.›

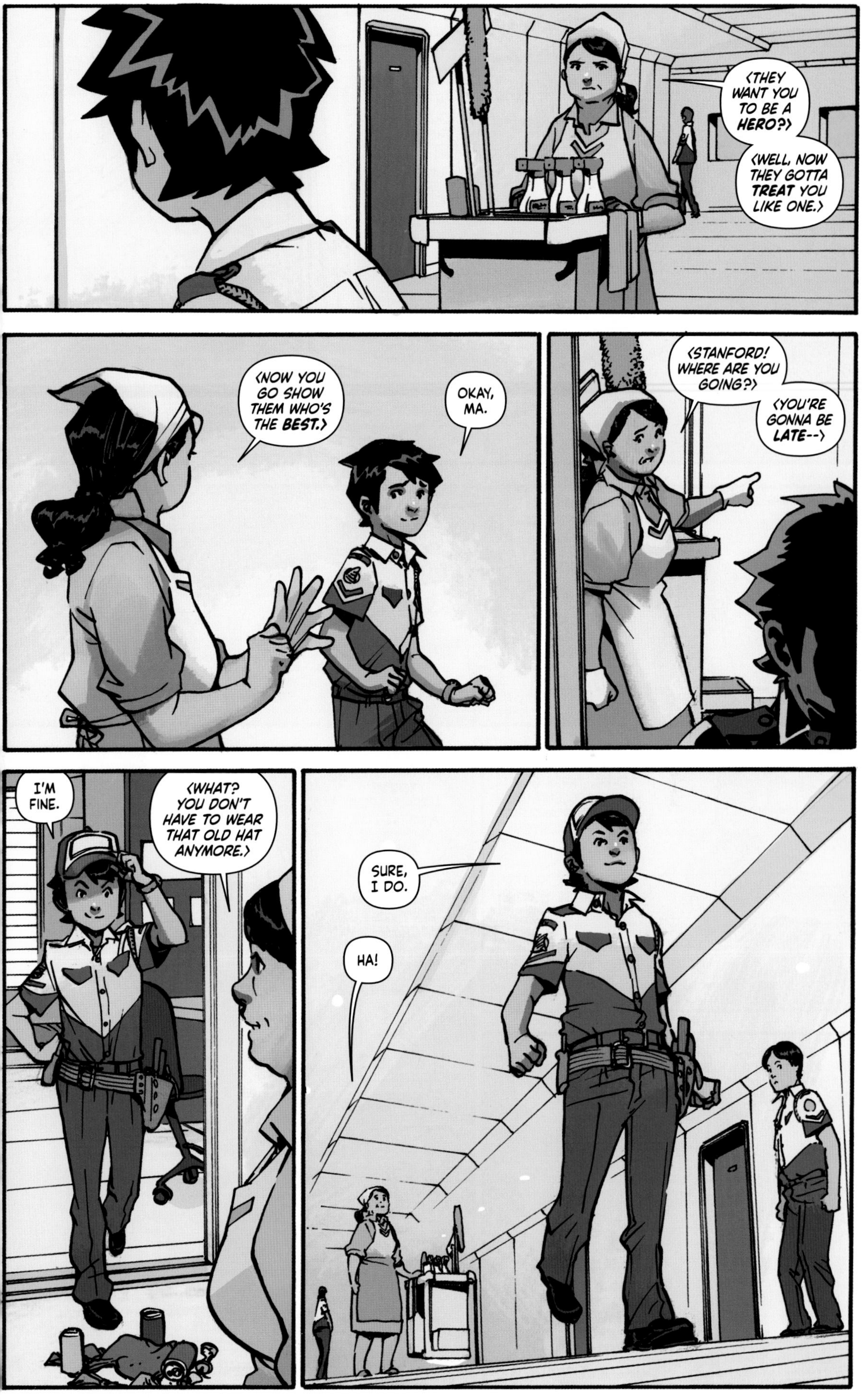
<THEY WANT YOU TO BE A HERO?>
<WELL, NOW THEY GOTTA TREAT YOU LIKE ONE.>
<NOW YOU GO SHOW THEM WHO'S THE BEST.>
OKAY, MA.
<STANFORD! WHERE ARE YOU GOING?>
<YOU'RE GONNA BE LATE-->
I'M FINE.
<WHAT? YOU DON'T HAVE TO WEAR THAT OLD HAT ANYMORE.>
SURE, I DO.
HA!

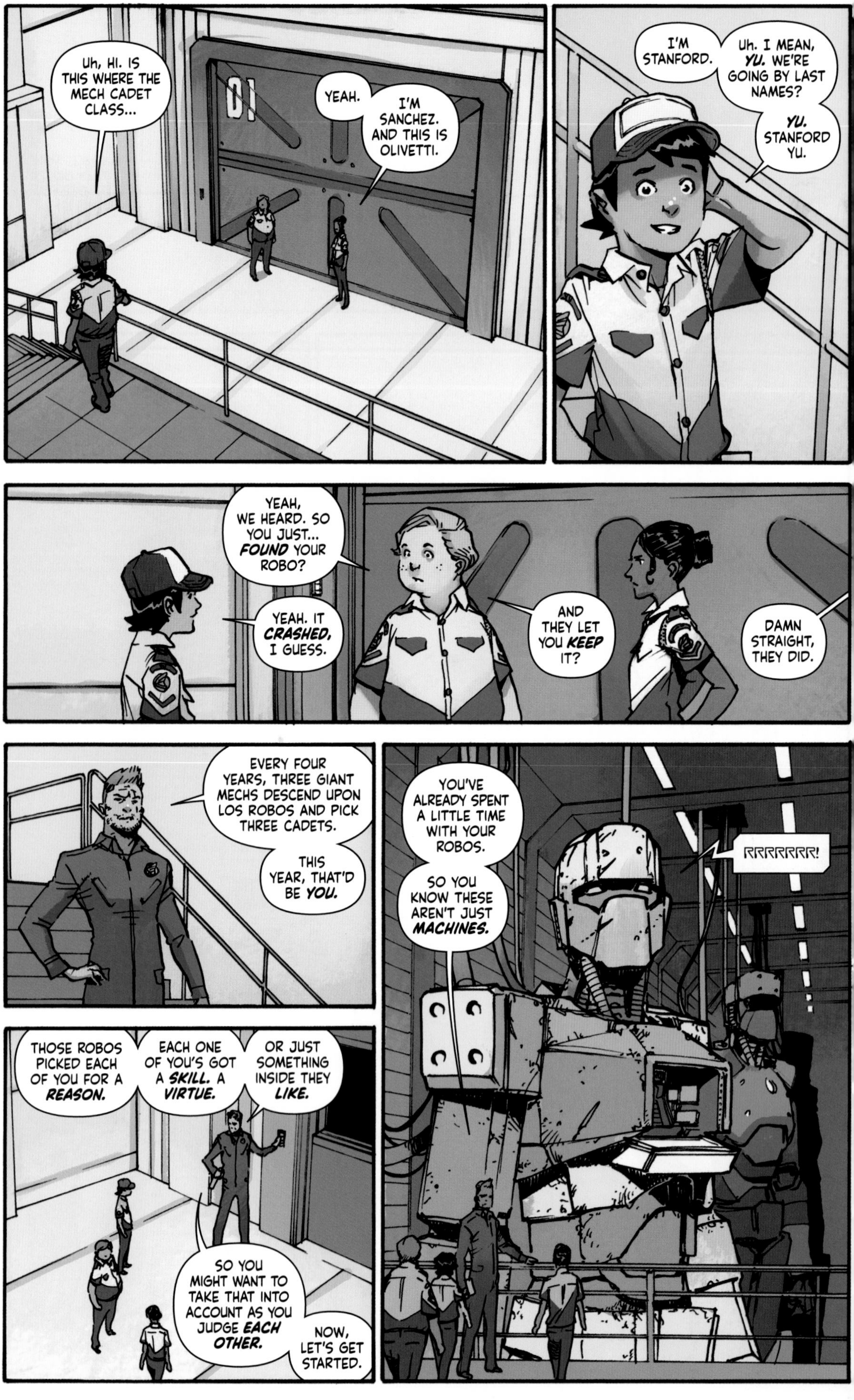
Uh, HI. IS THIS WHERE THE MECH CADET CLASS...
YEAH.
I'M SANCHEZ. AND THIS IS OLIVETTI.
I'M STANFORD.
Uh. I MEAN, YU. WE'RE GOING BY LAST NAMES?
YU. STANFORD YU.
YEAH, WE HEARD. SO YOU JUST... FOUND YOUR ROBO?
YEAH. IT CRASHED, I GUESS.
AND THEY LET YOU KEEP IT?
DAMN STRAIGHT, THEY DID.
EVERY FOUR YEARS, THREE GIANT MECHS DESCEND UPON LOS ROBOS AND PICK THREE CADETS.
THIS YEAR, THAT'D BE YOU.
THOSE ROBOS PICKED EACH OF YOU FOR A REASON.
EACH ONE OF YOU'S GOT A SKILL. A VIRTUE.
OR JUST SOMETHING INSIDE THEY LIKE.
SO YOU MIGHT WANT TO TAKE THAT INTO ACCOUNT AS YOU JUDGE EACH OTHER.
NOW, LET'S GET STARTED.
YOU'VE ALREADY SPENT A LITTLE TIME WITH YOUR ROBOS.
SO YOU KNOW THESE AREN'T JUST MACHINES.
RRRRRRRR!

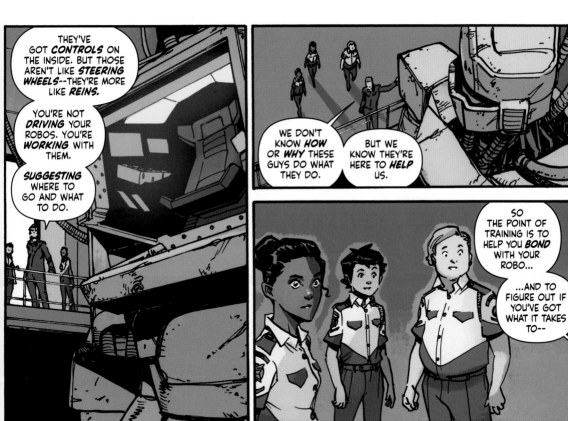

THEY'VE GOT **CONTROLS** ON THE INSIDE. BUT THOSE AREN'T LIKE **STEERING WHEELS**--THEY'RE MORE LIKE **REINS**.

YOU'RE NOT **DRIVING** YOUR ROBOS. YOU'RE **WORKING** WITH THEM.

SUGGESTING WHERE TO GO AND WHAT TO DO.

WE DON'T KNOW **HOW** OR **WHY** THESE GUYS DO WHAT THEY DO.

BUT WE KNOW THEY'RE HERE TO **HELP** US.

SO THE POINT OF TRAINING IS TO HELP YOU **BOND** WITH YOUR ROBO...

...AND TO FIGURE OUT IF YOU'VE GOT WHAT IT TAKES TO--

AHEM.

GENERAL. WHAT CAN I DO FOR YOU?

I HAVE ANOTHER STUDENT FOR YOU, CAPTAIN.

THIS IS **CADET PARK**. SHE'S BEEN APPROVED BY THE BOARD OF GOVERNORS FOR ADMITTANCE INTO THIS CLASS.

GENERAL...

...EVERY CADET IN THIS CLASS WAS CHOSEN BY A **ROBO MECH**.

I CAN'T TRAIN...YOUR **DAUGHTER**... IF SHE DOESN'T HAVE A **ROBO**.

THAT'S NOT A PROBLEM.

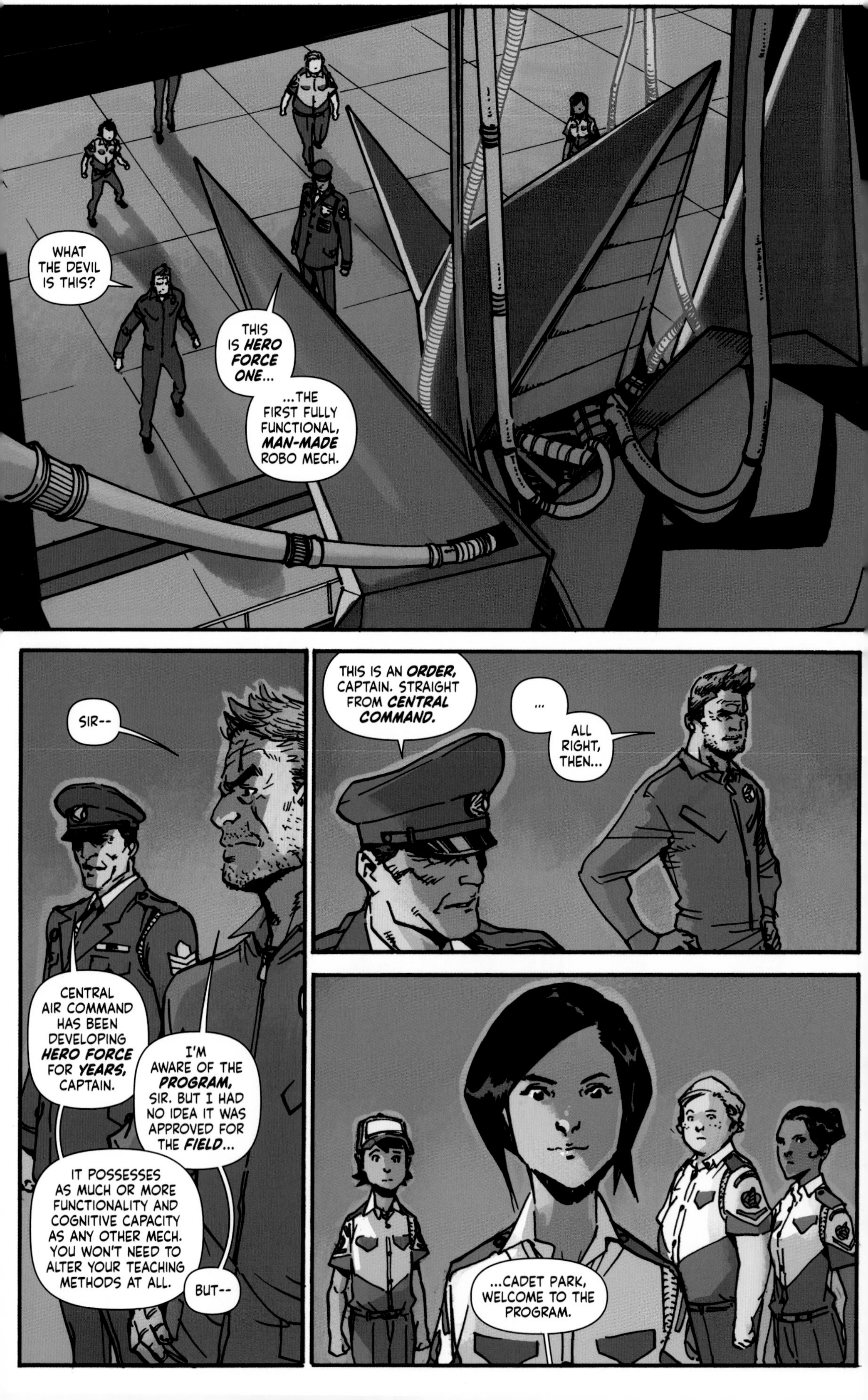
WHAT THE DEVIL IS THIS?
THIS IS HERO FORCE ONE...
...THE FIRST FULLY FUNCTIONAL, MAN-MADE ROBO MECH.
SIR--
CENTRAL AIR COMMAND HAS BEEN DEVELOPING HERO FORCE FOR YEARS, CAPTAIN.
I'M AWARE OF THE PROGRAM, SIR. BUT I HAD NO IDEA IT WAS APPROVED FOR THE FIELD...
IT POSSESSES AS MUCH OR MORE FUNCTIONALITY AND COGNITIVE CAPACITY AS ANY OTHER MECH. YOU WON'T NEED TO ALTER YOUR TEACHING METHODS AT ALL.
BUT--
THIS IS AN ORDER, CAPTAIN. STRAIGHT FROM CENTRAL COMMAND.
...
ALL RIGHT, THEN...
...CADET PARK, WELCOME TO THE PROGRAM.

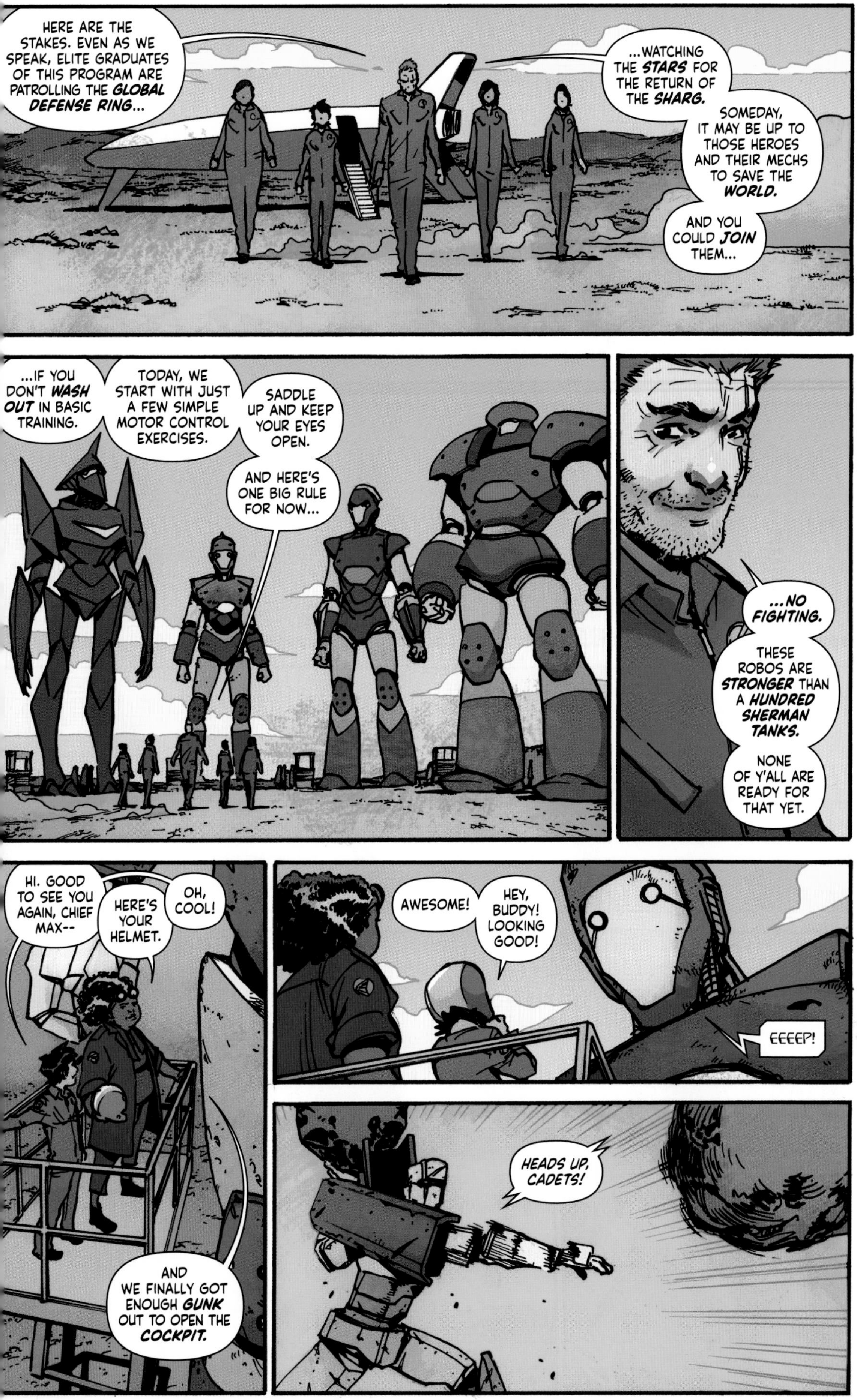
HERE ARE THE STAKES. EVEN AS WE SPEAK, ELITE GRADUATES OF THIS PROGRAM ARE PATROLLING THE GLOBAL DEFENSE RING...
...WATCHING THE STARS FOR THE RETURN OF THE SHARG.
SOMEDAY, IT MAY BE UP TO THOSE HEROES AND THEIR MECHS TO SAVE THE WORLD.
AND YOU COULD JOIN THEM...
...IF YOU DON'T WASH OUT IN BASIC TRAINING.
TODAY, WE START WITH JUST A FEW SIMPLE MOTOR CONTROL EXERCISES.
SADDLE UP AND KEEP YOUR EYES OPEN.
AND HERE'S ONE BIG RULE FOR NOW...
...NO FIGHTING.
THESE ROBOS ARE STRONGER THAN A HUNDRED SHERMAN TANKS.
NONE OF Y'ALL ARE READY FOR THAT YET.
HI. GOOD TO SEE YOU AGAIN, CHIEF MAX--
HERE'S YOUR HELMET.
OH, COOL!
AND WE FINALLY GOT ENOUGH GUNK OUT TO OPEN THE COCKPIT.
AWESOME!
HEY, BUDDY! LOOKING GOOD!
EEEEP!
HEADS UP, CADETS!

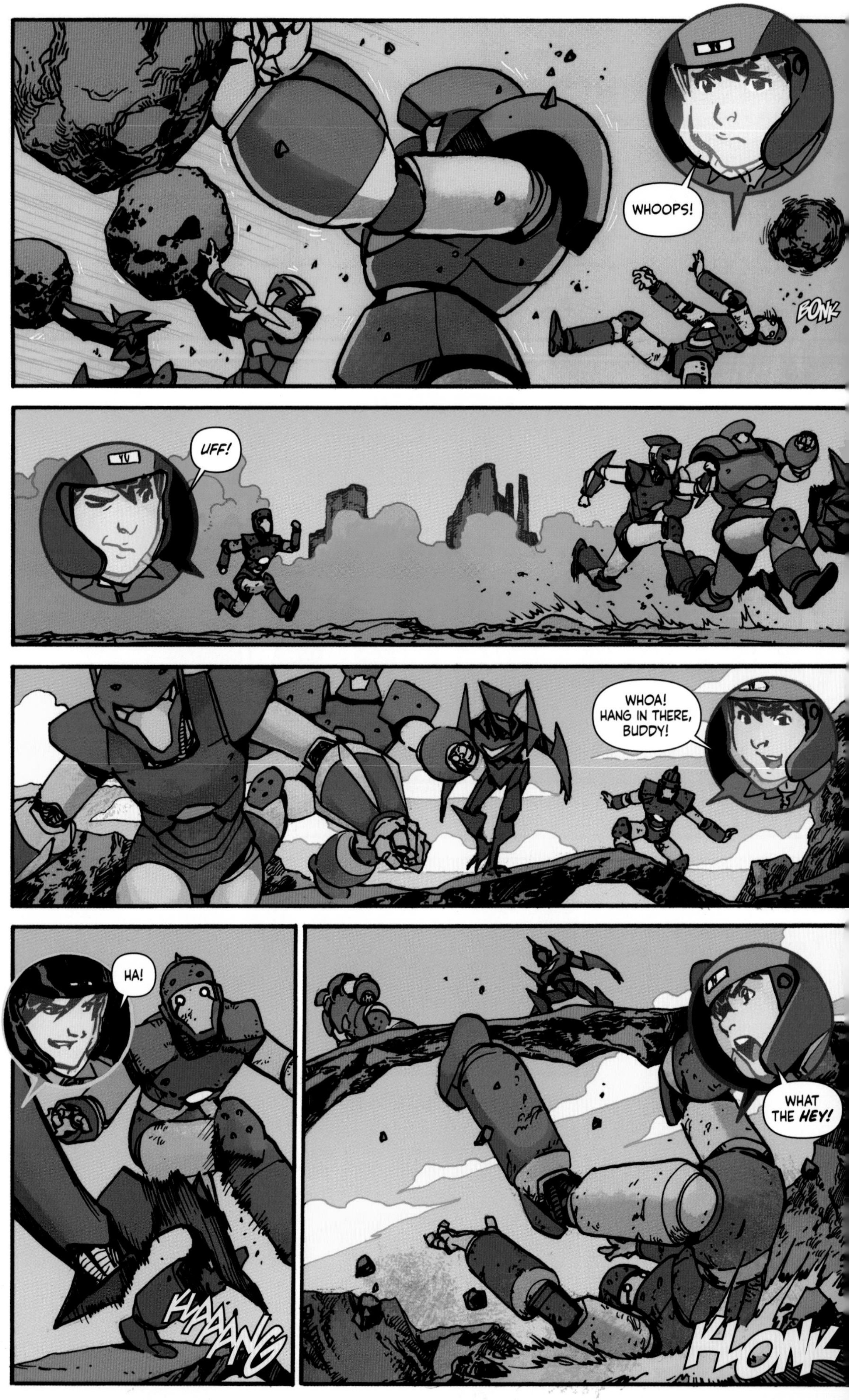
WHOOPS!
BONK
UFF!
WHOA! HANG IN THERE, BUDDY!
HA!
KWAAANG
WHAT THE HEY!
KLONK

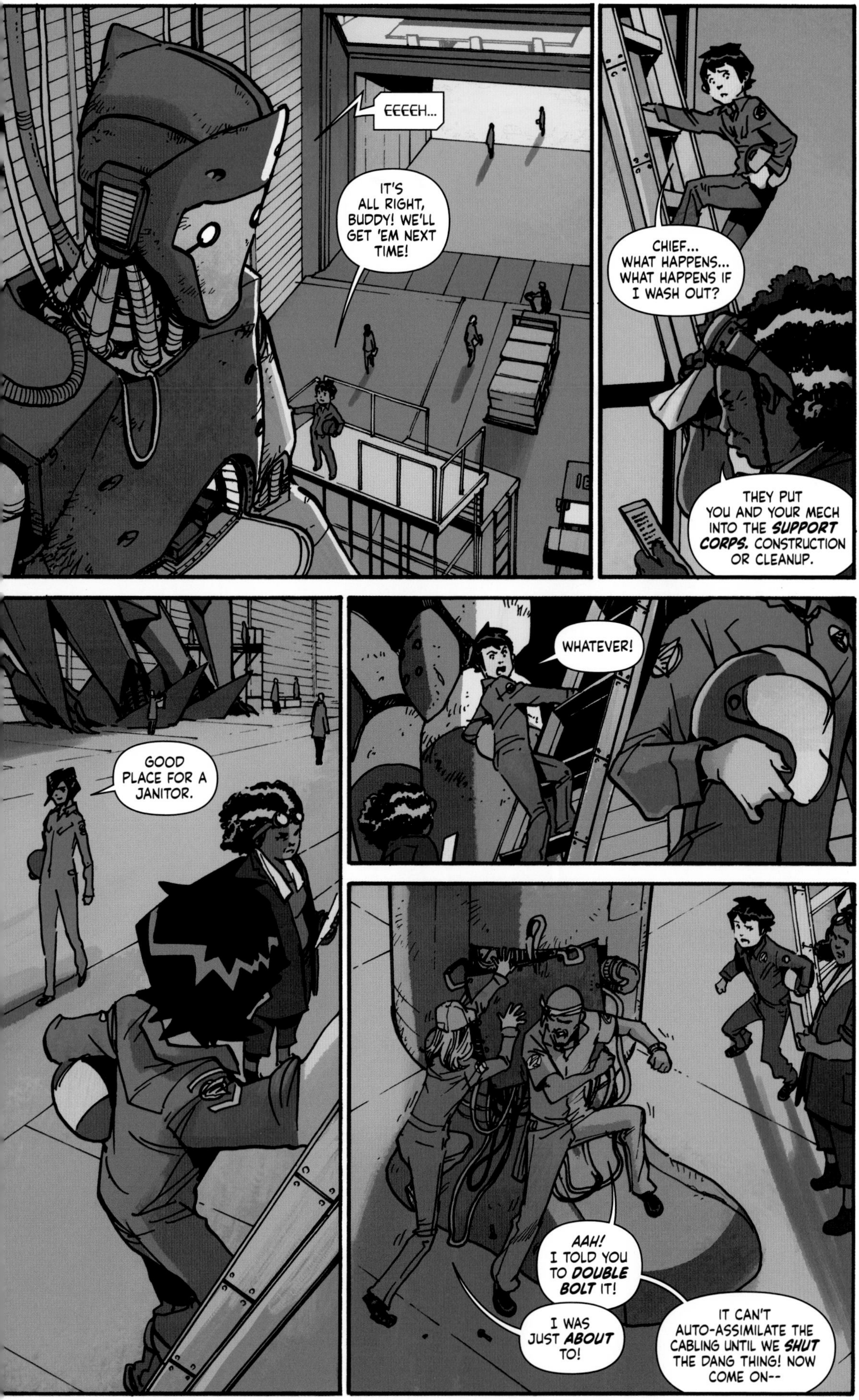
EEEEH...
IT'S ALL RIGHT, BUDDY! WE'LL GET 'EM NEXT TIME!
CHIEF... WHAT HAPPENS... WHAT HAPPENS IF I WASH OUT?
THEY PUT YOU AND YOUR MECH INTO THE SUPPORT CORPS. CONSTRUCTION OR CLEANUP.
GOOD PLACE FOR A JANITOR.
WHATEVER!
AAH! I TOLD YOU TO DOUBLE BOLT IT!
I WAS JUST ABOUT TO!
IT CAN'T AUTO-ASSIMILATE THE CABLING UNTIL WE SHUT THE DANG THING! NOW COME ON--

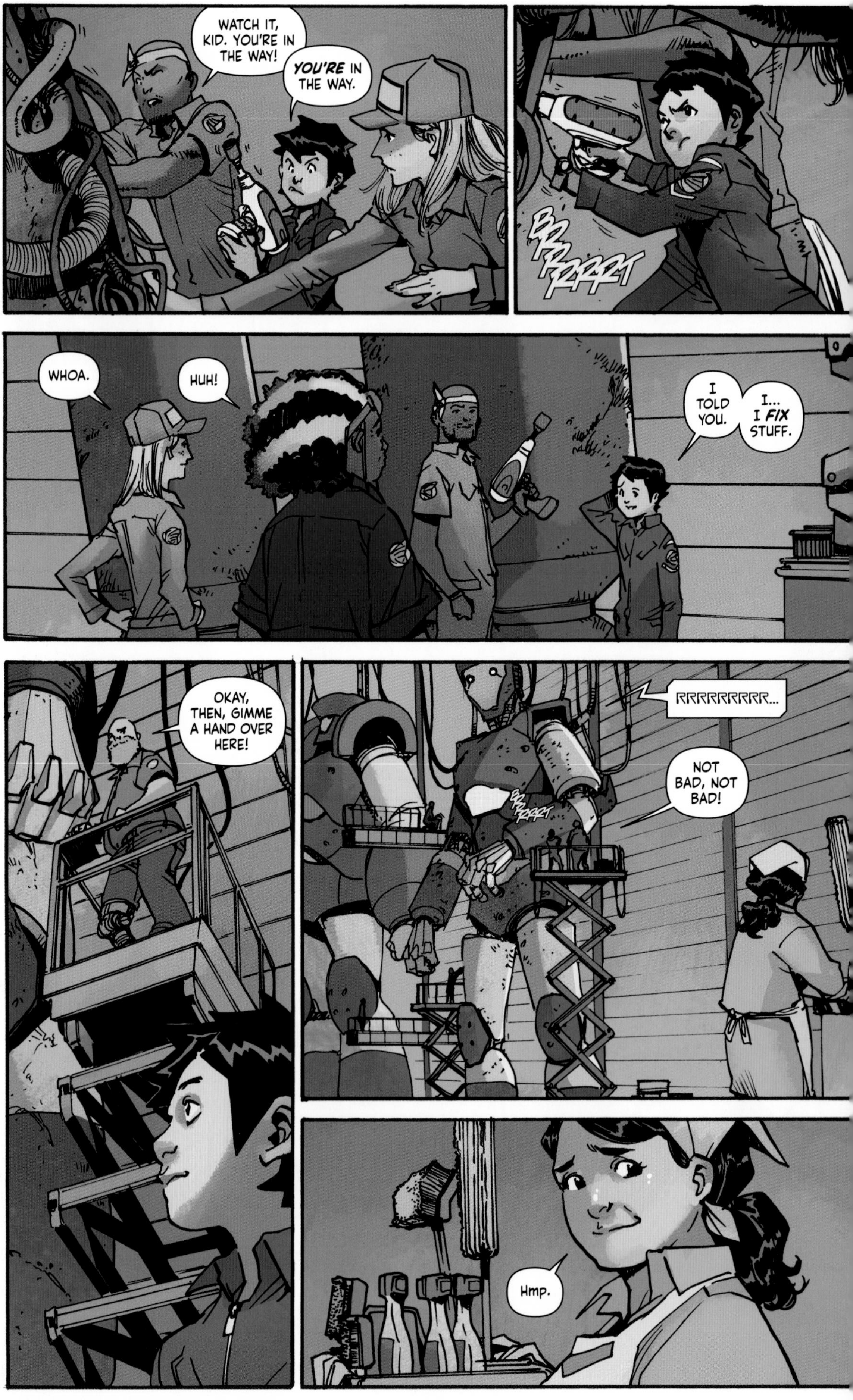
WATCH IT, KID. YOU'RE IN THE WAY!
YOU'RE IN THE WAY.
BRRRRRRRT
WHOA.
HUH!
I TOLD YOU.
I... I FIX STUFF.
OKAY, THEN, GIMME A HAND OVER HERE!
RRRRRRRRRR...
NOT BAD, NOT BAD!
Hmp.

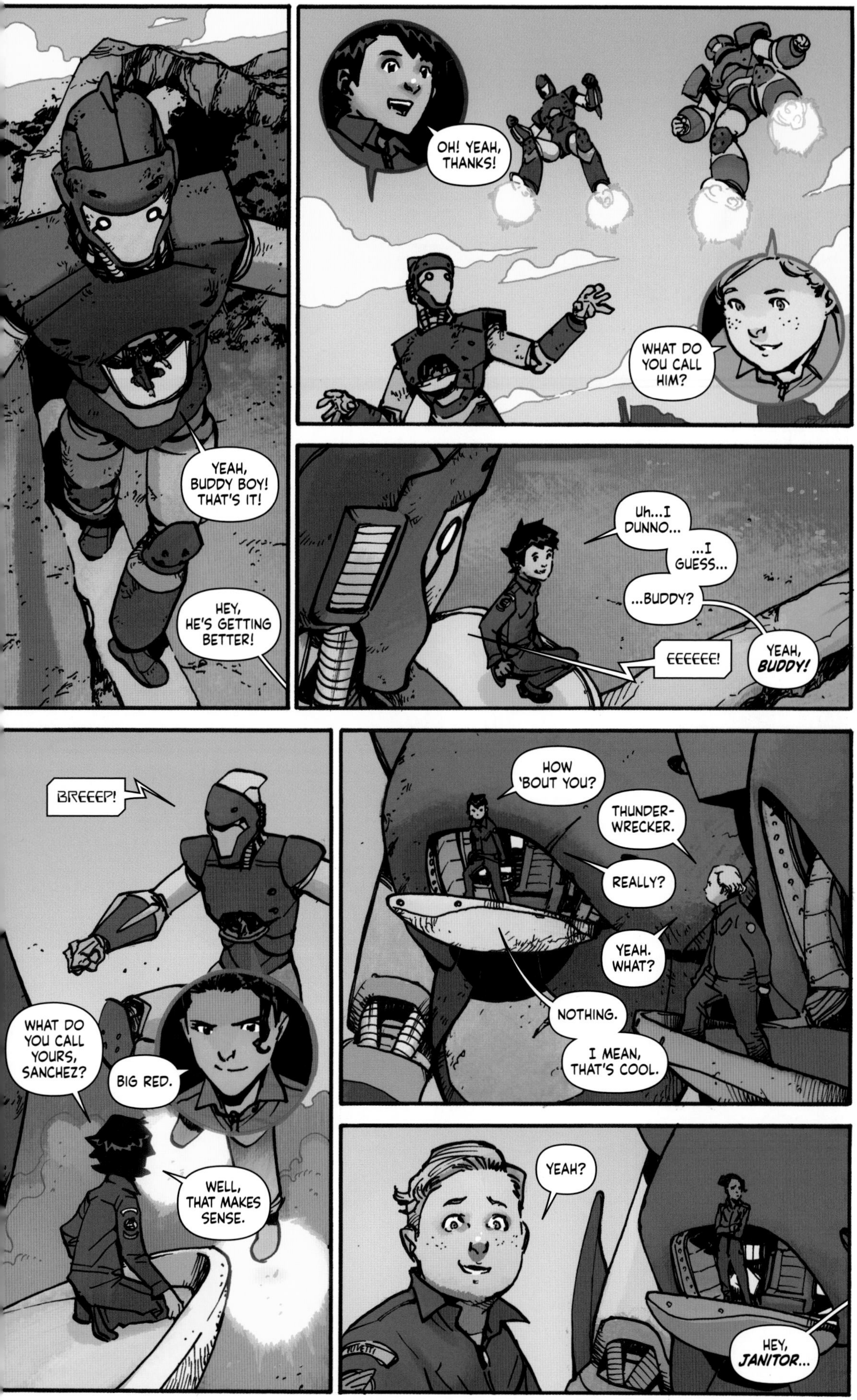

YEAH, BUDDY BOY! THAT'S IT!
HEY, HE'S GETTING BETTER!
OH! YEAH, THANKS!
WHAT DO YOU CALL HIM?
Uh...I DUNNO...
...I GUESS...
...BUDDY?
EEEEEE!
YEAH, *BUDDY!*
BREEEP!
WHAT DO YOU CALL YOURS, SANCHEZ?
BIG RED.
WELL, THAT MAKES SENSE.
HOW 'BOUT YOU?
THUNDER-WRECKER.
REALLY?
YEAH. WHAT?
NOTHING.
I MEAN, THAT'S COOL.
YEAH?
HEY, *JANITOR...*

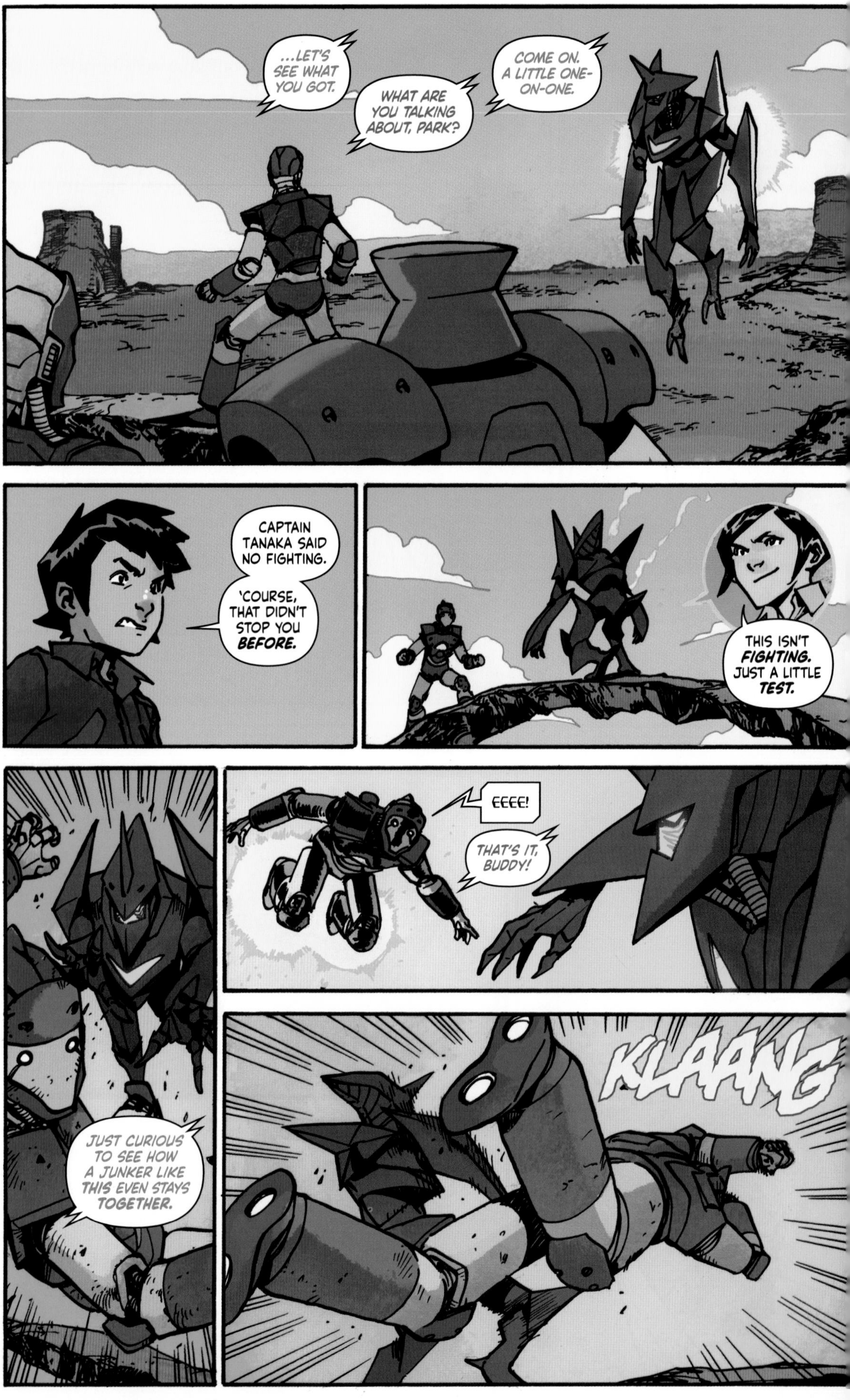
...LET'S SEE WHAT YOU GOT.
WHAT ARE YOU TALKING ABOUT, PARK?
COME ON. A LITTLE ONE-ON-ONE.
CAPTAIN TANAKA SAID NO FIGHTING.
'COURSE, THAT DIDN'T STOP YOU BEFORE.
THIS ISN'T FIGHTING. JUST A LITTLE TEST.
JUST CURIOUS TO SEE HOW A JUNKER LIKE THIS EVEN STAYS TOGETHER.
EEEE!
THAT'S IT, BUDDY!
KLAANG

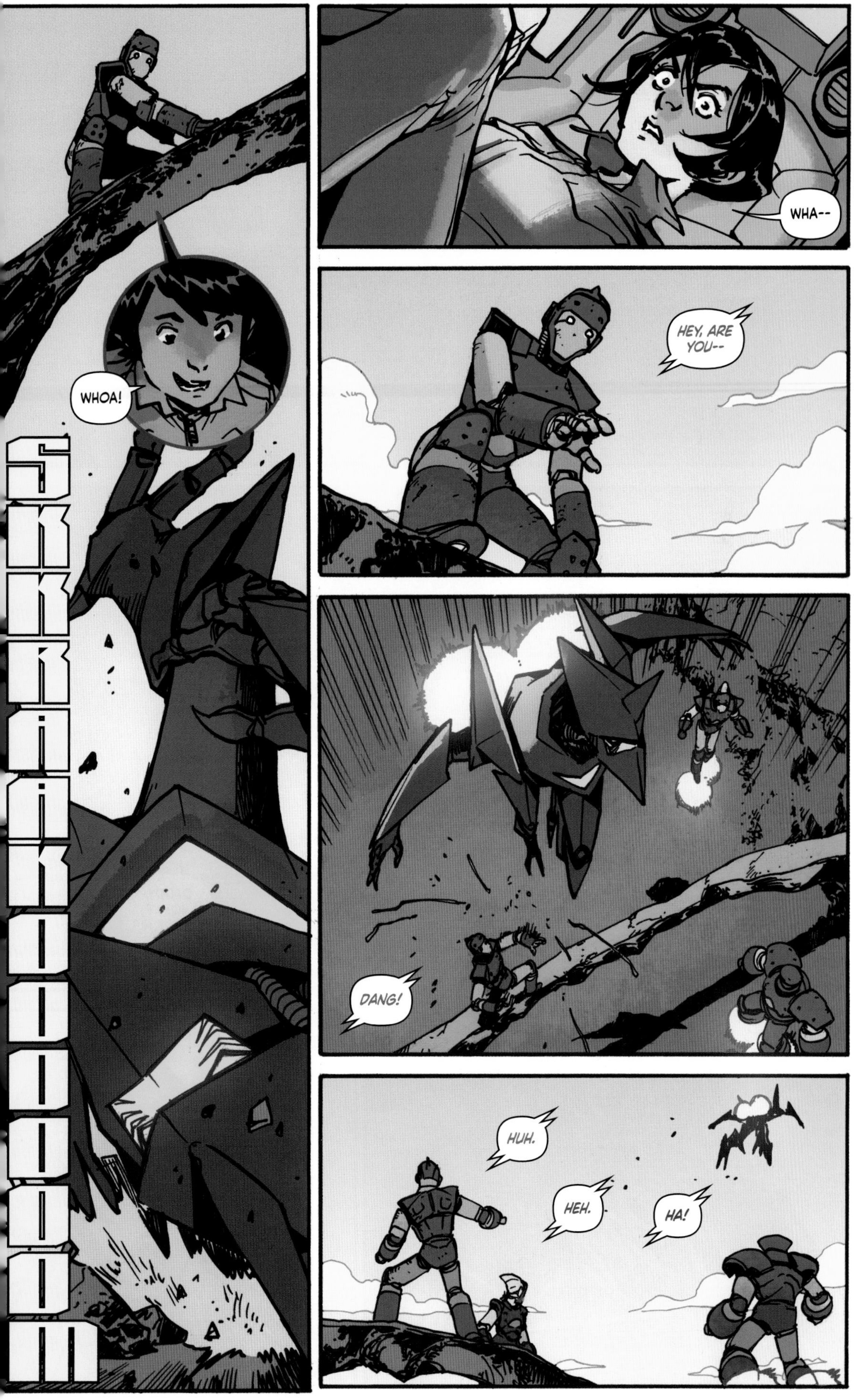
WHOA!
SKRAKOOOOOOM
WHA--
HEY, ARE YOU--
DANG!
HUH.
HEH.
HA!

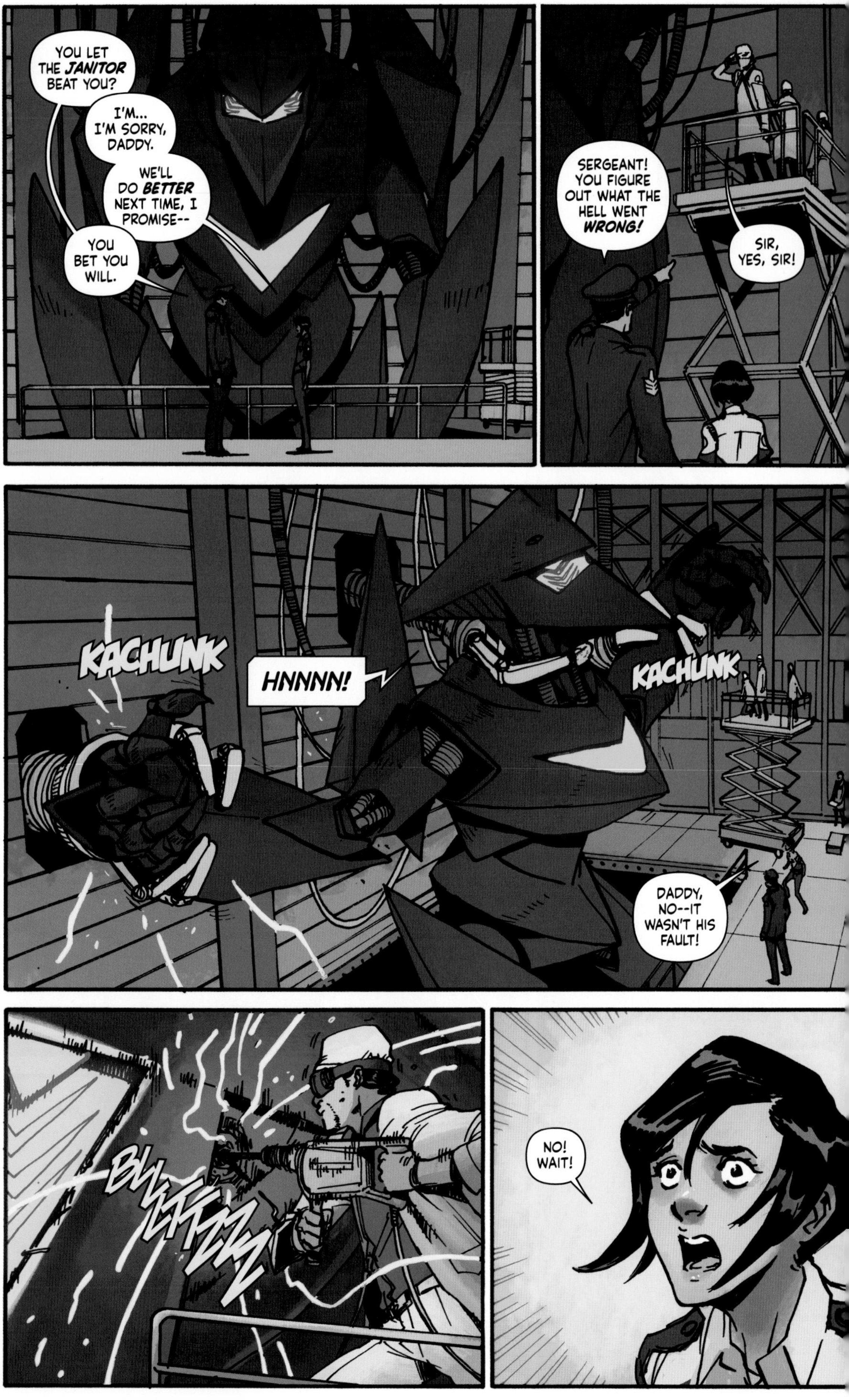
YOU LET THE JANITOR BEAT YOU?
I'M... I'M SORRY, DADDY.
WE'LL DO BETTER NEXT TIME, I PROMISE--
YOU BET YOU WILL.
SERGEANT! YOU FIGURE OUT WHAT THE HELL WENT WRONG!
SIR, YES, SIR!
KACHUNK
HNNNN!
KACHUNK
DADDY, NO--IT WASN'T HIS FAULT!
NO! WAIT!

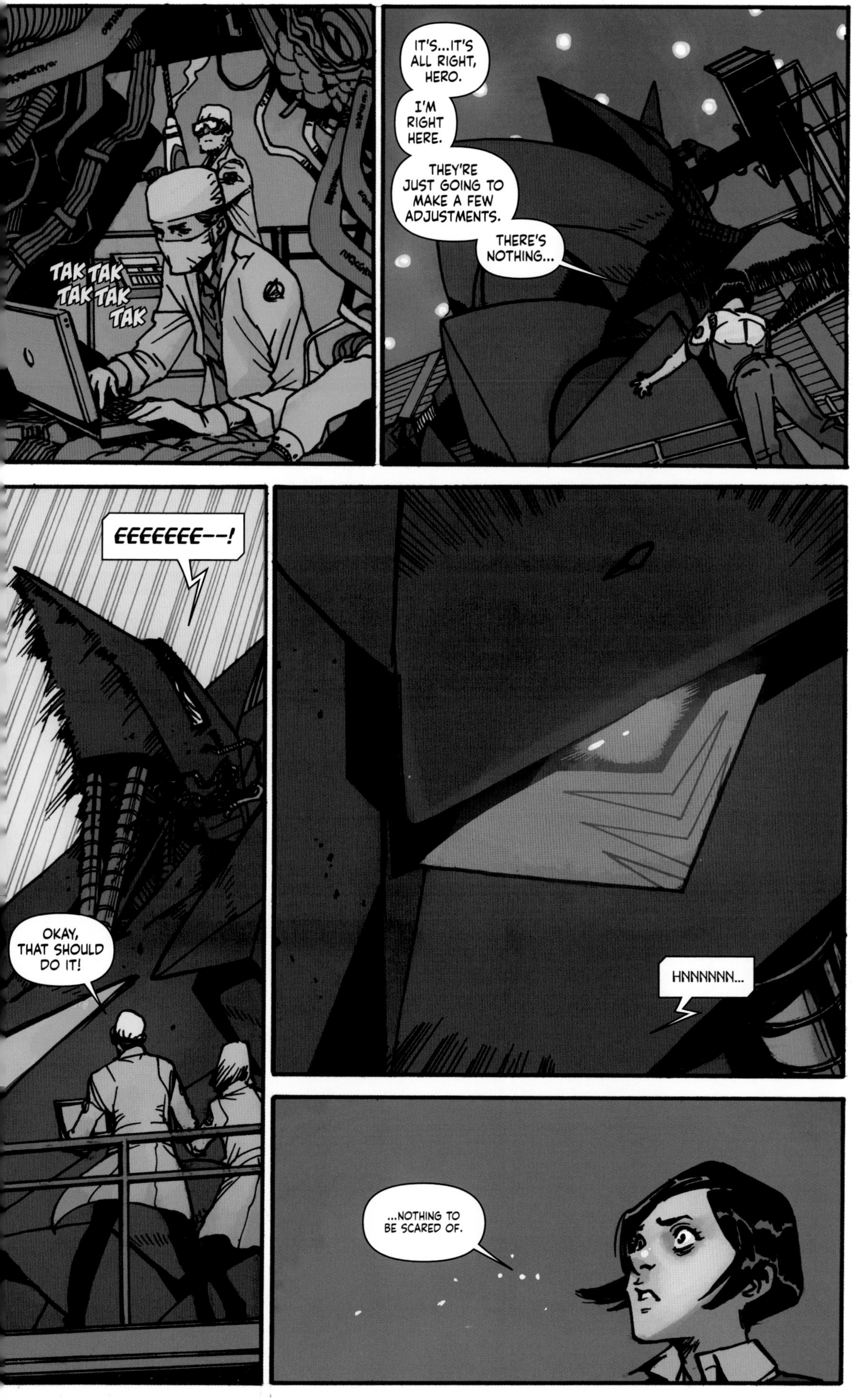
TAK TAK
TAK TAK
TAK
IT'S...IT'S ALL RIGHT, HERO.
I'M RIGHT HERE.
THEY'RE JUST GOING TO MAKE A FEW ADJUSTMENTS.
THERE'S NOTHING...
EEEEEEE--!
OKAY, THAT SHOULD DO IT!
HNNNNNN...
...NOTHING TO BE SCARED OF.

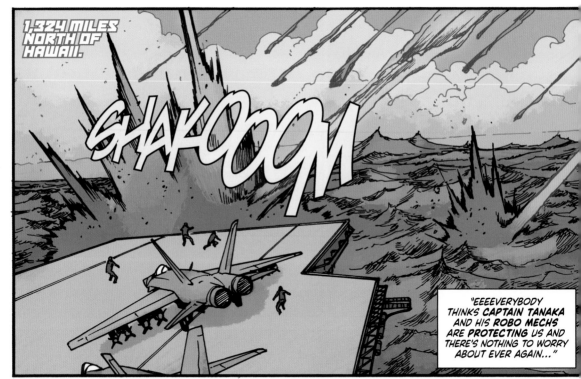

SHAK-OOOM

"EEEEVERYBODY THINKS **CAPTAIN TANAKA** AND HIS **ROBO MECHS** ARE **PROTECTING** US AND THERE'S NOTHING TO WORRY ABOUT EVER AGAIN..."

...BUT IN CASE ANYONE **FORGOT**...

...THE **WAR** NEVER REALLY **ENDED.** IT JUST MOVED **OFF-PLANET.** NO ONE'S **SAFE.**

SO THIS AFTERNOON, THREE **GLOBAL DEFENSE RING** SATELLITES CRASHED INTO THE **PACIFIC OCEAN.**

THE **SKY CORPS** HAS NOT YET MADE A FORMAL STATEMENT. BUT WE KNOW WHAT THIS MEANS...

...THE **SHARG** HAVE **RETURNED.**

STANFORD...

CHAPTER THREE

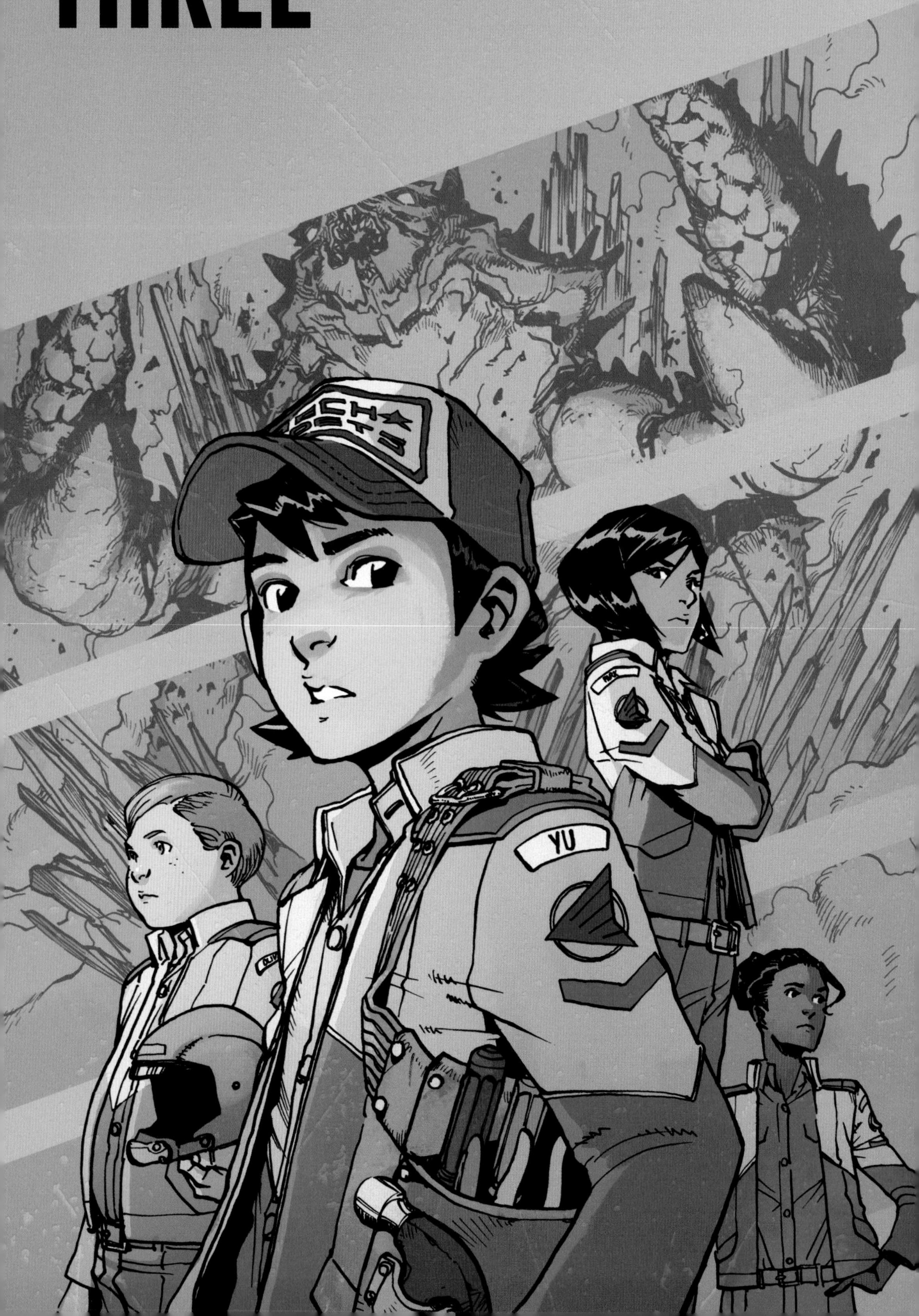
YU

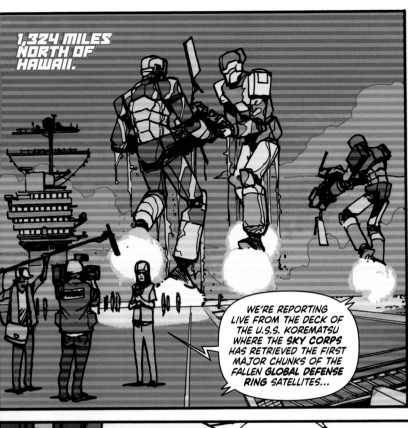

1,324 MILES NORTH OF HAWAII.

WE'RE REPORTING LIVE FROM THE DECK OF THE U.S.S. KOREMATSU WHERE THE **SKY CORPS** HAS RETRIEVED THE FIRST MAJOR CHUNKS OF THE FALLEN *GLOBAL DEFENSE RING* SATELLITES...

...AND AS FEARED, THOSE LOOK LIKE CLAW MARKS.

MY GOD. IT'S THE *SHARG.*

I DUNNO. THOSE ARE JUST *SCRATCHES*, PARK. THEY COULD HAVE BEEN MADE BY *ANYTHING--*

NO.

SANCHEZ--

JUST *LOOK*, OLIVETTI. THAT'S JUST LIKE WHAT PROFESSOR CAMPANELLI SHOWED IN HISTORY CLASS...

SKY CORPS ACADEMY. LOS ROBOS, ARIZONA.

...THE *SHARG* ARE *BACK.*

THIS...THIS IS IT. THIS IS WHAT WE'RE TRAINING FOR.

WHOA...

VREEEE VREEEE VREEEE

ALL CADETS REPORT TO THE GYMNASIUM!

ALL CADETS REPORT TO THE GYMNASIUM!

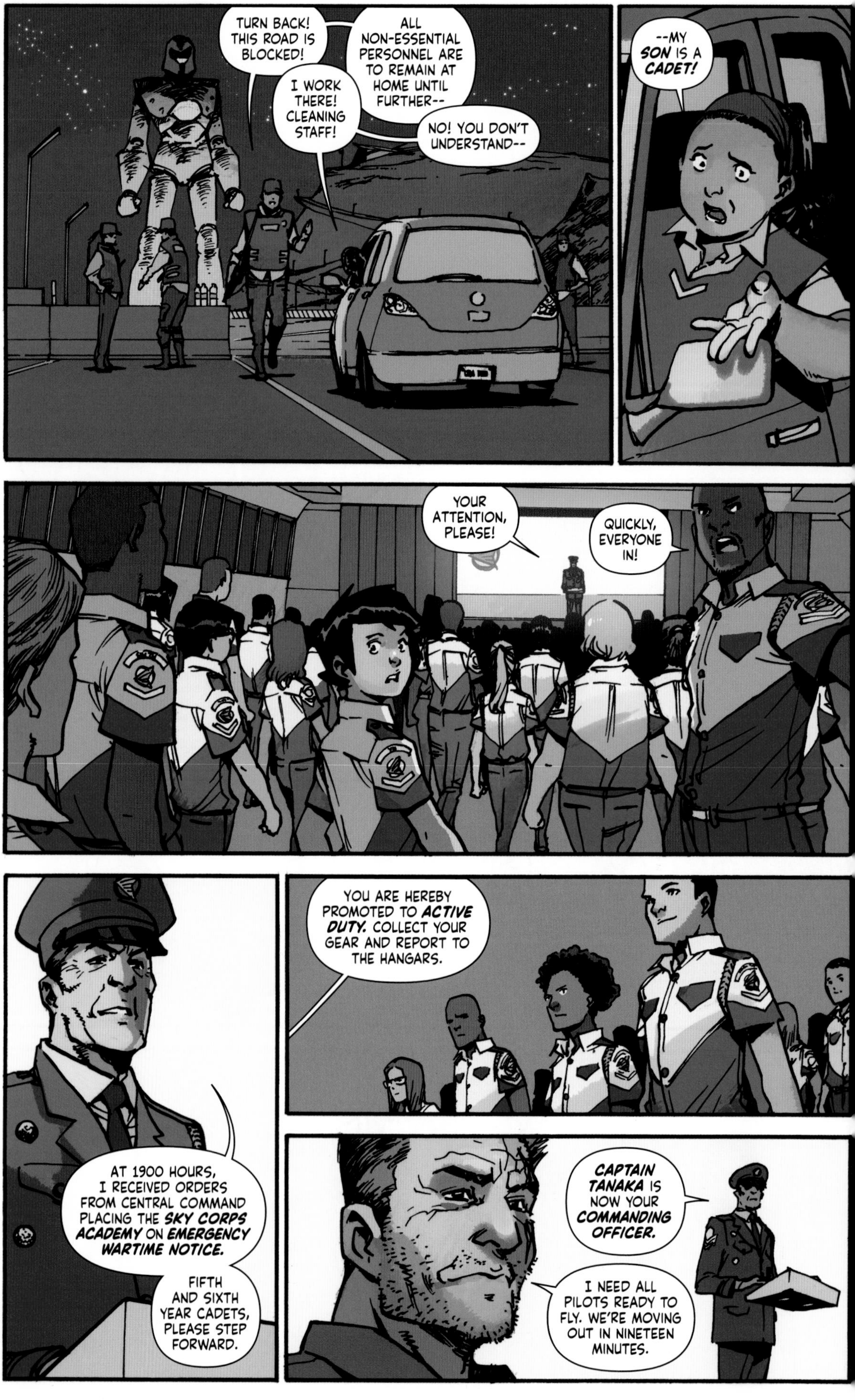
TURN BACK! THIS ROAD IS BLOCKED!
ALL NON-ESSENTIAL PERSONNEL ARE TO REMAIN AT HOME UNTIL FURTHER--
I WORK THERE! CLEANING STAFF!
NO! YOU DON'T UNDERSTAND--
--MY SON IS A CADET!
YOUR ATTENTION, PLEASE!
QUICKLY, EVERYONE IN!
AT 1900 HOURS, I RECEIVED ORDERS FROM CENTRAL COMMAND PLACING THE SKY CORPS ACADEMY ON EMERGENCY WARTIME NOTICE.
FIFTH AND SIXTH YEAR CADETS, PLEASE STEP FORWARD.
YOU ARE HEREBY PROMOTED TO ACTIVE DUTY. COLLECT YOUR GEAR AND REPORT TO THE HANGARS.
CAPTAIN TANAKA IS NOW YOUR COMMANDING OFFICER.
I NEED ALL PILOTS READY TO FLY. WE'RE MOVING OUT IN NINETEEN MINUTES.

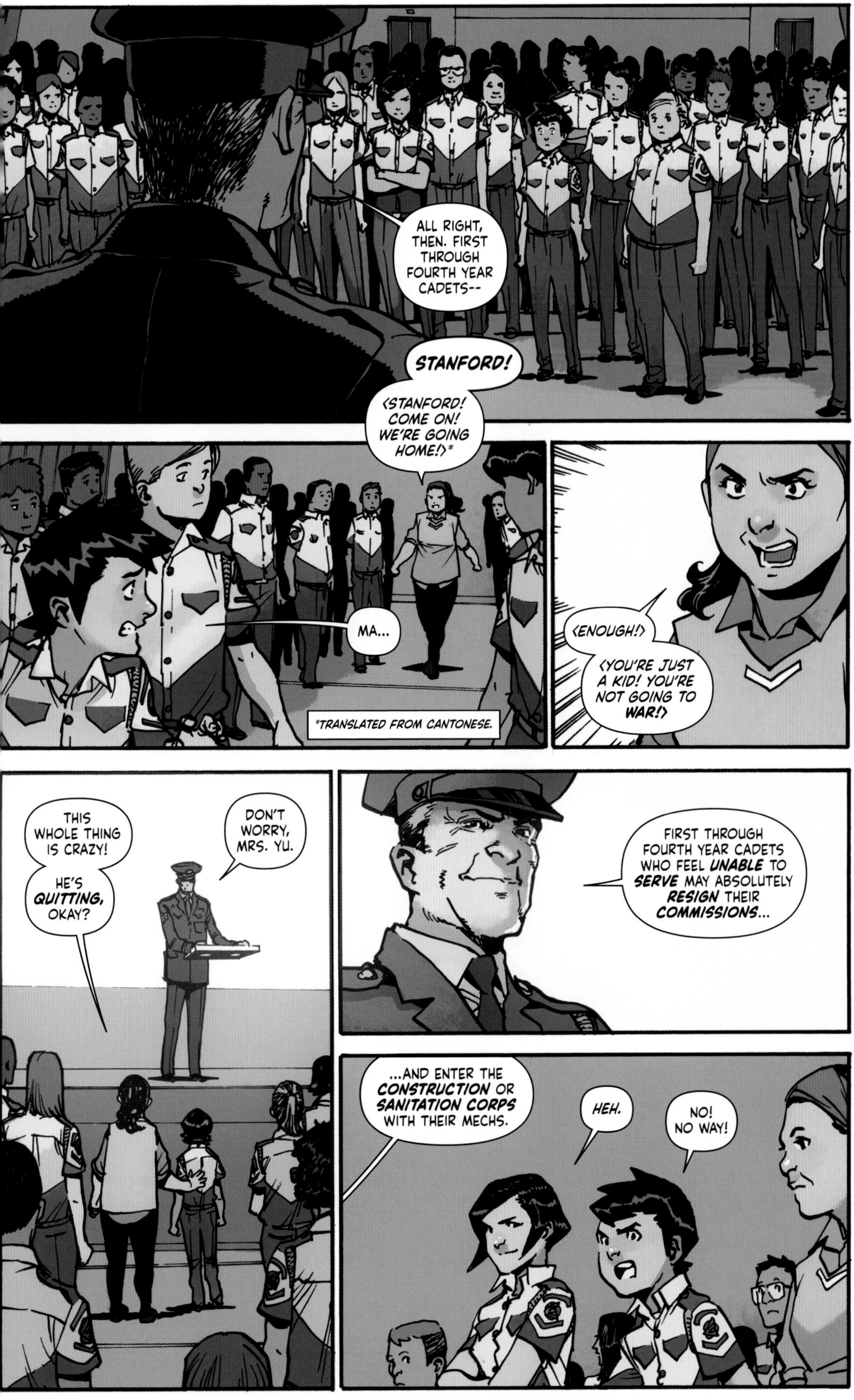
ALL RIGHT, THEN. FIRST THROUGH FOURTH YEAR CADETS--
STANFORD!
<STANFORD! COME ON! WE'RE GOING HOME!>*
MA...
*TRANSLATED FROM CANTONESE.
<ENOUGH!>
<YOU'RE JUST A KID! YOU'RE NOT GOING TO WAR!>
THIS WHOLE THING IS CRAZY!
HE'S QUITTING, OKAY?
DON'T WORRY, MRS. YU.
FIRST THROUGH FOURTH YEAR CADETS WHO FEEL UNABLE TO SERVE MAY ABSOLUTELY RESIGN THEIR COMMISSIONS...
...AND ENTER THE CONSTRUCTION OR SANITATION CORPS WITH THEIR MECHS.
HEH.
NO! NO WAY!

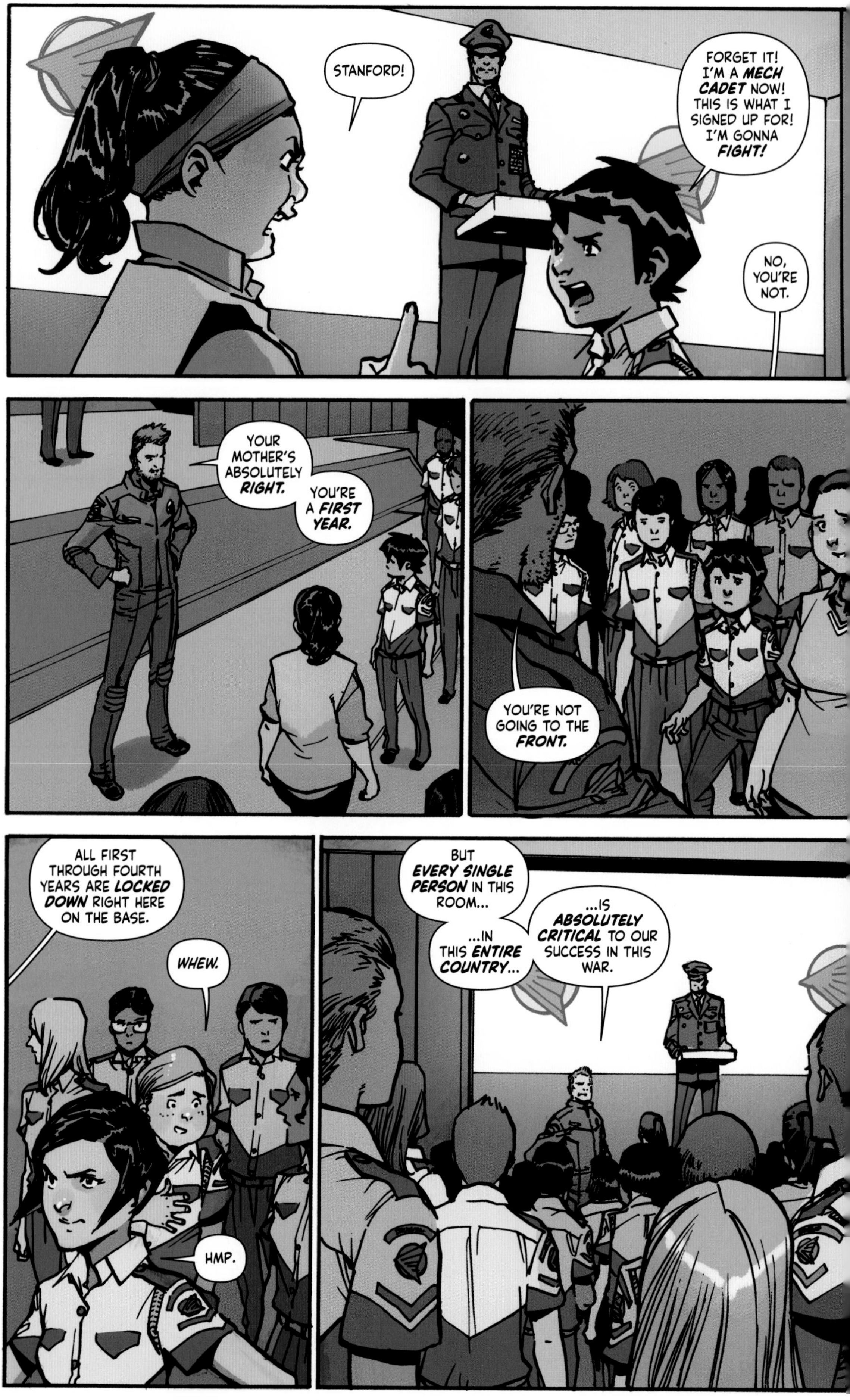
STANFORD!
FORGET IT! I'M A **MECH CADET** NOW! THIS IS WHAT I SIGNED UP FOR! I'M GONNA **FIGHT!**
NO, YOU'RE NOT.
YOUR MOTHER'S ABSOLUTELY **RIGHT.**
YOU'RE A **FIRST YEAR.**
YOU'RE NOT GOING TO THE **FRONT.**
ALL FIRST THROUGH FOURTH YEARS ARE **LOCKED DOWN** RIGHT HERE ON THE BASE.
WHEW.
HMP.
BUT **EVERY SINGLE PERSON** IN THIS ROOM...
...IN THIS **ENTIRE COUNTRY...**
...IS **ABSOLUTELY CRITICAL** TO OUR SUCCESS IN THIS WAR.

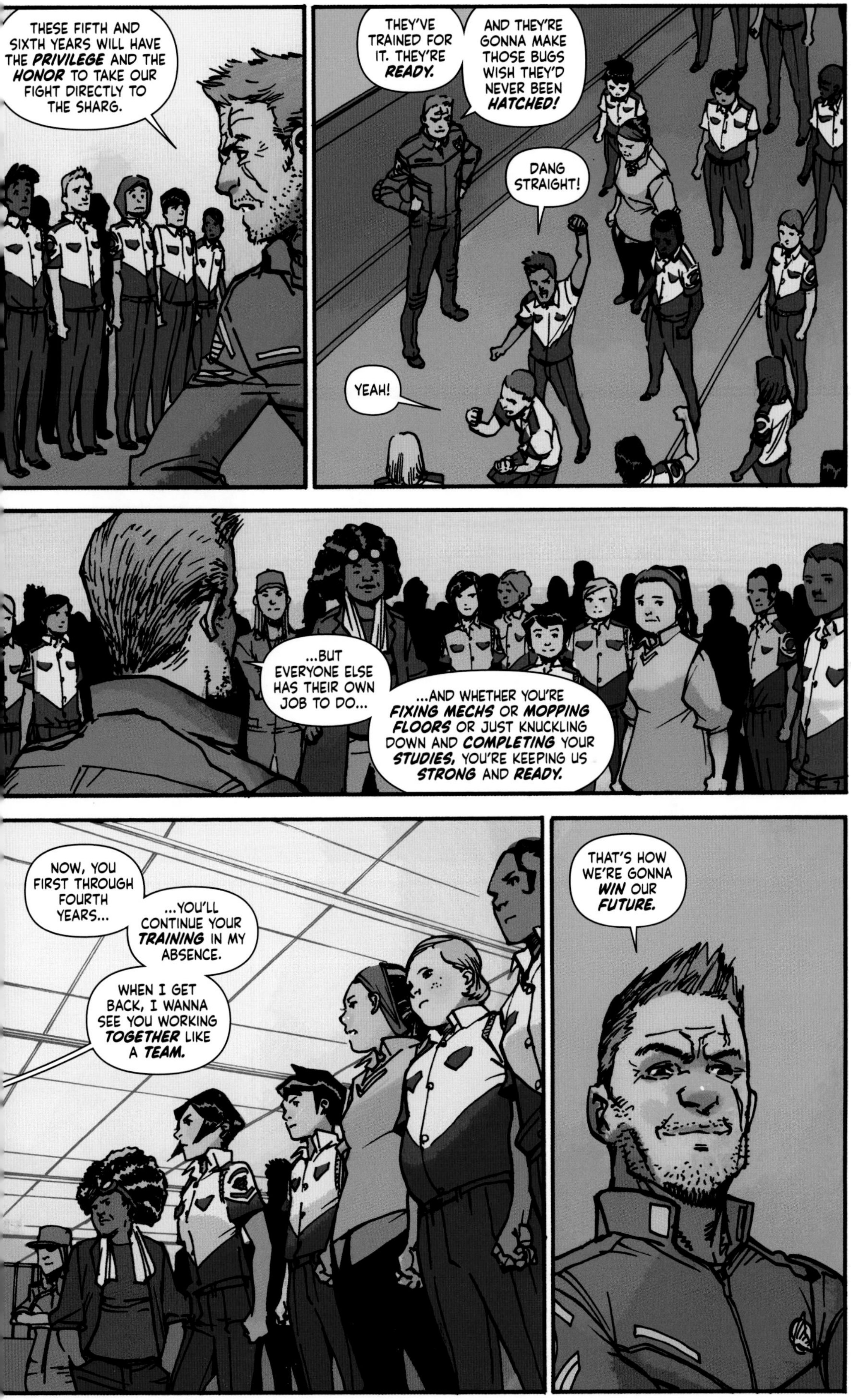
THESE FIFTH AND SIXTH YEARS WILL HAVE THE PRIVILEGE AND THE HONOR TO TAKE OUR FIGHT DIRECTLY TO THE SHARG.
THEY'VE TRAINED FOR IT. THEY'RE READY.
AND THEY'RE GONNA MAKE THOSE BUGS WISH THEY'D NEVER BEEN HATCHED!
DANG STRAIGHT!
YEAH!
...BUT EVERYONE ELSE HAS THEIR OWN JOB TO DO...
...AND WHETHER YOU'RE FIXING MECHS OR MOPPING FLOORS OR JUST KNUCKLING DOWN AND COMPLETING YOUR STUDIES, YOU'RE KEEPING US STRONG AND READY.
NOW, YOU FIRST THROUGH FOURTH YEARS...
...YOU'LL CONTINUE YOUR TRAINING IN MY ABSENCE.
WHEN I GET BACK, I WANNA SEE YOU WORKING TOGETHER LIKE A TEAM.
THAT'S HOW WE'RE GONNA WIN OUR FUTURE.

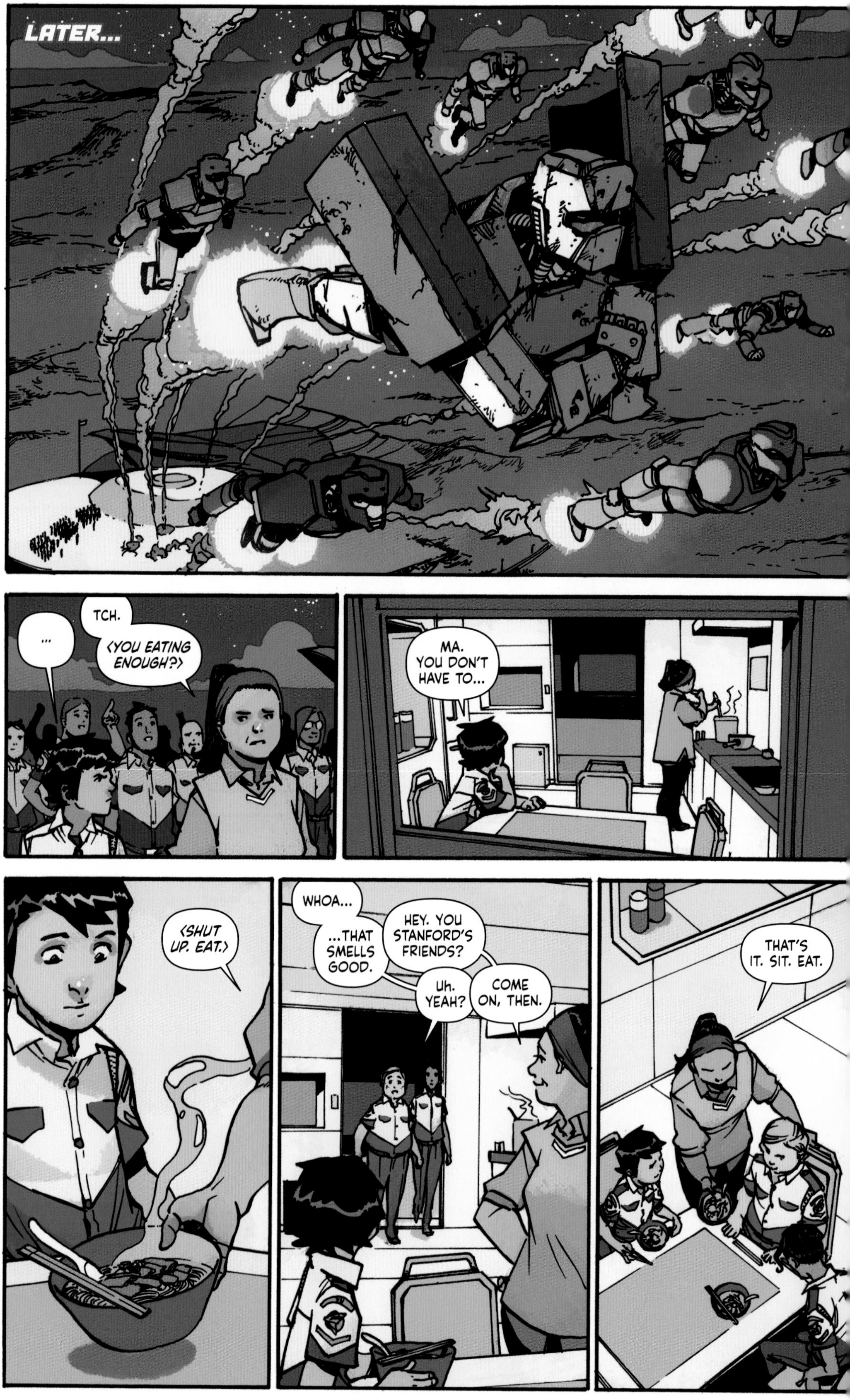
LATER...
...
TCH.
<YOU EATING ENOUGH?>
MA. YOU DON'T HAVE TO...
<SHUT UP. EAT.>
WHOA...
...THAT SMELLS GOOD.
HEY. YOU STANFORD'S FRIENDS?
Uh. YEAH?
COME ON, THEN.
THAT'S IT. SIT. EAT.

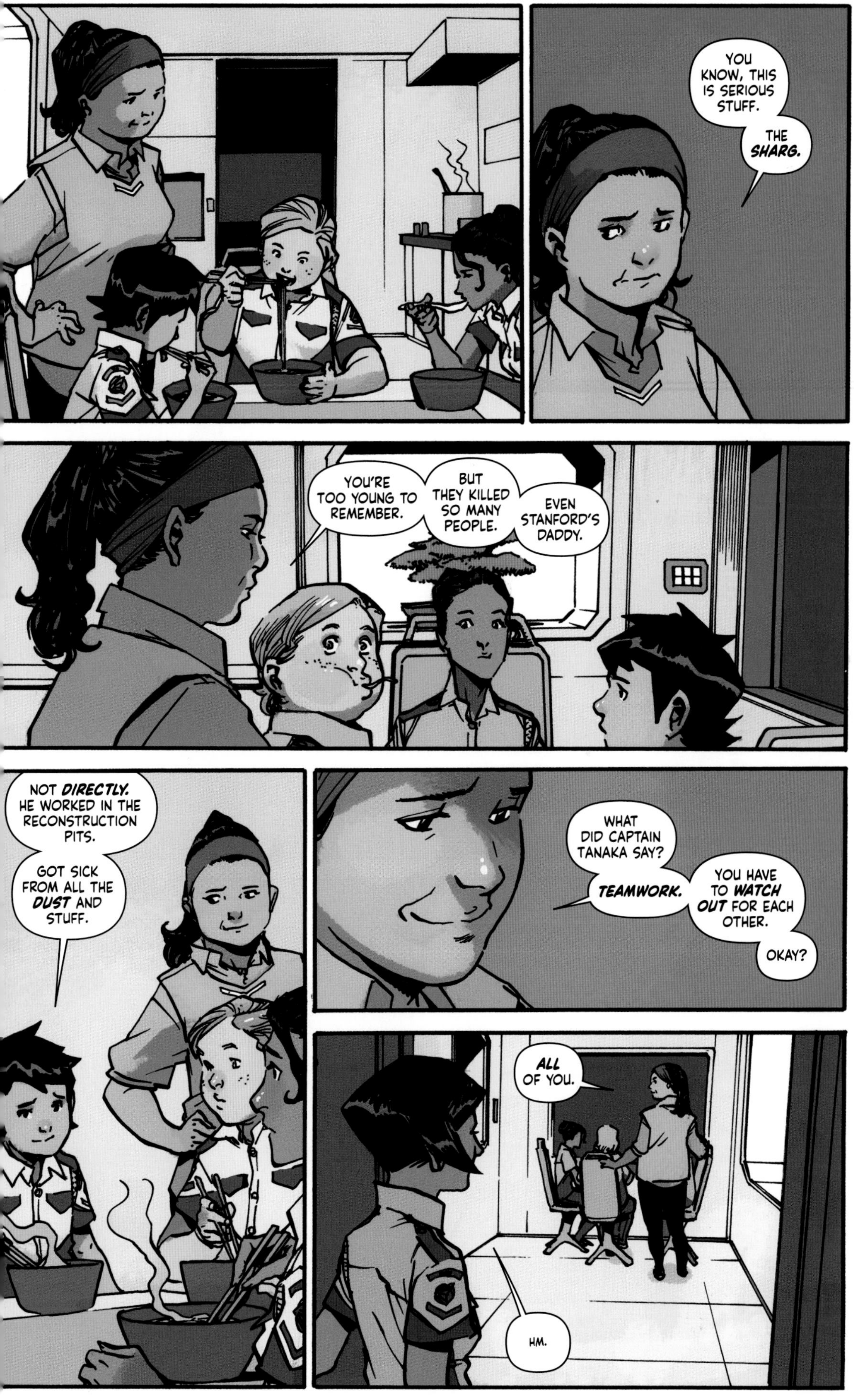

YOU KNOW, THIS IS SERIOUS STUFF.
THE *SHARG.*
YOU'RE TOO YOUNG TO REMEMBER.
BUT THEY KILLED SO MANY PEOPLE.
EVEN STANFORD'S DADDY.
NOT *DIRECTLY.* HE WORKED IN THE RECONSTRUCTION PITS.
GOT SICK FROM ALL THE *DUST* AND STUFF.
WHAT DID CAPTAIN TANAKA SAY?
TEAMWORK.
YOU HAVE TO *WATCH OUT* FOR EACH OTHER.
OKAY?
ALL OF YOU.
HM.

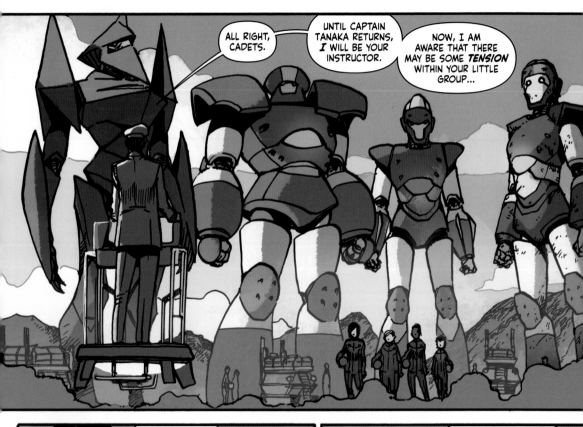

ALL RIGHT, CADETS.

UNTIL CAPTAIN TANAKA RETURNS, *I* WILL BE YOUR INSTRUCTOR.

NOW, I AM AWARE THAT THERE MAY BE SOME *TENSION* WITHIN YOUR LITTLE GROUP...

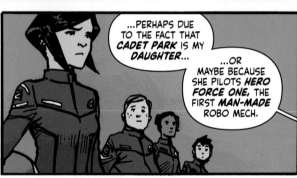

...PERHAPS DUE TO THE FACT THAT *CADET PARK* IS MY *DAUGHTER*...

...OR MAYBE BECAUSE SHE PILOTS *HERO FORCE ONE*, THE FIRST *MAN-MADE* ROBO MECH.

ON THE OTHER HAND, SOME OF YOU MAY RESENT *CADET YU*...

...WHO SOMEHOW *BONDED* WITH THE *ROBO* MANY THOUGHT *CADET PARK* SHOULD HAVE GOTTEN IN THE FIRST PLACE.

PLEASE BE ASSURED, THERE WILL BE NO *FAVORITISM* OR *RESENTMENT* IN THIS UNIT.

I WILL WORK *ALL* OF YOU *EQUALLY* HARD.

"NOW, I DON'T KNOW HOW WELL CAPTAIN TANAKA *PREPARED* YOU..."

"...SO TODAY LET'S JUST SEE WHERE YOU ARE AND WHAT YOU CAN DO."

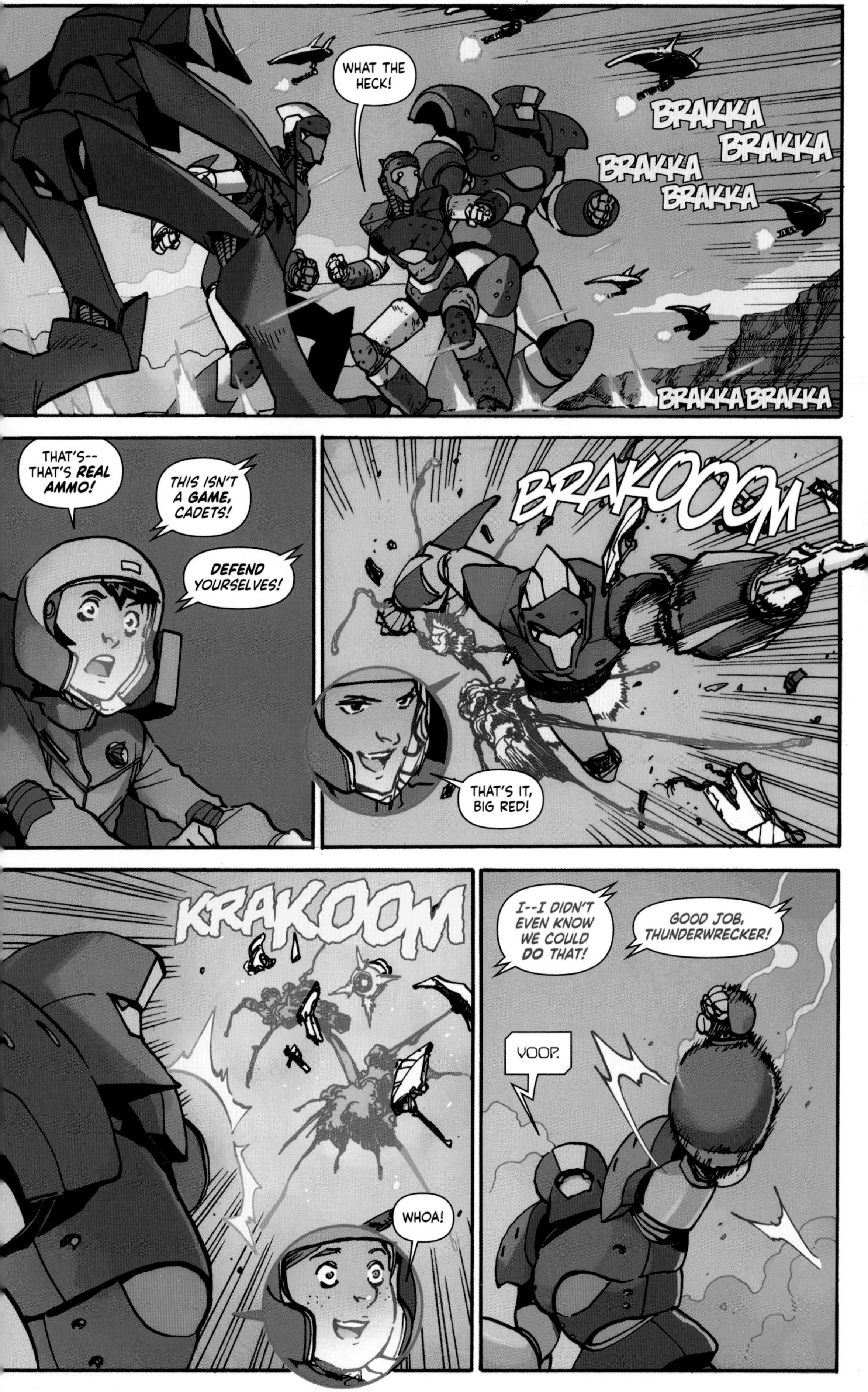
WHAT THE HECK!
BRAKKA
BRAKKA
BRAKKA
BRAKKA
BRAKKA BRAKKA
THAT'S-- THAT'S REAL AMMO!
THIS ISN'T A GAME, CADETS!
DEFEND YOURSELVES!
BRAKOOOM
THAT'S IT, BIG RED!
KRAKOOM
WHOA!
I--I DIDN'T EVEN KNOW WE COULD DO THAT!
GOOD JOB, THUNDERWRECKER!
VOOP.

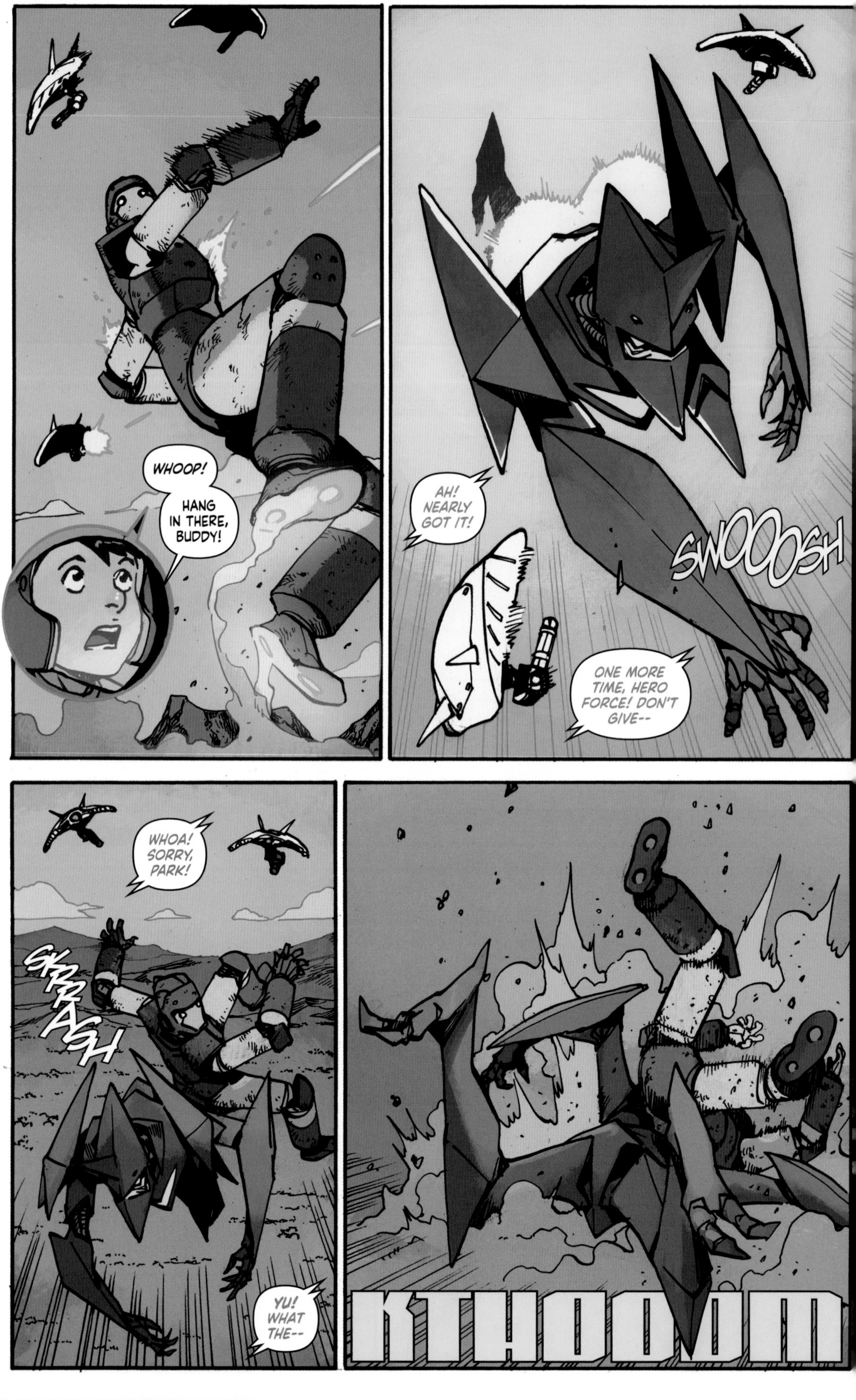
WHOOP!
HANG IN THERE, BUDDY!
AH! NEARLY GOT IT!
SWOOOOSH
ONE MORE TIME, HERO FORCE! DON'T GIVE--
WHOA! SORRY, PARK!
SKRRASH
YU! WHAT THE--
KTHOOOM

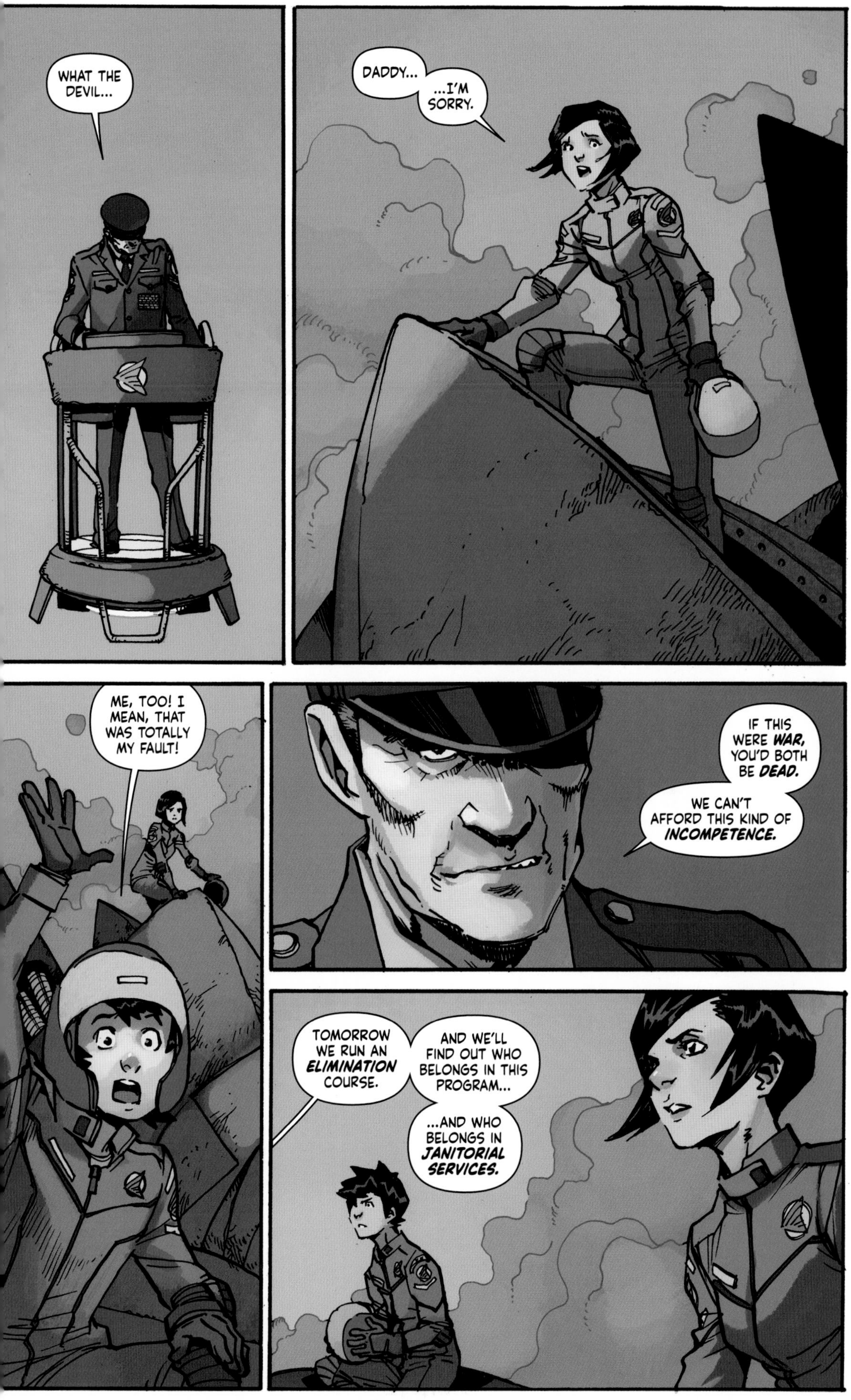
WHAT THE DEVIL...
DADDY...
...I'M SORRY.
ME, TOO! I MEAN, THAT WAS TOTALLY MY FAULT!
IF THIS WERE WAR, YOU'D BOTH BE DEAD.
WE CAN'T AFFORD THIS KIND OF INCOMPETENCE.
TOMORROW WE RUN AN ELIMINATION COURSE.
AND WE'LL FIND OUT WHO BELONGS IN THIS PROGRAM...
...AND WHO BELONGS IN JANITORIAL SERVICES.

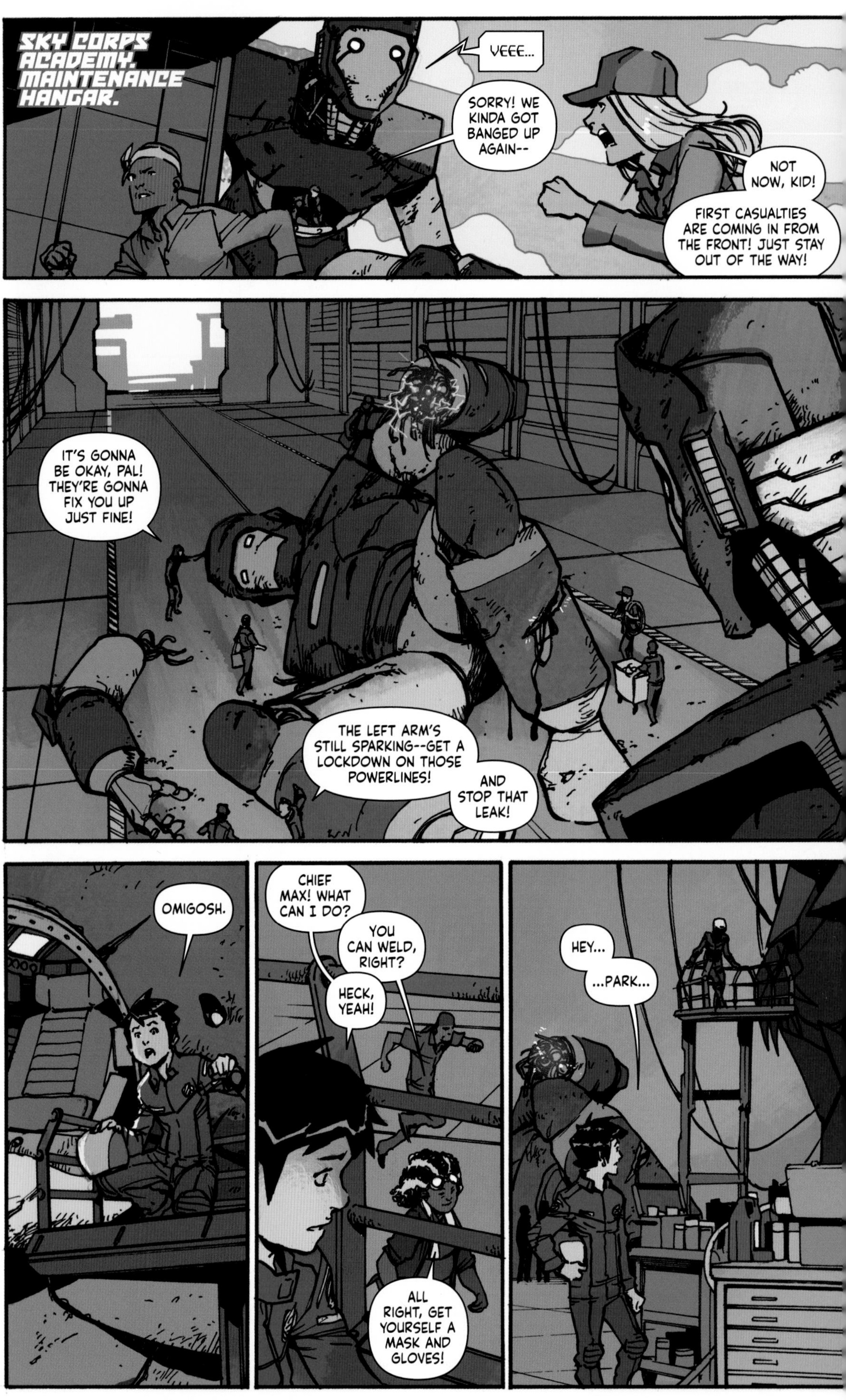
SKY CORPS ACADEMY. MAINTENANCE HANGAR.
VEEE...
SORRY! WE KINDA GOT BANGED UP AGAIN--
NOT NOW, KID!
FIRST CASUALTIES ARE COMING IN FROM THE FRONT! JUST STAY OUT OF THE WAY!
IT'S GONNA BE OKAY, PAL! THEY'RE GONNA FIX YOU UP JUST FINE!
THE LEFT ARM'S STILL SPARKING--GET A LOCKDOWN ON THOSE POWERLINES!
AND STOP THAT LEAK!
OMIGOSH.
CHIEF MAX! WHAT CAN I DO?
YOU CAN WELD, RIGHT?
HECK, YEAH!
ALL RIGHT, GET YOURSELF A MASK AND GLOVES!
HEY...
...PARK...

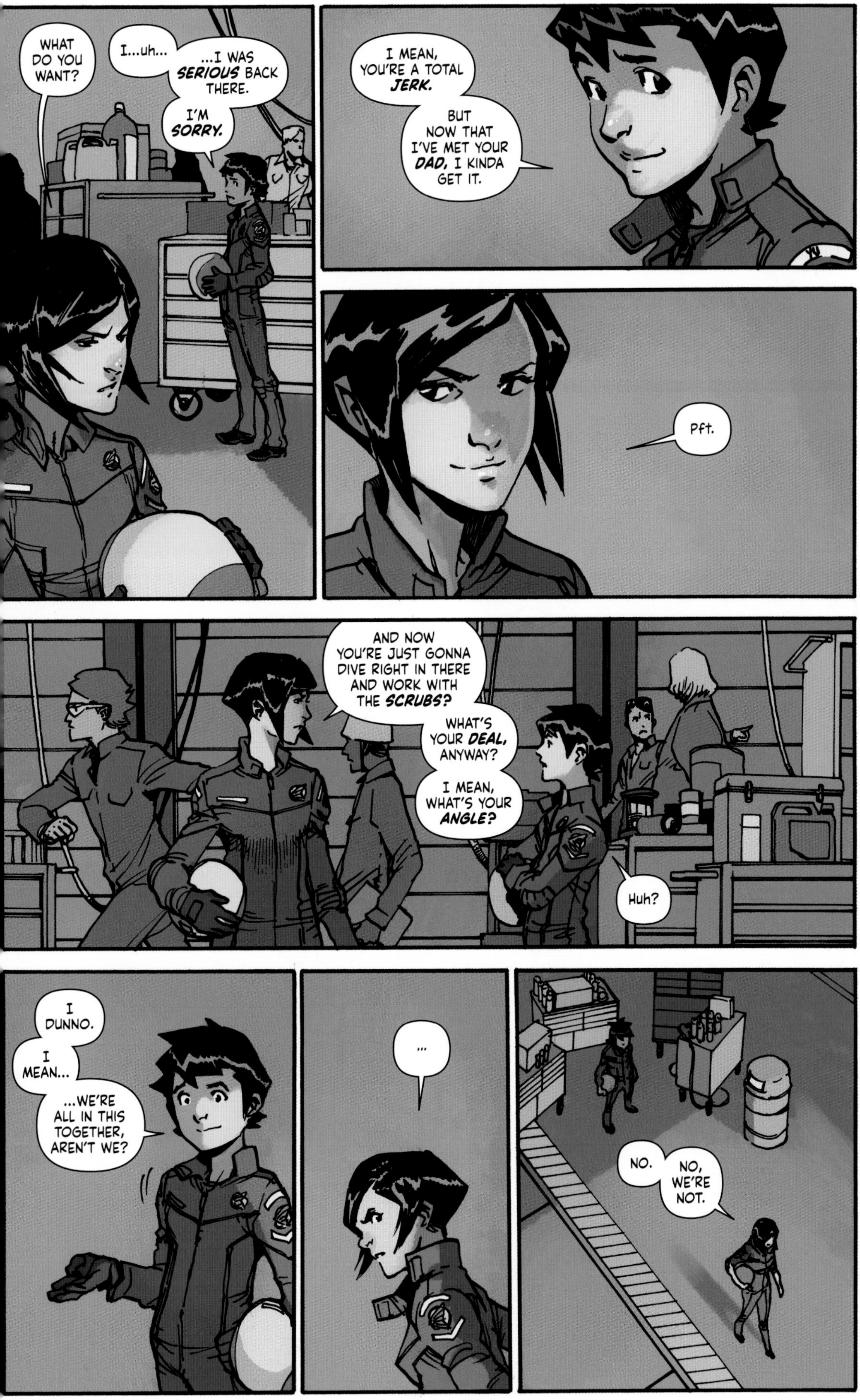
WHAT DO YOU WANT?
I...uh...
...I WAS SERIOUS BACK THERE.
I'M SORRY.
I MEAN, YOU'RE A TOTAL JERK.
BUT NOW THAT I'VE MET YOUR DAD, I KINDA GET IT.
Pft.
AND NOW YOU'RE JUST GONNA DIVE RIGHT IN THERE AND WORK WITH THE SCRUBS?
WHAT'S YOUR DEAL, ANYWAY?
I MEAN, WHAT'S YOUR ANGLE?
Huh?
I DUNNO.
I MEAN...
...WE'RE ALL IN THIS TOGETHER, AREN'T WE?
...
NO.
NO, WE'RE NOT.

VEE?
SHEESH, TELL ME ABOUT IT!
ALL RIGHT, THAT'S IT!
LOOKING GOOD!
THIS IS GONNA BE A LONG NIGHT...
...BUT YOU KNOW I LIKE THIS CREW!
VEE?
VOO...
BZZZT
OOOO

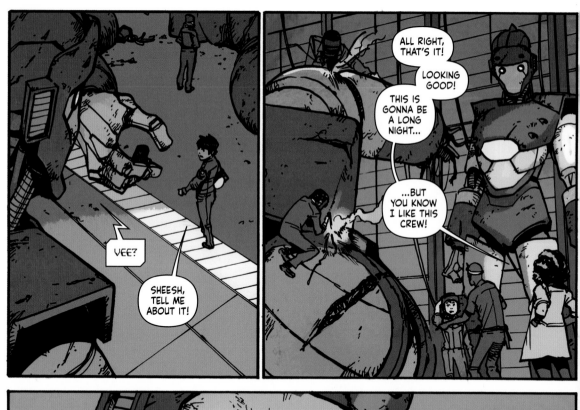

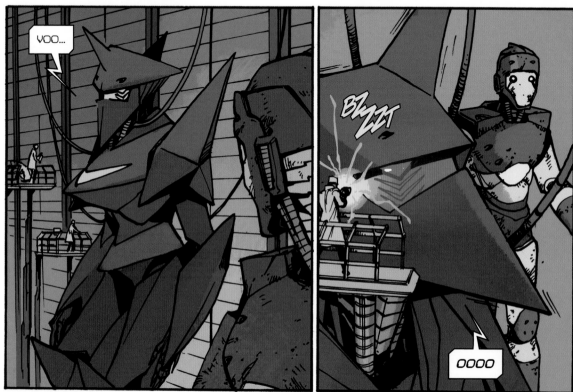

FOUR CADETS, FOUR ROBOS...

...BUT JUST *THREE* DRONES.

IF YOU WANT TO STAY IN THE PROGRAM...

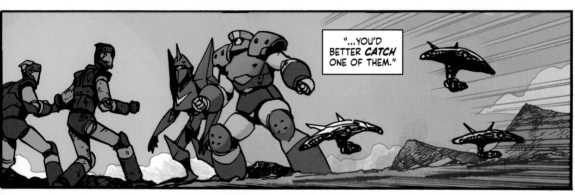

"...YOU'D BETTER *CATCH* ONE OF THEM."

HANG ON! THIS DOESN'T MAKE ANY SENSE!

CAPTAIN TANAKA SAID WE'RE SUPPOSED TO LEARN HOW TO WORK AS A *TEAM*, NOT--

HA!

SHING

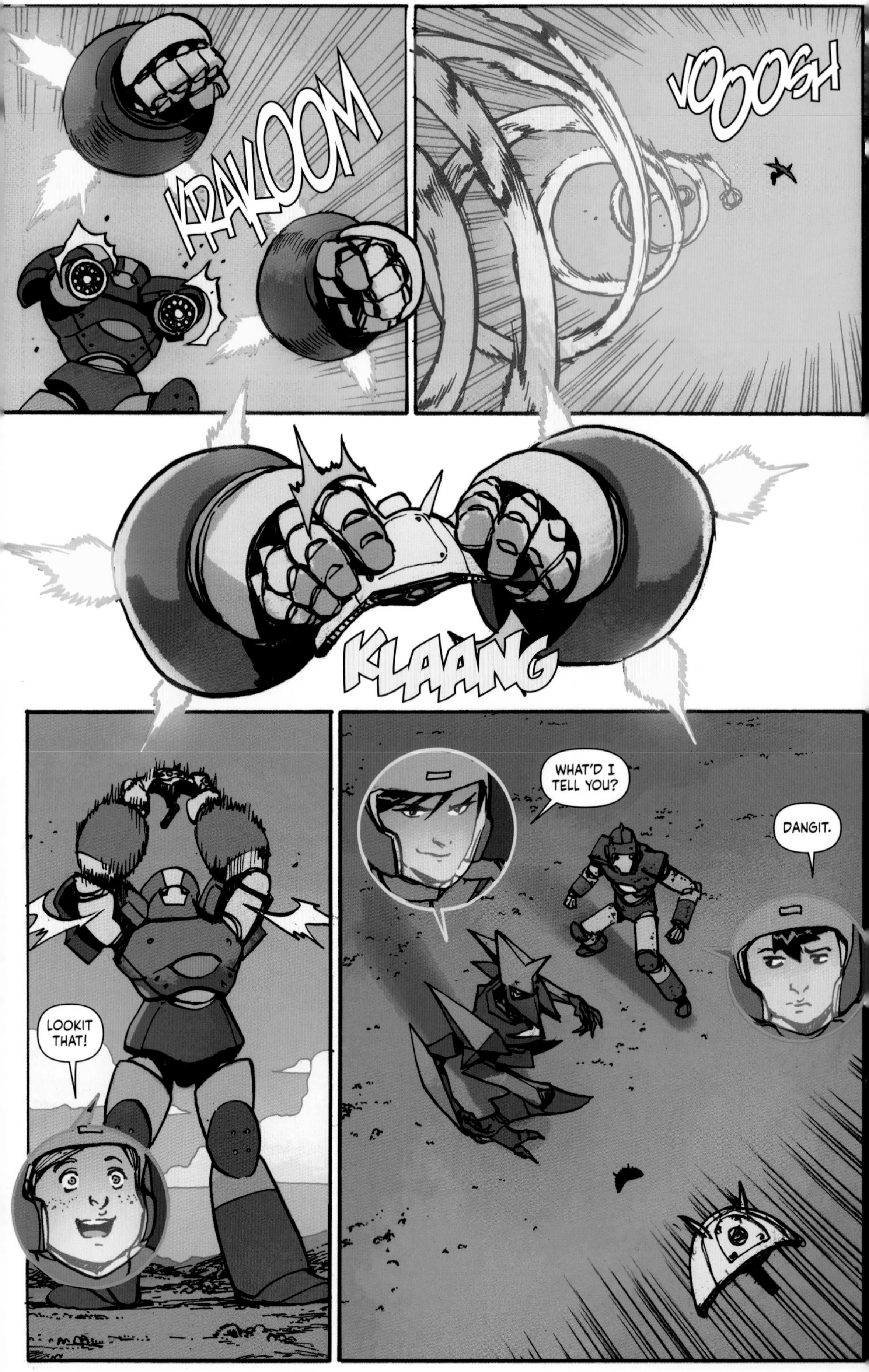
KRAKOOM
VOOOOSH
KLAANG
LOOKIT THAT!
WHAT'D I TELL YOU?
DANGIT.

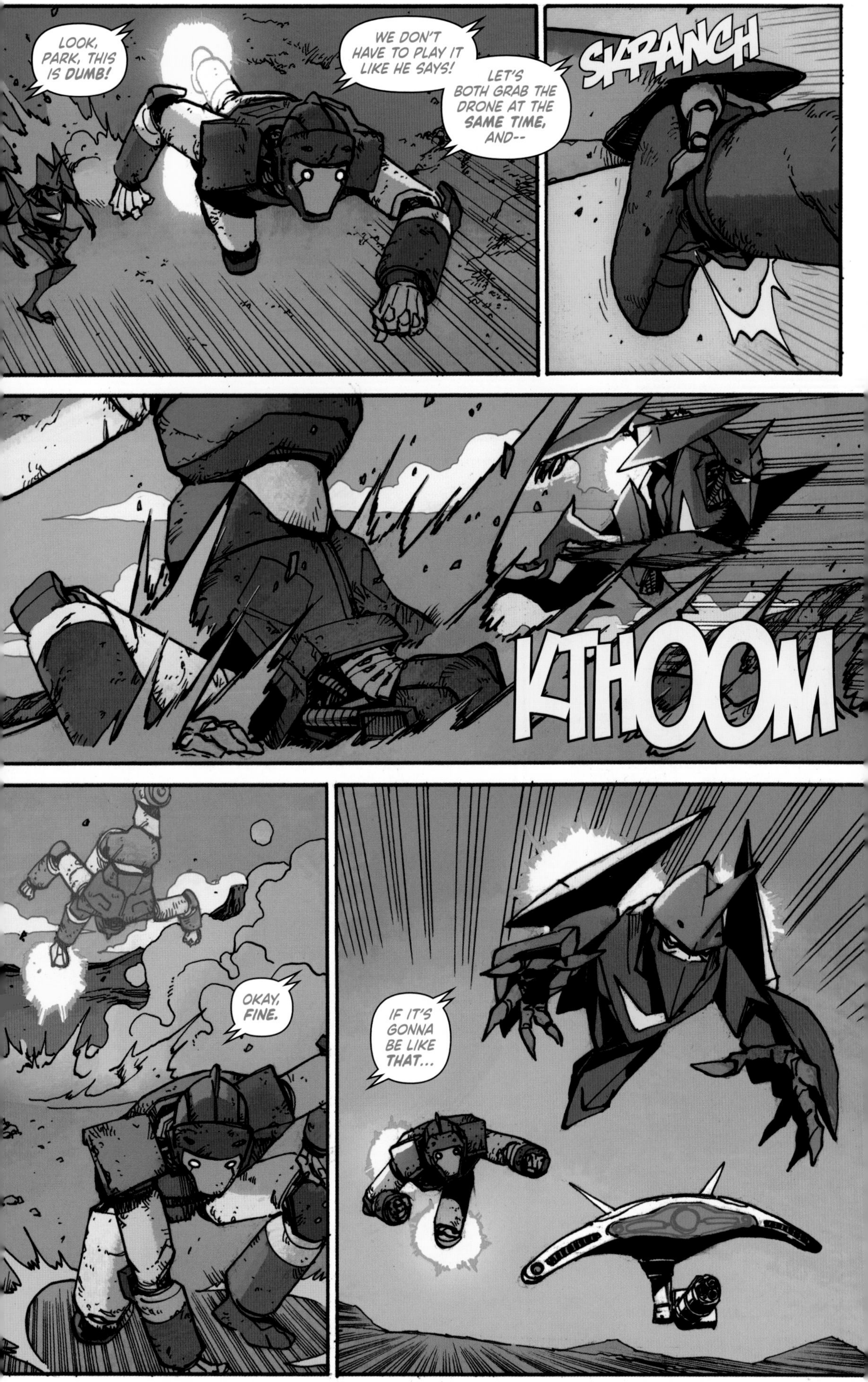
LOOK, PARK, THIS IS DUMB!
WE DON'T HAVE TO PLAY IT LIKE HE SAYS!
LET'S BOTH GRAB THE DRONE AT THE SAME TIME, AND--
SKRANCH
KTHOOM
OKAY, FINE.
IF IT'S GONNA BE LIKE THAT...

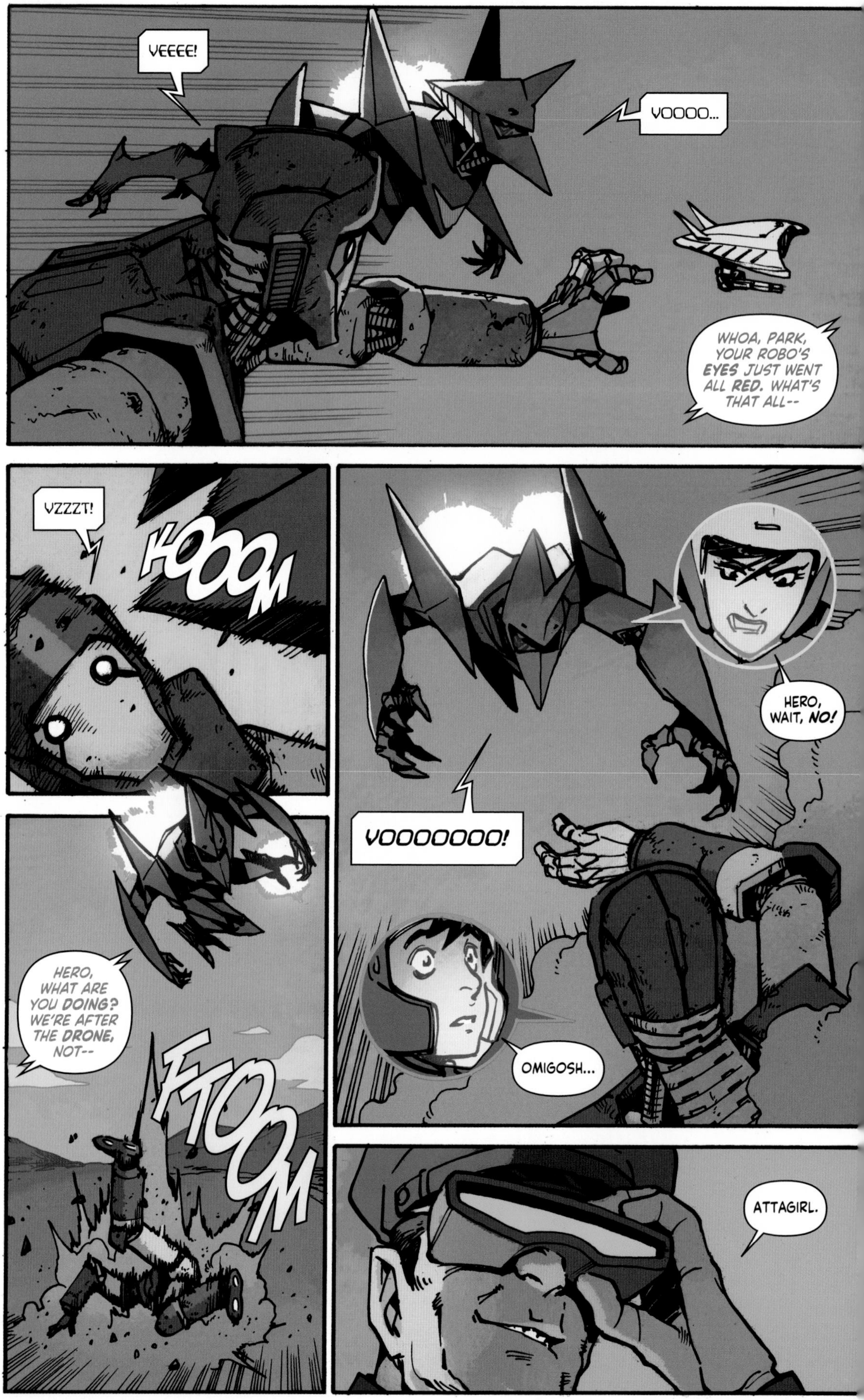
VEEEE!
VOOOO...
WHOA, PARK, YOUR ROBO'S EYES JUST WENT ALL RED. WHAT'S THAT ALL--
VZZZT!
KOOOM
HERO, WAIT, NO!
VOOOOOOO!
OMIGOSH...
HERO, WHAT ARE YOU DOING? WE'RE AFTER THE DRONE, NOT--
FTOOOM
ATTAGIRL.

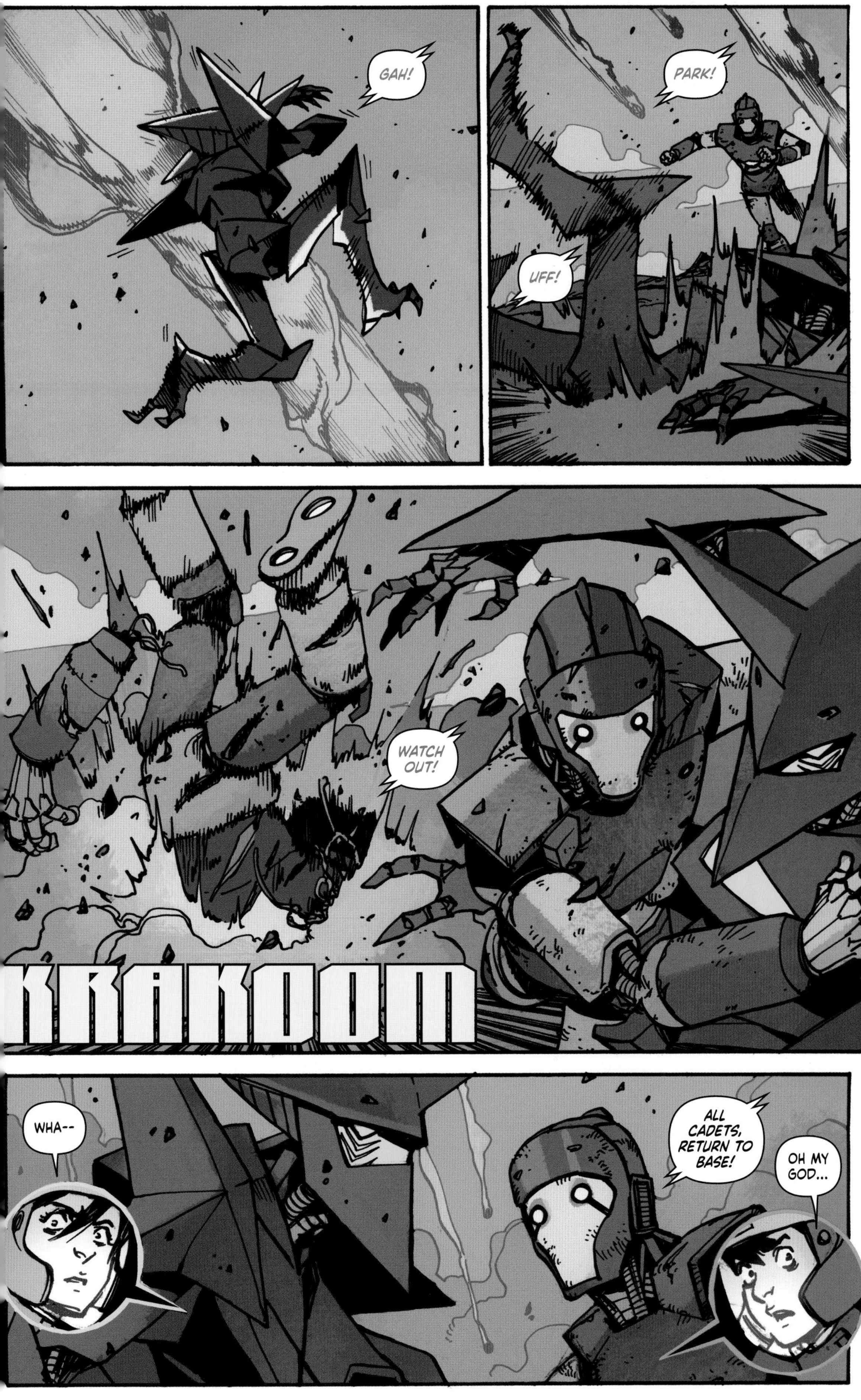
GAH!
PARK!
UFF!
WATCH OUT!
KRAKOOM
WHA--
ALL CADETS, RETURN TO BASE!
OH MY GOD...

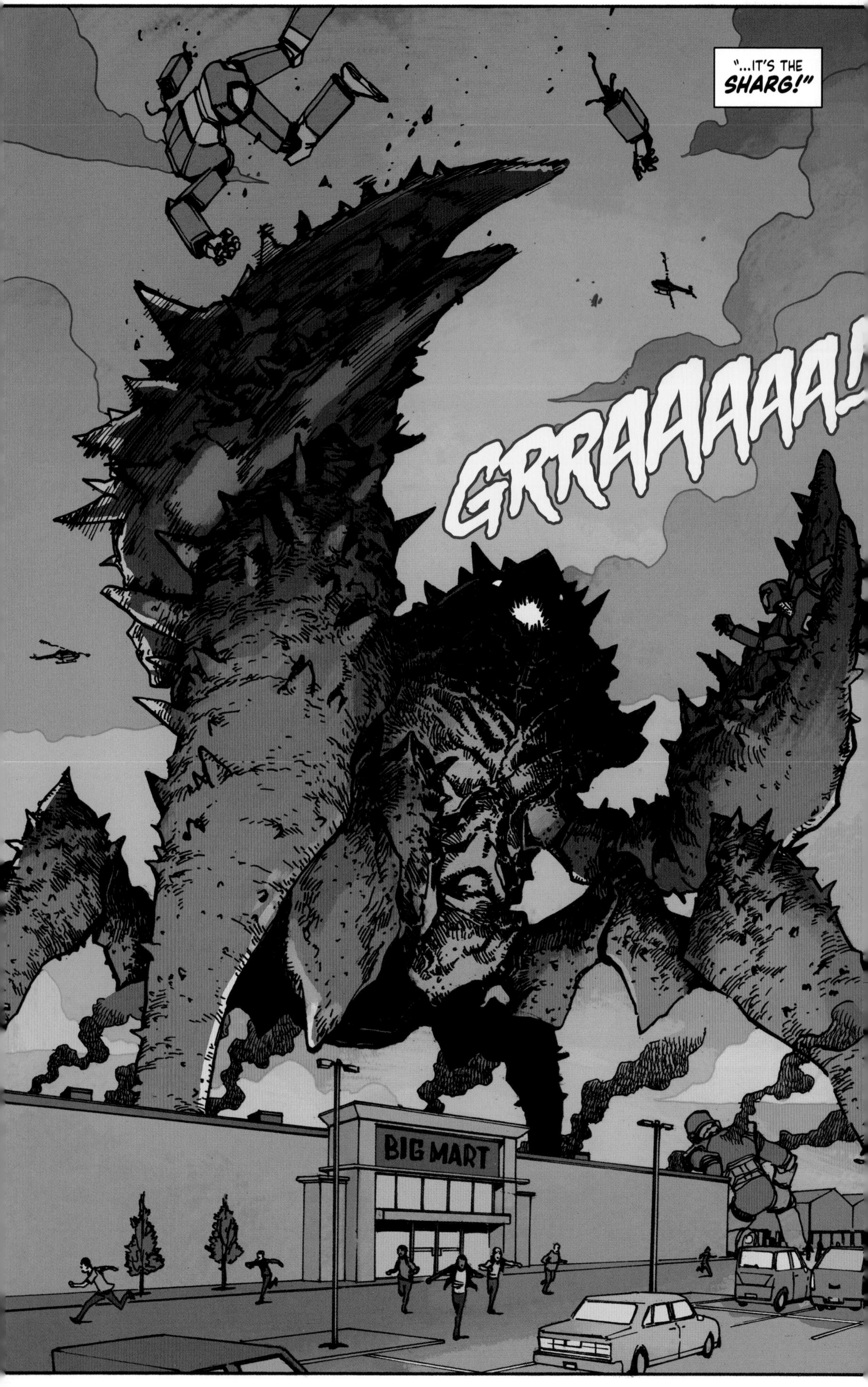
"...IT'S THE SHARG!"
GRRAAAAAA!
BIG MART

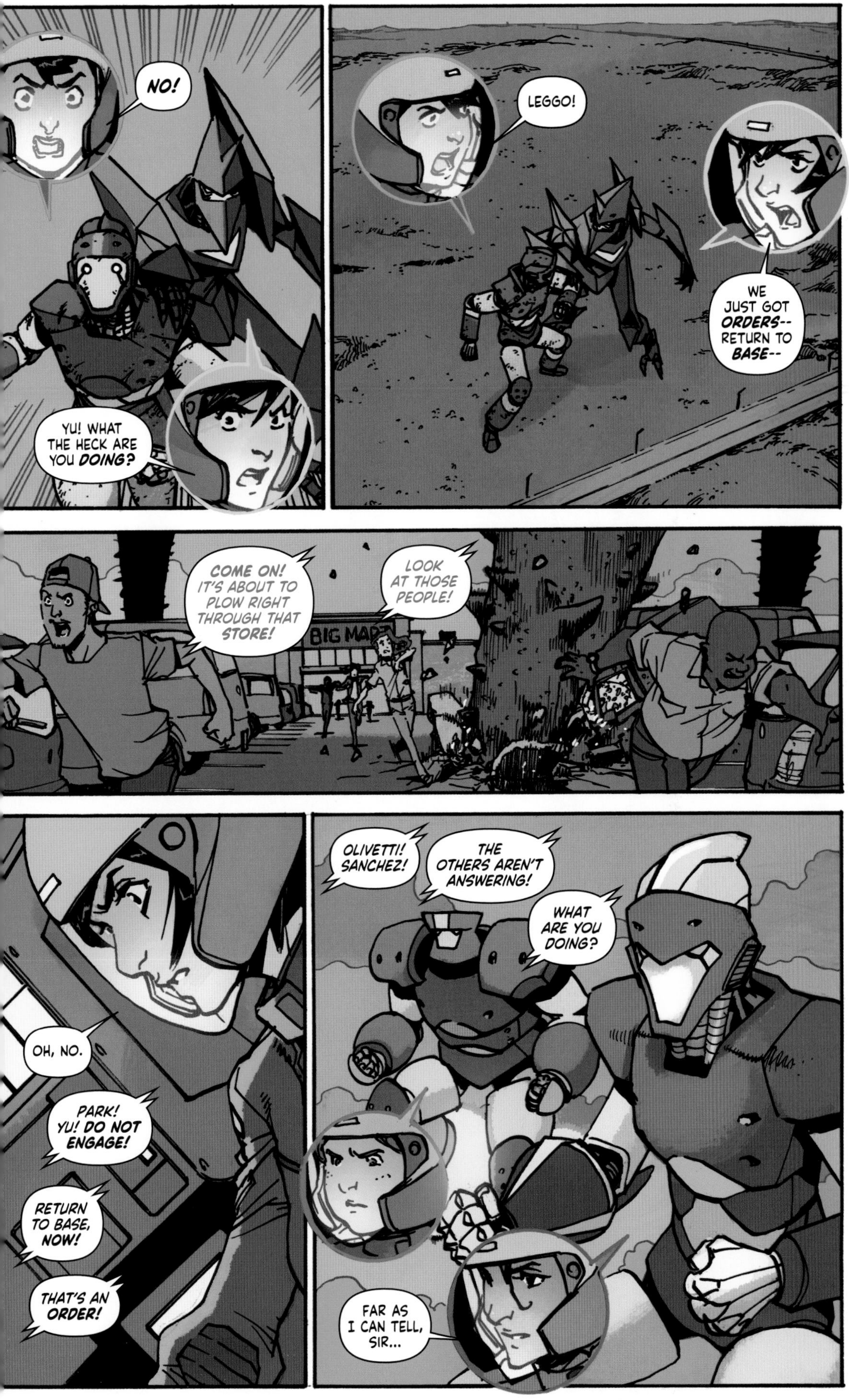
NO!
YU! WHAT THE HECK ARE YOU DOING?
LEGGO!
WE JUST GOT ORDERS-- RETURN TO BASE--
COME ON! IT'S ABOUT TO PLOW RIGHT THROUGH THAT STORE!
LOOK AT THOSE PEOPLE!
BIG MART
OH, NO.
PARK! YU! DO NOT ENGAGE!
RETURN TO BASE, NOW!
THAT'S AN ORDER!
OLIVETTI! SANCHEZ!
THE OTHERS AREN'T ANSWERING!
WHAT ARE YOU DOING?
FAR AS I CAN TELL, SIR...

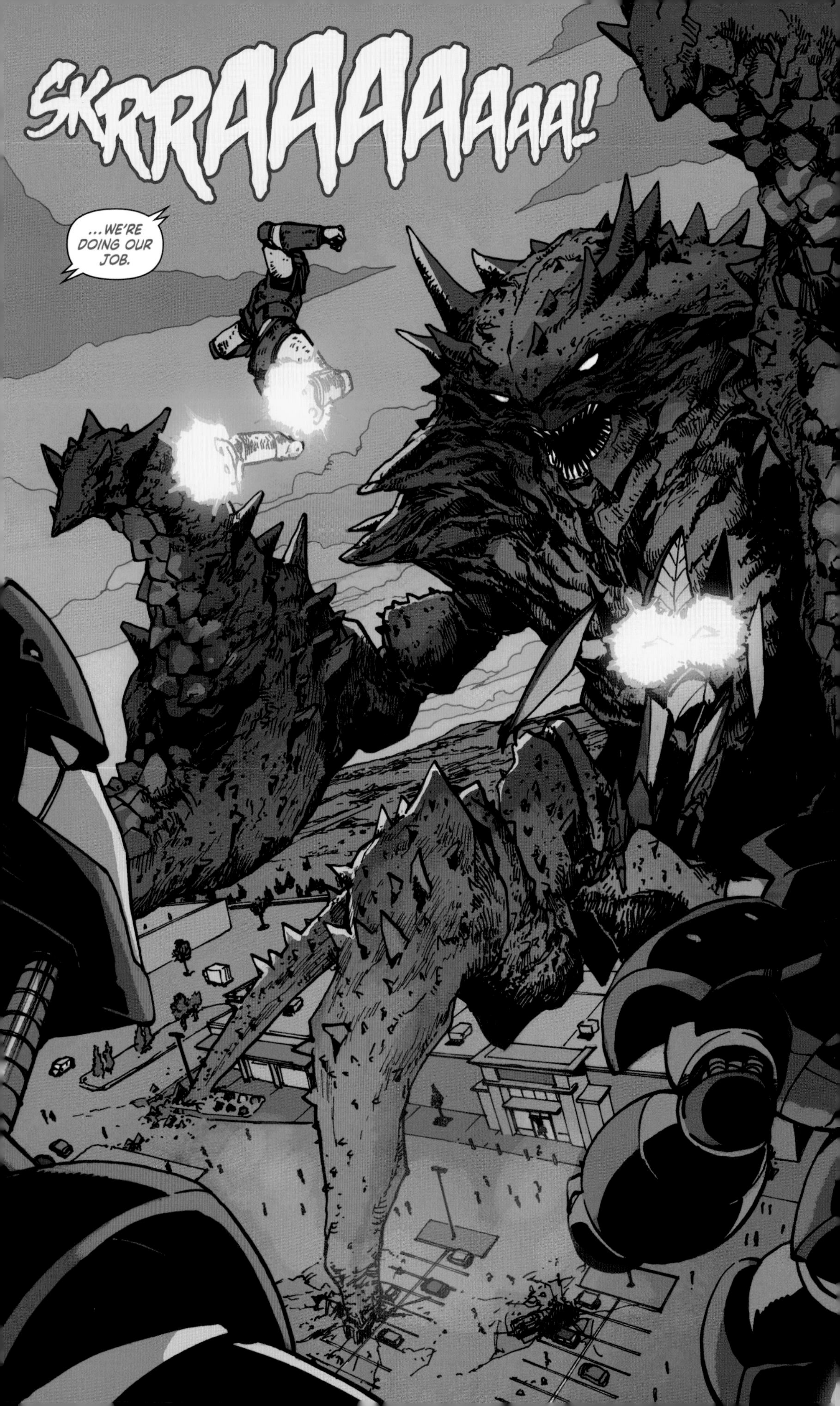
SKRRAAAAAaaa!
...WE'RE DOING OUR JOB.

CHAPTER **FOUR**

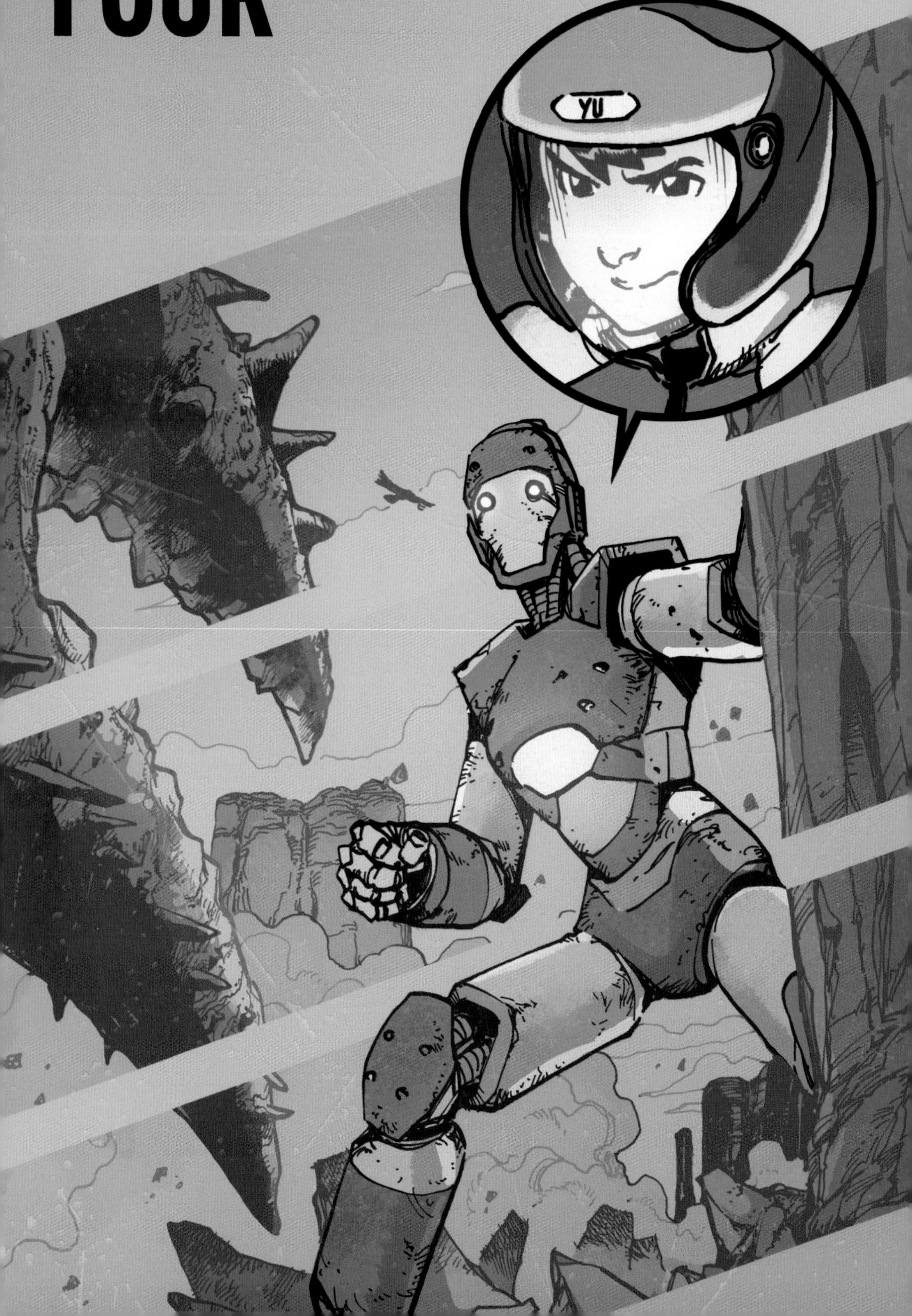
YU

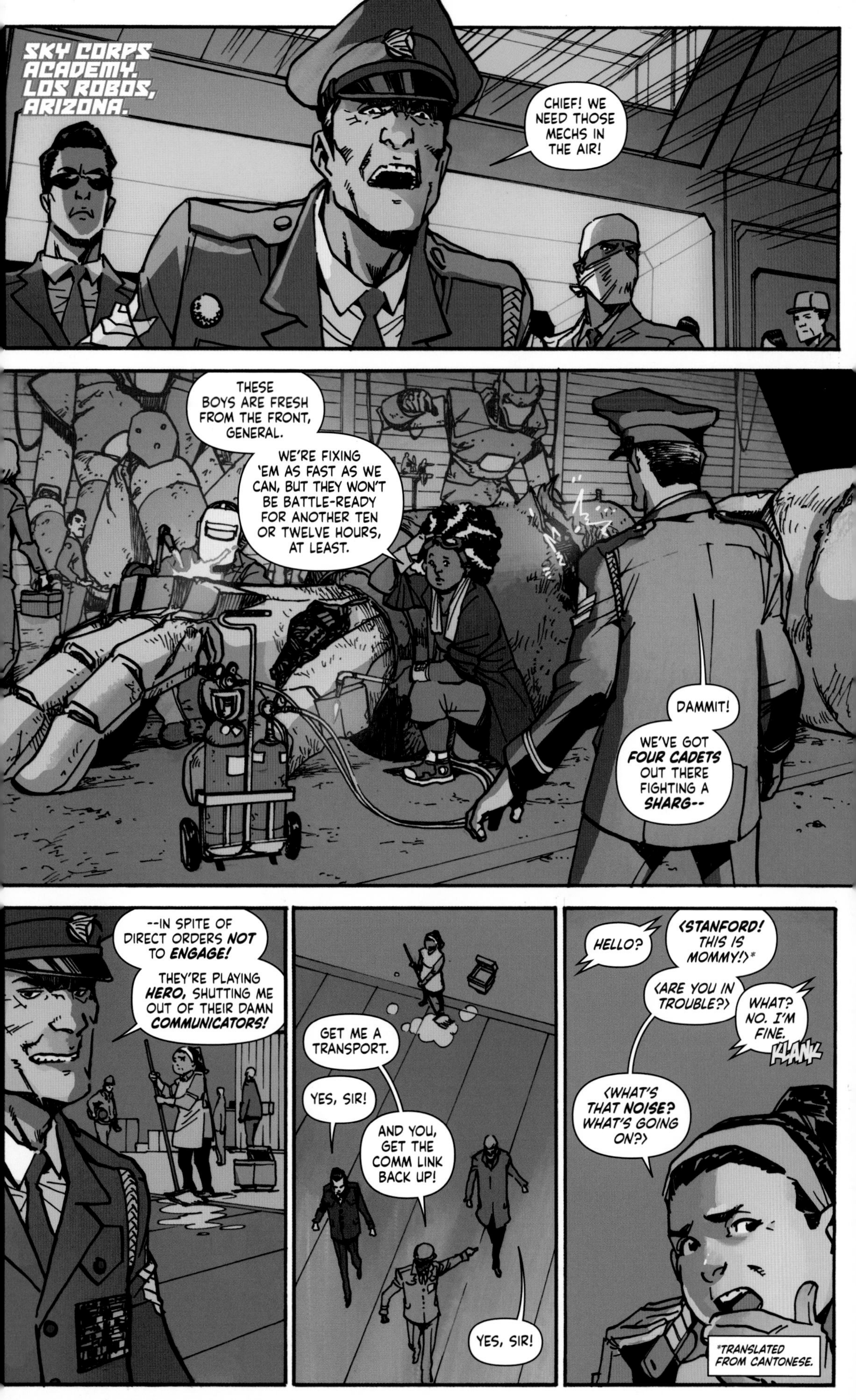
SKY CORPS ACADEMY. LOS ROBOS, ARIZONA.
CHIEF! WE NEED THOSE MECHS IN THE AIR!
THESE BOYS ARE FRESH FROM THE FRONT, GENERAL.
WE'RE FIXING 'EM AS FAST AS WE CAN, BUT THEY WON'T BE BATTLE-READY FOR ANOTHER TEN OR TWELVE HOURS, AT LEAST.
DAMMIT!
WE'VE GOT FOUR CADETS OUT THERE FIGHTING A SHARG--
--IN SPITE OF DIRECT ORDERS NOT TO ENGAGE!
THEY'RE PLAYING HERO, SHUTTING ME OUT OF THEIR DAMN COMMUNICATORS!
GET ME A TRANSPORT.
YES, SIR!
AND YOU, GET THE COMM LINK BACK UP!
YES, SIR!
HELLO?
‹STANFORD! THIS IS MOMMY!›*
‹ARE YOU IN TROUBLE?›
WHAT? NO. I'M FINE.
KLANK
‹WHAT'S THAT NOISE? WHAT'S GOING ON?›
*TRANSLATED FROM CANTONESE.

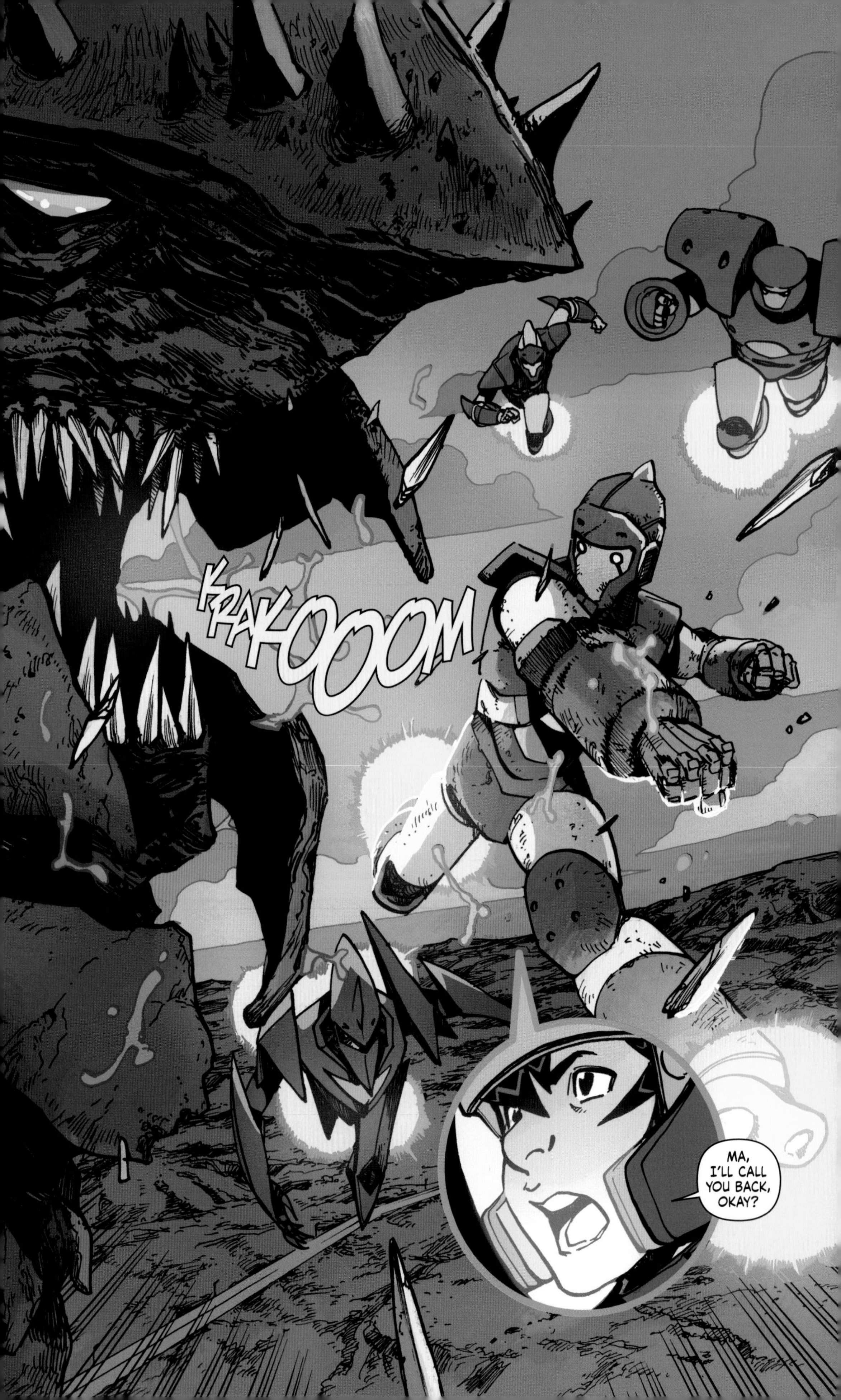
KRAKOOOOM
MA, I'LL CALL YOU BACK, OKAY?

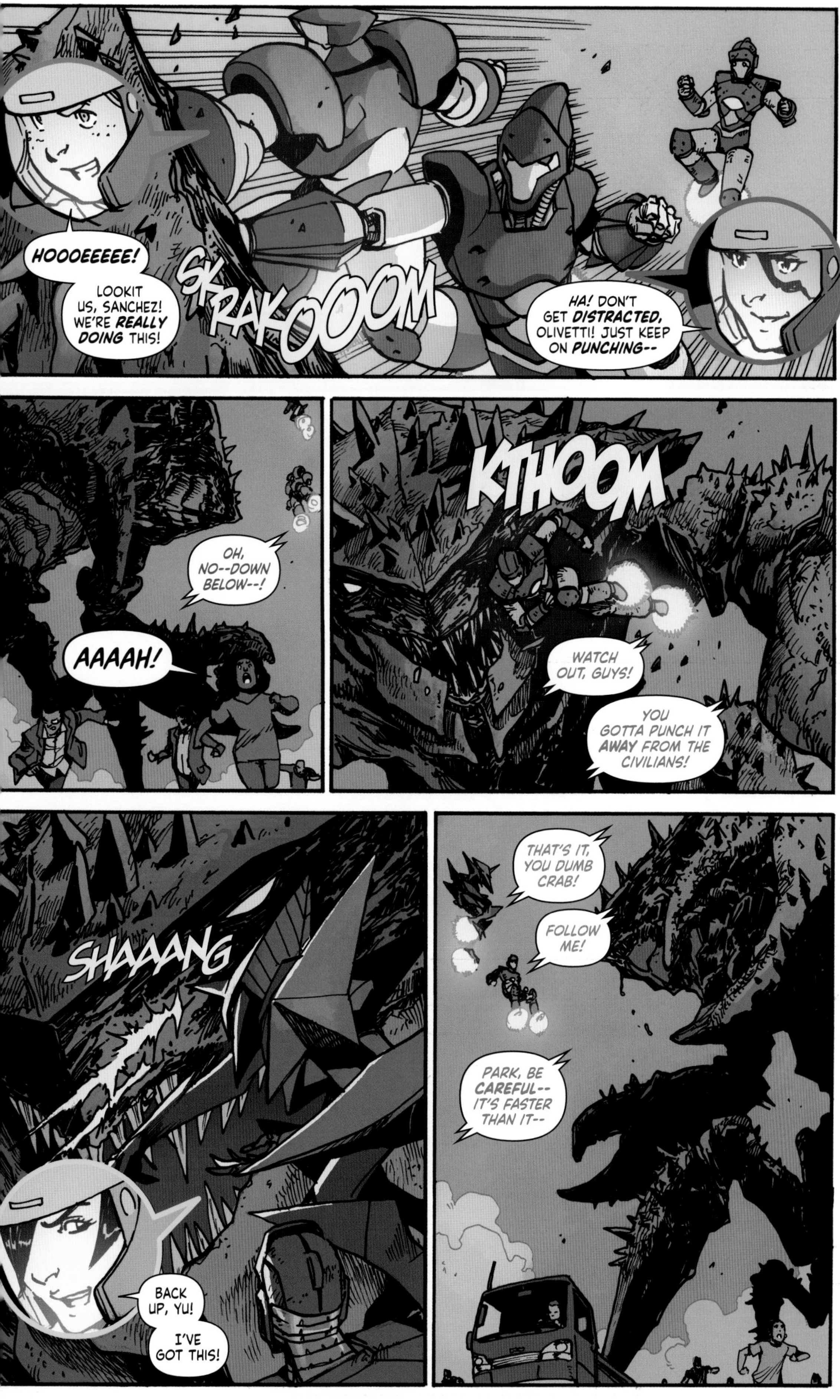
HOOOEEEEE!
LOOKIT US, SANCHEZ! WE'RE REALLY DOING THIS!
SKRAKOOOM
HA! DON'T GET DISTRACTED, OLIVETTI! JUST KEEP ON PUNCHING--
OH, NO--DOWN BELOW--!
AAAAH!
KTHOOM
WATCH OUT, GUYS!
YOU GOTTA PUNCH IT AWAY FROM THE CIVILIANS!
SHAAANG
BACK UP, YU!
I'VE GOT THIS!
THAT'S IT, YOU DUMB CRAB!
FOLLOW ME!
PARK, BE CAREFUL-- IT'S FASTER THAN IT--

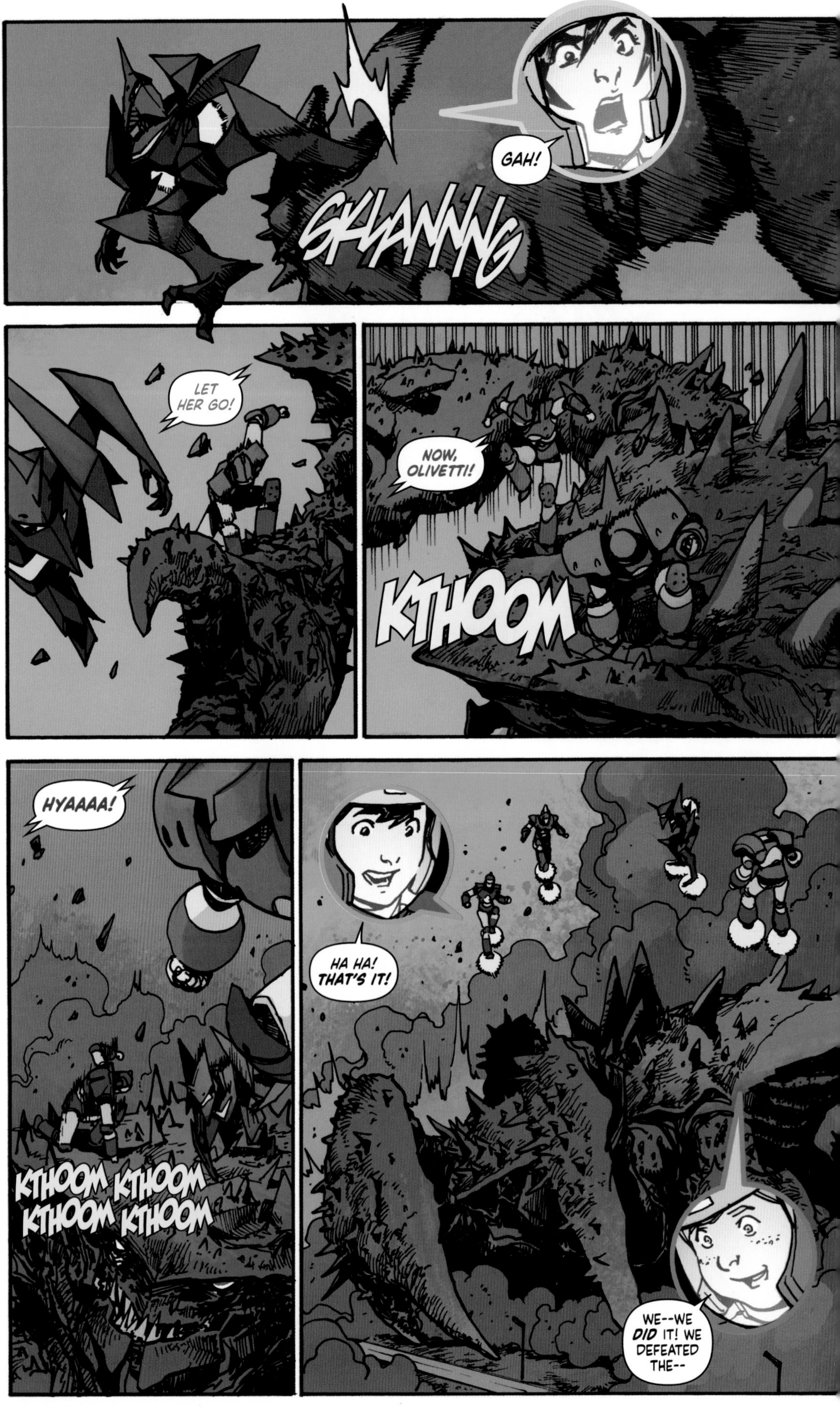
GAH!
SKLANNG
LET HER GO!
NOW, OLIVETTI!
KTHOOM
HYAAAA!
KTHOOM KTHOOM
KTHOOM KTHOOM
HA HA! THAT'S IT!
WE--WE DID IT! WE DEFEATED THE--

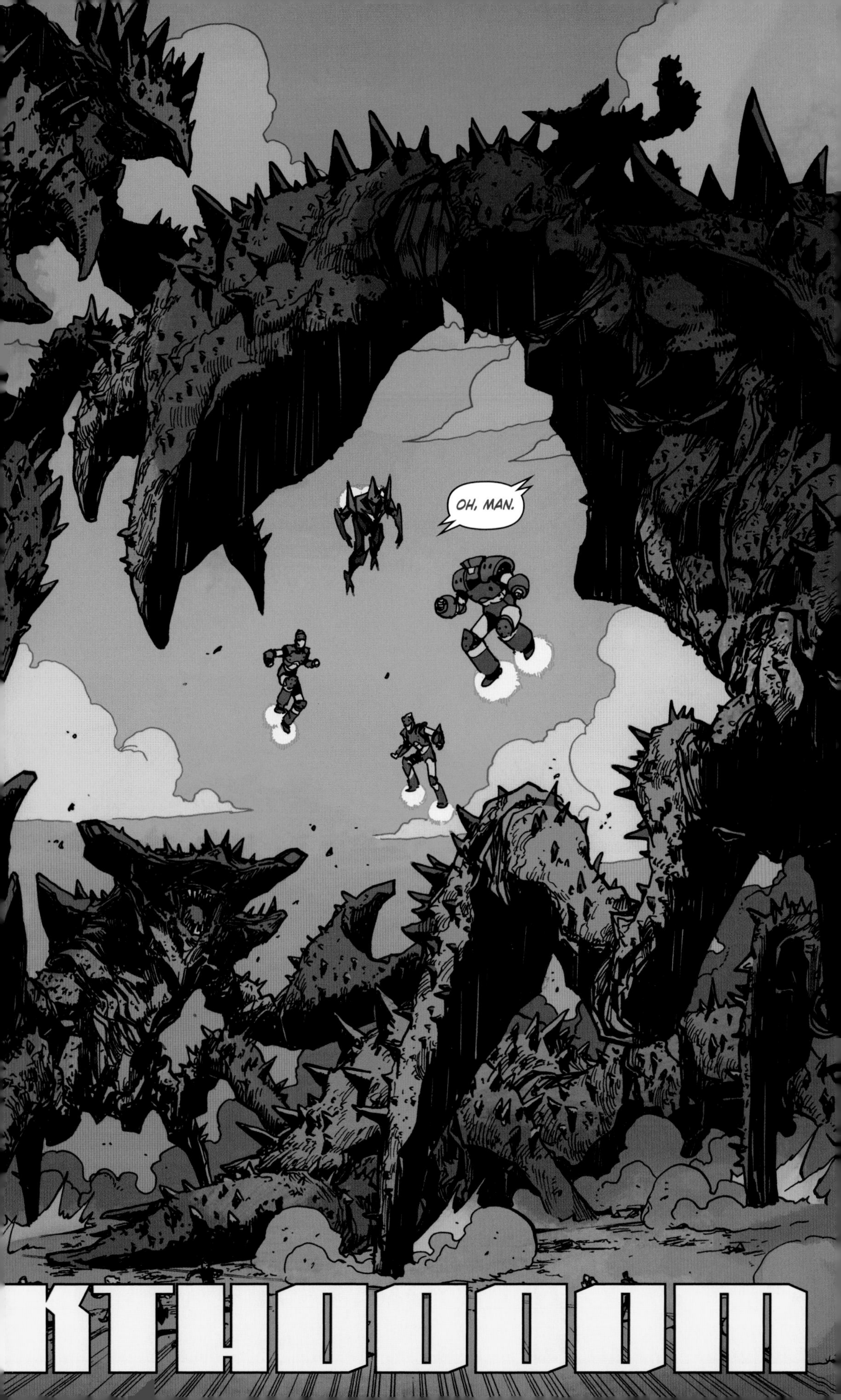
OH, MAN.
KTHOOOOM

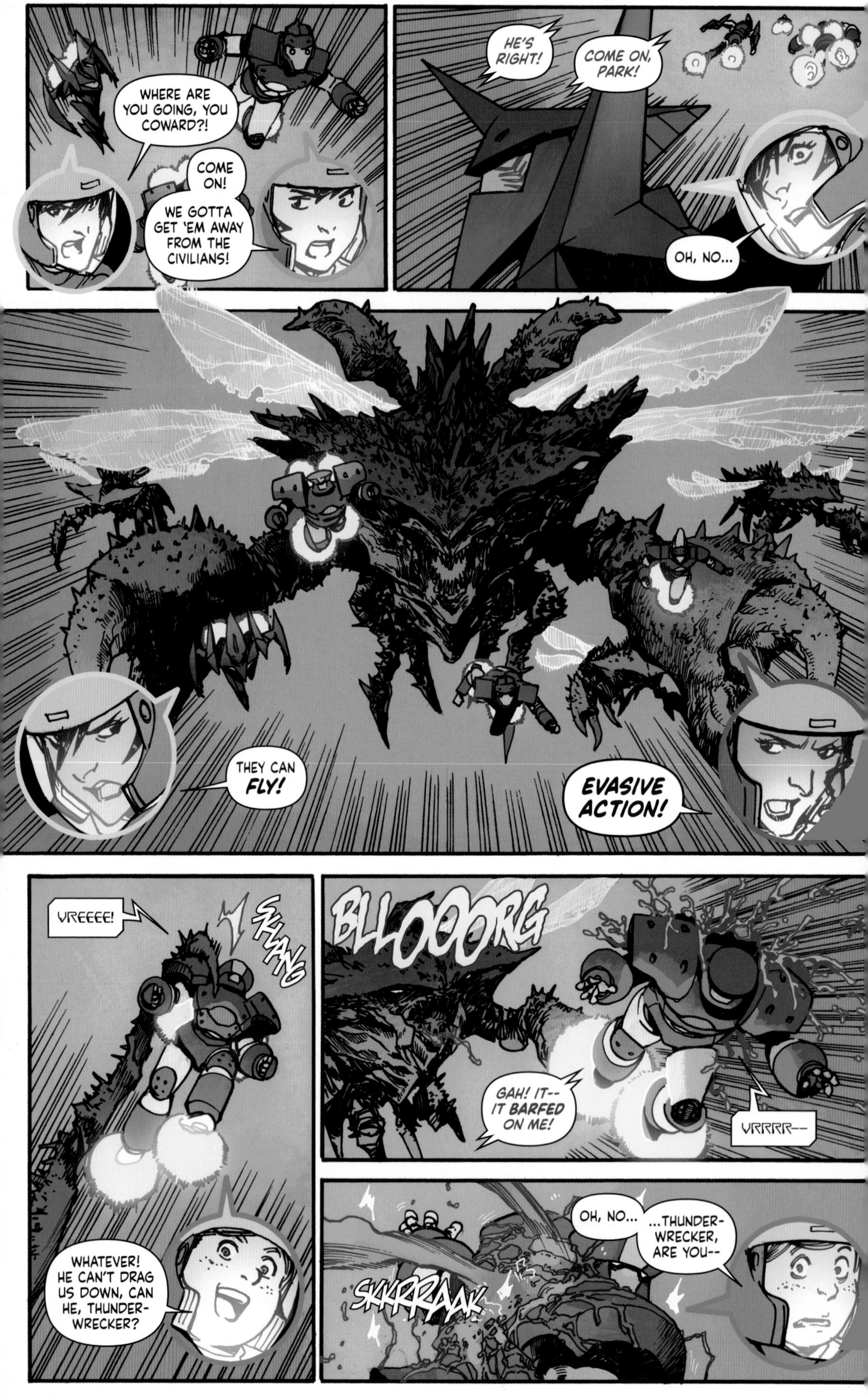
WHERE ARE YOU GOING, YOU COWARD?!
COME ON!
WE GOTTA GET 'EM AWAY FROM THE CIVILIANS!
HE'S RIGHT!
COME ON, PARK!
OH, NO...
THEY CAN FLY!
EVASIVE ACTION!
VREEEE!
SKLANG
BLLOOORG
GAH! IT-- IT BARFED ON ME!
VRRRRR--
WHATEVER! HE CAN'T DRAG US DOWN, CAN HE, THUNDER-WRECKER?
SKKRRAAK
OH, NO...
...THUNDER-WRECKER, ARE YOU--

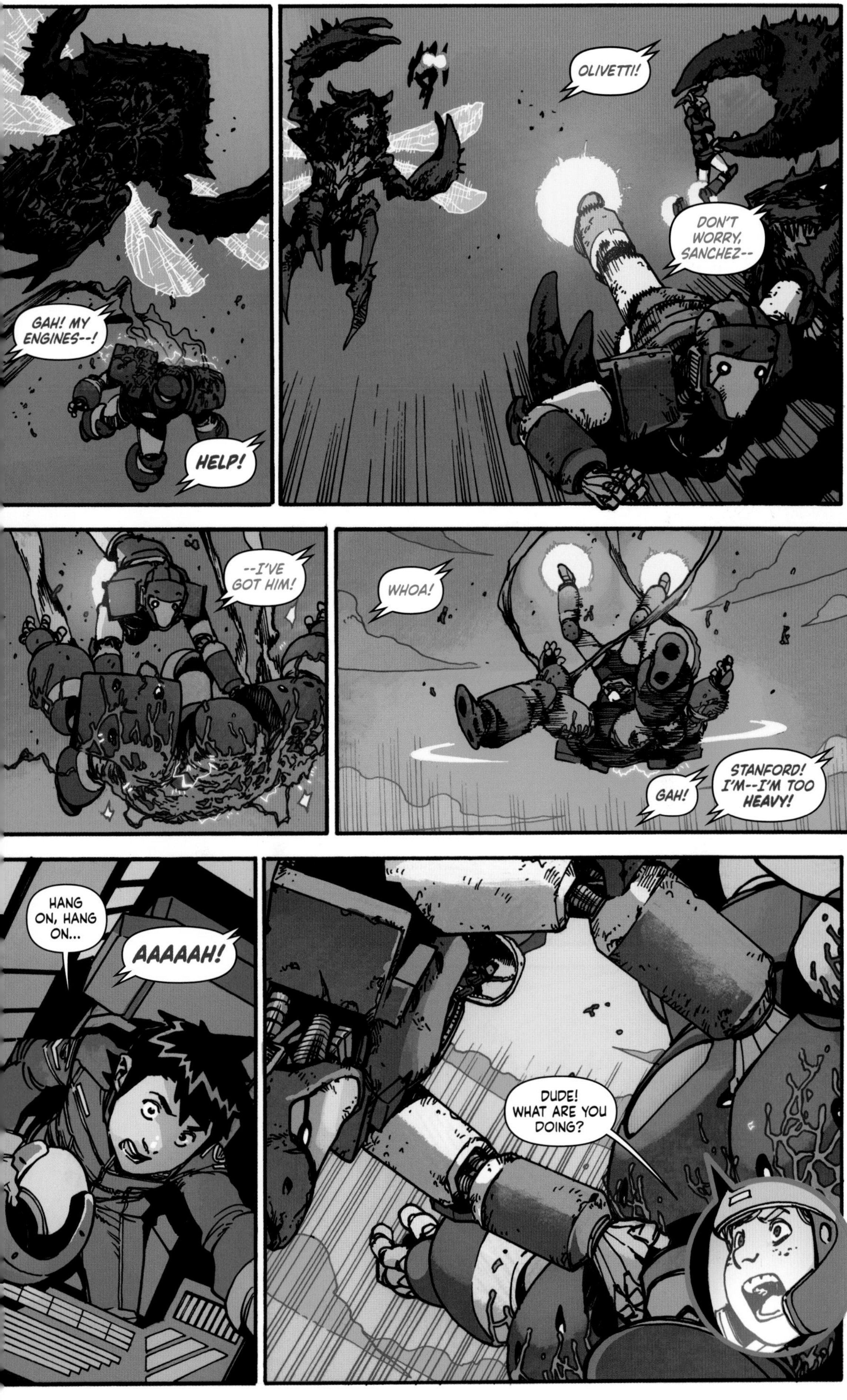
GAH! MY ENGINES--!
HELP!
OLIVETTI!
DON'T WORRY, SANCHEZ--
--I'VE GOT HIM!
WHOA!
GAH!
STANFORD! I'M--I'M TOO HEAVY!
HANG ON, HANG ON...
AAAAAH!
DUDE! WHAT ARE YOU DOING?

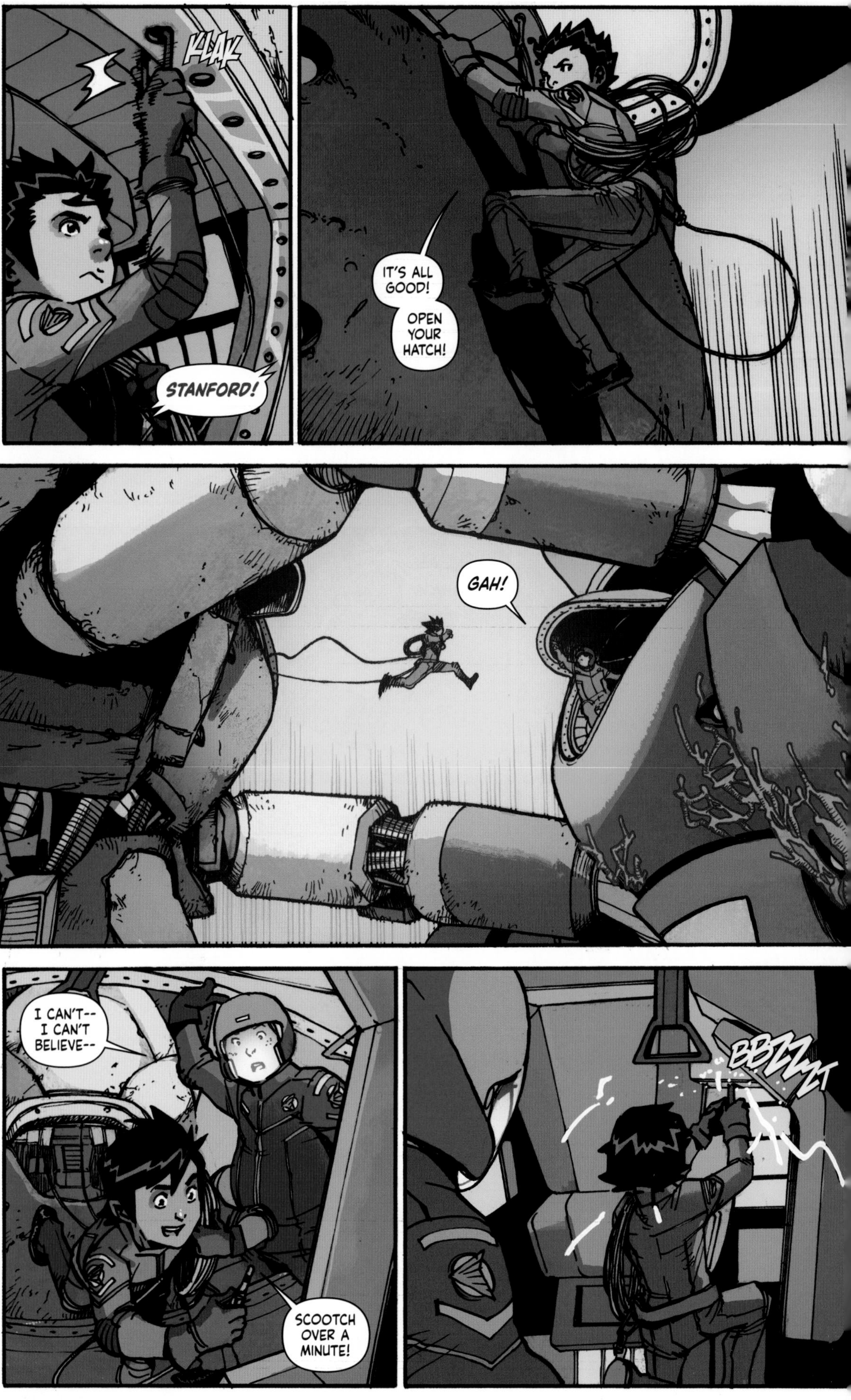
KLAK
STANFORD!
IT'S ALL GOOD!
OPEN YOUR HATCH!
GAH!
I CAN'T-- I CAN'T BELIEVE--
SCOOTCH OVER A MINUTE!
BBZZZT

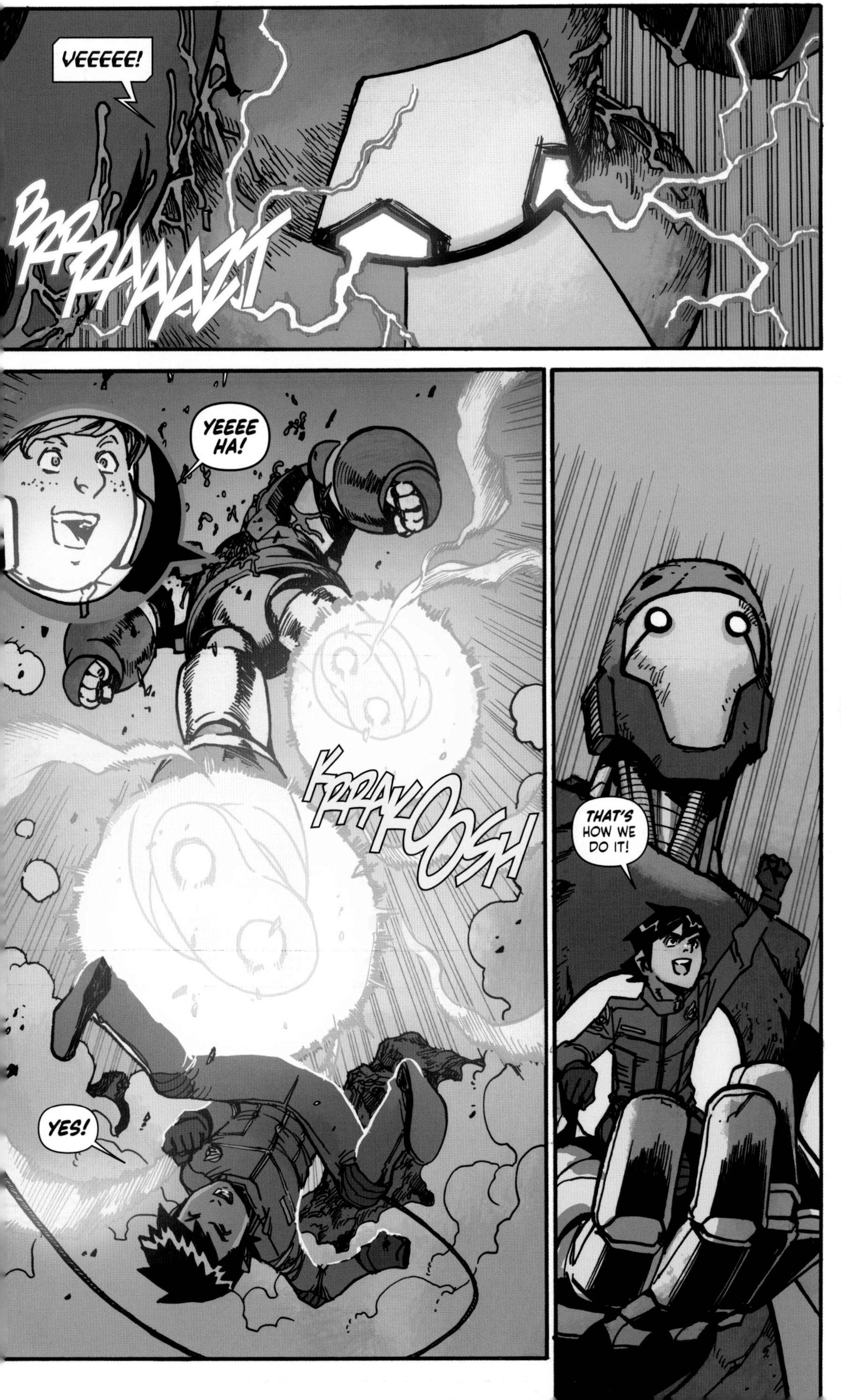
VEEEEE!
BRRRAAAZT
YEEEE HA!
KRRAKOOSH
YES!
THAT'S HOW WE DO IT!

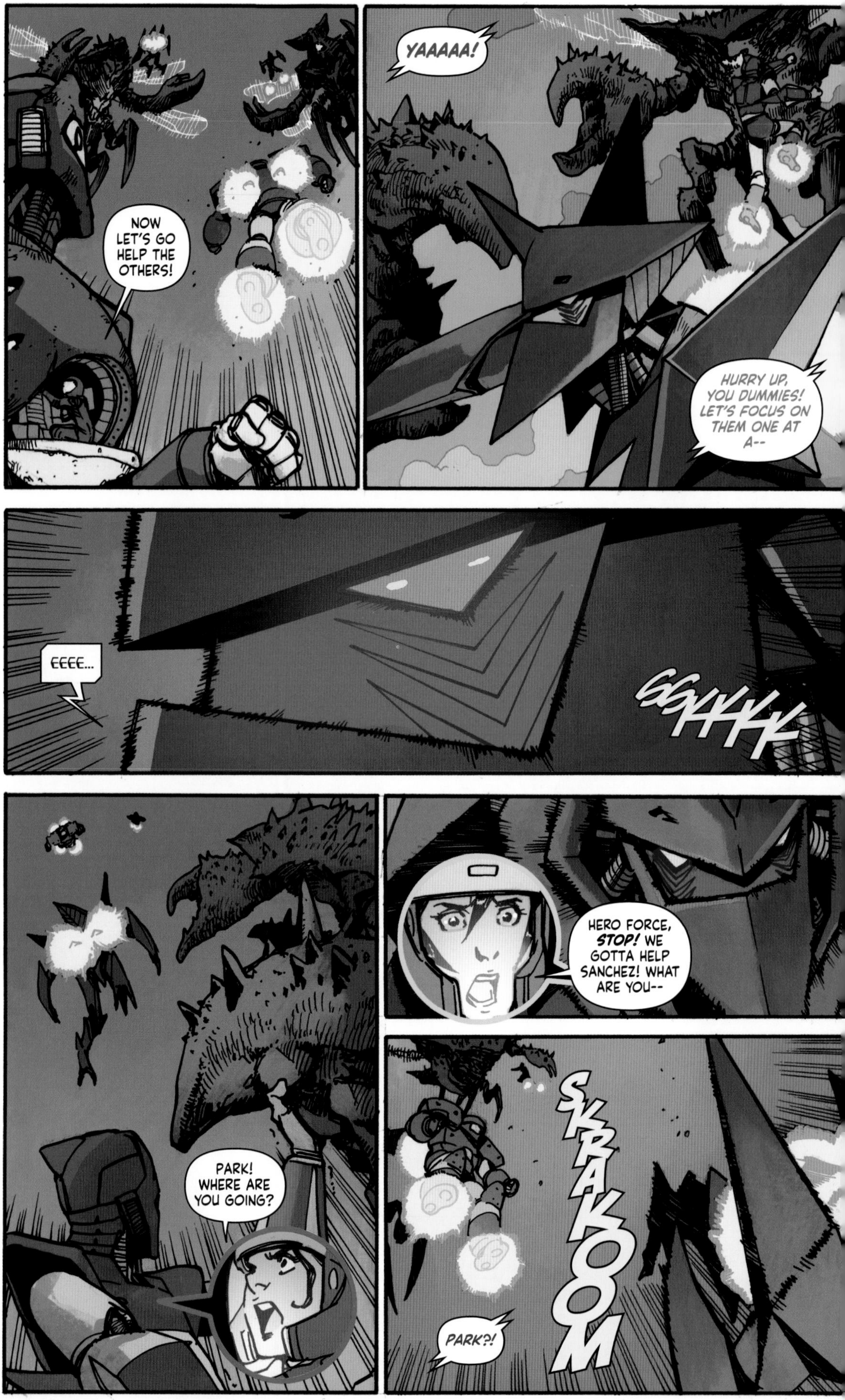
NOW LET'S GO HELP THE OTHERS!
YAAAAA!
HURRY UP, YOU DUMMIES! LET'S FOCUS ON THEM ONE AT A--
EEEE...
GGKKKK
PARK! WHERE ARE YOU GOING?
HERO FORCE, STOP! WE GOTTA HELP SANCHEZ! WHAT ARE YOU--
SKRAKOOM
PARK?!

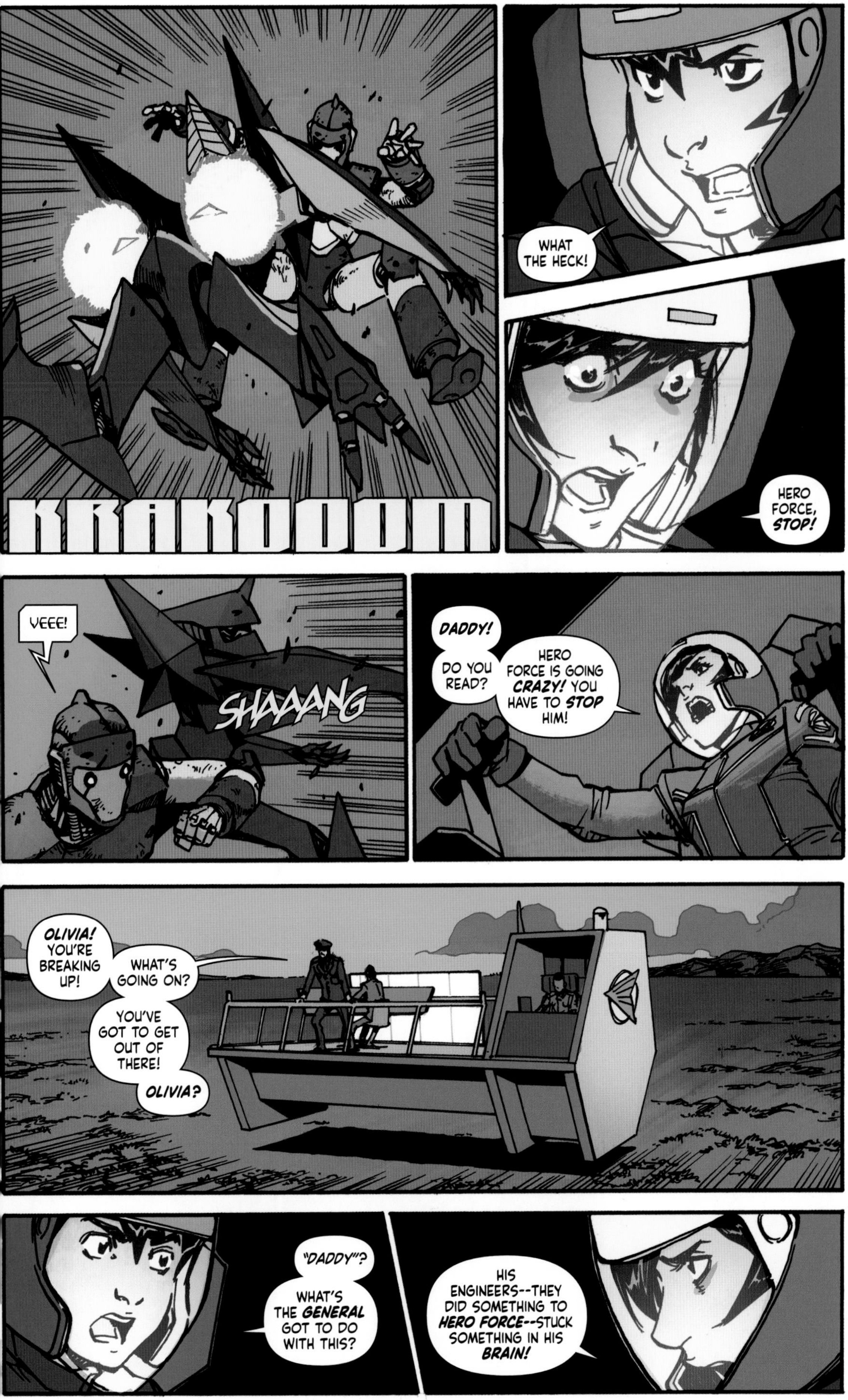

KRAKOOOM
WHAT THE HECK!
HERO FORCE, STOP!
VEEE!
SHAAAANG
DADDY!
DO YOU READ?
HERO FORCE IS GOING CRAZY! YOU HAVE TO STOP HIM!
OLIVIA! YOU'RE BREAKING UP!
WHAT'S GOING ON?
YOU'VE GOT TO GET OUT OF THERE!
OLIVIA?
"DADDY"?
WHAT'S THE GENERAL GOT TO DO WITH THIS?
HIS ENGINEERS--THEY DID SOMETHING TO HERO FORCE--STUCK SOMETHING IN HIS BRAIN!

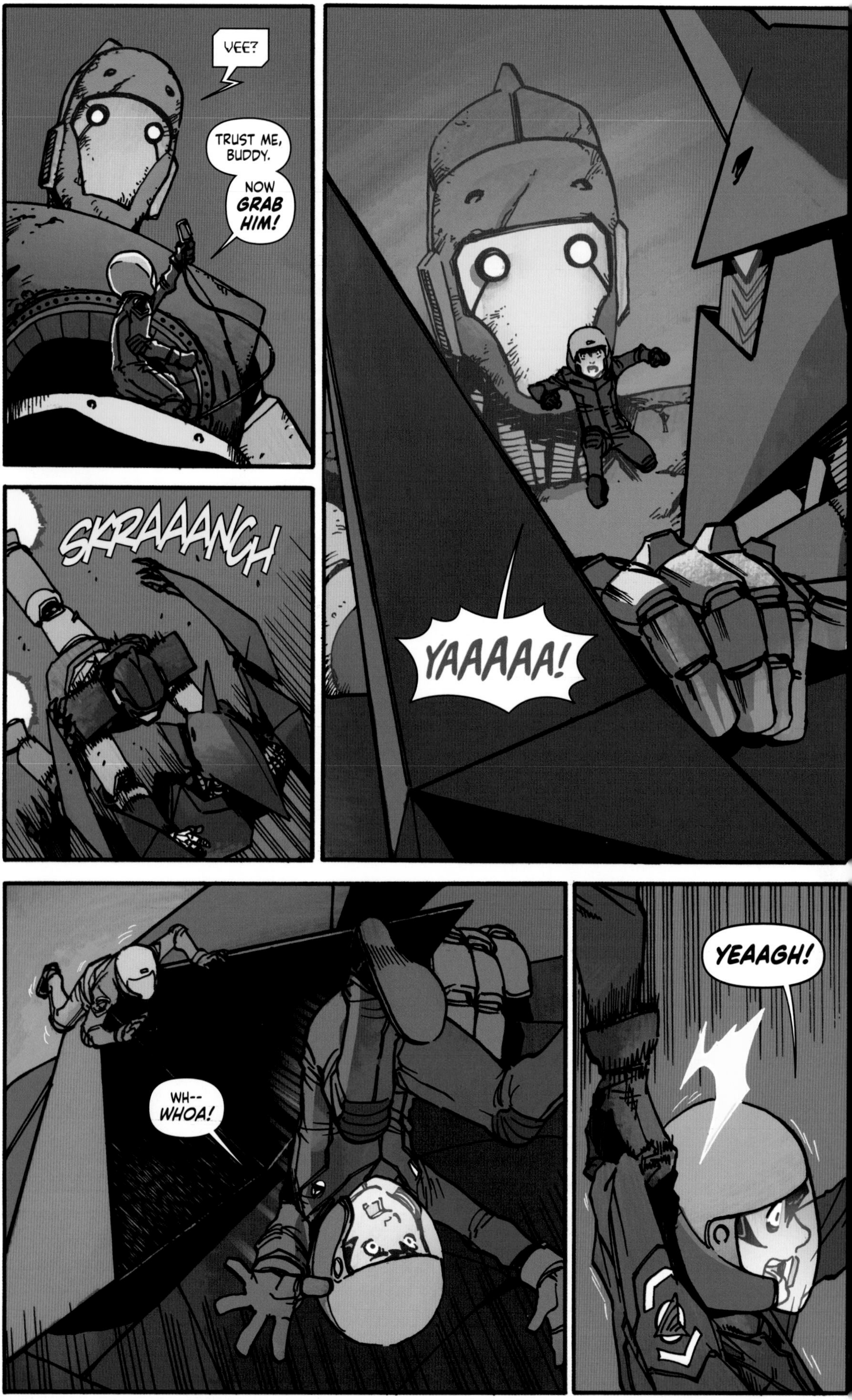
VEE?
TRUST ME, BUDDY.
NOW GRAB HIM!
YAAAAA!
SKRAAAANCH
WH-- WHOA!
YEAAGH!

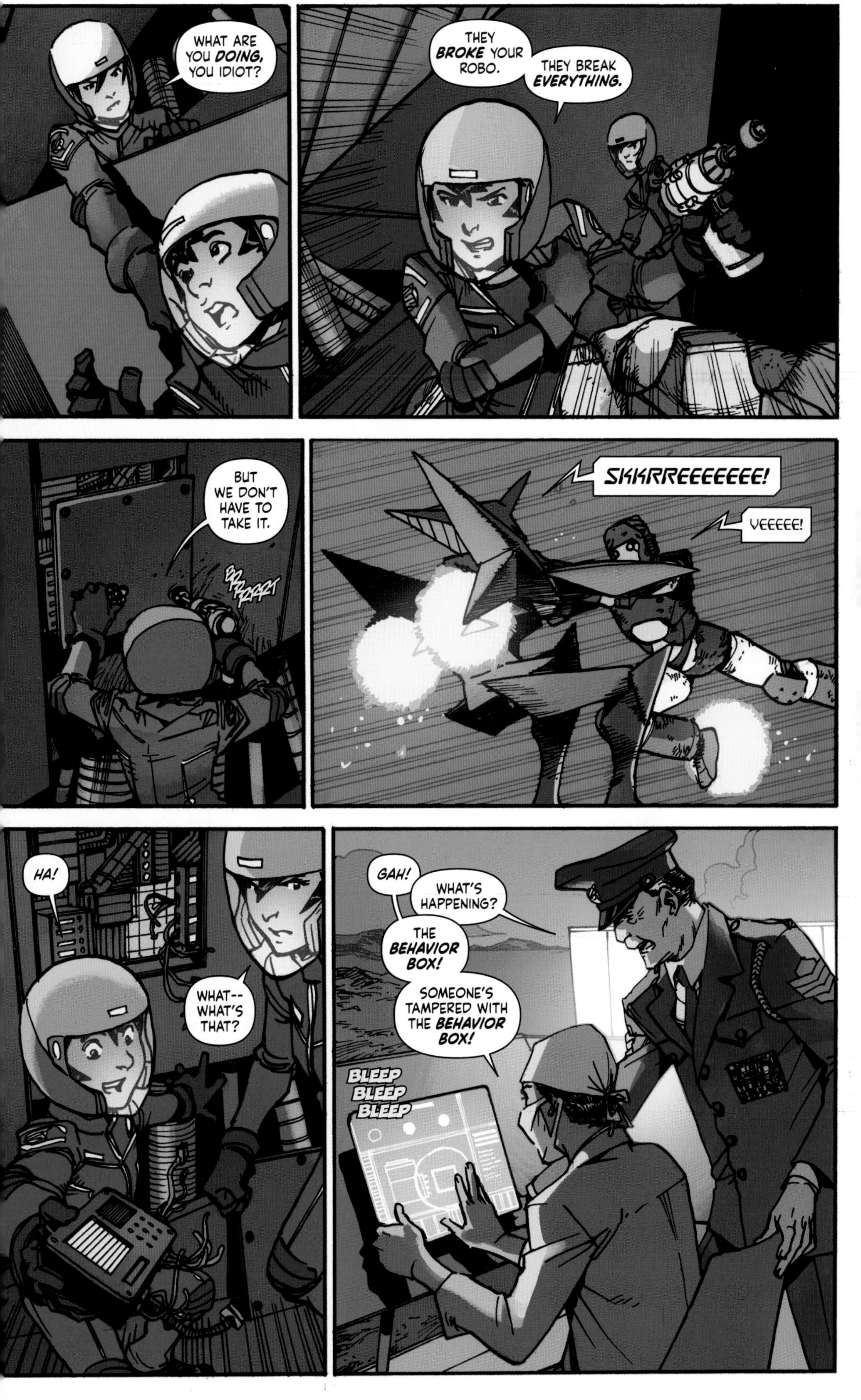

WHAT ARE YOU DOING, YOU IDIOT?
THEY BROKE YOUR ROBO.
THEY BREAK EVERYTHING.
BUT WE DON'T HAVE TO TAKE IT.
BRRRRRRT
SKKRREEEEEEEE!
VEEEEE!
HA!
WHAT-- WHAT'S THAT?
GAH!
WHAT'S HAPPENING?
THE BEHAVIOR BOX!
SOMEONE'S TAMPERED WITH THE BEHAVIOR BOX!
BLEEP BLEEP BLEEP

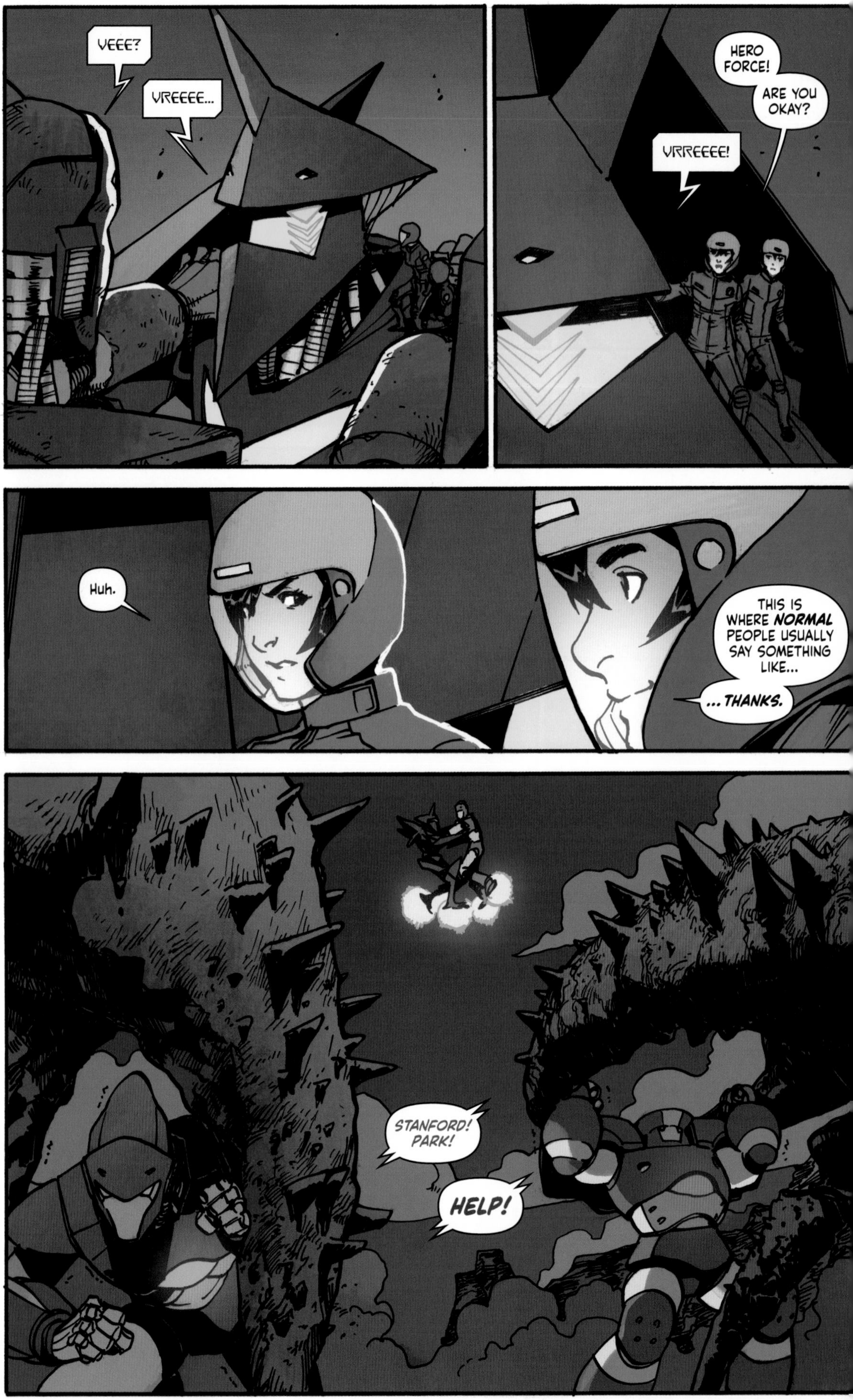
VEEE?
VREEEE...
HERO FORCE!
ARE YOU OKAY?
VRREEEE!
Huh.
THIS IS WHERE NORMAL PEOPLE USUALLY SAY SOMETHING LIKE...
...THANKS.
STANFORD! PARK!
HELP!

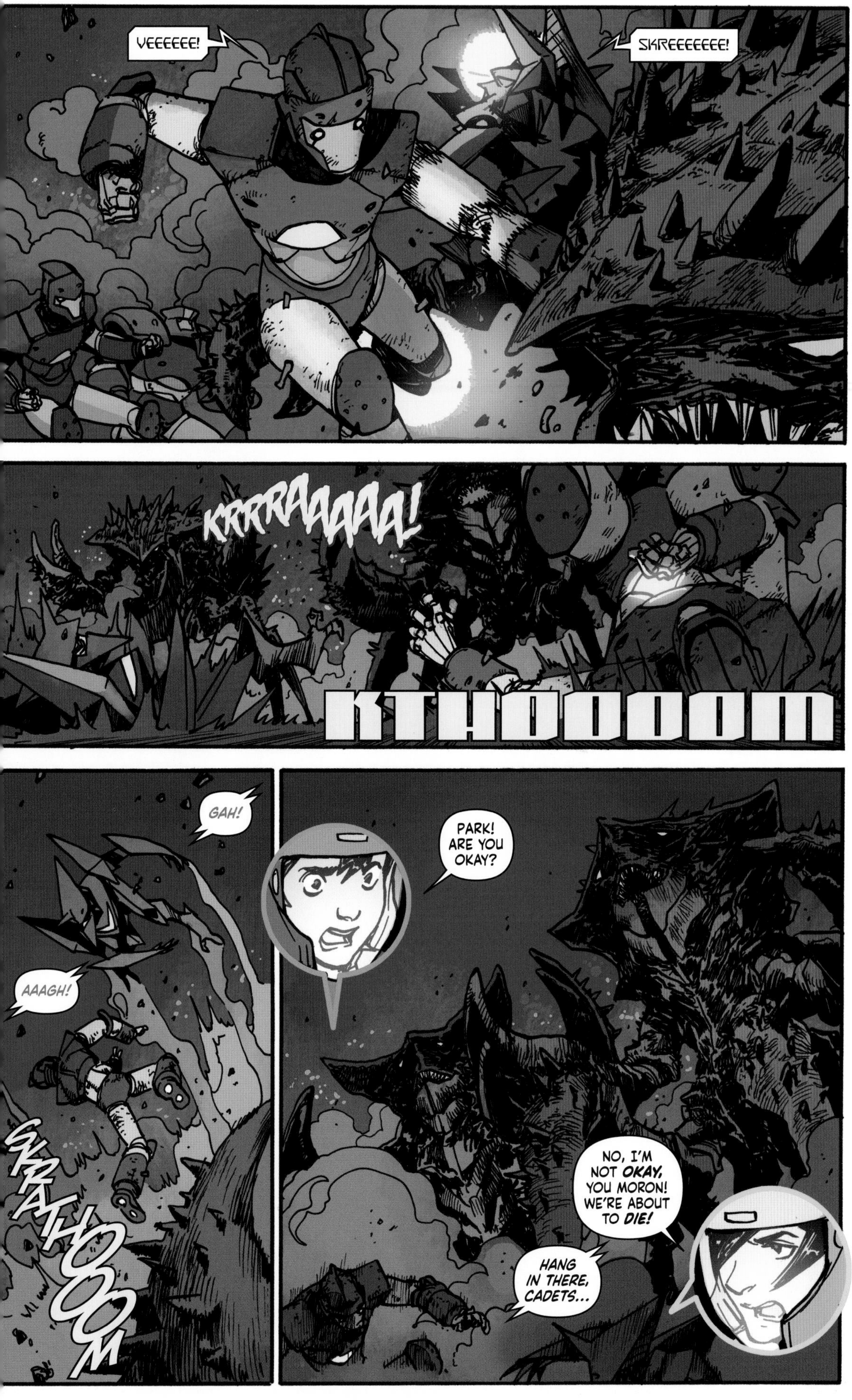
VEEEEEE!
SKREEEEEEE!
KRRRAAAAAA!
KTHOOOOOM
GAH!
AAAGH!
SKRAKHOOOOM
PARK! ARE YOU OKAY?
NO, I'M NOT *OKAY,* YOU MORON! WE'RE ABOUT TO *DIE!*
HANG IN THERE, CADETS...

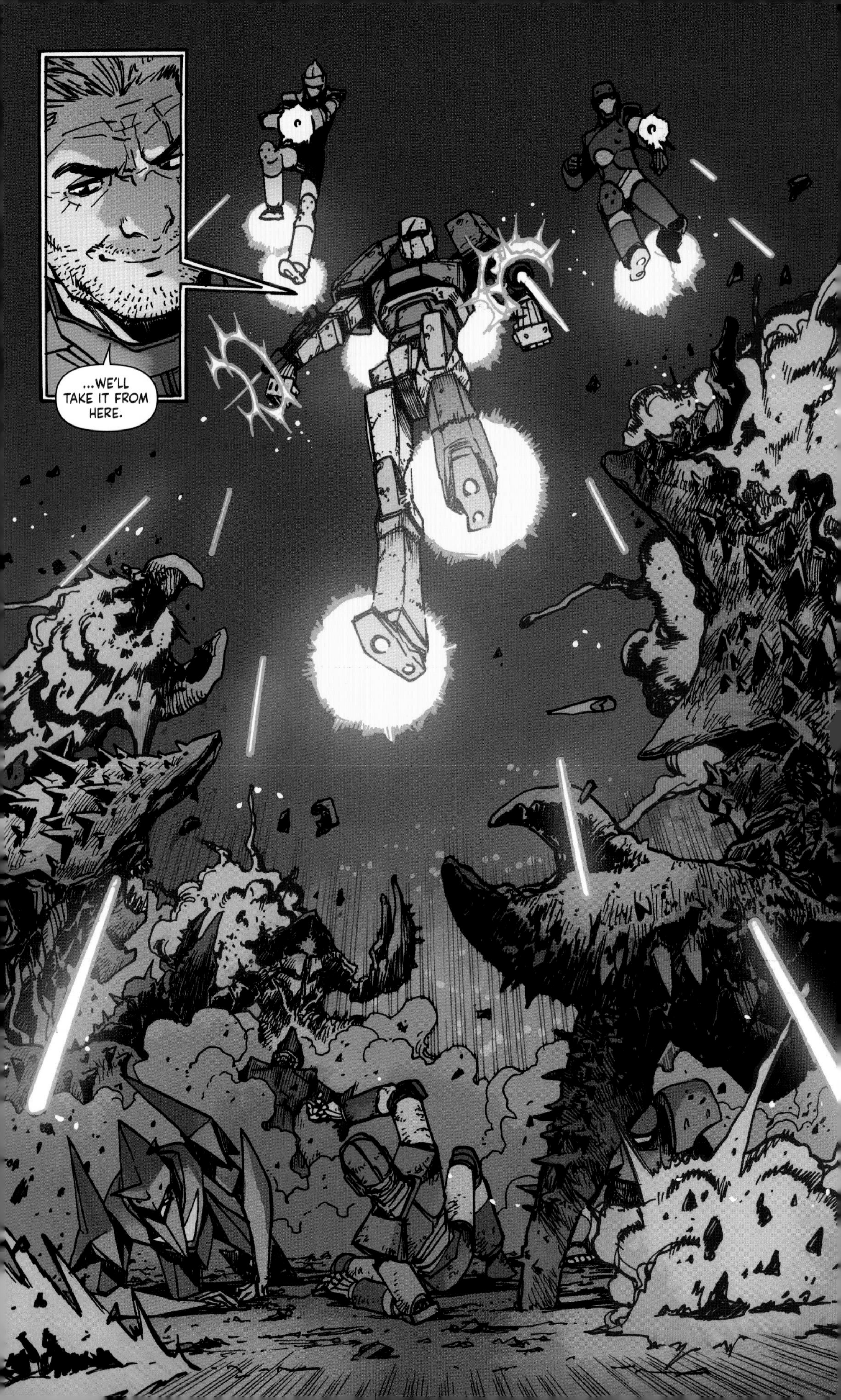
...WE'LL TAKE IT FROM HERE.

VEEE!

C-CAPTAIN TANAKA!

CADETS! FRONT AND CENTER!

YOU DISOBEYED ORDERS.

THAT'S NOT PERMISSIBLE.

THE *GENERAL'S* INCOMING.

I CAN ONLY IMAGINE WHAT HE'S GONNA SAY.

BUT I'M PRETTY DANG PROUD.

ATTEEEEN-- *HUT!*

UH, OH...

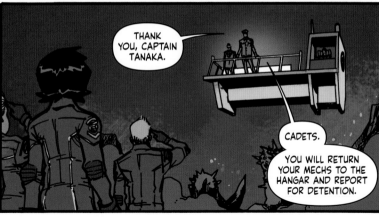

THANK YOU, CAPTAIN TANAKA.

CADETS.

YOU WILL RETURN YOUR MECHS TO THE HANGAR AND REPORT FOR DETENTION.

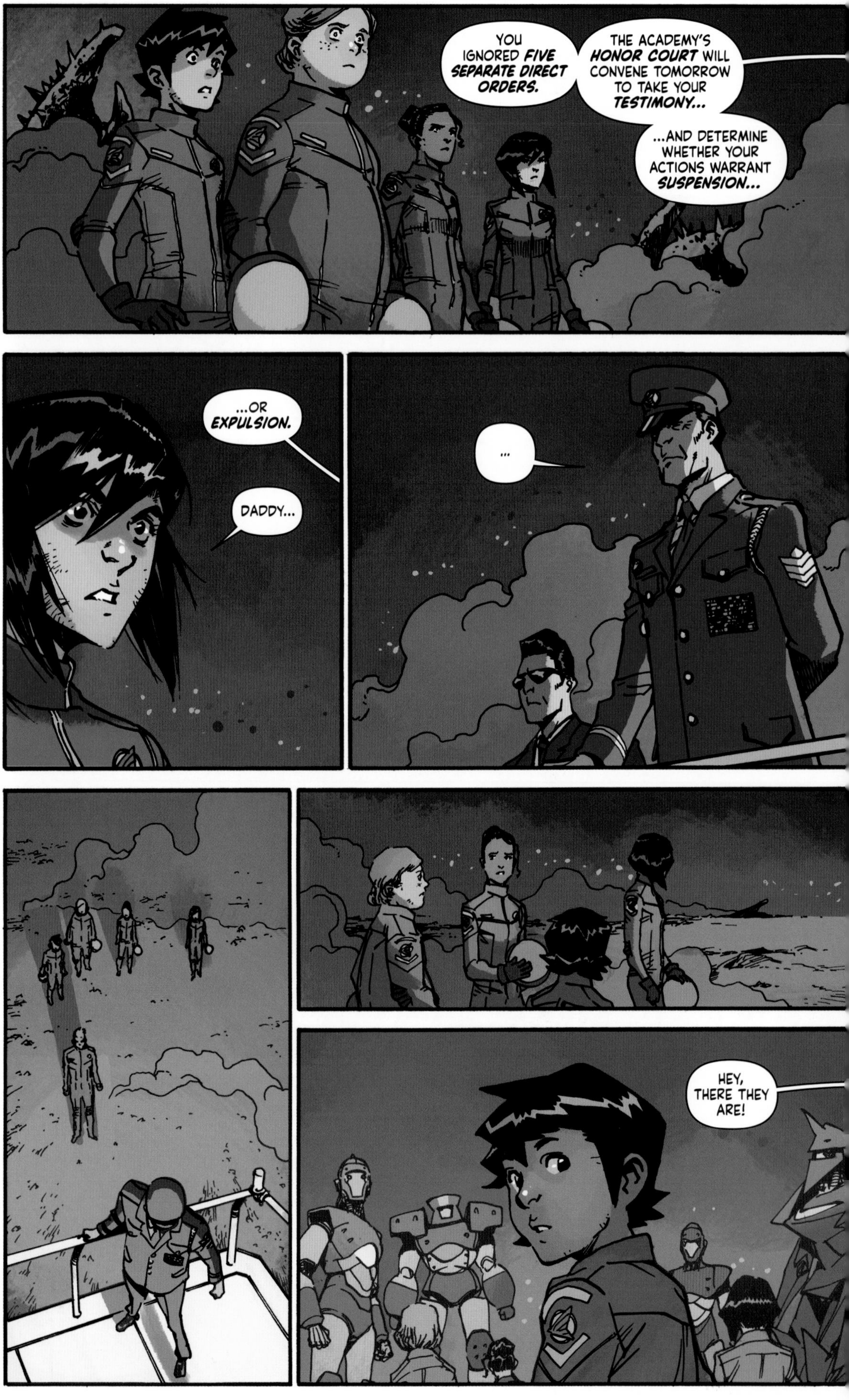
YOU IGNORED FIVE SEPARATE DIRECT ORDERS.
THE ACADEMY'S HONOR COURT WILL CONVENE TOMORROW TO TAKE YOUR TESTIMONY...
...AND DETERMINE WHETHER YOUR ACTIONS WARRANT SUSPENSION...
...OR EXPULSION.
DADDY...
...
HEY, THERE THEY ARE!

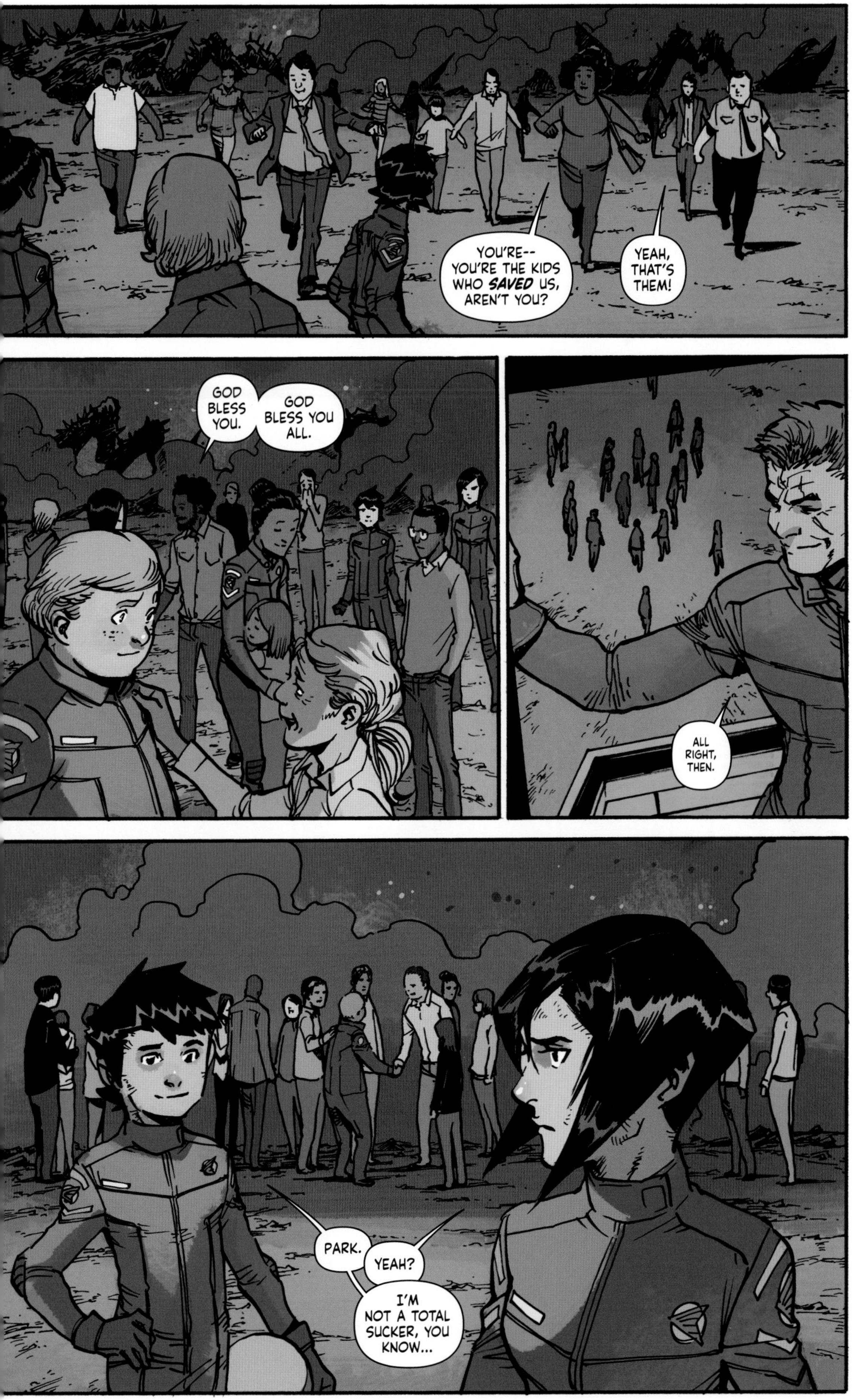
YOU'RE--
YOU'RE THE KIDS WHO *SAVED* US, AREN'T YOU?
YEAH, THAT'S THEM!
GOD BLESS YOU.
GOD BLESS YOU ALL.
ALL RIGHT, THEN.
PARK.
YEAH?
I'M NOT A TOTAL SUCKER, YOU KNOW...

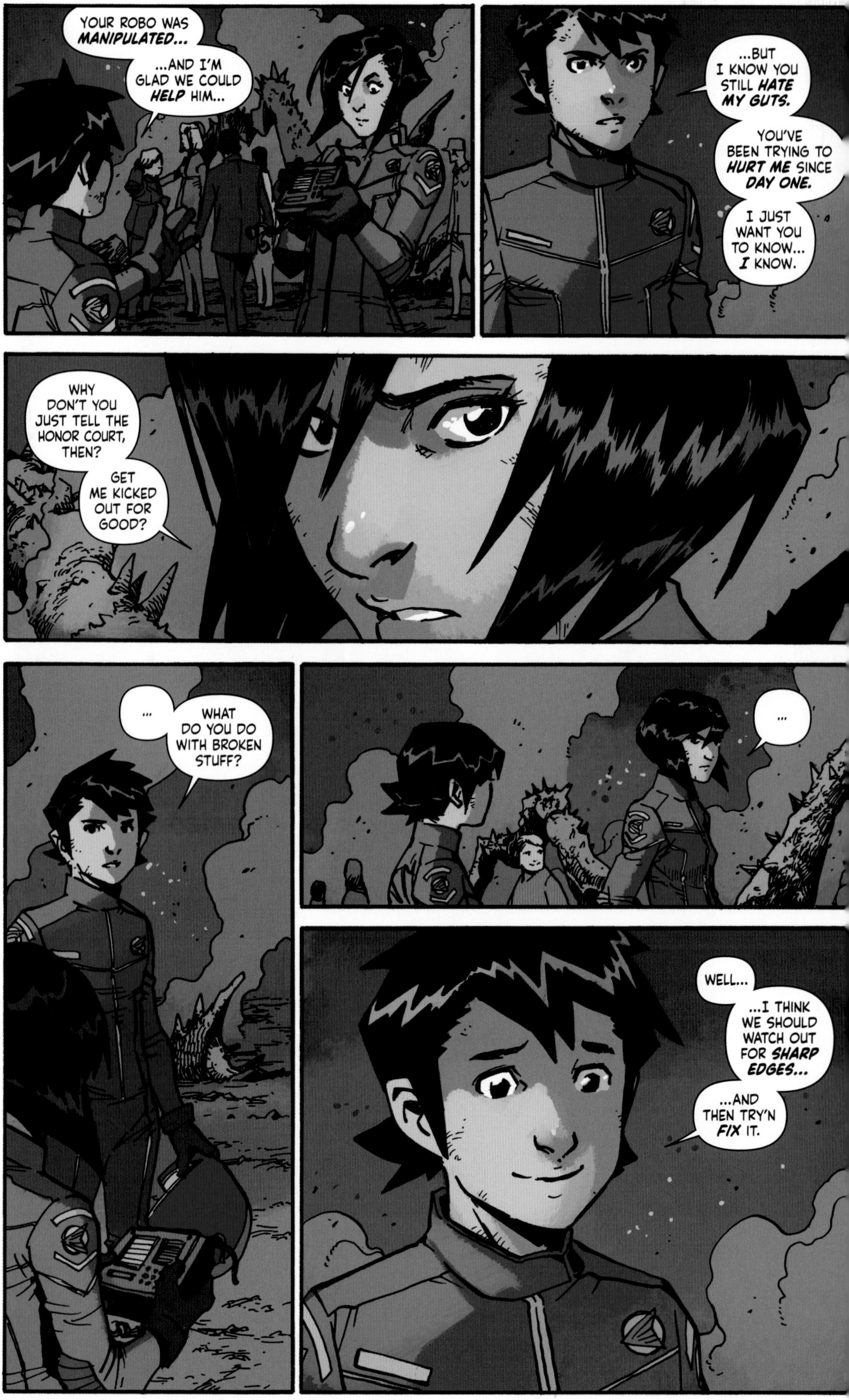
YOUR ROBO WAS MANIPULATED...
...AND I'M GLAD WE COULD HELP HIM...
...BUT I KNOW YOU STILL HATE MY GUTS.
YOU'VE BEEN TRYING TO HURT ME SINCE DAY ONE.
I JUST WANT YOU TO KNOW... I KNOW.
WHY DON'T YOU JUST TELL THE HONOR COURT, THEN?
GET ME KICKED OUT FOR GOOD?
...
WHAT DO YOU DO WITH BROKEN STUFF?
...
WELL...
...I THINK WE SHOULD WATCH OUT FOR SHARP EDGES...
...AND THEN TRY'N FIX IT.

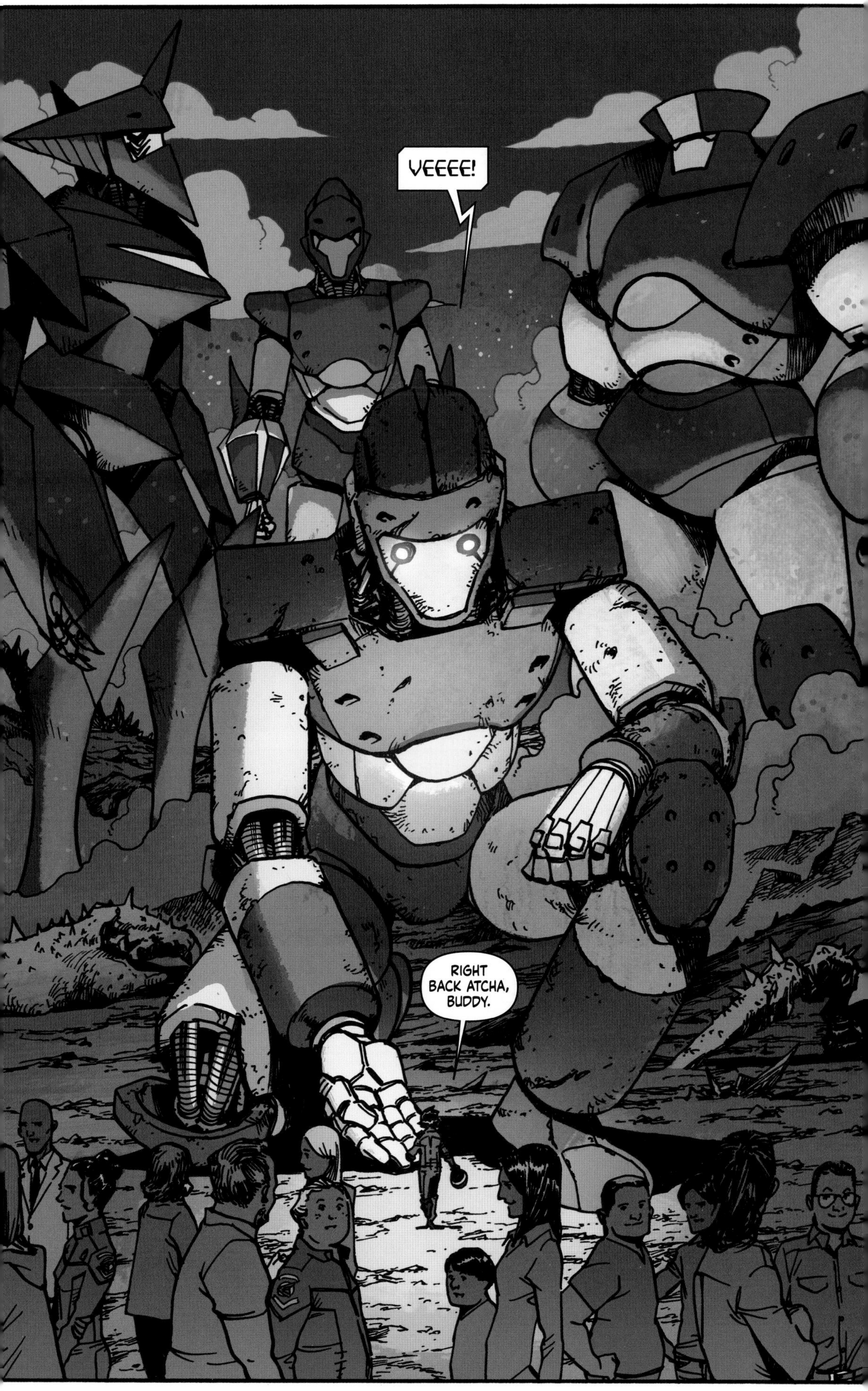
VEEEE!
RIGHT BACK ATCHA, BUDDY.

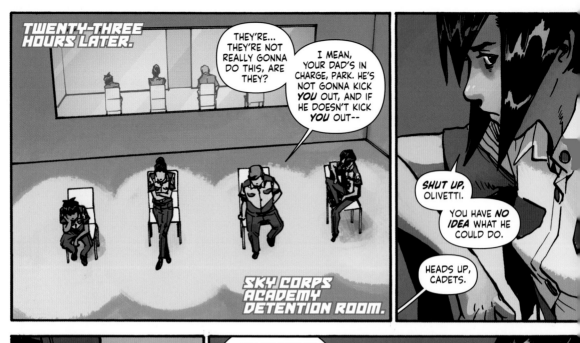

TWENTY-THREE HOURS LATER.

THEY'RE... THEY'RE NOT REALLY GONNA DO THIS, ARE THEY?

I MEAN, YOUR DAD'S IN CHARGE, PARK. HE'S NOT GONNA KICK *YOU* OUT, AND IF HE DOESN'T KICK *YOU* OUT--

SKY CORPS ACADEMY DETENTION ROOM.

SHUT UP, OLIVETTI.

YOU HAVE *NO IDEA* WHAT HE COULD DO.

HEADS UP, CADETS.

THE HONOR COURT'S ABOUT TO ISSUE ITS RULING.

BUT LISTEN CLOSELY, NOW.

AND DON'T TELL ANYONE ABOUT THIS...

...BUT THE WORLD'S GONNA NEED YOU IN THIS WAR FAR SOONER THAN ANYONE EVER ANTICIPATED.

NO CADETS ARE ALLOWED IN COMBAT BEFORE THE AGE OF *SEVENTEEN,* AND CENTRAL COMMAND ISN'T CHANGING THAT...

...BUT I'M NOT CENTRAL COMMAND.

I'VE GOT MY *OWN* PLANS.

AND YOU CAN BE PART OF 'EM...

...IF YOU'RE *WILLING* TO KEEP BREAKING A FEW *RULES.*

CHAPTER **FIVE**

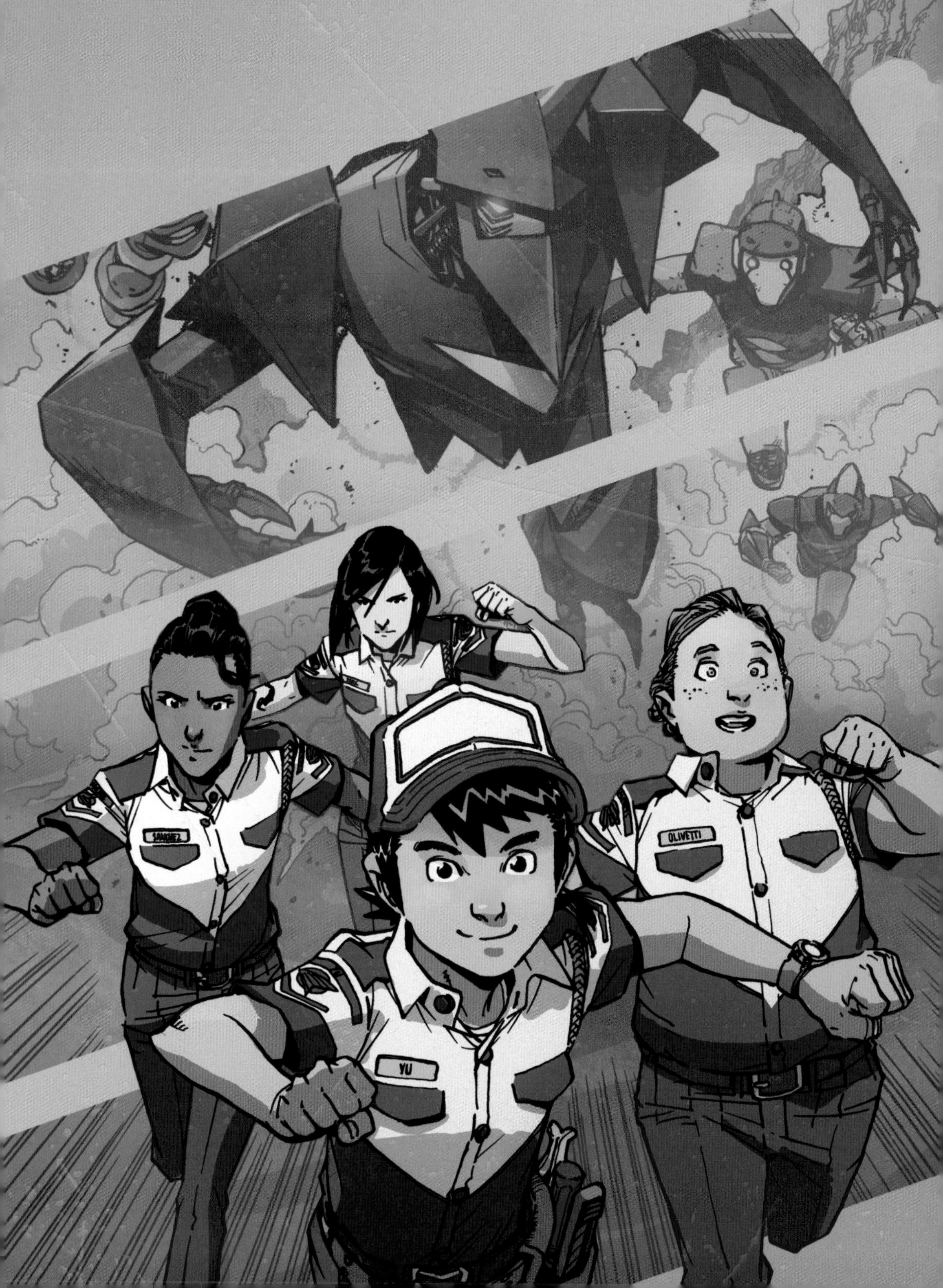
SANCHEZ
OLIVETTI
YU

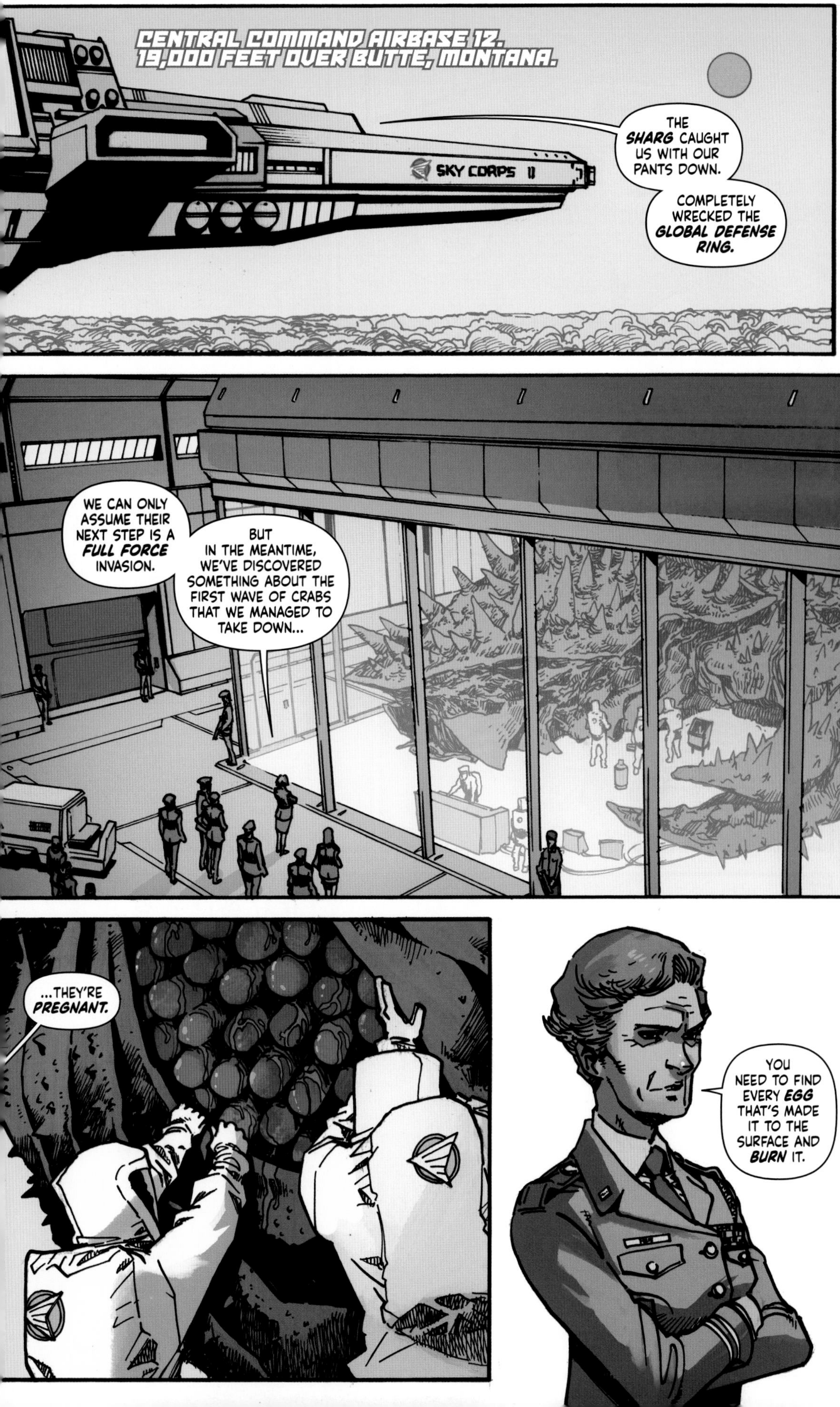
CENTRAL COMMAND AIRBASE 12.
19,000 FEET OVER BUTTE, MONTANA.
SKY CORPS 11
THE SHARG CAUGHT US WITH OUR PANTS DOWN.
COMPLETELY WRECKED THE GLOBAL DEFENSE RING.
WE CAN ONLY ASSUME THEIR NEXT STEP IS A FULL FORCE INVASION.
BUT IN THE MEANTIME, WE'VE DISCOVERED SOMETHING ABOUT THE FIRST WAVE OF CRABS THAT WE MANAGED TO TAKE DOWN...
...THEY'RE PREGNANT.
YOU NEED TO FIND EVERY EGG THAT'S MADE IT TO THE SURFACE AND BURN IT.

GENERAL PARK. A MOMENT.

YES, GENERAL FELIX?

IT'S MY UNDERSTANDING THAT YOUR CADETS FOUGHT A SHARG *AGAINST ORDERS.*

YES. THE WHOLE THING WAS INSTIGATED BY THE NEW CADET, STANFORD YU, AND THE DAMAGED ROBO THAT BONDED WITH HIM.

THE ACADEMY'S HONOR COURT IS DETERMINING THEIR PUNISHMENT--

FINE...

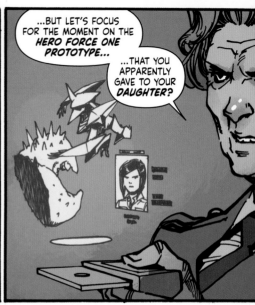

...BUT LET'S FOCUS FOR THE MOMENT ON THE *HERO FORCE ONE PROTOTYPE...*

...THAT YOU APPARENTLY GAVE TO YOUR *DAUGHTER?*

HERO FORCE NEEDED TO BE TESTED WITH A HUMAN PILOT. AND CADET PARK IS THE HIGHEST RANKED STUDENT IN HER YEAR.

TOP OF EVERY SUBJECT. FIRST IN EVERY SKILLS ASSESSMENT.

I'M SURE. AND YET SHE *DISOBEYED ORDERS* ALONG WITH THE REST...

...AND OUR *ONLY WORKING MAN-MADE MECH* FOLLOWED HER LEAD.

SHE... WILL SUFFER THE CONSEQUENCES.

I'M NOT CONCERNED ABOUT *HER,* GENERAL PARK.

I'M CONCERNED ABOUT THE *ROBO...*

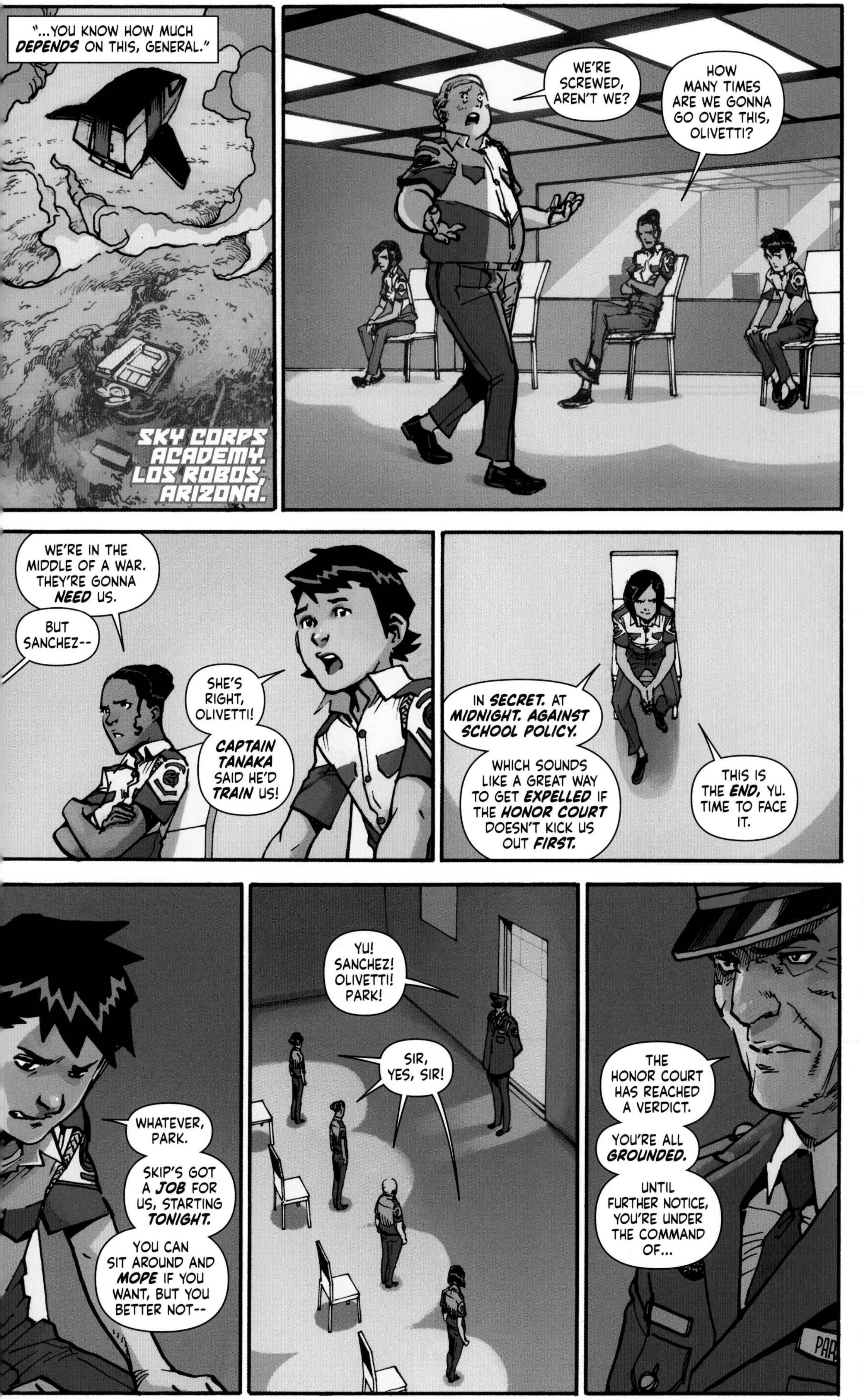

"...YOU KNOW HOW MUCH DEPENDS ON THIS, GENERAL."
SKY CORPS ACADEMY. LOS ROBOS, ARIZONA.
WE'RE SCREWED, AREN'T WE?
HOW MANY TIMES ARE WE GONNA GO OVER THIS, OLIVETTI?
WE'RE IN THE MIDDLE OF A WAR. THEY'RE GONNA NEED US.
BUT SANCHEZ--
SHE'S RIGHT, OLIVETTI!
CAPTAIN TANAKA SAID HE'D TRAIN US!
IN SECRET. AT MIDNIGHT. AGAINST SCHOOL POLICY.
WHICH SOUNDS LIKE A GREAT WAY TO GET EXPELLED IF THE HONOR COURT DOESN'T KICK US OUT FIRST.
THIS IS THE END, YU. TIME TO FACE IT.
WHATEVER, PARK.
SKIP'S GOT A JOB FOR US, STARTING TONIGHT.
YOU CAN SIT AROUND AND MOPE IF YOU WANT, BUT YOU BETTER NOT--
YU! SANCHEZ! OLIVETTI! PARK!
SIR, YES, SIR!
THE HONOR COURT HAS REACHED A VERDICT.
YOU'RE ALL GROUNDED.
UNTIL FURTHER NOTICE, YOU'RE UNDER THE COMMAND OF...

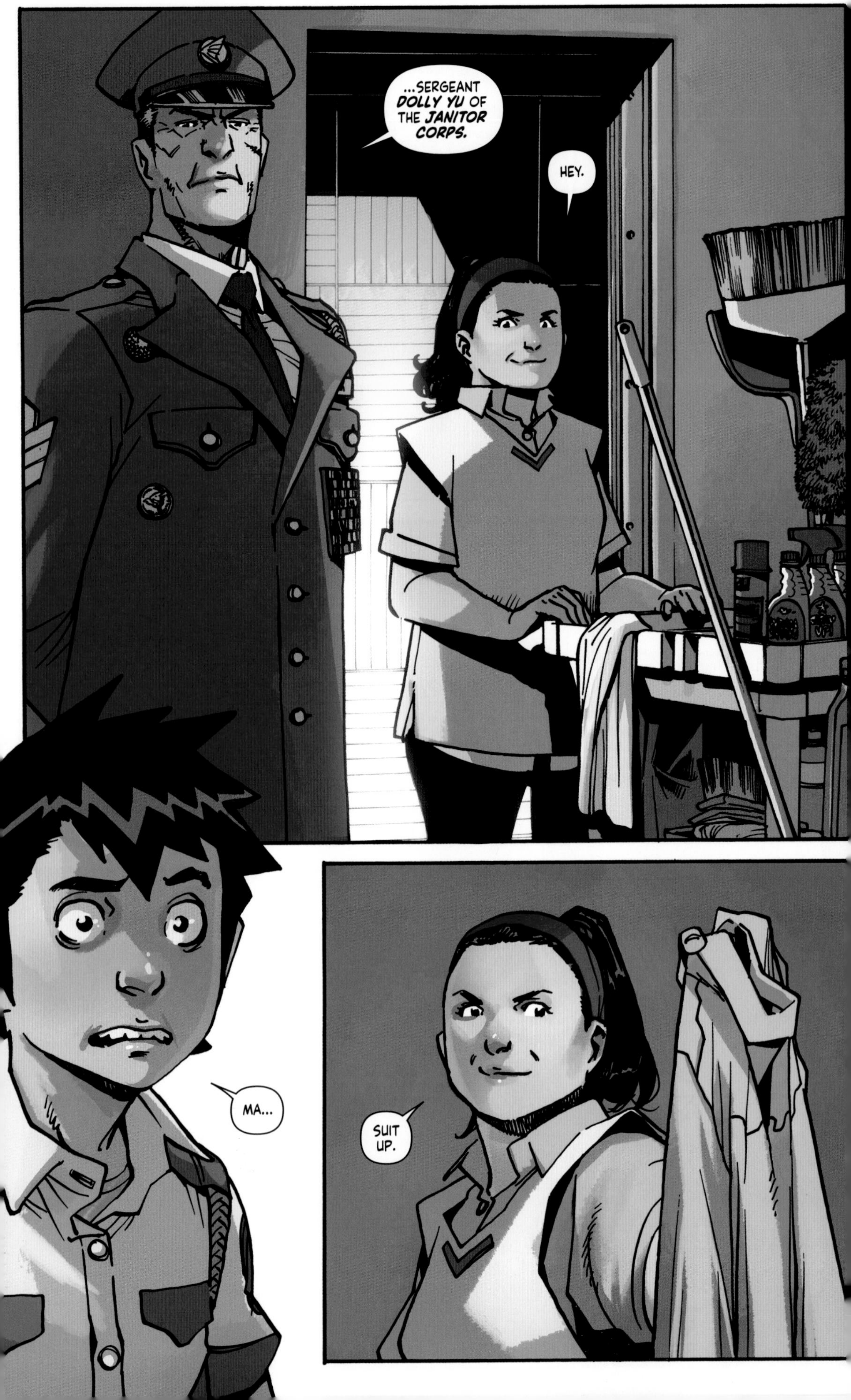
...SERGEANT DOLLY YU OF THE JANITOR CORPS.
HEY.
MA...
SUIT UP.

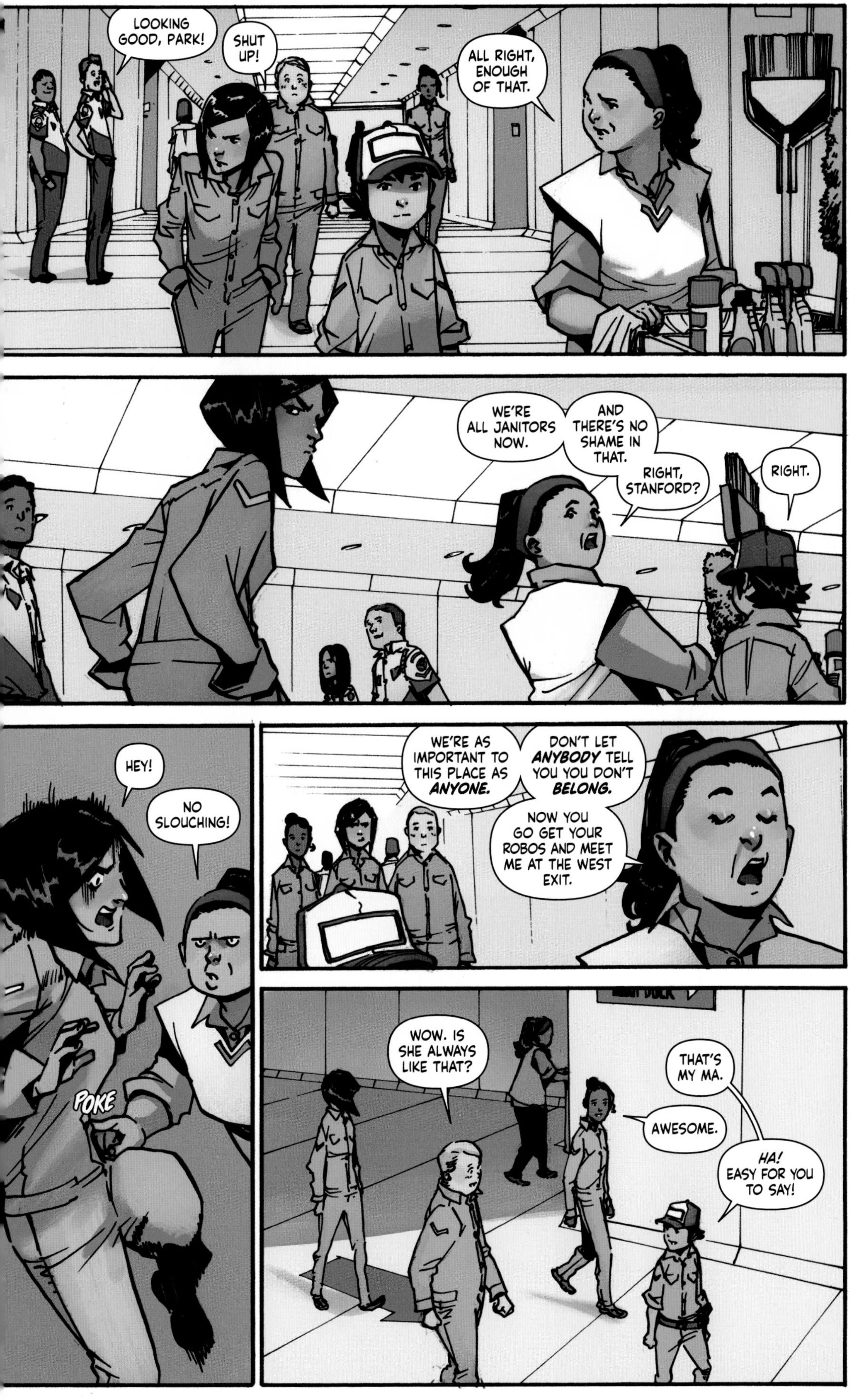

LOOKING GOOD, PARK!
SHUT UP!
ALL RIGHT, ENOUGH OF THAT.
WE'RE ALL JANITORS NOW.
AND THERE'S NO SHAME IN THAT.
RIGHT, STANFORD?
RIGHT.
HEY!
NO SLOUCHING!
POKE
WE'RE AS IMPORTANT TO THIS PLACE AS *ANYONE.*
DON'T LET *ANYBODY* TELL YOU YOU DON'T *BELONG.*
NOW YOU GO GET YOUR ROBOS AND MEET ME AT THE WEST EXIT.
WOW. IS SHE ALWAYS LIKE THAT?
THAT'S MY MA.
AWESOME.
HA! EASY FOR YOU TO SAY!

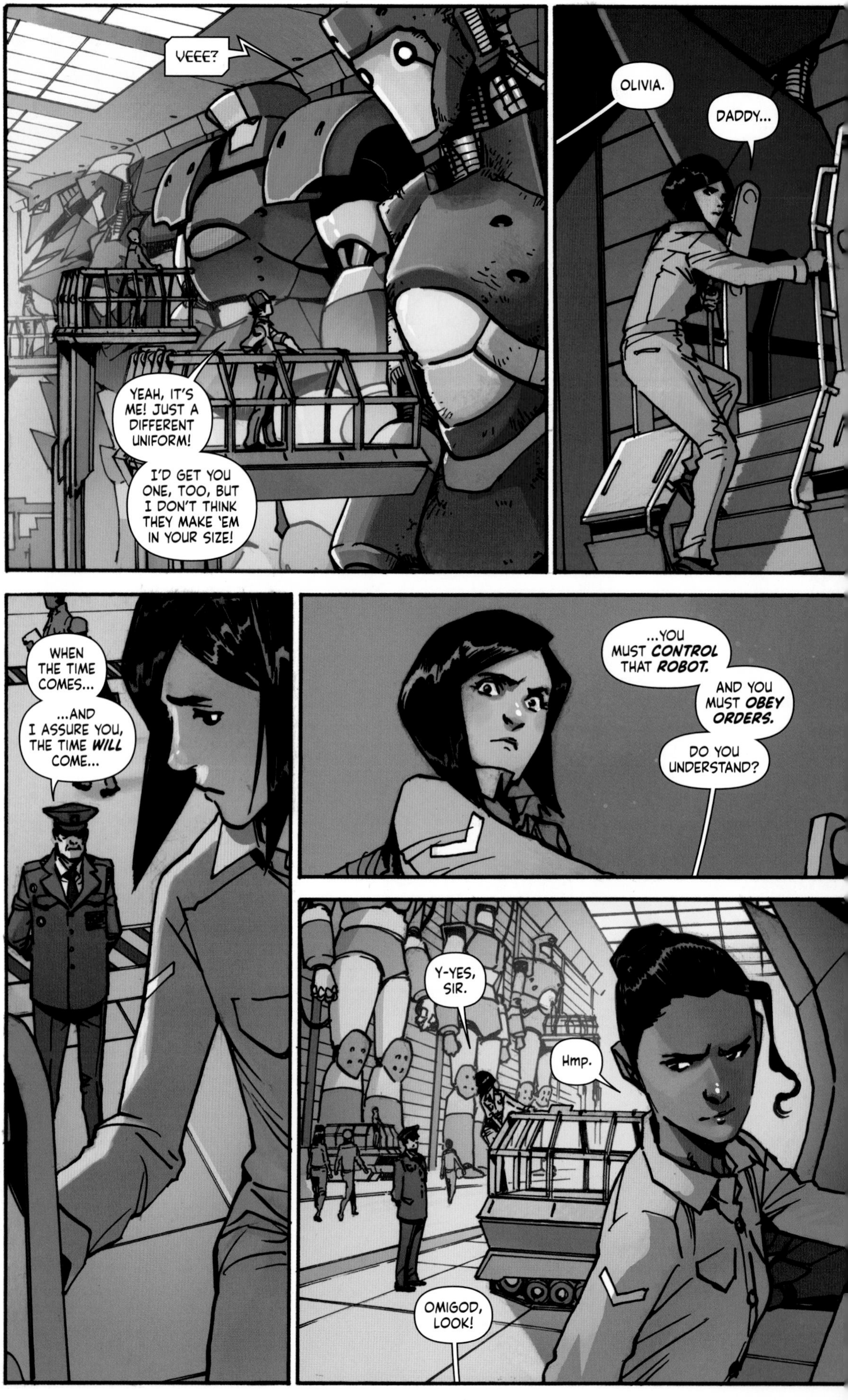
VEEE?
YEAH, IT'S ME! JUST A DIFFERENT UNIFORM!
I'D GET YOU ONE, TOO, BUT I DON'T THINK THEY MAKE 'EM IN YOUR SIZE!
OLIVIA.
DADDY...
WHEN THE TIME COMES...
...AND I ASSURE YOU, THE TIME *WILL* COME...
...YOU MUST *CONTROL* THAT *ROBOT.*
AND YOU MUST *OBEY ORDERS.*
DO YOU UNDERSTAND?
Y-YES, SIR.
Hmp.
OMIGOD, LOOK!

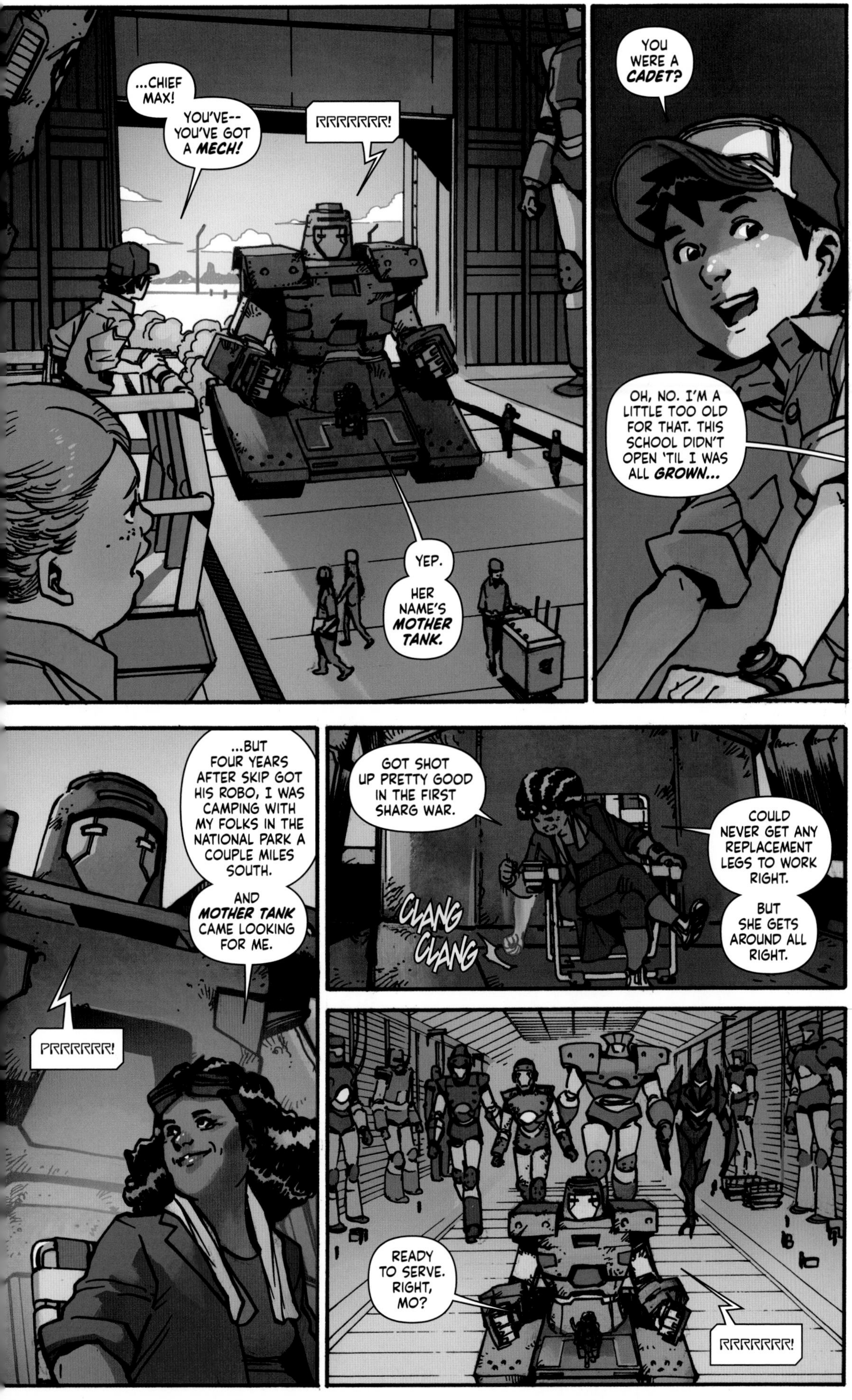

...CHIEF MAX!
YOU'VE-- YOU'VE GOT A MECH!
RRRRRRR!
YEP.
HER NAME'S MOTHER TANK.
YOU WERE A CADET?
OH, NO. I'M A LITTLE TOO OLD FOR THAT. THIS SCHOOL DIDN'T OPEN 'TIL I WAS ALL GROWN...
...BUT FOUR YEARS AFTER SKIP GOT HIS ROBO, I WAS CAMPING WITH MY FOLKS IN THE NATIONAL PARK A COUPLE MILES SOUTH.
AND MOTHER TANK CAME LOOKING FOR ME.
PRRRRRRR!
GOT SHOT UP PRETTY GOOD IN THE FIRST SHARG WAR.
COULD NEVER GET ANY REPLACEMENT LEGS TO WORK RIGHT.
BUT SHE GETS AROUND ALL RIGHT.
CLANG
CLANG
READY TO SERVE. RIGHT, MO?
RRRRRRR!

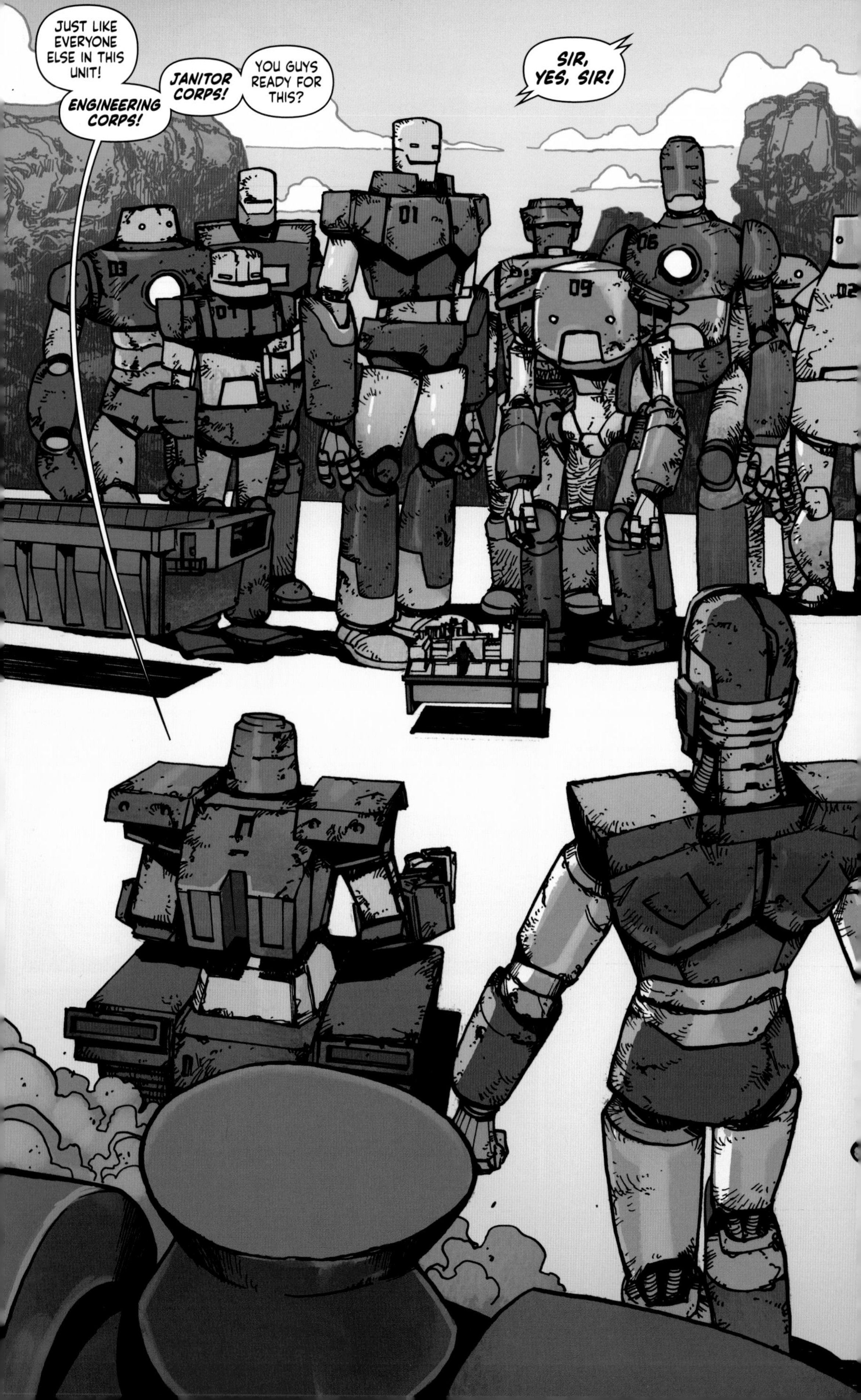

JUST LIKE EVERYONE ELSE IN THIS UNIT!
ENGINEERING CORPS!
JANITOR CORPS!
YOU GUYS READY FOR THIS?
SIR, YES, SIR!

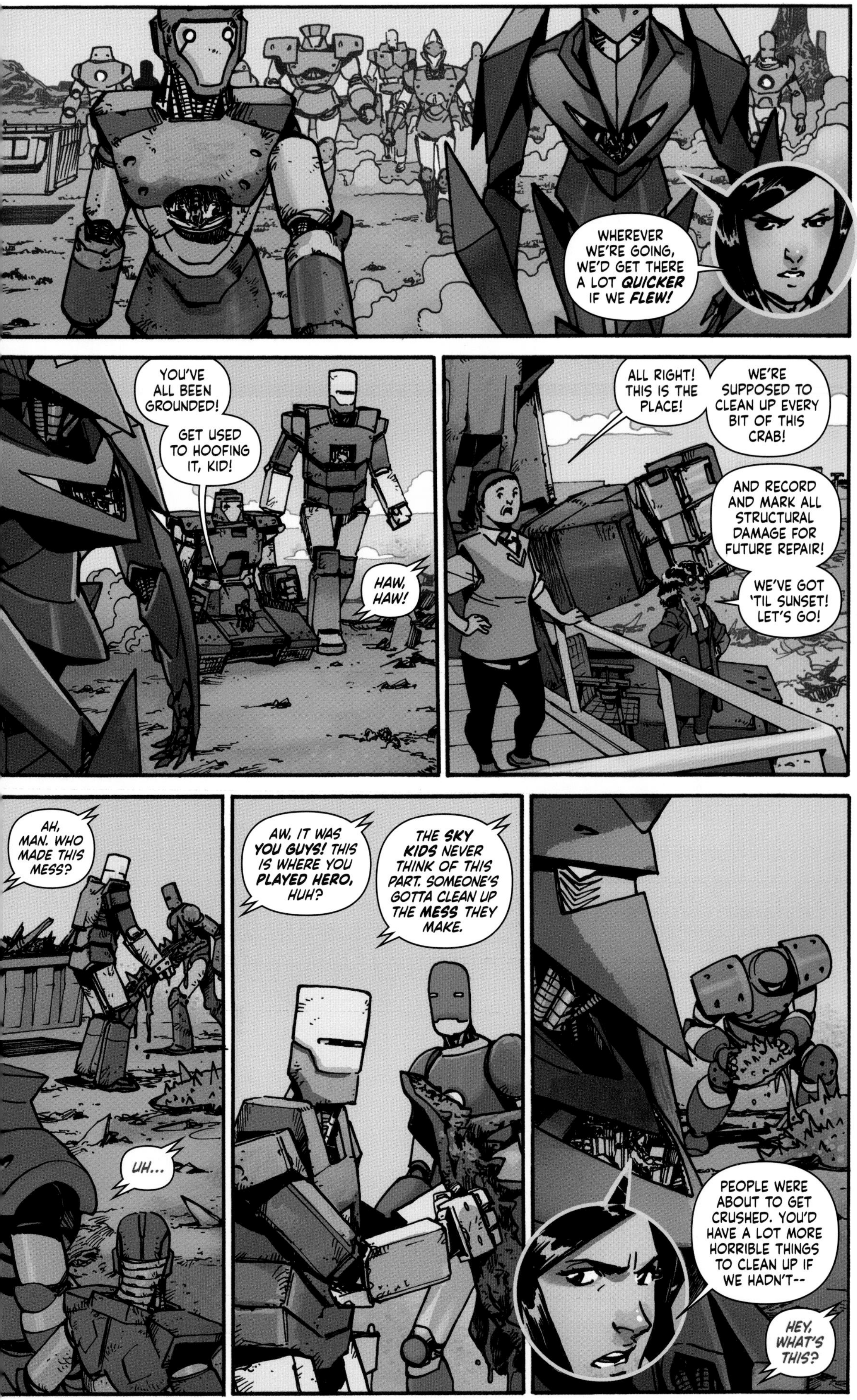
WHEREVER WE'RE GOING, WE'D GET THERE A LOT QUICKER IF WE FLEW!
YOU'VE ALL BEEN GROUNDED!
GET USED TO HOOFING IT, KID!
HAW, HAW!
ALL RIGHT! THIS IS THE PLACE!
WE'RE SUPPOSED TO CLEAN UP EVERY BIT OF THIS CRAB!
AND RECORD AND MARK ALL STRUCTURAL DAMAGE FOR FUTURE REPAIR!
WE'VE GOT 'TIL SUNSET! LET'S GO!
AH, MAN. WHO MADE THIS MESS?
UH...
AW, IT WAS YOU GUYS! THIS IS WHERE YOU PLAYED HERO, HUH?
THE SKY KIDS NEVER THINK OF THIS PART. SOMEONE'S GOTTA CLEAN UP THE MESS THEY MAKE.
PEOPLE WERE ABOUT TO GET CRUSHED. YOU'D HAVE A LOT MORE HORRIBLE THINGS TO CLEAN UP IF WE HADN'T--
HEY, WHAT'S THIS?

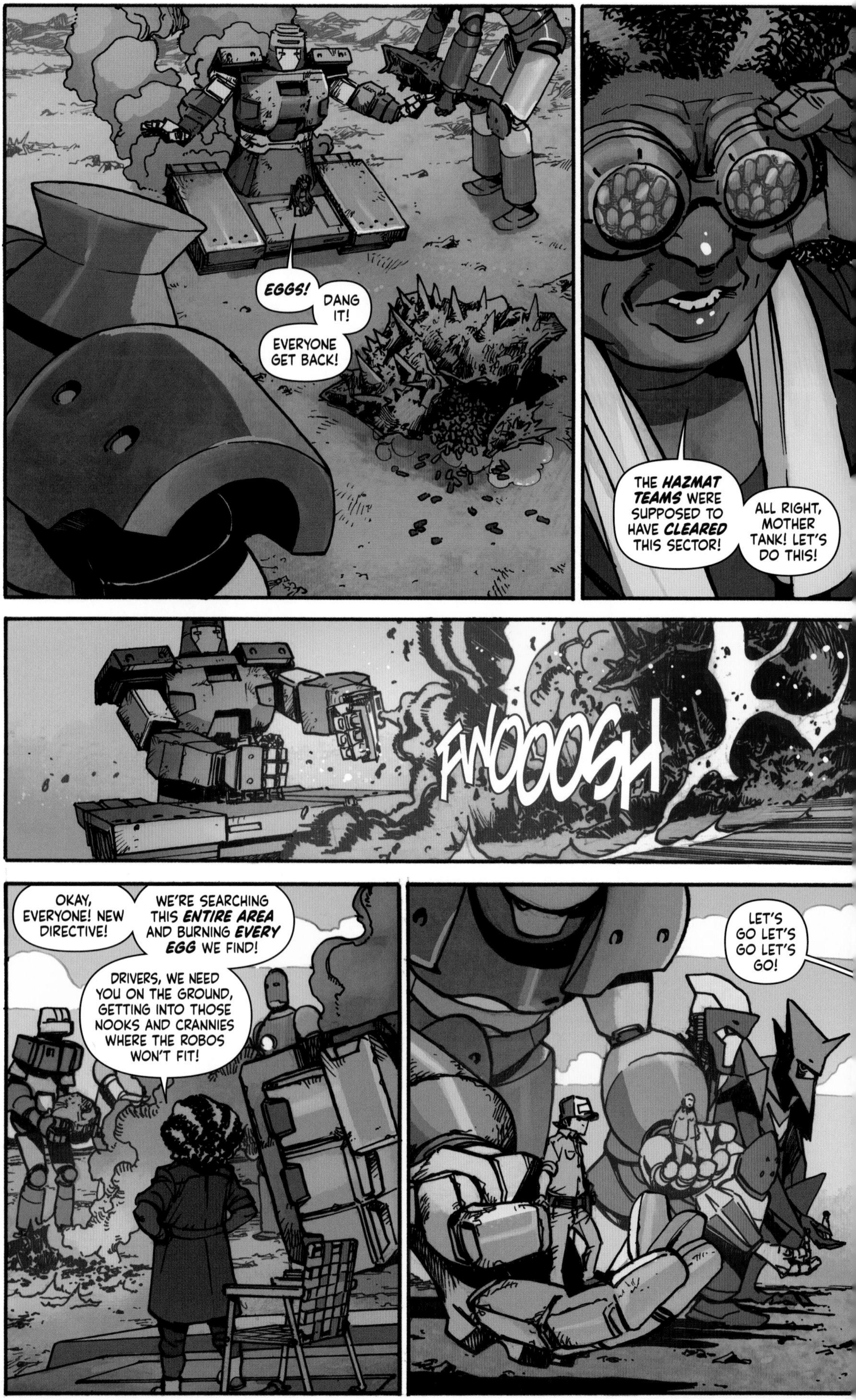
EGGS!
DANG IT!
EVERYONE GET BACK!
THE HAZMAT TEAMS WERE SUPPOSED TO HAVE CLEARED THIS SECTOR!
ALL RIGHT, MOTHER TANK! LET'S DO THIS!
FWOOOSH
OKAY, EVERYONE! NEW DIRECTIVE!
WE'RE SEARCHING THIS ENTIRE AREA AND BURNING EVERY EGG WE FIND!
DRIVERS, WE NEED YOU ON THE GROUND, GETTING INTO THOSE NOOKS AND CRANNIES WHERE THE ROBOS WON'T FIT!
LET'S GO LET'S GO LET'S GO!

HEY, OVER HERE!

AVERAGE EGG'S A COUPLE FEET ACROSS! BUT THEY COULD BE AS SMALL AS A FOOTBALL! EYES OPEN, PEOPLE!

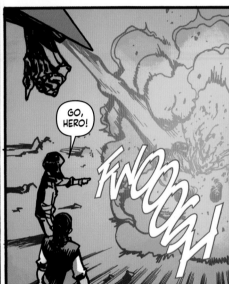

GO, HERO!

FWOOOGH

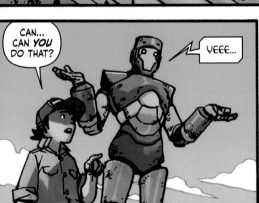

CAN... CAN *YOU* DO THAT?

VEEE...

UNNGH!

ALL CLEAR!

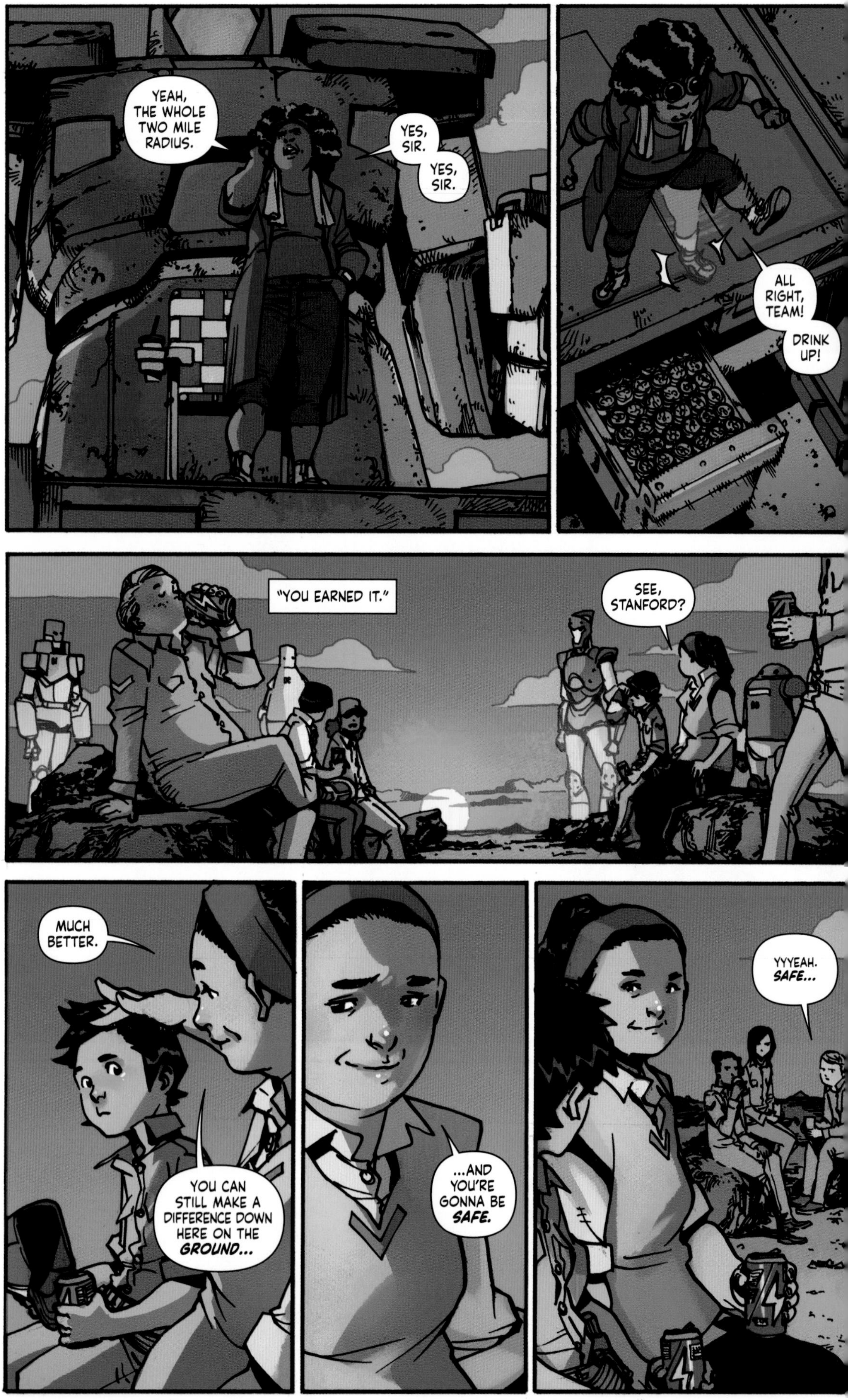
YEAH, THE WHOLE TWO MILE RADIUS.
YES, SIR.
YES, SIR.
ALL RIGHT, TEAM!
DRINK UP!
"YOU EARNED IT."
SEE, STANFORD?
MUCH BETTER.
YOU CAN STILL MAKE A DIFFERENCE DOWN HERE ON THE GROUND...
...AND YOU'RE GONNA BE SAFE.
YYYEAH. SAFE...

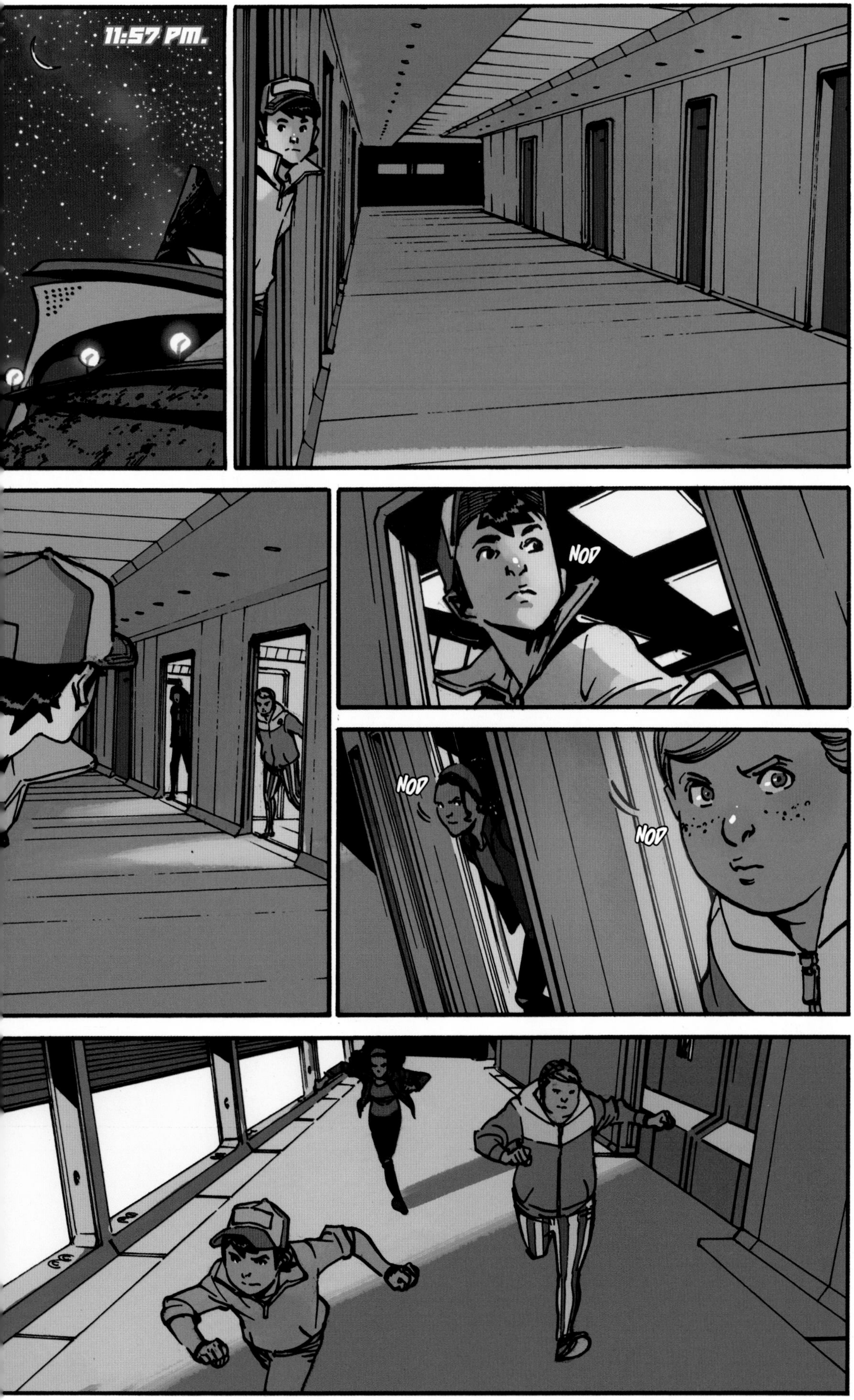
11:57 PM.
NOD
NOD
NOD

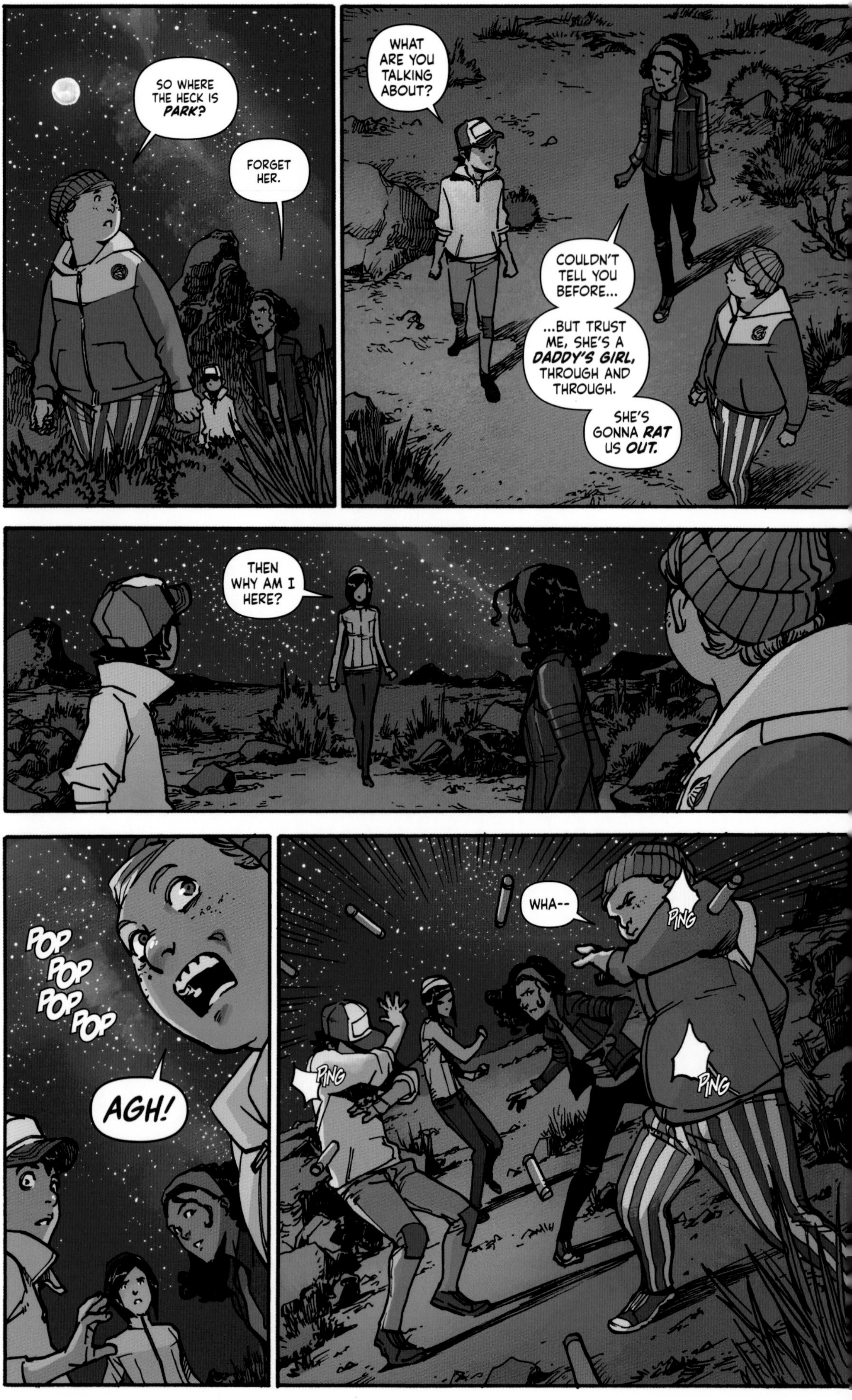

SO WHERE THE HECK IS PARK?
FORGET HER.
WHAT ARE YOU TALKING ABOUT?
COULDN'T TELL YOU BEFORE...
...BUT TRUST ME, SHE'S A DADDY'S GIRL, THROUGH AND THROUGH.
SHE'S GONNA RAT US OUT.
THEN WHY AM I HERE?
POP POP POP POP
AGH!
WHA--
PING
PING
PING

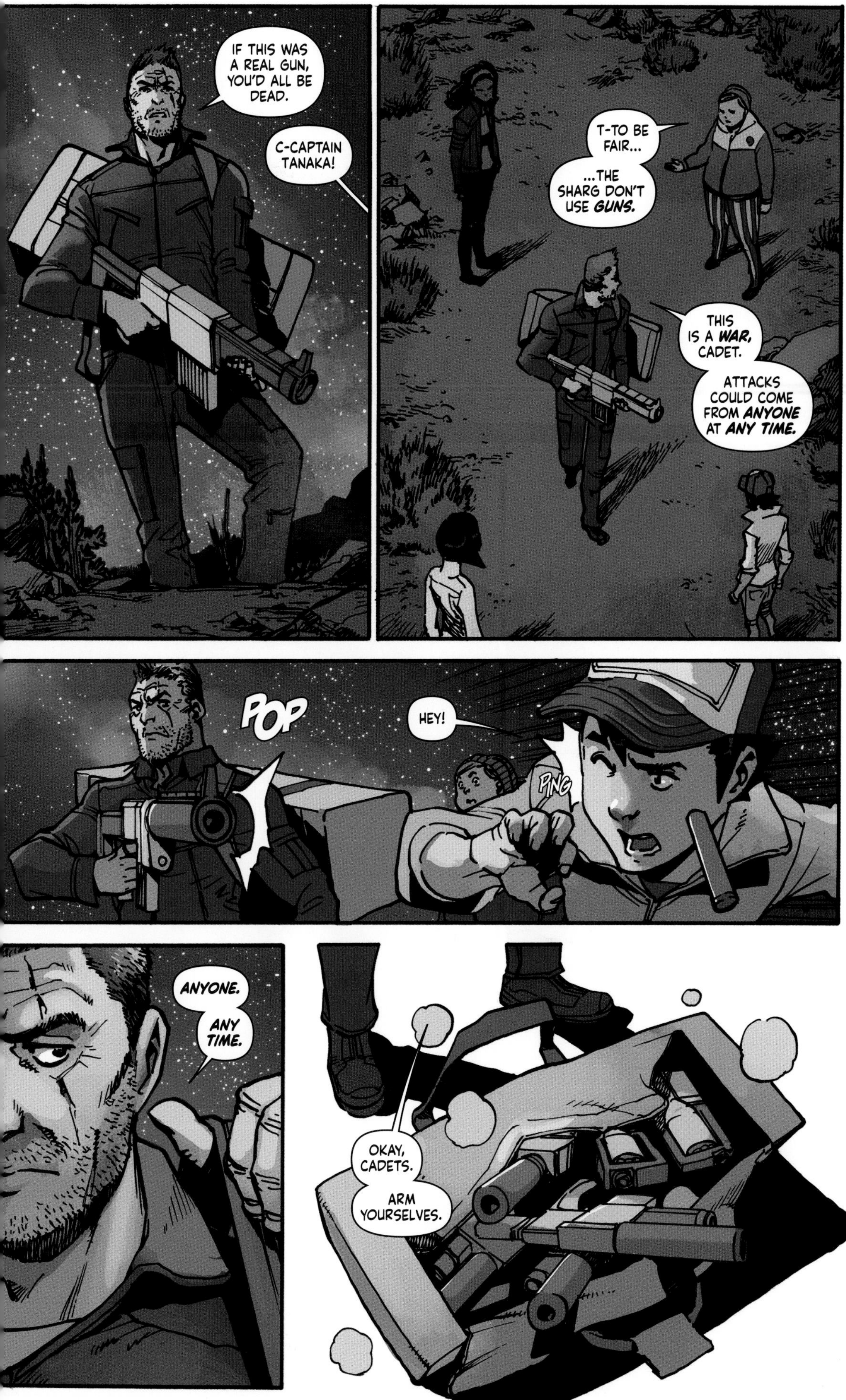

IF THIS WAS A REAL GUN, YOU'D ALL BE DEAD.
C-CAPTAIN TANAKA!
T-TO BE FAIR...
...THE SHARG DON'T USE **GUNS.**
THIS IS A **WAR,** CADET.
ATTACKS COULD COME FROM **ANYONE** AT **ANY TIME.**
POP
HEY!
PING
ANYONE.
ANY TIME.
OKAY, CADETS.
ARM YOURSELVES.

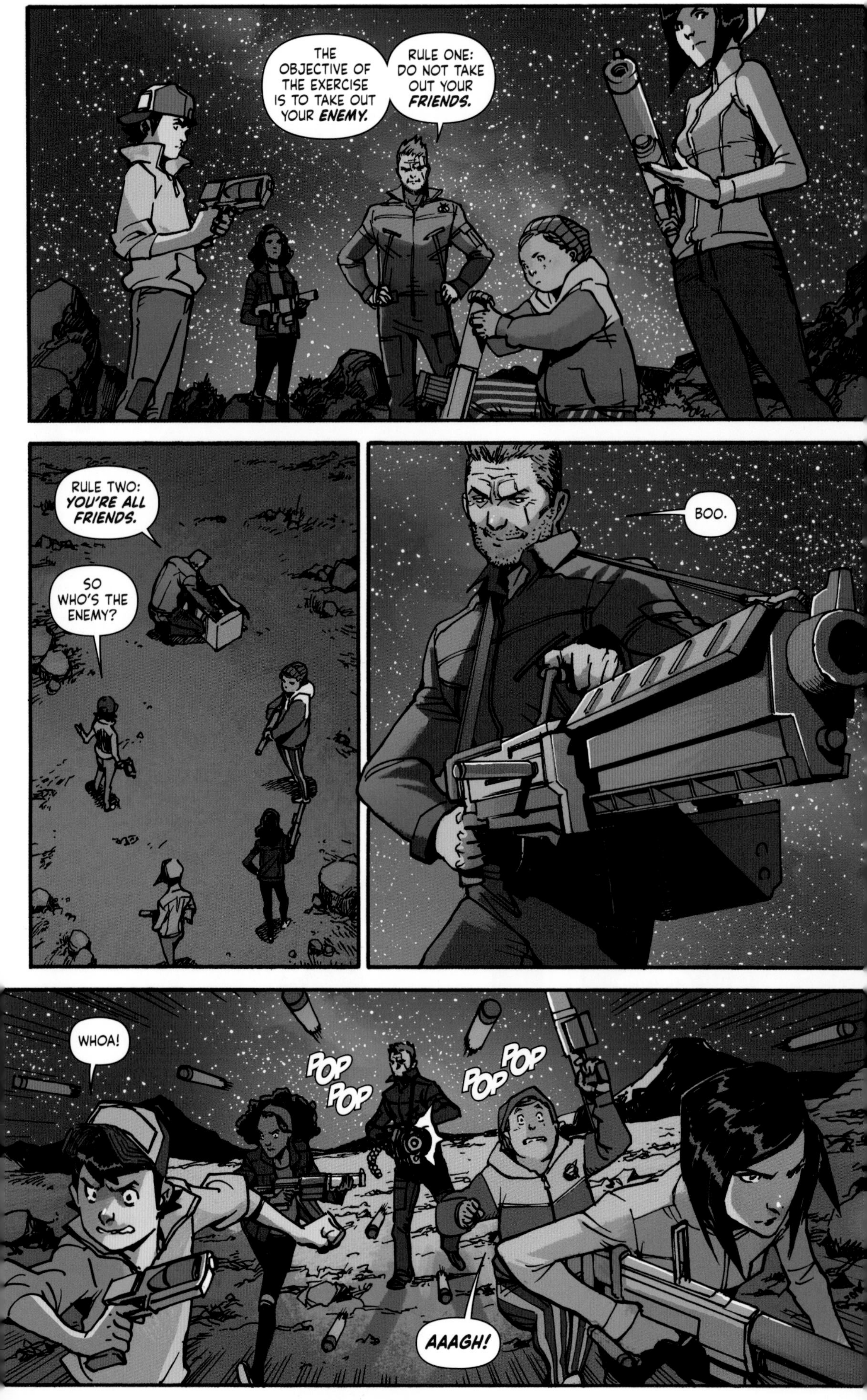
THE OBJECTIVE OF THE EXERCISE IS TO TAKE OUT YOUR ENEMY.
RULE ONE: DO NOT TAKE OUT YOUR FRIENDS.
RULE TWO: YOU'RE ALL FRIENDS.
SO WHO'S THE ENEMY?
BOO.
WHOA!
POP POP
POP POP POP
AAAGH!

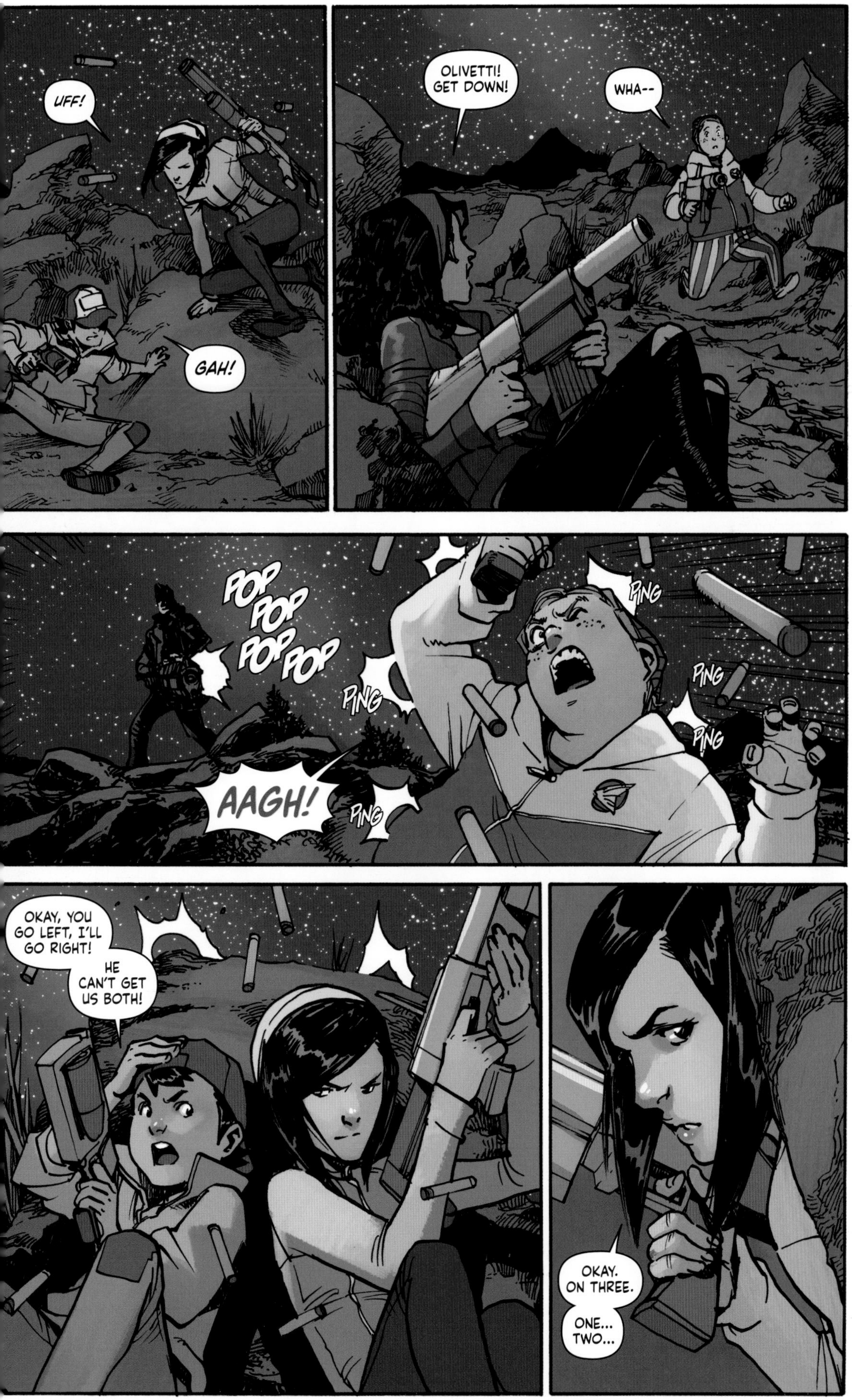
UFF!
GAH!
OLIVETTI! GET DOWN!
WHA--
POP POP POP POP
PING
PING
PING
PING
PING
AAGH!
OKAY, YOU GO LEFT, I'LL GO RIGHT!
HE CAN'T GET US BOTH!
OKAY. ON THREE.
ONE... TWO...

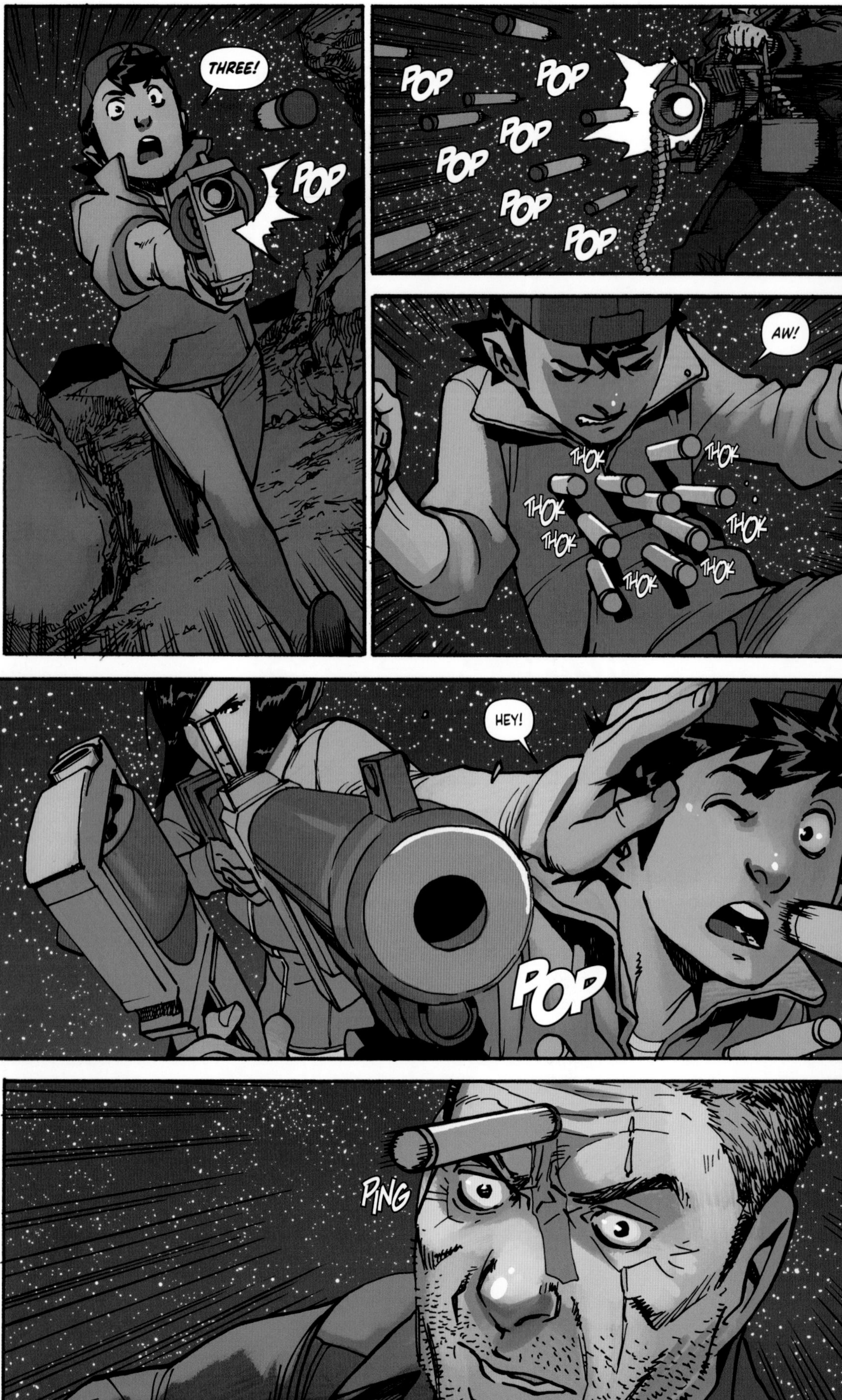
THREE!
POP
POP
POP
POP
POP
POP
POP
AW!
THOK
THOK
THOK
THOK
THOK
THOK
THOK
HEY!
POP
PING

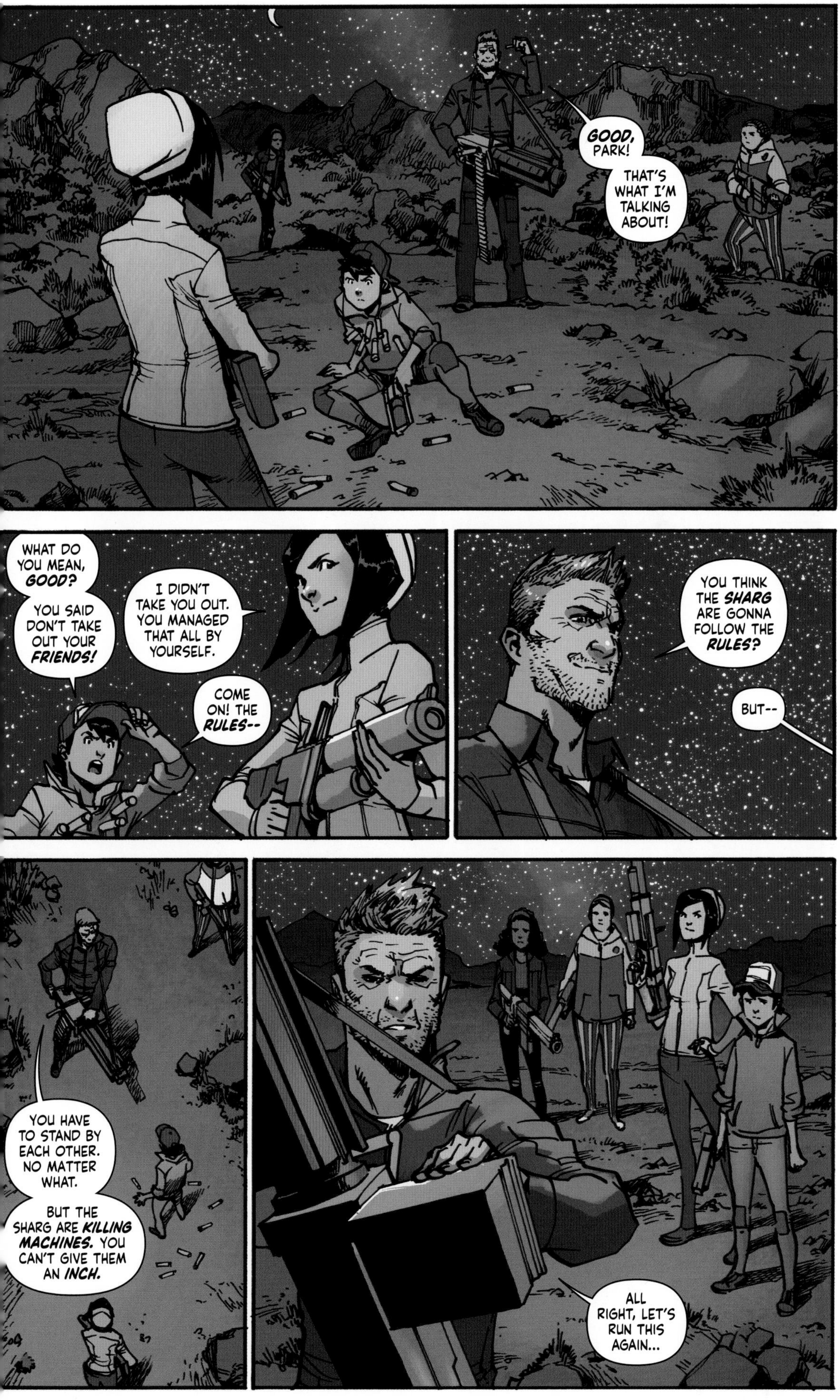
GOOD, PARK!
THAT'S WHAT I'M TALKING ABOUT!
WHAT DO YOU MEAN, GOOD?
YOU SAID DON'T TAKE OUT YOUR FRIENDS!
I DIDN'T TAKE YOU OUT. YOU MANAGED THAT ALL BY YOURSELF.
COME ON! THE RULES--
YOU THINK THE SHARG ARE GONNA FOLLOW THE RULES?
BUT--
YOU HAVE TO STAND BY EACH OTHER. NO MATTER WHAT.
BUT THE SHARG ARE KILLING MACHINES. YOU CAN'T GIVE THEM AN INCH.
ALL RIGHT, LET'S RUN THIS AGAIN...

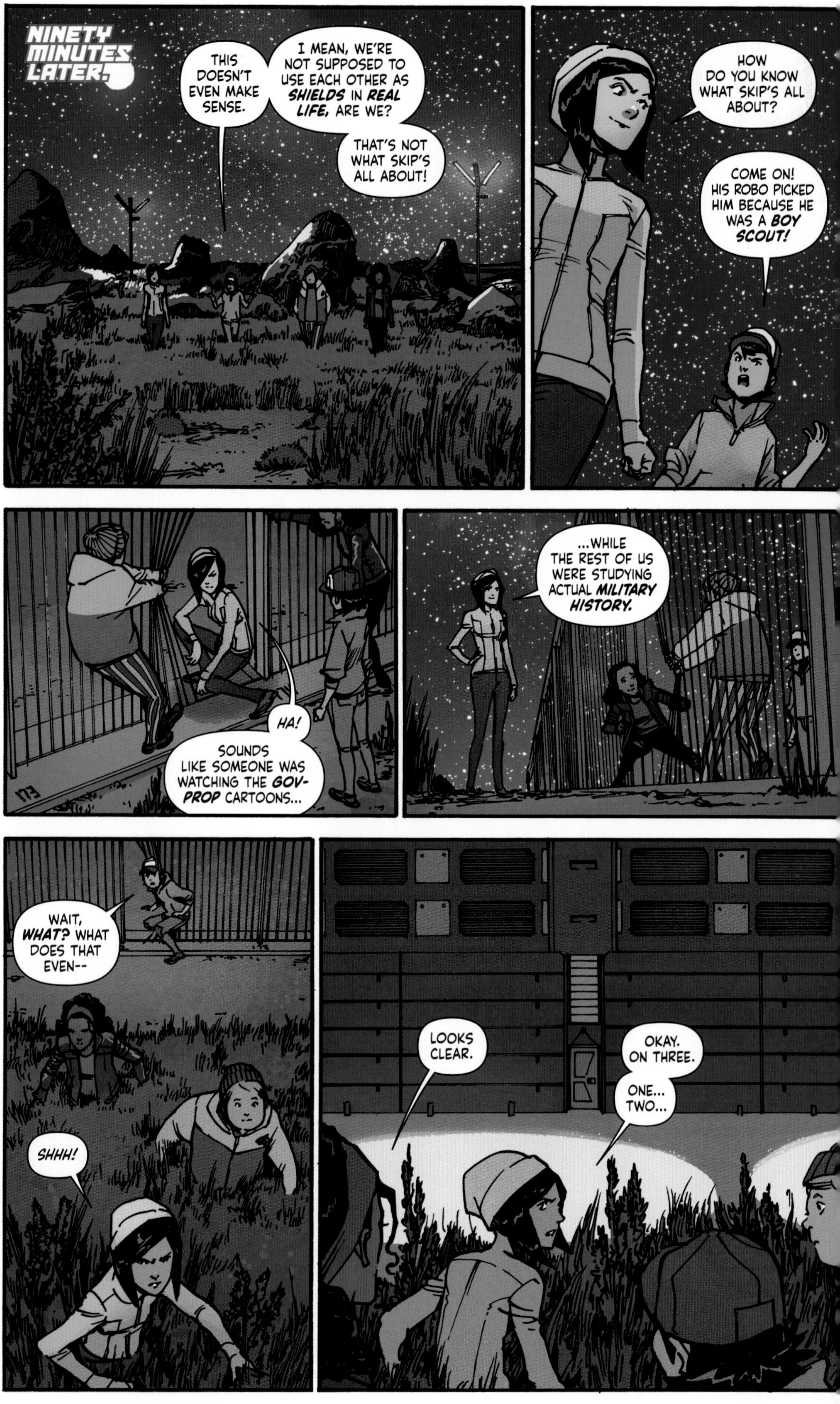
NINETY MINUTES LATER.
THIS DOESN'T EVEN MAKE SENSE.
I MEAN, WE'RE NOT SUPPOSED TO USE EACH OTHER AS SHIELDS IN REAL LIFE, ARE WE?
THAT'S NOT WHAT SKIP'S ALL ABOUT!
HOW DO YOU KNOW WHAT SKIP'S ALL ABOUT?
COME ON! HIS ROBO PICKED HIM BECAUSE HE WAS A BOY SCOUT!
HA!
SOUNDS LIKE SOMEONE WAS WATCHING THE GOV-PROP CARTOONS...
...WHILE THE REST OF US WERE STUDYING ACTUAL MILITARY HISTORY.
WAIT, WHAT? WHAT DOES THAT EVEN--
SHHH!
LOOKS CLEAR.
OKAY. ON THREE.
ONE... TWO...

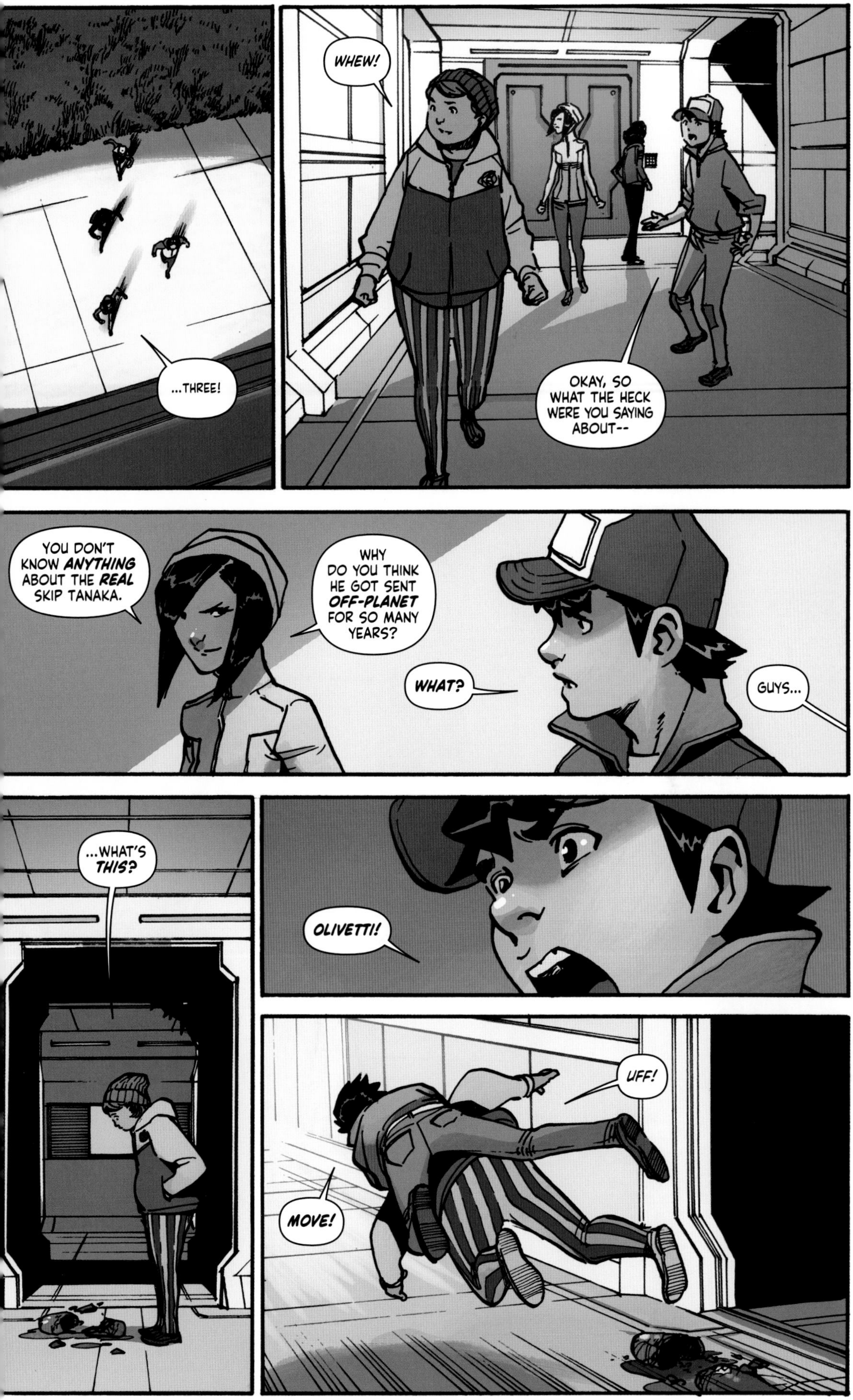
...THREE!
WHEW!
OKAY, SO WHAT THE HECK WERE YOU SAYING ABOUT--
YOU DON'T KNOW **ANYTHING** ABOUT THE **REAL** SKIP TANAKA.
WHY DO YOU THINK HE GOT SENT **OFF-PLANET** FOR SO MANY YEARS?
WHAT?
GUYS...
...WHAT'S **THIS?**
OLIVETTI!
UFF!
MOVE!

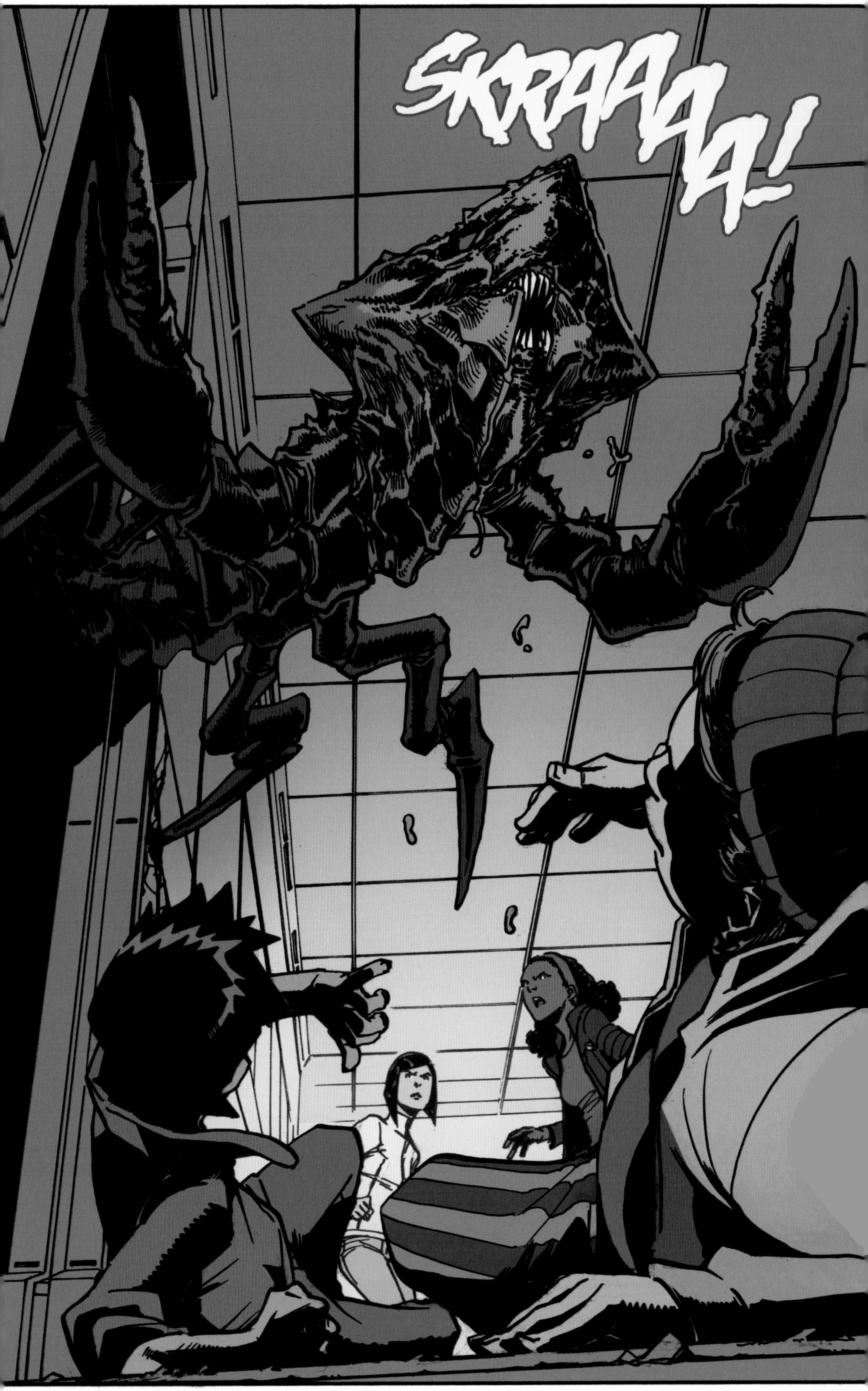
SKRAAAAA!

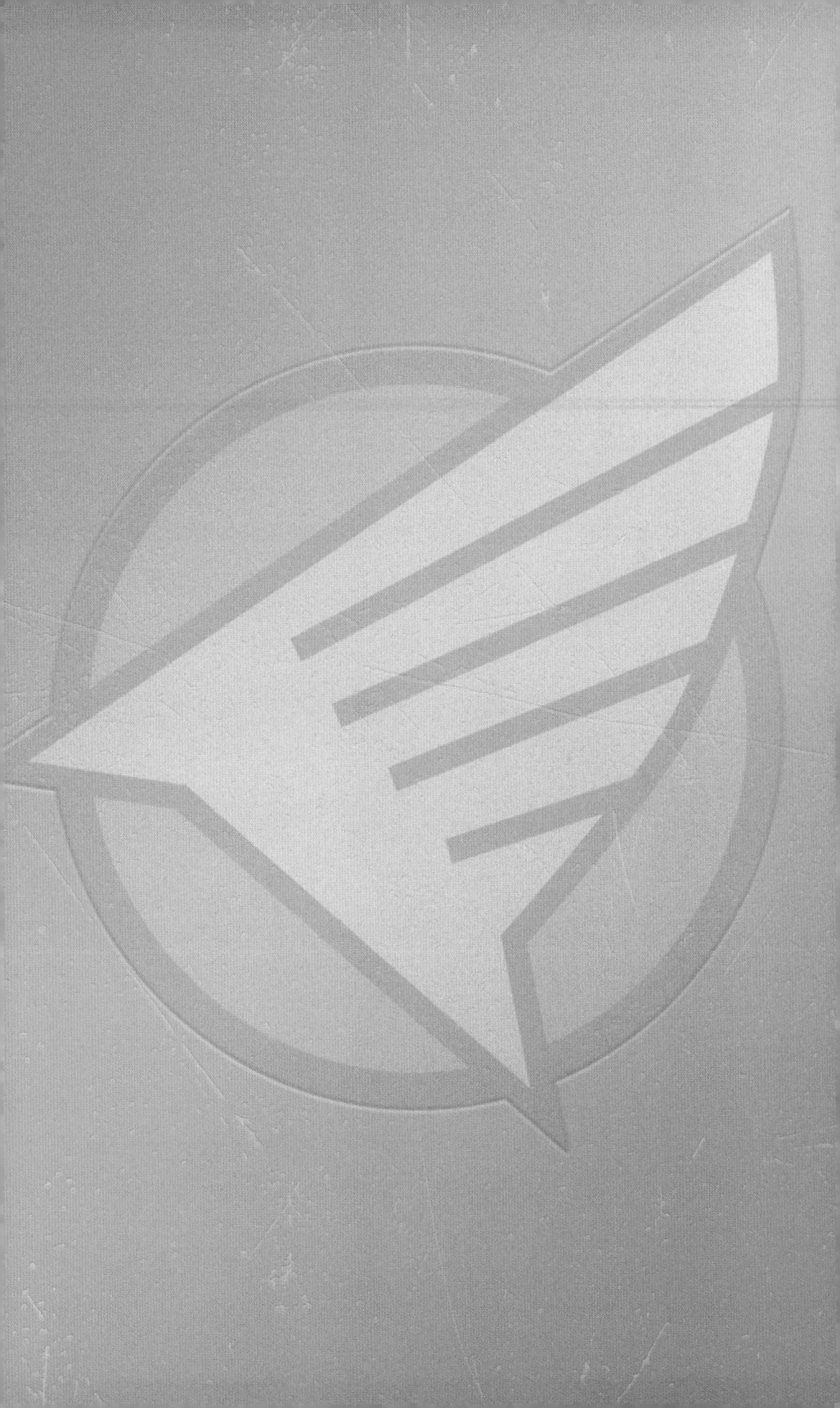

CHAPTER
SIX

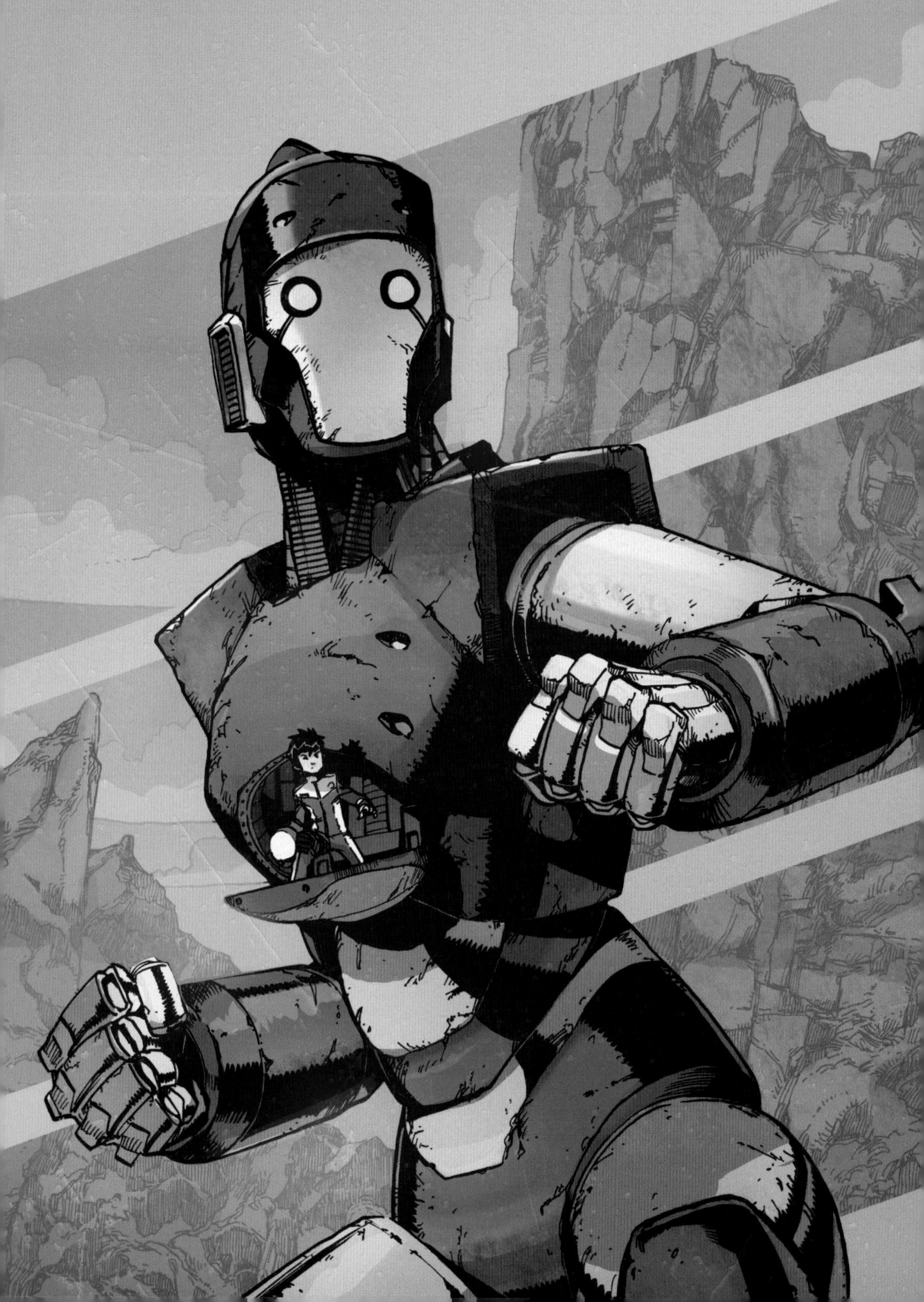

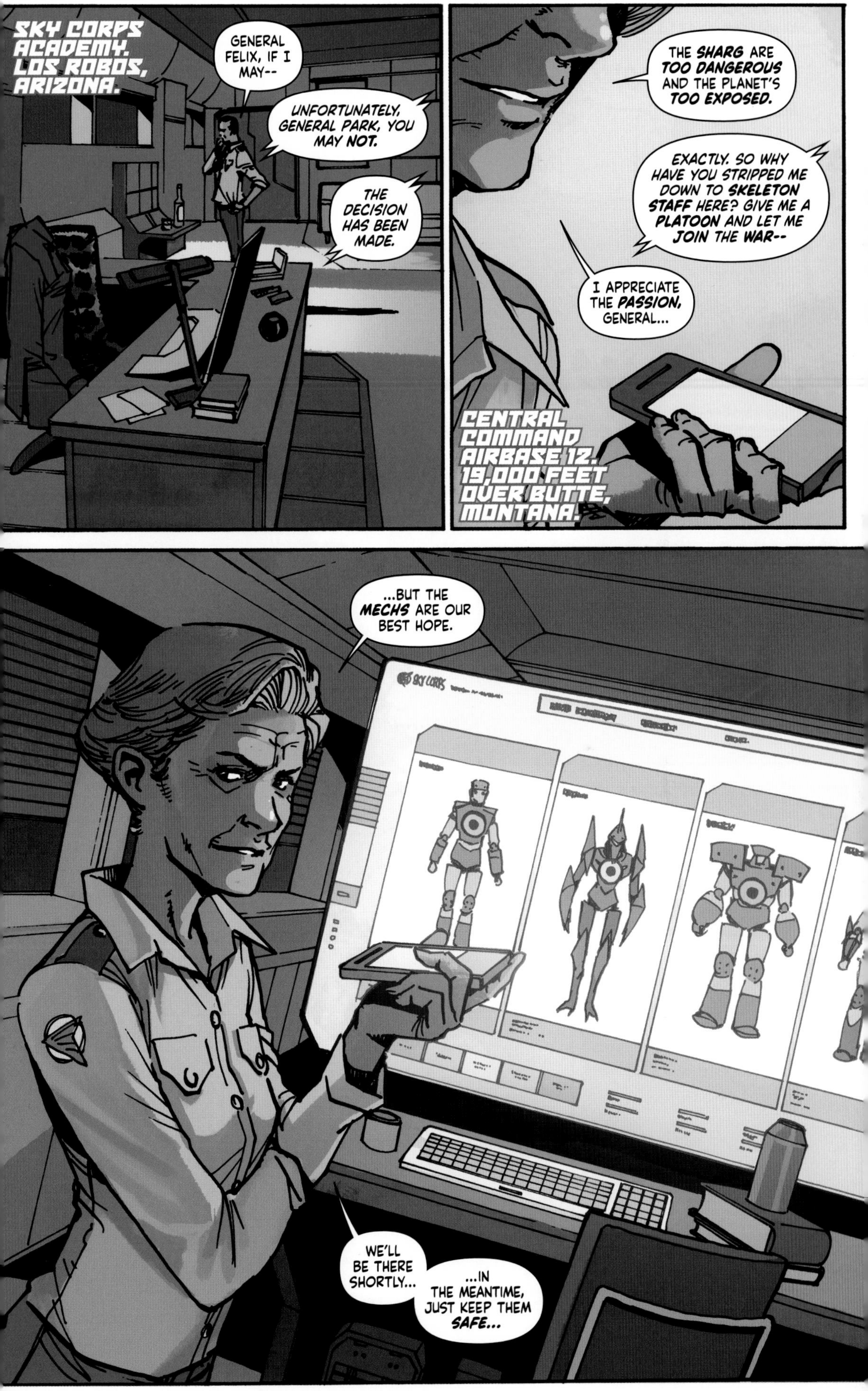
SKY CORPS ACADEMY. LOS ROBOS, ARIZONA.
GENERAL FELIX, IF I MAY--
UNFORTUNATELY, GENERAL PARK, YOU MAY NOT.
THE DECISION HAS BEEN MADE.
THE SHARG ARE TOO DANGEROUS AND THE PLANET'S TOO EXPOSED.
EXACTLY. SO WHY HAVE YOU STRIPPED ME DOWN TO SKELETON STAFF HERE? GIVE ME A PLATOON AND LET ME JOIN THE WAR--
I APPRECIATE THE PASSION, GENERAL...
CENTRAL COMMAND AIRBASE 12. 19,000 FEET OVER BUTTE, MONTANA.
...BUT THE MECHS ARE OUR BEST HOPE.
SKY CORPS
WE'LL BE THERE SHORTLY...
...IN THE MEANTIME, JUST KEEP THEM SAFE...

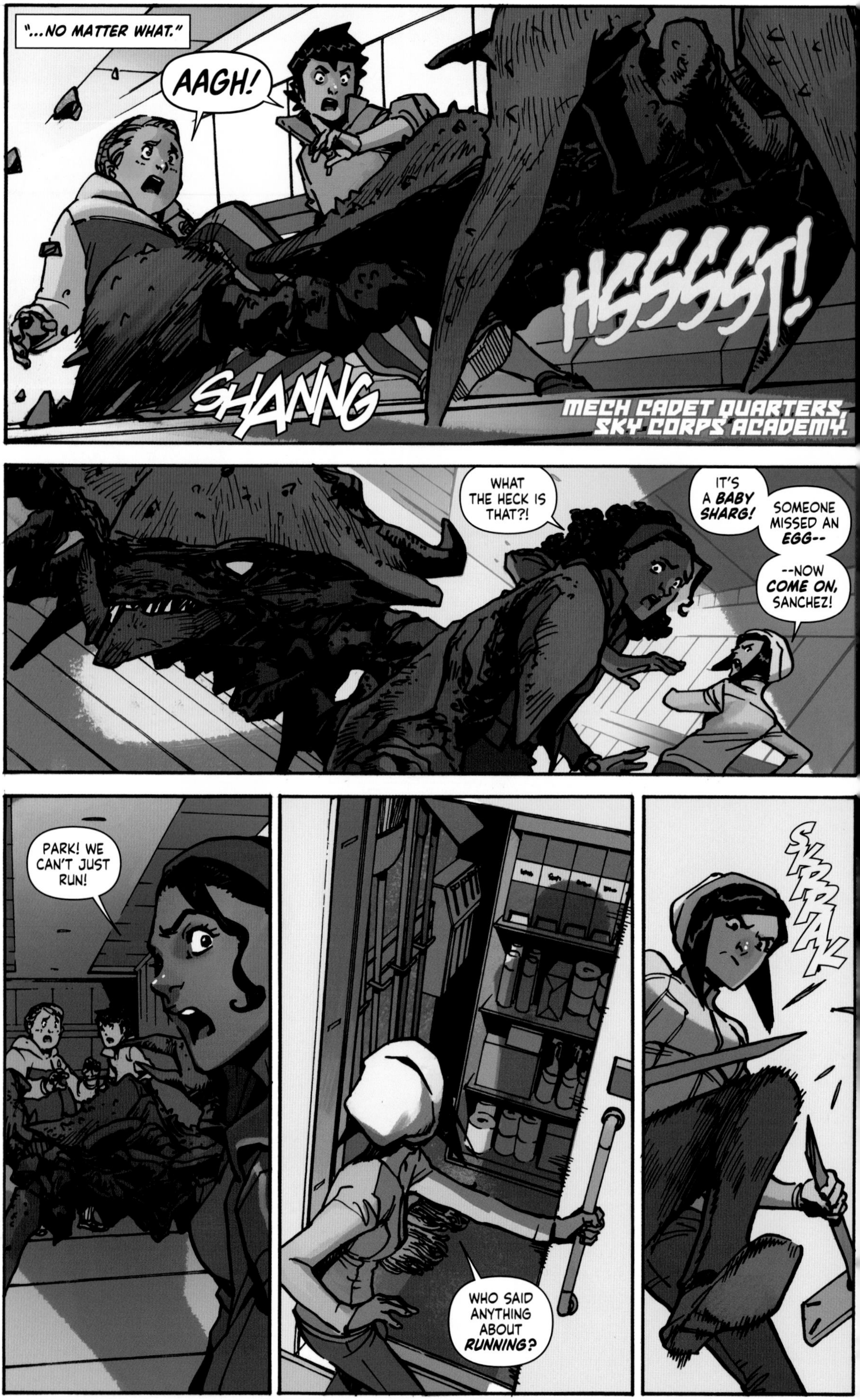
"...NO MATTER WHAT."
AAGH!
HSSSST!
SHANNG
MECH CADET QUARTERS, SKY CORPS ACADEMY.
WHAT THE HECK IS THAT?!
IT'S A BABY SHARG!
SOMEONE MISSED AN EGG--
--NOW COME ON, SANCHEZ!
PARK! WE CAN'T JUST RUN!
WHO SAID ANYTHING ABOUT RUNNING?
SKRAK

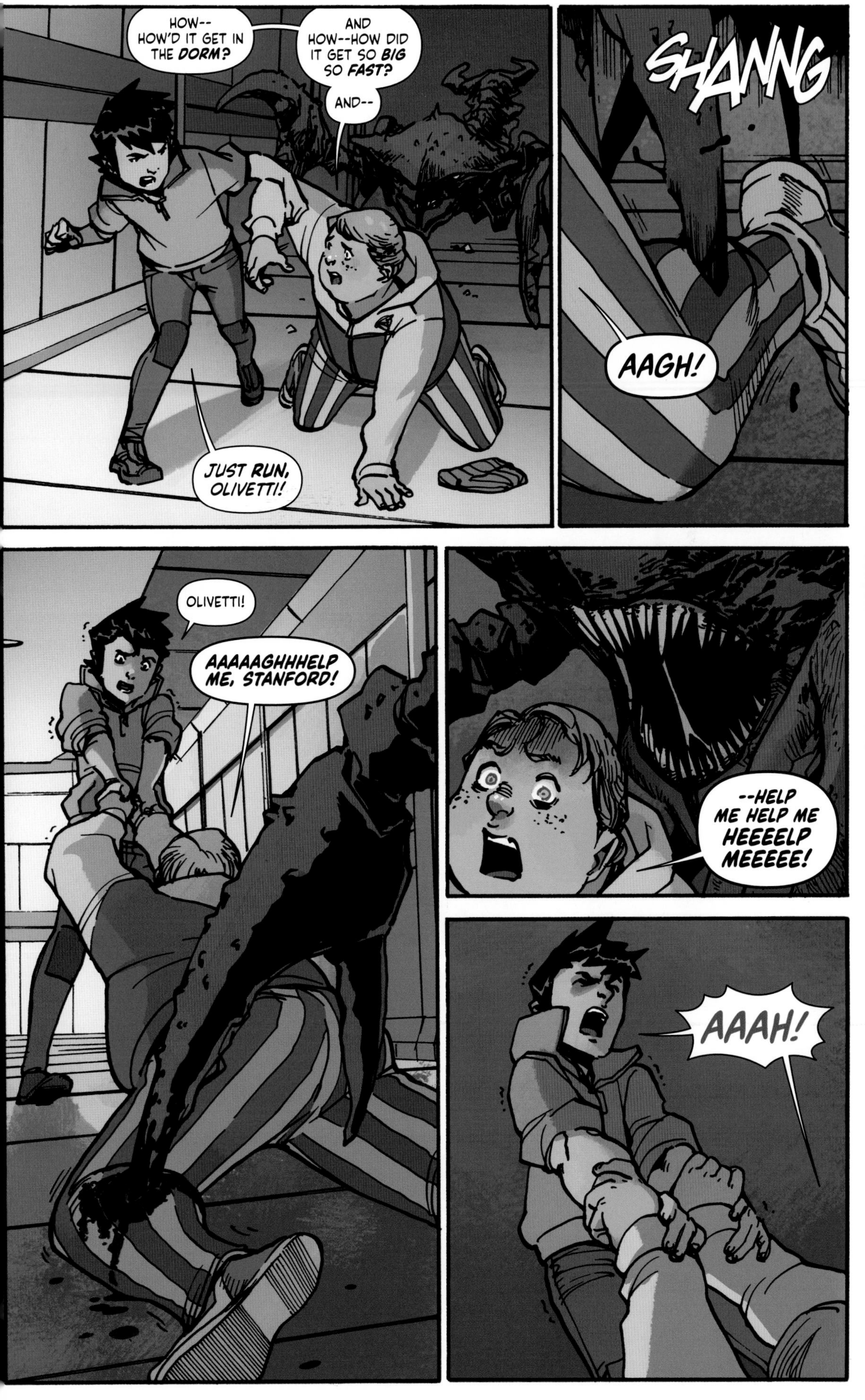
HOW-- HOW'D IT GET IN THE DORM?
AND HOW--HOW DID IT GET SO BIG SO FAST?
AND--
JUST RUN, OLIVETTI!
SHANNG
AAGH!
OLIVETTI!
AAAAAGHHHELP ME, STANFORD!
--HELP ME HELP ME HEEEELP MEEEEE!
AAAH!

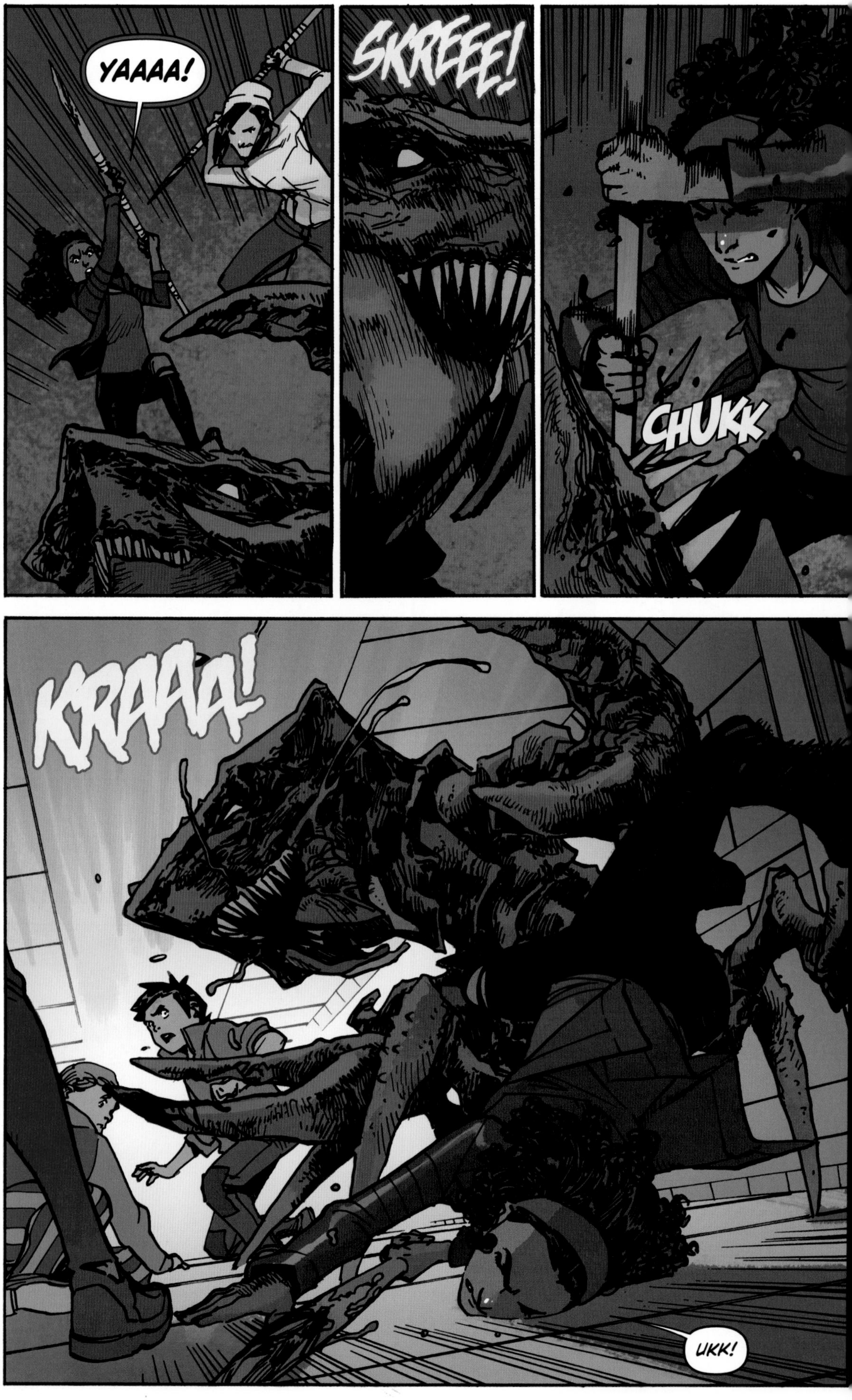
YAAAA!
SKREEE!
CHUKK
KRAAA!
UKK!

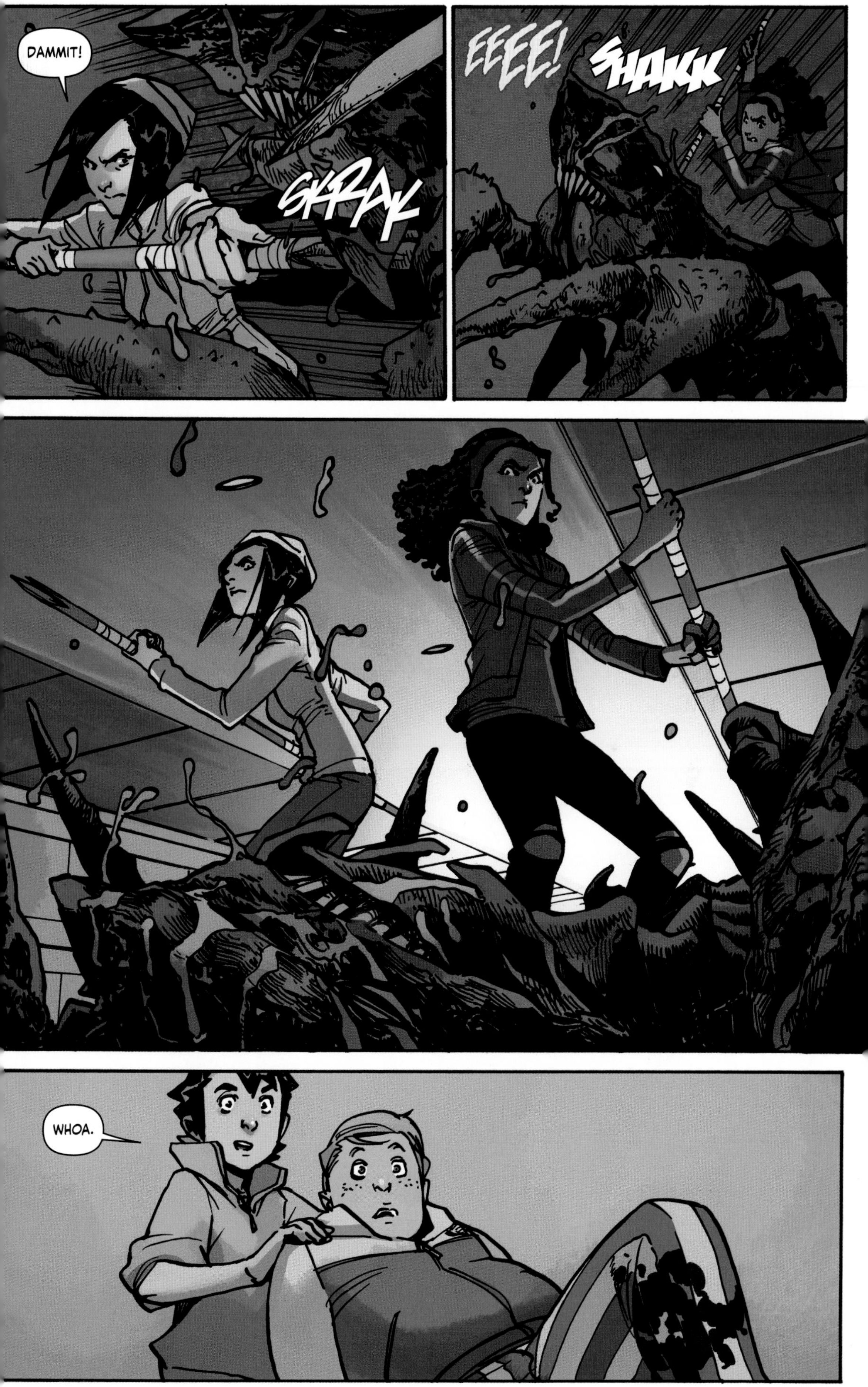
DAMMIT!
SKRAK
EEEE!
SHAKK
WHOA.

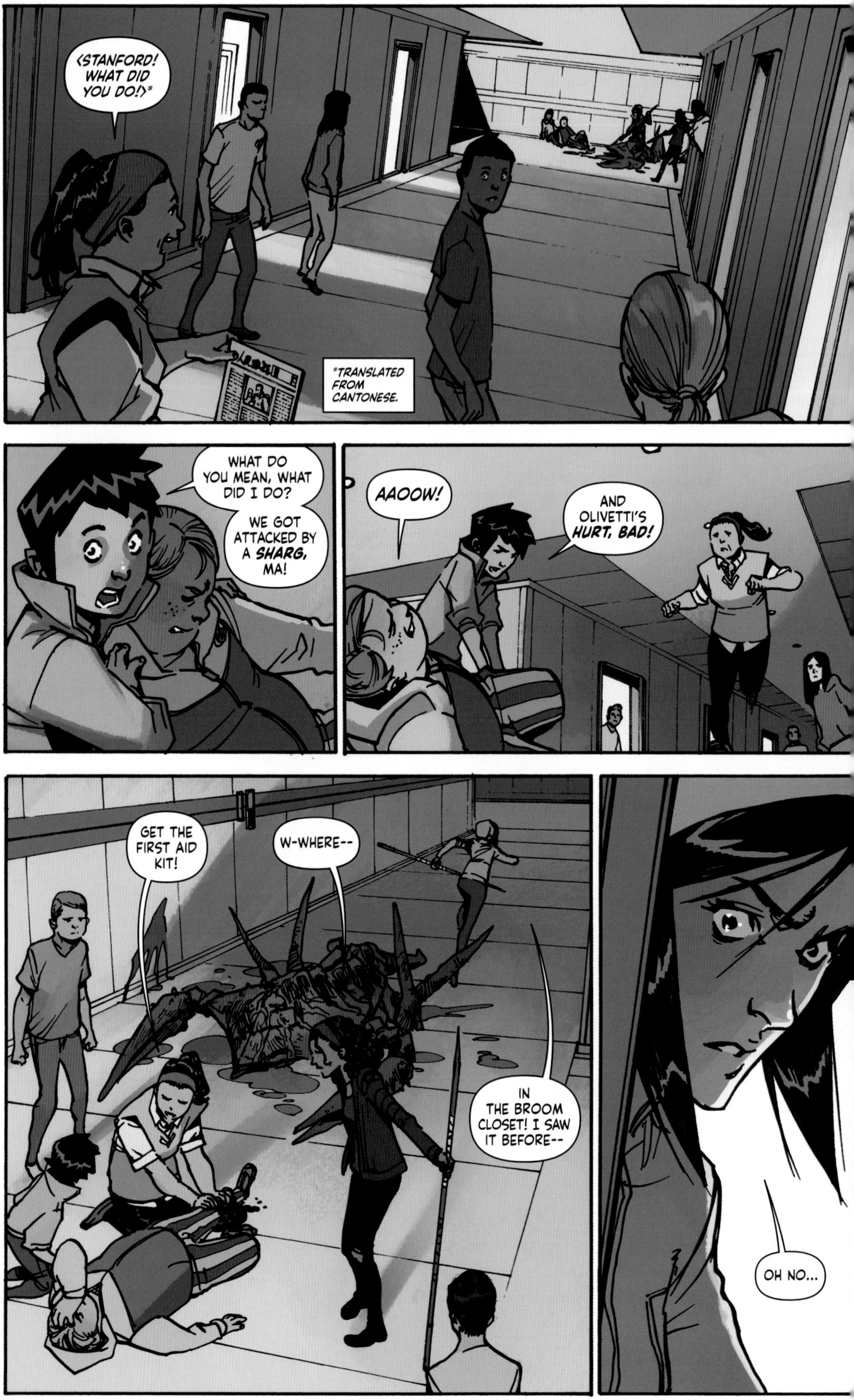

<STANFORD! WHAT DID YOU DO!>*
*TRANSLATED FROM CANTONESE.
WHAT DO YOU MEAN, WHAT DID I DO?
WE GOT ATTACKED BY A SHARG, MA!
AAOOW!
AND OLIVETTI'S HURT, BAD!
GET THE FIRST AID KIT!
W-WHERE--
IN THE BROOM CLOSET! I SAW IT BEFORE--
OH NO...

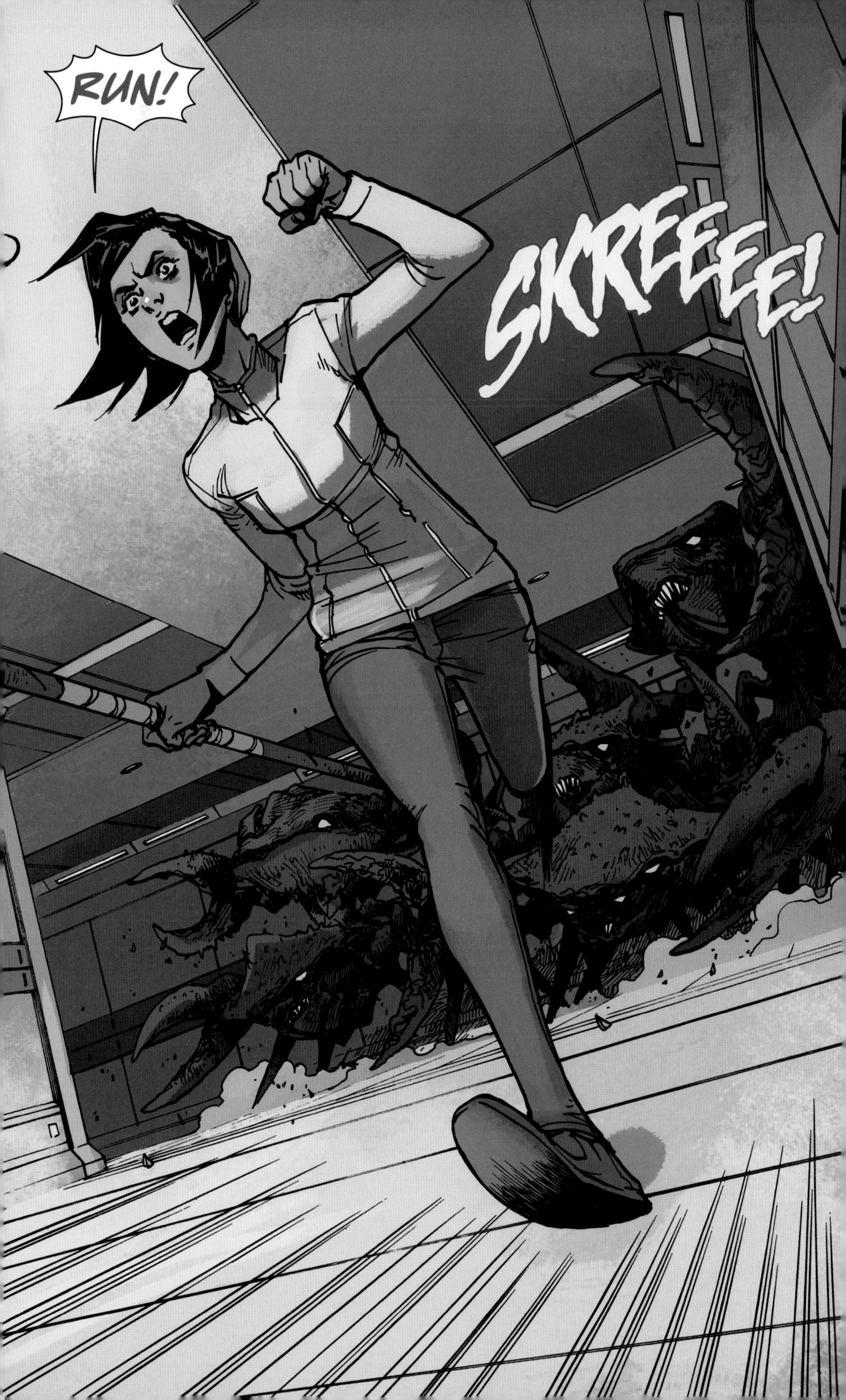
RUN!
SKREEEEE!

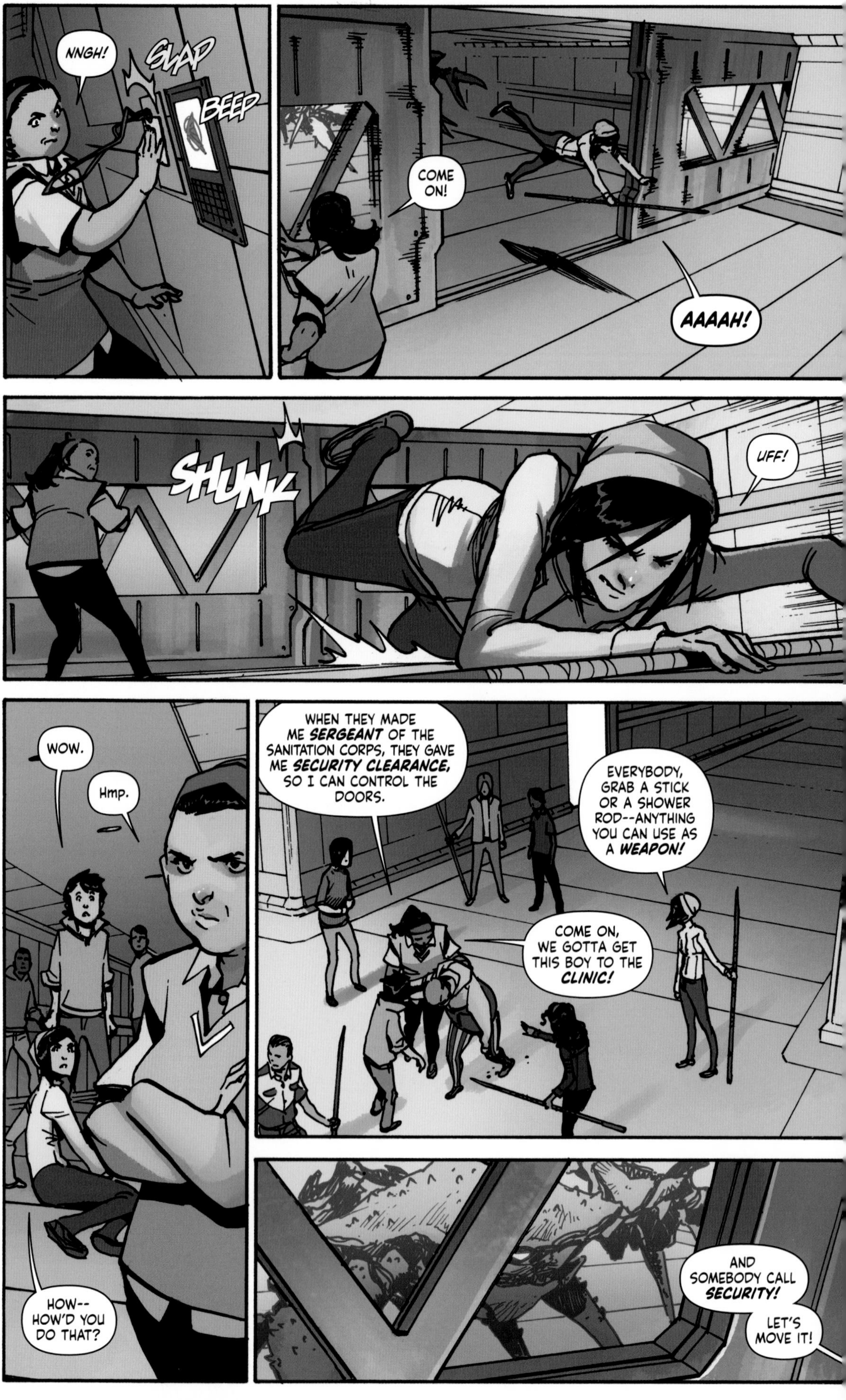
NNGH!
SLAP
BEEP
COME ON!
AAAAH!
SHUNK
UFF!
WOW.
Hmp.
HOW-- HOW'D YOU DO THAT?
WHEN THEY MADE ME SERGEANT OF THE SANITATION CORPS, THEY GAVE ME SECURITY CLEARANCE, SO I CAN CONTROL THE DOORS.
EVERYBODY, GRAB A STICK OR A SHOWER ROD--ANYTHING YOU CAN USE AS A WEAPON!
COME ON, WE GOTTA GET THIS BOY TO THE CLINIC!
AND SOMEBODY CALL SECURITY!
LET'S MOVE IT!

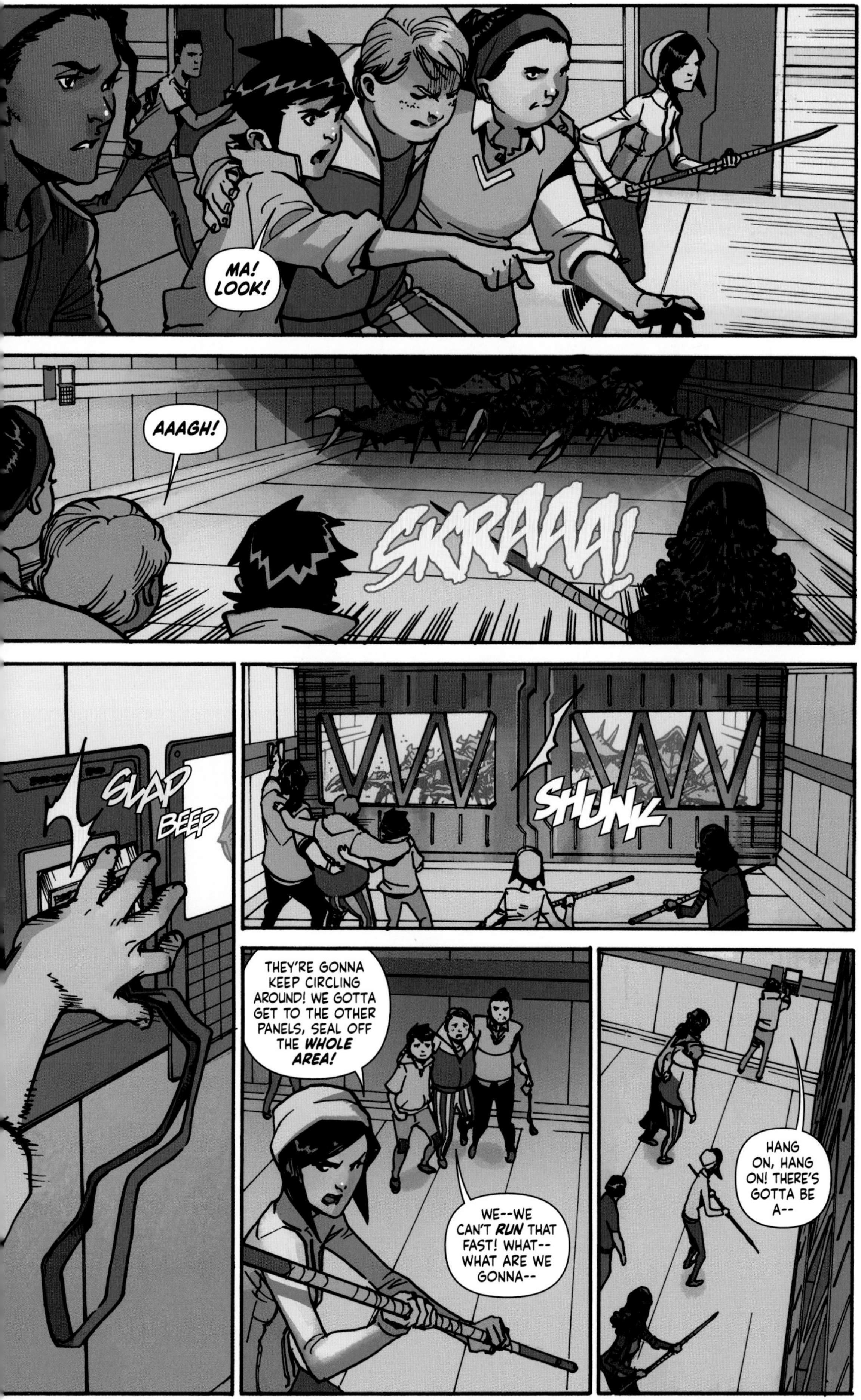
MA! LOOK!
AAAGH!
SKRAAAA!
SLAP
BEEP
SHUNK
THEY'RE GONNA KEEP CIRCLING AROUND! WE GOTTA GET TO THE OTHER PANELS, SEAL OFF THE WHOLE AREA!
WE--WE CAN'T RUN THAT FAST! WHAT-- WHAT ARE WE GONNA--
HANG ON, HANG ON! THERE'S GOTTA BE A--

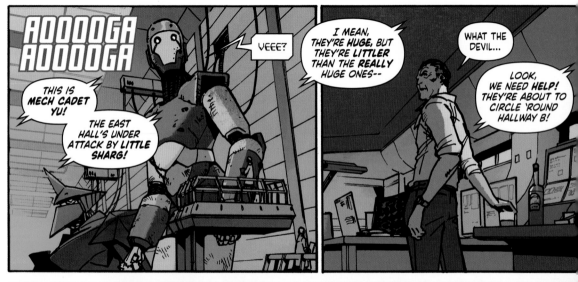

AOOOOGA
AOOOOGA

THIS IS MECH CADET YU!

THE EAST HALL'S UNDER ATTACK BY LITTLE SHARG!

VEEE?

I MEAN, THEY'RE HUGE, BUT THEY'RE LITTLER THAN THE REALLY HUGE ONES--

WHAT THE DEVIL...

LOOK, WE NEED HELP! THEY'RE ABOUT TO CIRCLE 'ROUND HALLWAY B!

SOMEBODY, SEAL OFF THE WHOLE EAST HALL!

SIR?

DO IT!

SKRAAA!

BEEP

SHUNK

SHUNK

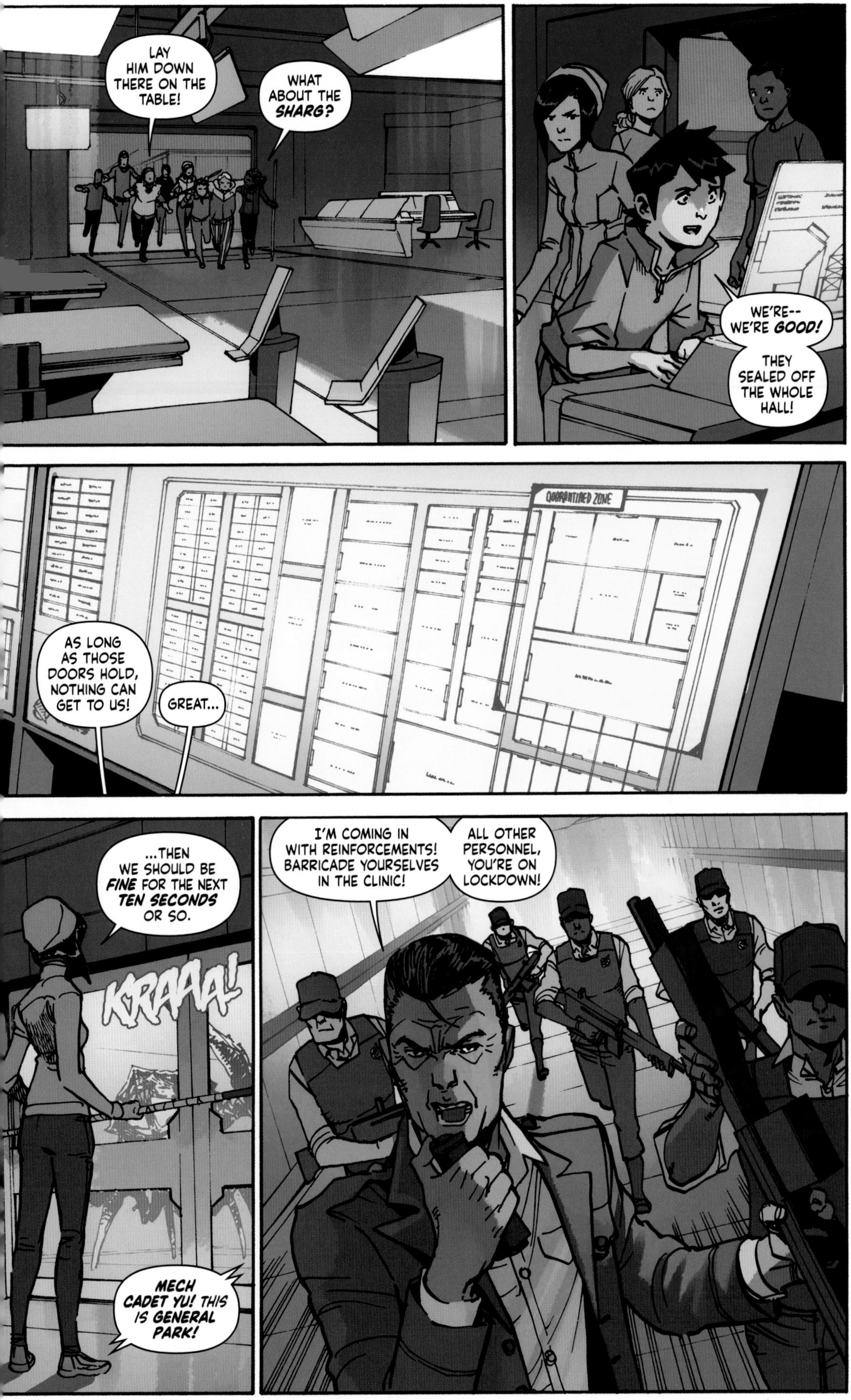

LAY HIM DOWN THERE ON THE TABLE!
WHAT ABOUT THE SHARG?
WE'RE-- WE'RE GOOD!
THEY SEALED OFF THE WHOLE HALL!
QUARANTINED ZONE
AS LONG AS THOSE DOORS HOLD, NOTHING CAN GET TO US!
GREAT...
...THEN WE SHOULD BE FINE FOR THE NEXT TEN SECONDS OR SO.
KRAAA!
MECH CADET YU! THIS IS GENERAL PARK!
I'M COMING IN WITH REINFORCEMENTS! BARRICADE YOURSELVES IN THE CLINIC!
ALL OTHER PERSONNEL, YOU'RE ON LOCKDOWN!

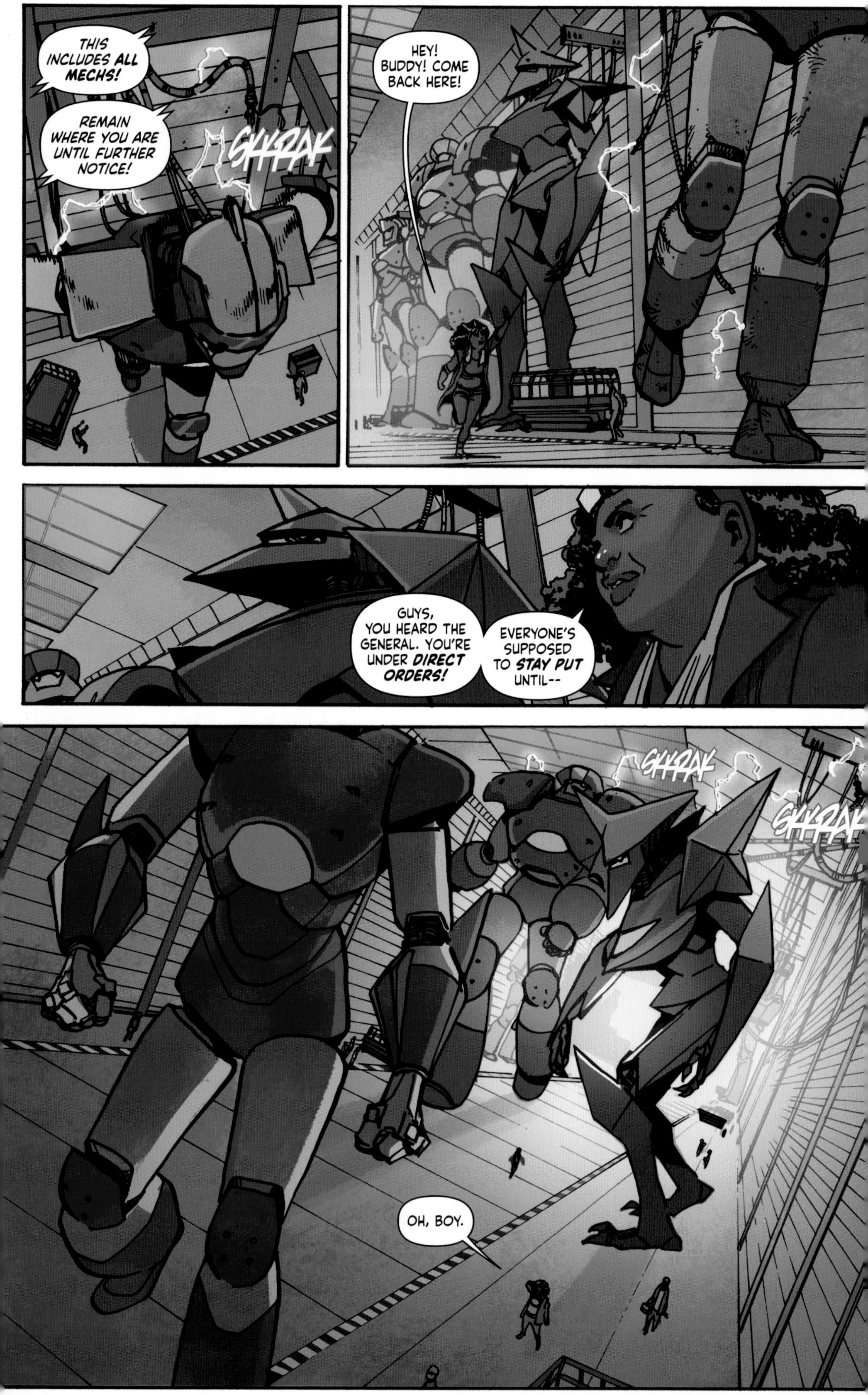
THIS INCLUDES ALL MECHS!
REMAIN WHERE YOU ARE UNTIL FURTHER NOTICE!
SKKRAK
HEY! BUDDY! COME BACK HERE!
GUYS, YOU HEARD THE GENERAL. YOU'RE UNDER DIRECT ORDERS!
EVERYONE'S SUPPOSED TO STAY PUT UNTIL--
SKKRAK
SKKRAK
OH, BOY.

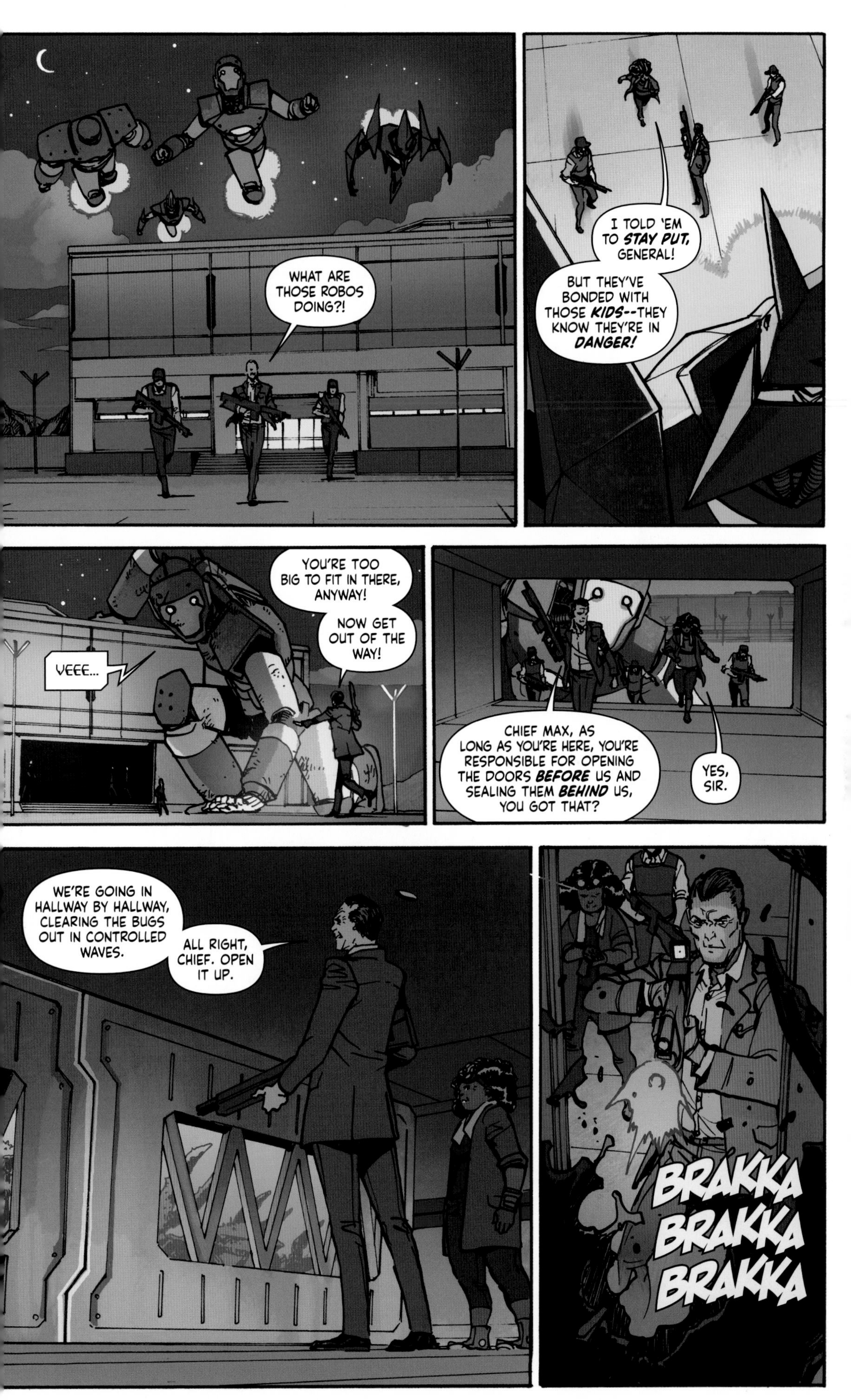

WHAT ARE THOSE ROBOS DOING?!
I TOLD 'EM TO STAY PUT, GENERAL!
BUT THEY'VE BONDED WITH THOSE KIDS--THEY KNOW THEY'RE IN DANGER!
YOU'RE TOO BIG TO FIT IN THERE, ANYWAY!
NOW GET OUT OF THE WAY!
VEEE...
CHIEF MAX, AS LONG AS YOU'RE HERE, YOU'RE RESPONSIBLE FOR OPENING THE DOORS BEFORE US AND SEALING THEM BEHIND US, YOU GOT THAT?
YES, SIR.
WE'RE GOING IN HALLWAY BY HALLWAY, CLEARING THE BUGS OUT IN CONTROLLED WAVES.
ALL RIGHT, CHIEF. OPEN IT UP.
BRAKKA BRAKKA BRAKKA

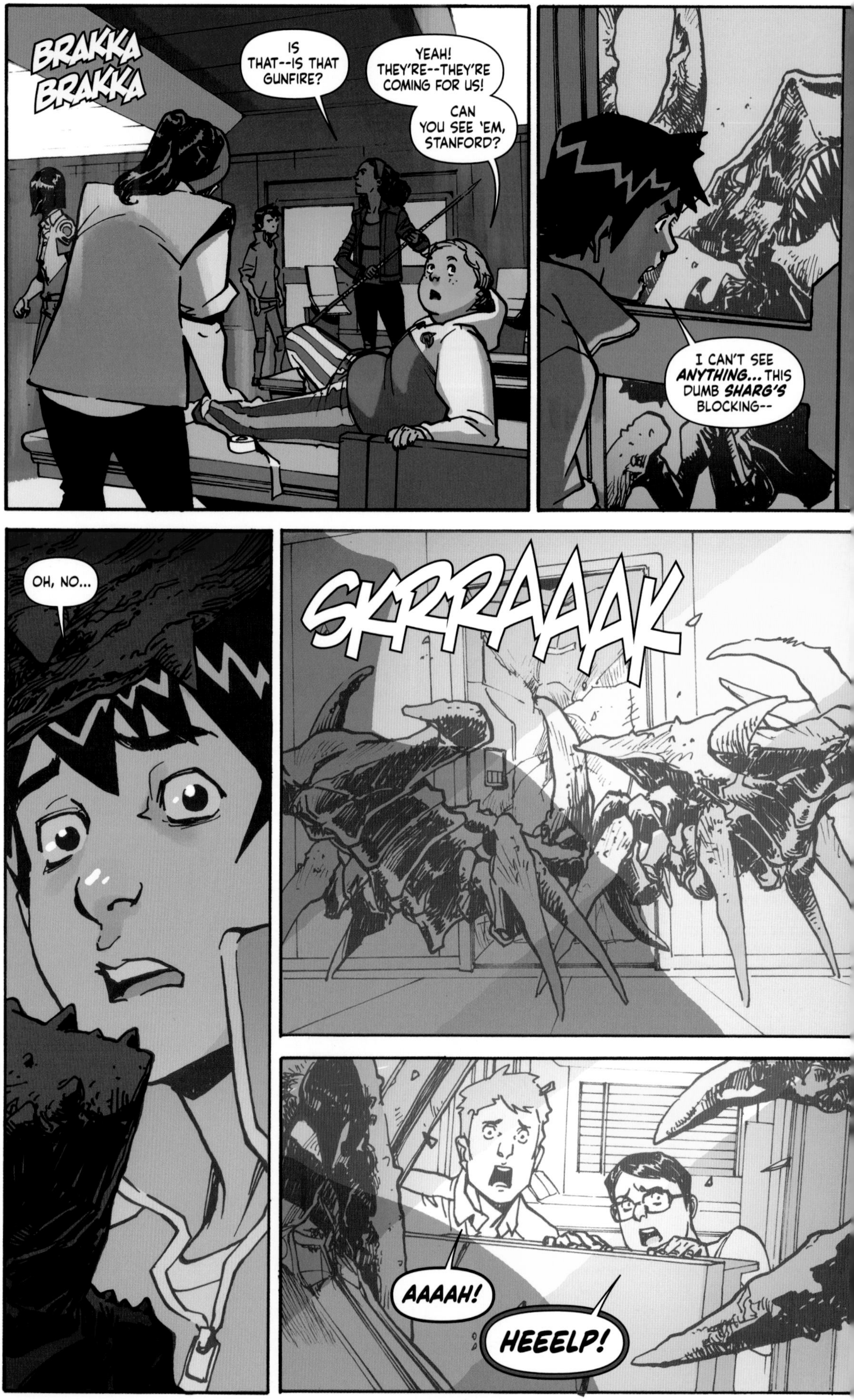
BRAKKA BRAKKA
IS THAT--IS THAT GUNFIRE?
YEAH! THEY'RE--THEY'RE COMING FOR US!
CAN YOU SEE 'EM, STANFORD?
I CAN'T SEE ANYTHING... THIS DUMB SHARG'S BLOCKING--
OH, NO...
SKRRAAAK
AAAAH!
HEEELP!

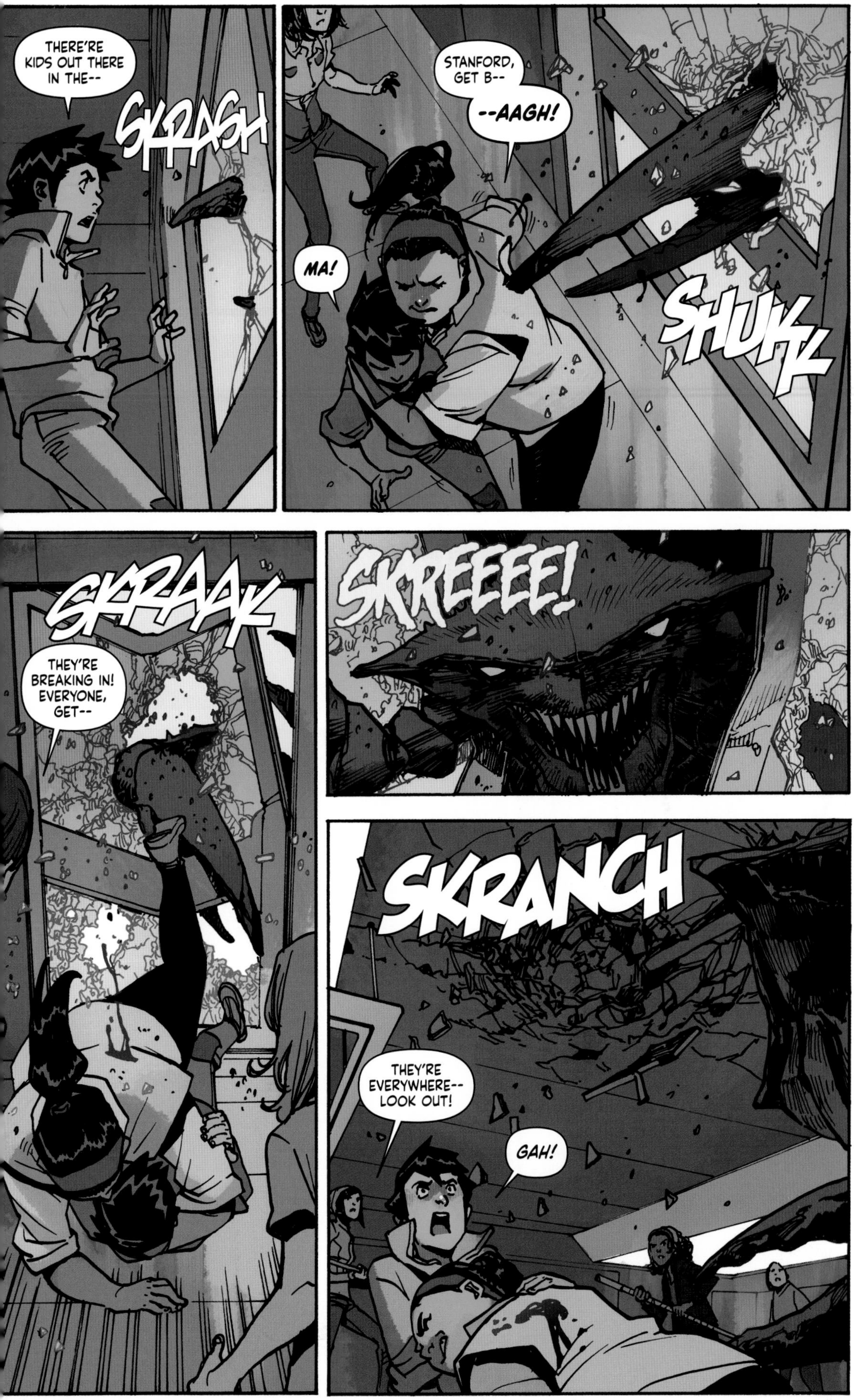
THERE'RE KIDS OUT THERE IN THE--
SKRASH
STANFORD, GET B--
--AAGH!
MA!
SHUKK
SKRAAK
THEY'RE BREAKING IN! EVERYONE, GET--
SKREEEE!
SKRANCH
THEY'RE EVERYWHERE-- LOOK OUT!
GAH!

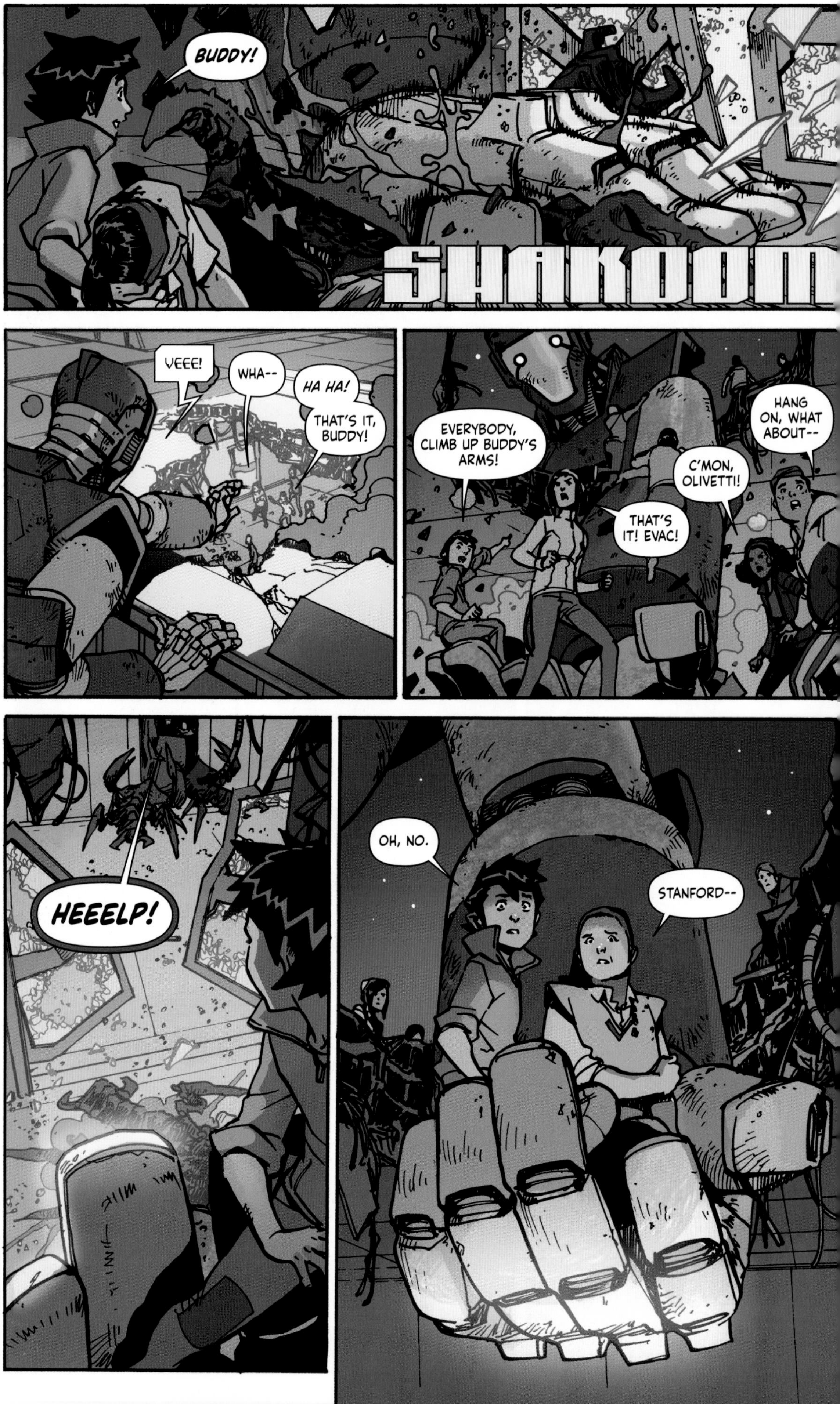
BUDDY!
SHAKOOM
VEEE!
WHA--
HA HA!
THAT'S IT, BUDDY!
EVERYBODY, CLIMB UP BUDDY'S ARMS!
THAT'S IT! EVAC!
C'MON, OLIVETTI!
HANG ON, WHAT ABOUT--
HEEELP!
OH, NO.
STANFORD--

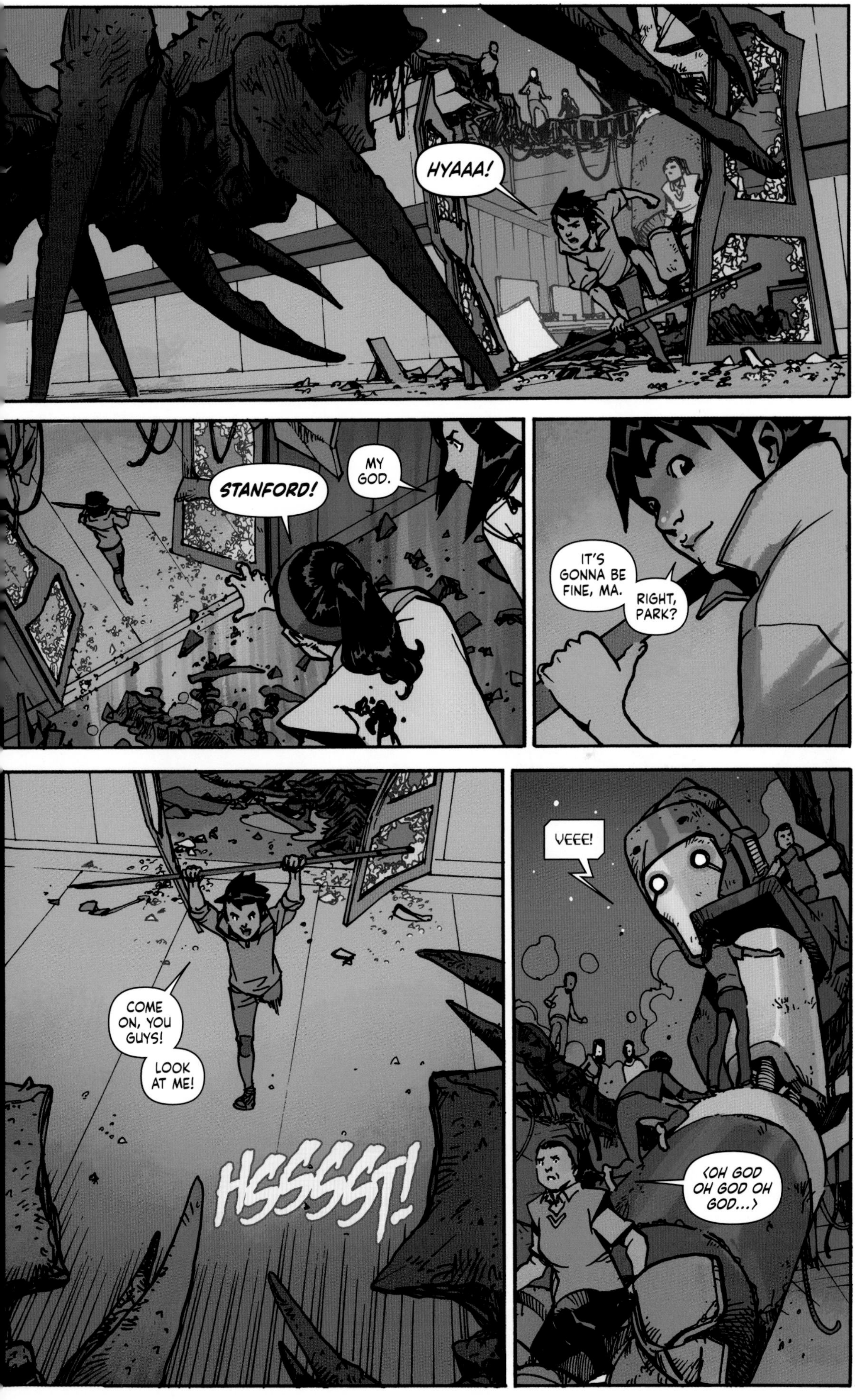
HYAAA!
STANFORD!
MY GOD.
IT'S GONNA BE FINE, MA.
RIGHT, PARK?
COME ON, YOU GUYS!
LOOK AT ME!
HSSSST!
VEEE!
<OH GOD OH GOD OH GOD...>

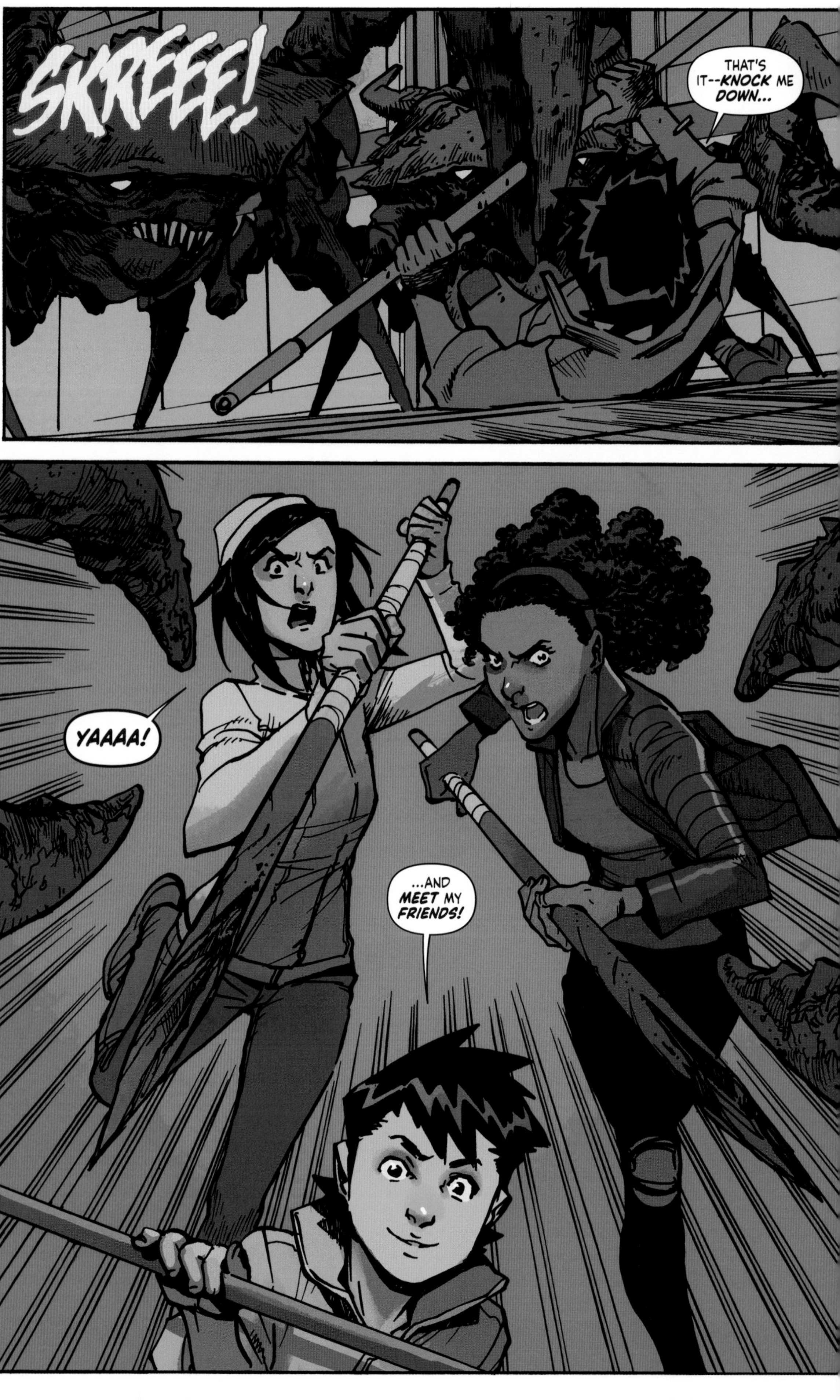
SKREEE!
THAT'S IT--KNOCK ME DOWN...
YAAAA!
...AND MEET MY FRIENDS!

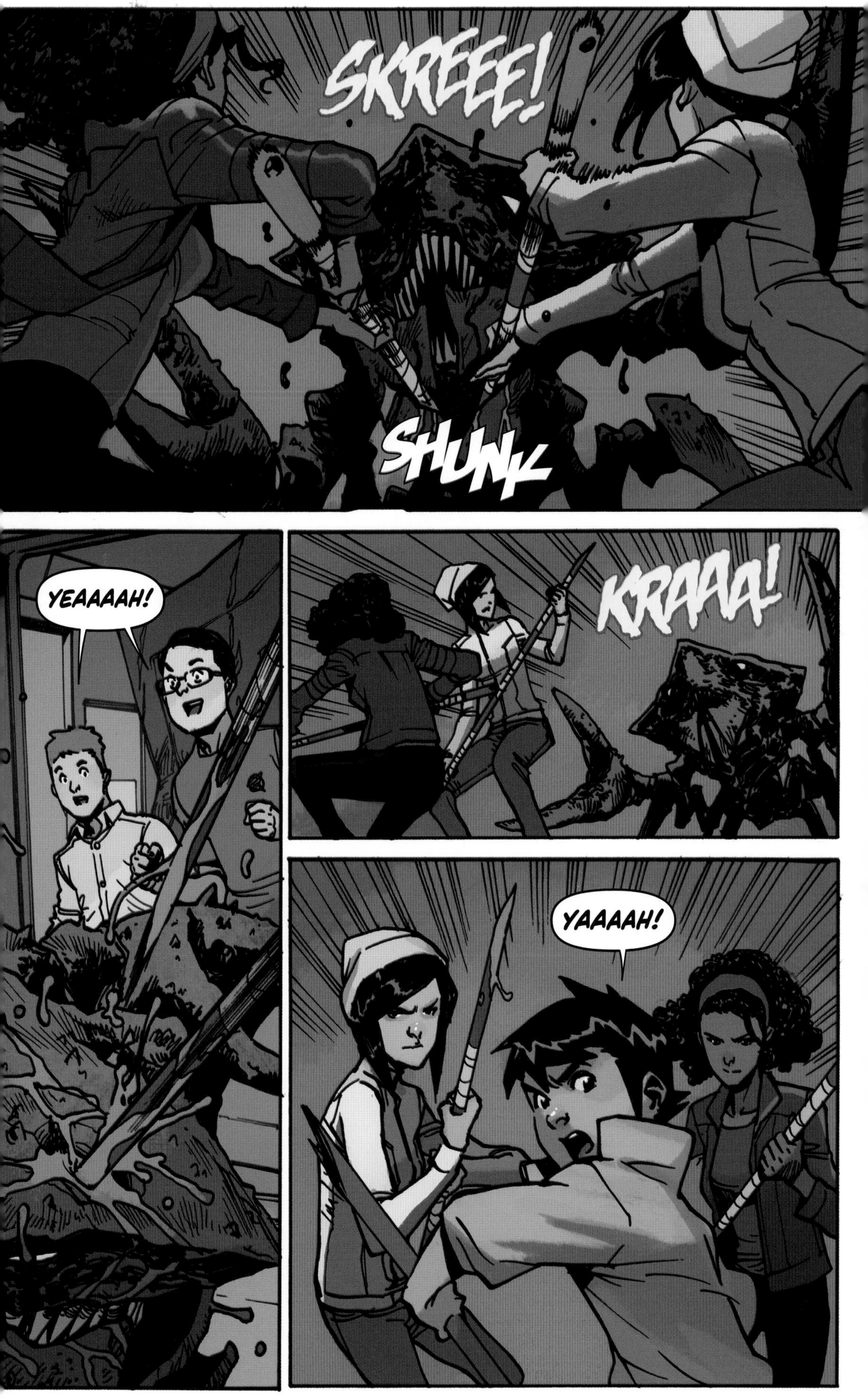
SKREEE!
SHUNK
YEAAAAH!
KRAAA!
YAAAAH!

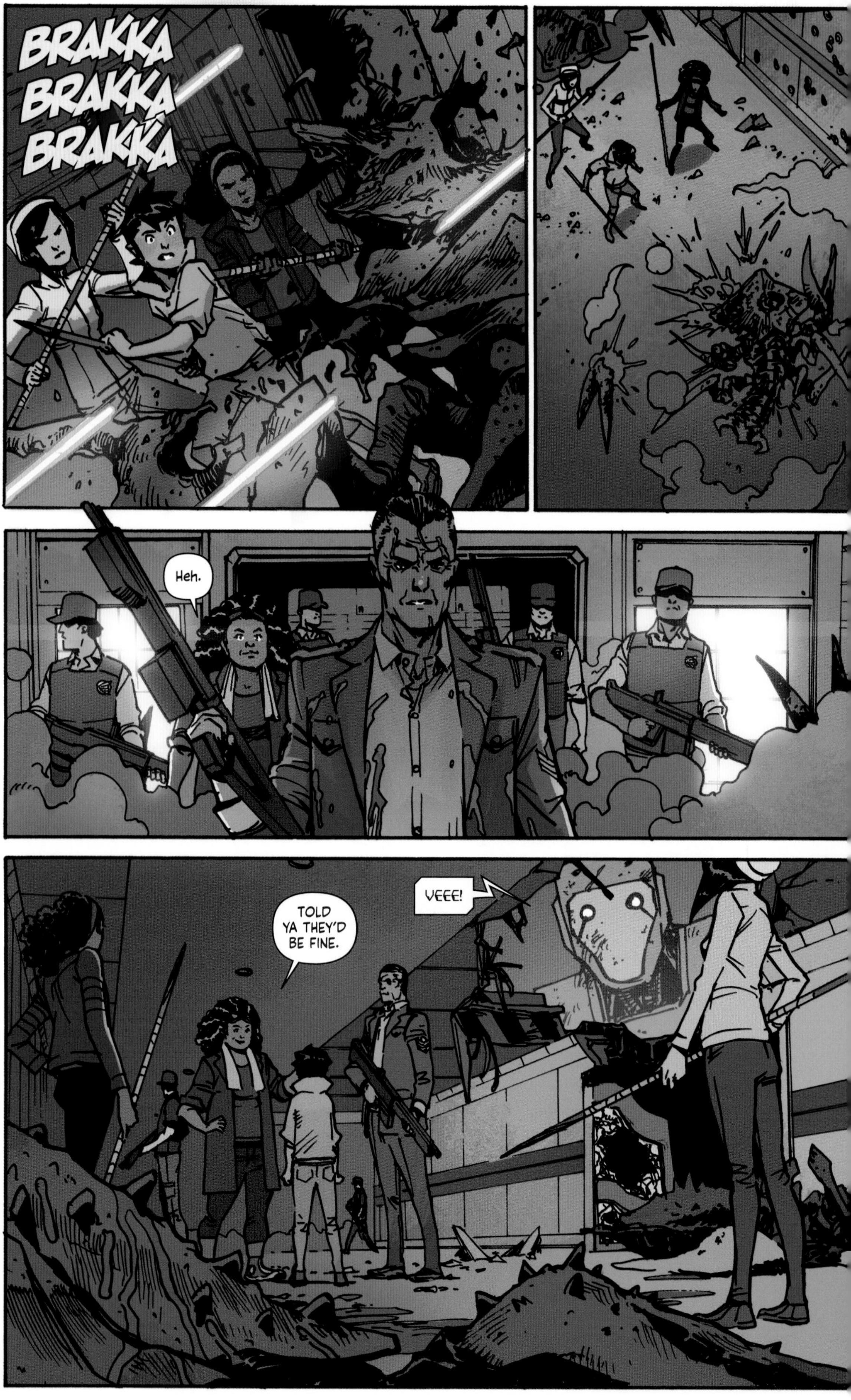
BRAKKA
BRAKKA
BRAKKA
Heh.
TOLD YA THEY'D BE FINE.
VEEE!

YOU... DID WELL.

TH-THANK YOU.

ROLL CALL'S GOOD, GENERAL! ALL STUDENTS AND STAFF ACCOUNTED FOR!

GENERAL, SIR! CAN WE GET THE *WOUNDED* BACK INTO THE *CLINIC* NOW?

NO. THEY'LL BE TAKEN CARE OF ELSEWHERE.

ALL ROBOS, INTO THE TRANSPORT!

WAIT, WHAT'S GOING ON?

ALL MECHS HAVE BEEN ORDERED TO REPORT TO CENTRAL COMMAND.

PILOTS CAN ACCOMPANY THEM, IF THEY DESIRE.

"IF THEY DESIRE"? ARE YOU *KIDDING?* WE'RE *MECH CADETS!*

I'M SORRY, SON...

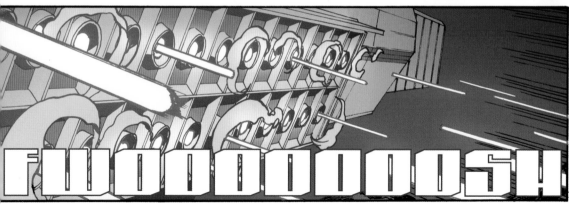

FWOOOOOOOSH

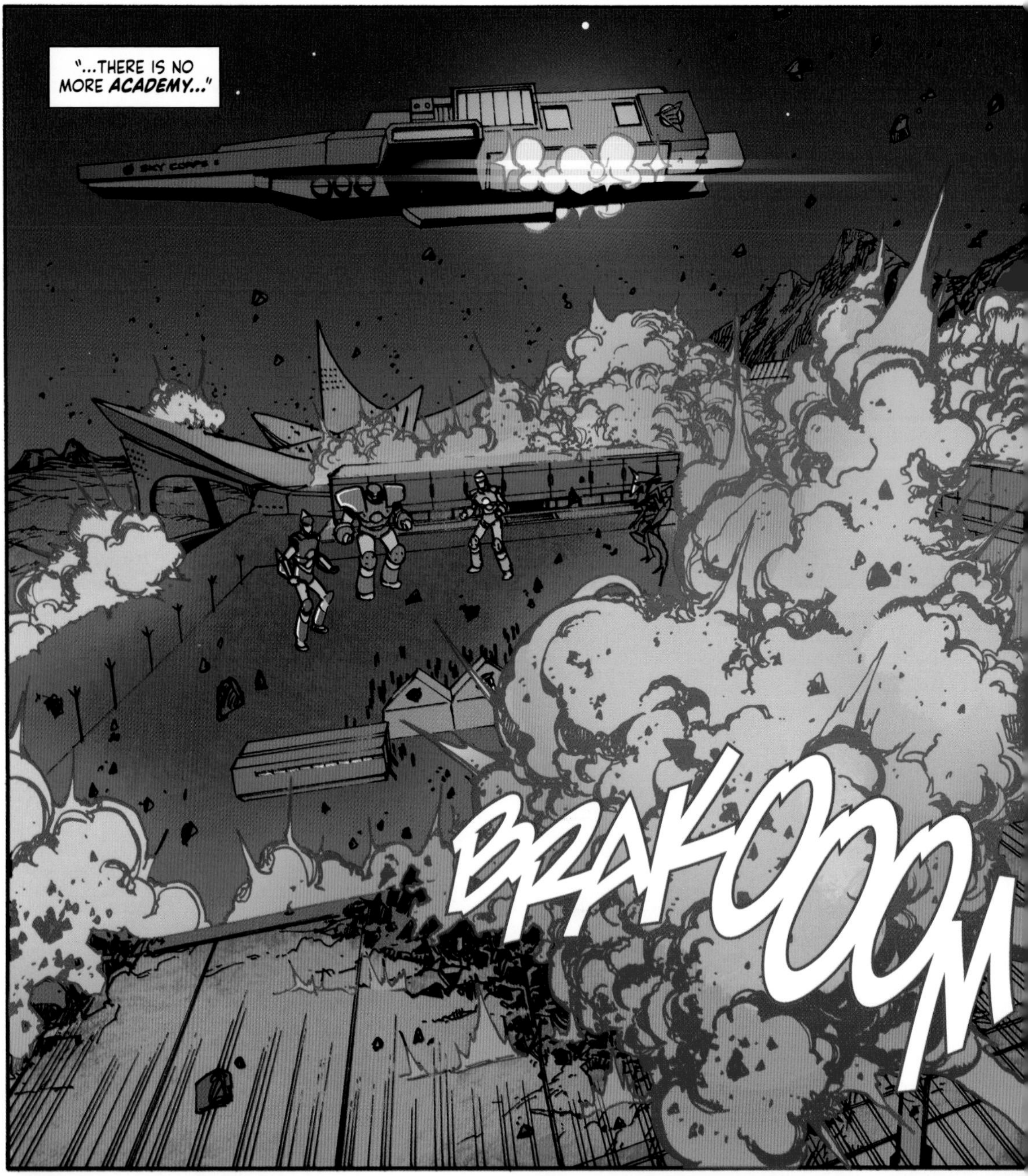
"...THERE IS NO MORE *ACADEMY*..."
SKY CORPS
BRAKOOOOM

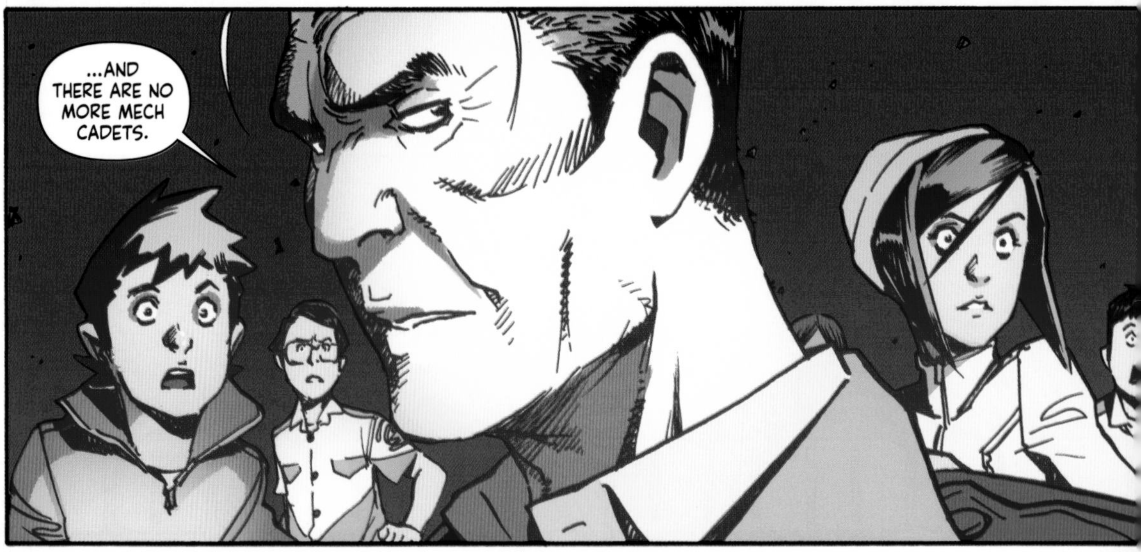
...AND THERE ARE NO MORE MECH CADETS.

CHAPTER **SEVEN**

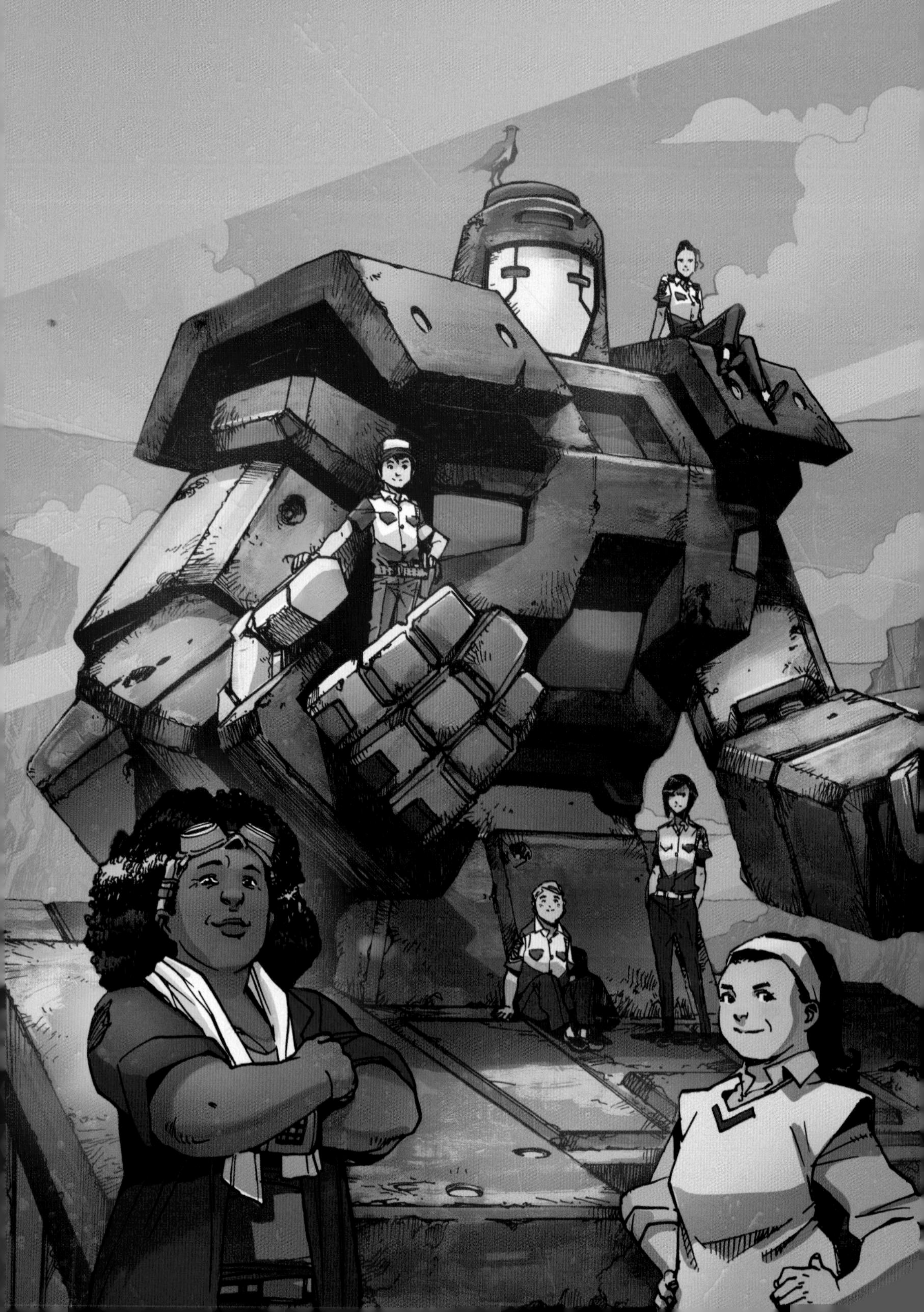

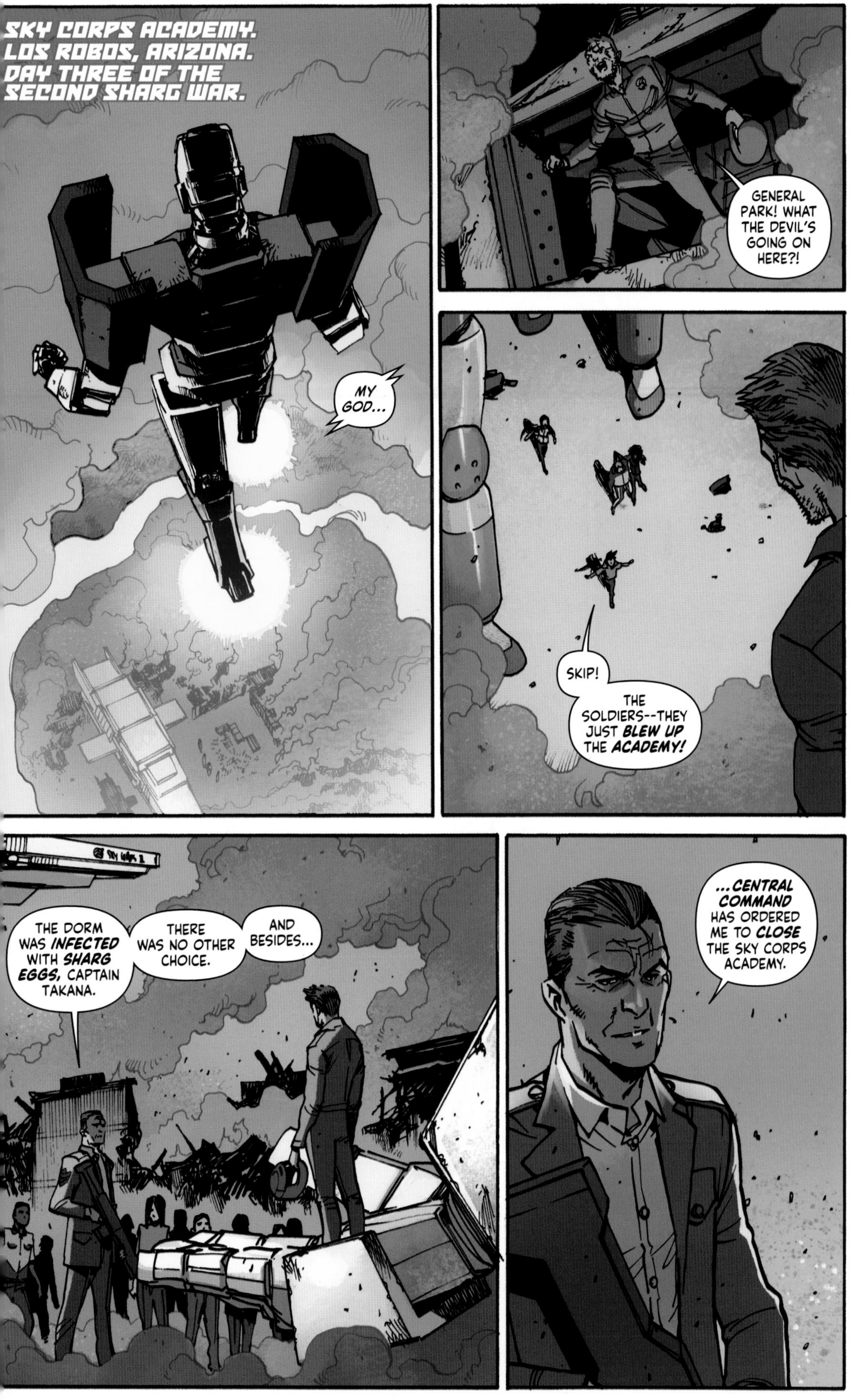
SKY CORPS ACADEMY.
LOS ROBOS, ARIZONA.
DAY THREE OF THE
SECOND SHARG WAR.
MY GOD...
GENERAL PARK! WHAT THE DEVIL'S GOING ON HERE?!
SKIP!
THE SOLDIERS--THEY JUST BLEW UP THE ACADEMY!
THE DORM WAS INFECTED WITH SHARG EGGS, CAPTAIN TAKANA.
THERE WAS NO OTHER CHOICE.
AND BESIDES...
...CENTRAL COMMAND HAS ORDERED ME TO CLOSE THE SKY CORPS ACADEMY.

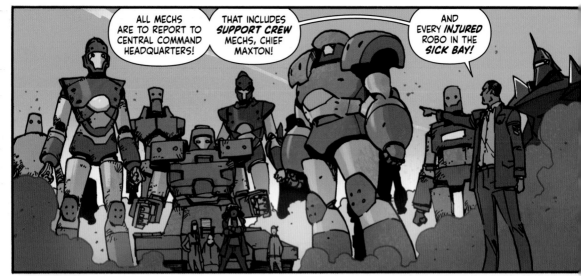

ALL MECHS ARE TO REPORT TO CENTRAL COMMAND HEADQUARTERS!

THAT INCLUDES *SUPPORT CREW* MECHS, CHIEF MAXTON!

AND EVERY *INJURED* ROBO IN THE *SICK BAY!*

WHAT HAPPENS AT CENTRAL COMMAND, SIR?

WE'LL FIND OUT WHEN WE GET THERE, CHIEF.

LET'S DO THIS! TRANSPORT DEPARTS IN FIFTEEN MINUTES!

EVERYONE INSIDE!

KRREEE

WHY DON'T THE MECHS JUST *FLY?*

...

...SIR.

WE'RE SAVING ENERGY AND TRAVELING UNDER RADAR, CAPTAIN.

YOU SPENT A LOT OF TIME IN THE WILDERNESS...

...HAVEN'T YOU LEARNED TO FOLLOW *ORDERS* YET?

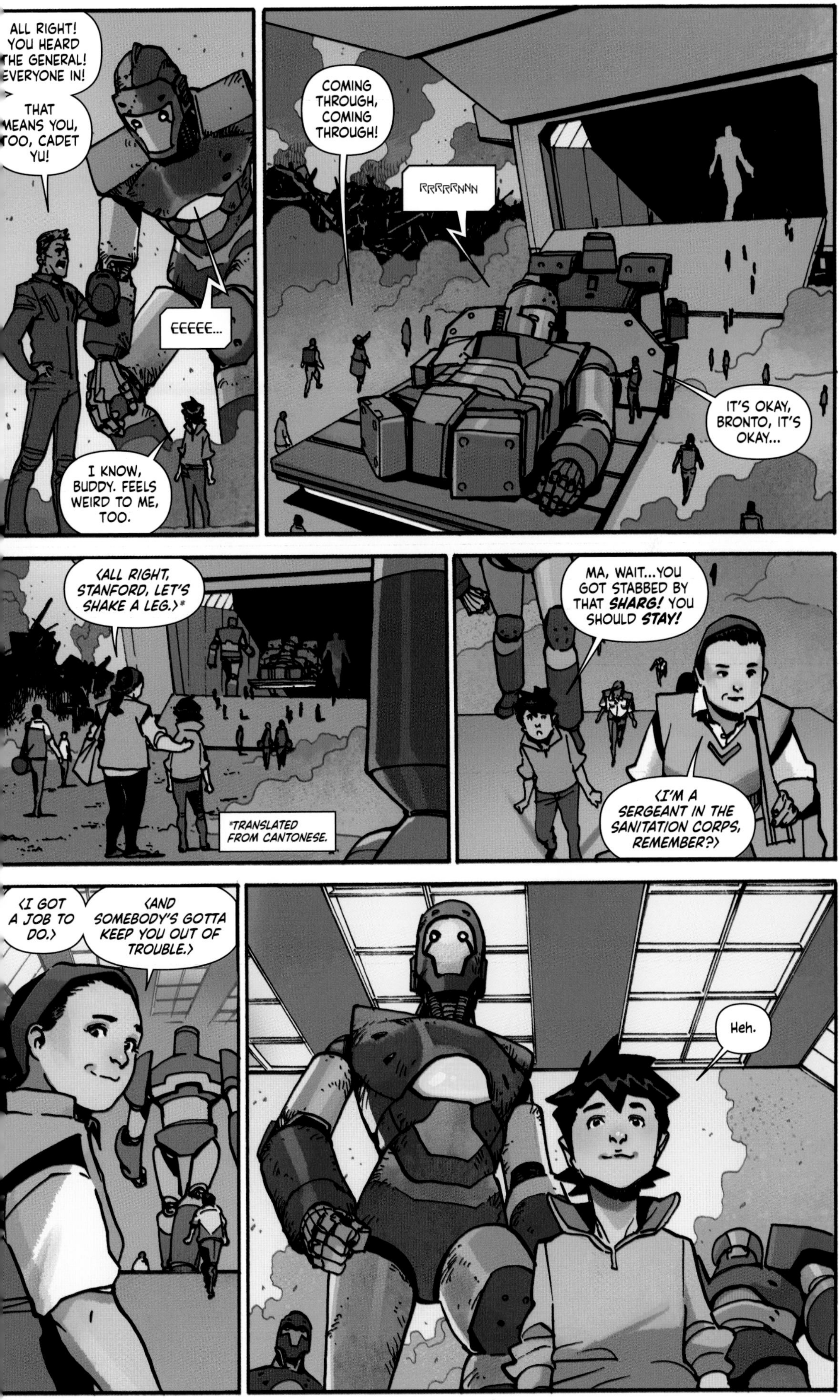
ALL RIGHT! YOU HEARD THE GENERAL! EVERYONE IN!
THAT MEANS YOU, TOO, CADET YU!
EEEEE...
I KNOW, BUDDY. FEELS WEIRD TO ME, TOO.
COMING THROUGH, COMING THROUGH!
RRRRRNNN
IT'S OKAY, BRONTO, IT'S OKAY...
‹ALL RIGHT, STANFORD, LET'S SHAKE A LEG.›*
*TRANSLATED FROM CANTONESE.
MA, WAIT...YOU GOT STABBED BY THAT SHARG! YOU SHOULD STAY!
‹I'M A SERGEANT IN THE SANITATION CORPS, REMEMBER?›
‹I GOT A JOB TO DO.›
‹AND SOMEBODY'S GOTTA KEEP YOU OUT OF TROUBLE.›
Heh.

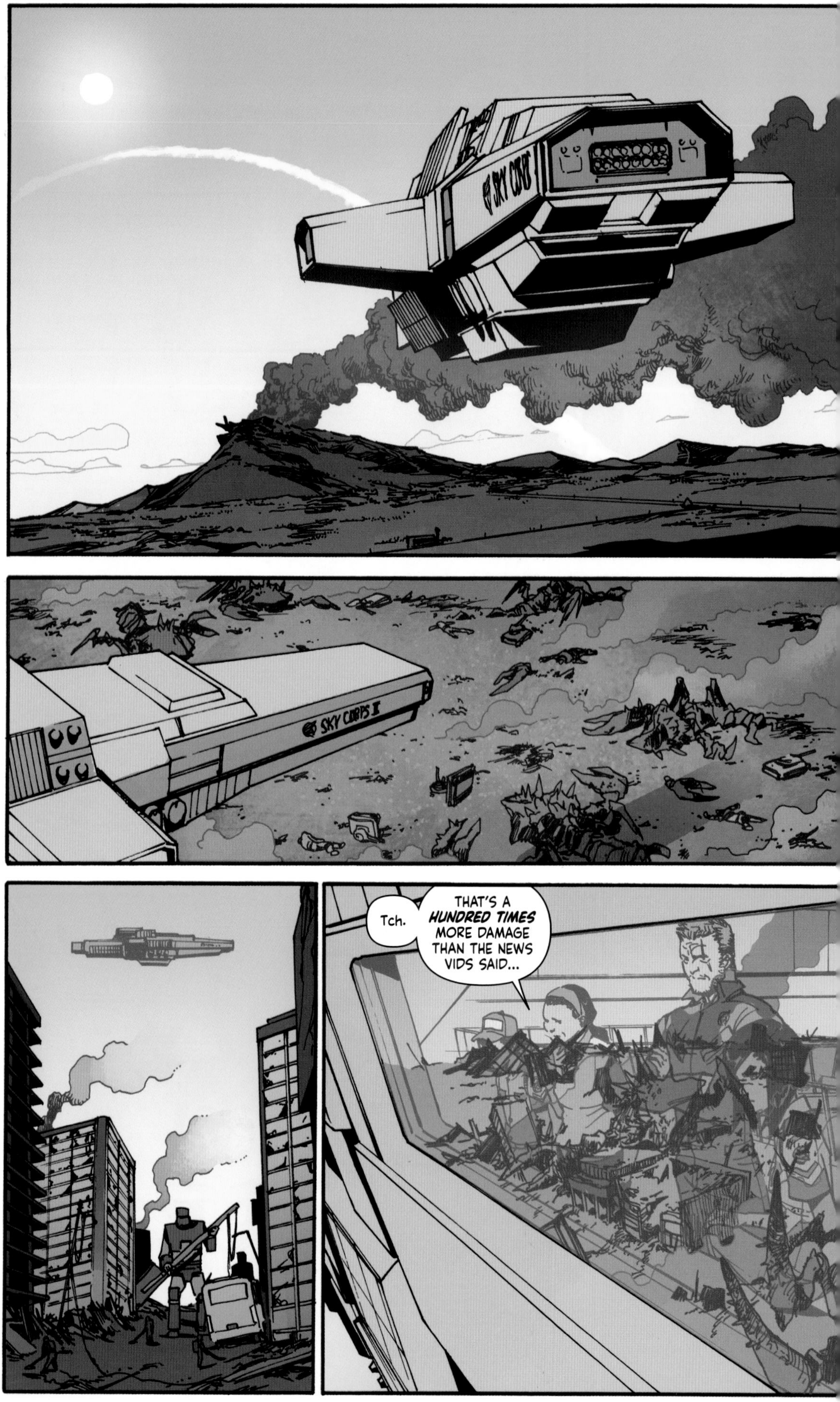
SKY CORPS
SKY CORPS II
Tch.
THAT'S A *HUNDRED TIMES* MORE DAMAGE THAN THE NEWS VIDS SAID...

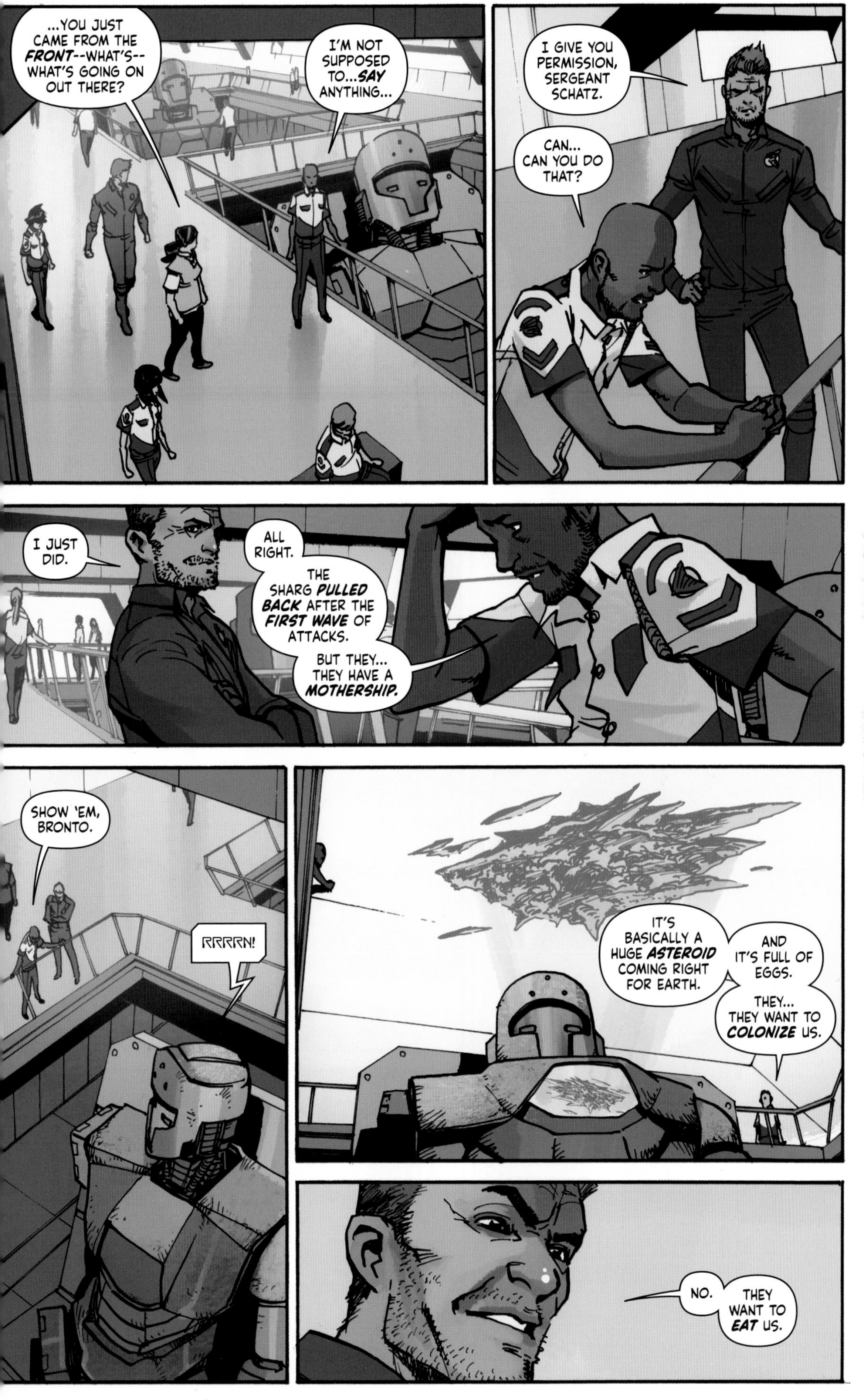
...YOU JUST CAME FROM THE FRONT--WHAT'S--WHAT'S GOING ON OUT THERE?
I'M NOT SUPPOSED TO...SAY ANYTHING...
I GIVE YOU PERMISSION, SERGEANT SCHATZ.
CAN... CAN YOU DO THAT?
I JUST DID.
ALL RIGHT.
THE SHARG PULLED BACK AFTER THE FIRST WAVE OF ATTACKS.
BUT THEY... THEY HAVE A MOTHERSHIP.
SHOW 'EM, BRONTO.
RRRRN!
IT'S BASICALLY A HUGE ASTEROID COMING RIGHT FOR EARTH.
AND IT'S FULL OF EGGS.
THEY... THEY WANT TO COLONIZE US.
NO.
THEY WANT TO EAT US.

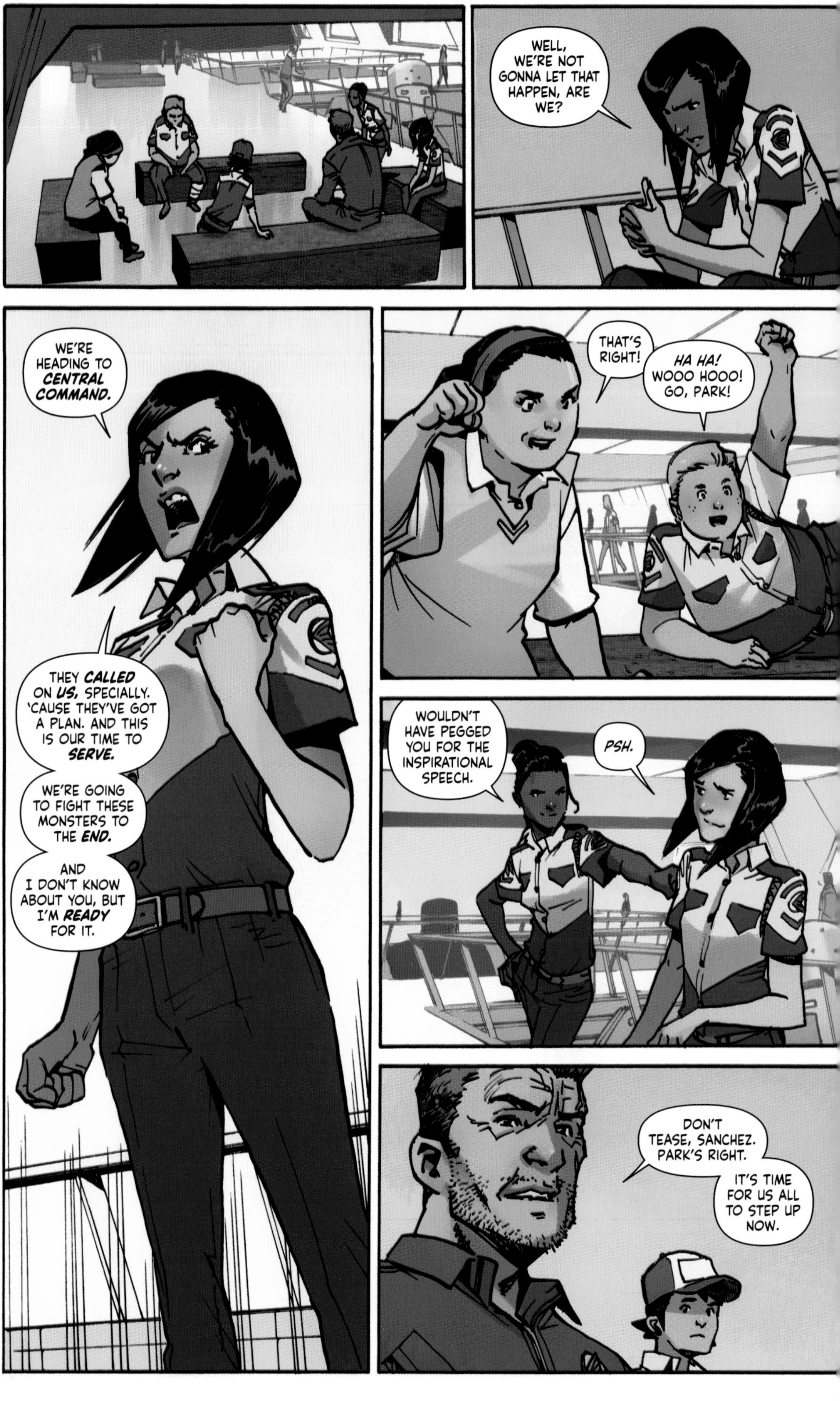
WELL, WE'RE NOT GONNA LET THAT HAPPEN, ARE WE?
WE'RE HEADING TO **CENTRAL COMMAND.**
THEY **CALLED** ON **US,** SPECIALLY. 'CAUSE THEY'VE GOT A PLAN. AND THIS IS OUR TIME TO **SERVE.**
WE'RE GOING TO FIGHT THESE MONSTERS TO THE **END.**
AND I DON'T KNOW ABOUT YOU, BUT I'M **READY** FOR IT.
THAT'S RIGHT!
HA HA! WOOO HOOO! GO, PARK!
WOULDN'T HAVE PEGGED YOU FOR THE INSPIRATIONAL SPEECH.
PSH.
DON'T TEASE, SANCHEZ. PARK'S RIGHT.
IT'S TIME FOR US ALL TO STEP UP NOW.

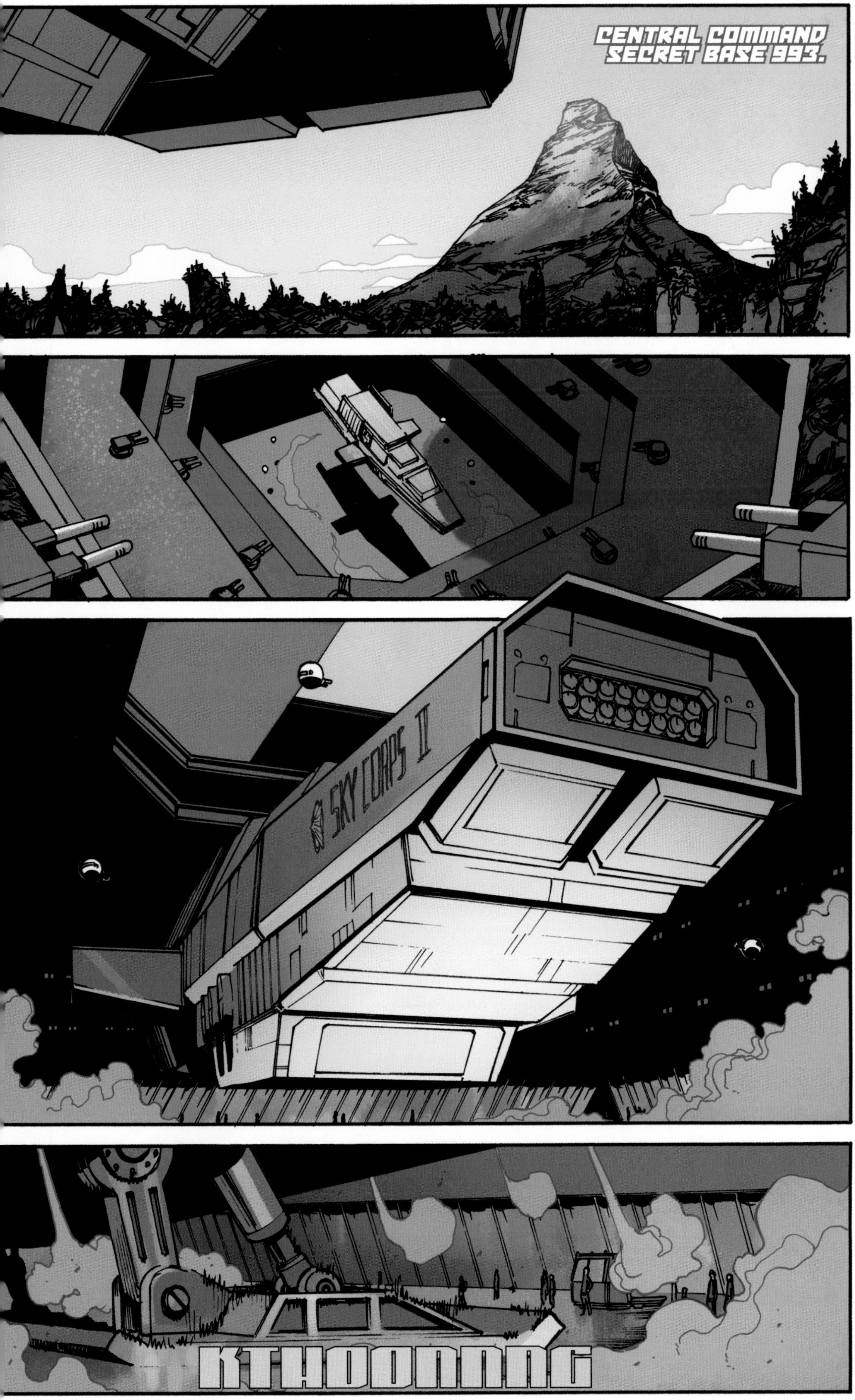
CENTRAL COMMAND
SECRET BASE 993.
SKY CORPS II
KTHOONNNG

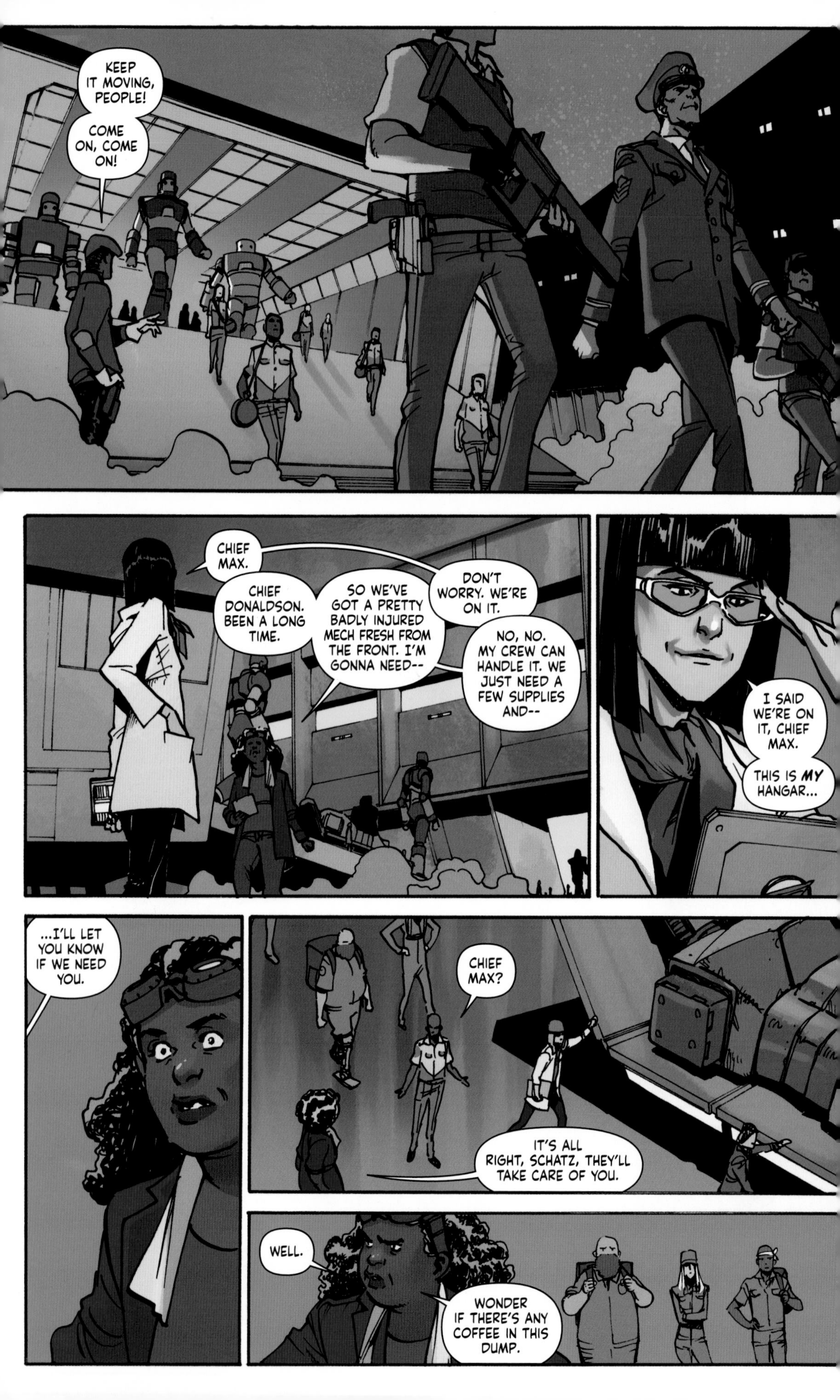

KEEP IT MOVING, PEOPLE!
COME ON, COME ON!
CHIEF MAX.
CHIEF DONALDSON. BEEN A LONG TIME.
SO WE'VE GOT A PRETTY BADLY INJURED MECH FRESH FROM THE FRONT. I'M GONNA NEED--
DON'T WORRY. WE'RE ON IT.
NO, NO. MY CREW CAN HANDLE IT. WE JUST NEED A FEW SUPPLIES AND--
I SAID WE'RE ON IT, CHIEF MAX.
THIS IS **MY** HANGAR...
...I'LL LET YOU KNOW IF WE NEED YOU.
CHIEF MAX?
IT'S ALL RIGHT, SCHATZ, THEY'LL TAKE CARE OF YOU.
WELL.
WONDER IF THERE'S ANY COFFEE IN THIS DUMP.

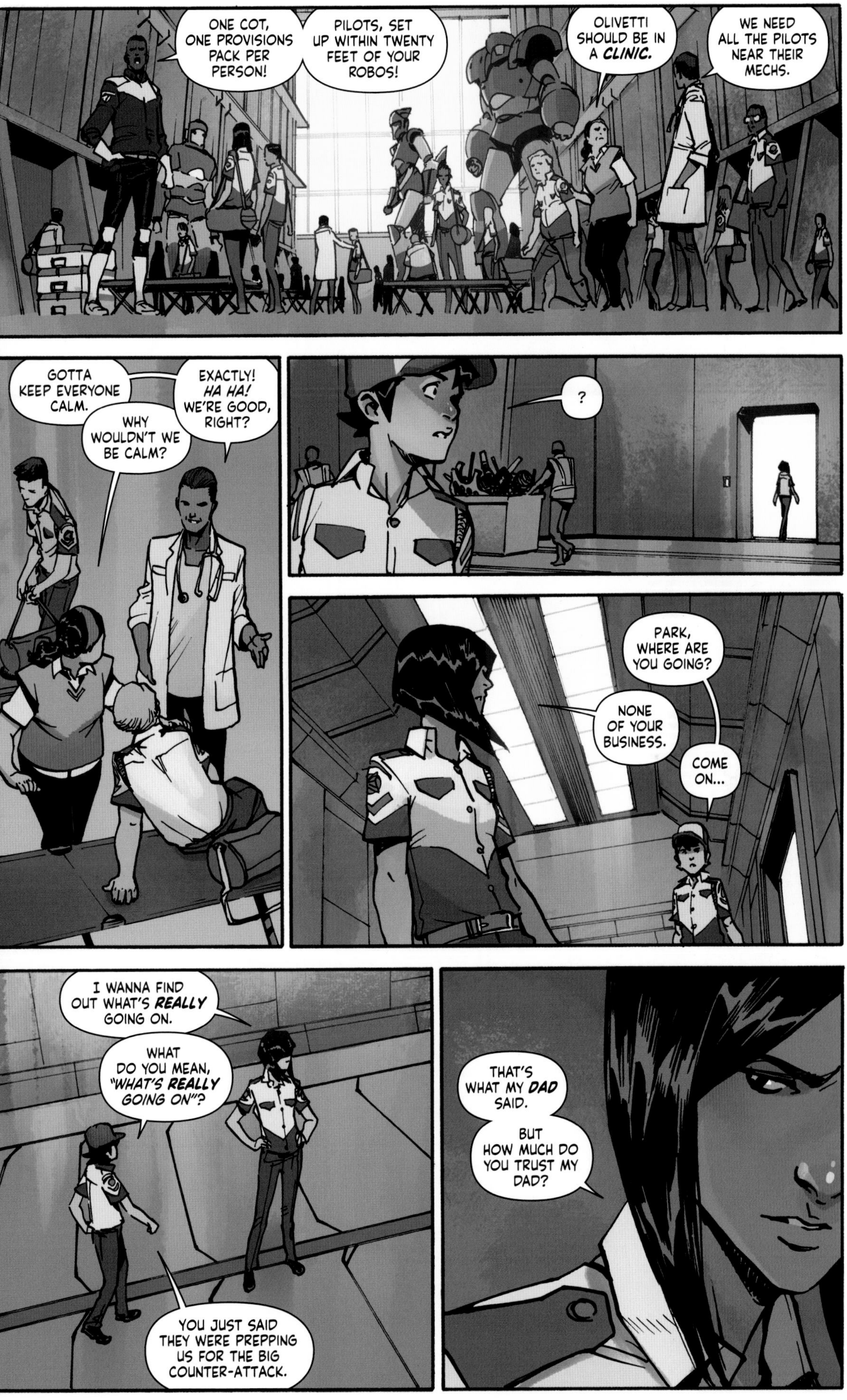
ONE COT, ONE PROVISIONS PACK PER PERSON!
PILOTS, SET UP WITHIN TWENTY FEET OF YOUR ROBOS!
OLIVETTI SHOULD BE IN A *CLINIC.*
WE NEED ALL THE PILOTS NEAR THEIR MECHS.
GOTTA KEEP EVERYONE CALM.
WHY WOULDN'T WE BE CALM?
EXACTLY! *HA HA!* WE'RE GOOD, RIGHT?
?
PARK, WHERE ARE YOU GOING?
NONE OF YOUR BUSINESS.
COME ON...
I WANNA FIND OUT WHAT'S *REALLY* GOING ON.
WHAT DO YOU MEAN, *"WHAT'S REALLY GOING ON"*?
YOU JUST SAID THEY WERE PREPPING US FOR THE BIG COUNTER-ATTACK.
THAT'S WHAT MY *DAD* SAID.
BUT HOW MUCH DO YOU TRUST MY DAD?

HEY, WHAT ARE YOU GUYS DOING?

I'M *GENERAL PARK'S* DAUGHTER.

HE TOLD ME TO MEET HIM AT 1900 HOURS.

OH, RIGHT. YOU KNOW THE WAY?

OF COURSE.

PRETTY SLICK.

HEY, LOOK...

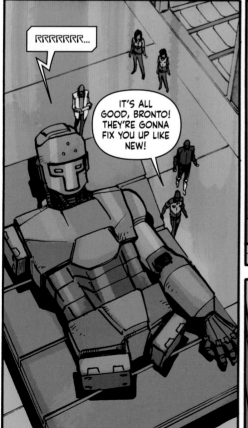

RRRRRRR...

IT'S ALL GOOD, BRONTO! THEY'RE GONNA FIX YOU UP LIKE NEW!

MECH COMING THROUGH!

LET'S GO, LET'S GO!

Whoa.

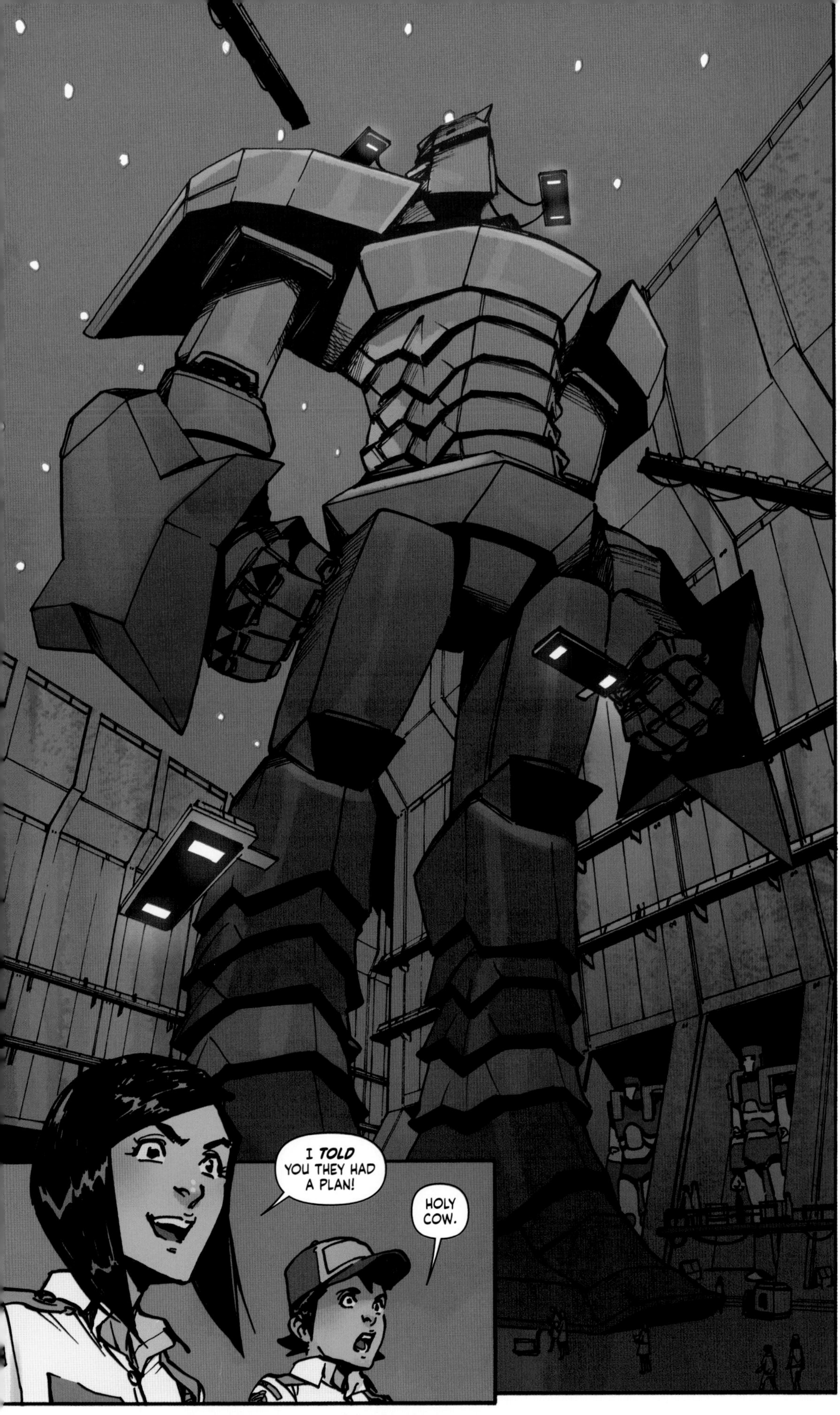
I TOLD YOU THEY HAD A PLAN!
HOLY COW.

THIS...THIS IS INCREDIBLE.

STEP AWAY FROM THE MECH, SERGEANT SCHATZ.

WAIT, WHAT?

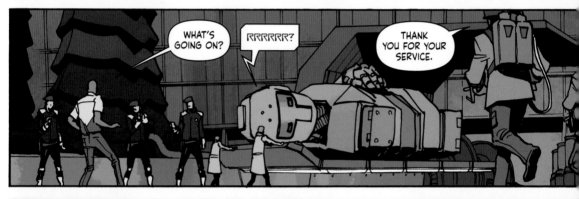

WHAT'S GOING ON?

RRRRRRR?

THANK YOU FOR YOUR SERVICE.

RRREEEEEE!

SKRRRAKK

NO!

SKRRAK

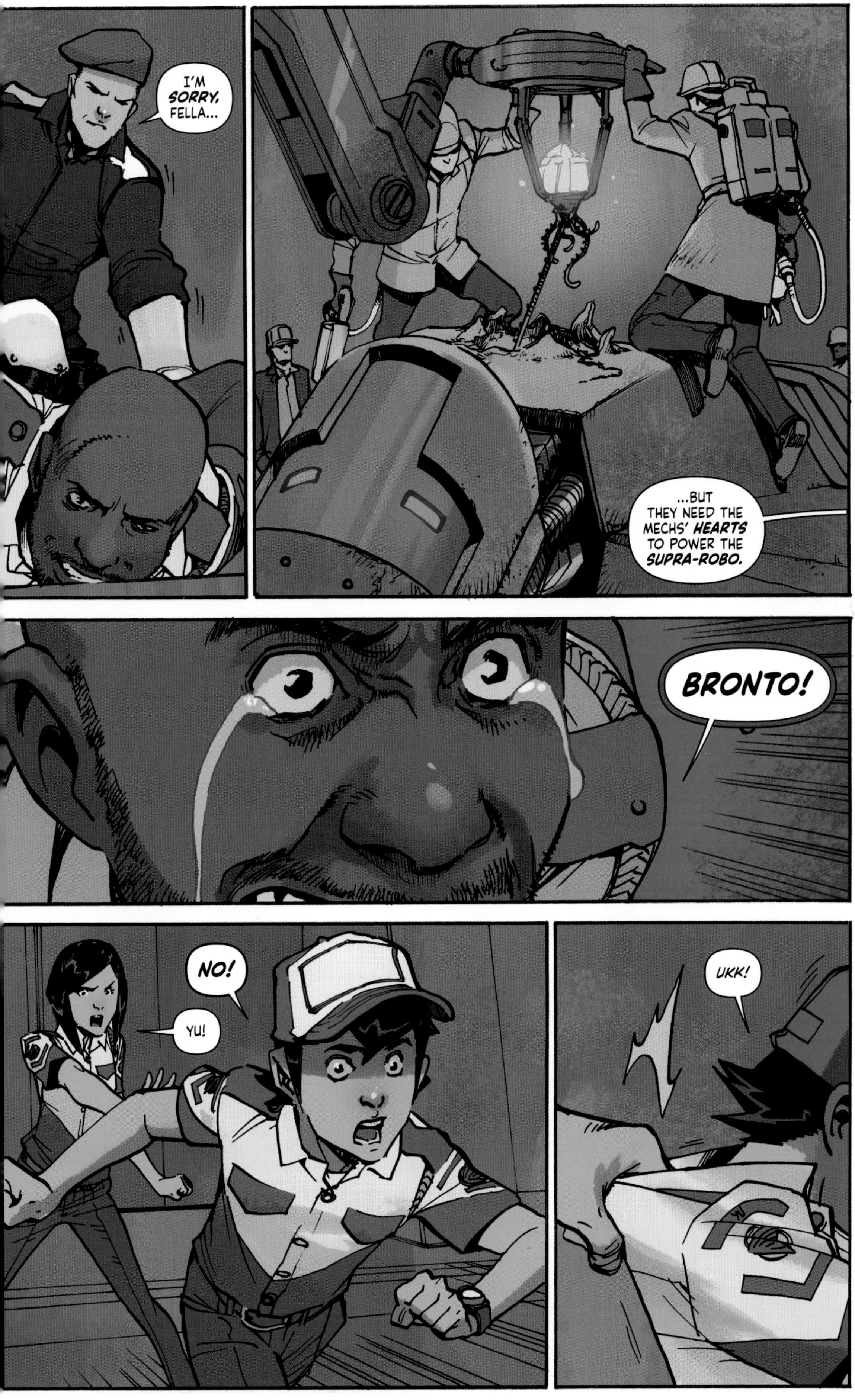
I'M SORRY, FELLA...
...BUT THEY NEED THE MECHS' HEARTS TO POWER THE SUPRA-ROBO.
BRONTO!
NO!
YU!
UKK!

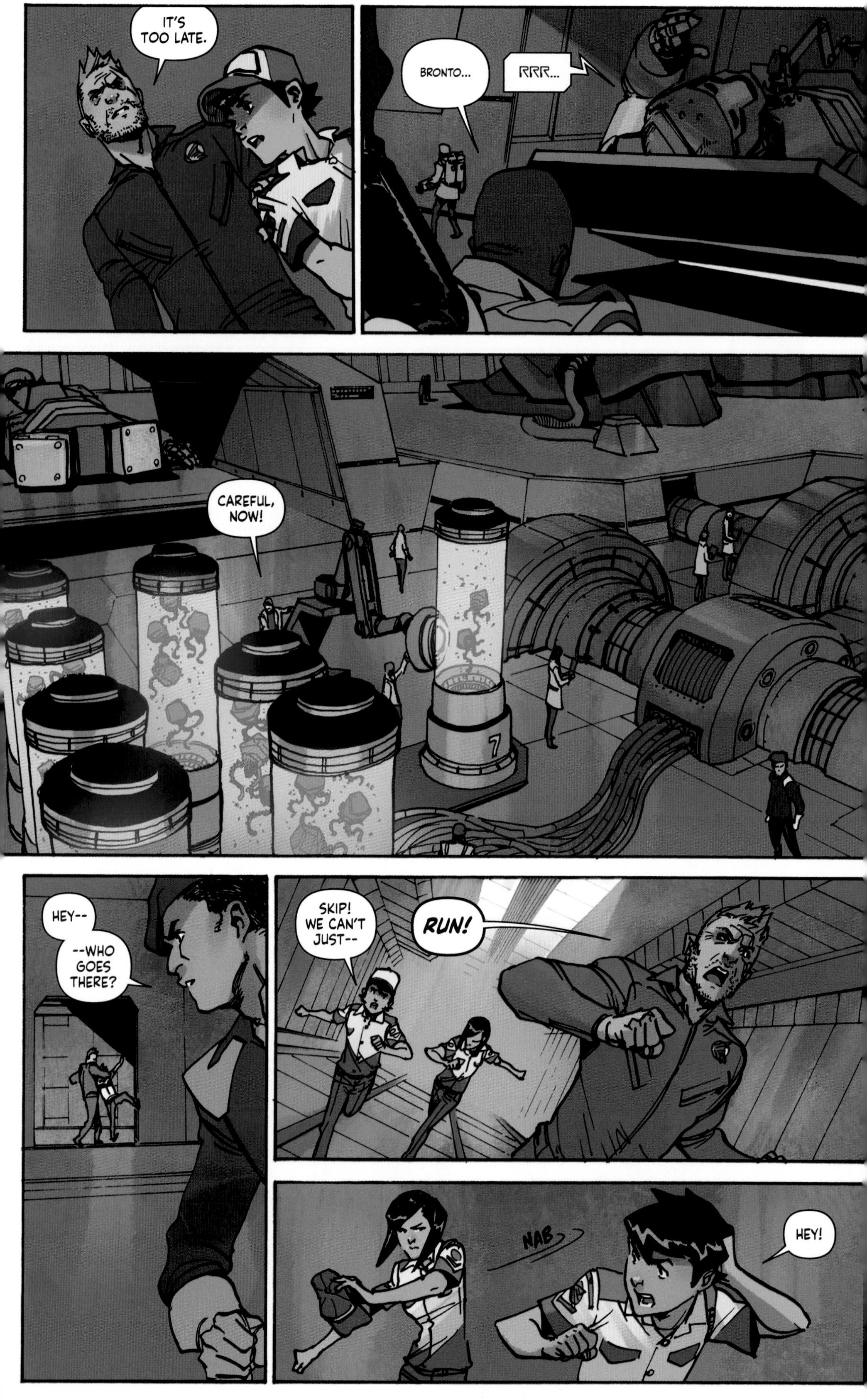

IT'S TOO LATE.
BRONTO...
RRR...
CAREFUL, NOW!
7
HEY--
--WHO GOES THERE?
SKIP! WE CAN'T JUST--
RUN!
NAB
HEY!

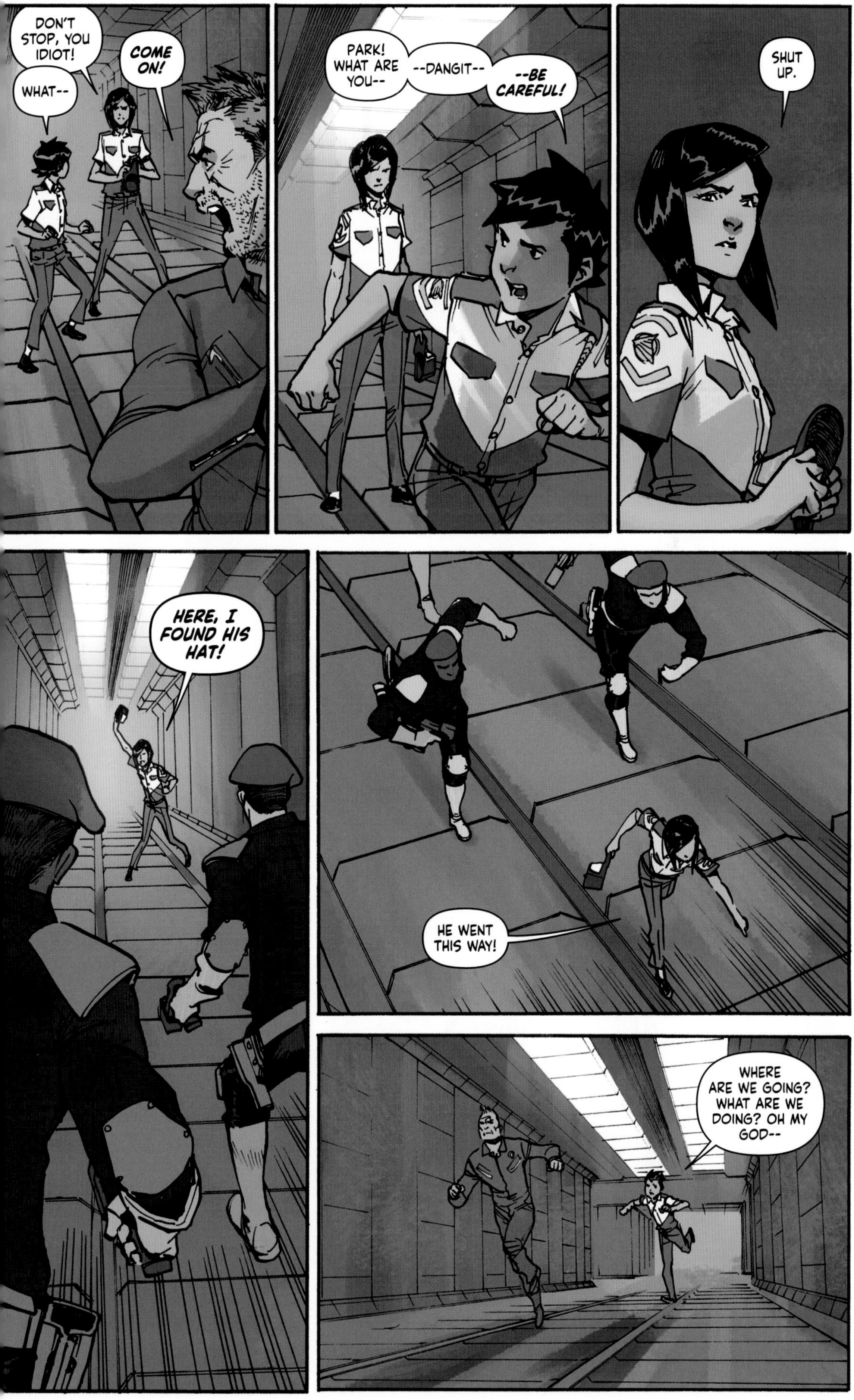

DON'T STOP, YOU IDIOT!
WHAT--
COME ON!
PARK! WHAT ARE YOU--
--DANGIT--
--BE CAREFUL!
SHUT UP.
HERE, I FOUND HIS HAT!
HE WENT THIS WAY!
WHERE ARE WE GOING? WHAT ARE WE DOING? OH MY GOD--

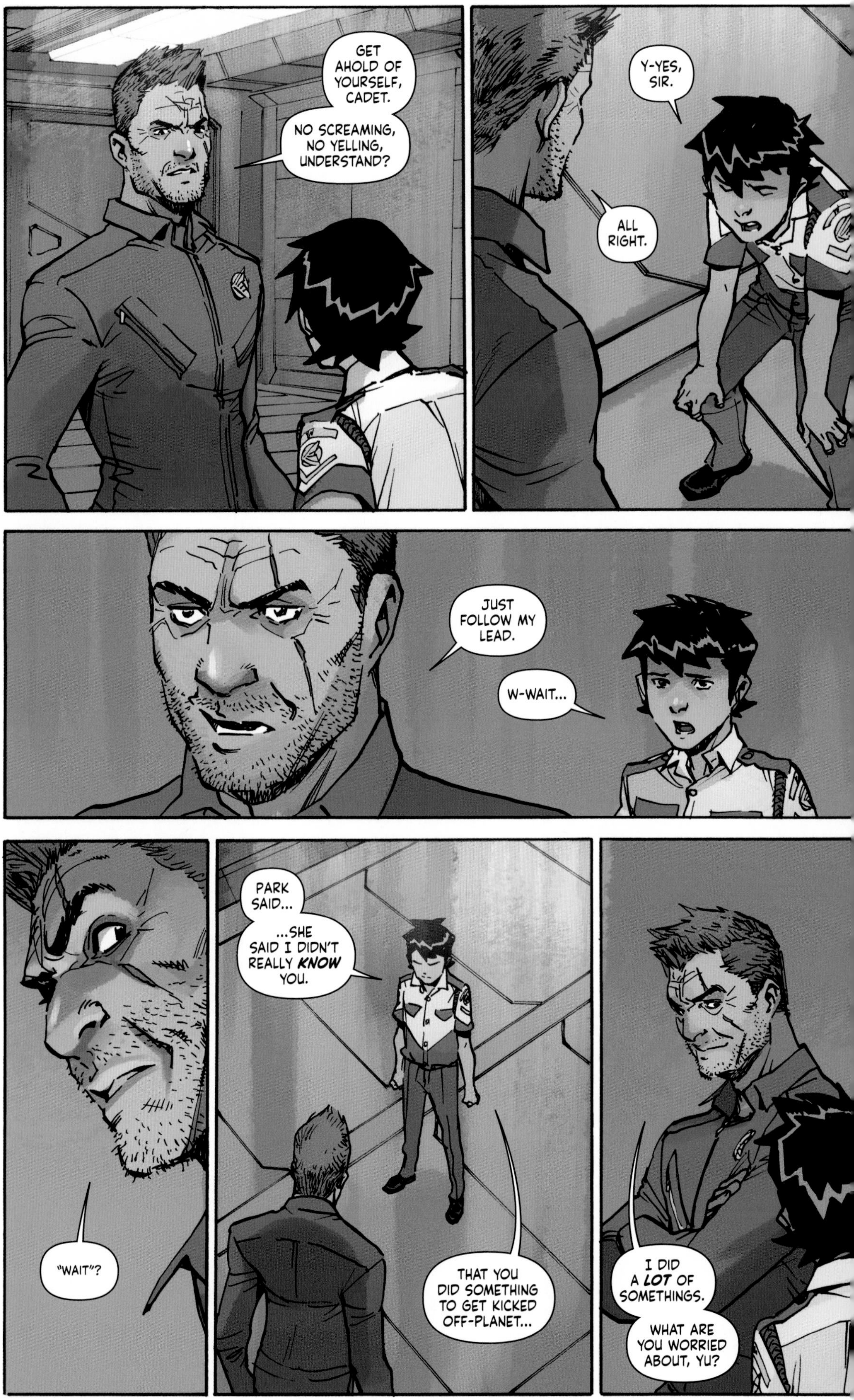
GET AHOLD OF YOURSELF, CADET.
NO SCREAMING, NO YELLING, UNDERSTAND?
Y-YES, SIR.
ALL RIGHT.
JUST FOLLOW MY LEAD.
W-WAIT...
"WAIT"?
PARK SAID...
...SHE SAID I DIDN'T REALLY KNOW YOU.
THAT YOU DID SOMETHING TO GET KICKED OFF-PLANET...
I DID A LOT OF SOMETHINGS.
WHAT ARE YOU WORRIED ABOUT, YU?

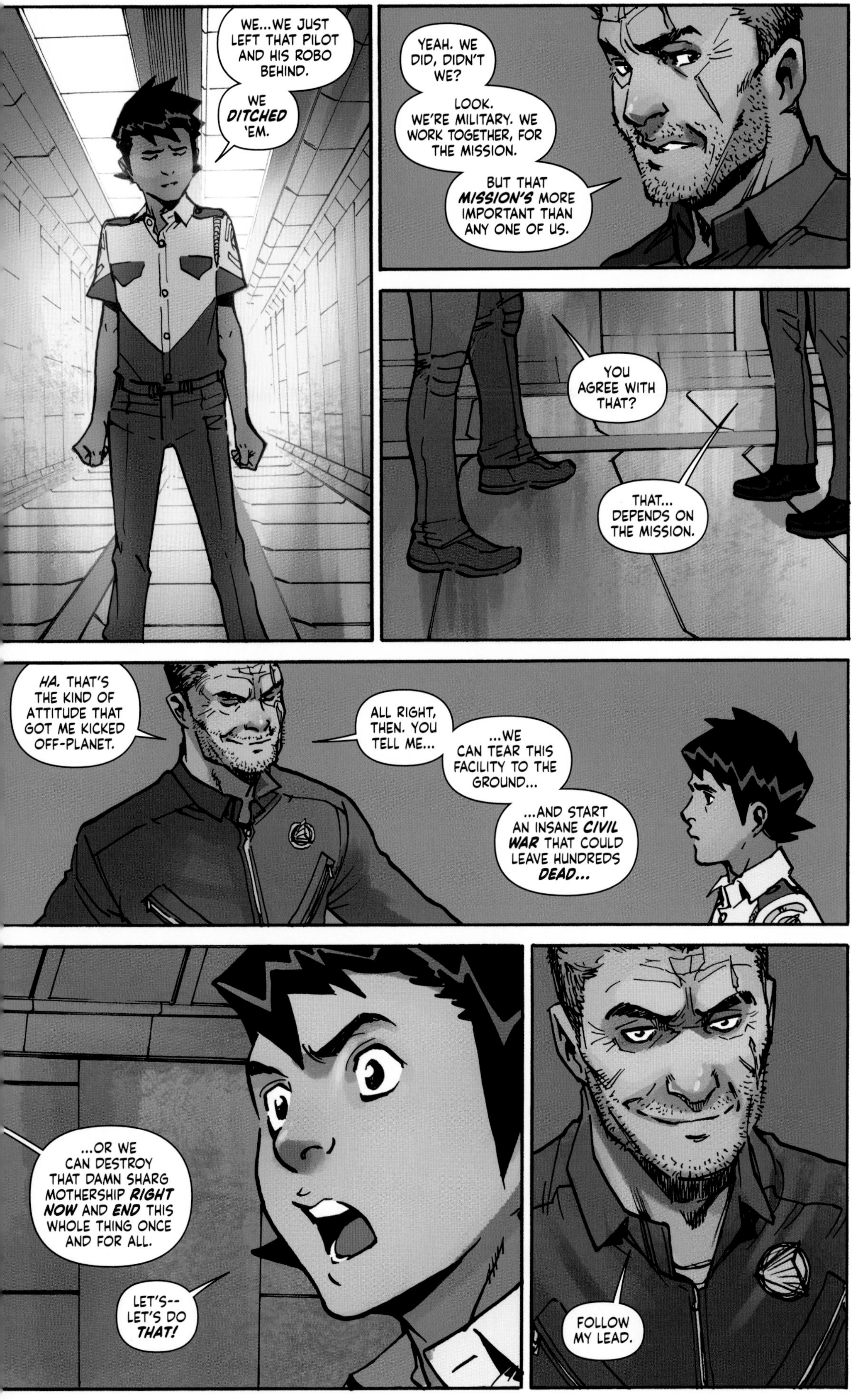
WE...WE JUST LEFT THAT PILOT AND HIS ROBO BEHIND.
WE *DITCHED* 'EM.
YEAH. WE DID, DIDN'T WE?
LOOK. WE'RE MILITARY. WE WORK TOGETHER, FOR THE MISSION.
BUT THAT *MISSION'S* MORE IMPORTANT THAN ANY ONE OF US.
YOU AGREE WITH THAT?
THAT... DEPENDS ON THE MISSION.
HA. THAT'S THE KIND OF ATTITUDE THAT GOT ME KICKED OFF-PLANET.
ALL RIGHT, THEN. YOU TELL ME...
...WE CAN TEAR THIS FACILITY TO THE GROUND...
...AND START AN INSANE *CIVIL WAR* THAT COULD LEAVE HUNDREDS *DEAD...*
...OR WE CAN DESTROY THAT DAMN SHARG MOTHERSHIP *RIGHT NOW* AND *END* THIS WHOLE THING ONCE AND FOR ALL.
LET'S-- LET'S DO *THAT!*
FOLLOW MY LEAD.

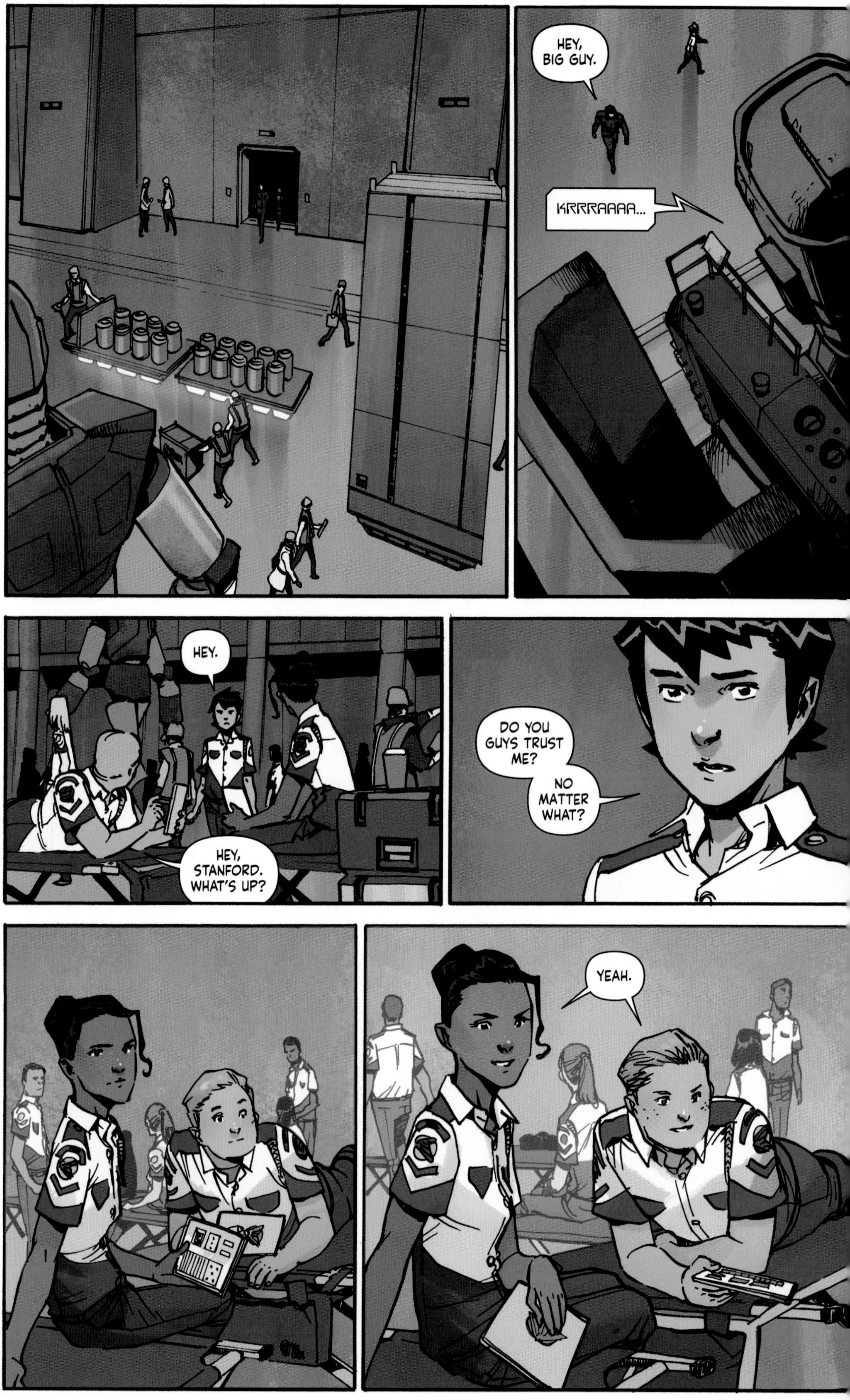

HEY, BIG GUY.
KRRRAAAA...
HEY.
HEY, STANFORD. WHAT'S UP?
DO YOU GUYS TRUST ME?
NO MATTER WHAT?
YEAH.

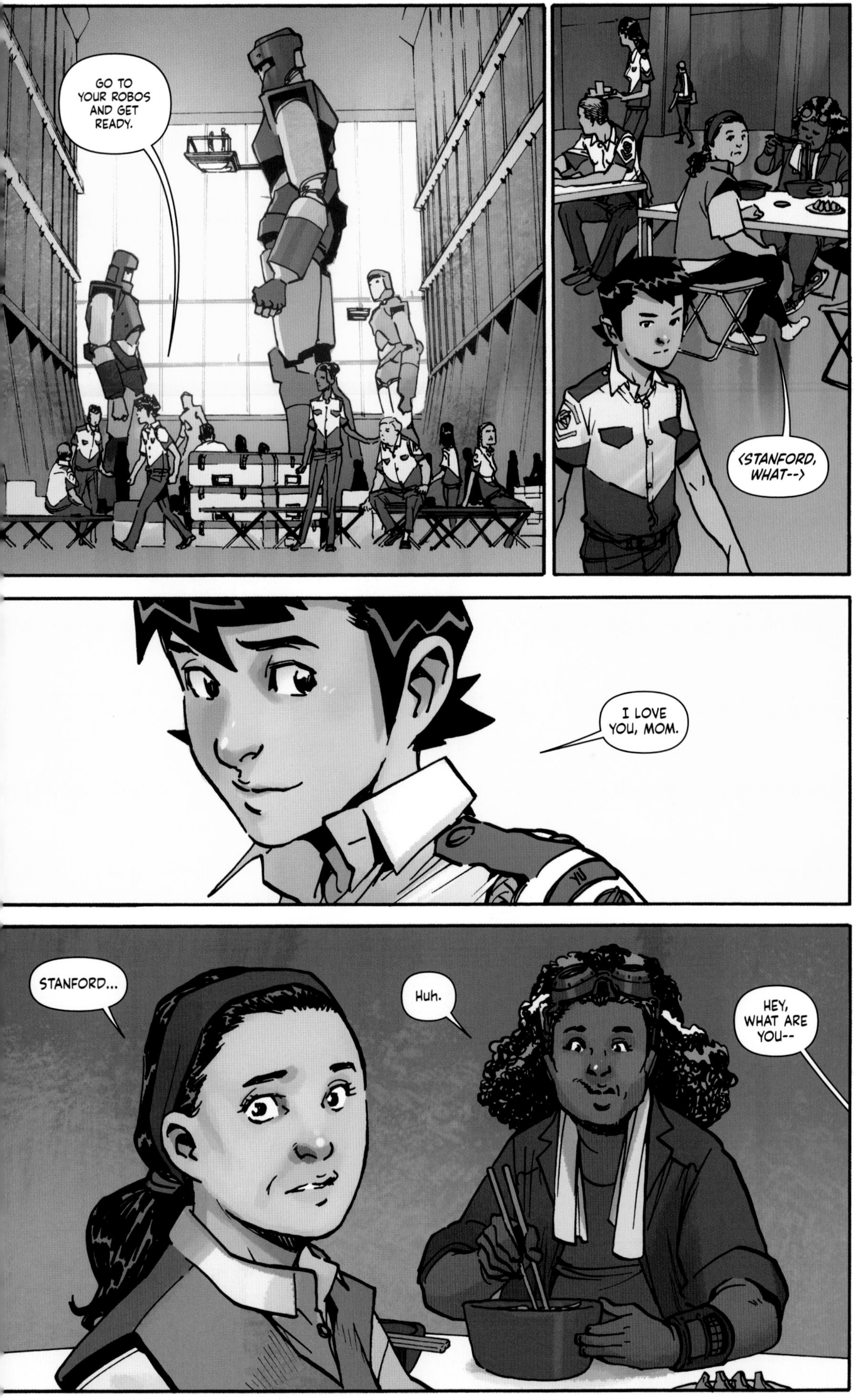
GO TO YOUR ROBOS AND GET READY.
<STANFORD, WHAT-->
I LOVE YOU, MOM.
STANFORD...
Huh.
HEY, WHAT ARE YOU--

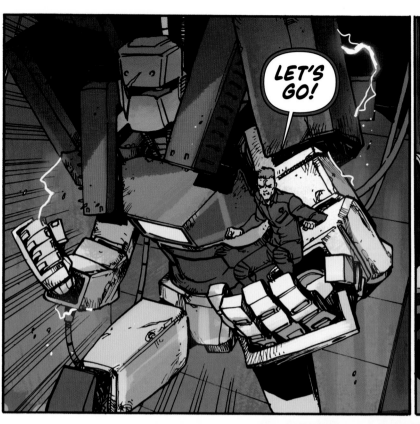

LET'S GO!

WHAT THE HECK--

SKRRRRRAAANNCH!

STAND DOWN, SIR!

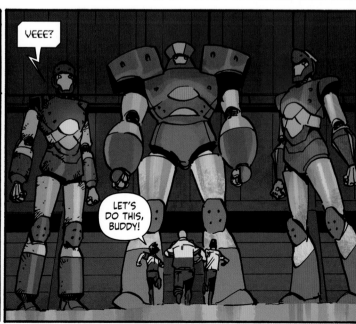

VEEE?

LET'S DO THIS, BUDDY!

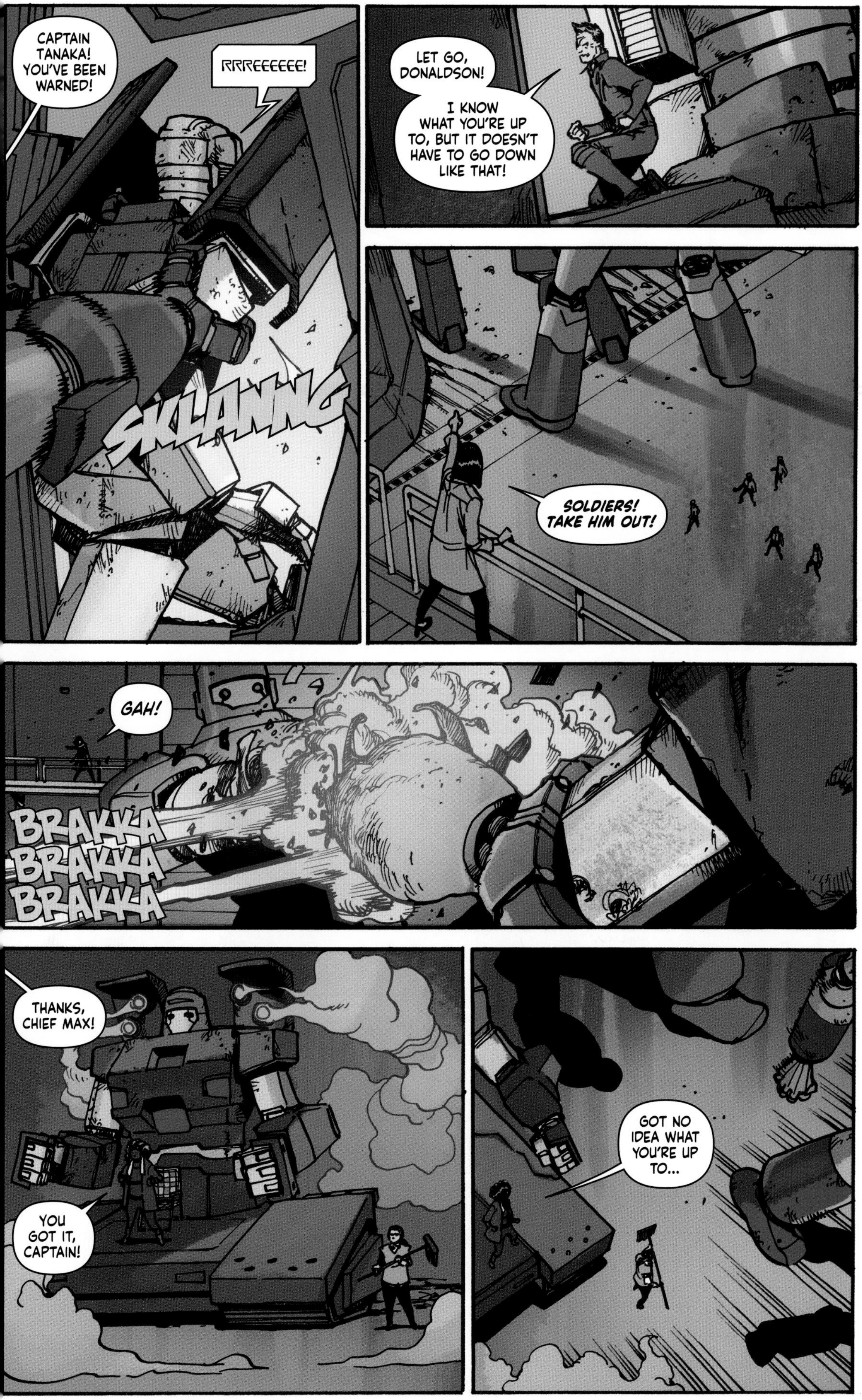
CAPTAIN TANAKA! YOU'VE BEEN WARNED!
RRRREEEEEEE!
SKLANNG
LET GO, DONALDSON!
I KNOW WHAT YOU'RE UP TO, BUT IT DOESN'T HAVE TO GO DOWN LIKE THAT!
SOLDIERS! TAKE HIM OUT!
GAH!
BRAKKA BRAKKA BRAKKA
THANKS, CHIEF MAX!
YOU GOT IT, CAPTAIN!
GOT NO IDEA WHAT YOU'RE UP TO...

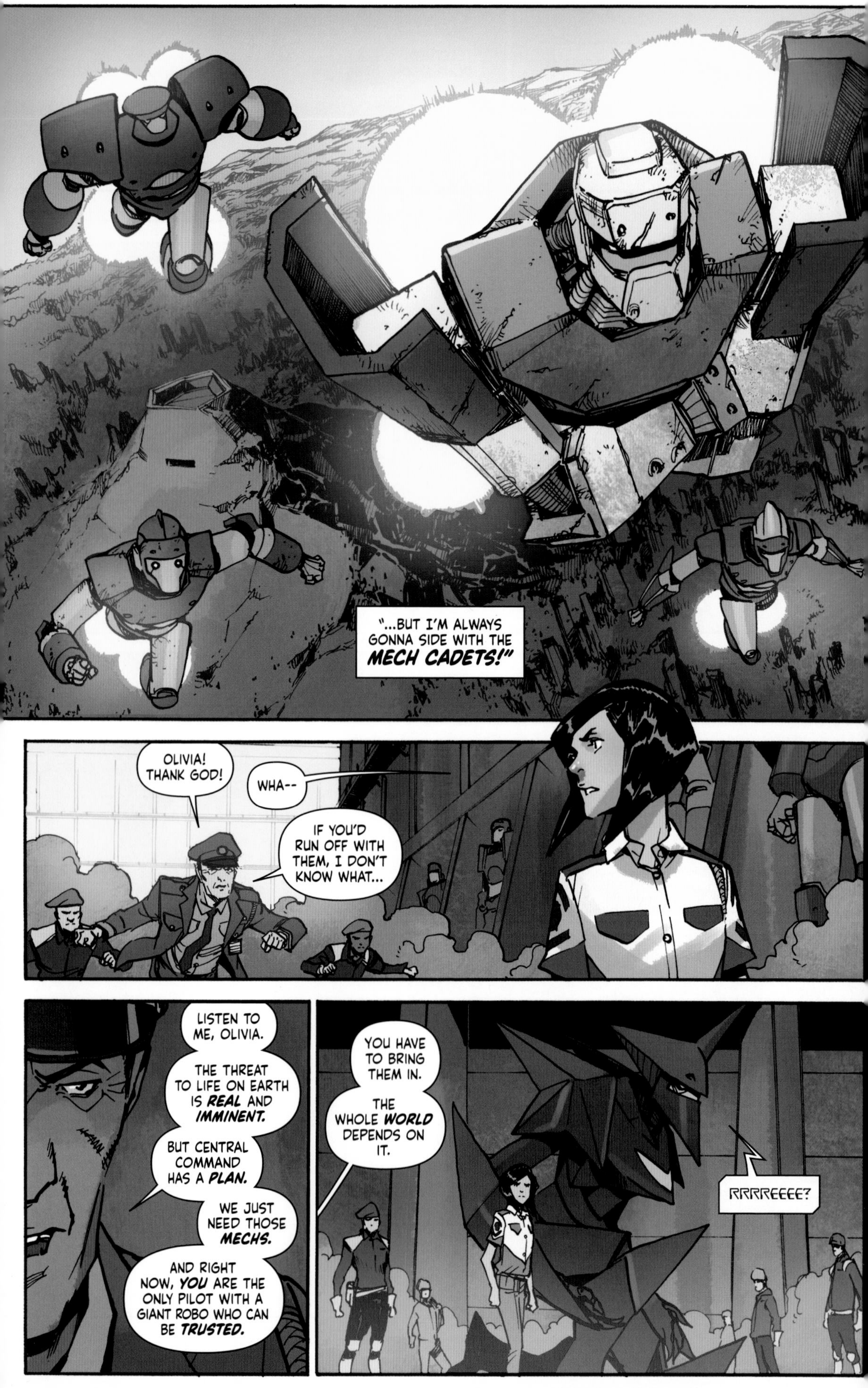
"...BUT I'M ALWAYS GONNA SIDE WITH THE ***MECH CADETS!***"
OLIVIA! THANK GOD!
WHA--
IF YOU'D RUN OFF WITH THEM, I DON'T KNOW WHAT...
LISTEN TO ME, OLIVIA.
THE THREAT TO LIFE ON EARTH IS ***REAL*** AND ***IMMINENT.***
BUT CENTRAL COMMAND HAS A ***PLAN.***
WE JUST NEED THOSE ***MECHS.***
AND RIGHT NOW, ***YOU*** ARE THE ONLY PILOT WITH A GIANT ROBO WHO CAN BE ***TRUSTED.***
YOU HAVE TO BRING THEM IN.
THE WHOLE ***WORLD*** DEPENDS ON IT.
RRRREEEE?

CHAPTER
EIGHT

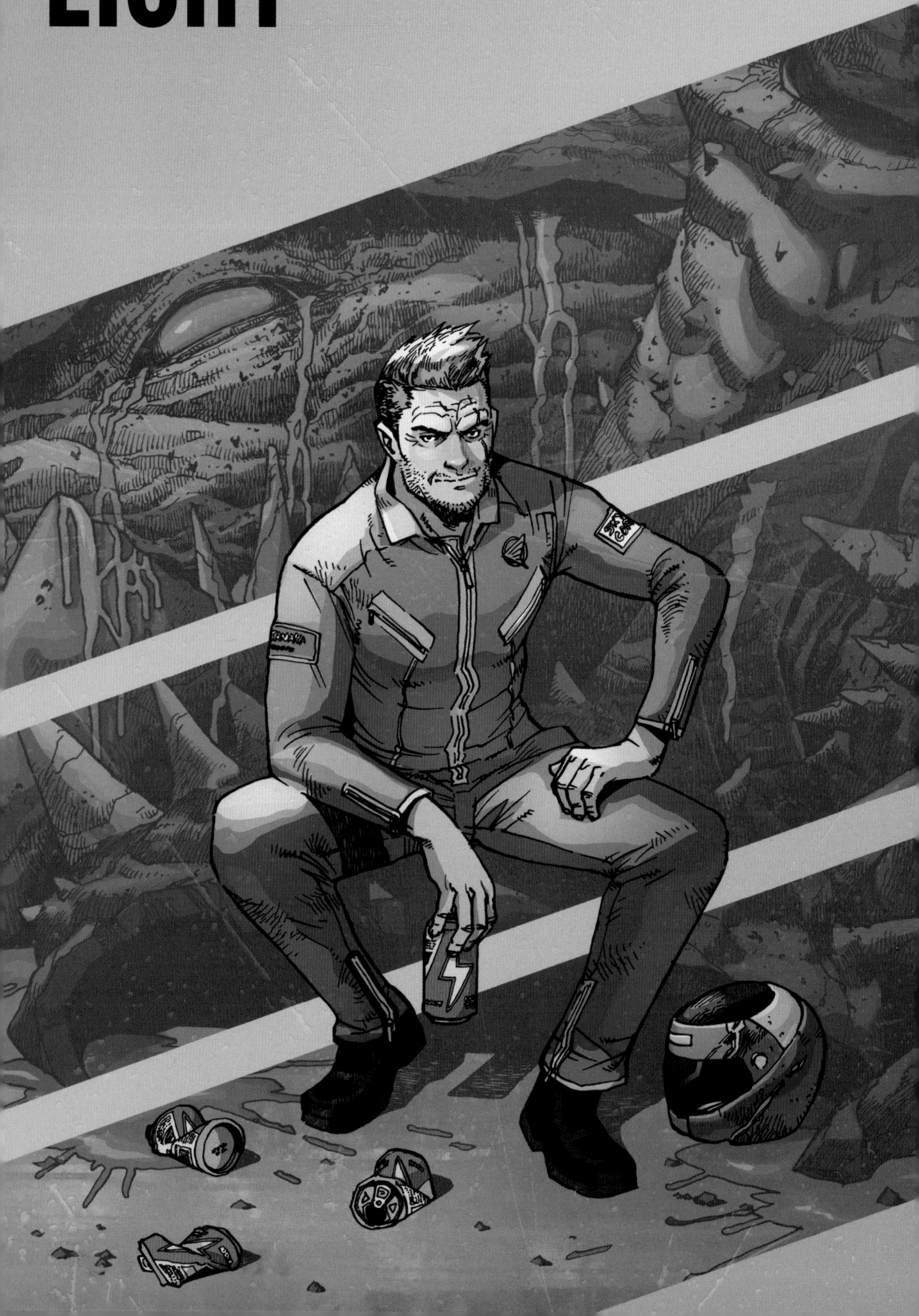

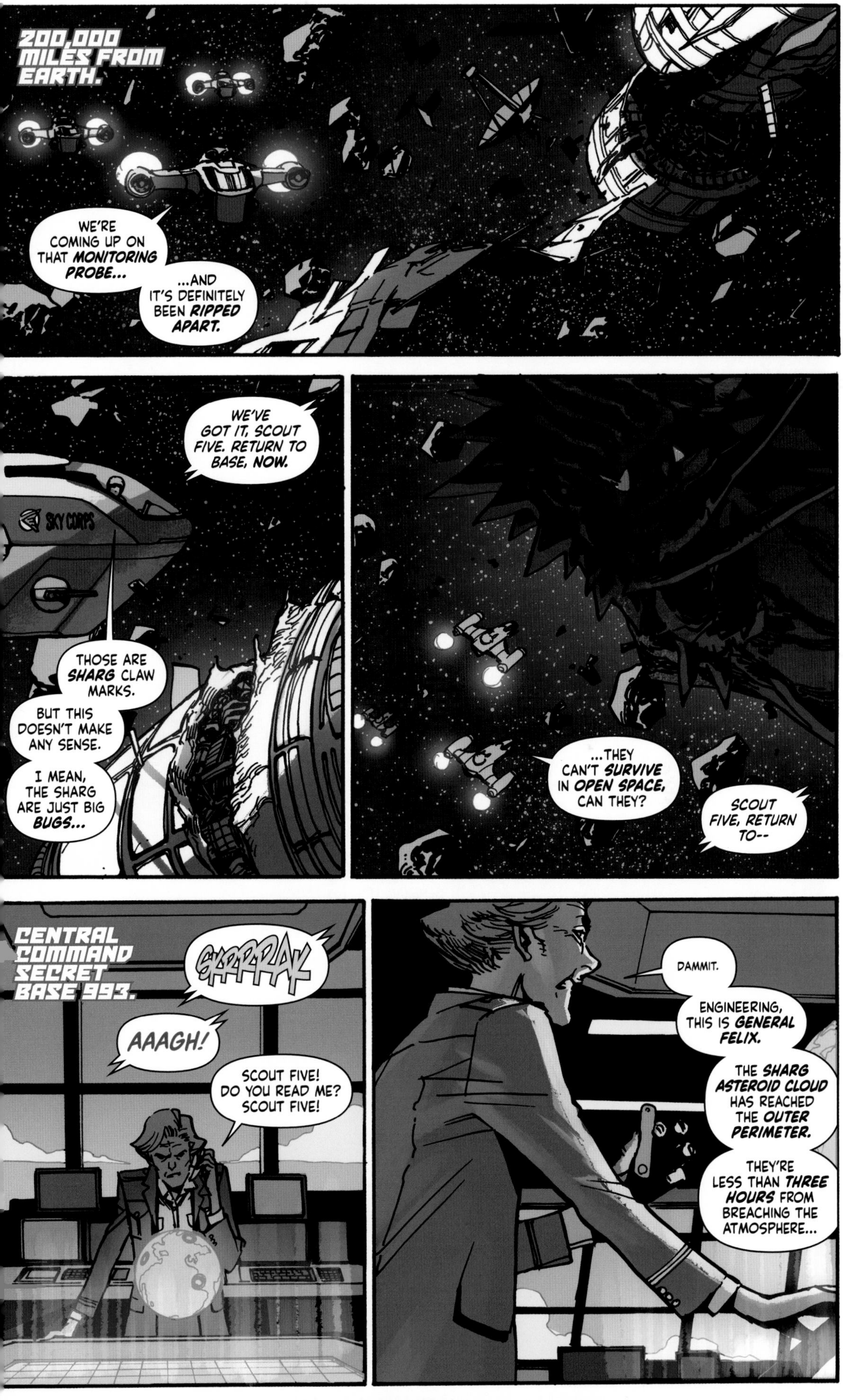

200,000 MILES FROM EARTH.
WE'RE COMING UP ON THAT MONITORING PROBE...
...AND IT'S DEFINITELY BEEN RIPPED APART.
WE'VE GOT IT, SCOUT FIVE. RETURN TO BASE, NOW.
SKY CORPS
THOSE ARE SHARG CLAW MARKS.
BUT THIS DOESN'T MAKE ANY SENSE.
I MEAN, THE SHARG ARE JUST BIG BUGS...
...THEY CAN'T SURVIVE IN OPEN SPACE, CAN THEY?
SCOUT FIVE, RETURN TO--
CENTRAL COMMAND SECRET BASE 993.
SKRRRAK
AAAGH!
SCOUT FIVE! DO YOU READ ME? SCOUT FIVE!
DAMMIT.
ENGINEERING, THIS IS GENERAL FELIX.
THE SHARG ASTEROID CLOUD HAS REACHED THE OUTER PERIMETER.
THEY'RE LESS THAN THREE HOURS FROM BREACHING THE ATMOSPHERE...

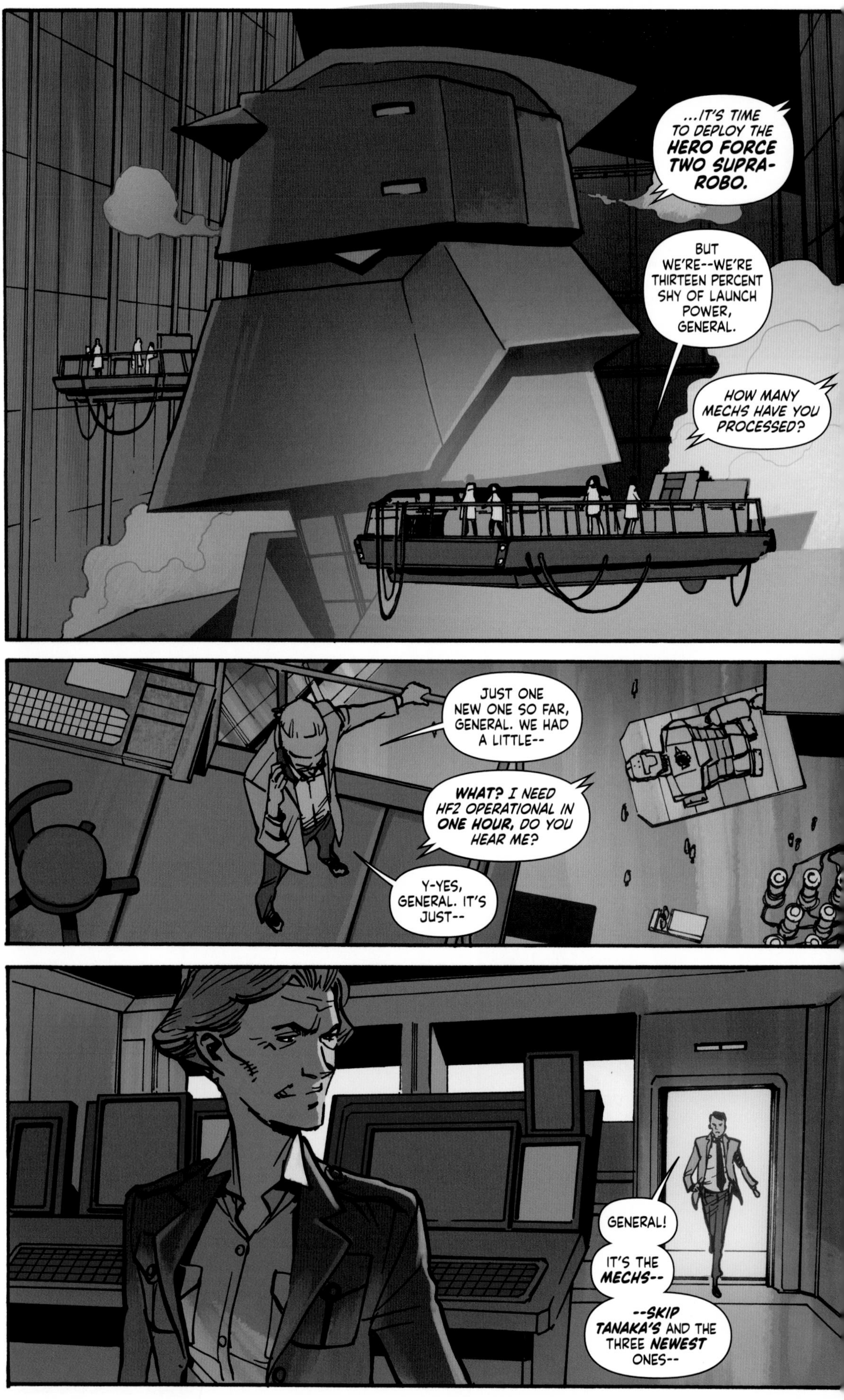
...IT'S TIME TO DEPLOY THE **HERO FORCE TWO SUPRA-ROBO.**
BUT WE'RE--WE'RE THIRTEEN PERCENT SHY OF LAUNCH POWER, GENERAL.
HOW MANY MECHS HAVE YOU PROCESSED?
JUST ONE NEW ONE SO FAR, GENERAL. WE HAD A LITTLE--
WHAT? *I NEED HF2 OPERATIONAL IN* ***ONE HOUR,*** *DO YOU HEAR ME?*
Y-YES, GENERAL. IT'S JUST--
GENERAL!
IT'S THE ***MECHS--***
--SKIP TANAKA'S AND THE THREE ***NEWEST*** ONES--

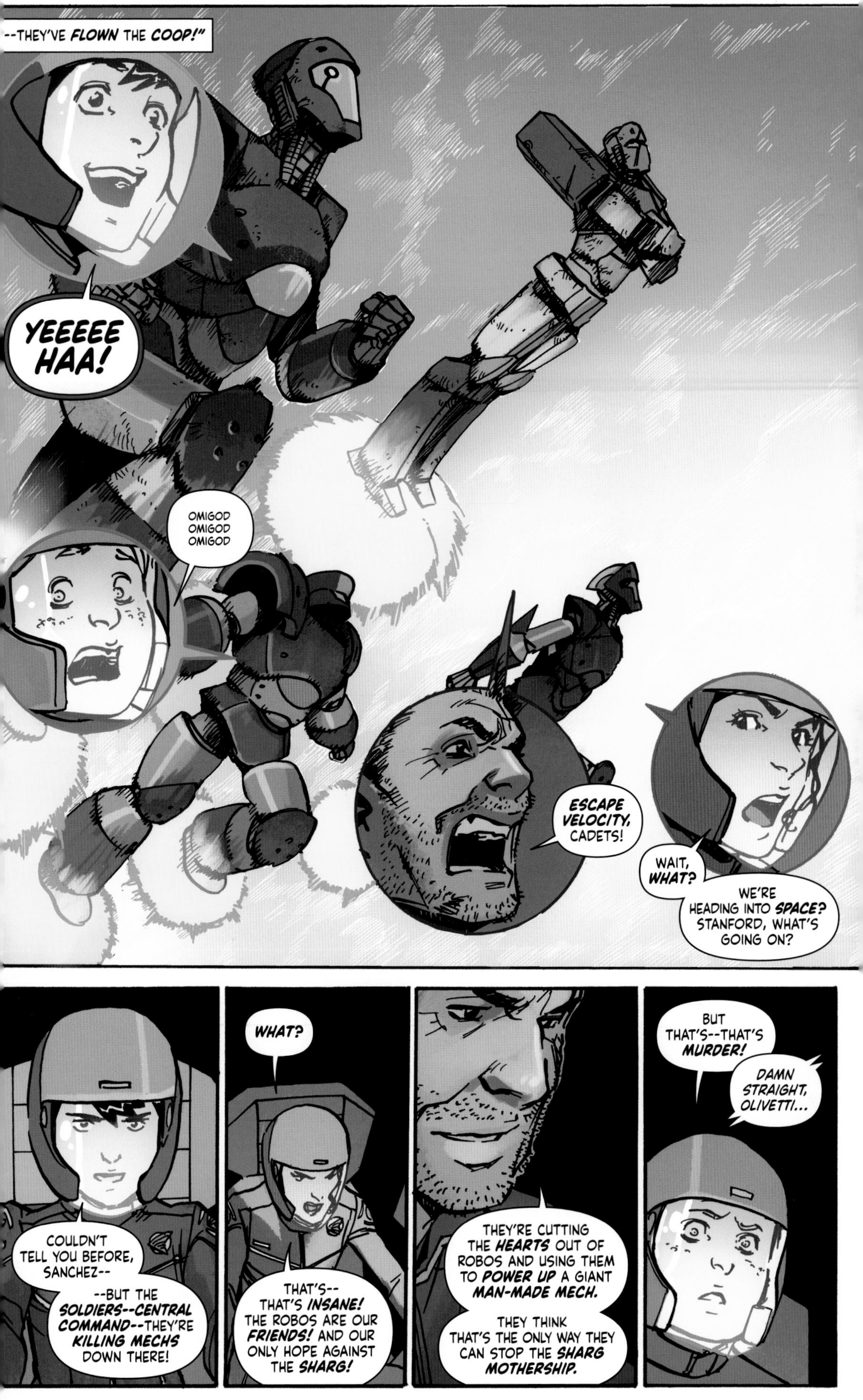
--THEY'VE FLOWN THE COOP!"
YEEEEE HAA!
OMIGOD OMIGOD OMIGOD
ESCAPE VELOCITY, CADETS!
WAIT, WHAT?
WE'RE HEADING INTO SPACE? STANFORD, WHAT'S GOING ON?
COULDN'T TELL YOU BEFORE, SANCHEZ--
--BUT THE SOLDIERS--CENTRAL COMMAND--THEY'RE KILLING MECHS DOWN THERE!
WHAT?
THAT'S-- THAT'S INSANE! THE ROBOS ARE OUR FRIENDS! AND OUR ONLY HOPE AGAINST THE SHARG!
THEY'RE CUTTING THE HEARTS OUT OF ROBOS AND USING THEM TO POWER UP A GIANT MAN-MADE MECH.
THEY THINK THAT'S THE ONLY WAY THEY CAN STOP THE SHARG MOTHERSHIP.
BUT THAT'S--THAT'S MURDER!
DAMN STRAIGHT, OLIVETTI...

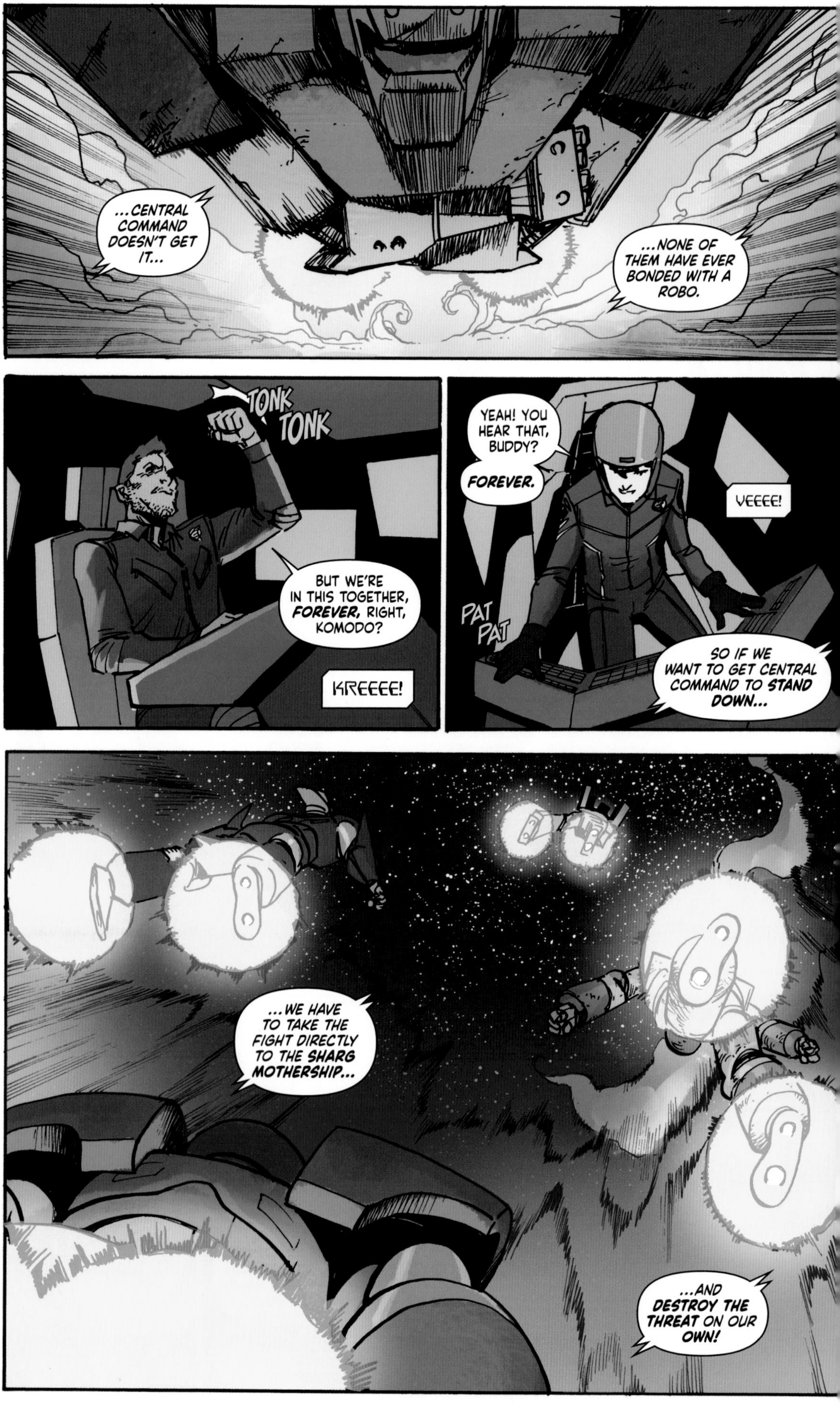
...CENTRAL COMMAND DOESN'T GET IT...
...NONE OF THEM HAVE EVER BONDED WITH A ROBO.
TONK TONK
BUT WE'RE IN THIS TOGETHER, FOREVER, RIGHT, KOMODO?
KREEEE!
YEAH! YOU HEAR THAT, BUDDY?
FOREVER.
VEEEE!
PAT PAT
SO IF WE WANT TO GET CENTRAL COMMAND TO STAND DOWN...
...WE HAVE TO TAKE THE FIGHT DIRECTLY TO THE SHARG MOTHERSHIP...
...AND DESTROY THE THREAT ON OUR OWN!

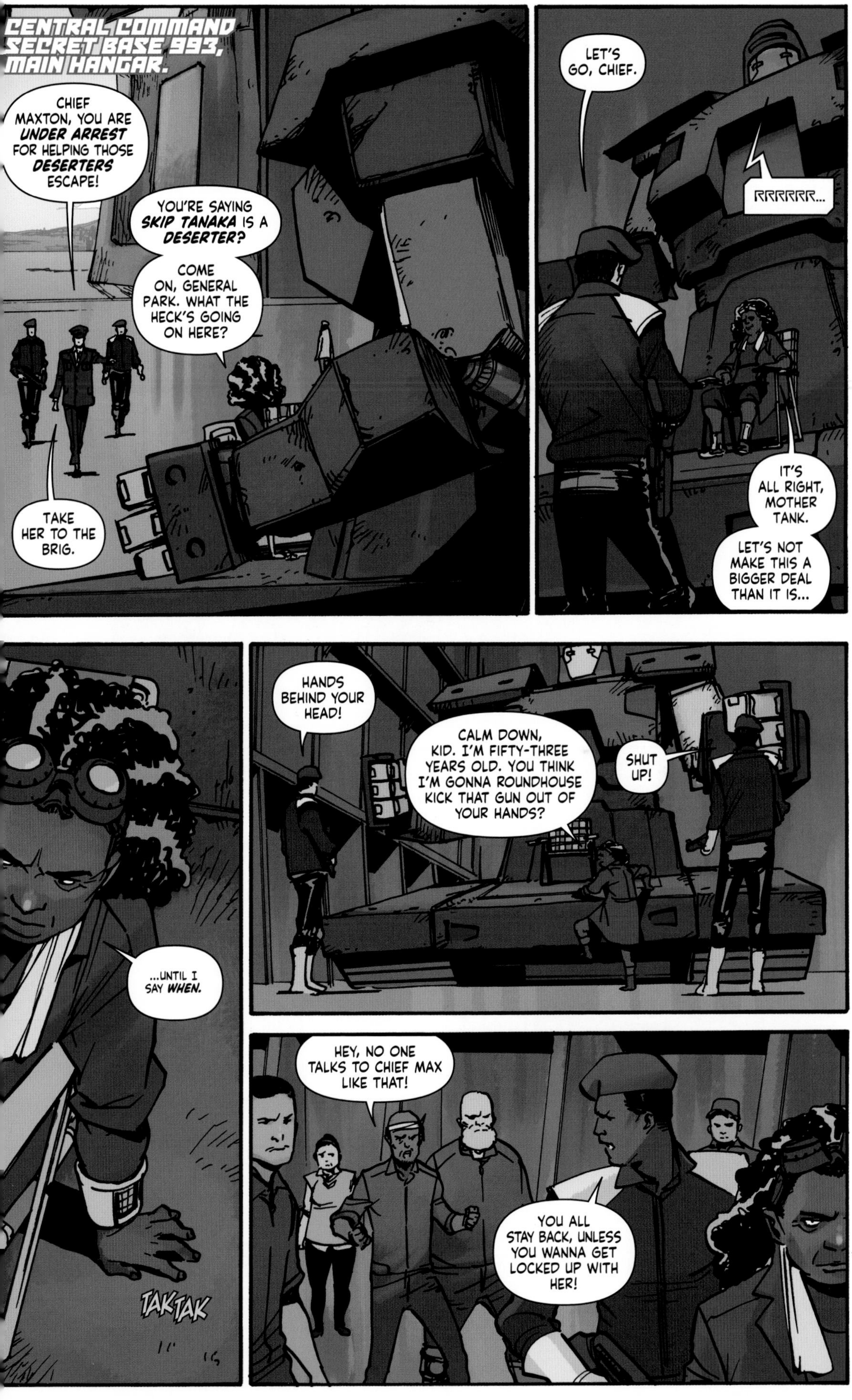
CENTRAL COMMAND SECRET BASE 993, MAIN HANGAR.
CHIEF MAXTON, YOU ARE UNDER ARREST FOR HELPING THOSE DESERTERS ESCAPE!
YOU'RE SAYING SKIP TANAKA IS A DESERTER?
COME ON, GENERAL PARK. WHAT THE HECK'S GOING ON HERE?
TAKE HER TO THE BRIG.
LET'S GO, CHIEF.
RRRRRRR...
IT'S ALL RIGHT, MOTHER TANK.
LET'S NOT MAKE THIS A BIGGER DEAL THAN IT IS...
...UNTIL I SAY WHEN.
TAKTAK
HANDS BEHIND YOUR HEAD!
CALM DOWN, KID. I'M FIFTY-THREE YEARS OLD. YOU THINK I'M GONNA ROUNDHOUSE KICK THAT GUN OUT OF YOUR HANDS?
SHUT UP!
HEY, NO ONE TALKS TO CHIEF MAX LIKE THAT!
YOU ALL STAY BACK, UNLESS YOU WANNA GET LOCKED UP WITH HER!

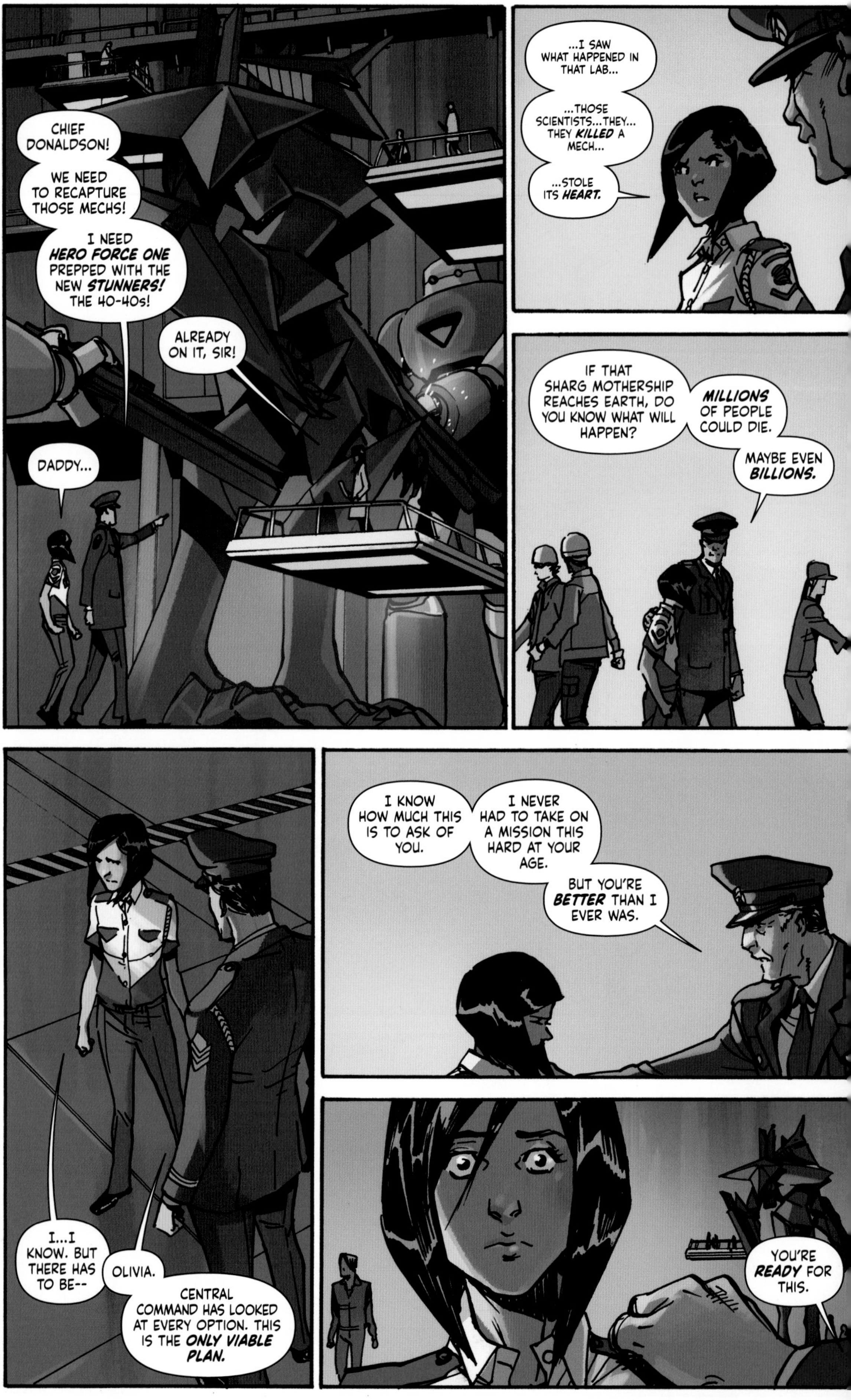
CHIEF DONALDSON!
WE NEED TO RECAPTURE THOSE MECHS!
I NEED HERO FORCE ONE PREPPED WITH THE NEW STUNNERS! THE 40-40s!
ALREADY ON IT, SIR!
DADDY...
...I SAW WHAT HAPPENED IN THAT LAB...
...THOSE SCIENTISTS...THEY... THEY KILLED A MECH...
...STOLE ITS HEART.
IF THAT SHARG MOTHERSHIP REACHES EARTH, DO YOU KNOW WHAT WILL HAPPEN?
MILLIONS OF PEOPLE COULD DIE.
MAYBE EVEN BILLIONS.
I...I KNOW. BUT THERE HAS TO BE--
OLIVIA.
CENTRAL COMMAND HAS LOOKED AT EVERY OPTION. THIS IS THE ONLY VIABLE PLAN.
I KNOW HOW MUCH THIS IS TO ASK OF YOU.
I NEVER HAD TO TAKE ON A MISSION THIS HARD AT YOUR AGE.
BUT YOU'RE BETTER THAN I EVER WAS.
YOU'RE READY FOR THIS.

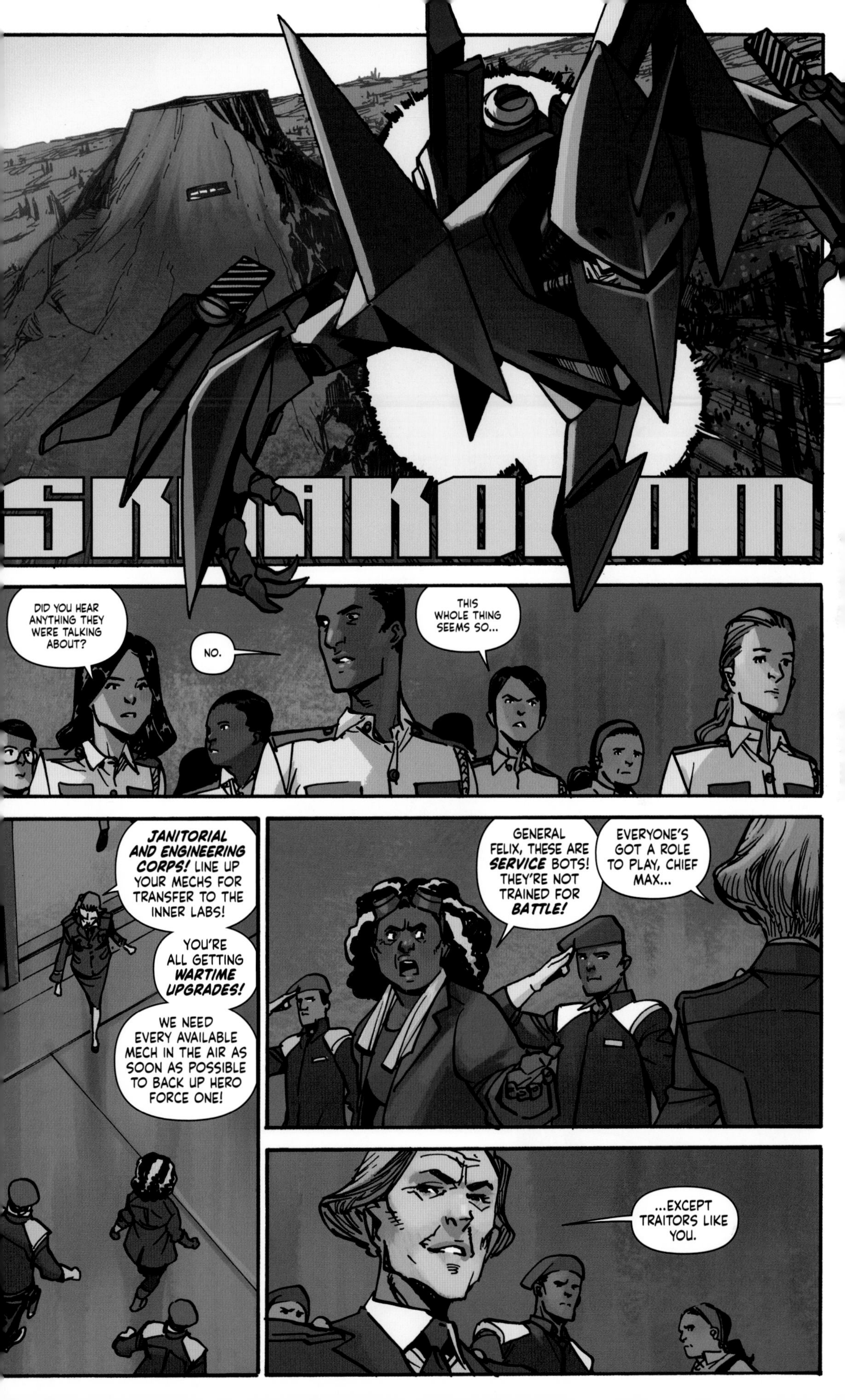
DID YOU HEAR ANYTHING THEY WERE TALKING ABOUT?
NO.
THIS WHOLE THING SEEMS SO...
JANITORIAL AND ENGINEERING CORPS! LINE UP YOUR MECHS FOR TRANSFER TO THE INNER LABS!
YOU'RE ALL GETTING WARTIME UPGRADES!
WE NEED EVERY AVAILABLE MECH IN THE AIR AS SOON AS POSSIBLE TO BACK UP HERO FORCE ONE!
GENERAL FELIX, THESE ARE SERVICE BOTS! THEY'RE NOT TRAINED FOR BATTLE!
EVERYONE'S GOT A ROLE TO PLAY, CHIEF MAX...
...EXCEPT TRAITORS LIKE YOU.

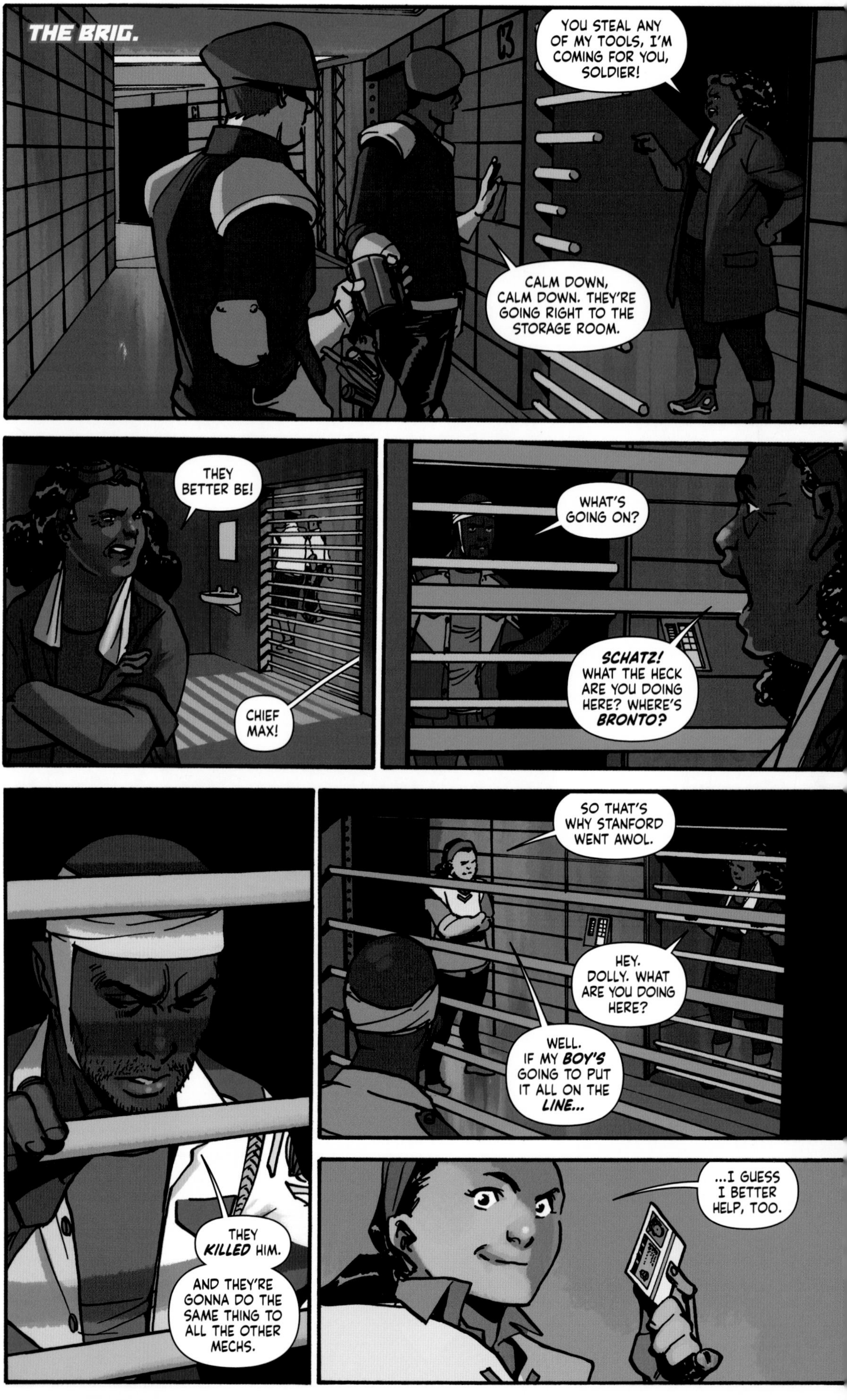
THE BRIG.
YOU STEAL ANY OF MY TOOLS, I'M COMING FOR YOU, SOLDIER!
CALM DOWN, CALM DOWN. THEY'RE GOING RIGHT TO THE STORAGE ROOM.
THEY BETTER BE!
CHIEF MAX!
WHAT'S GOING ON?
SCHATZ! WHAT THE HECK ARE YOU DOING HERE? WHERE'S BRONTO?
THEY KILLED HIM.
AND THEY'RE GONNA DO THE SAME THING TO ALL THE OTHER MECHS.
SO THAT'S WHY STANFORD WENT AWOL.
HEY. DOLLY. WHAT ARE YOU DOING HERE?
WELL. IF MY BOY'S GOING TO PUT IT ALL ON THE LINE...
...I GUESS I BETTER HELP, TOO.

OH, NO...

TRAINING'S OVER, CADETS...

...THIS IS A *REAL* MISSION, NOW.

I CAN'T PROMISE TO KEEP YOU SAFE.

I CAN'T PROMISE WE'RE ALL GOING TO MAKE IT OUT ALIVE.

I'M GOING TO GIVE YOU ORDERS AND I EXPECT YOU TO OBEY THEM INSTANTLY.

IN FACT...

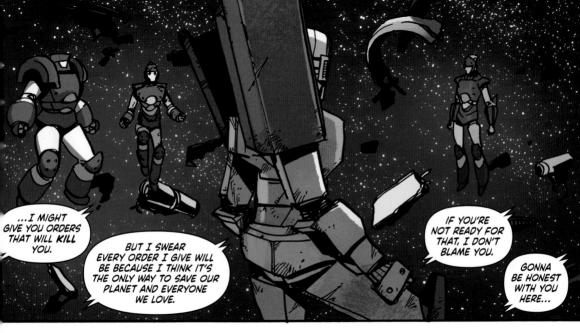

...I MIGHT GIVE YOU ORDERS THAT WILL *KILL* YOU.

BUT I SWEAR EVERY ORDER I GIVE WILL BE BECAUSE I THINK IT'S THE ONLY WAY TO SAVE OUR PLANET AND EVERYONE WE LOVE.

IF YOU'RE NOT READY FOR THAT, I DON'T BLAME YOU.

GONNA BE HONEST WITH YOU HERE...

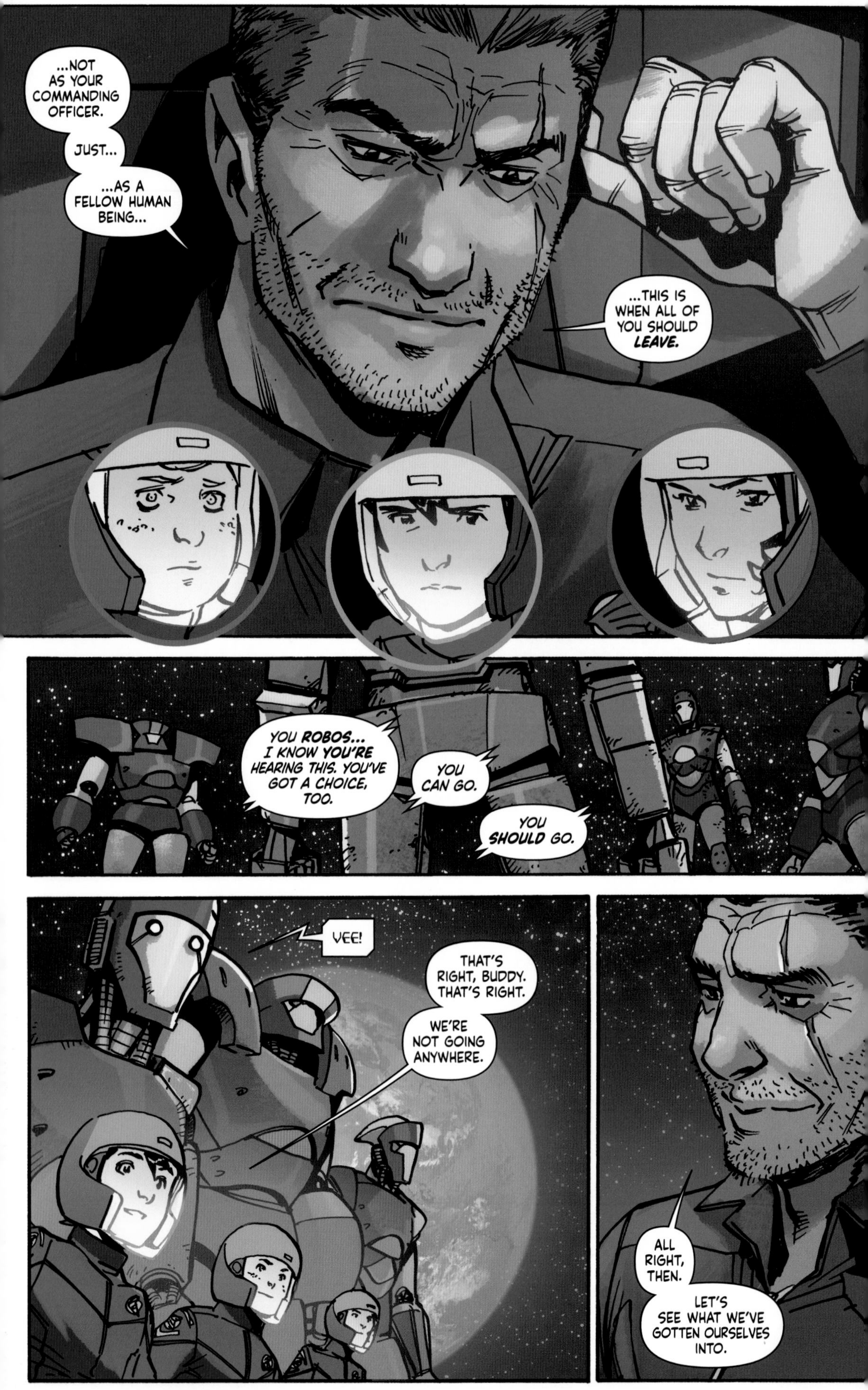
...NOT AS YOUR COMMANDING OFFICER.
JUST...
...AS A FELLOW HUMAN BEING...
...THIS IS WHEN ALL OF YOU SHOULD **LEAVE.**
YOU **ROBOS...** I KNOW **YOU'RE** HEARING THIS. YOU'VE GOT A CHOICE, TOO.
YOU CAN GO.
YOU **SHOULD** GO.
VEE!
THAT'S RIGHT, BUDDY. THAT'S RIGHT.
WE'RE NOT GOING ANYWHERE.
ALL RIGHT, THEN.
LET'S SEE WHAT WE'VE GOTTEN OURSELVES INTO.

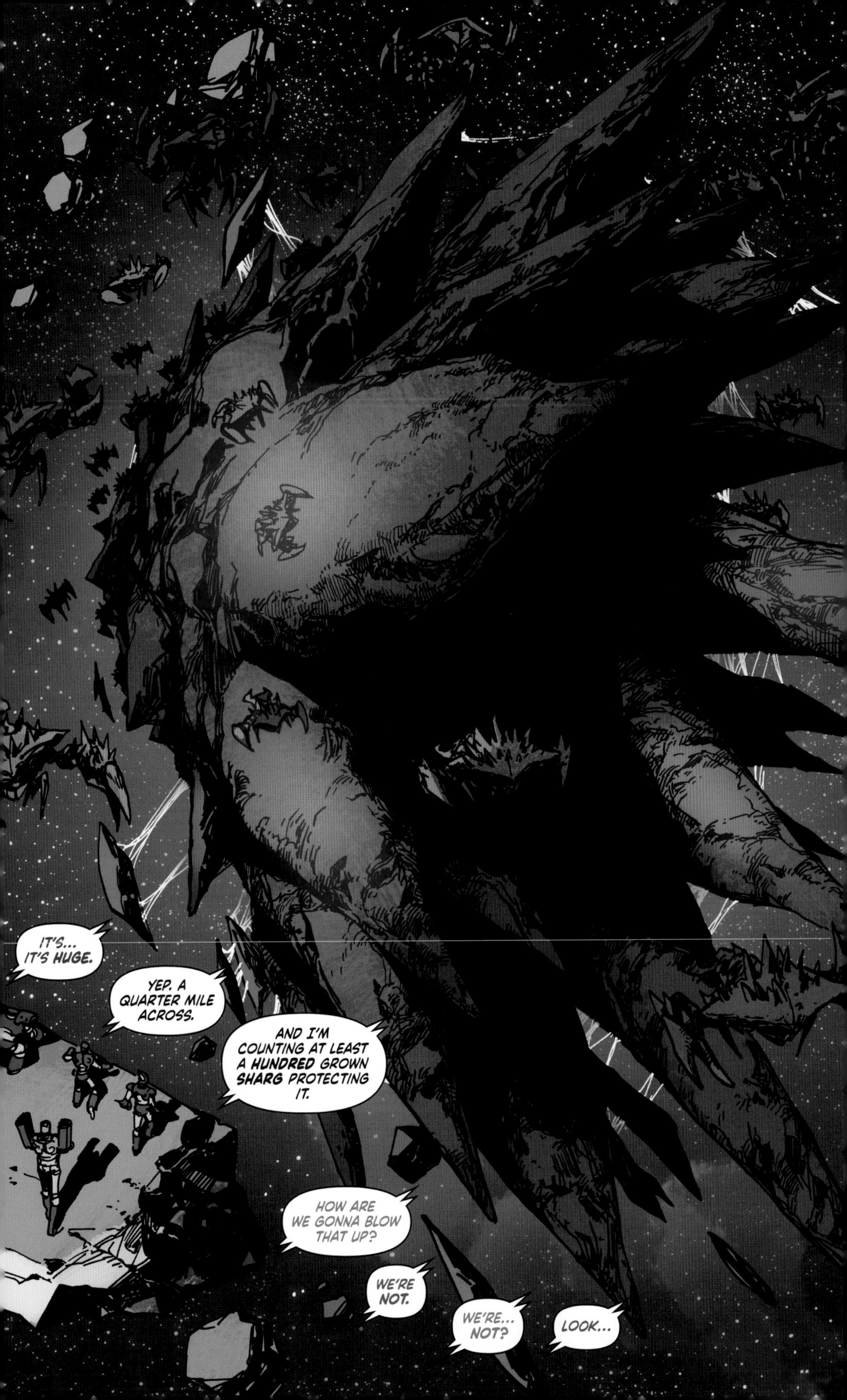
IT'S... IT'S **HUGE.**
YEP. A QUARTER MILE ACROSS.
AND I'M COUNTING AT LEAST A **HUNDRED** GROWN **SHARG** PROTECTING IT.
HOW ARE WE GONNA BLOW THAT UP?
WE'RE **NOT.**
WE'RE... **NOT?**
LOOK...

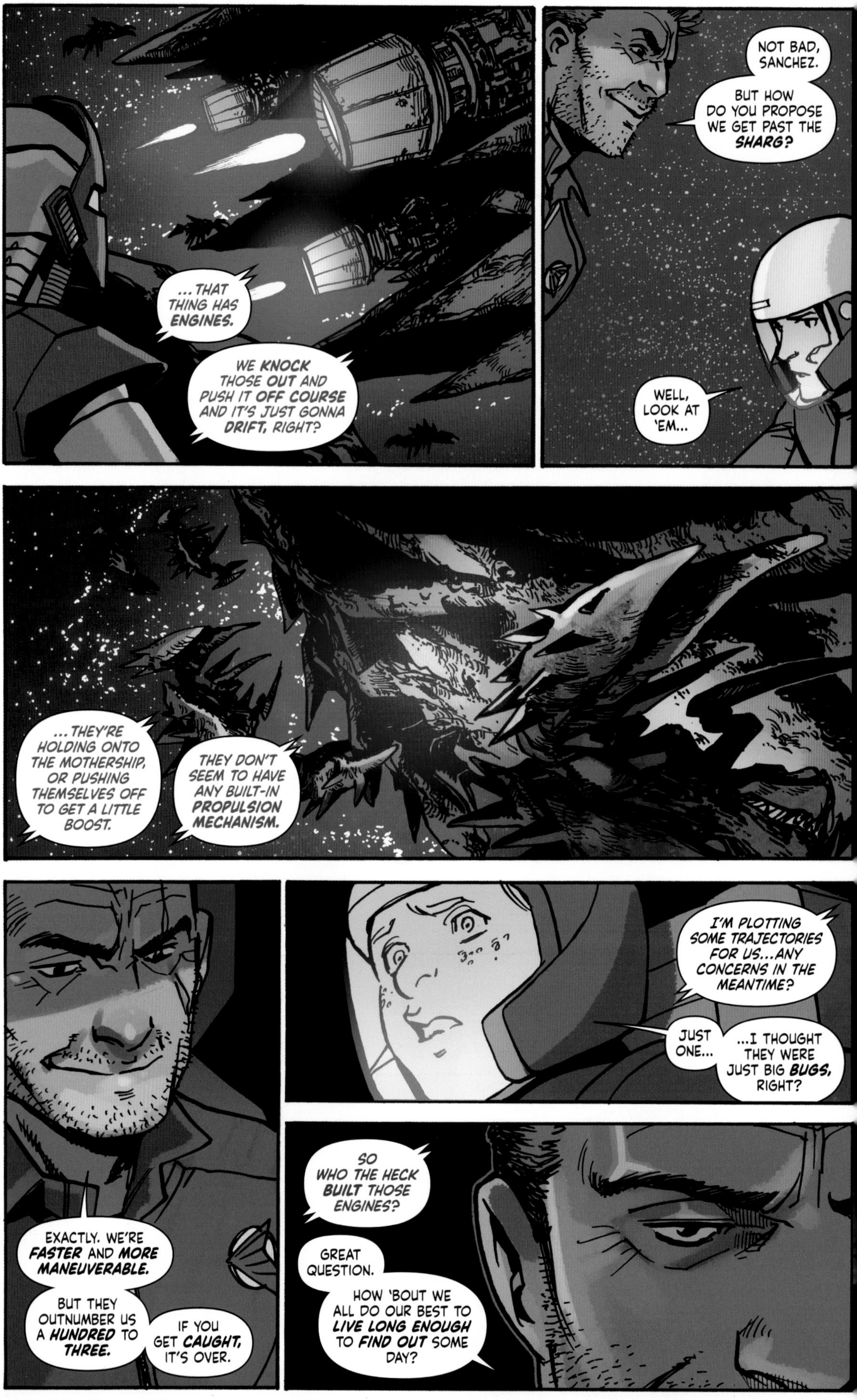
...THAT THING HAS ENGINES.
WE KNOCK THOSE OUT AND PUSH IT OFF COURSE AND IT'S JUST GONNA DRIFT, RIGHT?
NOT BAD, SANCHEZ.
BUT HOW DO YOU PROPOSE WE GET PAST THE SHARG?
WELL, LOOK AT 'EM...
...THEY'RE HOLDING ONTO THE MOTHERSHIP, OR PUSHING THEMSELVES OFF TO GET A LITTLE BOOST.
THEY DON'T SEEM TO HAVE ANY BUILT-IN PROPULSION MECHANISM.
EXACTLY. WE'RE FASTER AND MORE MANEUVERABLE.
BUT THEY OUTNUMBER US A HUNDRED TO THREE.
IF YOU GET CAUGHT, IT'S OVER.
I'M PLOTTING SOME TRAJECTORIES FOR US...ANY CONCERNS IN THE MEANTIME?
JUST ONE...
...I THOUGHT THEY WERE JUST BIG BUGS, RIGHT?
SO WHO THE HECK BUILT THOSE ENGINES?
GREAT QUESTION.
HOW 'BOUT WE ALL DO OUR BEST TO LIVE LONG ENOUGH TO FIND OUT SOME DAY?

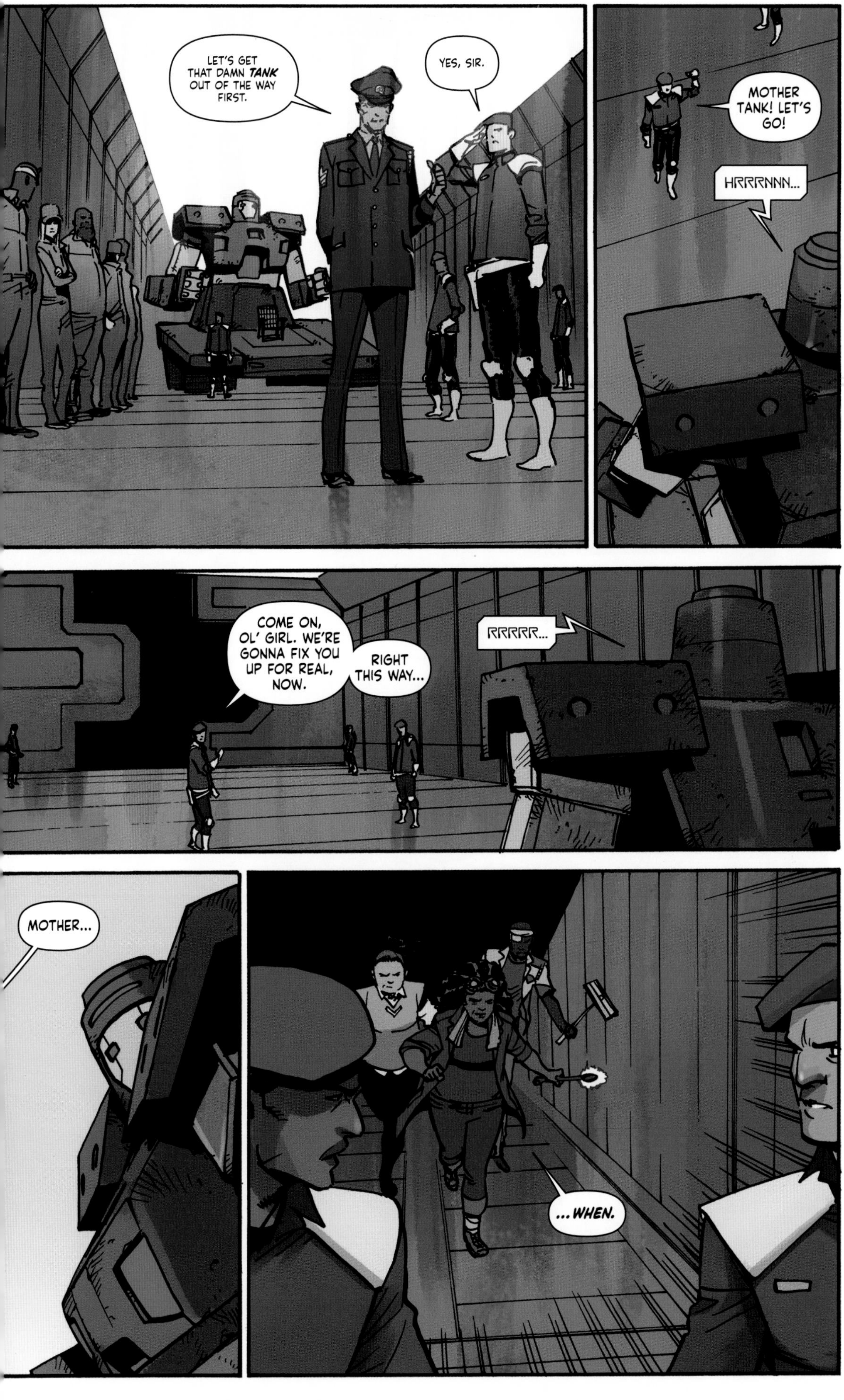
LET'S GET THAT DAMN TANK OUT OF THE WAY FIRST.
YES, SIR.
MOTHER TANK! LET'S GO!
HRRRNNN...
COME ON, OL' GIRL. WE'RE GONNA FIX YOU UP FOR REAL, NOW.
RIGHT THIS WAY...
RRRRR...
MOTHER...
...WHEN.

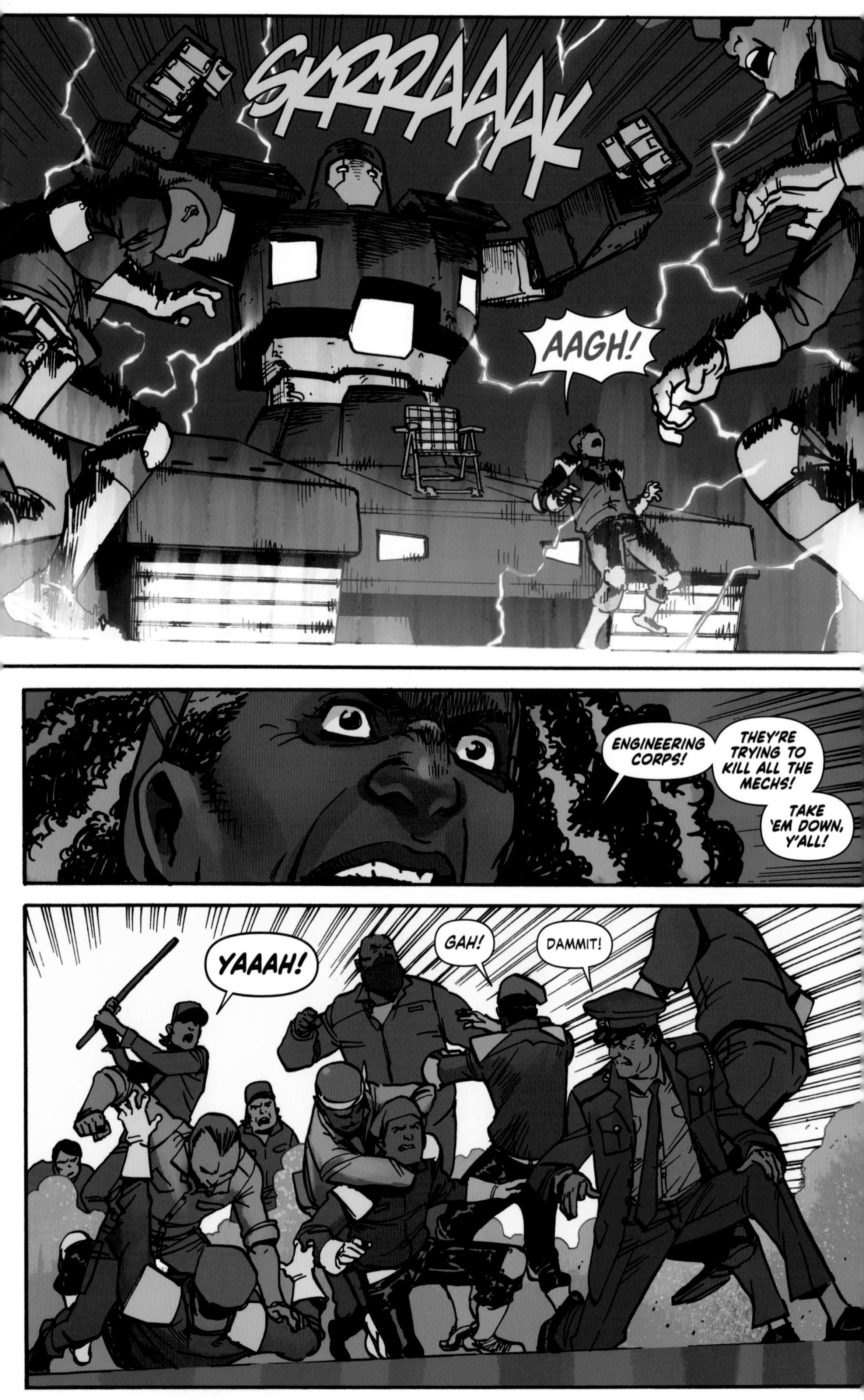
SKRRAAAK
AAGH!
ENGINEERING CORPS!
THEY'RE TRYING TO KILL ALL THE MECHS!
TAKE 'EM DOWN, Y'ALL!
YAAAH!
GAH!
DAMMIT!

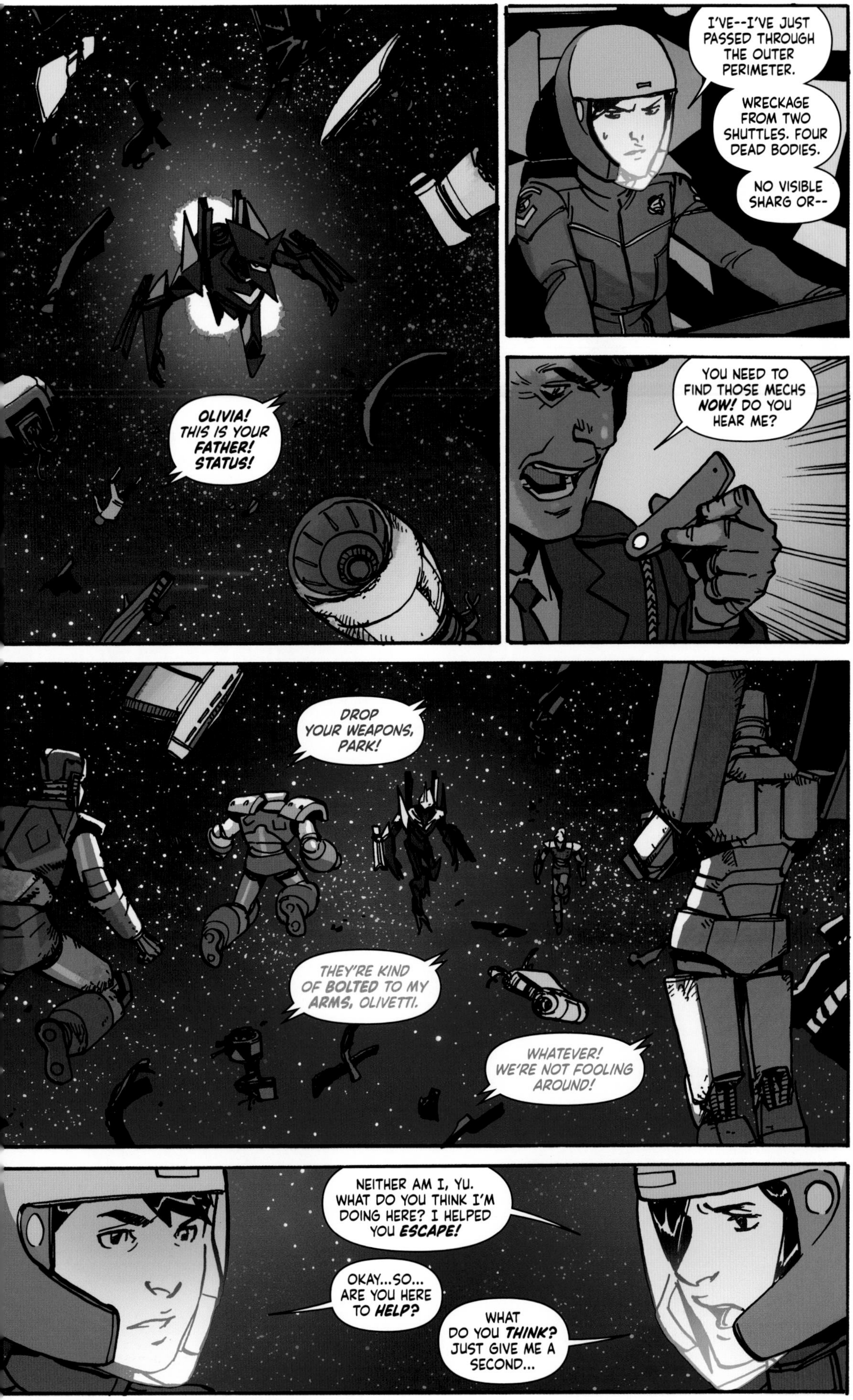
OLIVIA! THIS IS YOUR FATHER! STATUS!
I'VE--I'VE JUST PASSED THROUGH THE OUTER PERIMETER.
WRECKAGE FROM TWO SHUTTLES. FOUR DEAD BODIES.
NO VISIBLE SHARG OR--
YOU NEED TO FIND THOSE MECHS NOW! DO YOU HEAR ME?
DROP YOUR WEAPONS, PARK!
THEY'RE KIND OF BOLTED TO MY ARMS, OLIVETTI.
WHATEVER! WE'RE NOT FOOLING AROUND!
NEITHER AM I, YU. WHAT DO YOU THINK I'M DOING HERE? I HELPED YOU ESCAPE!
OKAY...SO... ARE YOU HERE TO HELP?
WHAT DO YOU THINK? JUST GIVE ME A SECOND...

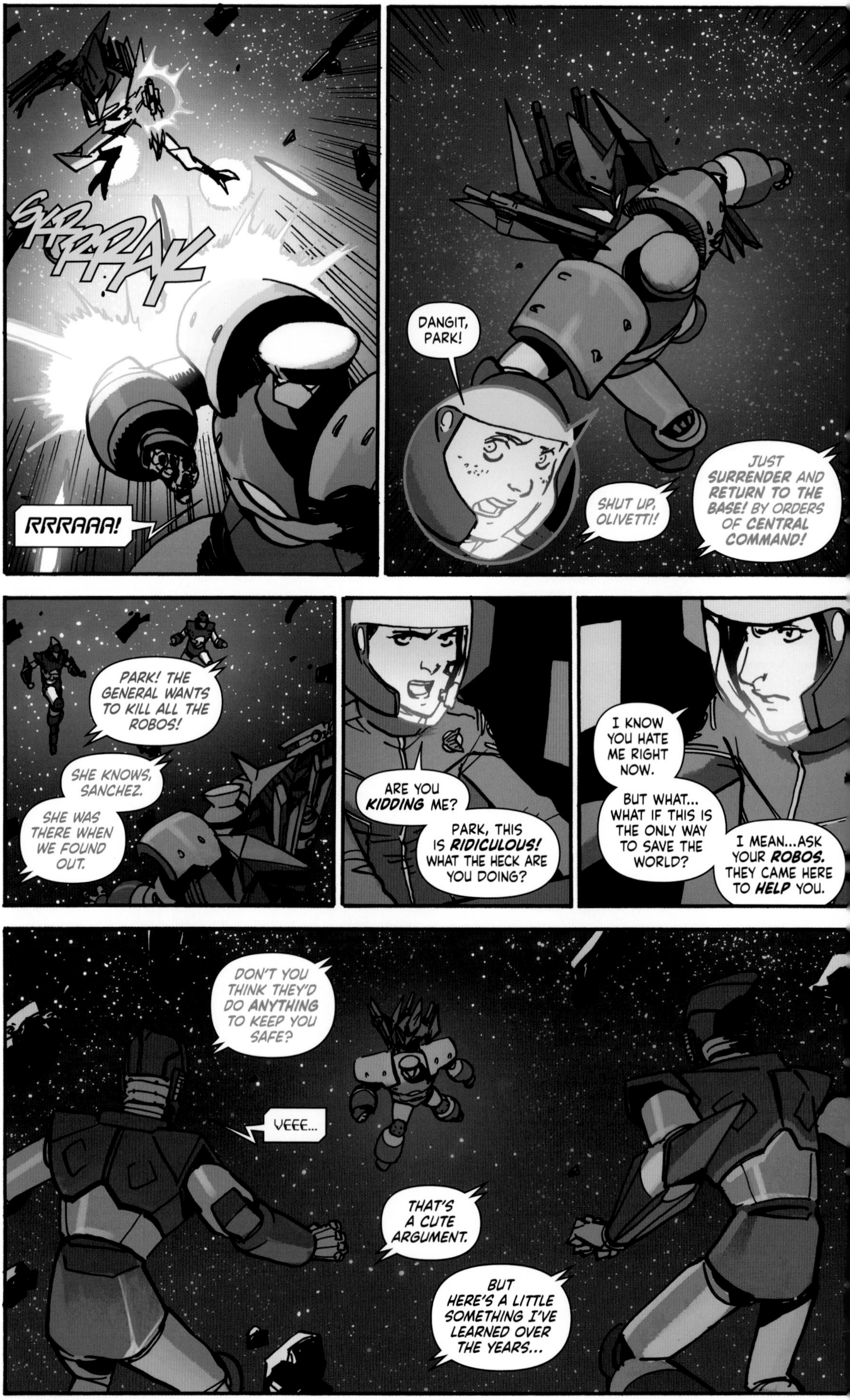
SKRRRAK
RRRRAAA!
DANGIT, PARK!
JUST SURRENDER AND RETURN TO THE BASE! BY ORDERS OF CENTRAL COMMAND!
SHUT UP, OLIVETTI!
PARK! THE GENERAL WANTS TO KILL ALL THE ROBOS!
SHE KNOWS, SANCHEZ.
SHE WAS THERE WHEN WE FOUND OUT.
ARE YOU KIDDING ME?
PARK, THIS IS RIDICULOUS! WHAT THE HECK ARE YOU DOING?
I KNOW YOU HATE ME RIGHT NOW.
BUT WHAT... WHAT IF THIS IS THE ONLY WAY TO SAVE THE WORLD?
I MEAN...ASK YOUR ROBOS. THEY CAME HERE TO HELP YOU.
DON'T YOU THINK THEY'D DO ANYTHING TO KEEP YOU SAFE?
VEEE...
THAT'S A CUTE ARGUMENT.
BUT HERE'S A LITTLE SOMETHING I'VE LEARNED OVER THE YEARS...

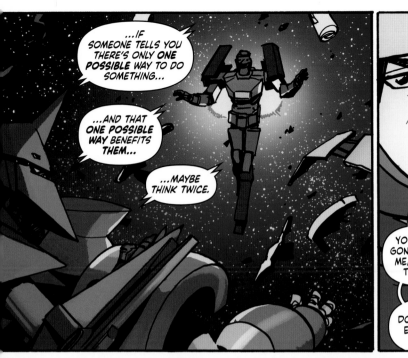

...IF SOMEONE TELLS YOU THERE'S ONLY **ONE** POSSIBLE WAY TO DO SOMETHING...

...AND THAT **ONE** POSSIBLE WAY BENEFITS **THEM**...

...MAYBE THINK TWICE.

YOU'RE NOT GONNA **TRICK** ME, CAPTAIN TANAKA.

YOUR **DAD** SENT YOU HERE, PARK. JUST **THINK** FOR ONE MINUTE--

MY DAD'S A **GENERAL.** THIS DOESN'T BENEFIT HIM OR ANYONE ELSE DOWN THERE--EXCEPT BY **SAVING** THE **WORLD.**

IN MY EXPERIENCE, THE ONLY THING GENERALS LIKE MORE THAN **SAVING** THE WORLD...

...IS **RUNNING** IT.

AND WITH THE **ROBOS** GONE, THERE'LL BE NO ONE **POWERFUL ENOUGH** LEFT STANDING TO TELL THEM **NO--**

YOU DON'T GET TO TALK THAT WAY ABOUT MY FATHER! HE'S NOT LIKE THAT--

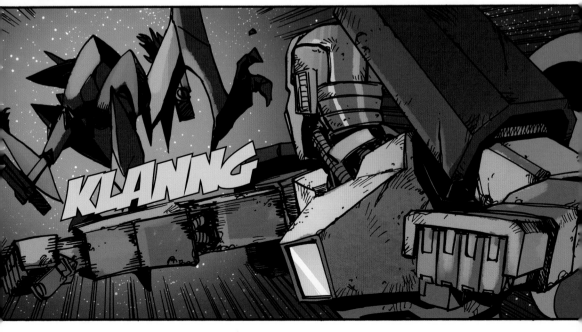

KLANNG

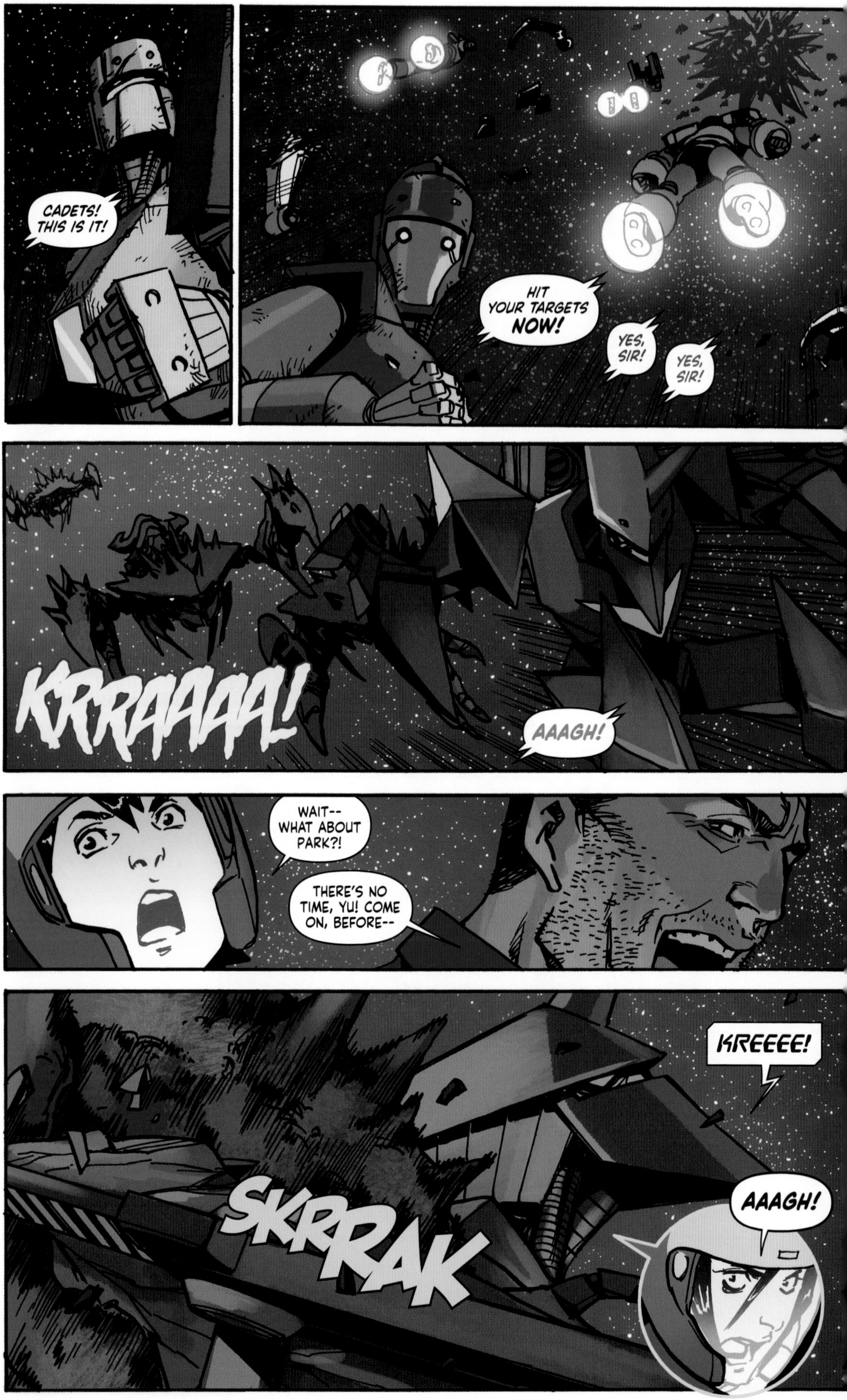
CADETS! THIS IS IT!
HIT YOUR TARGETS NOW!
YES, SIR!
YES, SIR!
KRRAAAAL!
AAAGH!
WAIT-- WHAT ABOUT PARK?!
THERE'S NO TIME, YU! COME ON, BEFORE--
KREEEE!
SKRRAK
AAAGH!

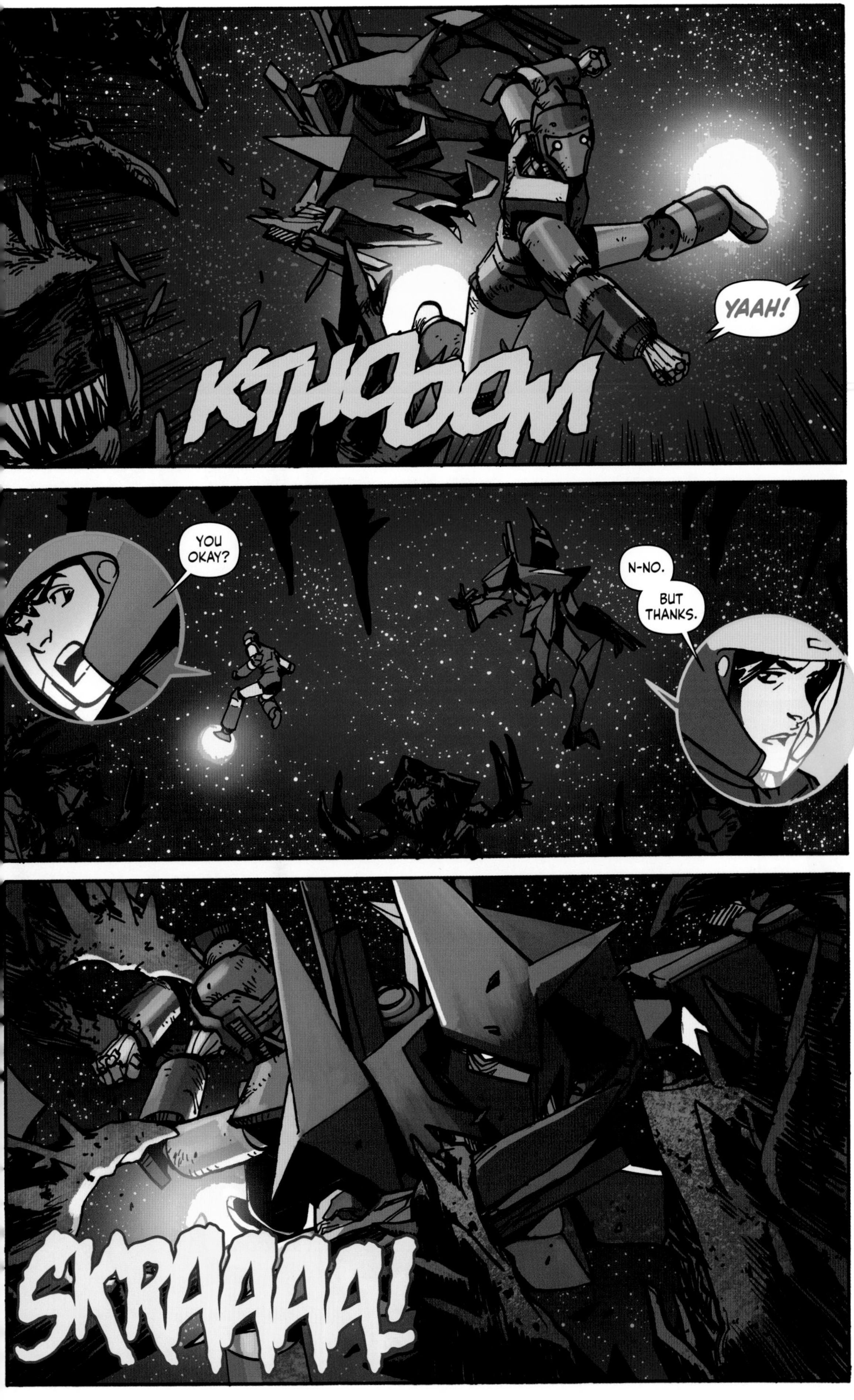
YAAH!
KTHOOOM
YOU OKAY?
N-NO.
BUT THANKS.
SKRAAAA!

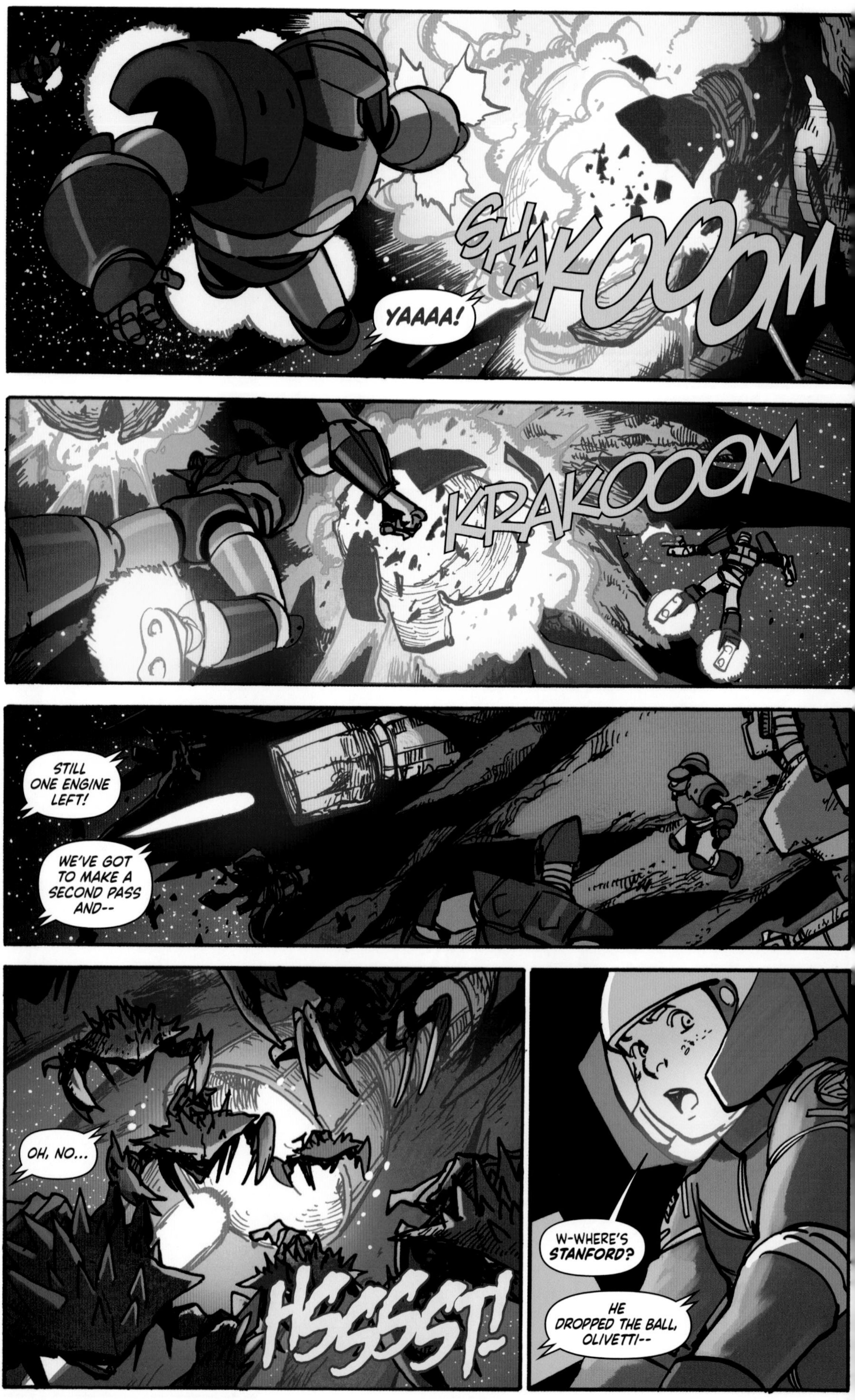
SHAKOOOOM
YAAAA!
KRAKOOOOM
STILL ONE ENGINE LEFT!
WE'VE GOT TO MAKE A SECOND PASS AND--
OH, NO...
HSSSST!
W-WHERE'S STANFORD?
HE DROPPED THE BALL, OLIVETTI--

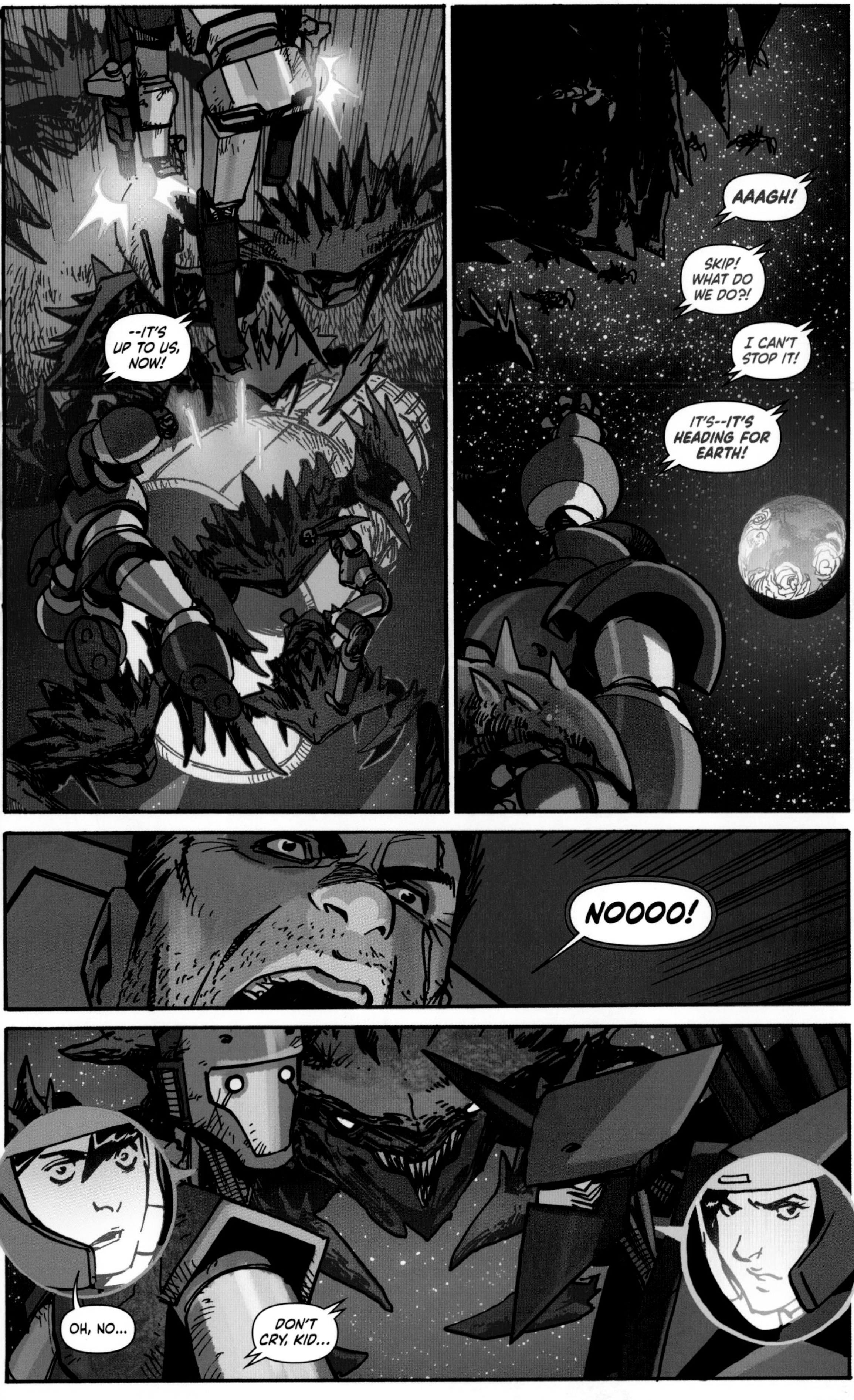
--IT'S UP TO US, NOW!
AAAGH!
SKIP! WHAT DO WE DO?!
I CAN'T STOP IT!
IT'S--IT'S HEADING FOR EARTH!
NOOOO!
OH, NO...
DON'T CRY, KID...

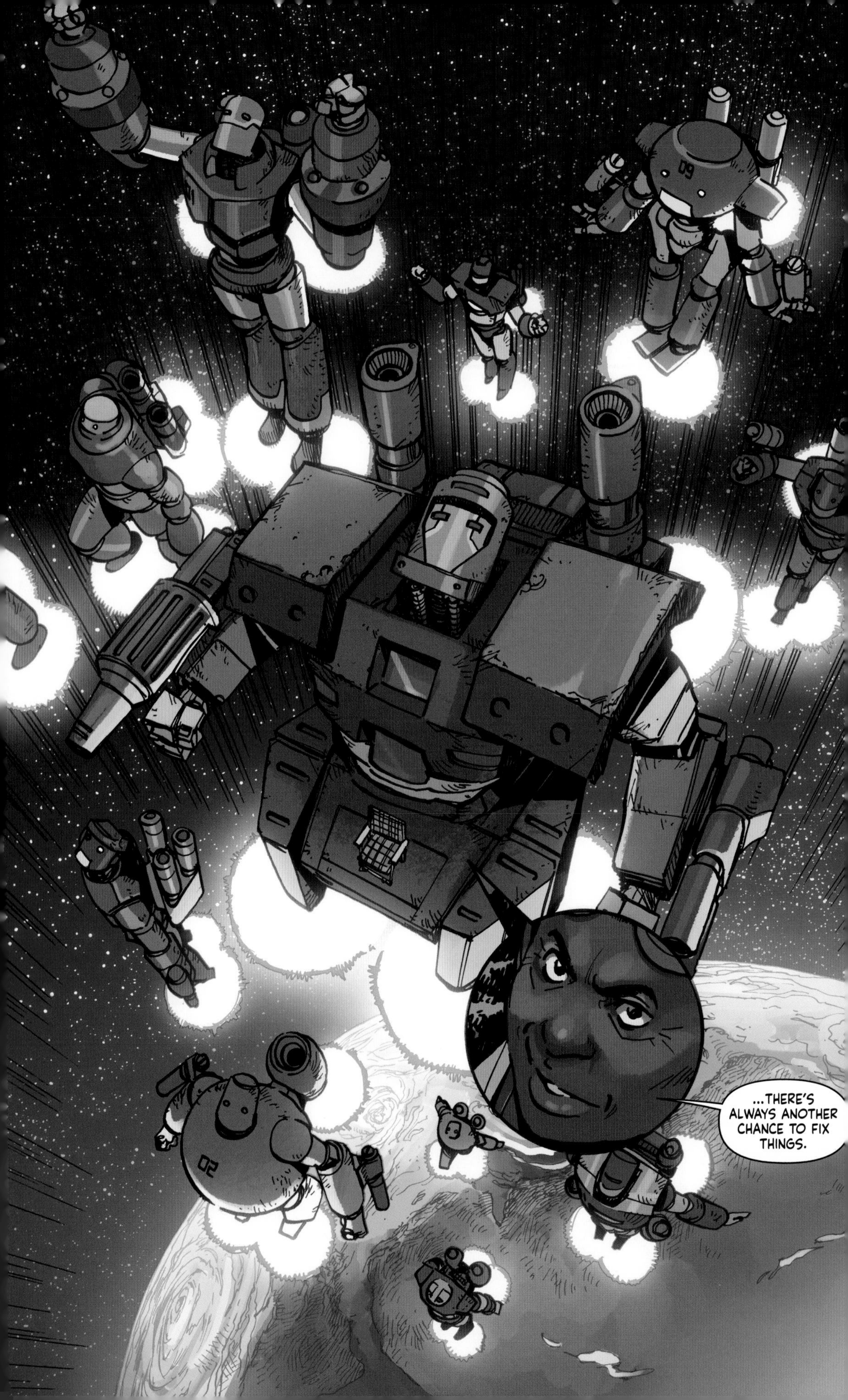
...THERE'S ALWAYS ANOTHER CHANCE TO FIX THINGS.

CHAPTER
NINE

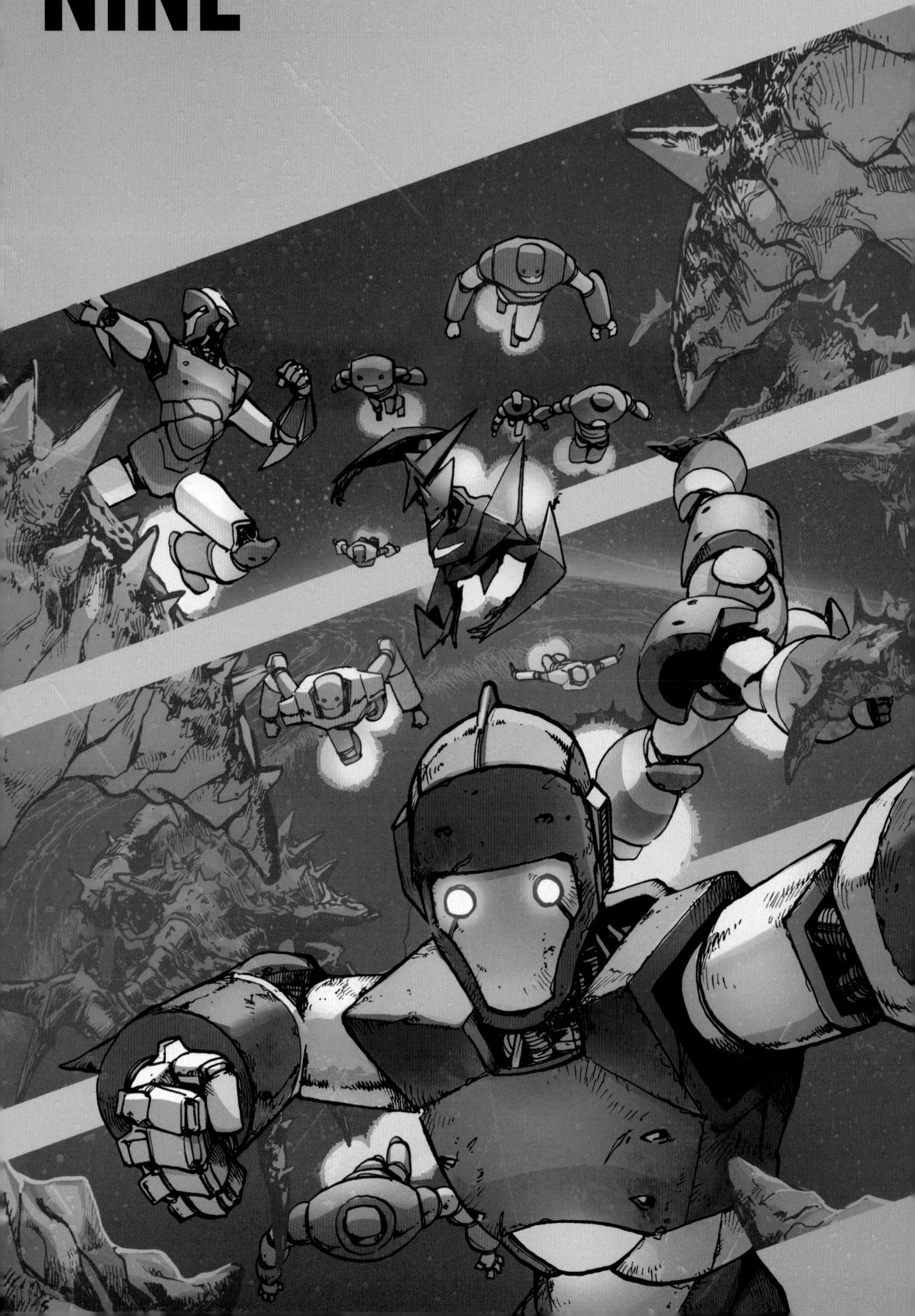

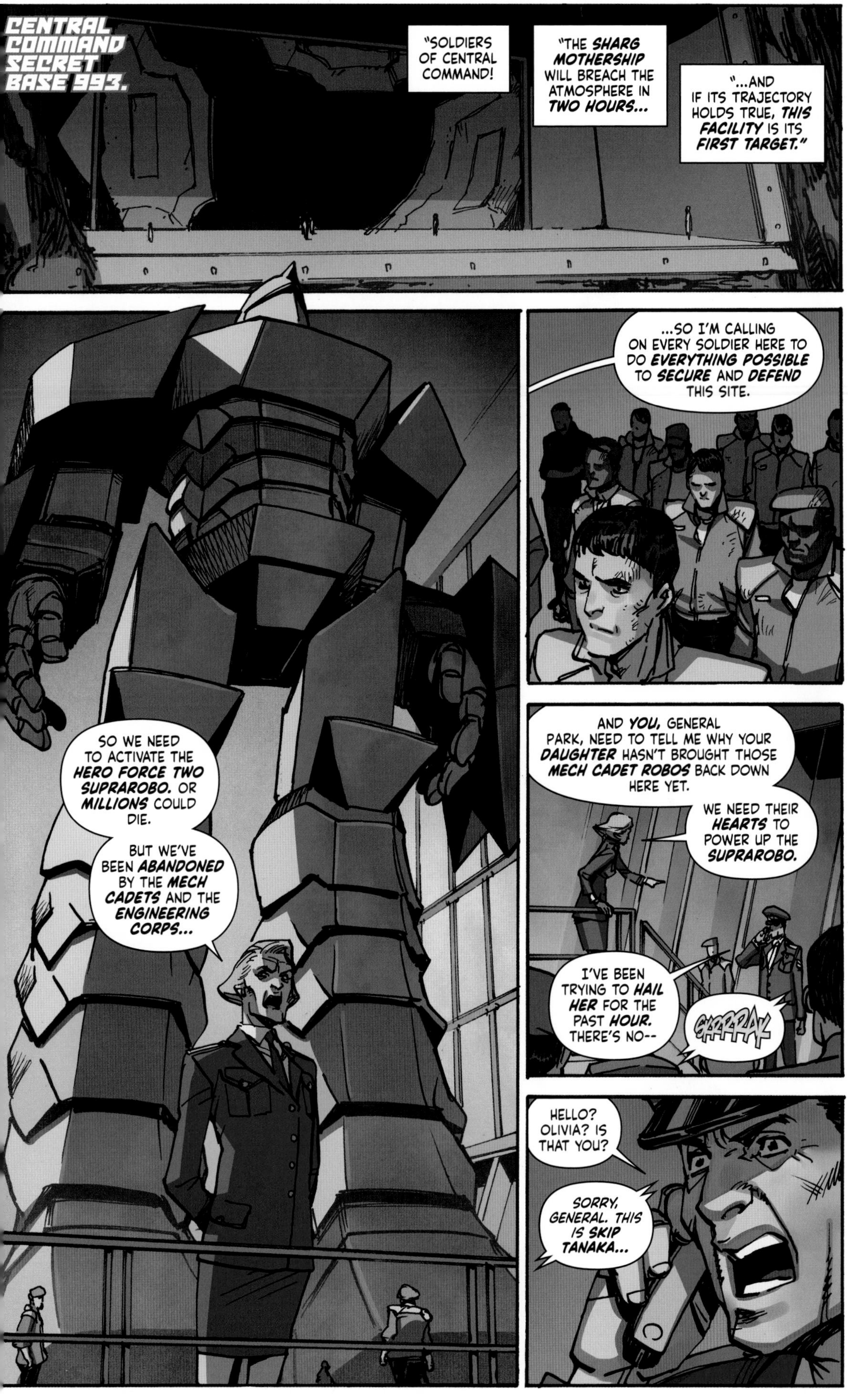
CENTRAL COMMAND SECRET BASE 993.
"SOLDIERS OF CENTRAL COMMAND!
"THE SHARG MOTHERSHIP WILL BREACH THE ATMOSPHERE IN TWO HOURS...
"...AND IF ITS TRAJECTORY HOLDS TRUE, THIS FACILITY IS ITS FIRST TARGET."
SO WE NEED TO ACTIVATE THE HERO FORCE TWO SUPRAROBO. OR MILLIONS COULD DIE.
BUT WE'VE BEEN ABANDONED BY THE MECH CADETS AND THE ENGINEERING CORPS...
...SO I'M CALLING ON EVERY SOLDIER HERE TO DO EVERYTHING POSSIBLE TO SECURE AND DEFEND THIS SITE.
AND YOU, GENERAL PARK, NEED TO TELL ME WHY YOUR DAUGHTER HASN'T BROUGHT THOSE MECH CADET ROBOS BACK DOWN HERE YET.
WE NEED THEIR HEARTS TO POWER UP THE SUPRAROBO.
I'VE BEEN TRYING TO HAIL HER FOR THE PAST HOUR. THERE'S NO--
SKRRRAK
HELLO? OLIVIA? IS THAT YOU?
SORRY, GENERAL. THIS IS SKIP TANAKA...

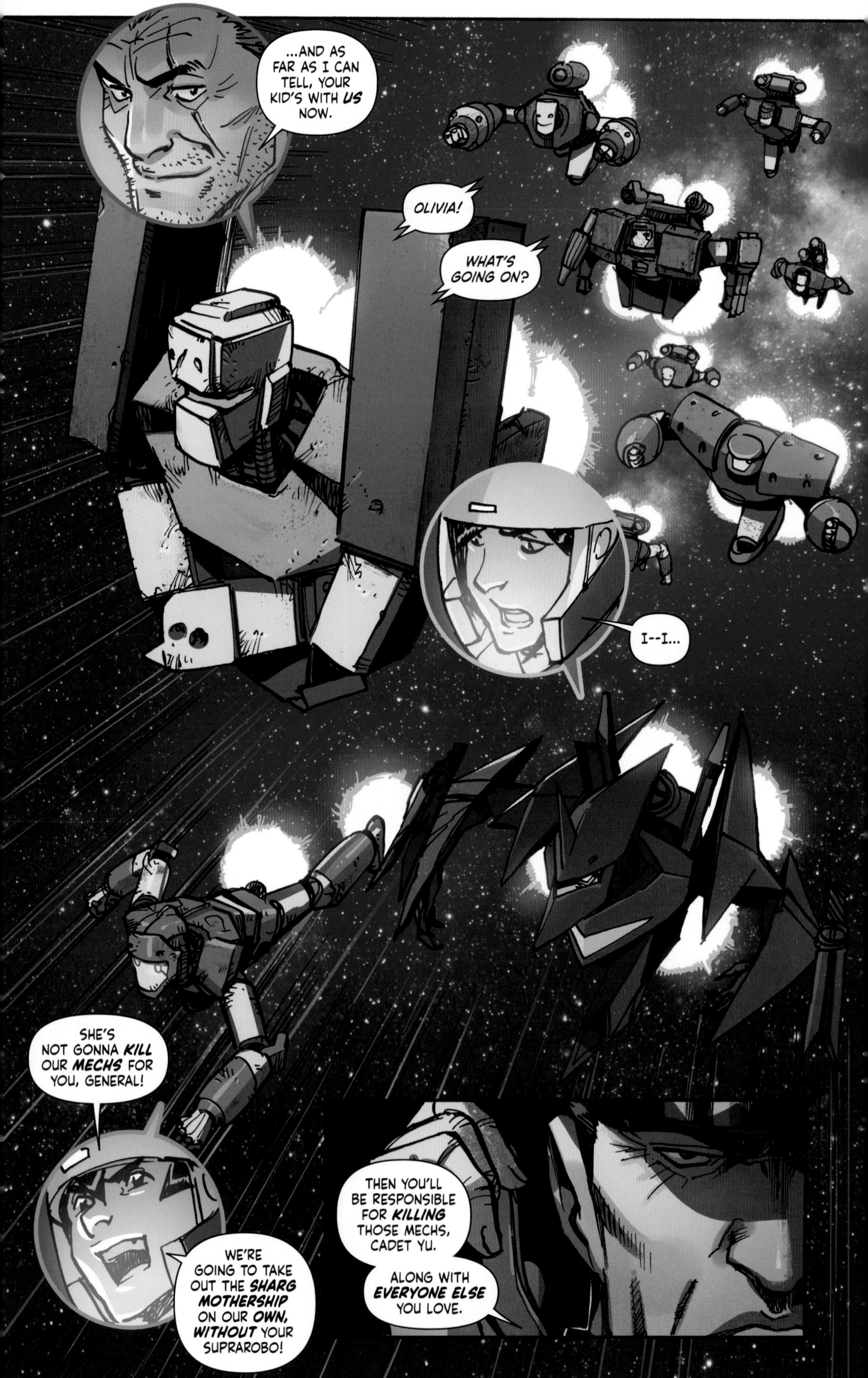
...AND AS FAR AS I CAN TELL, YOUR KID'S WITH US NOW.
OLIVIA!
WHAT'S GOING ON?
I--I...
SHE'S NOT GONNA KILL OUR MECHS FOR YOU, GENERAL!
WE'RE GOING TO TAKE OUT THE SHARG MOTHERSHIP ON OUR OWN, WITHOUT YOUR SUPRAROBO!
THEN YOU'LL BE RESPONSIBLE FOR KILLING THOSE MECHS, CADET YU.
ALONG WITH EVERYONE ELSE YOU LOVE.

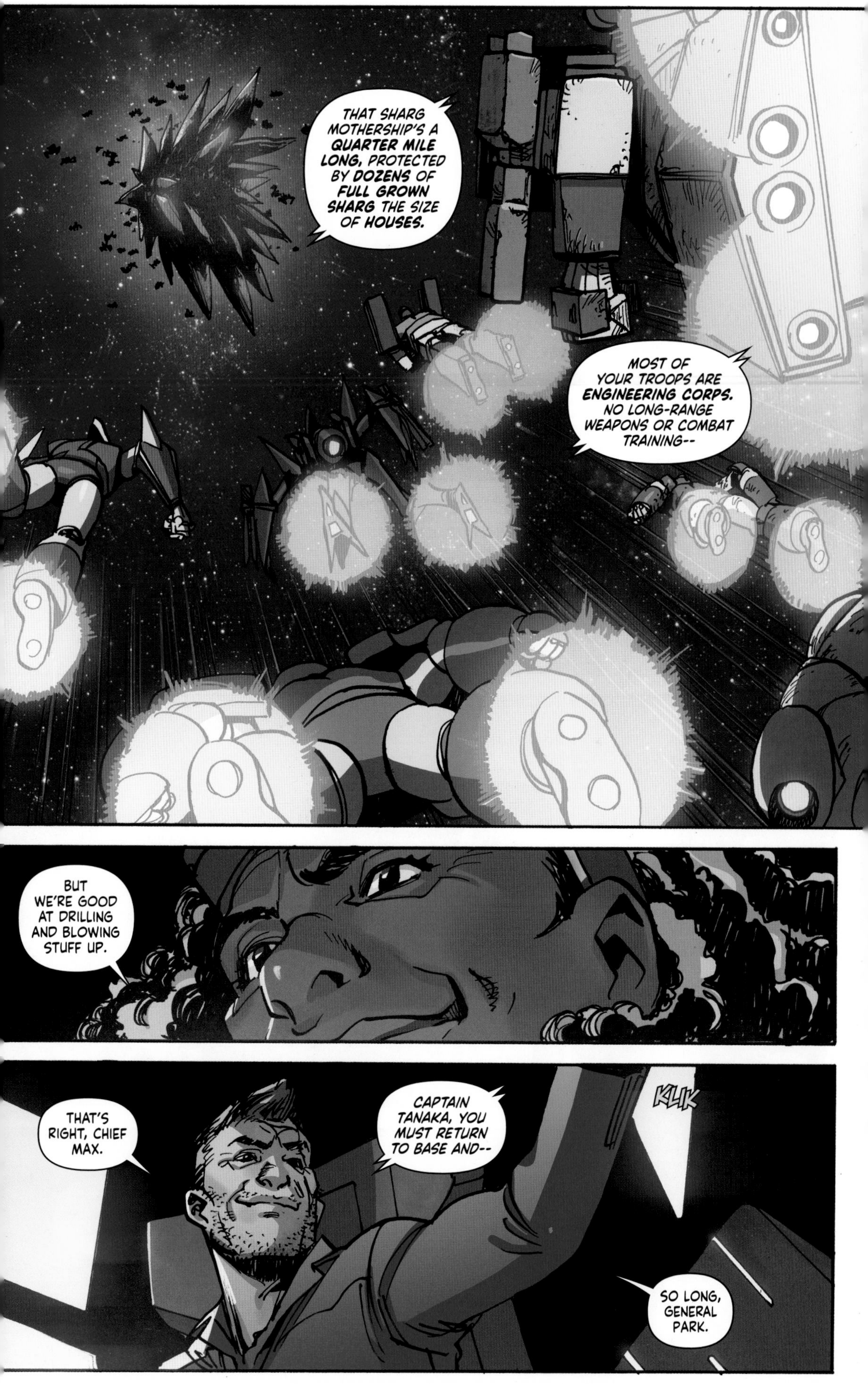
THAT SHARG MOTHERSHIP'S A QUARTER MILE LONG, PROTECTED BY DOZENS OF FULL GROWN SHARG THE SIZE OF HOUSES.
MOST OF YOUR TROOPS ARE ENGINEERING CORPS. NO LONG-RANGE WEAPONS OR COMBAT TRAINING--
BUT WE'RE GOOD AT DRILLING AND BLOWING STUFF UP.
THAT'S RIGHT, CHIEF MAX.
CAPTAIN TANAKA, YOU MUST RETURN TO BASE AND--
KLIK
SO LONG, GENERAL PARK.

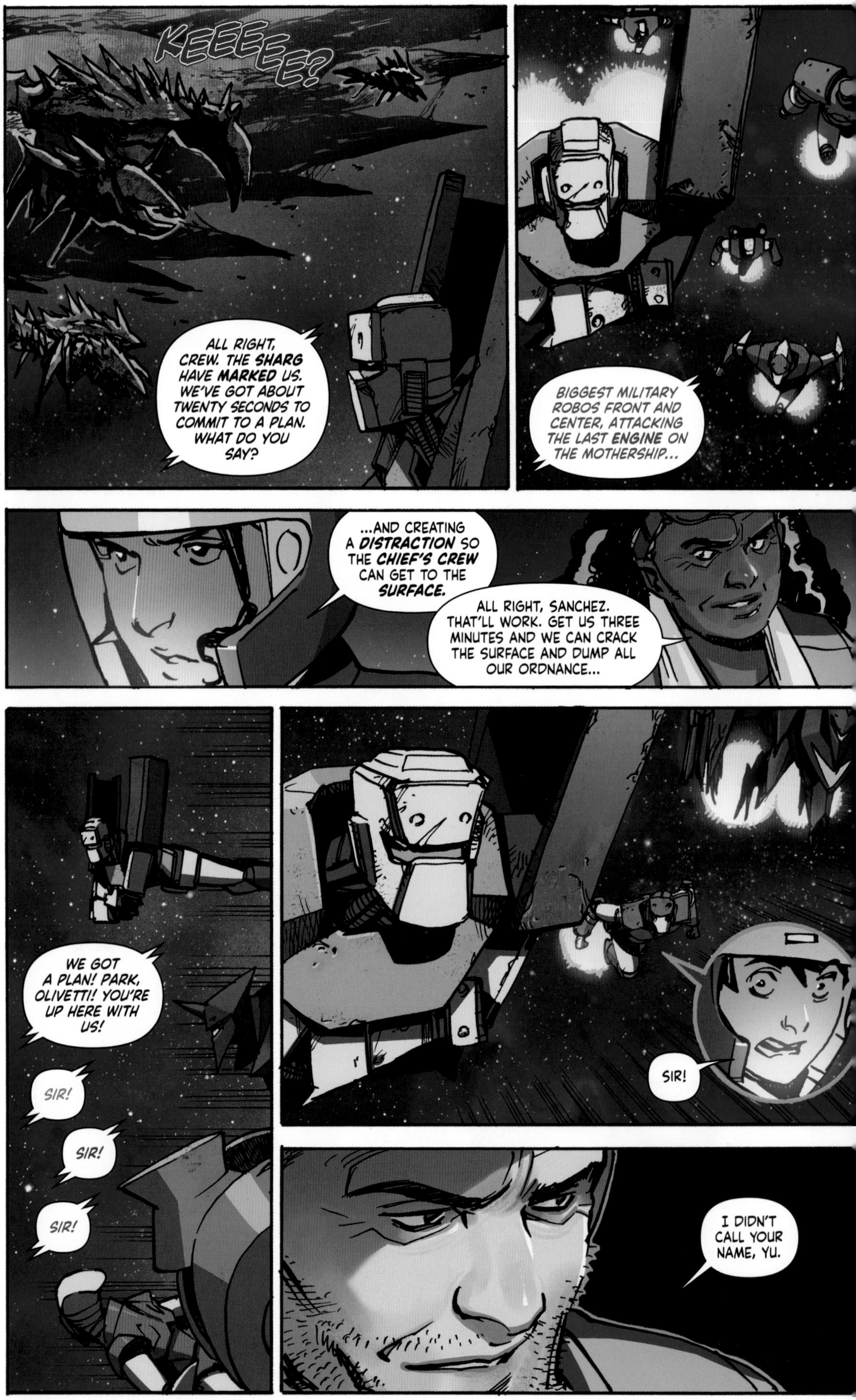
KEEEEEE?
ALL RIGHT, CREW. THE SHARG HAVE MARKED US. WE'VE GOT ABOUT TWENTY SECONDS TO COMMIT TO A PLAN. WHAT DO YOU SAY?
BIGGEST MILITARY ROBOS FRONT AND CENTER, ATTACKING THE LAST ENGINE ON THE MOTHERSHIP...
...AND CREATING A DISTRACTION SO THE CHIEF'S CREW CAN GET TO THE SURFACE.
ALL RIGHT, SANCHEZ. THAT'LL WORK. GET US THREE MINUTES AND WE CAN CRACK THE SURFACE AND DUMP ALL OUR ORDNANCE...
WE GOT A PLAN! PARK, OLIVETTI! YOU'RE UP HERE WITH US!
SIR!
SIR!
SIR!
SIR!
I DIDN'T CALL YOUR NAME, YU.

WHAT ARE YOU TALKING ABOUT? I'M A *MECH CADET!* ME AND BUDDY ARE DOING WHATEVER EVERYONE ELSE IS DOING!

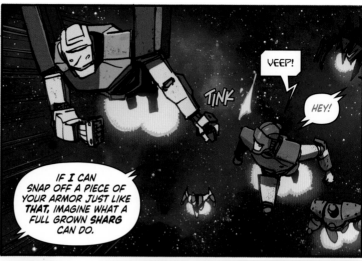

VEEP!

HEY!

TINK

IF *I* CAN SNAP OFF A PIECE OF YOUR ARMOR JUST LIKE *THAT,* IMAGINE WHAT A FULL GROWN *SHARG* CAN DO.

YOUR ROBO'S TOO *SMALL,* YU. AND TOO *FRAGILE.* HE'S BEEN ON THE VERGE OF *FALLING APART* SINCE YOU GOT HIM.

COME ON! WE'VE FOUGHT IN EVERY DANG BATTLE RIGHT BY YOUR SIDE!

AND OLIVETTI'S HURT FROM THE BABY SHARG ATTACK!

HIS LEG'S PROBABLY STILL BLEEDING!

HE HAD A *FEVER* THE LAST TIME HE GOT CHECKED!

I'M-- I'M FINE!

C'MON! YOU GUYS NEED ALL THE HELP YOU CAN GET!

EXACTLY. THAT'S WHY YOU'RE RIDING WITH *CHIEF MAX.*

THEY'LL NEED SOMEONE WATCHING THEIR BACKS.

AND YOU KNOW HOW TO *FIX* THINGS BETTER THAN ANY OF THESE OTHER CADETS.

WE NEED YOU, KID.

...

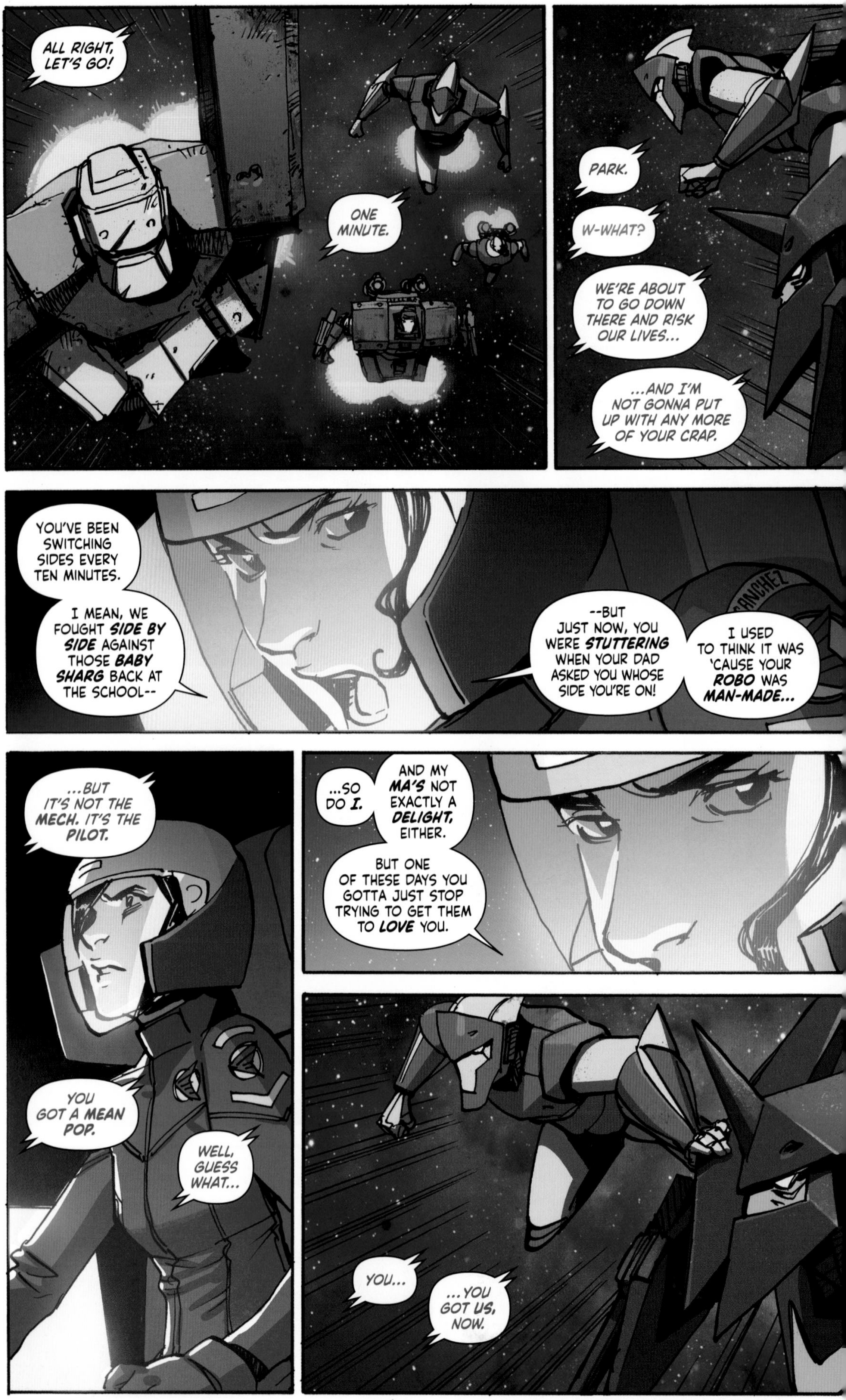
ALL RIGHT, LET'S GO!
ONE MINUTE.
PARK.
W-WHAT?
WE'RE ABOUT TO GO DOWN THERE AND RISK OUR LIVES...
...AND I'M NOT GONNA PUT UP WITH ANY MORE OF YOUR CRAP.
YOU'VE BEEN SWITCHING SIDES EVERY TEN MINUTES.
I MEAN, WE FOUGHT SIDE BY SIDE AGAINST THOSE BABY SHARG BACK AT THE SCHOOL--
--BUT JUST NOW, YOU WERE STUTTERING WHEN YOUR DAD ASKED YOU WHOSE SIDE YOU'RE ON!
I USED TO THINK IT WAS 'CAUSE YOUR ROBO WAS MAN-MADE...
...BUT IT'S NOT THE MECH. IT'S THE PILOT.
YOU GOT A MEAN POP.
WELL, GUESS WHAT...
...SO DO I.
AND MY MA'S NOT EXACTLY A DELIGHT, EITHER.
BUT ONE OF THESE DAYS YOU GOTTA JUST STOP TRYING TO GET THEM TO LOVE YOU.
YOU...
...YOU GOT US, NOW.

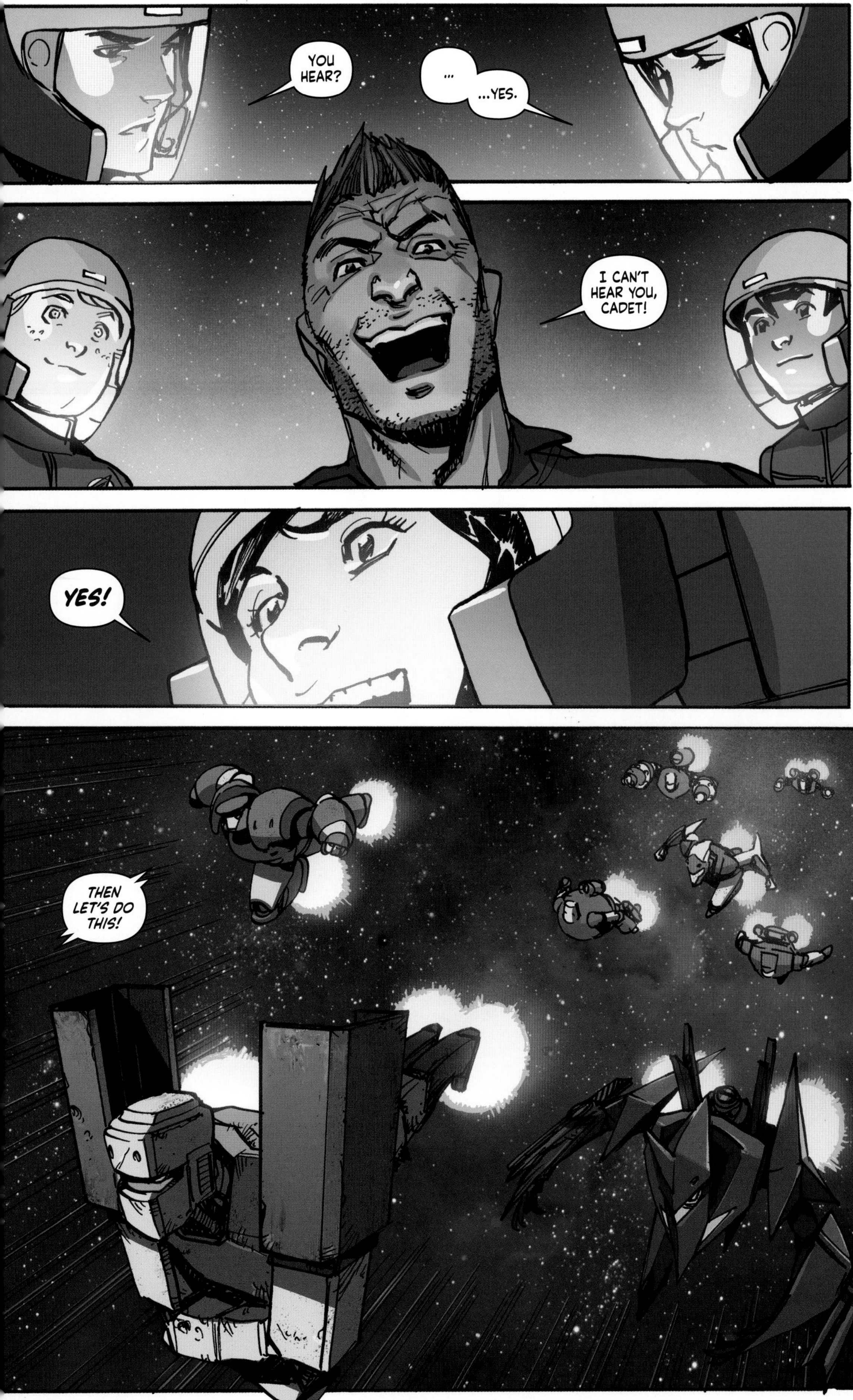
YOU HEAR?
...
...YES.
I CAN'T HEAR YOU, CADET!
YES!
THEN LET'S DO THIS!

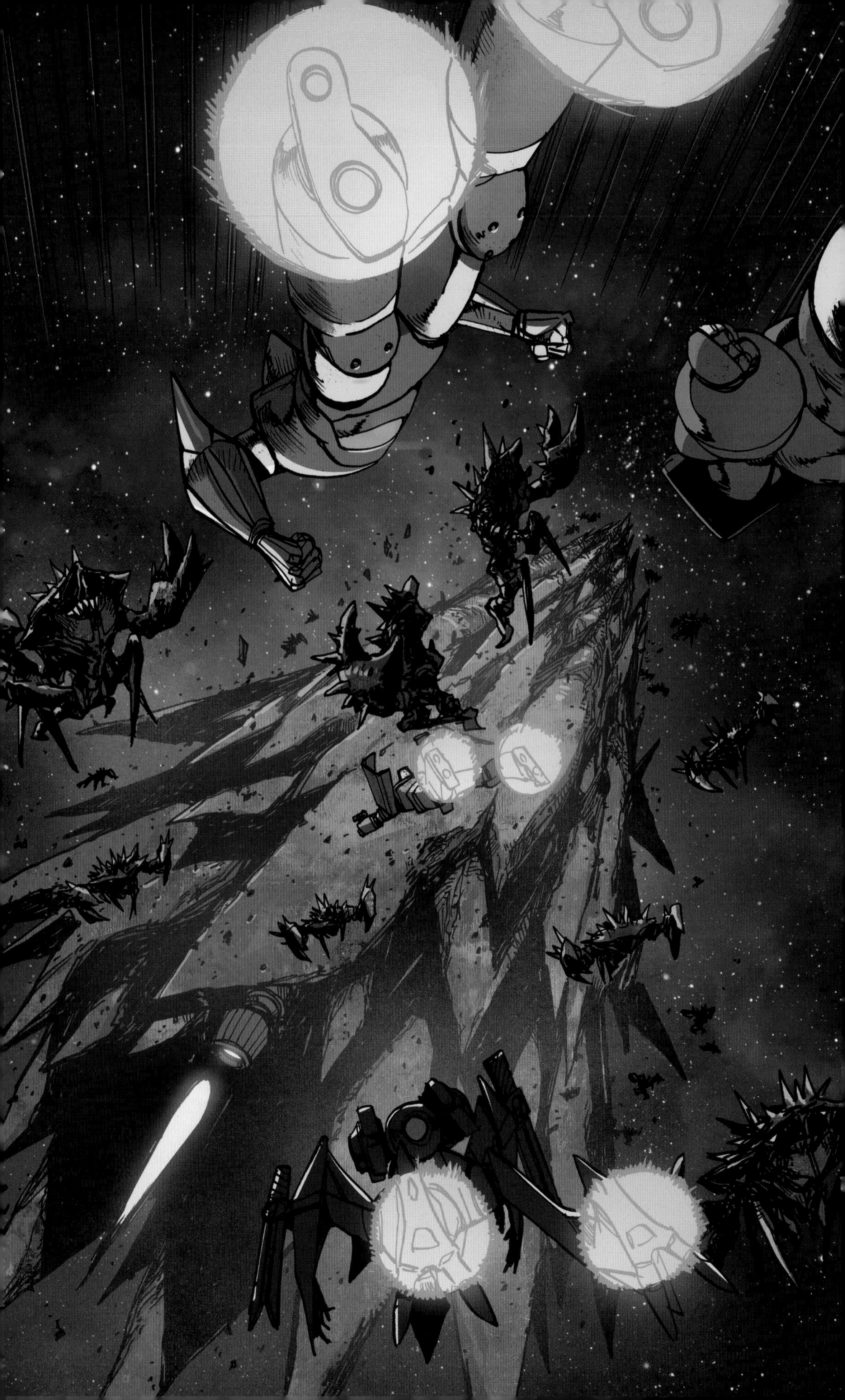

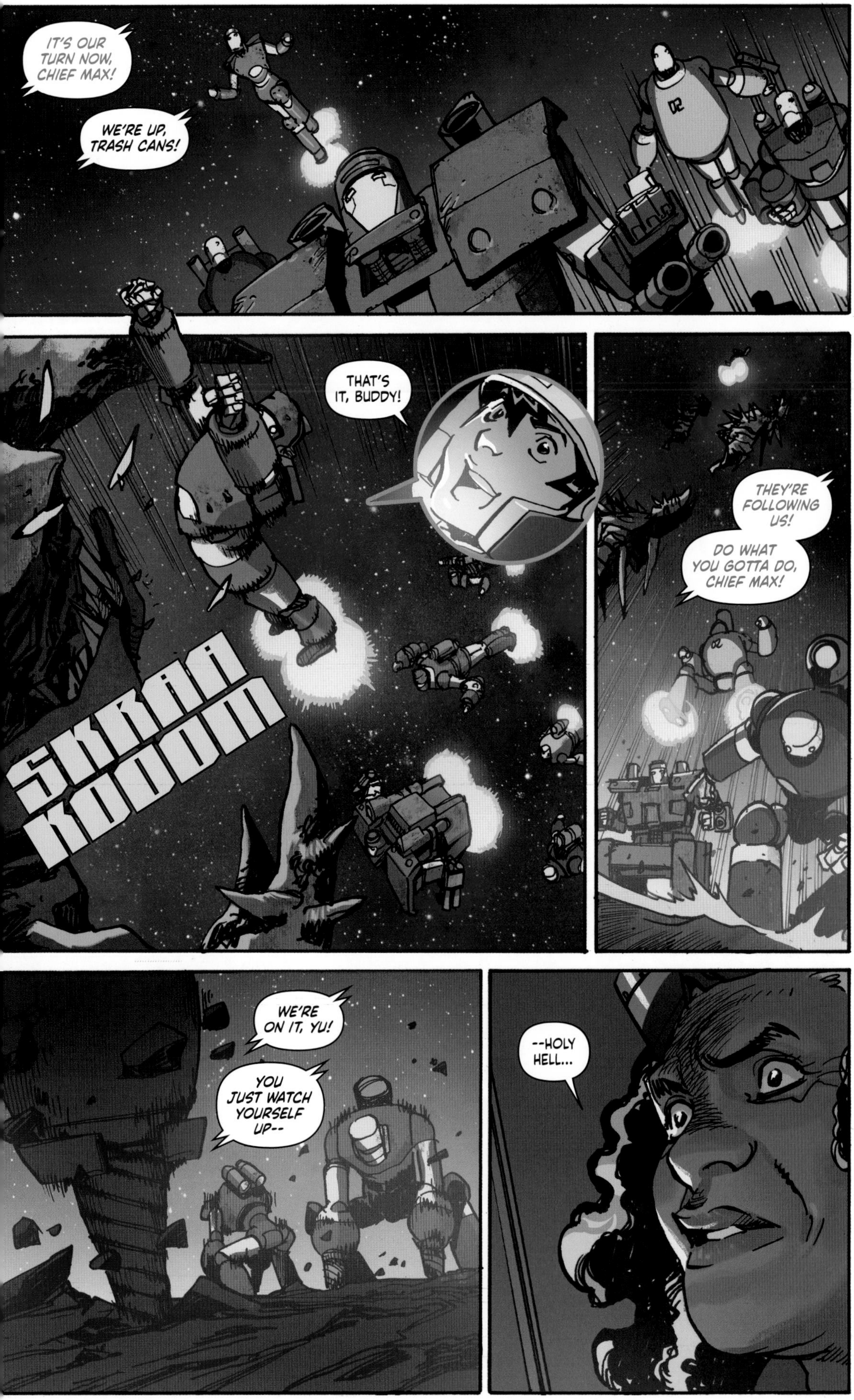
IT'S OUR TURN NOW, CHIEF MAX!
WE'RE UP, TRASH CANS!
THAT'S IT, BUDDY!
SKRAA KOOOM
THEY'RE FOLLOWING US!
DO WHAT YOU GOTTA DO, CHIEF MAX!
WE'RE ON IT, YU!
YOU JUST WATCH YOURSELF UP--
--HOLY HELL...

IT'S FULL OF EGGS!
IF THESE MAKE IT TO GROUND, THE WHOLE PLANET'LL BE INFESTED!
DUMP ALL THE MINING ORDNANCE YOU GOT, RIGHT IN HERE, AND--
KTOOOM KTOOOM
WHAT THE--
MY GOD...

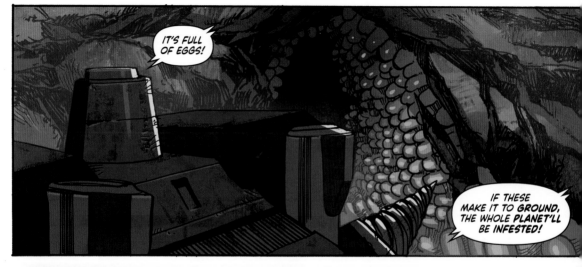

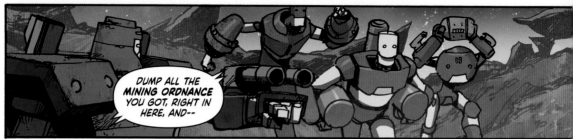

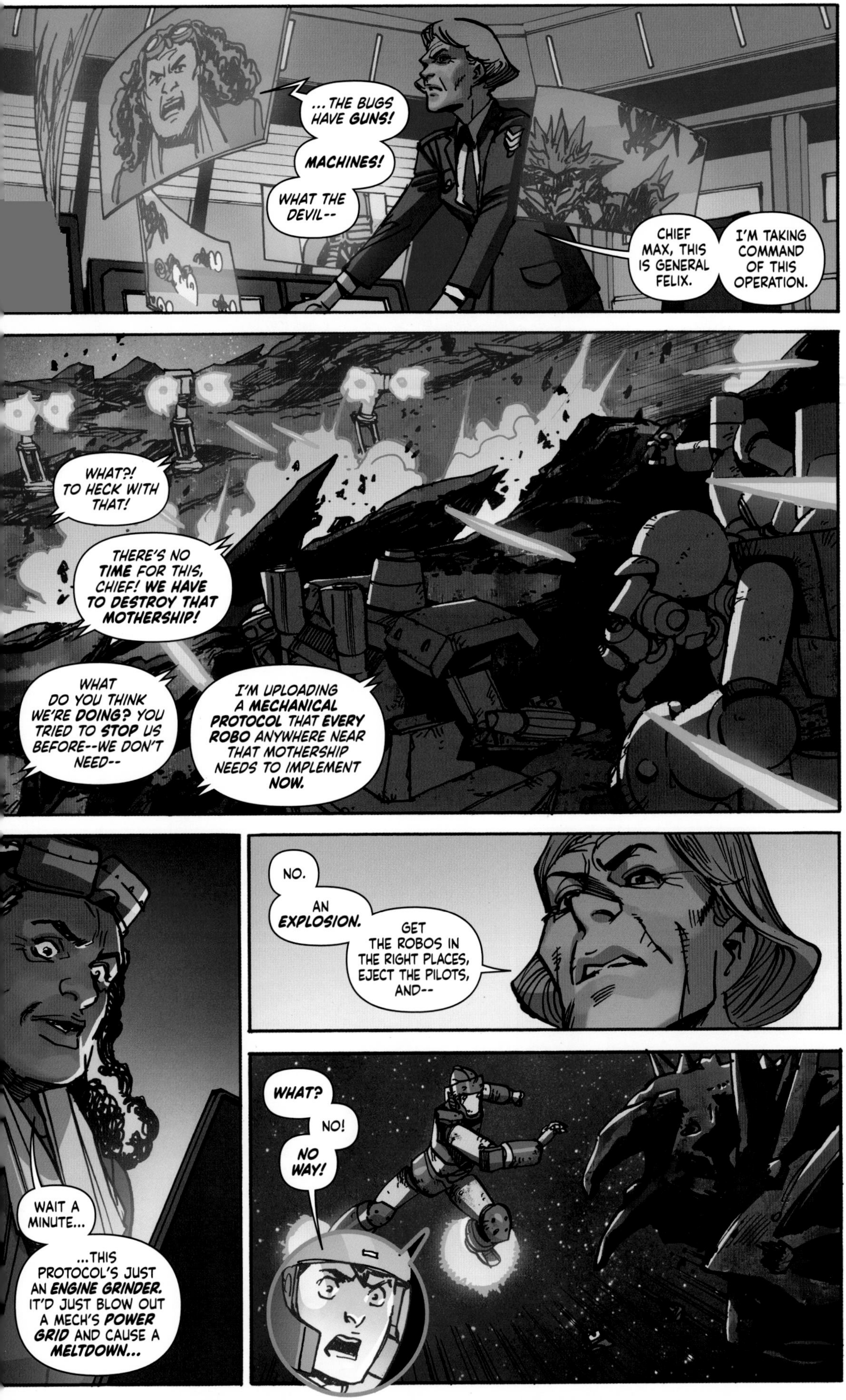
...THE BUGS HAVE GUNS!
MACHINES!
WHAT THE DEVIL--
CHIEF MAX, THIS IS GENERAL FELIX.
I'M TAKING COMMAND OF THIS OPERATION.
WHAT?! TO HECK WITH THAT!
THERE'S NO TIME FOR THIS, CHIEF! WE HAVE TO DESTROY THAT MOTHERSHIP!
WHAT DO YOU THINK WE'RE DOING? YOU TRIED TO STOP US BEFORE--WE DON'T NEED--
I'M UPLOADING A MECHANICAL PROTOCOL THAT EVERY ROBO ANYWHERE NEAR THAT MOTHERSHIP NEEDS TO IMPLEMENT NOW.
WAIT A MINUTE...
...THIS PROTOCOL'S JUST AN ENGINE GRINDER. IT'D JUST BLOW OUT A MECH'S POWER GRID AND CAUSE A MELTDOWN...
NO.
AN EXPLOSION.
GET THE ROBOS IN THE RIGHT PLACES, EJECT THE PILOTS, AND--
WHAT?
NO!
NO WAY!

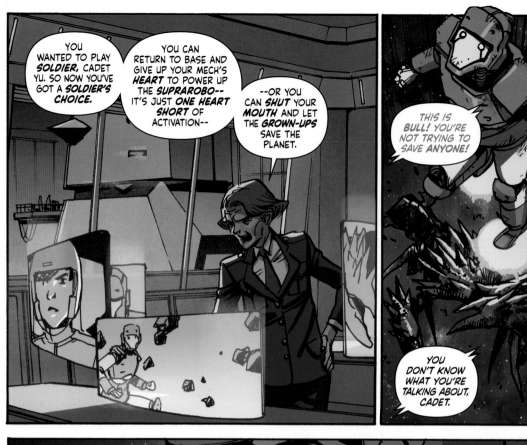

YOU WANTED TO PLAY *SOLDIER*, CADET YU. SO NOW YOU'VE GOT A *SOLDIER'S CHOICE*.

YOU CAN RETURN TO BASE AND GIVE UP YOUR MECH'S *HEART* TO POWER UP THE *SUPRAROBO*-- IT'S JUST *ONE HEART SHORT* OF ACTIVATION--

--OR YOU CAN *SHUT* YOUR *MOUTH* AND LET THE *GROWN-UPS* SAVE THE PLANET.

THIS IS *BULL!* YOU'RE NOT TRYING TO SAVE *ANYONE!*

YOU DON'T KNOW WHAT YOU'RE TALKING ABOUT, CADET.

OH, YEAH?

HOW COME *EVERY SINGLE PLAN* YOU COME UP WITH INVOLVES *KILLING OUR ROBOS?*

ALL RIGHT, FINE. LISTEN UP. ALL OF YOU.

THAT *SHARG MOTHERSHIP* IS POWERED BY *ENGINES* AND EQUIPPED WITH *WEAPONS*...

...AND AS FAR AS OUR SENSORS CAN DETERMINE, THAT *SHARG TECH* IS MADE FROM THE SAME MATERIAL AS YOUR *MECHS.*

SO THE SAME THING THAT SENT *YOUR ROBOS* MAY HAVE SENT THE *SHARG.*

WE HUMANS HAVE TO TAKE CONTROL OF *OUR OWN DESTINY.* WE CAN'T TRUST--

WITH ALL DUE RESPECT, GENERAL...

...*YOU* CAN SHUT YOUR MOUTH!

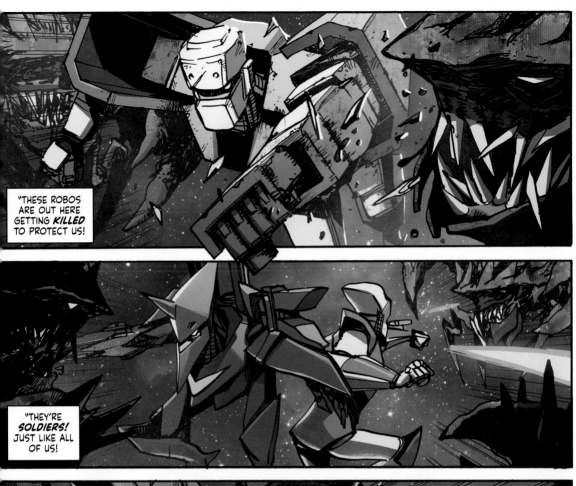

"THESE ROBOS ARE OUT HERE GETTING *KILLED* TO PROTECT US!"

"THEY'RE *SOLDIERS!* JUST LIKE ALL OF US!"

"DON'T YOU *DARE* QUESTION THEIR ALLEGIANCE!"

KTOOOM KTOOOM KTOOOM

NOW *COME ON,* YOU GUYS!

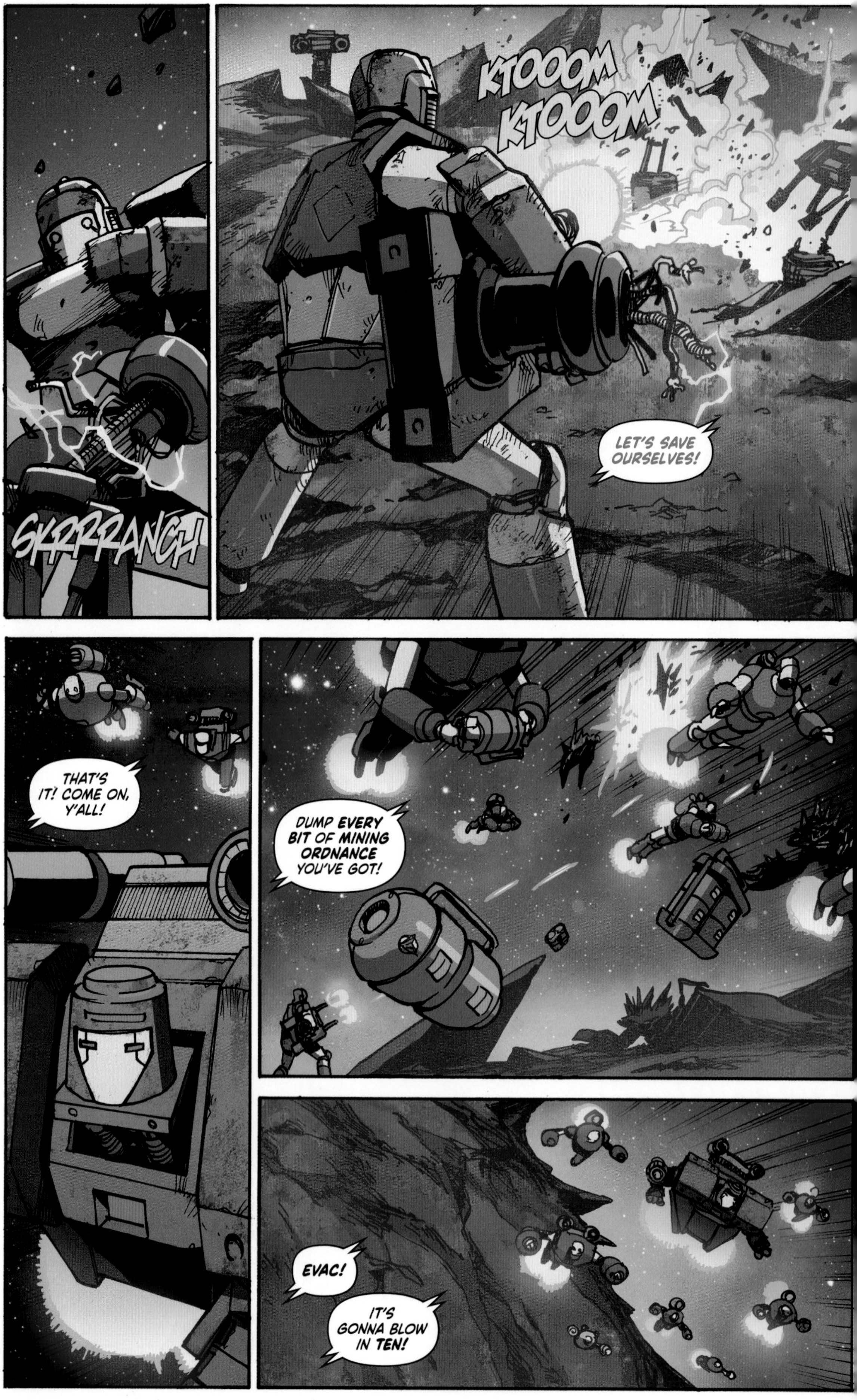
SKRRRANCH
KTOOOM
KTOOOM
LET'S SAVE OURSELVES!
THAT'S IT! COME ON, Y'ALL!
DUMP EVERY BIT OF MINING ORDNANCE YOU'VE GOT!
EVAC!
IT'S GONNA BLOW IN TEN!

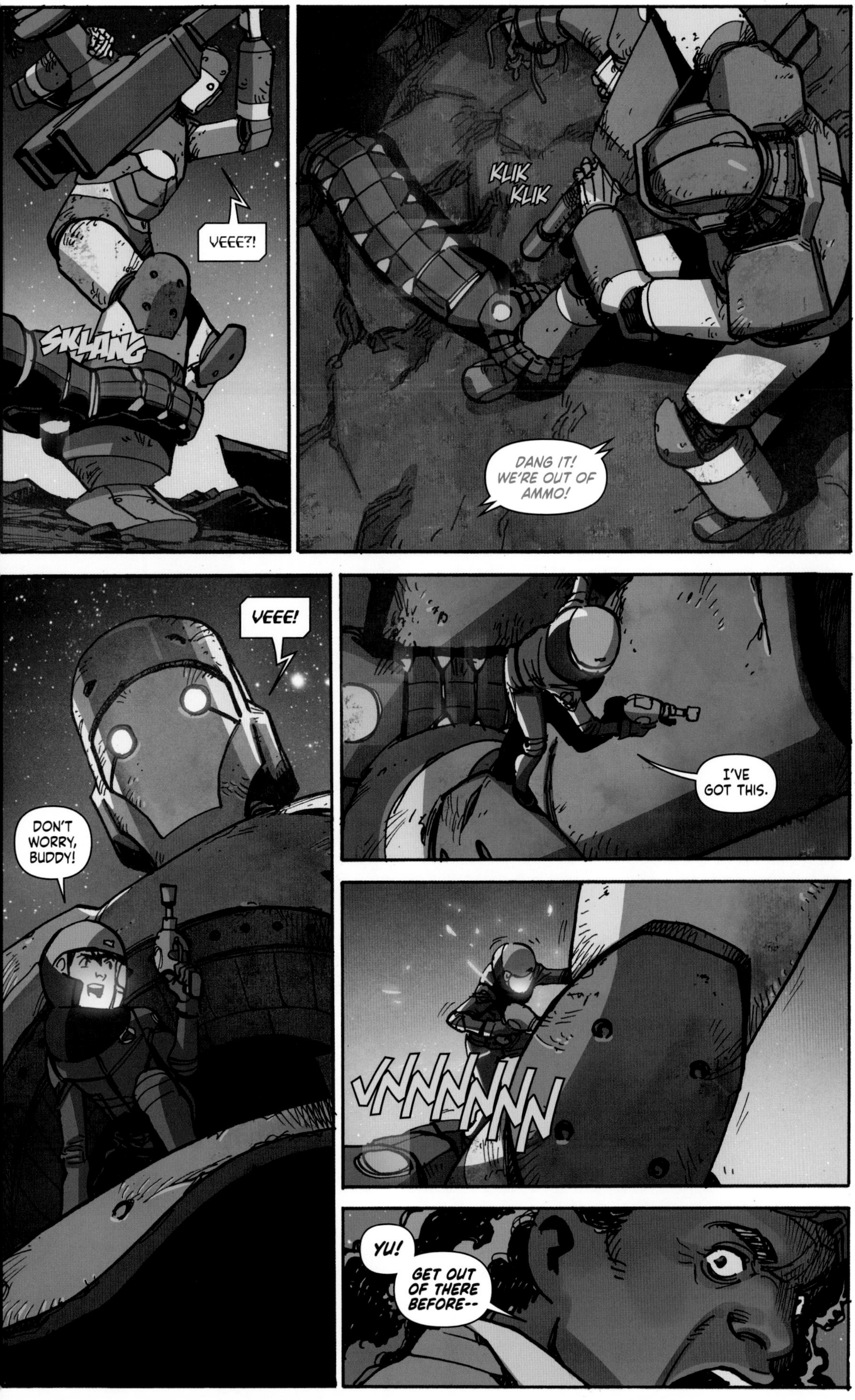
VEEE?!
SKLANG
KLIK
KLIK
DANG IT! WE'RE OUT OF AMMO!
VEEE!
DON'T WORRY, BUDDY!
I'VE GOT THIS.
VNNNNNN
YU!
GET OUT OF THERE BEFORE--

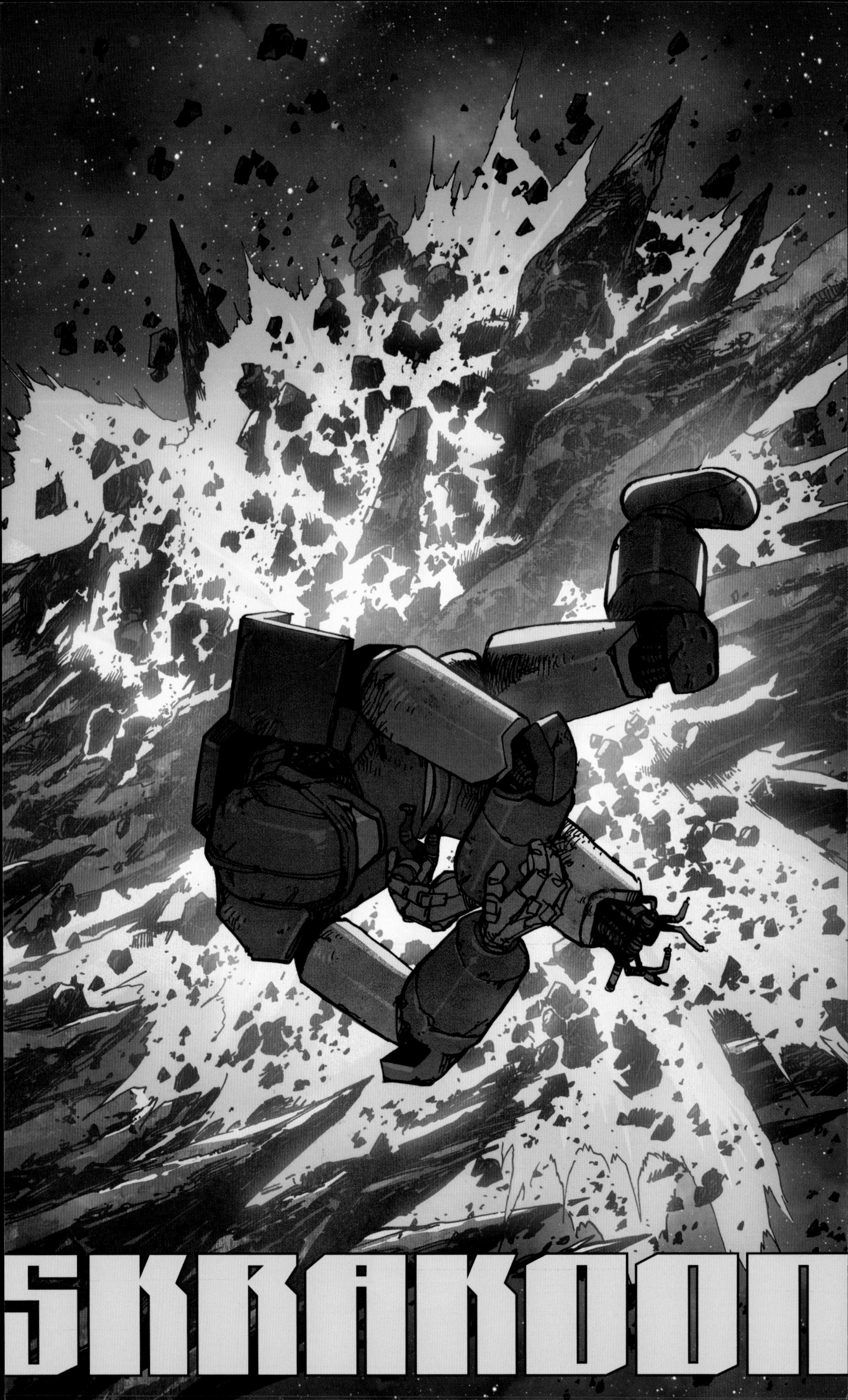
SKRAKOON

OH MY GOSH...

KRRAAAAA!

HA HA! *THE SHARG--*

THEY'RE *BURNING UP* IN THE ATMOSPHERE.

THEY DID IT.

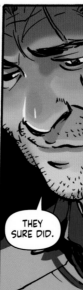

THEY SURE DID.

VEE?

OH, NO...

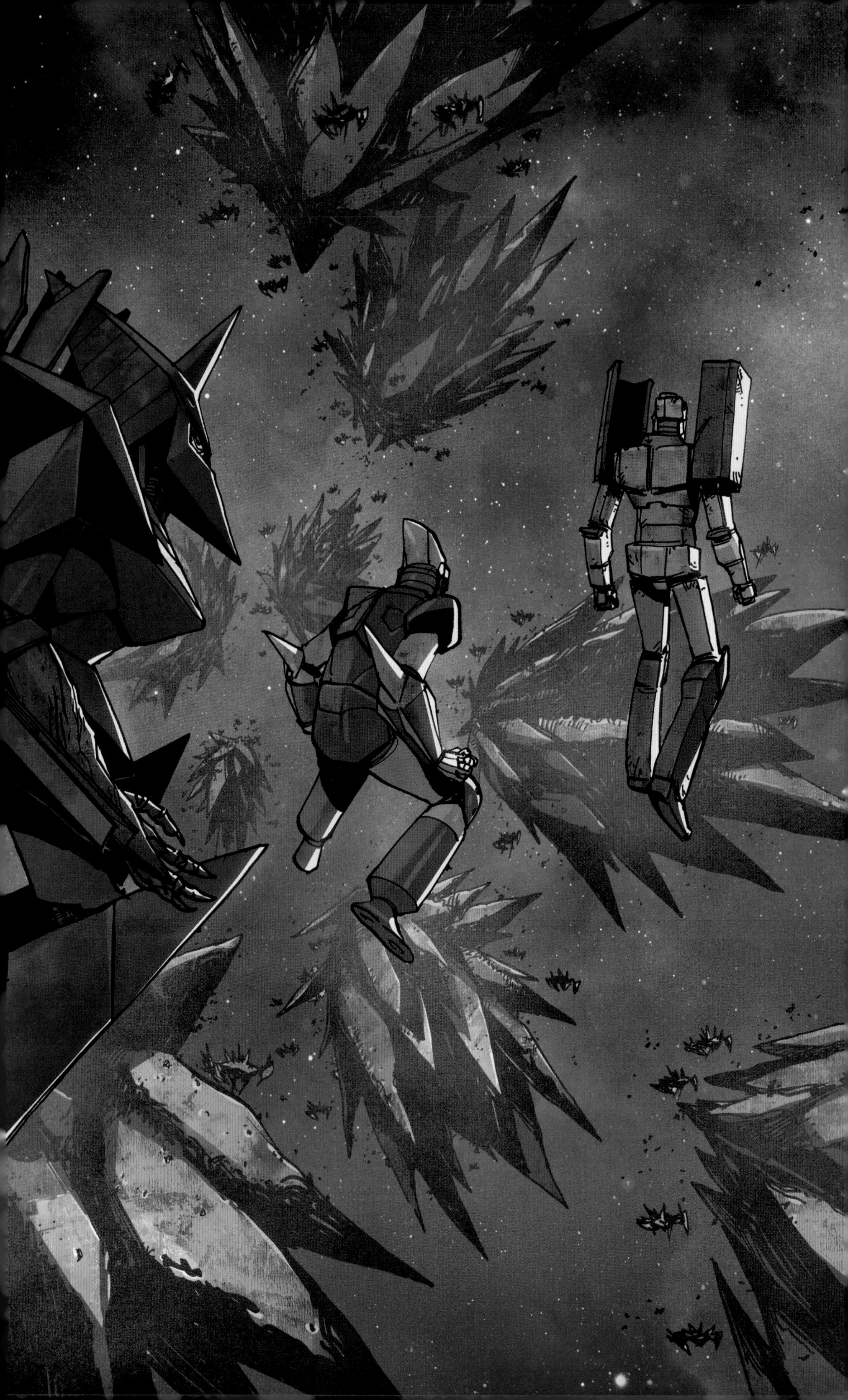

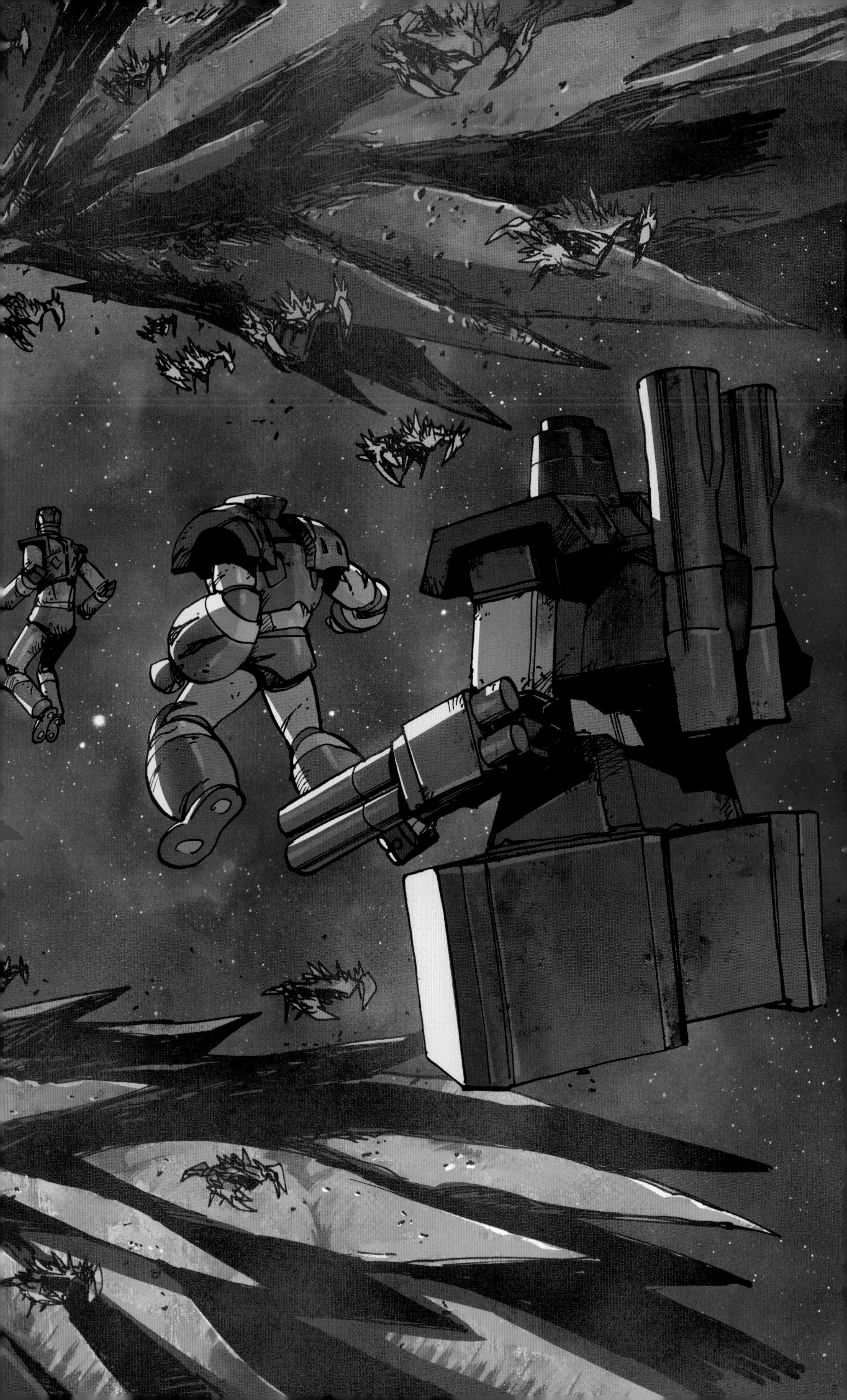

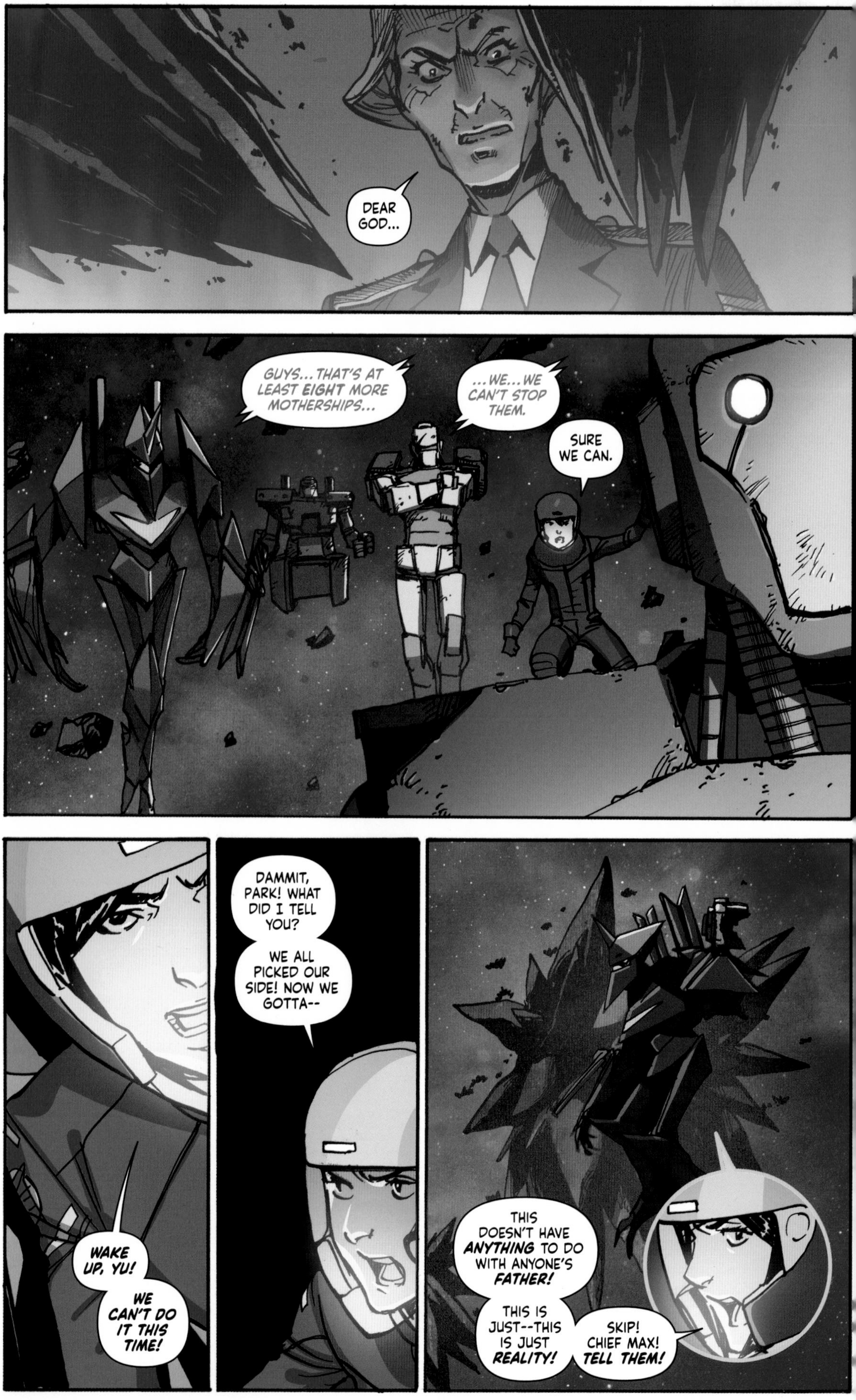
DEAR GOD...
GUYS... THAT'S AT LEAST EIGHT MORE MOTHERSHIPS...
...WE... WE CAN'T STOP THEM.
SURE WE CAN.
WAKE UP, YU!
WE CAN'T DO IT THIS TIME!
DAMMIT, PARK! WHAT DID I TELL YOU?
WE ALL PICKED OUR SIDE! NOW WE GOTTA--
THIS DOESN'T HAVE ANYTHING TO DO WITH ANYONE'S FATHER!
THIS IS JUST--THIS IS JUST REALITY!
SKIP! CHIEF MAX! TELL THEM!

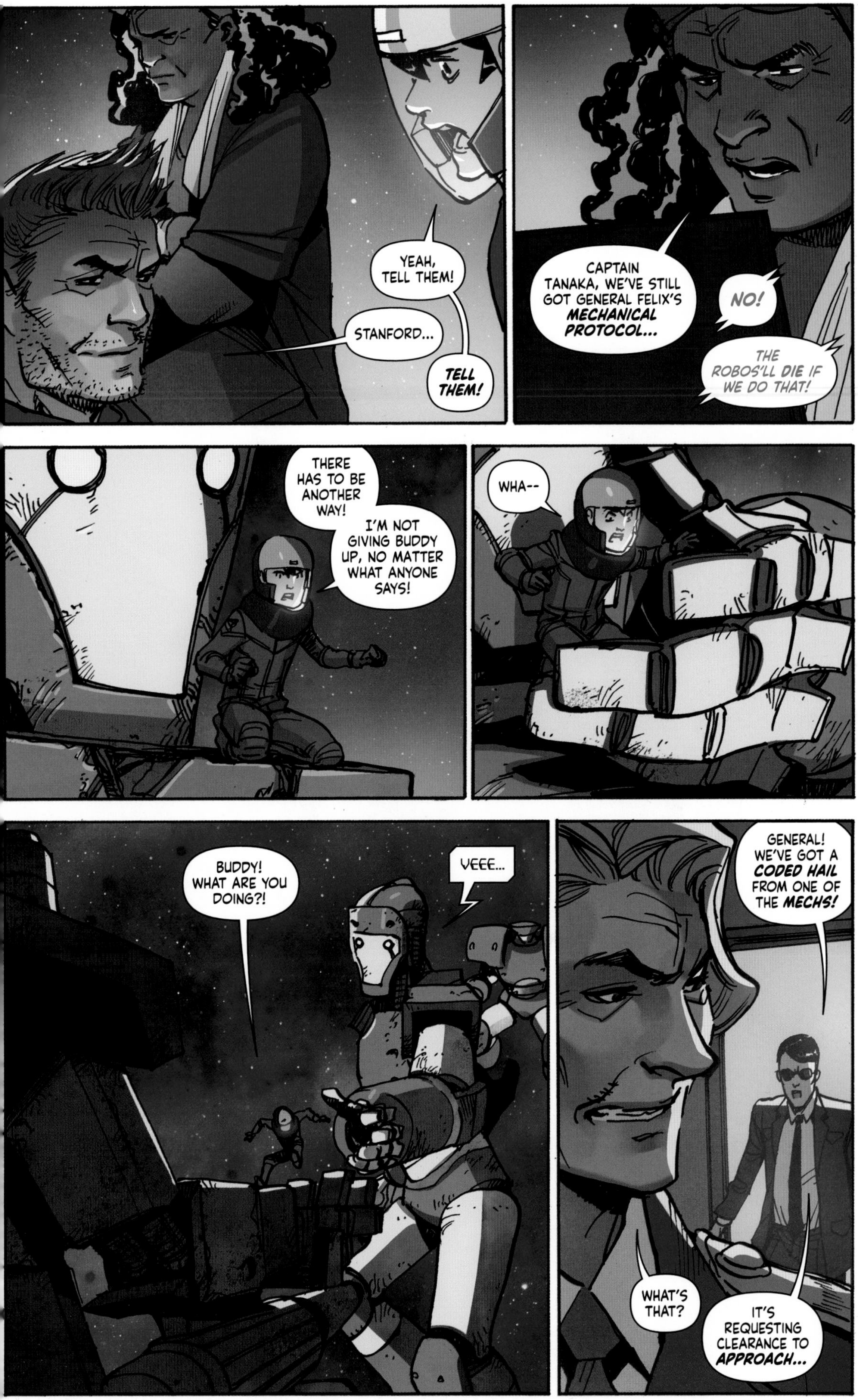
YEAH, TELL THEM!
STANFORD...
TELL THEM!
CAPTAIN TANAKA, WE'VE STILL GOT GENERAL FELIX'S MECHANICAL PROTOCOL...
NO!
THE ROBOS'LL DIE IF WE DO THAT!
THERE HAS TO BE ANOTHER WAY!
I'M NOT GIVING BUDDY UP, NO MATTER WHAT ANYONE SAYS!
WHA--
BUDDY! WHAT ARE YOU DOING?!
VEEE...
GENERAL! WE'VE GOT A CODED HAIL FROM ONE OF THE MECHS!
WHAT'S THAT?
IT'S REQUESTING CLEARANCE TO APPROACH...

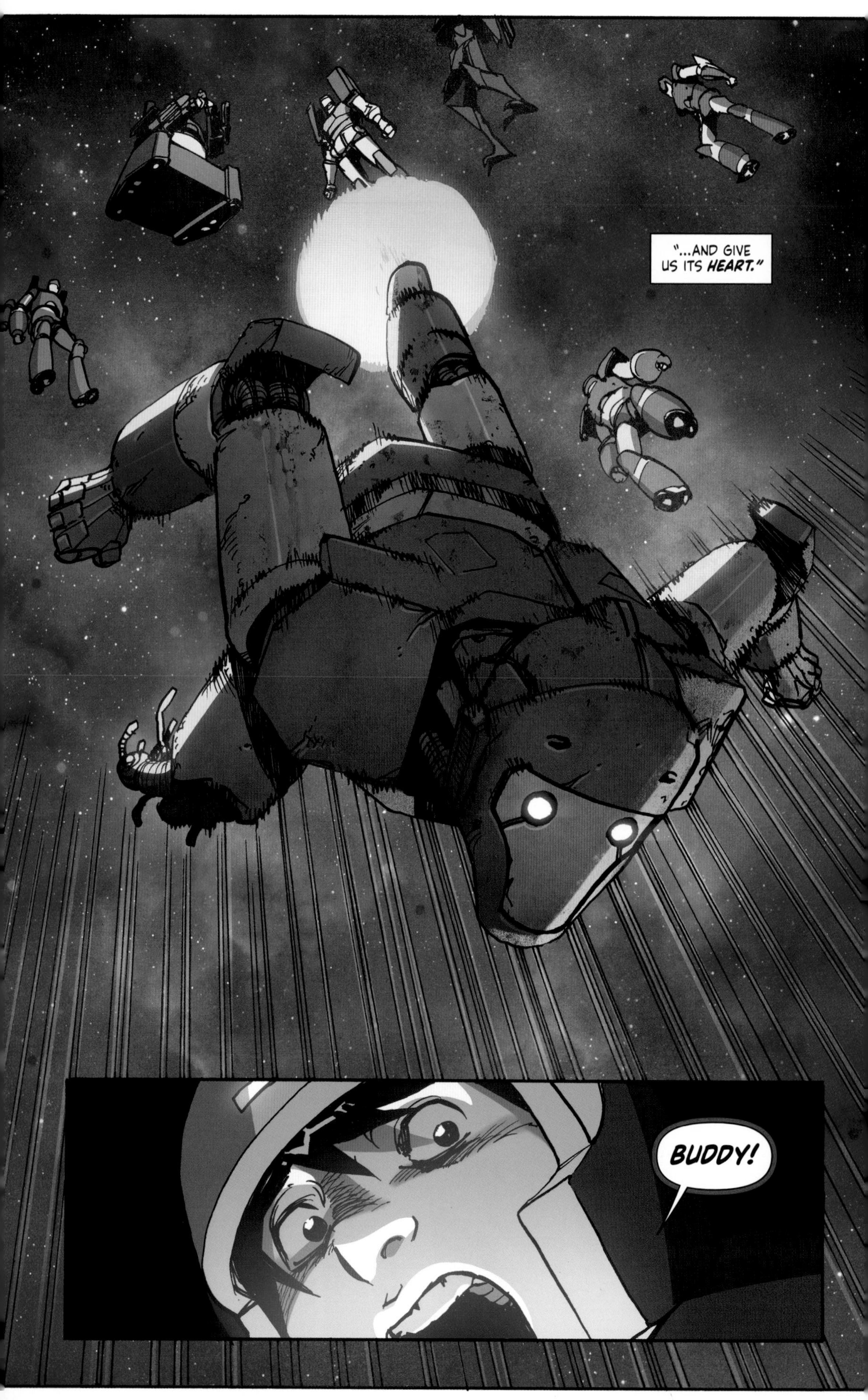
"...AND GIVE US ITS HEART."
BUDDY!

CHAPTER
TEN

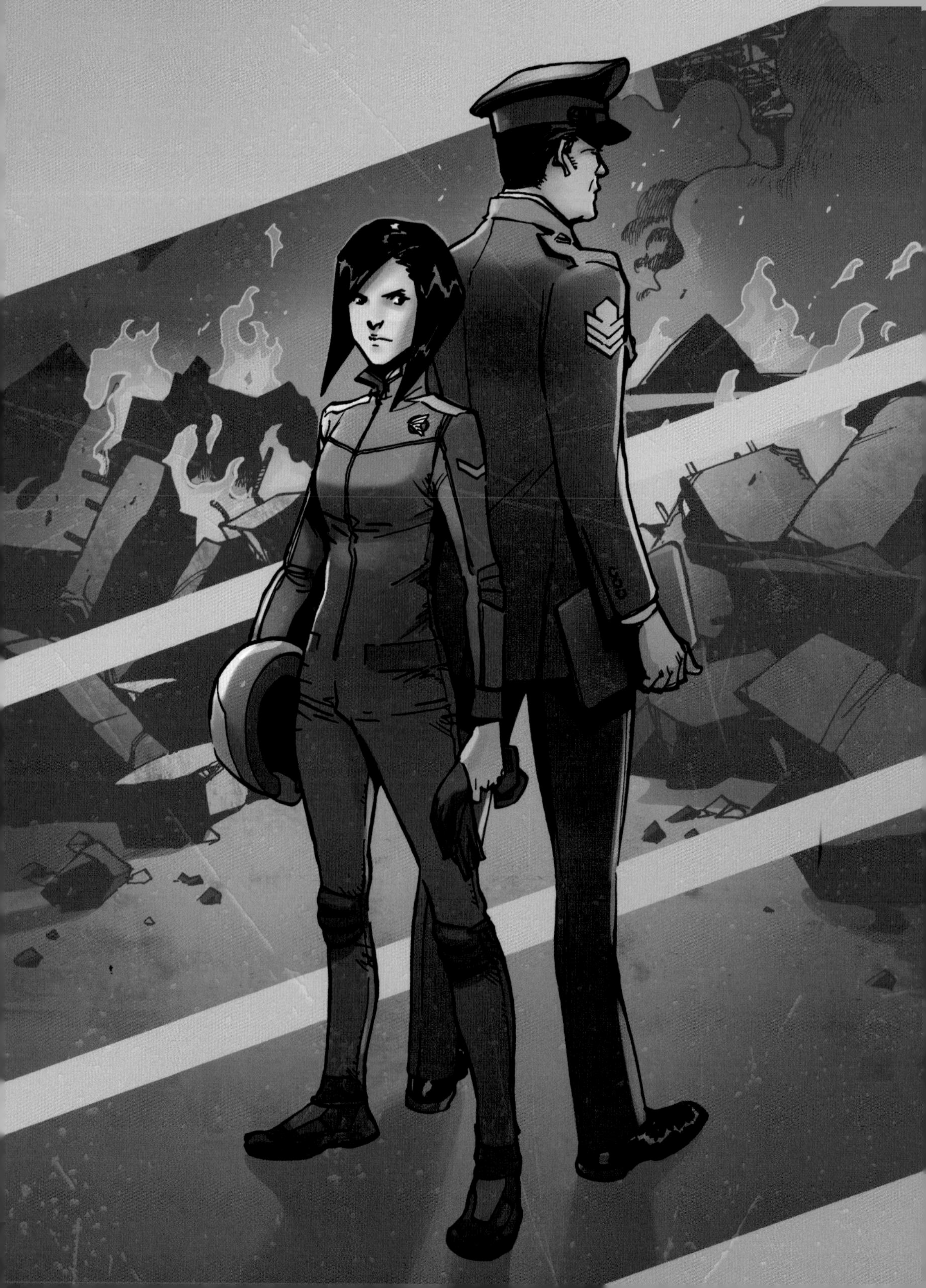

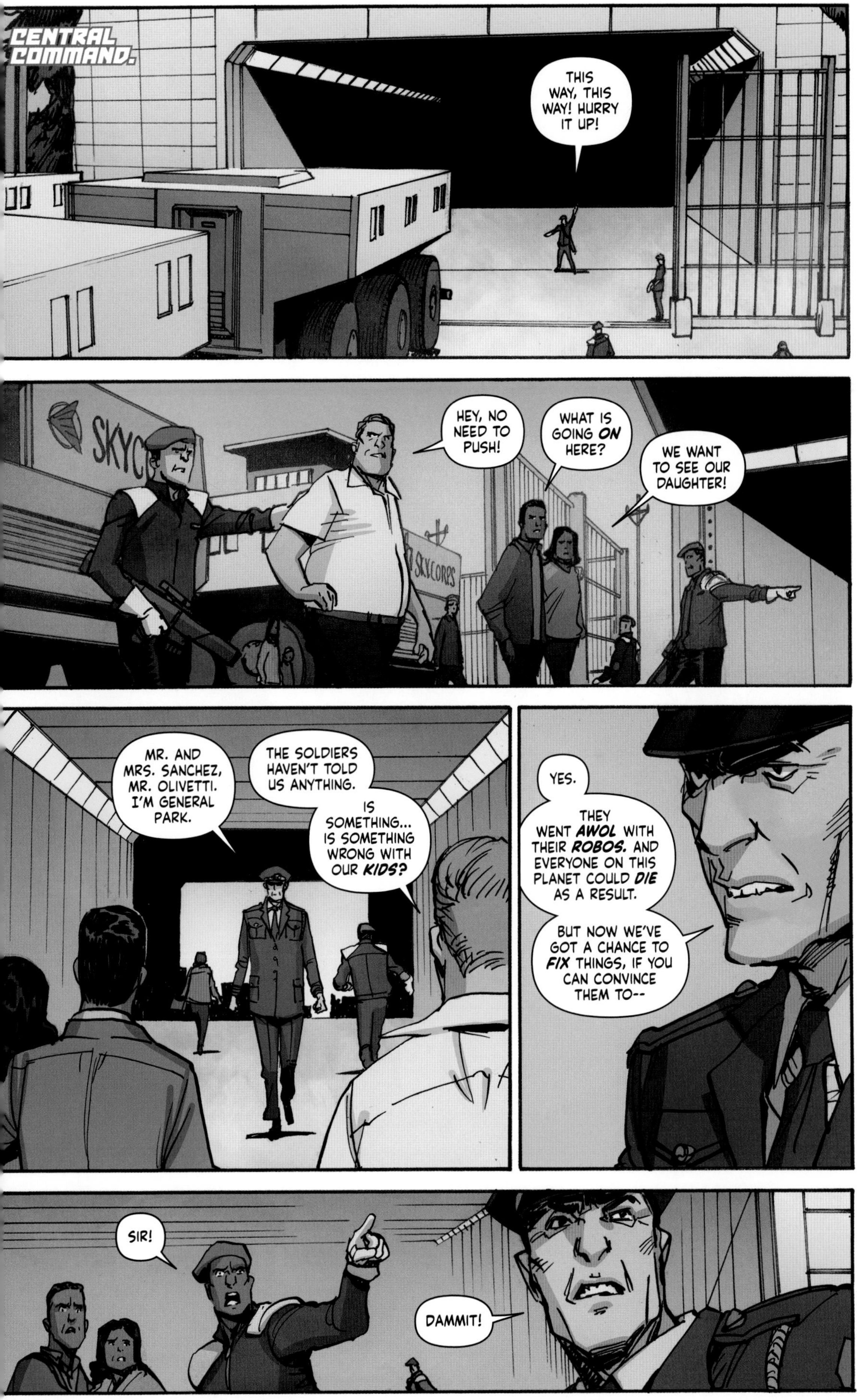
CENTRAL COMMAND.
THIS WAY, THIS WAY! HURRY IT UP!
SKYC
SKYCORPS
HEY, NO NEED TO PUSH!
WHAT IS GOING ON HERE?
WE WANT TO SEE OUR DAUGHTER!
MR. AND MRS. SANCHEZ, MR. OLIVETTI. I'M GENERAL PARK.
THE SOLDIERS HAVEN'T TOLD US ANYTHING.
IS SOMETHING... IS SOMETHING WRONG WITH OUR KIDS?
YES.
THEY WENT AWOL WITH THEIR ROBOS. AND EVERYONE ON THIS PLANET COULD DIE AS A RESULT.
BUT NOW WE'VE GOT A CHANCE TO FIX THINGS, IF YOU CAN CONVINCE THEM TO--
SIR!
DAMMIT!

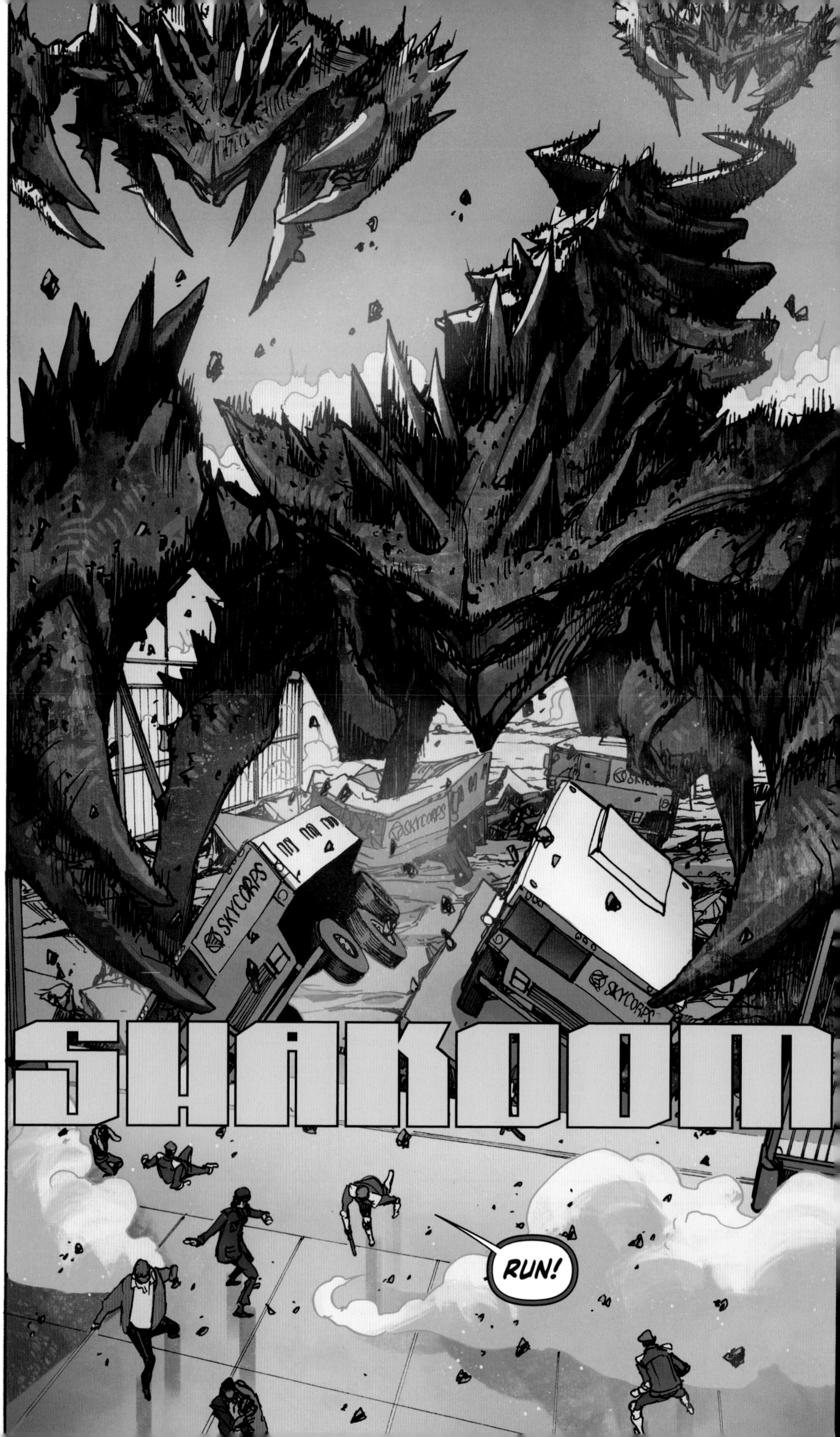
SKYCORPS
SKYCORPS
SKYCORPS
SHAKOOM
RUN!

SIXTY-TWO MILES ABOVE.

CADETS! THIS IS GENERAL PARK!

YOUR PARENTS ARE NOW AT THE FACILITY--

--AND WE ARE UNDER ATTACK BY THE SHARG!

WHAT?

DID I STUTTER, OLIVETTI?

OUR PARENTS?

YES, SANCHEZ! YOU NEED TO RETURN TO BASE IMMEDIATELY!

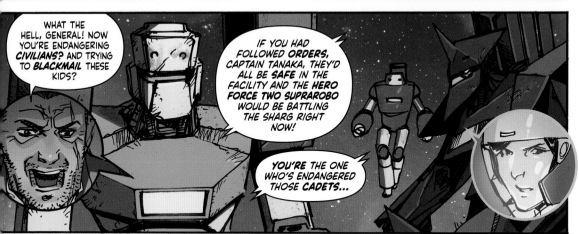

WHAT THE HELL, GENERAL! NOW YOU'RE ENDANGERING CIVILIANS? AND TRYING TO BLACKMAIL THESE KIDS?

IF YOU HAD FOLLOWED ORDERS, CAPTAIN TANAKA, THEY'D ALL BE SAFE IN THE FACILITY AND THE HERO FORCE TWO SUPRAROBO WOULD BE BATTLING THE SHARG RIGHT NOW!

YOU'RE THE ONE WHO'S ENDANGERED THOSE CADETS...

...INCLUDING MY OWN DAUGHTER!

DADDY...

I THOUGHT YOU KNEW YOUR DUTY BETTER THAN THIS, OLIVIA! GET BACK TO THE BASE, NOW, AND BRING YOUR FRIENDS WITH YOU!

WE NEED THOSE MECHS' POWER CORES OR WE'RE ALL DOOMED!

IT'S TOO LATE, DADDY...

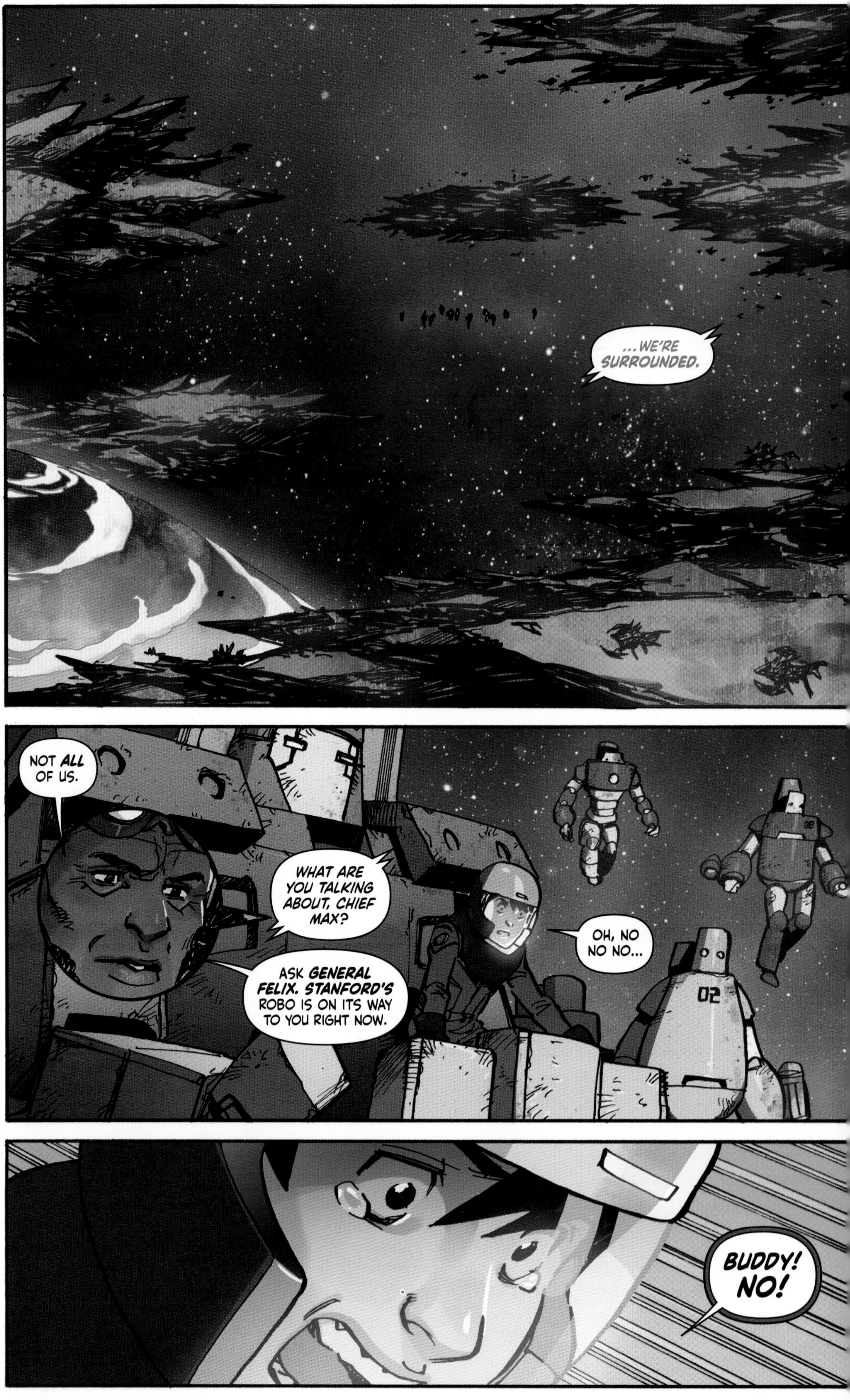
...WE'RE SURROUNDED.
NOT ALL OF US.
WHAT ARE YOU TALKING ABOUT, CHIEF MAX?
ASK GENERAL FELIX. STANFORD'S ROBO IS ON ITS WAY TO YOU RIGHT NOW.
OH, NO NO NO...
02
BUDDY! NO!

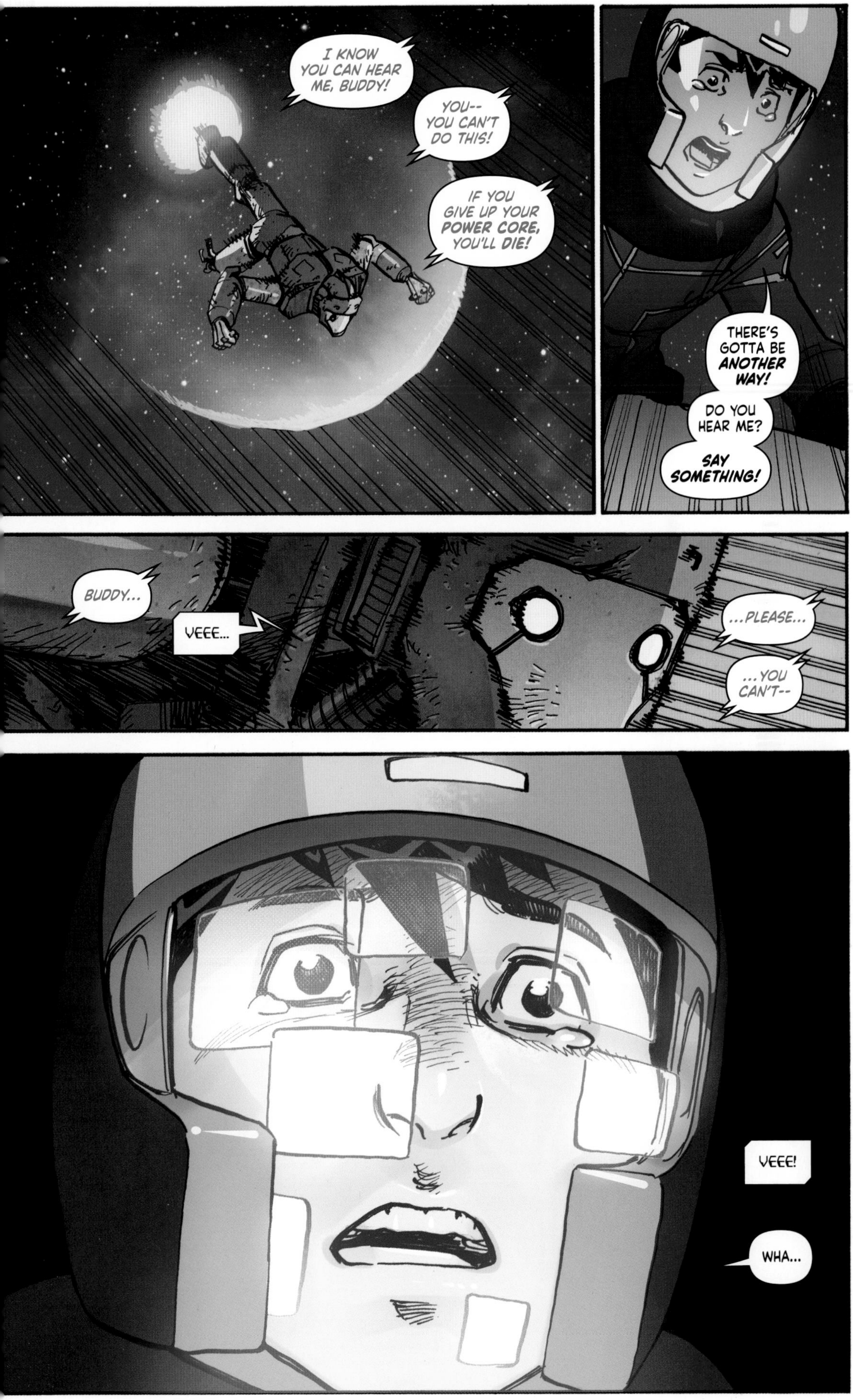
I KNOW YOU CAN HEAR ME, BUDDY!
YOU-- YOU CAN'T DO THIS!
IF YOU GIVE UP YOUR POWER CORE, YOU'LL DIE!
THERE'S GOTTA BE ANOTHER WAY!
DO YOU HEAR ME?
SAY SOMETHING!
BUDDY...
VEEE...
...PLEASE...
...YOU CAN'T--
VEEE!
WHA...

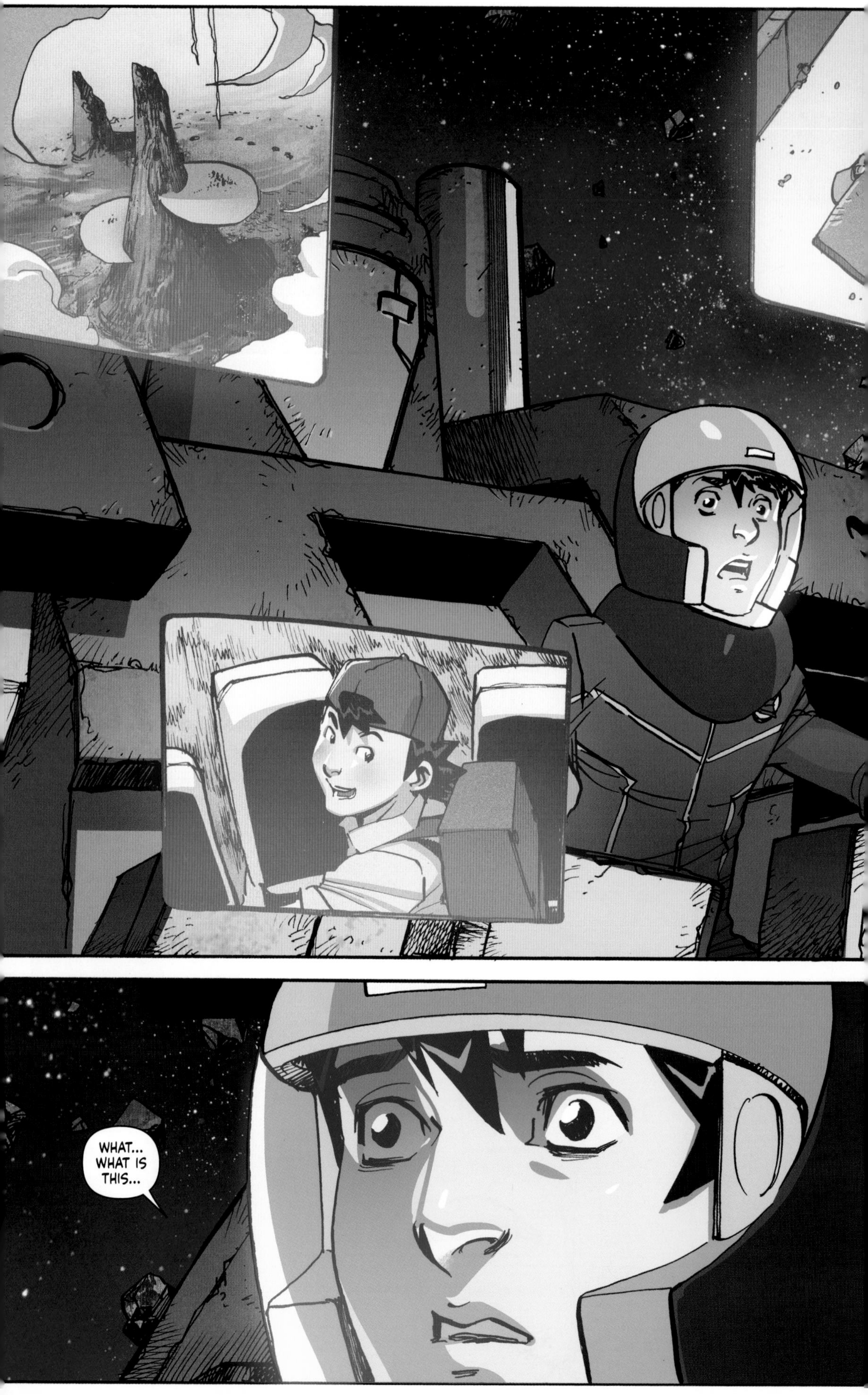
WHAT... WHAT IS THIS...

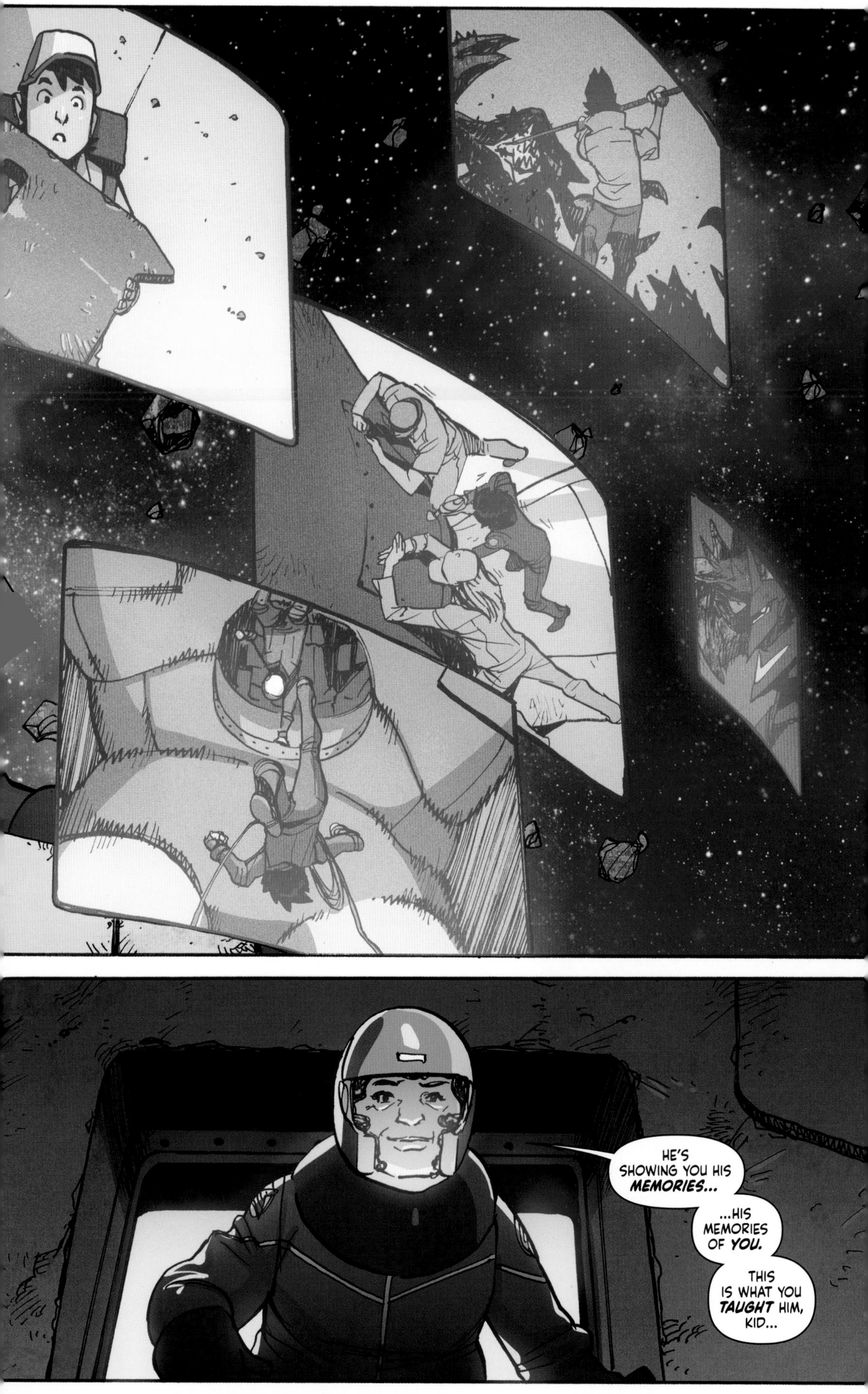
HE'S SHOWING YOU HIS *MEMORIES...*
...HIS MEMORIES OF *YOU.*
THIS IS WHAT YOU *TAUGHT* HIM, KID...

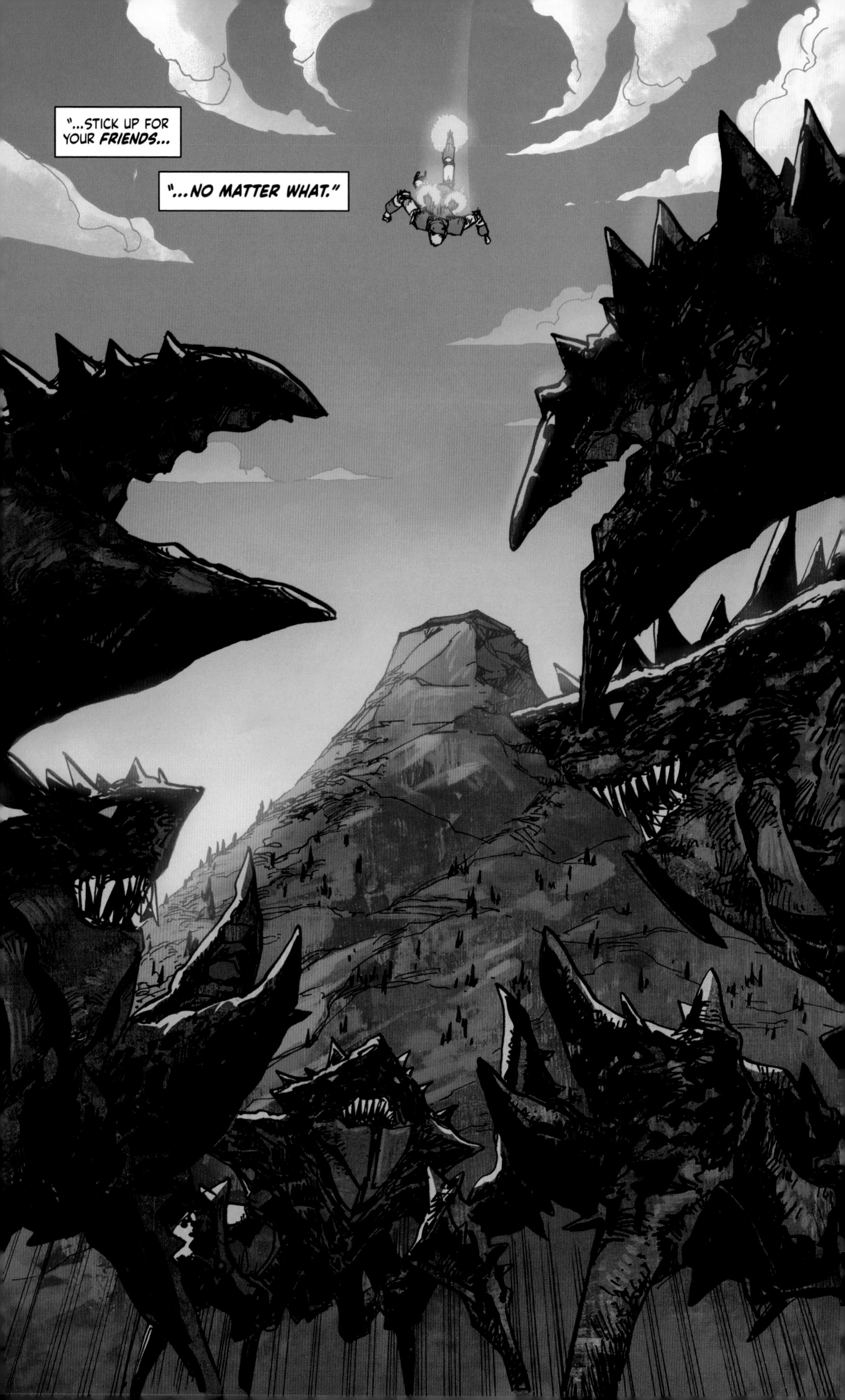
"...STICK UP FOR YOUR FRIENDS...
"...NO MATTER WHAT."

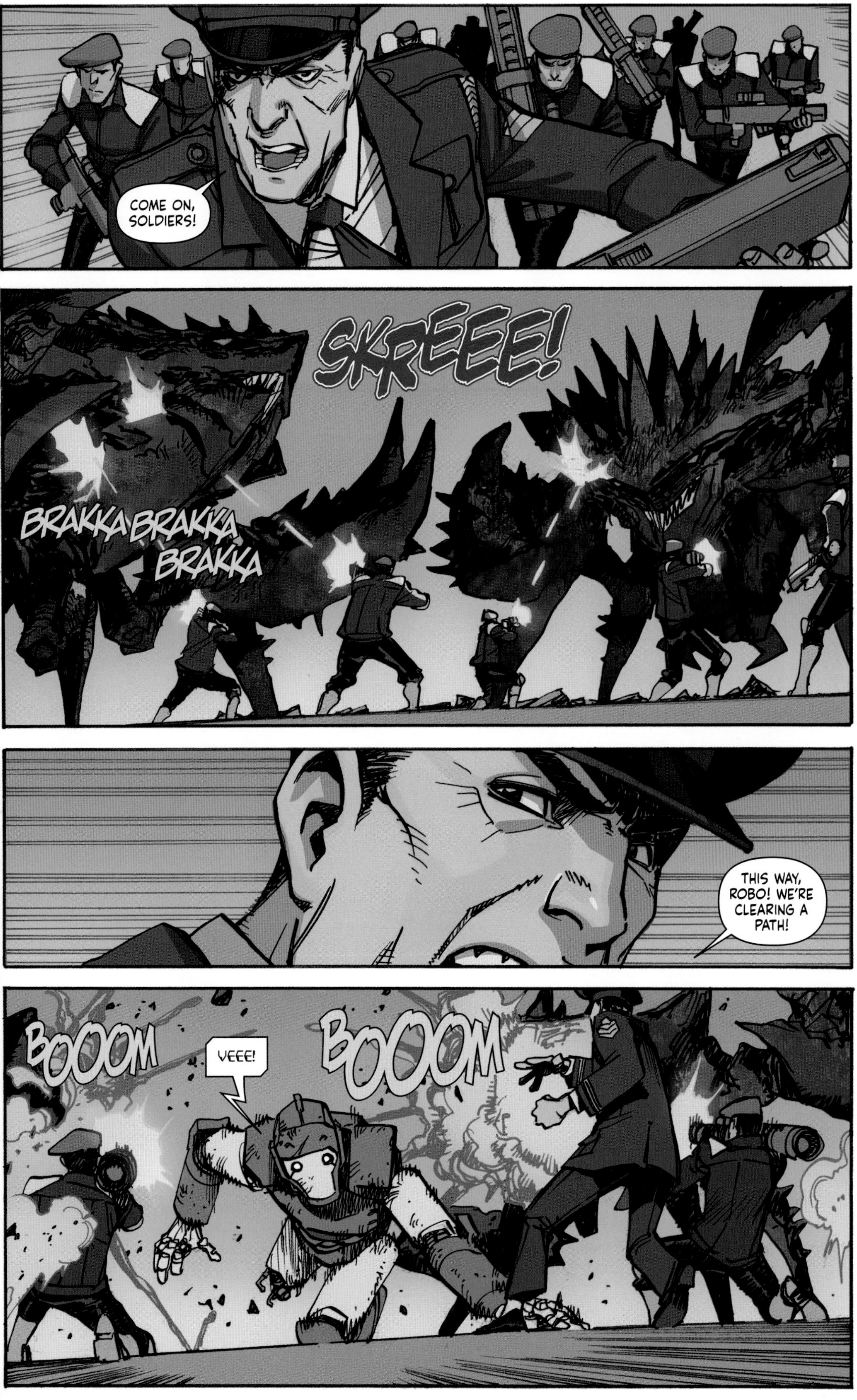
COME ON, SOLDIERS!
SKREEE!
BRAKKA BRAKKA BRAKKA
THIS WAY, ROBO! WE'RE CLEARING A PATH!
BOOOM
VEEE!
BOOOM

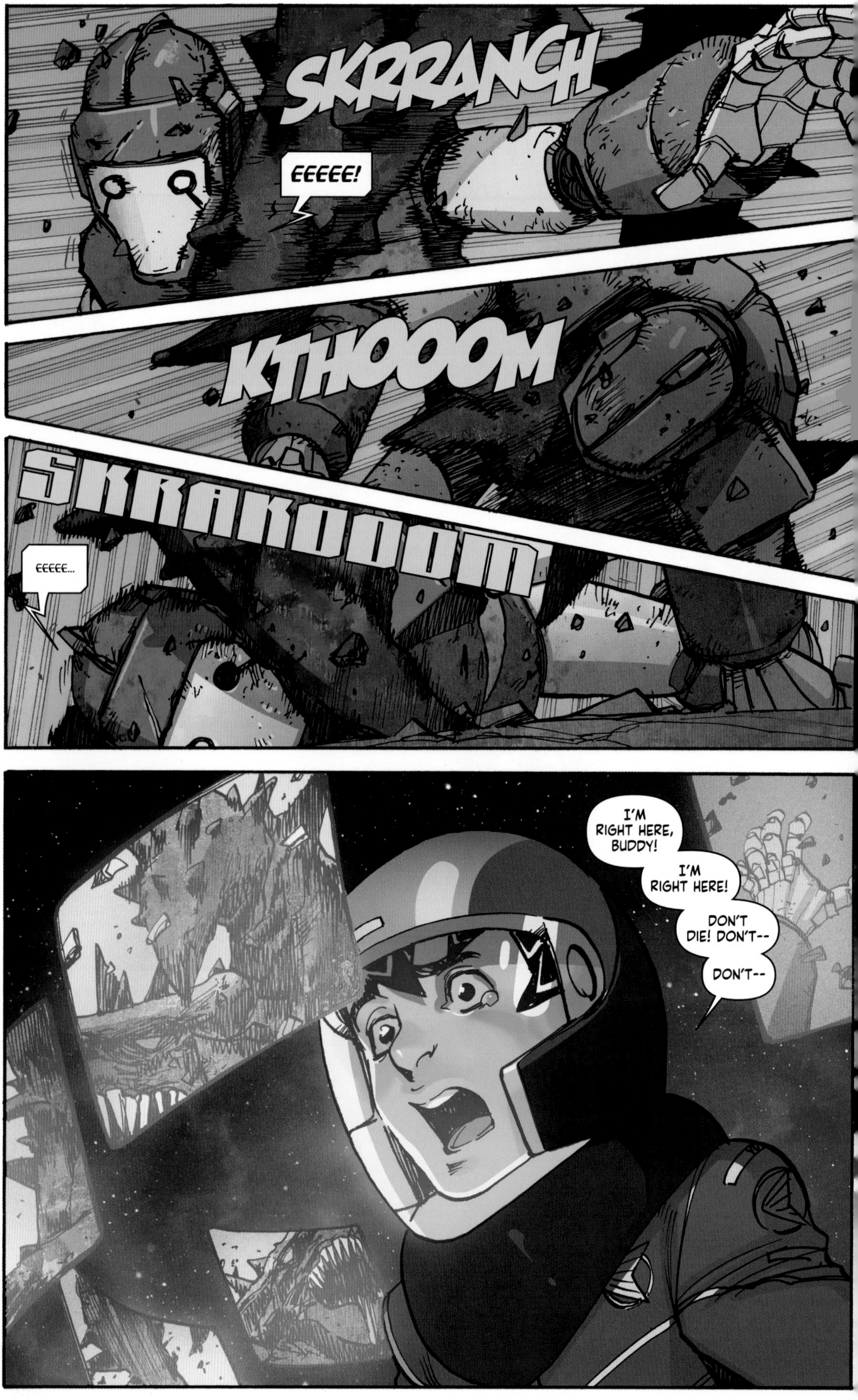
SKRRANCH
EEEEE!
KTHOOOM
SKRAKOOOM
EEEEE...
I'M RIGHT HERE, BUDDY!
I'M RIGHT HERE!
DON'T DIE! DON'T--
DON'T--

CHIEF MAX! YOU AND YOUR CREW FOLLOW ME!

RIGHT BEHIND YOU, CAPTAIN!

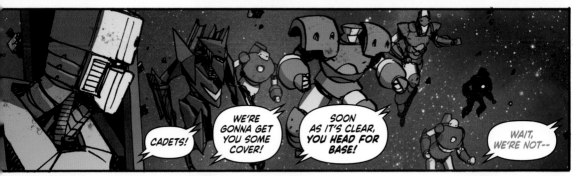

CADETS!

WE'RE GONNA GET YOU SOME COVER!

SOON AS IT'S CLEAR, *YOU HEAD FOR BASE!*

WAIT, WE'RE NOT--

HERE, PARK. WATCH OUT FOR STANFORD.

HEY, WHAT--

WAIT A MINUTE, WE'RE NOT--

NO *ARGUING*, PARK. THIS ISN'T ABOUT *RUNNING AWAY.*

WE'RE ALL DOING WHAT WE HAVE TO DO, AND THIS IS YOUR *JOB.*

THAT'S EXACTLY IT.

IF THINGS DON'T WORK OUT *UP HERE...*

...IT'S UP TO YOU CADETS TO SAVE THE WORLD *DOWN THERE.*

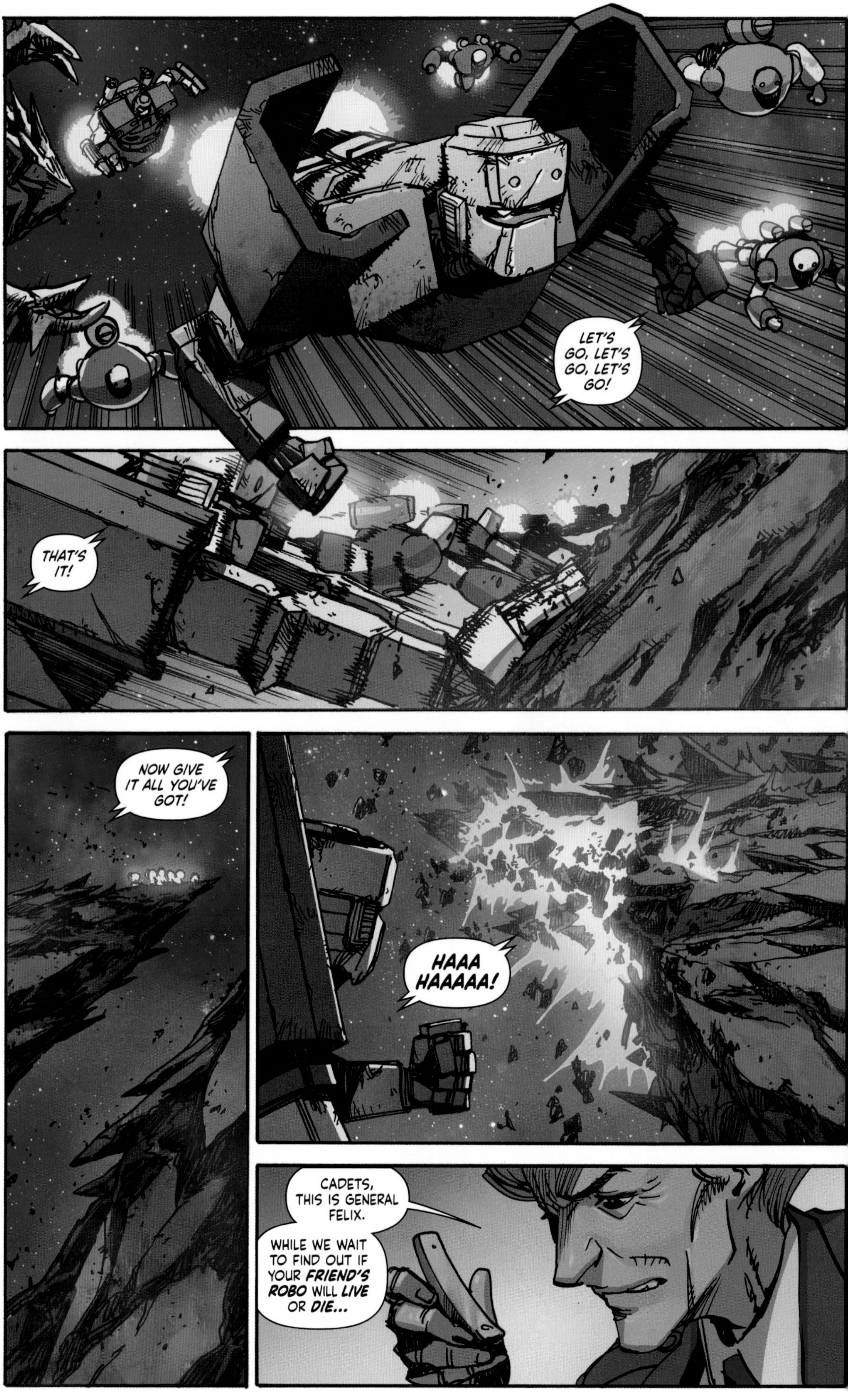
LET'S GO, LET'S GO, LET'S GO!
THAT'S IT!
NOW GIVE IT ALL YOU'VE GOT!
HAAA HAAAAA!
CADETS, THIS IS GENERAL FELIX.
WHILE WE WAIT TO FIND OUT IF YOUR FRIEND'S ROBO WILL LIVE OR DIE...

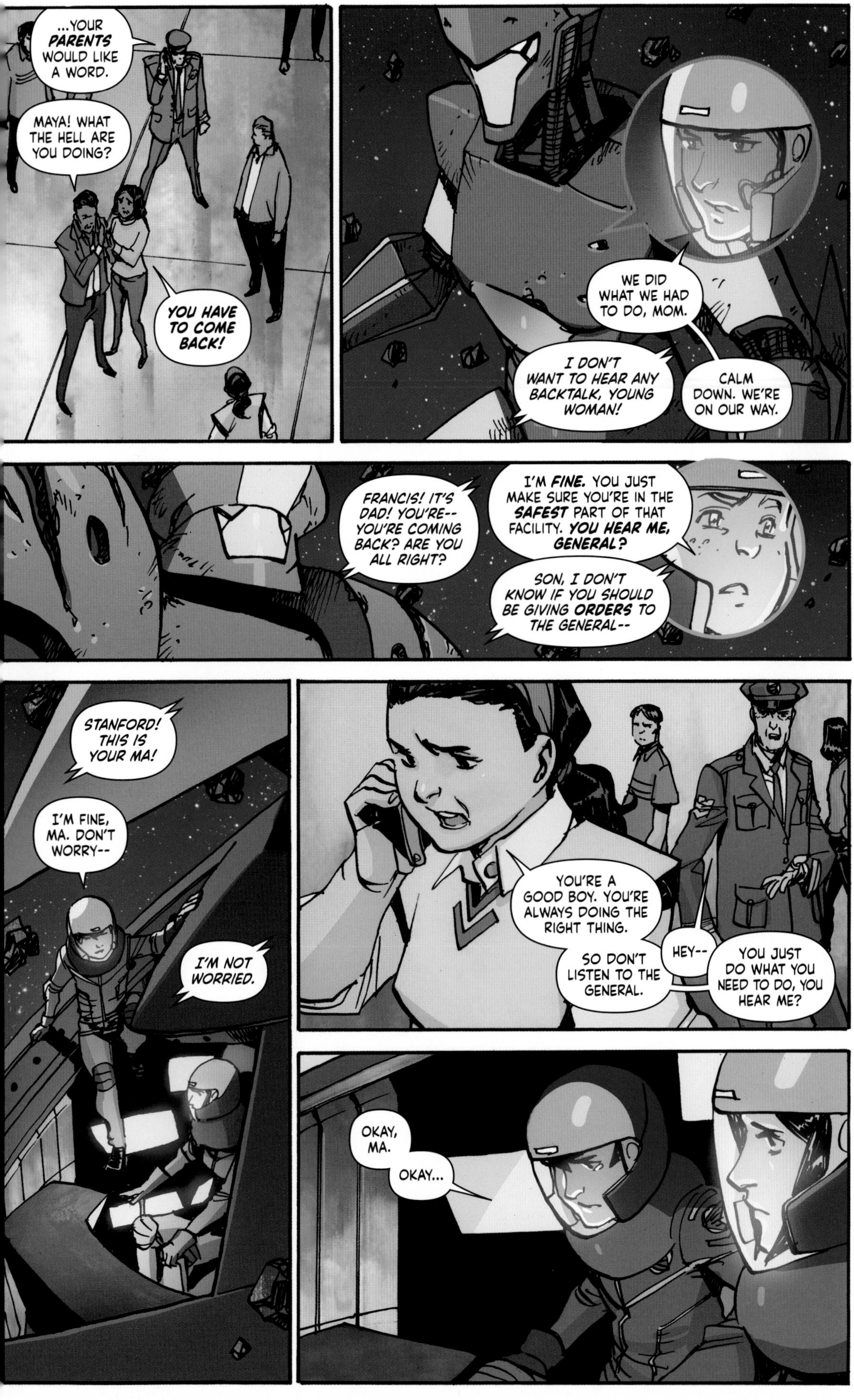
...YOUR PARENTS WOULD LIKE A WORD.
MAYA! WHAT THE HELL ARE YOU DOING?
YOU HAVE TO COME BACK!
WE DID WHAT WE HAD TO DO, MOM.
I DON'T WANT TO HEAR ANY BACKTALK, YOUNG WOMAN!
CALM DOWN. WE'RE ON OUR WAY.
FRANCIS! IT'S DAD! YOU'RE-- YOU'RE COMING BACK? ARE YOU ALL RIGHT?
I'M FINE. YOU JUST MAKE SURE YOU'RE IN THE SAFEST PART OF THAT FACILITY. YOU HEAR ME, GENERAL?
SON, I DON'T KNOW IF YOU SHOULD BE GIVING ORDERS TO THE GENERAL--
STANFORD! THIS IS YOUR MA!
I'M FINE, MA. DON'T WORRY--
I'M NOT WORRIED.
YOU'RE A GOOD BOY. YOU'RE ALWAYS DOING THE RIGHT THING.
SO DON'T LISTEN TO THE GENERAL.
HEY--
YOU JUST DO WHAT YOU NEED TO DO, YOU HEAR ME?
OKAY, MA.
OKAY...

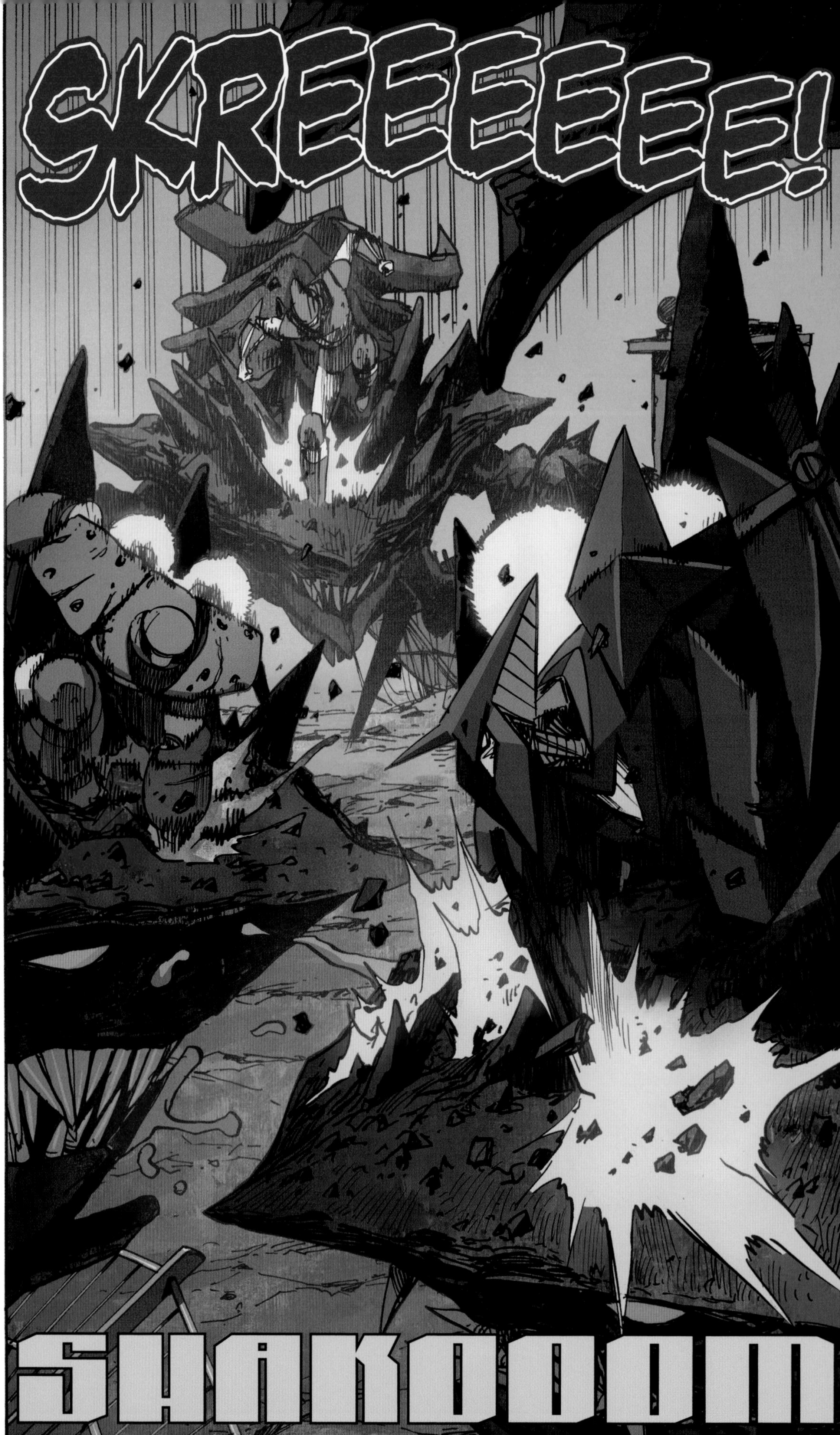
SKREEEEEEE!
SHAKOOOM

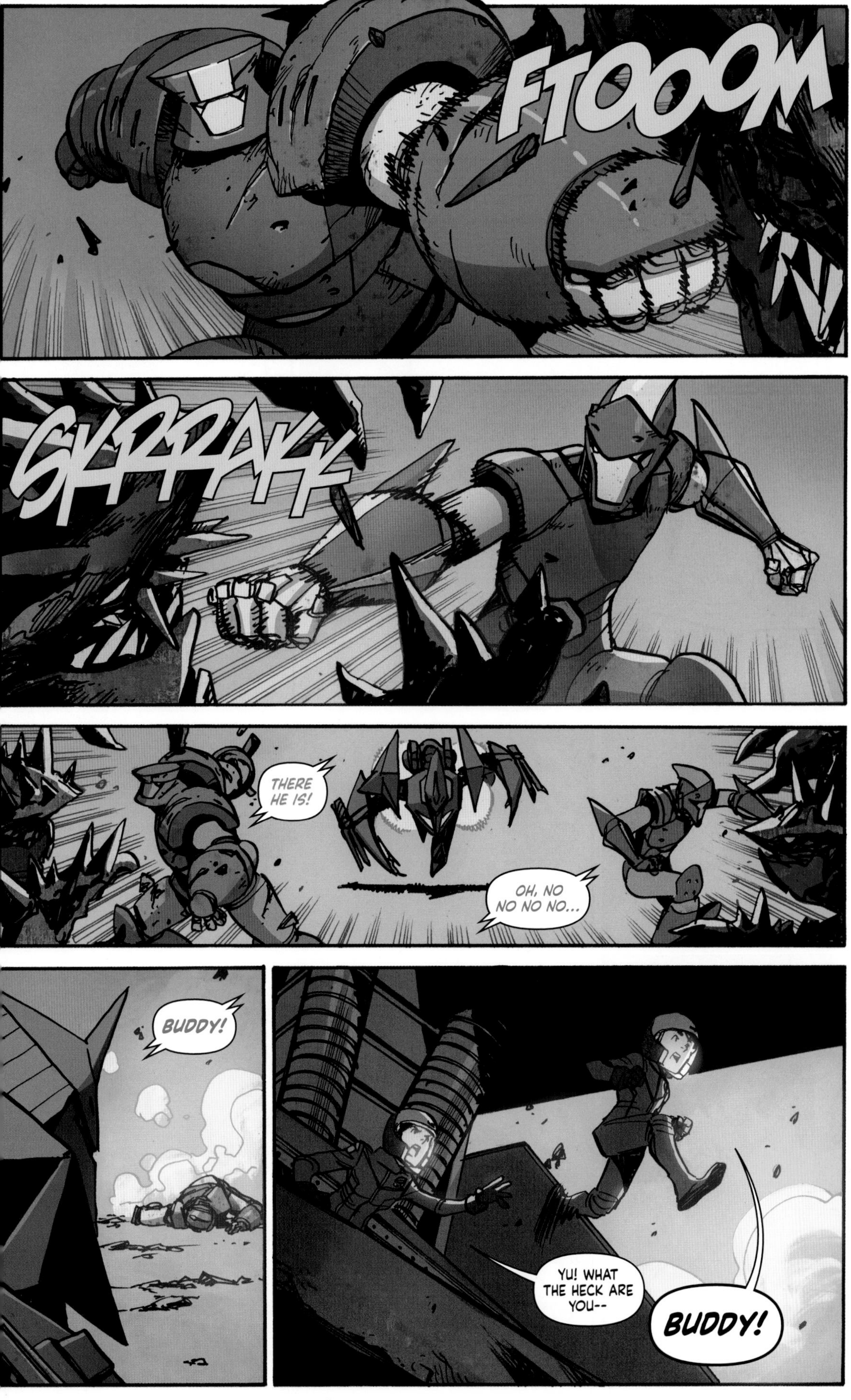
FTOOOM
SKRRAKK
THERE HE IS!
OH, NO NO NO NO...
BUDDY!
YU! WHAT THE HECK ARE YOU--
BUDDY!

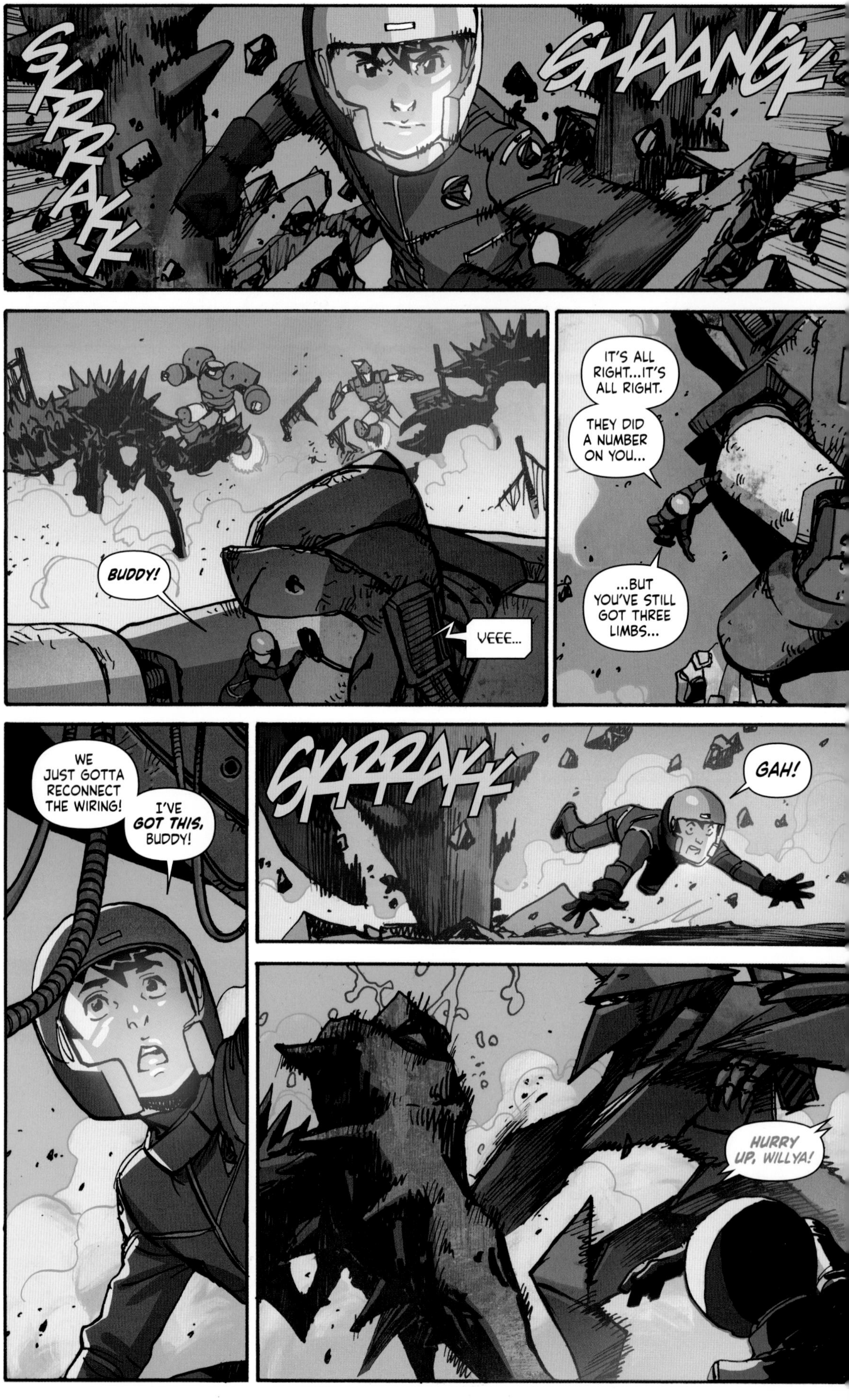
SKRRAKK
SHAANGK
BUDDY!
VEEE...
IT'S ALL RIGHT...IT'S ALL RIGHT.
THEY DID A NUMBER ON YOU...
...BUT YOU'VE STILL GOT THREE LIMBS...
WE JUST GOTTA RECONNECT THE WIRING!
I'VE GOT THIS, BUDDY!
SKRRAKK
GAH!
HURRY UP, WILLYA!

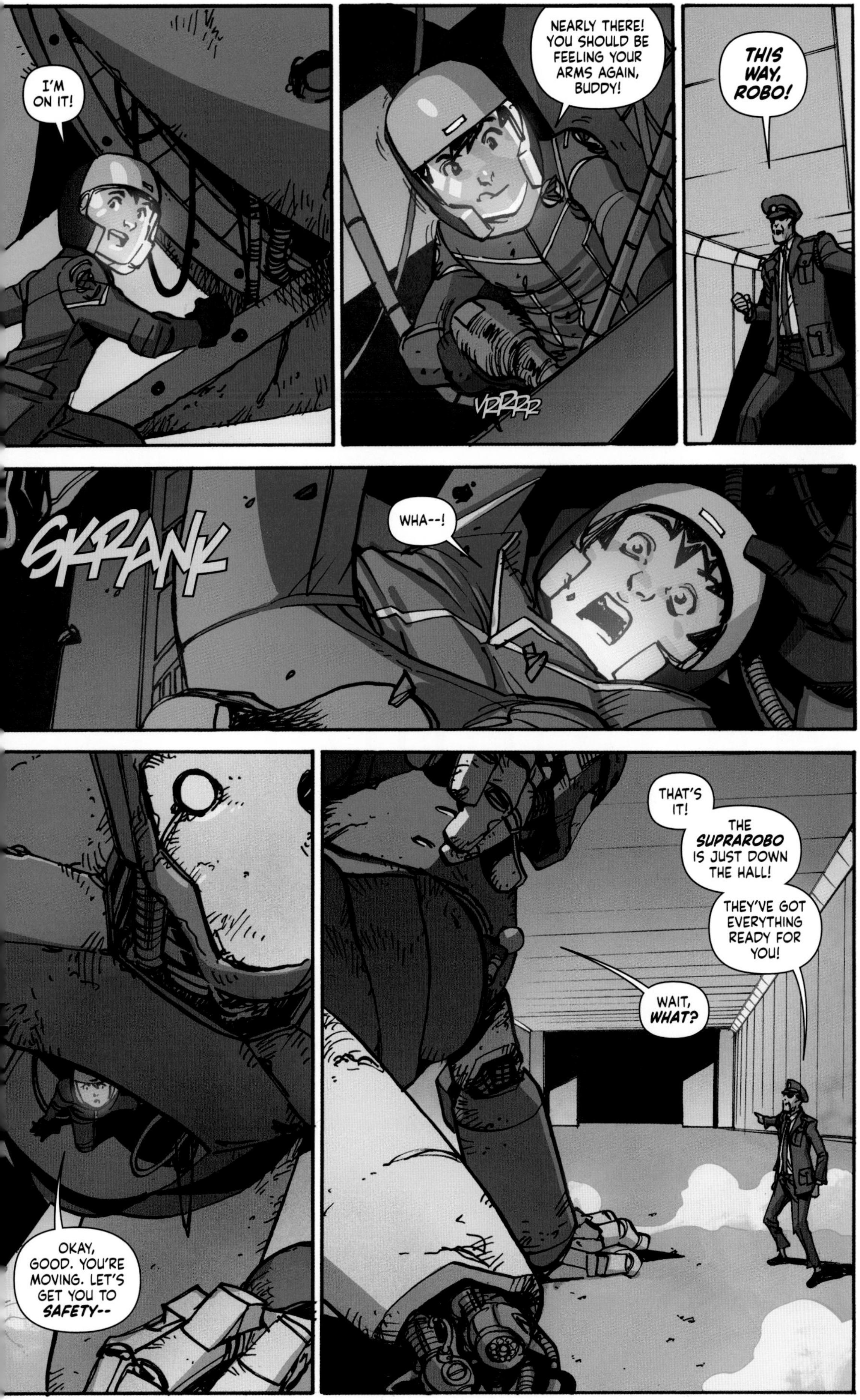
I'M ON IT!
NEARLY THERE! YOU SHOULD BE FEELING YOUR ARMS AGAIN, BUDDY!
VRRRR
THIS WAY, ROBO!
SKRANK
WHA--!
OKAY, GOOD. YOU'RE MOVING. LET'S GET YOU TO SAFETY--
THAT'S IT!
THE SUPRAROBO IS JUST DOWN THE HALL!
THEY'VE GOT EVERYTHING READY FOR YOU!
WAIT, WHAT?

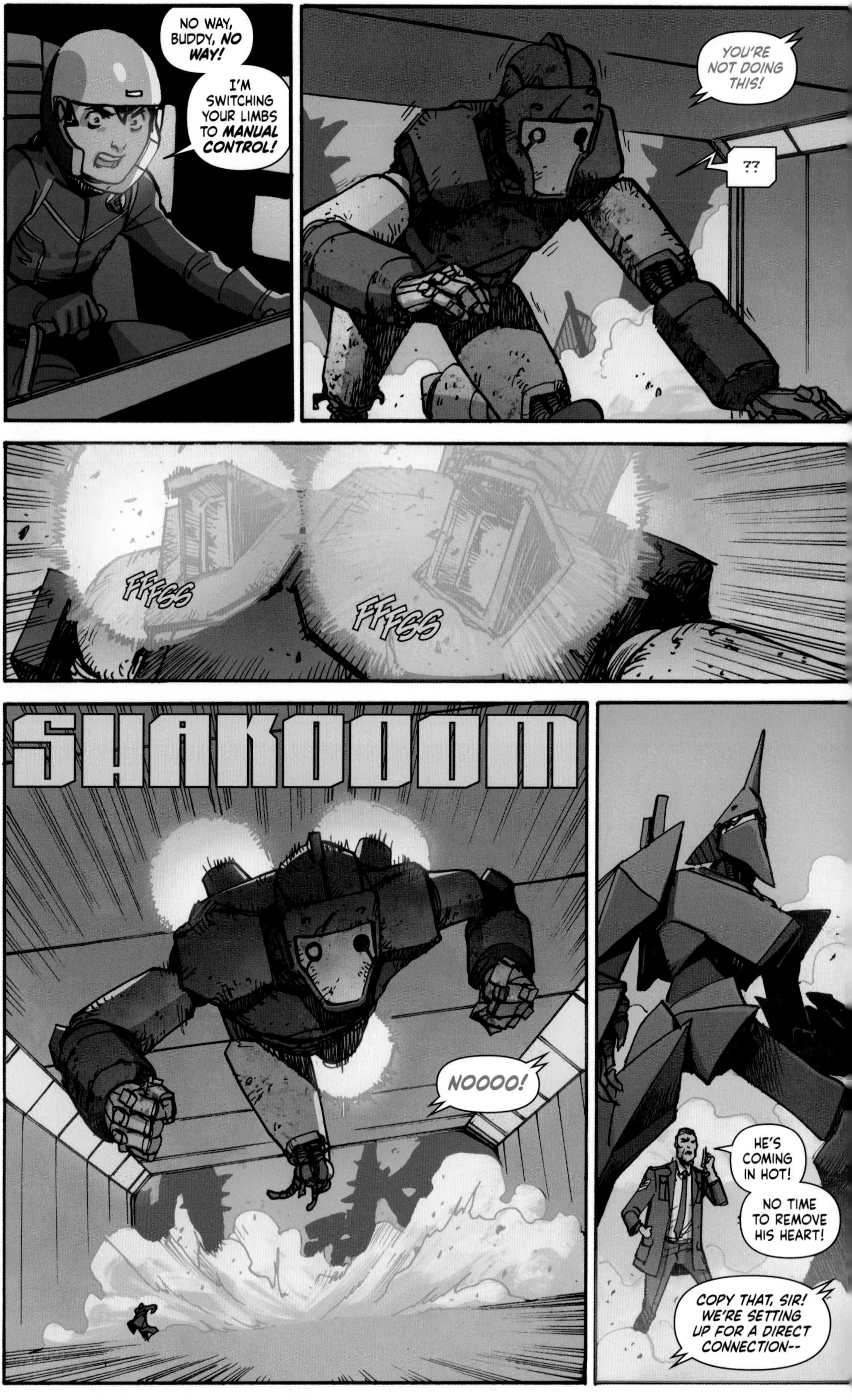
NO WAY, BUDDY, NO WAY!
I'M SWITCHING YOUR LIMBS TO MANUAL CONTROL!
YOU'RE NOT DOING THIS!
??
FFFSS
FFFSS
SHAKOOOM
NOOOO!
HE'S COMING IN HOT!
NO TIME TO REMOVE HIS HEART!
COPY THAT, SIR! WE'RE SETTING UP FOR A DIRECT CONNECTION--

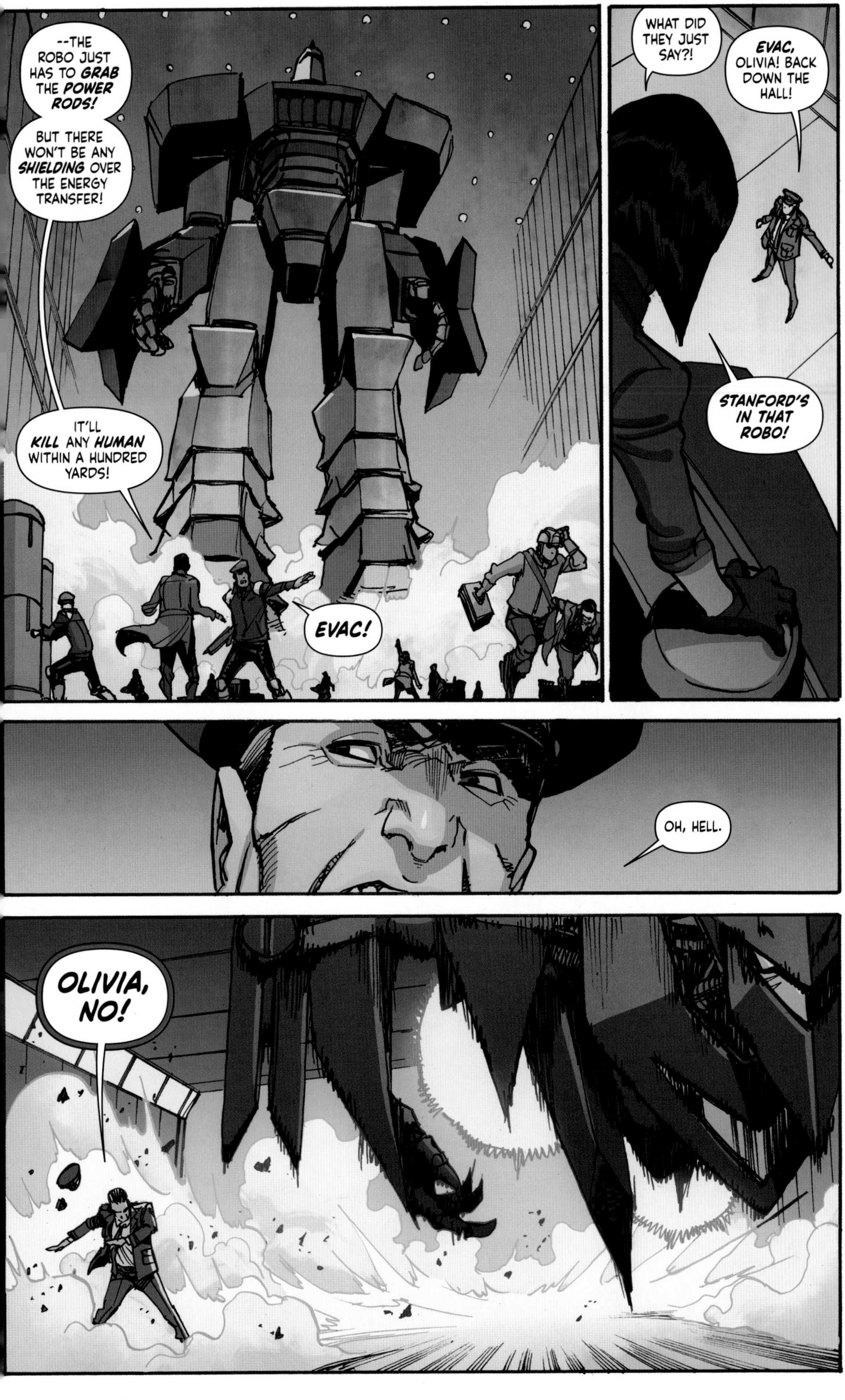
--THE ROBO JUST HAS TO GRAB THE POWER RODS!
BUT THERE WON'T BE ANY SHIELDING OVER THE ENERGY TRANSFER!
IT'LL KILL ANY HUMAN WITHIN A HUNDRED YARDS!
EVAC!
WHAT DID THEY JUST SAY?!
EVAC, OLIVIA! BACK DOWN THE HALL!
STANFORD'S IN THAT ROBO!
OH, HELL.
OLIVIA, NO!

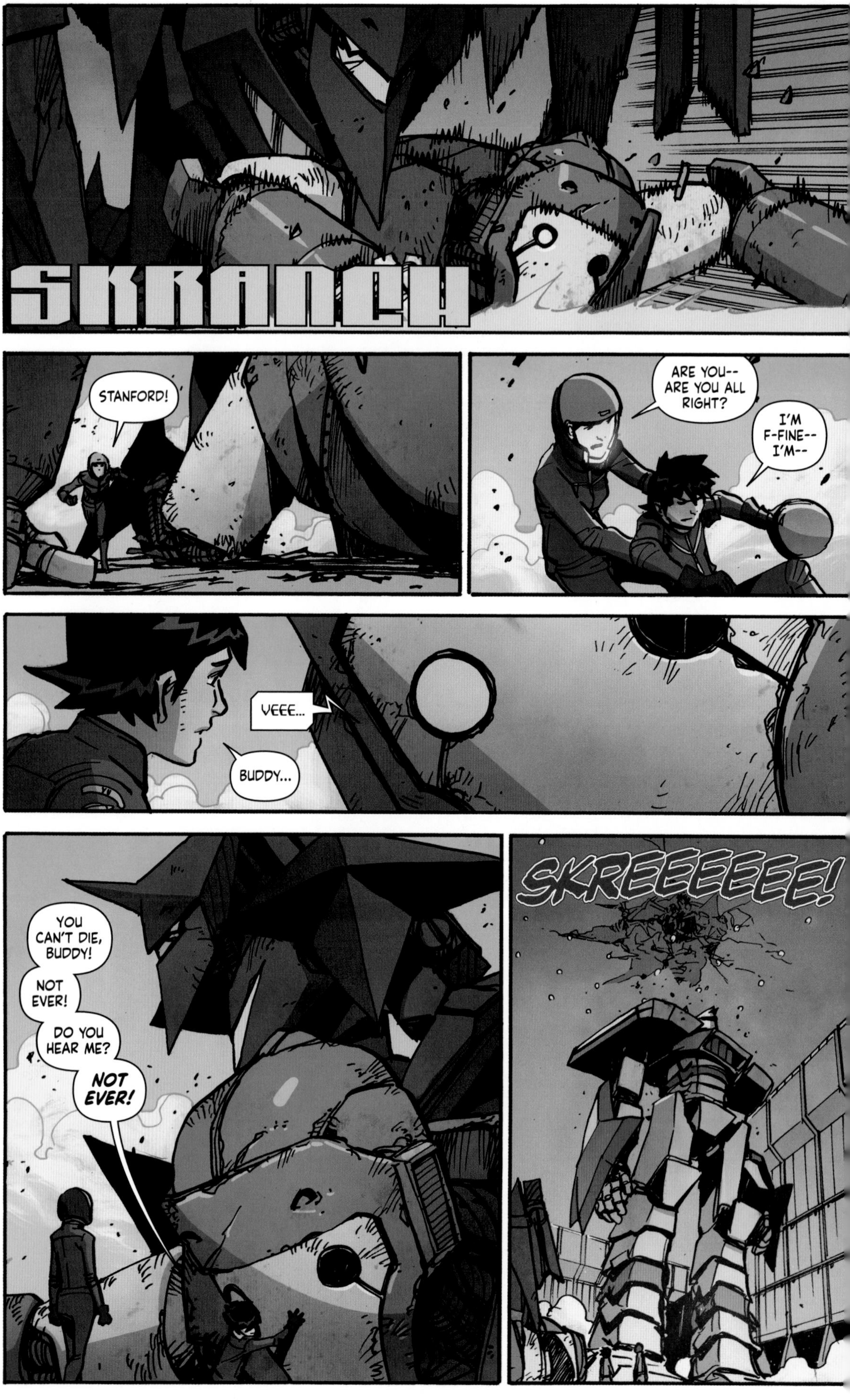
SKRANCH
STANFORD!
ARE YOU-- ARE YOU ALL RIGHT?
I'M F-FINE-- I'M--
VEEE...
BUDDY...
YOU CAN'T DIE, BUDDY!
NOT EVER!
DO YOU HEAR ME?
NOT EVER!
SKREEEEEEE!

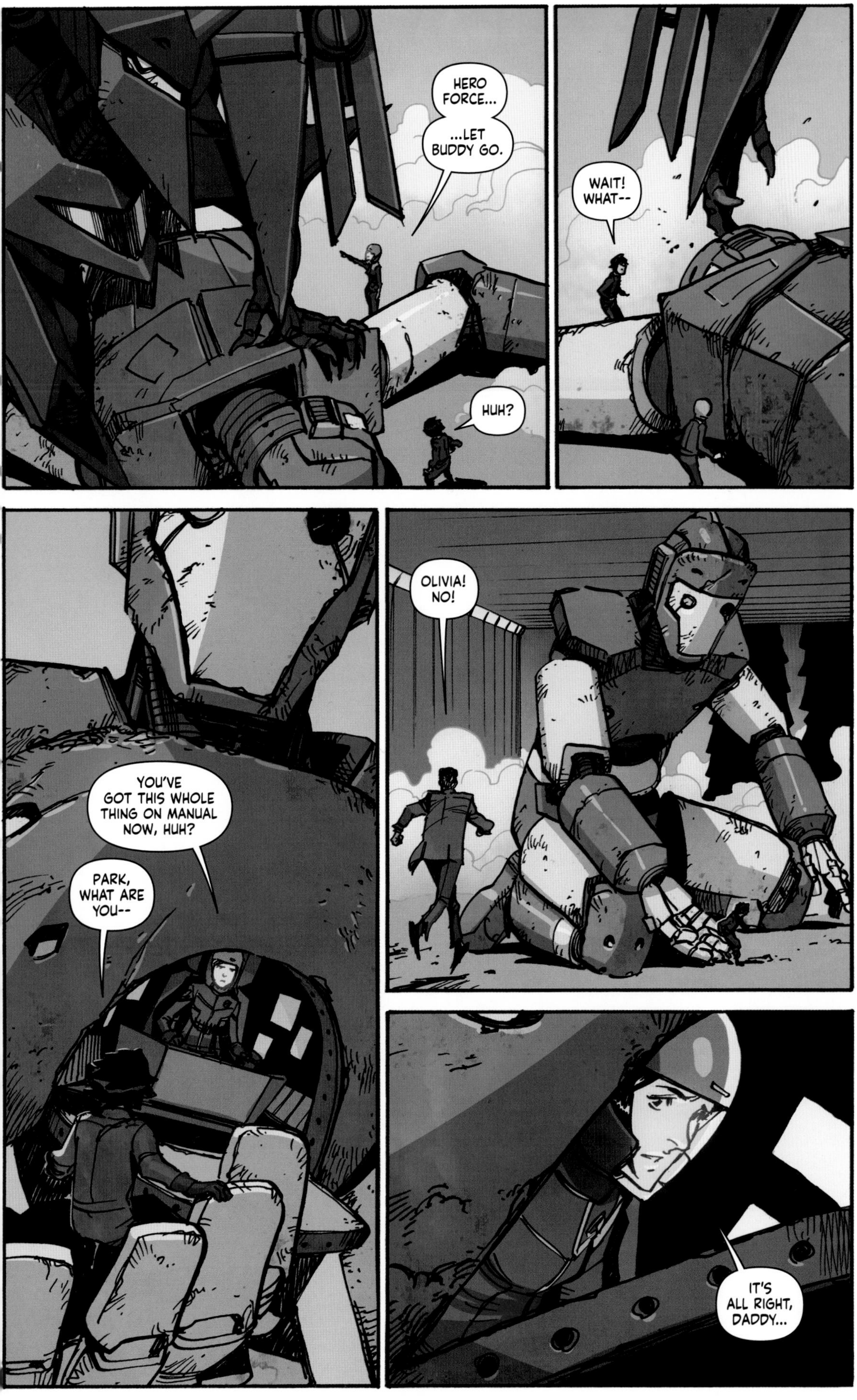
HERO FORCE...
...LET BUDDY GO.
HUH?
WAIT! WHAT--
YOU'VE GOT THIS WHOLE THING ON MANUAL NOW, HUH?
PARK, WHAT ARE YOU--
OLIVIA! NO!
IT'S ALL RIGHT, DADDY...

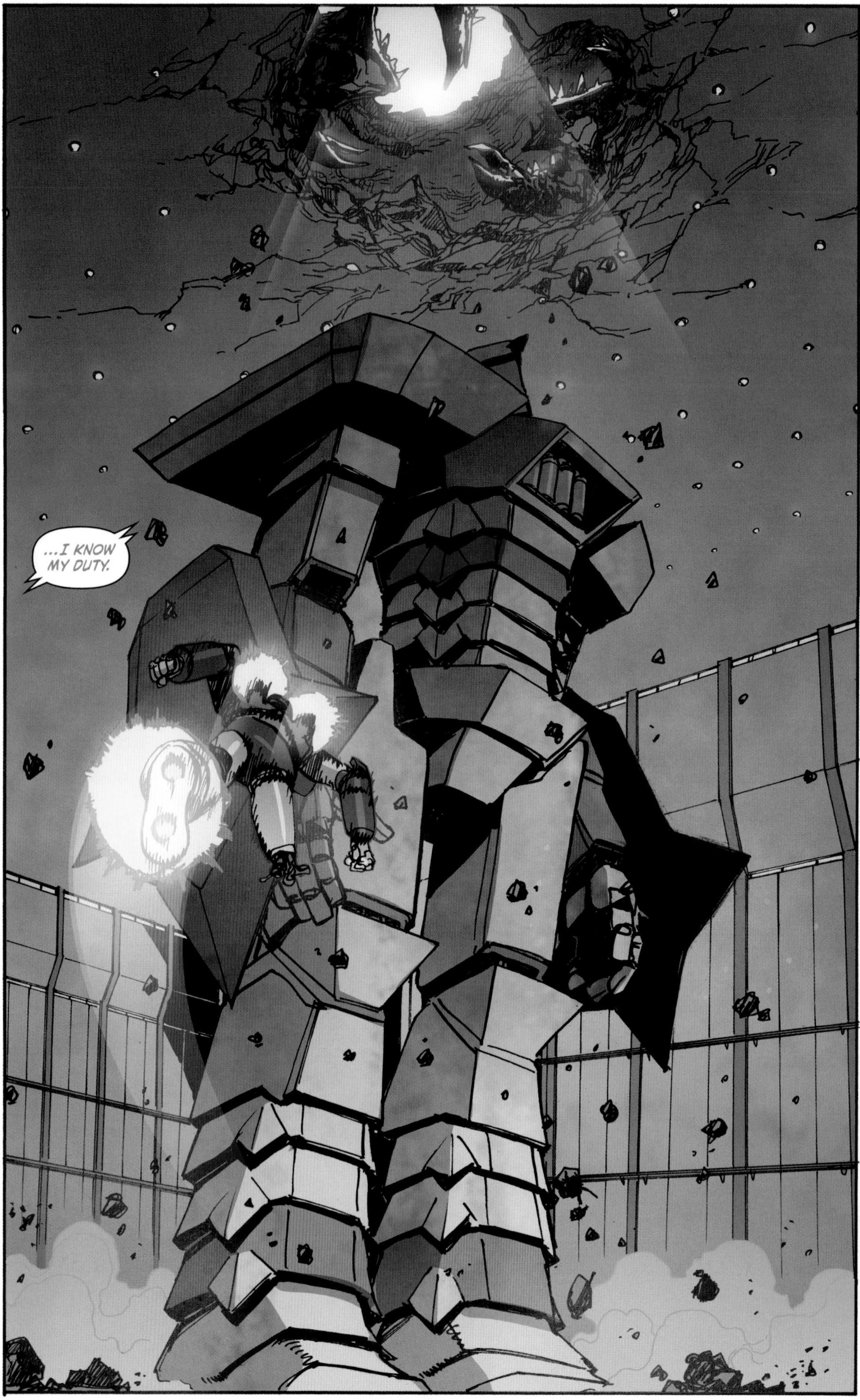
...I KNOW MY DUTY.

CHAPTER **ELEVEN**

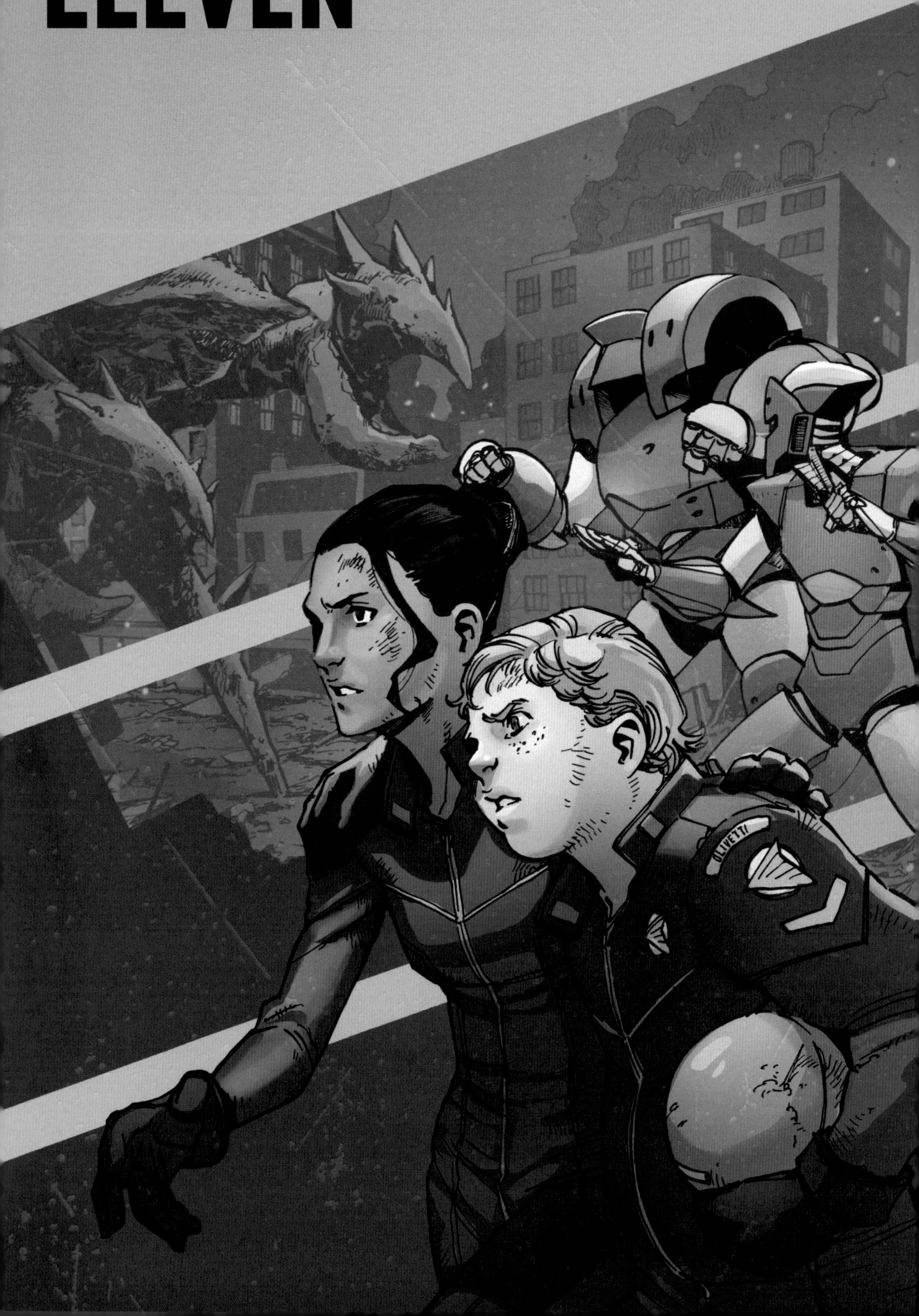
OLIVETTI

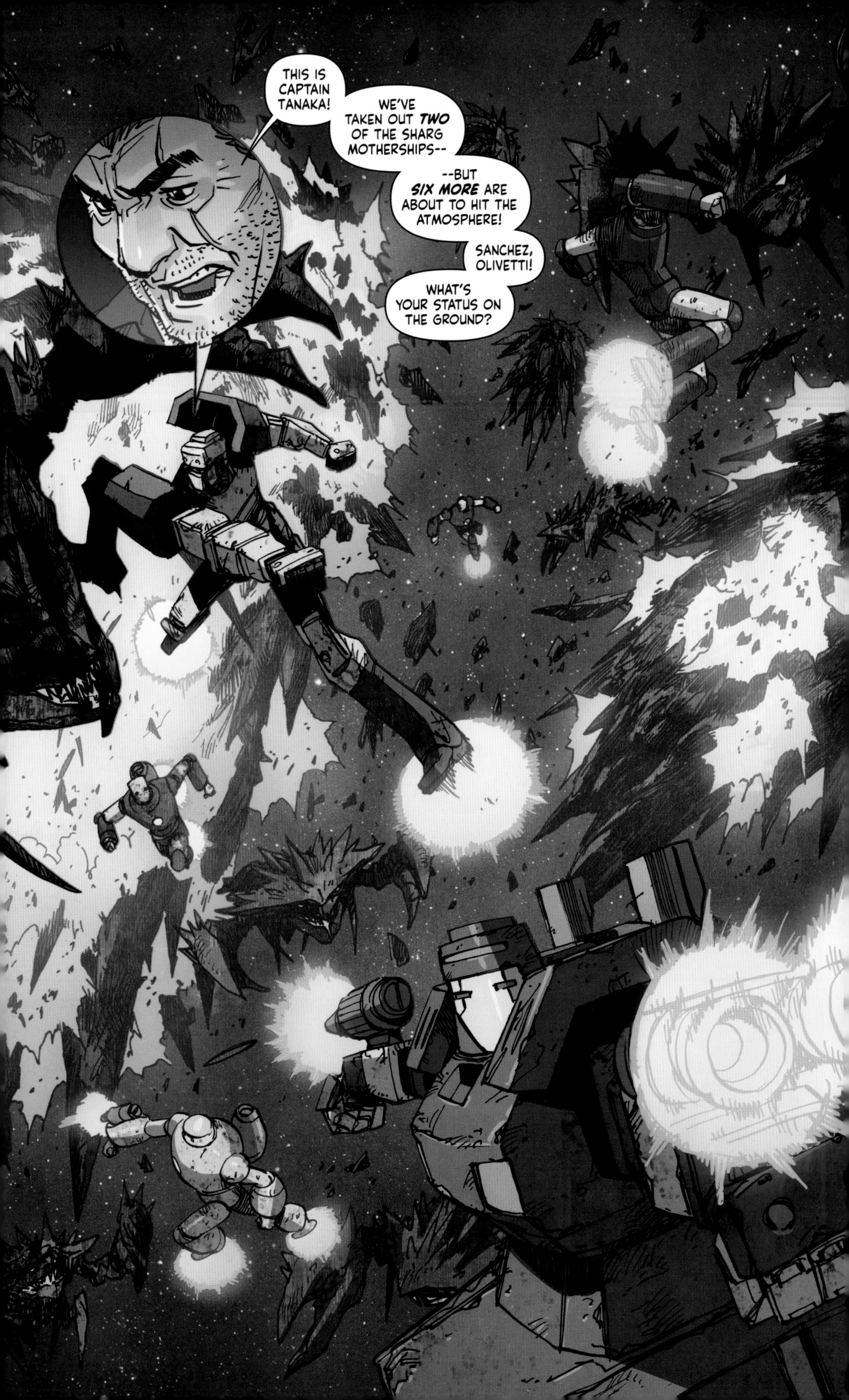
THIS IS CAPTAIN TANAKA!
WE'VE TAKEN OUT ***TWO*** OF THE SHARG MOTHERSHIPS--
--BUT ***SIX MORE*** ARE ABOUT TO HIT THE ATMOSPHERE!
SANCHEZ, OLIVETTI!
WHAT'S YOUR STATUS ON THE GROUND?

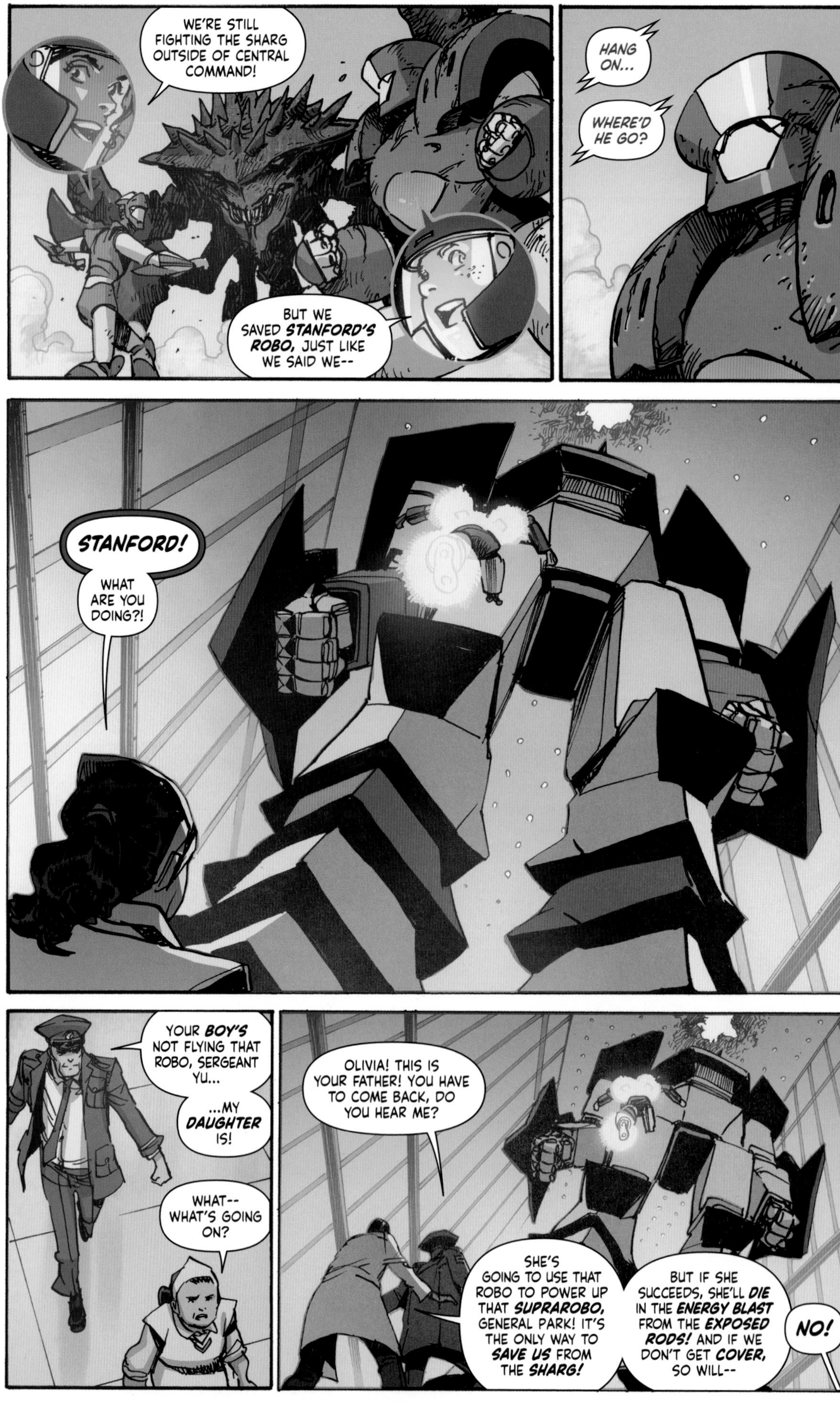
WE'RE STILL FIGHTING THE SHARG OUTSIDE OF CENTRAL COMMAND!
BUT WE SAVED STANFORD'S ROBO, JUST LIKE WE SAID WE--
HANG ON...
WHERE'D HE GO?
STANFORD!
WHAT ARE YOU DOING?!
YOUR BOY'S NOT FLYING THAT ROBO, SERGEANT YU...
...MY DAUGHTER IS!
WHAT-- WHAT'S GOING ON?
OLIVIA! THIS IS YOUR FATHER! YOU HAVE TO COME BACK, DO YOU HEAR ME?
SHE'S GOING TO USE THAT ROBO TO POWER UP THAT SUPRAROBO, GENERAL PARK! IT'S THE ONLY WAY TO SAVE US FROM THE SHARG!
BUT IF SHE SUCCEEDS, SHE'LL DIE IN THE ENERGY BLAST FROM THE EXPOSED RODS! AND IF WE DON'T GET COVER, SO WILL--
NO!

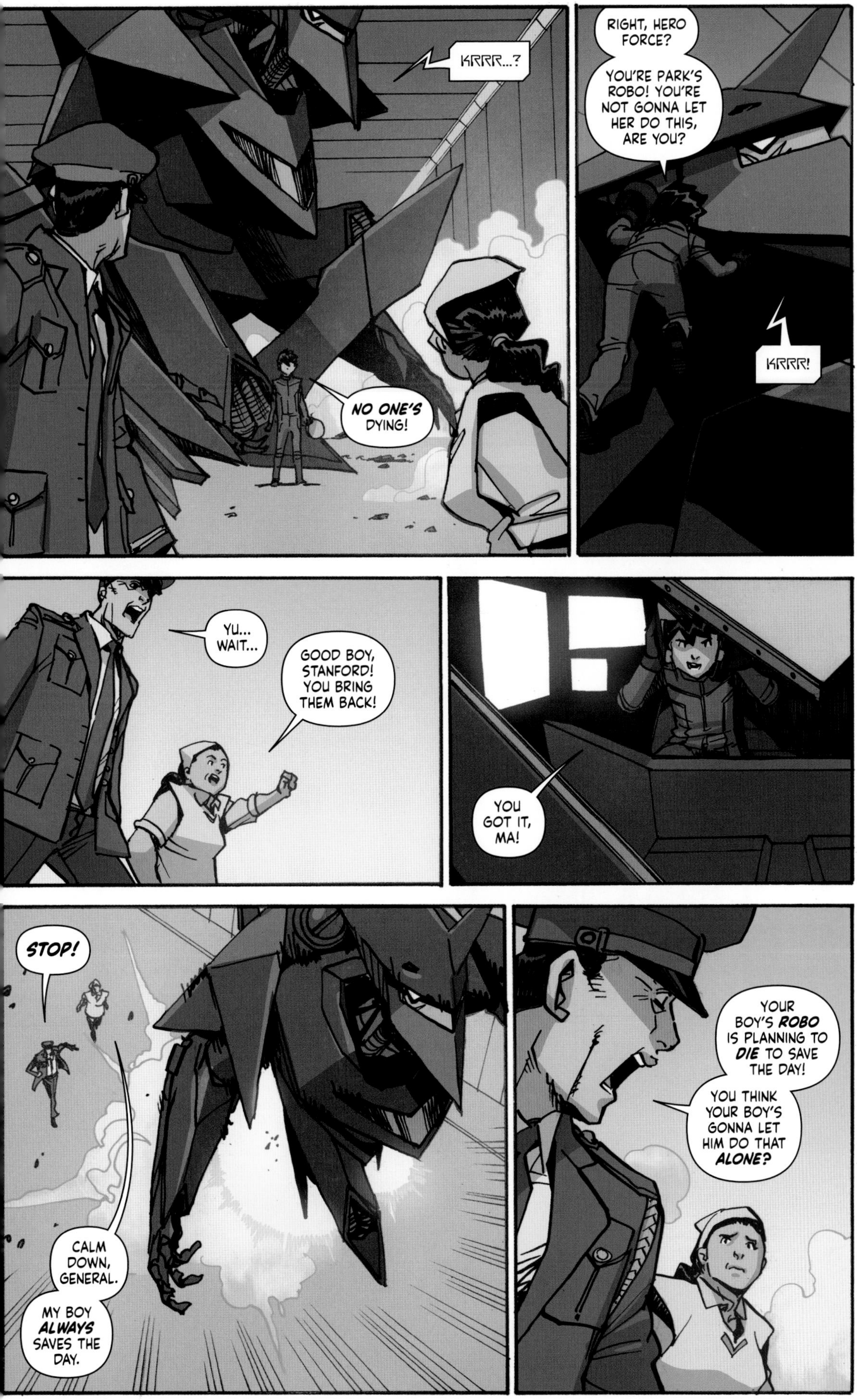
KRRR...?
NO ONE'S DYING!
RIGHT, HERO FORCE?
YOU'RE PARK'S ROBO! YOU'RE NOT GONNA LET HER DO THIS, ARE YOU?
KRRR!
YU... WAIT...
GOOD BOY, STANFORD! YOU BRING THEM BACK!
YOU GOT IT, MA!
STOP!
CALM DOWN, GENERAL.
MY BOY ALWAYS SAVES THE DAY.
YOUR BOY'S ROBO IS PLANNING TO DIE TO SAVE THE DAY!
YOU THINK YOUR BOY'S GONNA LET HIM DO THAT ALONE?

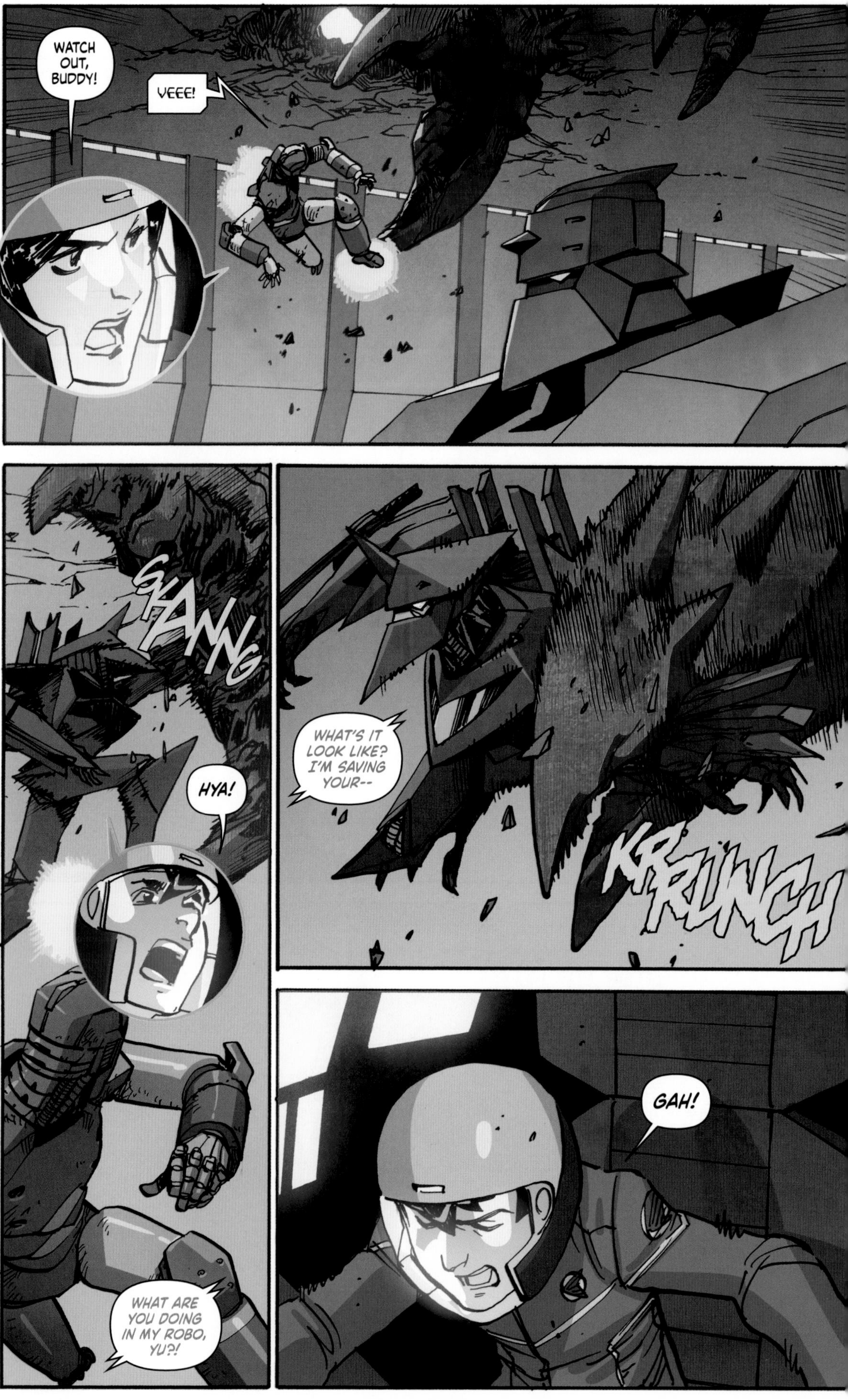
WATCH OUT, BUDDY!
VEEE!
SKANNG
HYA!
WHAT'S IT LOOK LIKE? I'M SAVING YOUR--
KR-RUNCH
WHAT ARE YOU DOING IN MY ROBO, YU?!
GAH!

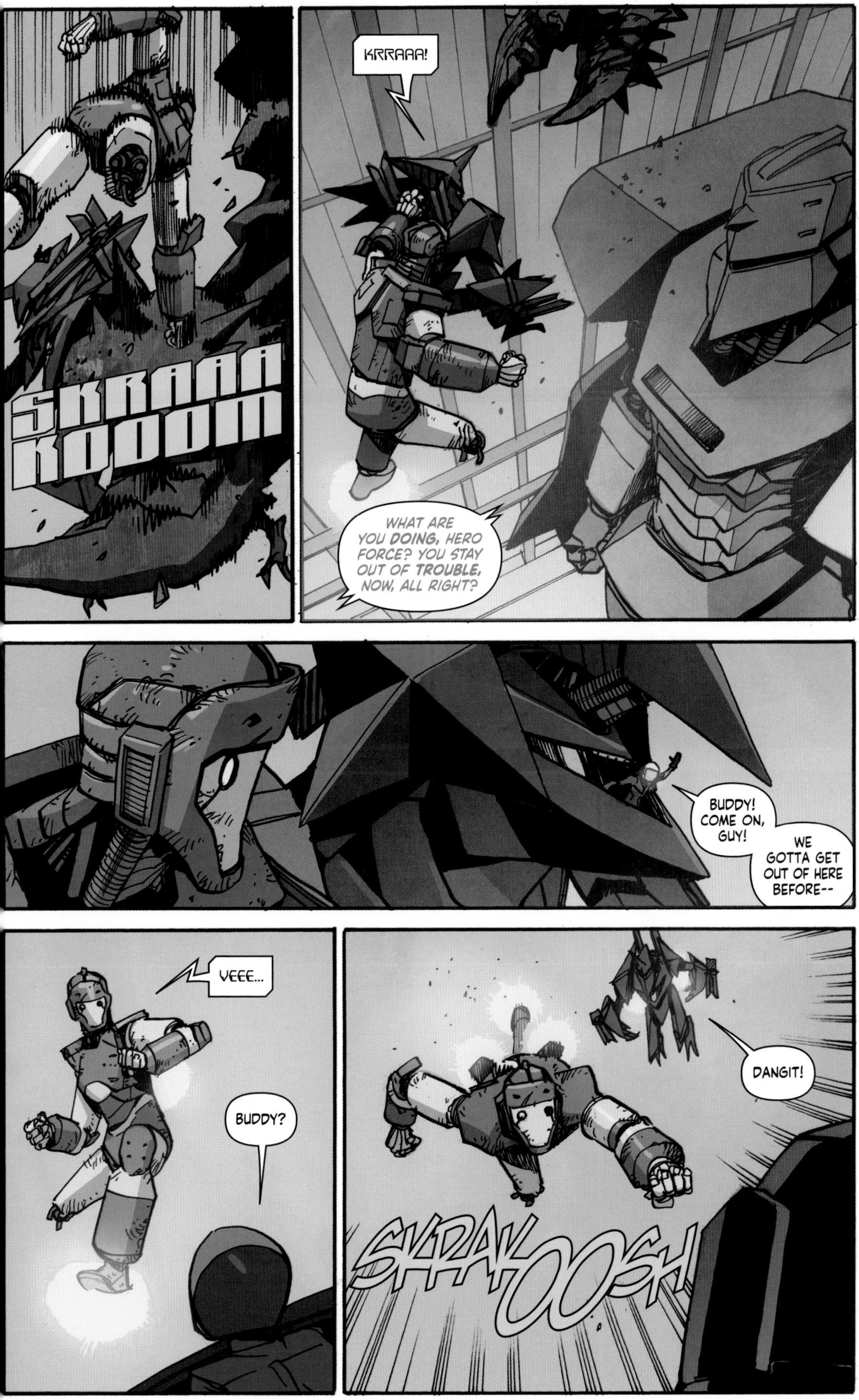
SKRAAA KOOOM
KRRAAA!
WHAT ARE YOU DOING, HERO FORCE? YOU STAY OUT OF TROUBLE, NOW, ALL RIGHT?
BUDDY! COME ON, GUY!
WE GOTTA GET OUT OF HERE BEFORE--
VEEE...
BUDDY?
DANGIT!
SKRAKOOSH

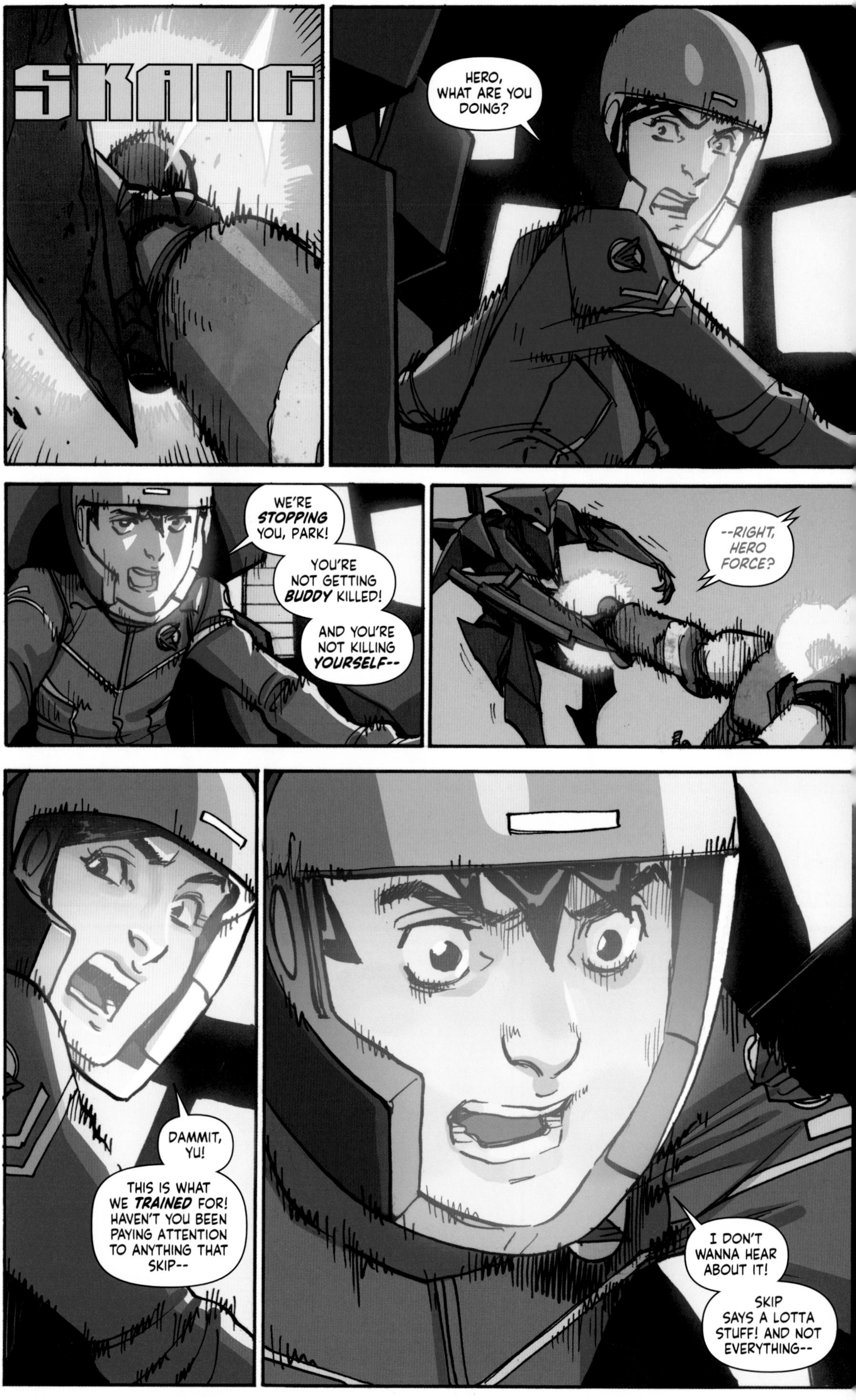
SKANG
HERO, WHAT ARE YOU DOING?
WE'RE STOPPING YOU, PARK!
YOU'RE NOT GETTING BUDDY KILLED!
AND YOU'RE NOT KILLING YOURSELF--
--RIGHT, HERO FORCE?
DAMMIT, YU!
THIS IS WHAT WE TRAINED FOR! HAVEN'T YOU BEEN PAYING ATTENTION TO ANYTHING THAT SKIP--
I DON'T WANNA HEAR ABOUT IT!
SKIP SAYS A LOTTA STUFF! AND NOT EVERYTHING--

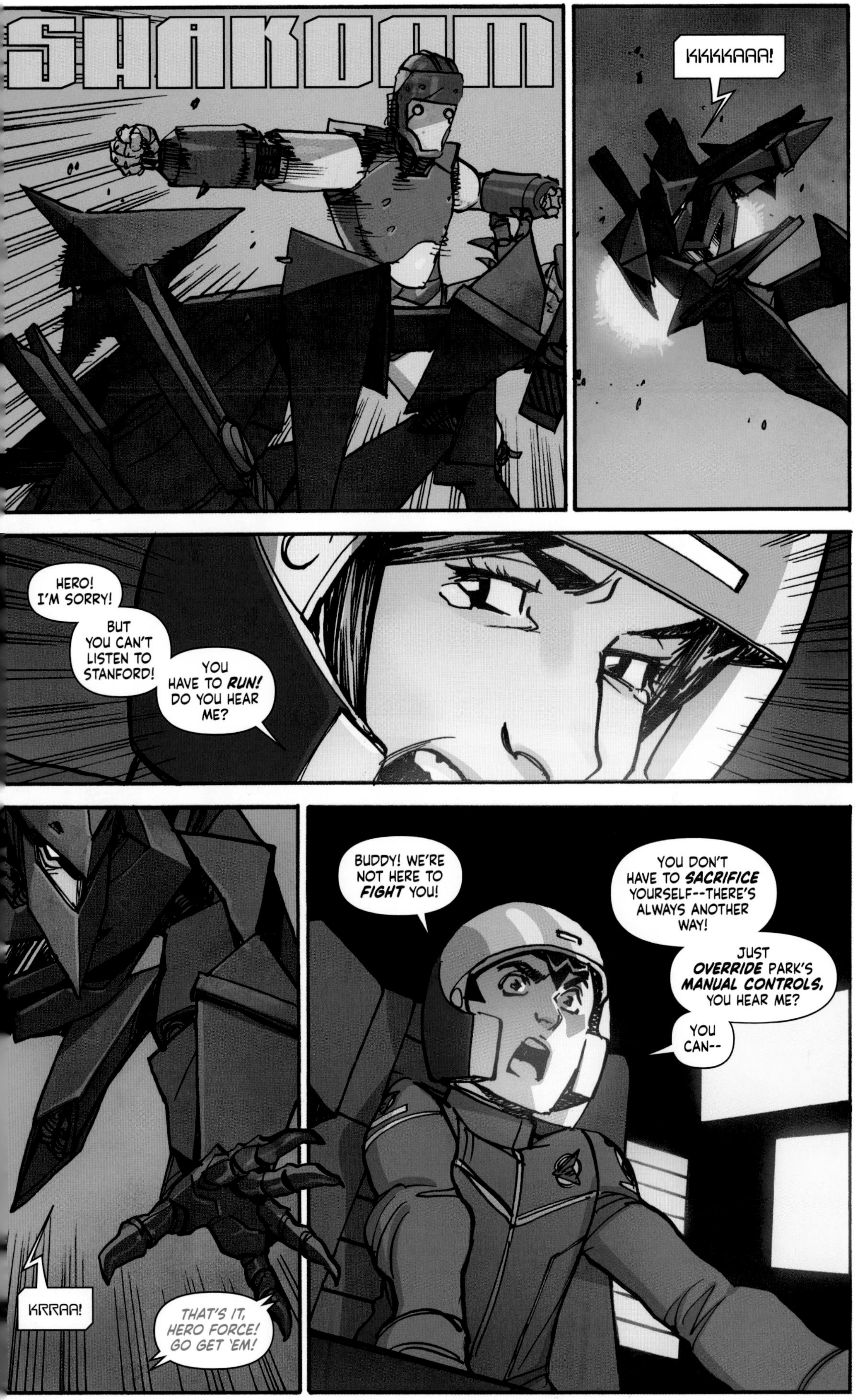
SHAKOOM
KKKKAAA!
HERO! I'M SORRY!
BUT YOU CAN'T LISTEN TO STANFORD!
YOU HAVE TO *RUN!* DO YOU HEAR ME?
BUDDY! WE'RE NOT HERE TO *FIGHT* YOU!
YOU DON'T HAVE TO *SACRIFICE* YOURSELF--THERE'S ALWAYS ANOTHER WAY!
JUST *OVERRIDE* PARK'S *MANUAL CONTROLS,* YOU HEAR ME?
YOU CAN--
KRRAA!
THAT'S IT, HERO FORCE! GO GET 'EM!

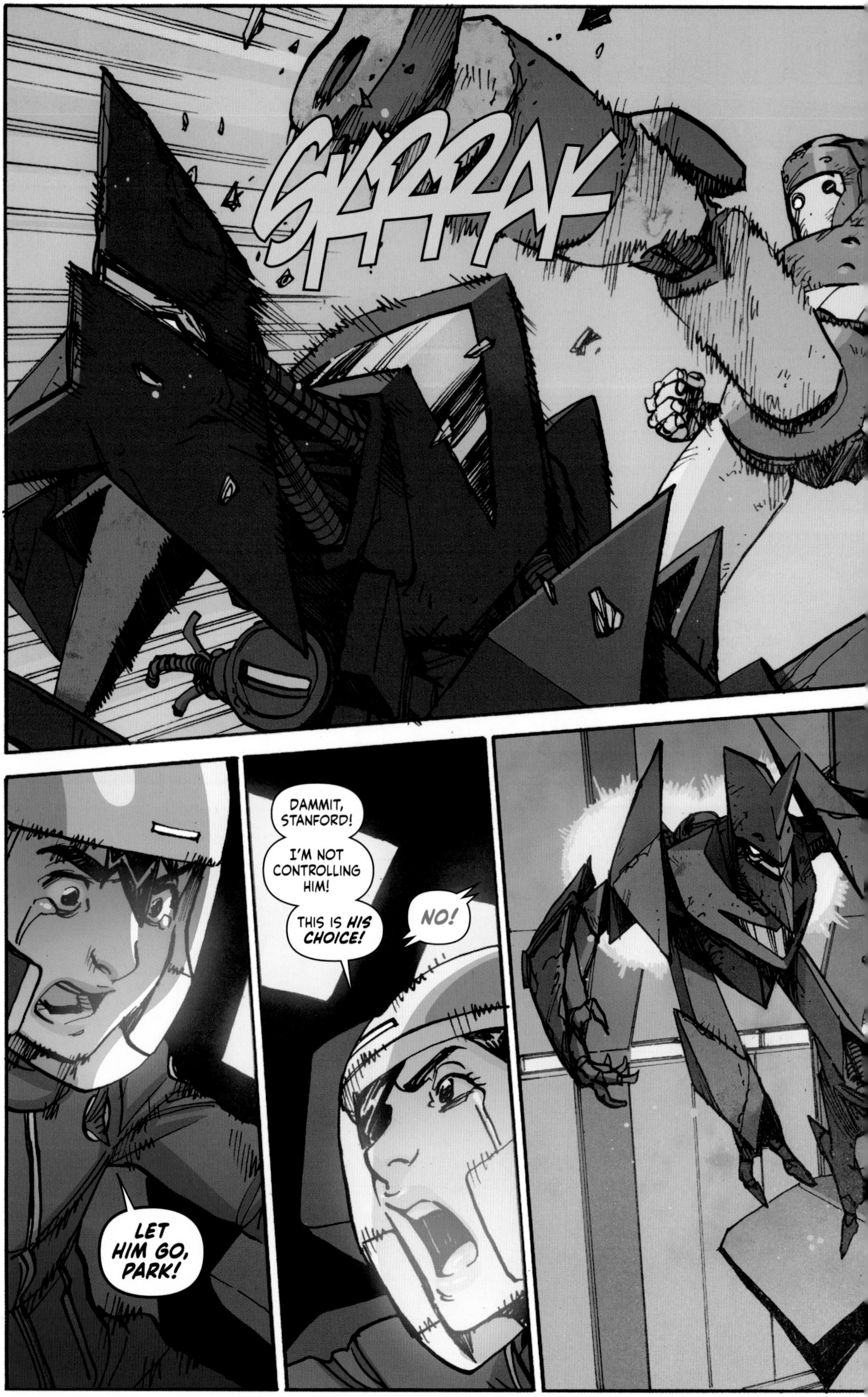
SKRRAK
LET HIM GO, PARK!
DAMMIT, STANFORD!
I'M NOT CONTROLLING HIM!
THIS IS HIS CHOICE!
NO!

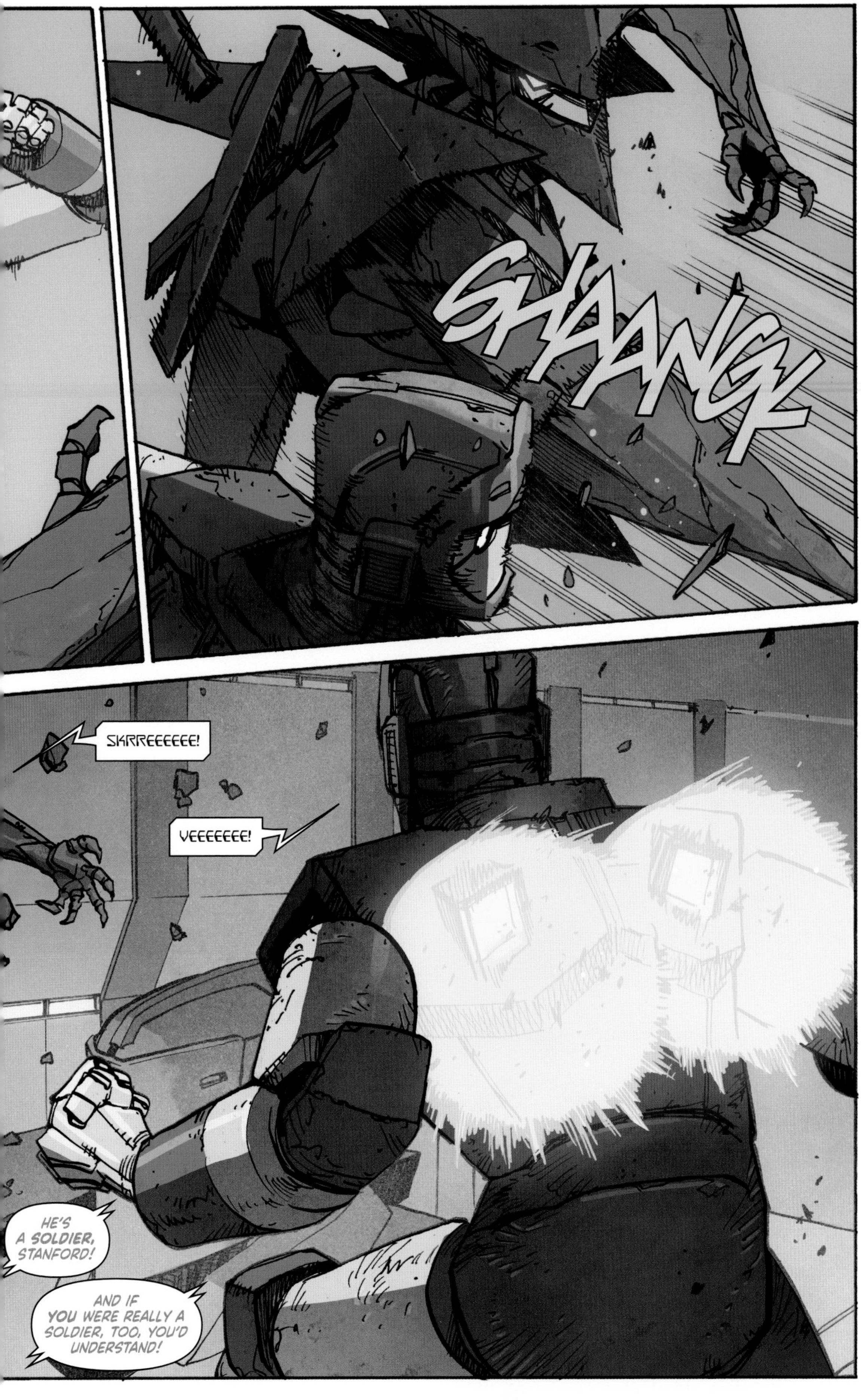
SHAANGK
SKRREEEEEEE!
VEEEEEEE!
HE'S A SOLDIER, STANFORD!
AND IF YOU WERE REALLY A SOLDIER, TOO, YOU'D UNDERSTAND!

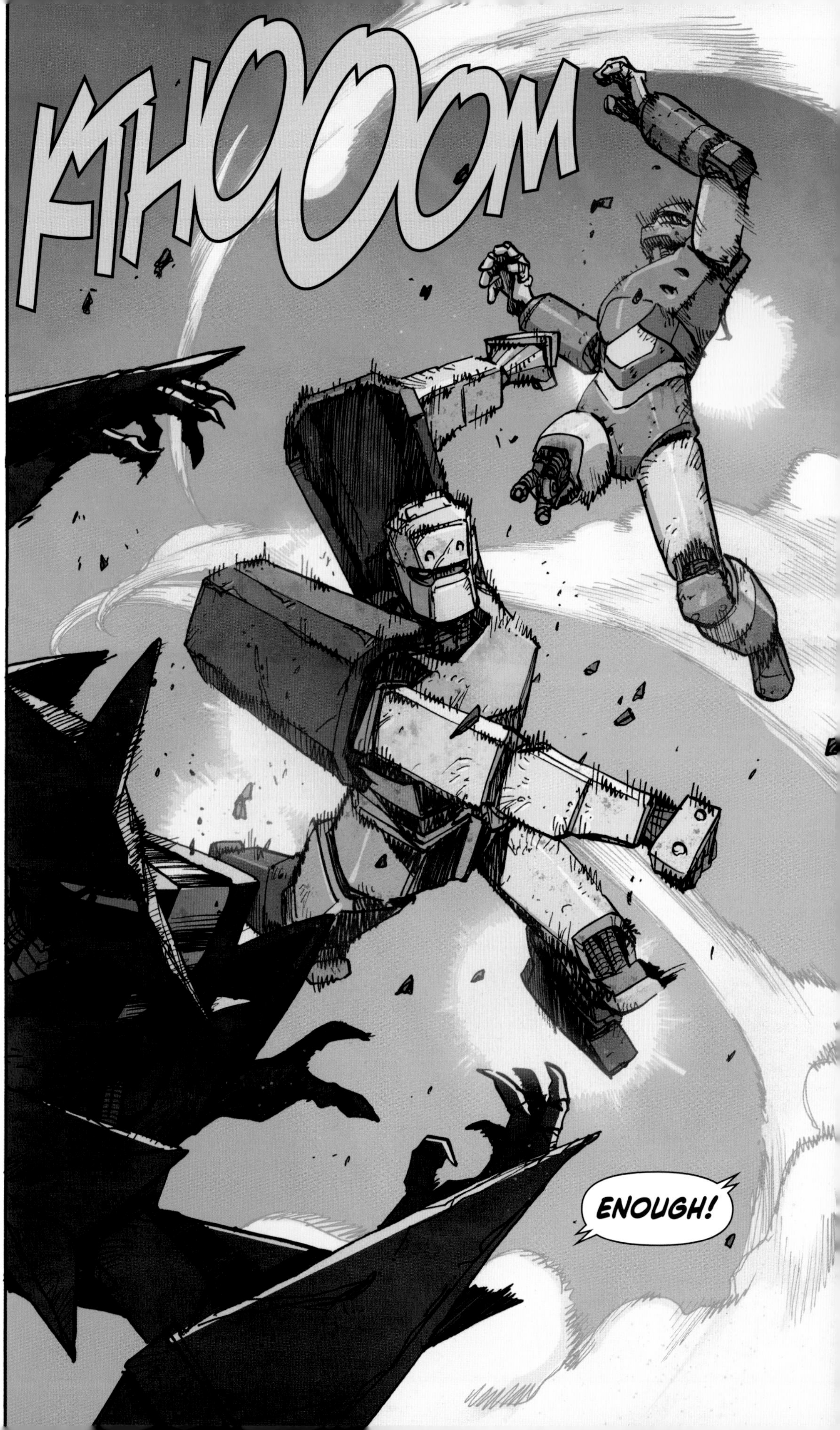
KTHOOOM
ENOUGH!

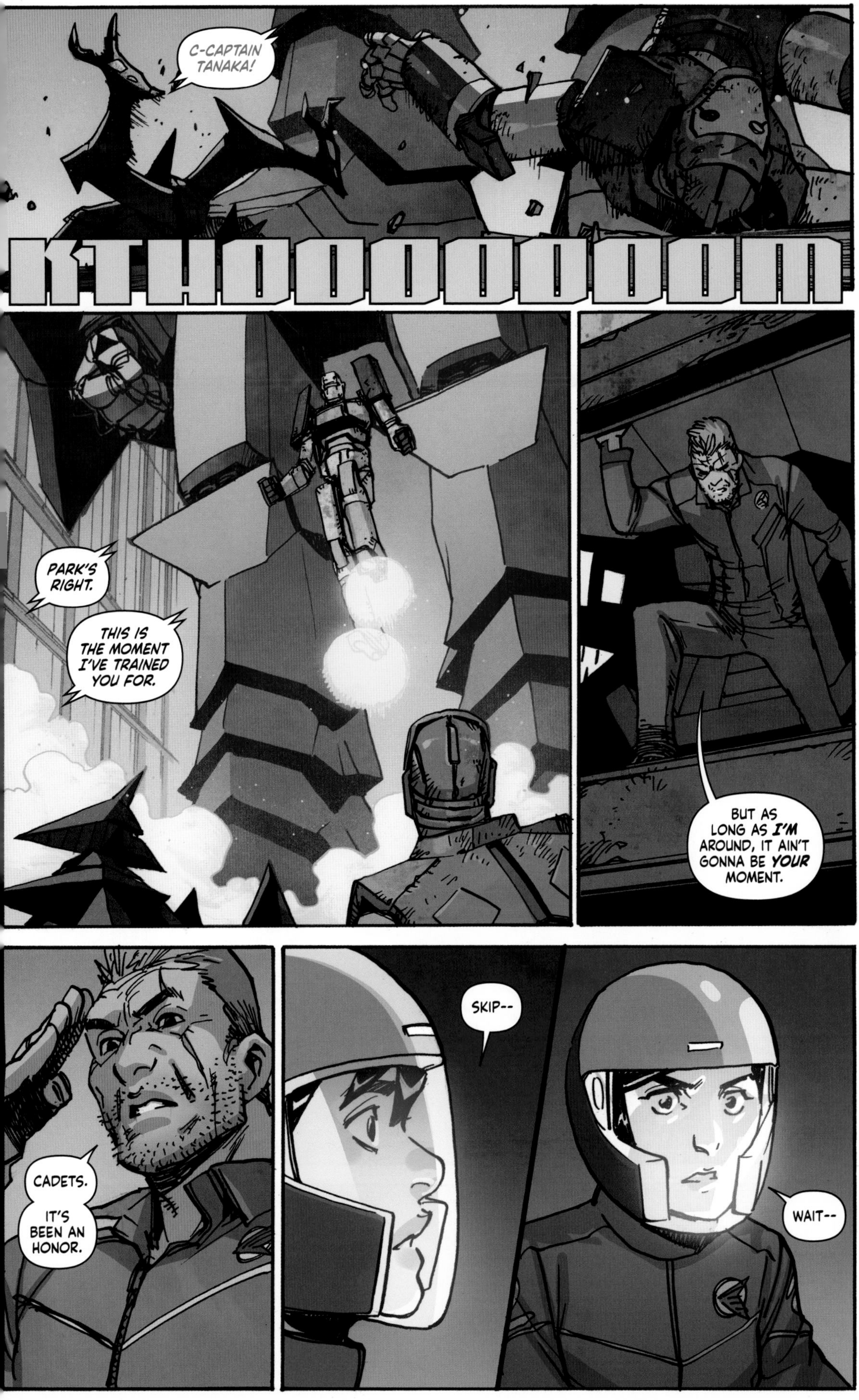
C-CAPTAIN TANAKA!
KTHOOOOOOOM
PARK'S RIGHT.
THIS IS THE MOMENT I'VE TRAINED YOU FOR.
BUT AS LONG AS I'M AROUND, IT AIN'T GONNA BE YOUR MOMENT.
CADETS.
IT'S BEEN AN HONOR.
SKIP--
WAIT--

CAPTAIN TANAKA'S APPROACHING THE NODES, GENERAL!

I THINK--I THINK HE'S--

SKEEEEEE!

BRRRRZT

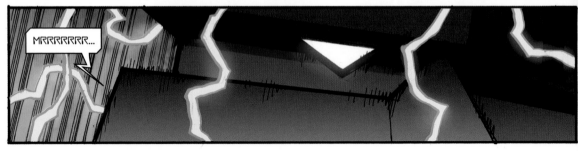

MRRRRRRR...

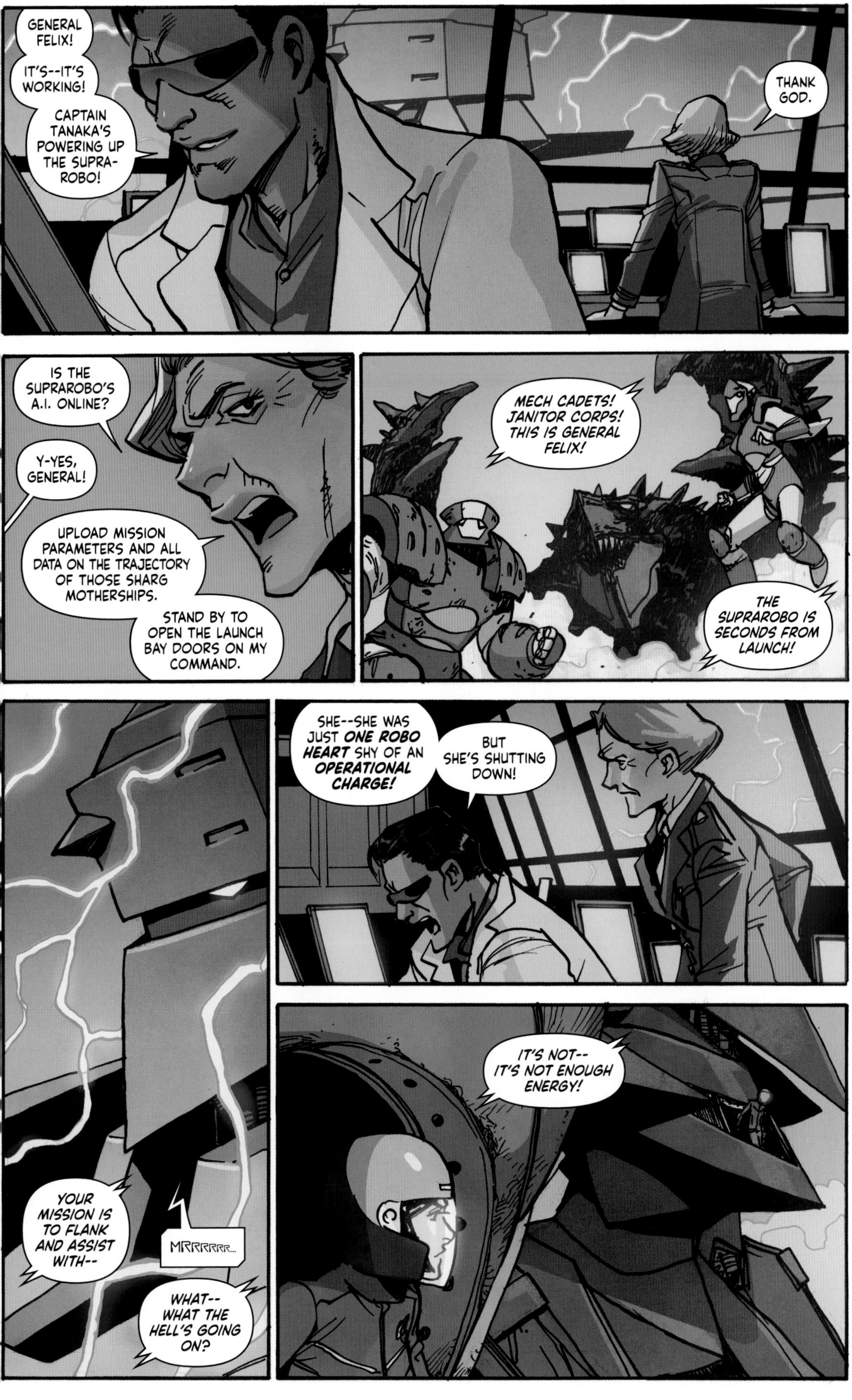
GENERAL FELIX!
IT'S--IT'S WORKING!
CAPTAIN TANAKA'S POWERING UP THE SUPRA-ROBO!
THANK GOD.
IS THE SUPRAROBO'S A.I. ONLINE?
Y-YES, GENERAL!
UPLOAD MISSION PARAMETERS AND ALL DATA ON THE TRAJECTORY OF THOSE SHARG MOTHERSHIPS.
STAND BY TO OPEN THE LAUNCH BAY DOORS ON MY COMMAND.
MECH CADETS! JANITOR CORPS! THIS IS GENERAL FELIX!
THE SUPRAROBO IS SECONDS FROM LAUNCH!
YOUR MISSION IS TO FLANK AND ASSIST WITH--
MRRRRRRR...
WHAT--WHAT THE HELL'S GOING ON?
SHE--SHE WAS JUST ONE ROBO HEART SHY OF AN OPERATIONAL CHARGE!
BUT SHE'S SHUTTING DOWN!
IT'S NOT--IT'S NOT ENOUGH ENERGY!

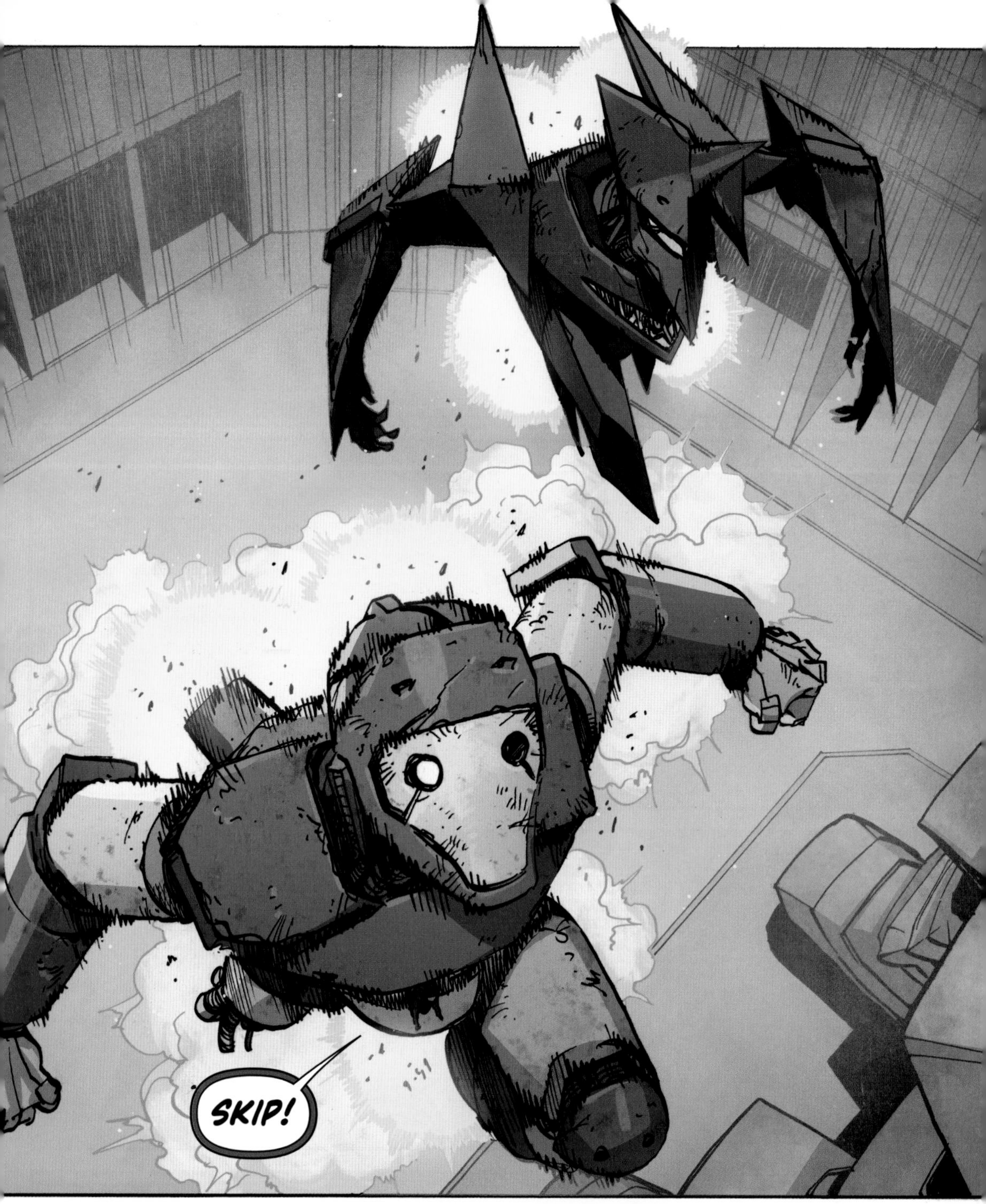
SKIP!

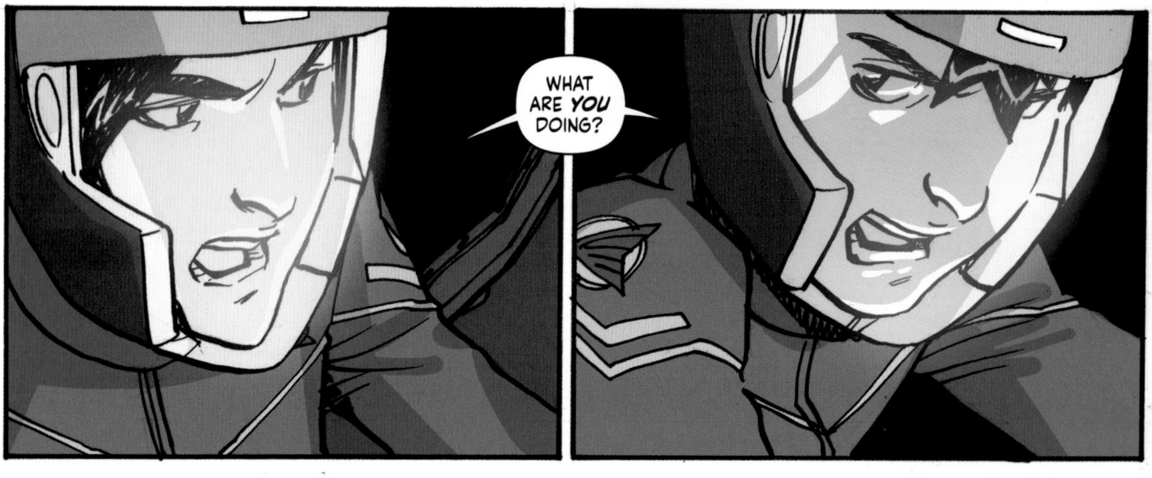
WHAT ARE YOU DOING?

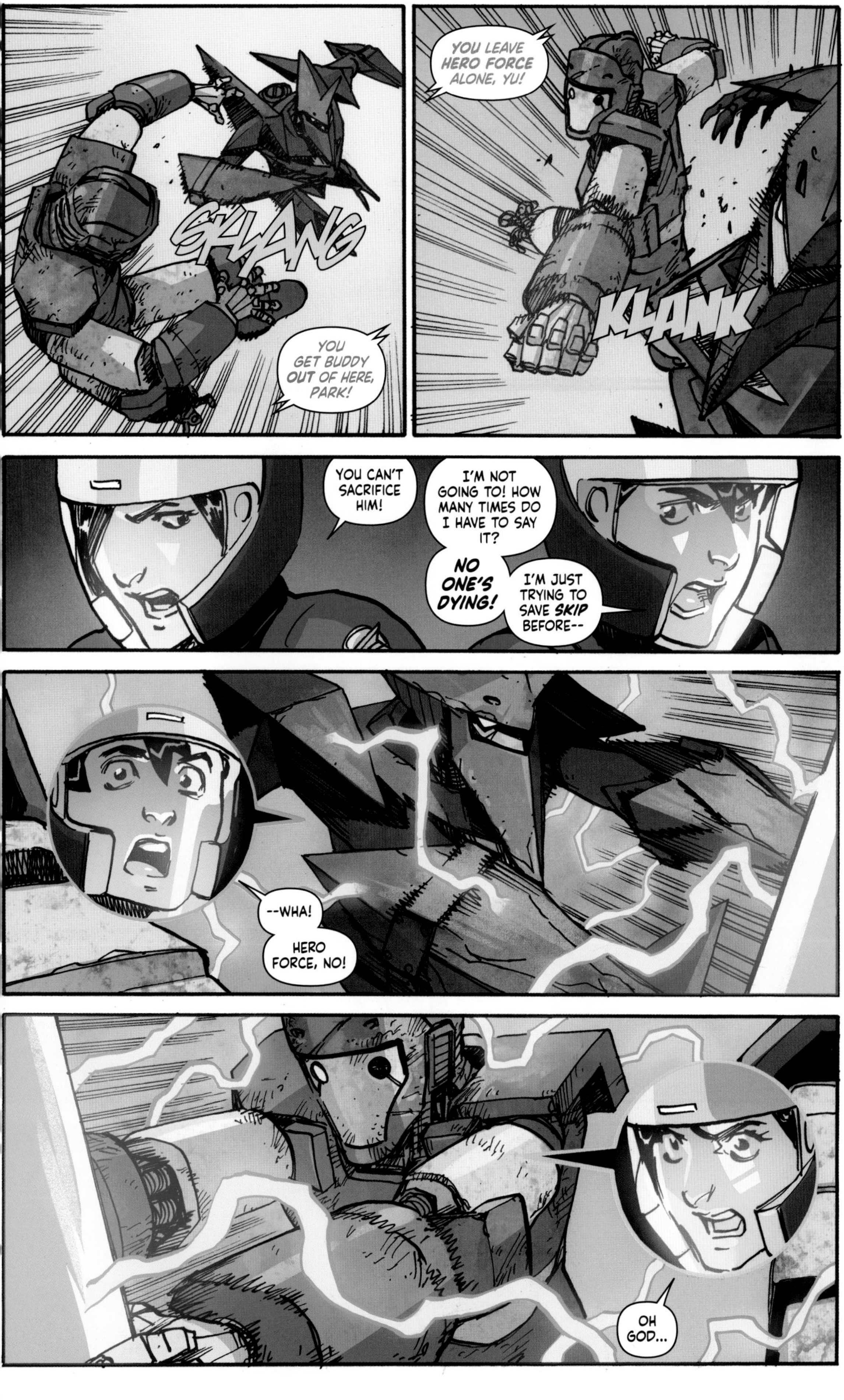
SKYANG
YOU GET BUDDY OUT OF HERE, PARK!
YOU LEAVE HERO FORCE ALONE, YU!
KLANK
YOU CAN'T SACRIFICE HIM!
I'M NOT GOING TO! HOW MANY TIMES DO I HAVE TO SAY IT?
NO ONE'S DYING!
I'M JUST TRYING TO SAVE SKIP BEFORE--
--WHA!
HERO FORCE, NO!
OH GOD...

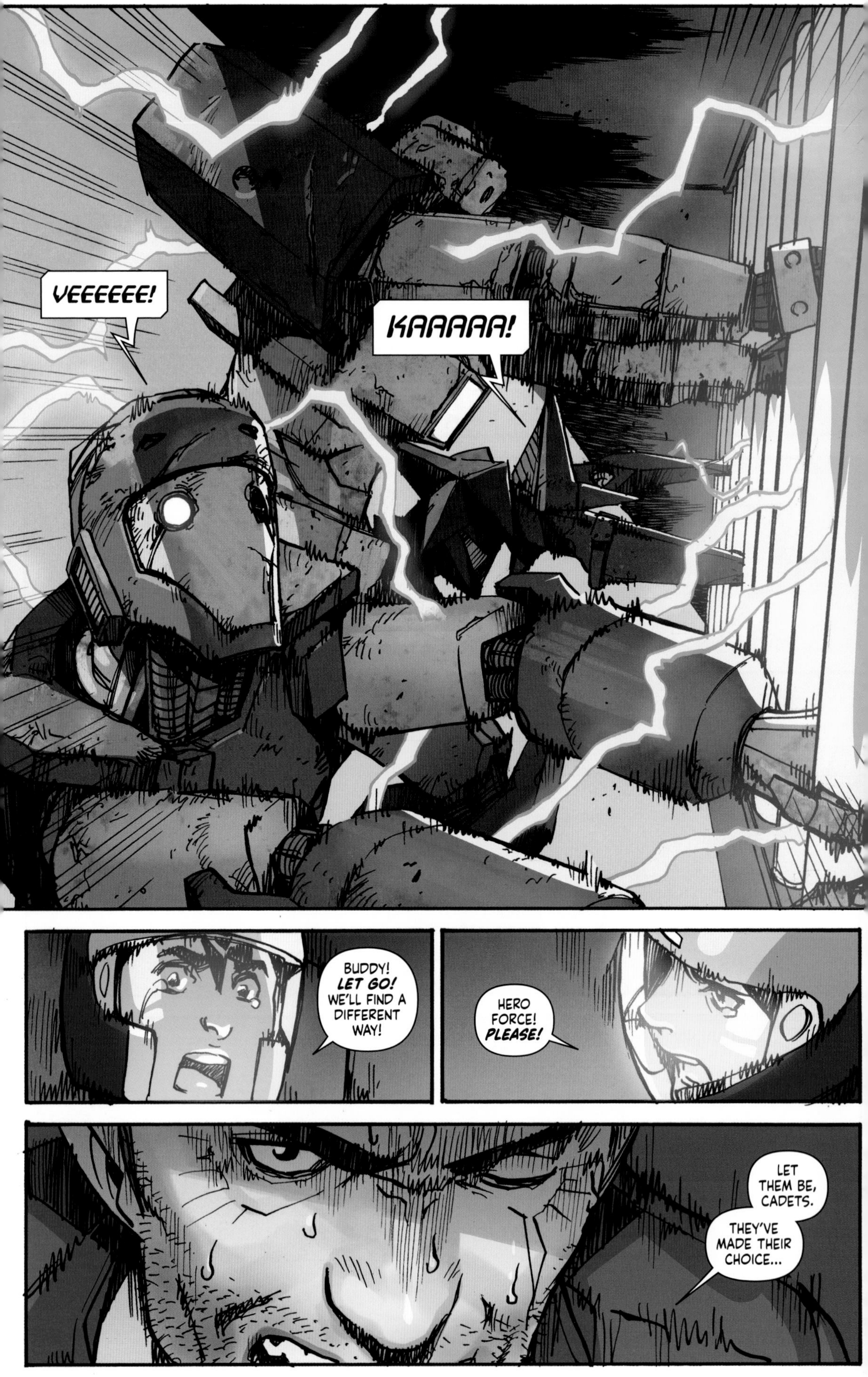
VEEEEEE!
KAAAAA!
BUDDY! LET GO! WE'LL FIND A DIFFERENT WAY!
HERO FORCE! PLEASE!
LET THEM BE, CADETS.
THEY'VE MADE THEIR CHOICE...

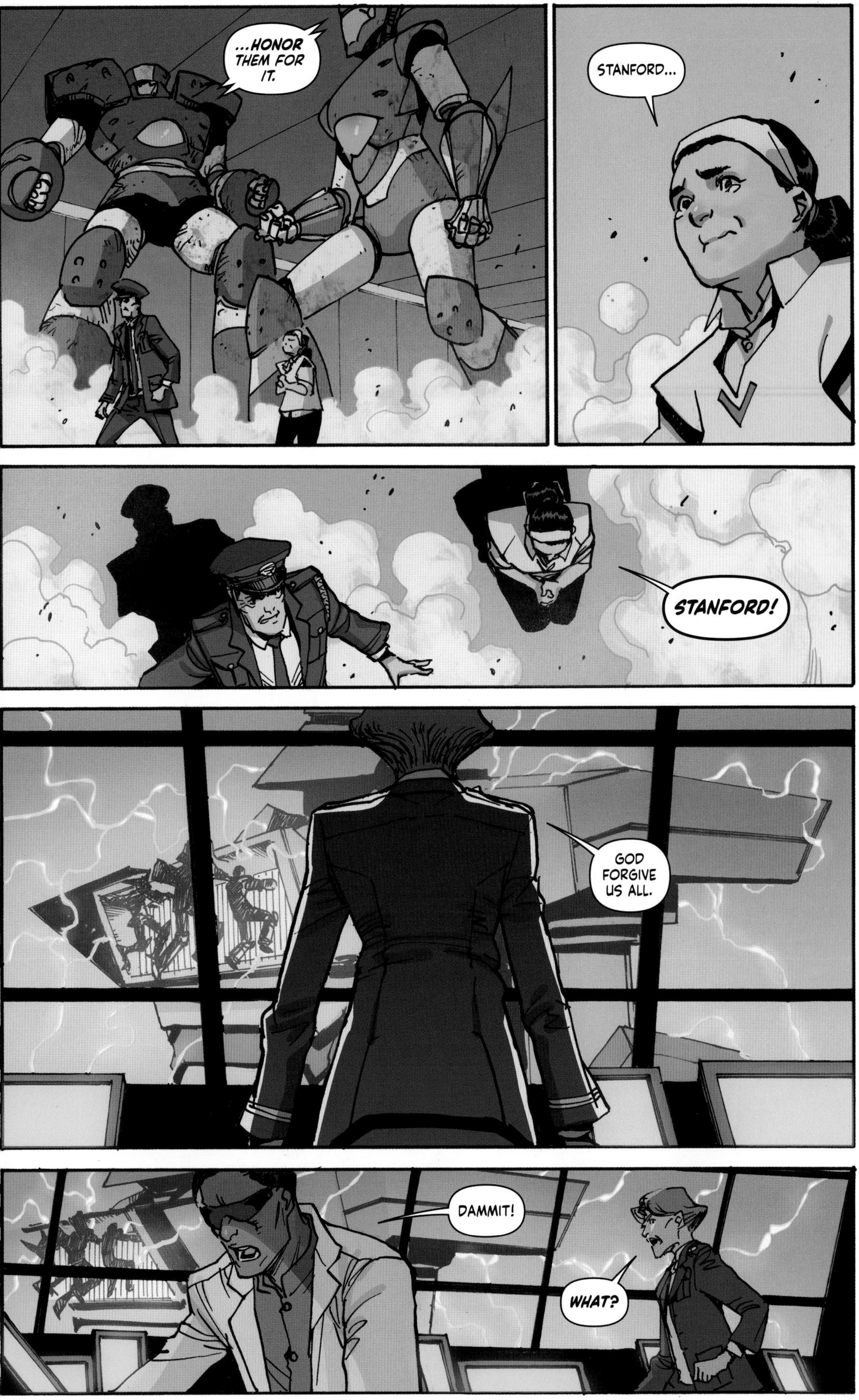
...HONOR THEM FOR IT.
STANFORD...
STANFORD!
GOD FORGIVE US ALL.
DAMMIT!
WHAT?

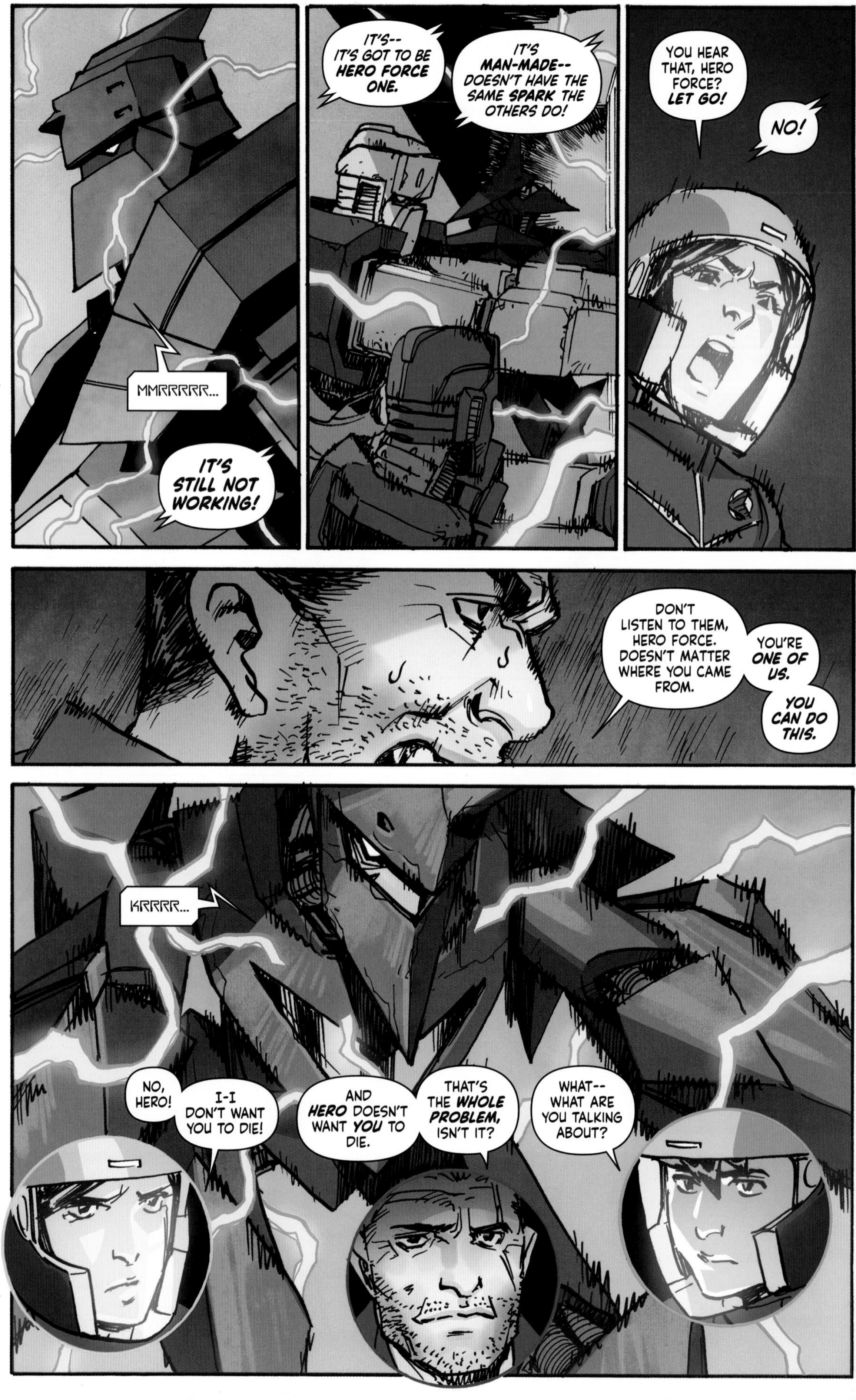
MMRRRRRR...
IT'S STILL NOT WORKING!
IT'S-- IT'S GOT TO BE HERO FORCE ONE.
IT'S MAN-MADE-- DOESN'T HAVE THE SAME SPARK THE OTHERS DO!
YOU HEAR THAT, HERO FORCE? LET GO!
NO!
DON'T LISTEN TO THEM, HERO FORCE. DOESN'T MATTER WHERE YOU CAME FROM.
YOU'RE ONE OF US.
YOU CAN DO THIS.
KRRRR...
NO, HERO!
I-I DON'T WANT YOU TO DIE!
AND HERO DOESN'T WANT YOU TO DIE.
THAT'S THE WHOLE PROBLEM, ISN'T IT?
WHAT-- WHAT ARE YOU TALKING ABOUT?

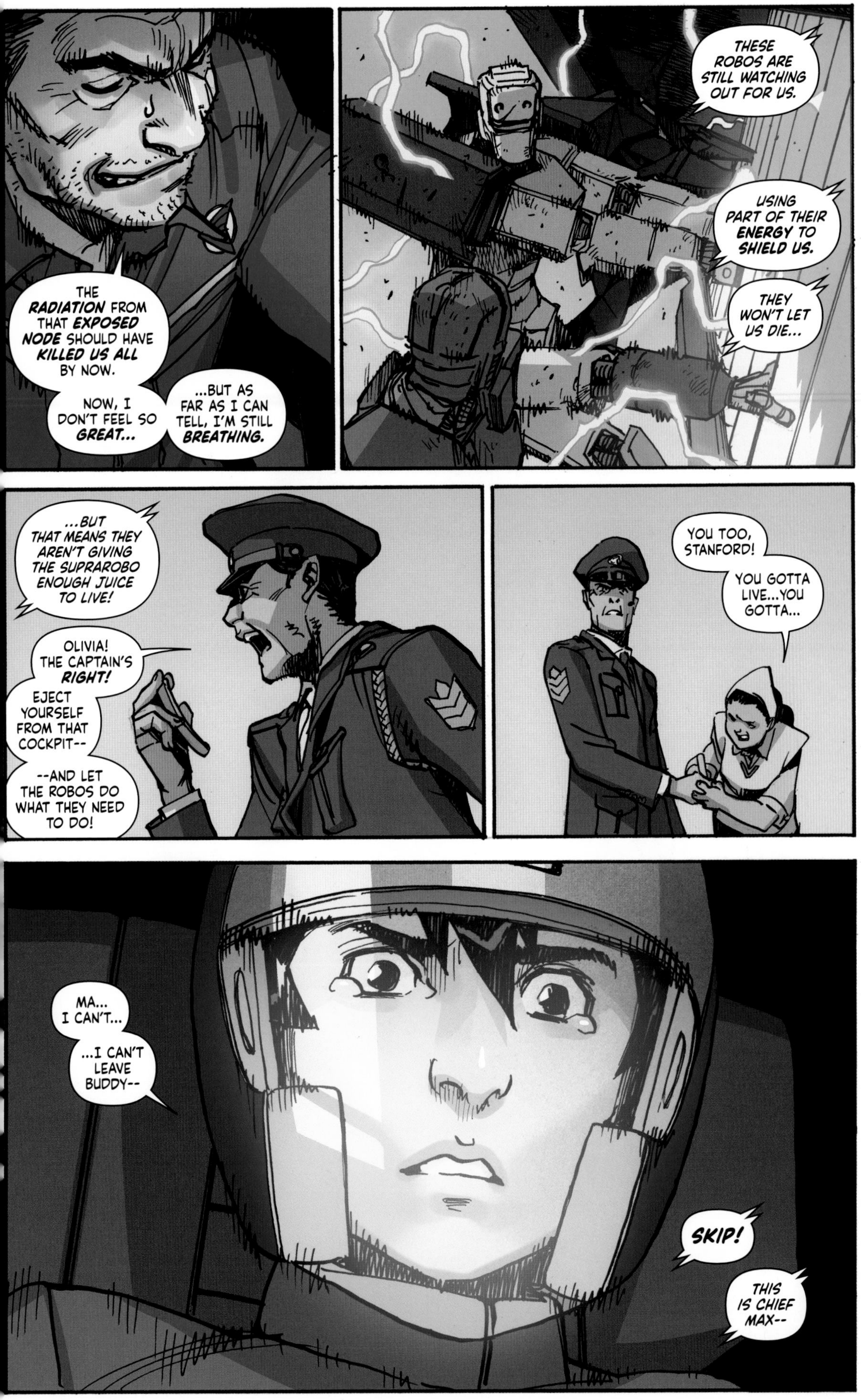
THE RADIATION FROM THAT EXPOSED NODE SHOULD HAVE KILLED US ALL BY NOW.
NOW, I DON'T FEEL SO GREAT...
...BUT AS FAR AS I CAN TELL, I'M STILL BREATHING.
THESE ROBOS ARE STILL WATCHING OUT FOR US.
USING PART OF THEIR ENERGY TO SHIELD US.
THEY WON'T LET US DIE...
...BUT THAT MEANS THEY AREN'T GIVING THE SUPRAROBO ENOUGH JUICE TO LIVE!
OLIVIA! THE CAPTAIN'S RIGHT!
EJECT YOURSELF FROM THAT COCKPIT--
--AND LET THE ROBOS DO WHAT THEY NEED TO DO!
YOU TOO, STANFORD!
YOU GOTTA LIVE...YOU GOTTA...
MA... I CAN'T...
...I CAN'T LEAVE BUDDY--
SKIP!
THIS IS CHIEF MAX--

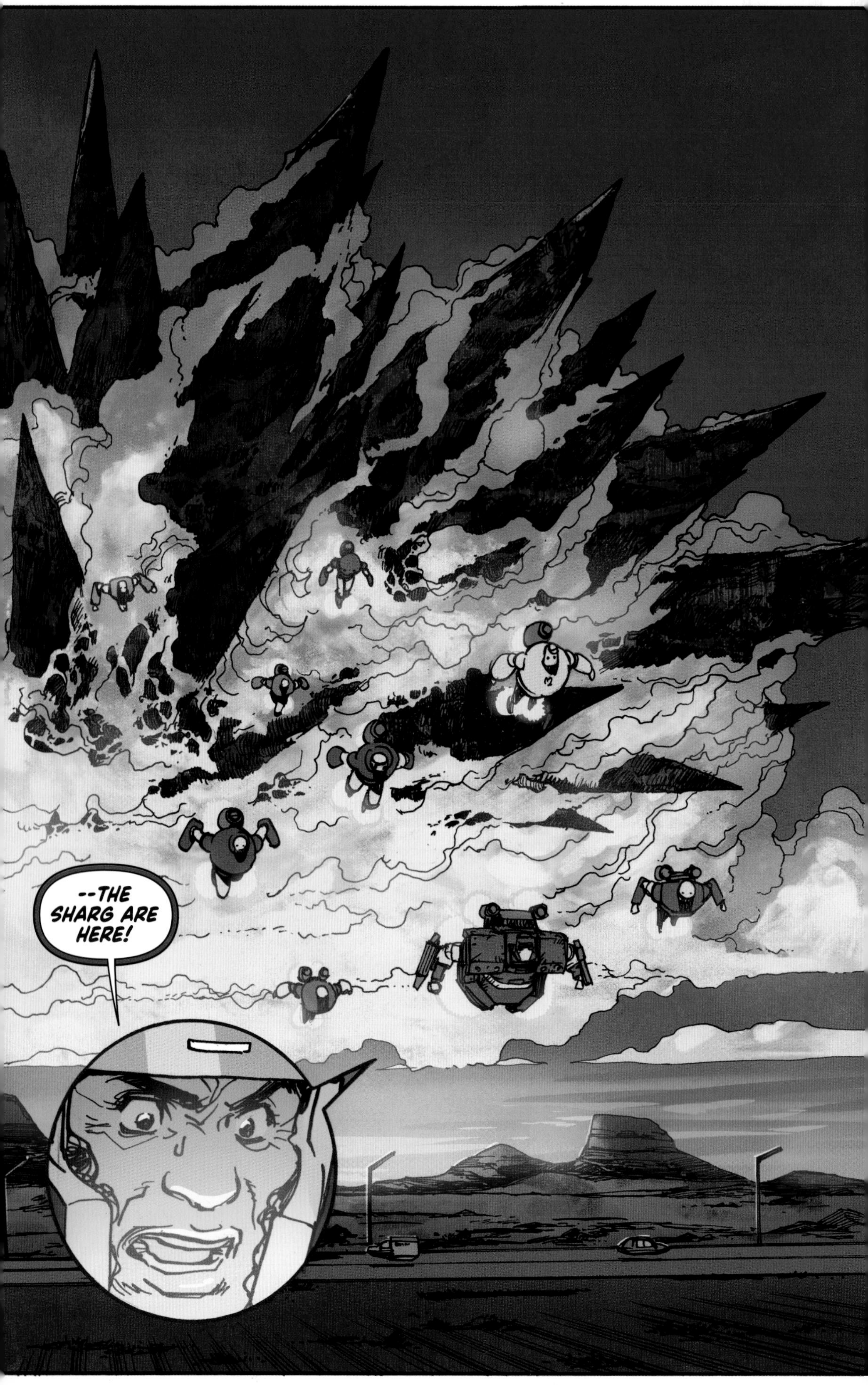
--THE SHARG ARE HERE!

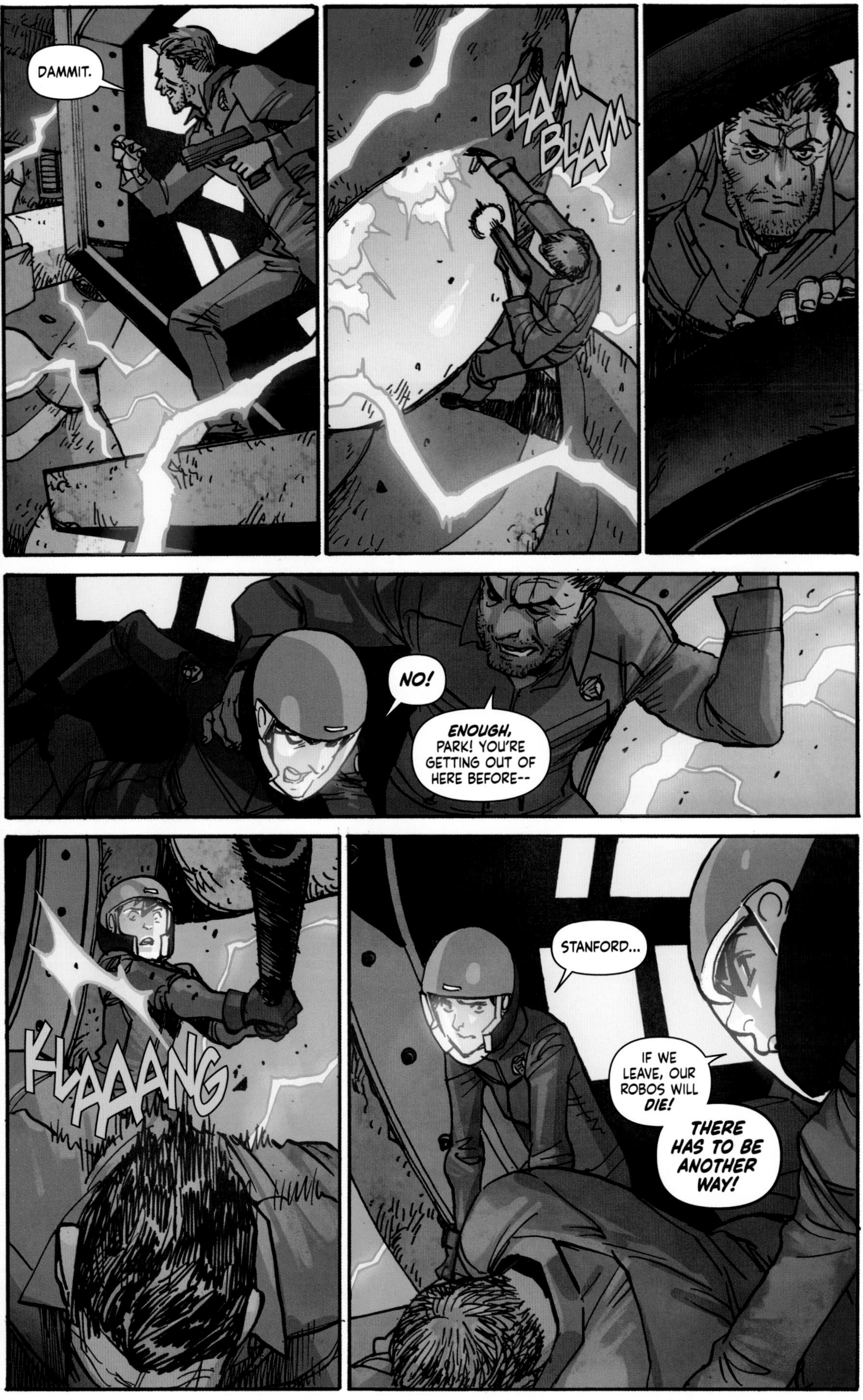
DAMMIT.
BLAM BLAM
NO!
ENOUGH, PARK! YOU'RE GETTING OUT OF HERE BEFORE--
KLAAANG
STANFORD...
IF WE LEAVE, OUR ROBOS WILL DIE!
THERE HAS TO BE ANOTHER WAY!

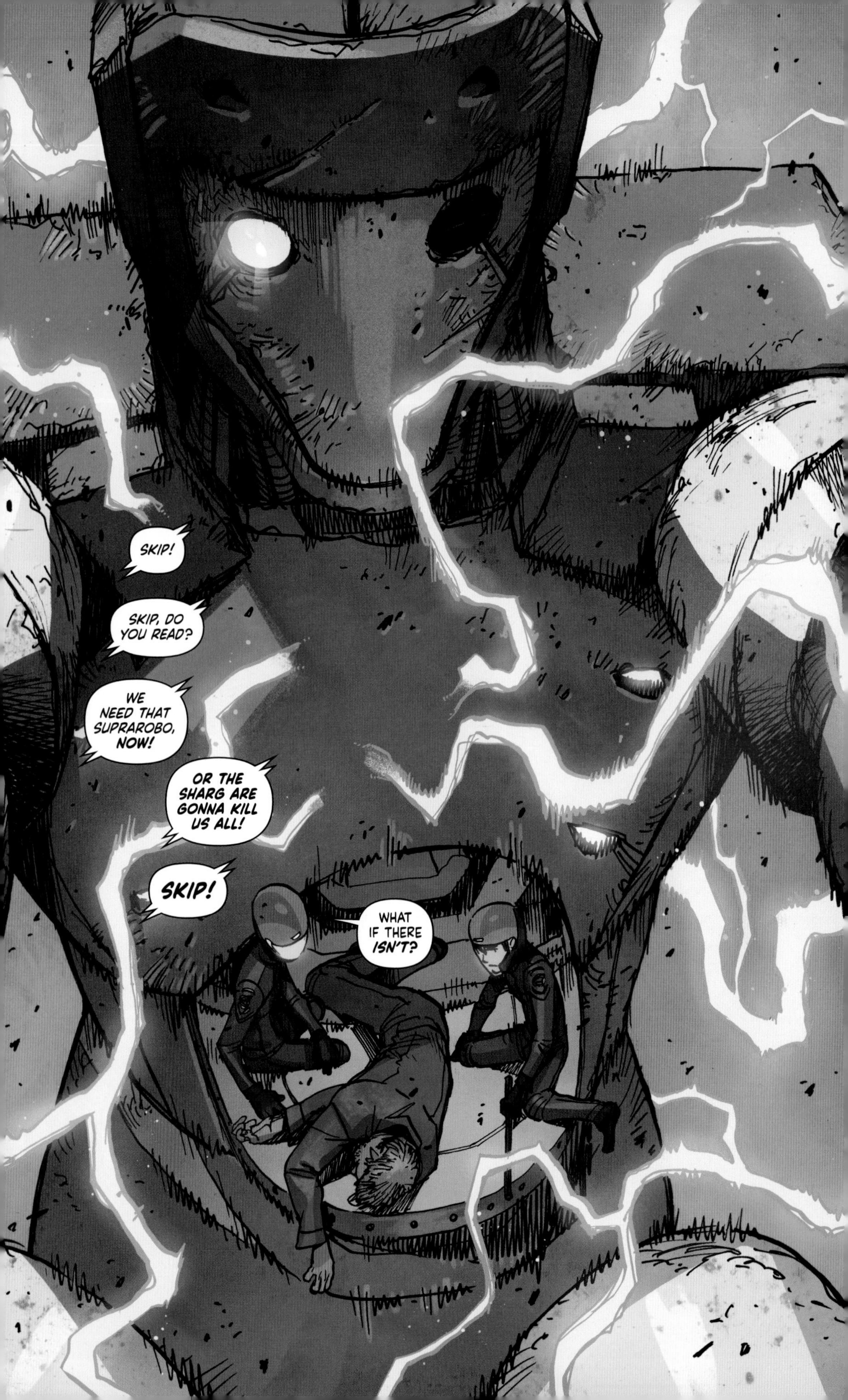
SKIP!
SKIP, DO YOU READ?
WE NEED THAT SUPRAROBO, NOW!
OR THE SHARG ARE GONNA KILL US ALL!
SKIP!
WHAT IF THERE ISN'T?

CHAPTER TWELVE

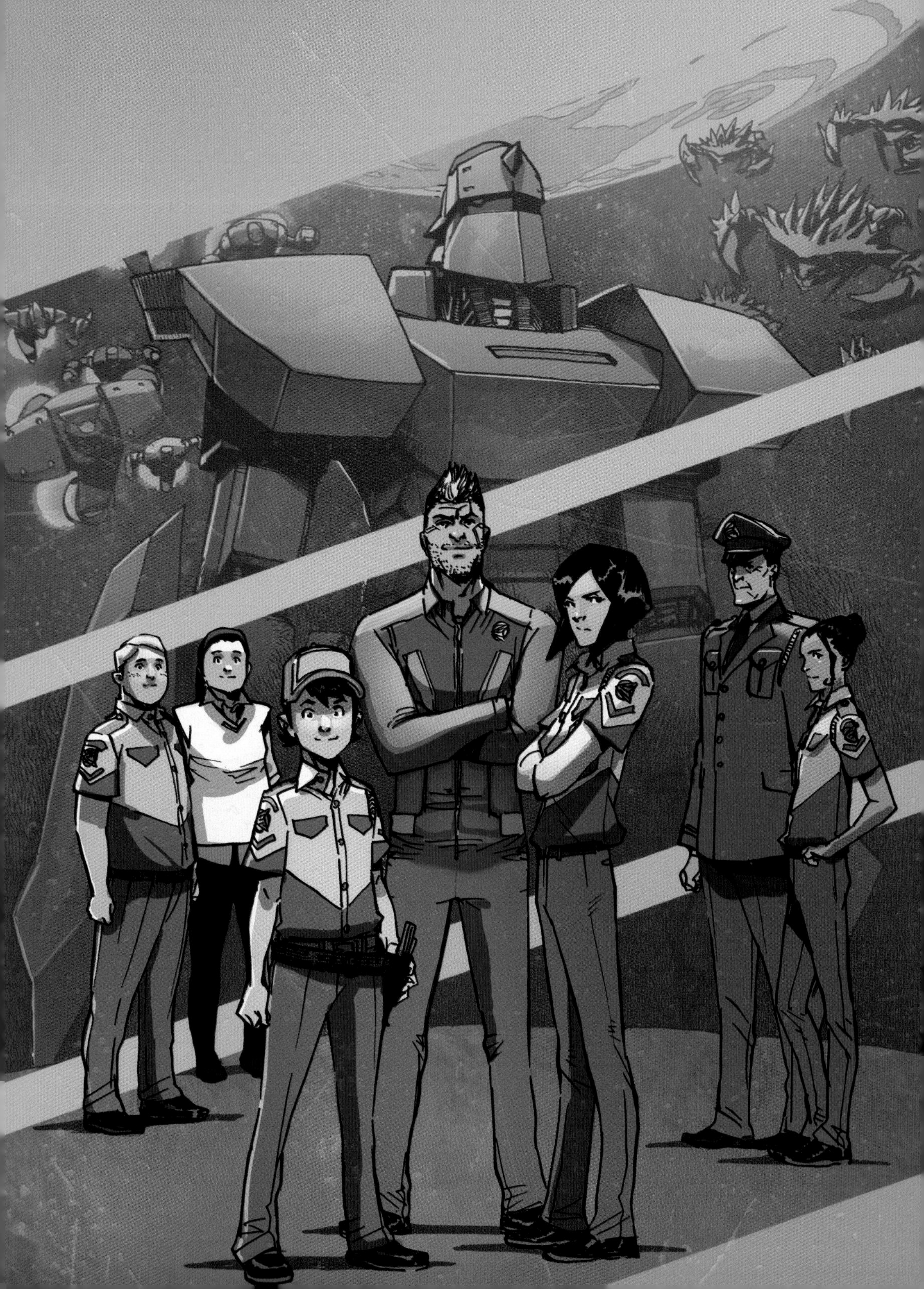

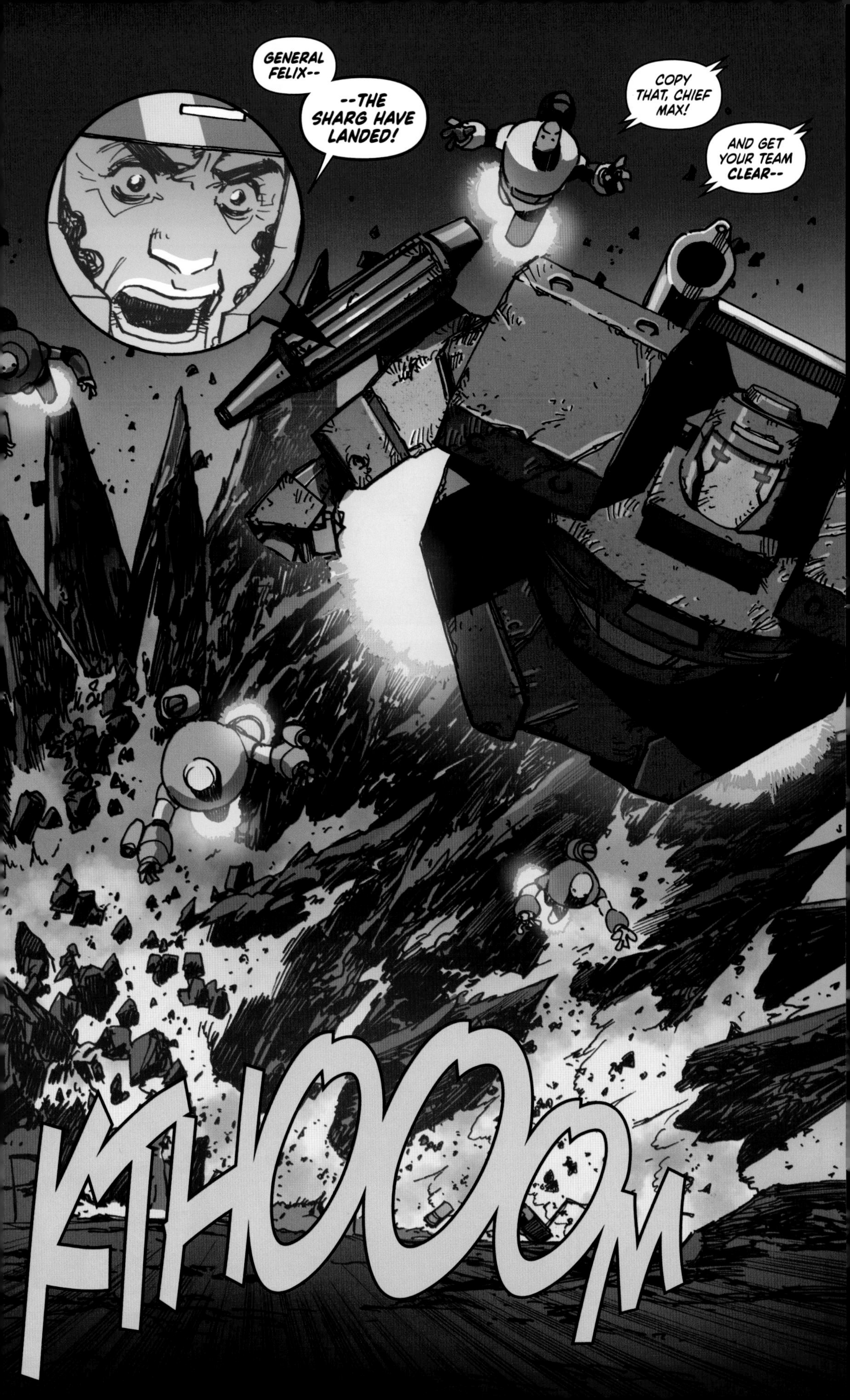
GENERAL FELIX--
--THE SHARG HAVE LANDED!
COPY THAT, CHIEF MAX!
AND GET YOUR TEAM CLEAR--
KTHOOOM

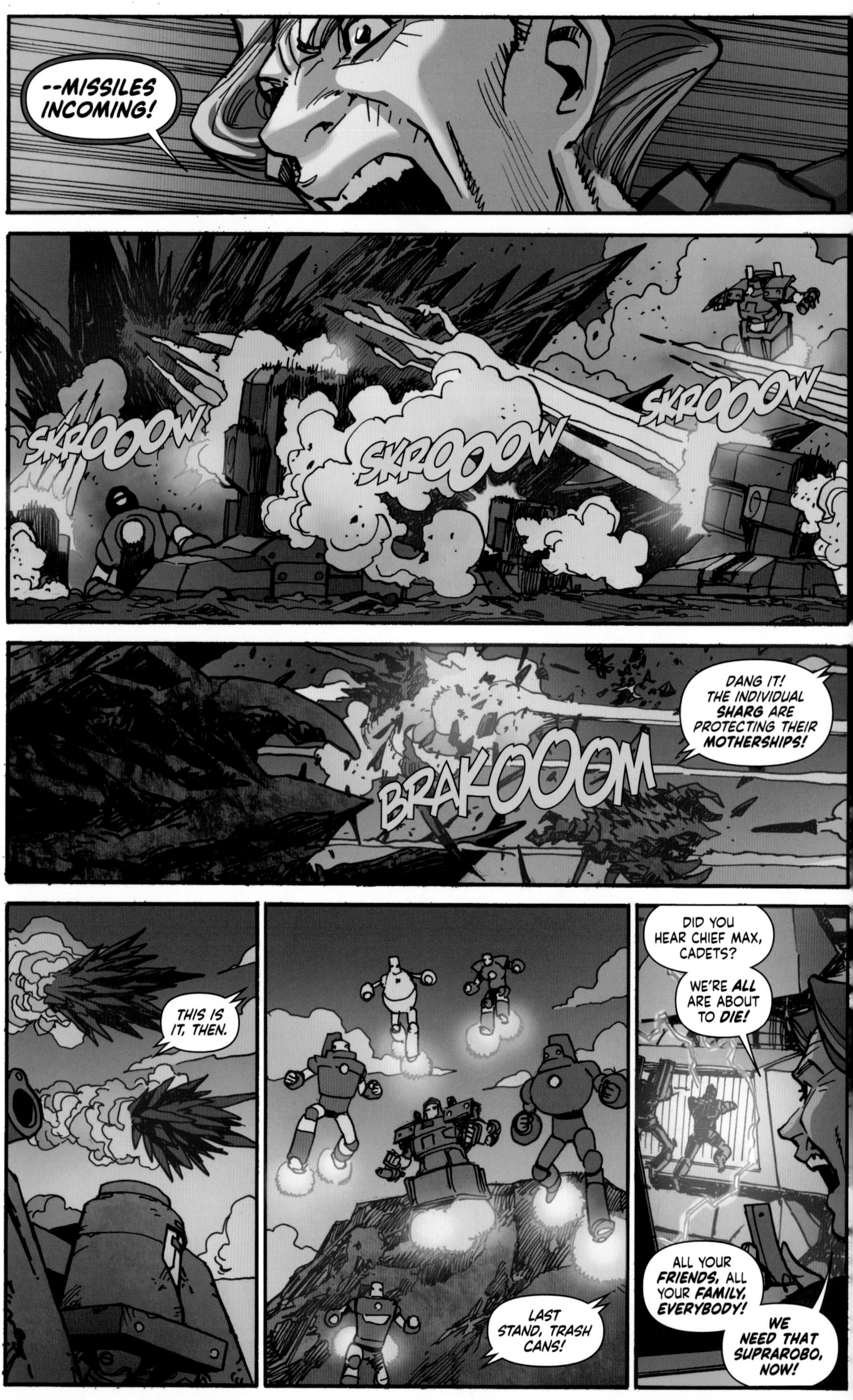
--MISSILES INCOMING!
SKROOOW
SKROOOW
SKROOOW
DANG IT! THE INDIVIDUAL SHARG ARE PROTECTING THEIR MOTHERSHIPS!
BRAKOOOM
THIS IS IT, THEN.
LAST STAND, TRASH CANS!
DID YOU HEAR CHIEF MAX, CADETS?
WE'RE ALL ARE ABOUT TO DIE!
ALL YOUR FRIENDS, ALL YOUR FAMILY, EVERYBODY!
WE NEED THAT SUPRAROBO, NOW!

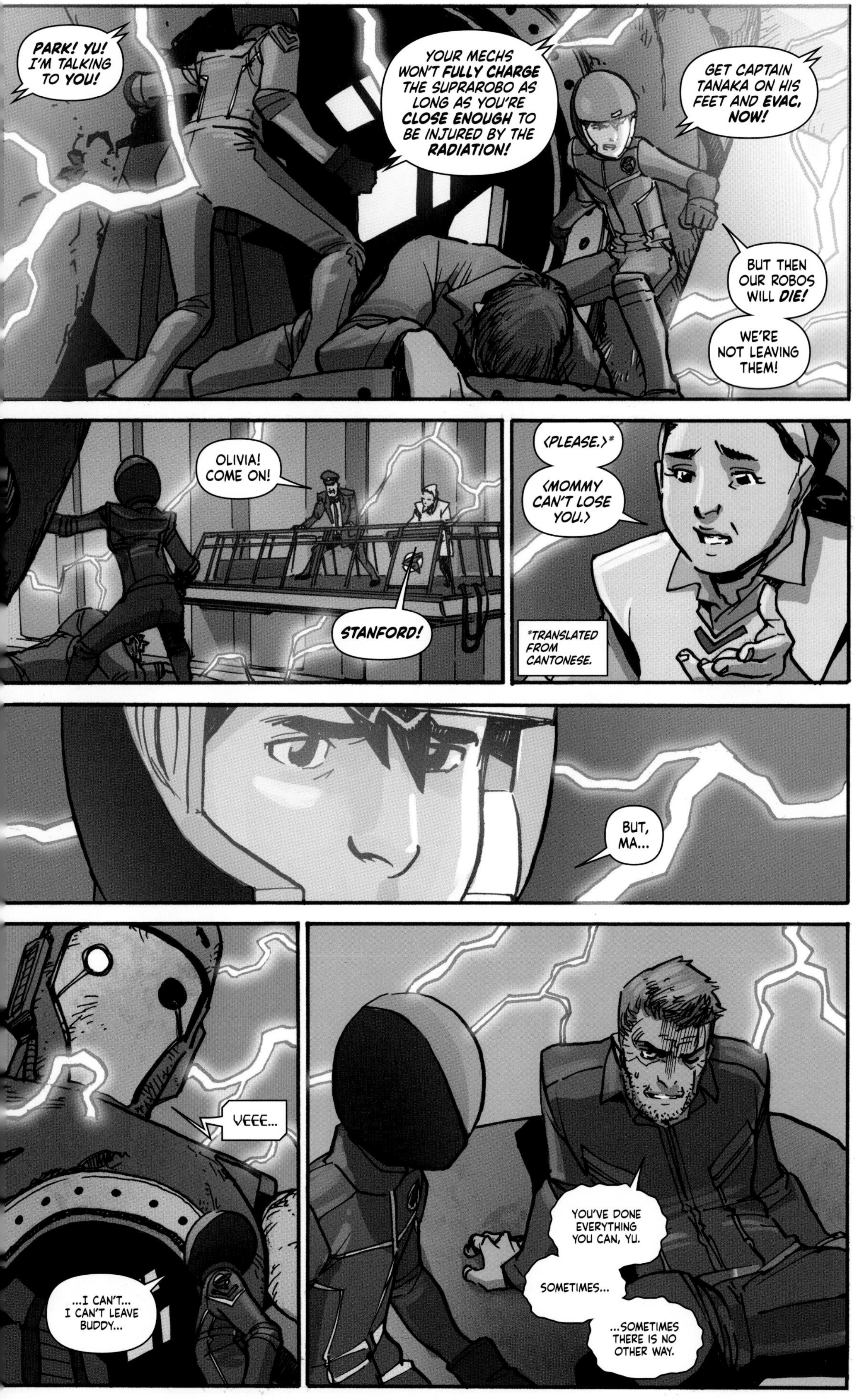
PARK! YU! I'M TALKING TO YOU!
YOUR MECHS WON'T FULLY CHARGE THE SUPRAROBO AS LONG AS YOU'RE CLOSE ENOUGH TO BE INJURED BY THE RADIATION!
GET CAPTAIN TANAKA ON HIS FEET AND EVAC, NOW!
BUT THEN OUR ROBOS WILL DIE!
WE'RE NOT LEAVING THEM!
OLIVIA! COME ON!
STANFORD!
‹PLEASE.›*
‹MOMMY CAN'T LOSE YOU.›
*TRANSLATED FROM CANTONESE.
BUT, MA...
VEEE...
...I CAN'T... I CAN'T LEAVE BUDDY...
YOU'VE DONE EVERYTHING YOU CAN, YU.
SOMETIMES...
...SOMETIMES THERE IS NO OTHER WAY.

AND THEN SOMETIMES THERE *IS!*

OLIVETTI! SANCHEZ! WHAT ARE YOU DOING--

PARDON ME, SERGEANT YU!

SORRY! COMING THROUGH!

WE JUST GOTTA FIGURE OUT WHERE TO PLUG IN...

KAAAA!

KACHUK KACHUK

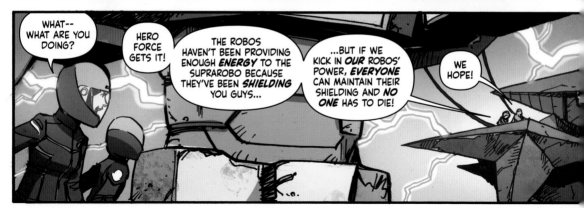

WHAT-- WHAT ARE YOU DOING?

HERO FORCE GETS IT!

THE ROBOS HAVEN'T BEEN PROVIDING ENOUGH *ENERGY* TO THE SUPRAROBO BECAUSE THEY'VE BEEN *SHIELDING* YOU GUYS...

...BUT IF WE KICK IN *OUR* ROBOS' POWER, *EVERYONE* CAN MAINTAIN THEIR SHIELDING AND *NO ONE* HAS TO DIE!

WE HOPE!

YOU GUYS...

YOU DID IT FOR *ME* ONCE, STANFORD.

OKAY, ROBOS!

YOU'RE HOOKED UP!

GIVE IT WHAT YOU GOT!

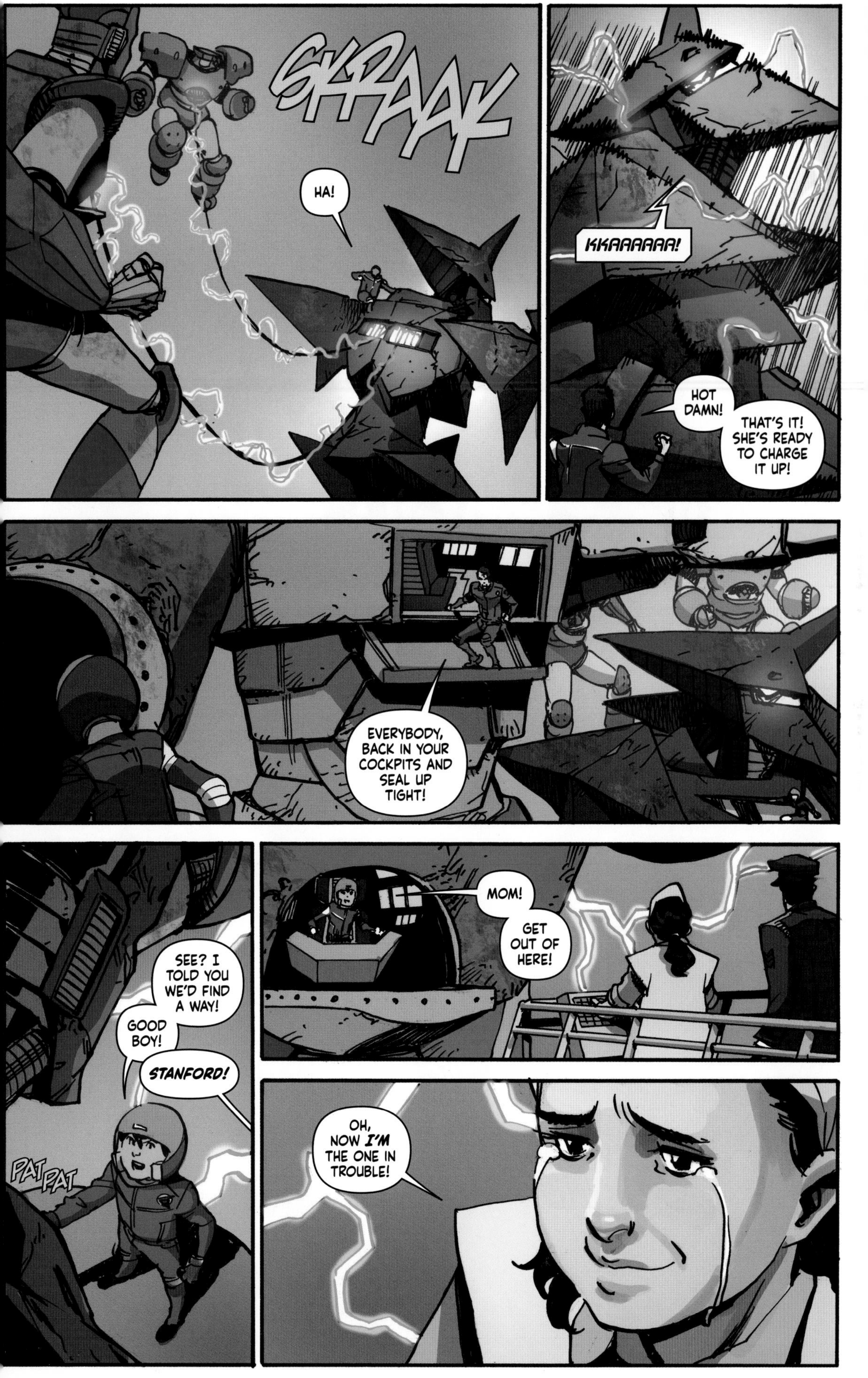
SKRAAK
HA!
KKAAAAAAA!
HOT DAMN!
THAT'S IT! SHE'S READY TO CHARGE IT UP!
EVERYBODY, BACK IN YOUR COCKPITS AND SEAL UP TIGHT!
SEE? I TOLD YOU WE'D FIND A WAY!
GOOD BOY!
STANFORD!
PAT PAT
MOM!
GET OUT OF HERE!
OH, NOW I'M THE ONE IN TROUBLE!

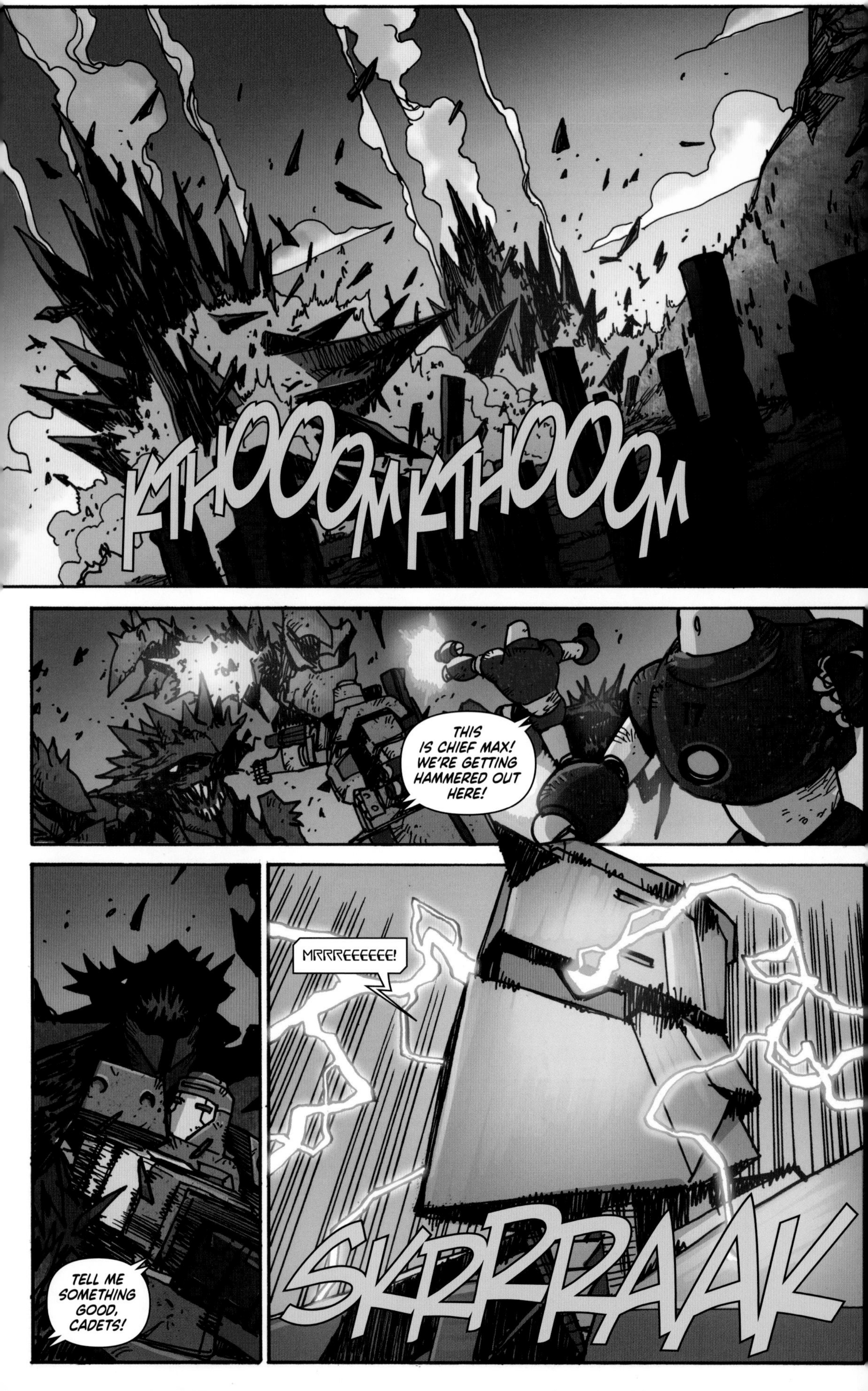
KTHOOOM KTHOOOM
THIS IS CHIEF MAX! WE'RE GETTING HAMMERED OUT HERE!
TELL ME SOMETHING GOOD, CADETS!
MRRREEEEEE!
SKRRRAAK

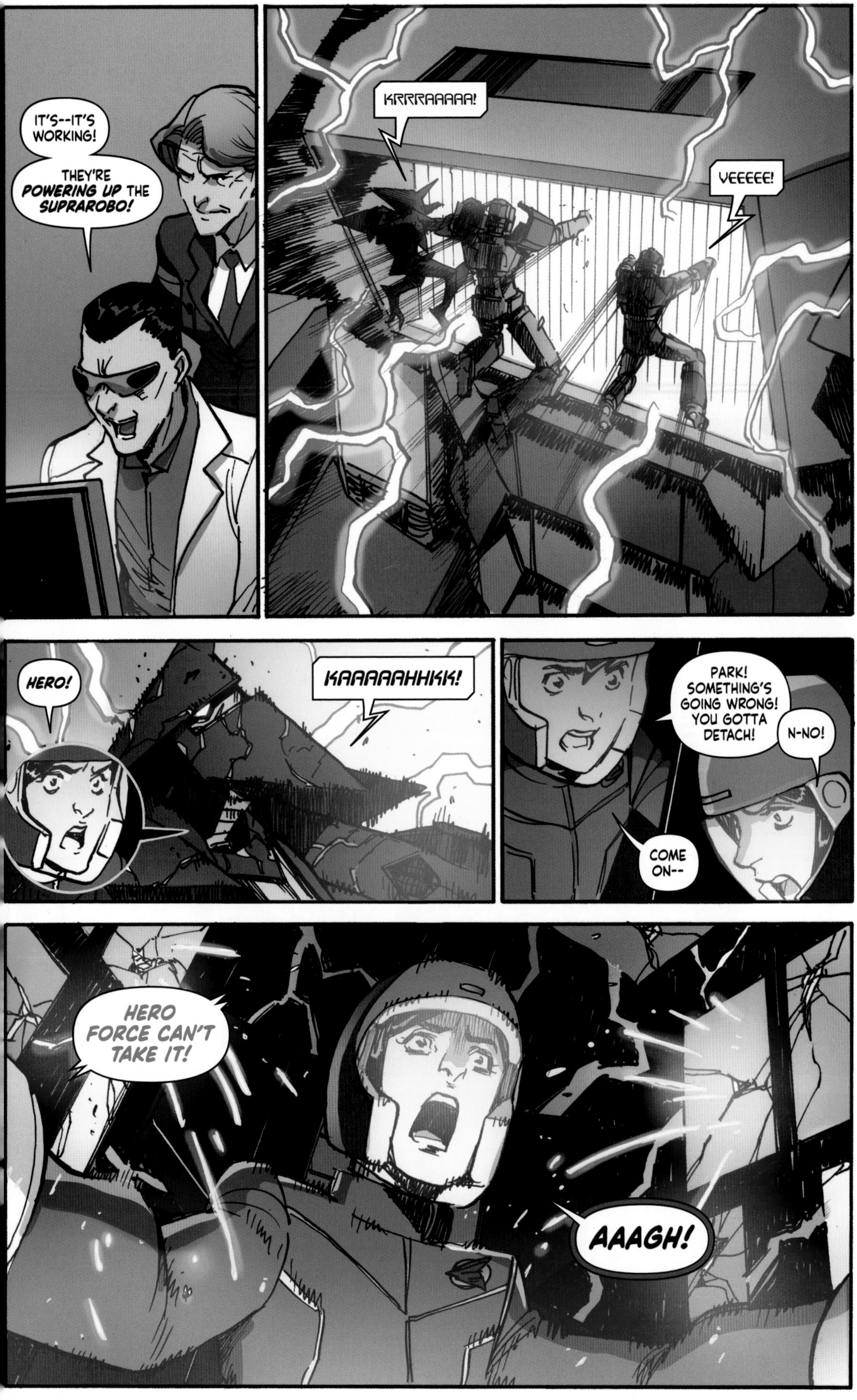

IT'S--IT'S WORKING!
THEY'RE POWERING UP THE SUPRAROBO!
KRRRAAAAA!
VEEEEE!
HERO!
KAAAAAHHKK!
PARK! SOMETHING'S GOING WRONG! YOU GOTTA DETACH!
N-NO!
COME ON--
HERO FORCE CAN'T TAKE IT!
AAAGH!

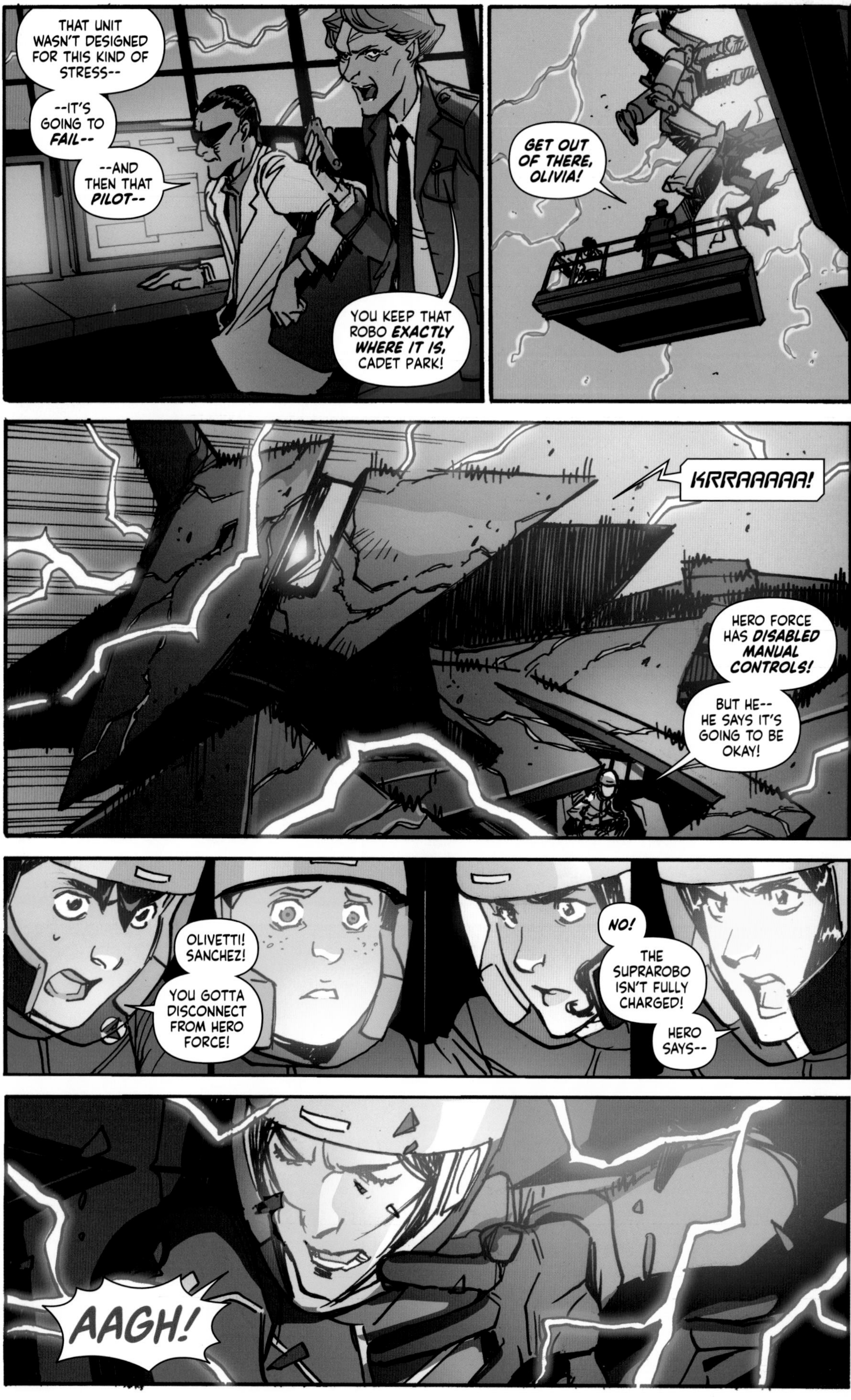
THAT UNIT WASN'T DESIGNED FOR THIS KIND OF STRESS--
--IT'S GOING TO FAIL--
--AND THEN THAT PILOT--
YOU KEEP THAT ROBO EXACTLY WHERE IT IS, CADET PARK!
GET OUT OF THERE, OLIVIA!
KRRAAAAA!
HERO FORCE HAS DISABLED MANUAL CONTROLS!
BUT HE-- HE SAYS IT'S GOING TO BE OKAY!
OLIVETTI! SANCHEZ!
YOU GOTTA DISCONNECT FROM HERO FORCE!
NO!
THE SUPRAROBO ISN'T FULLY CHARGED!
HERO SAYS--
AAGH!

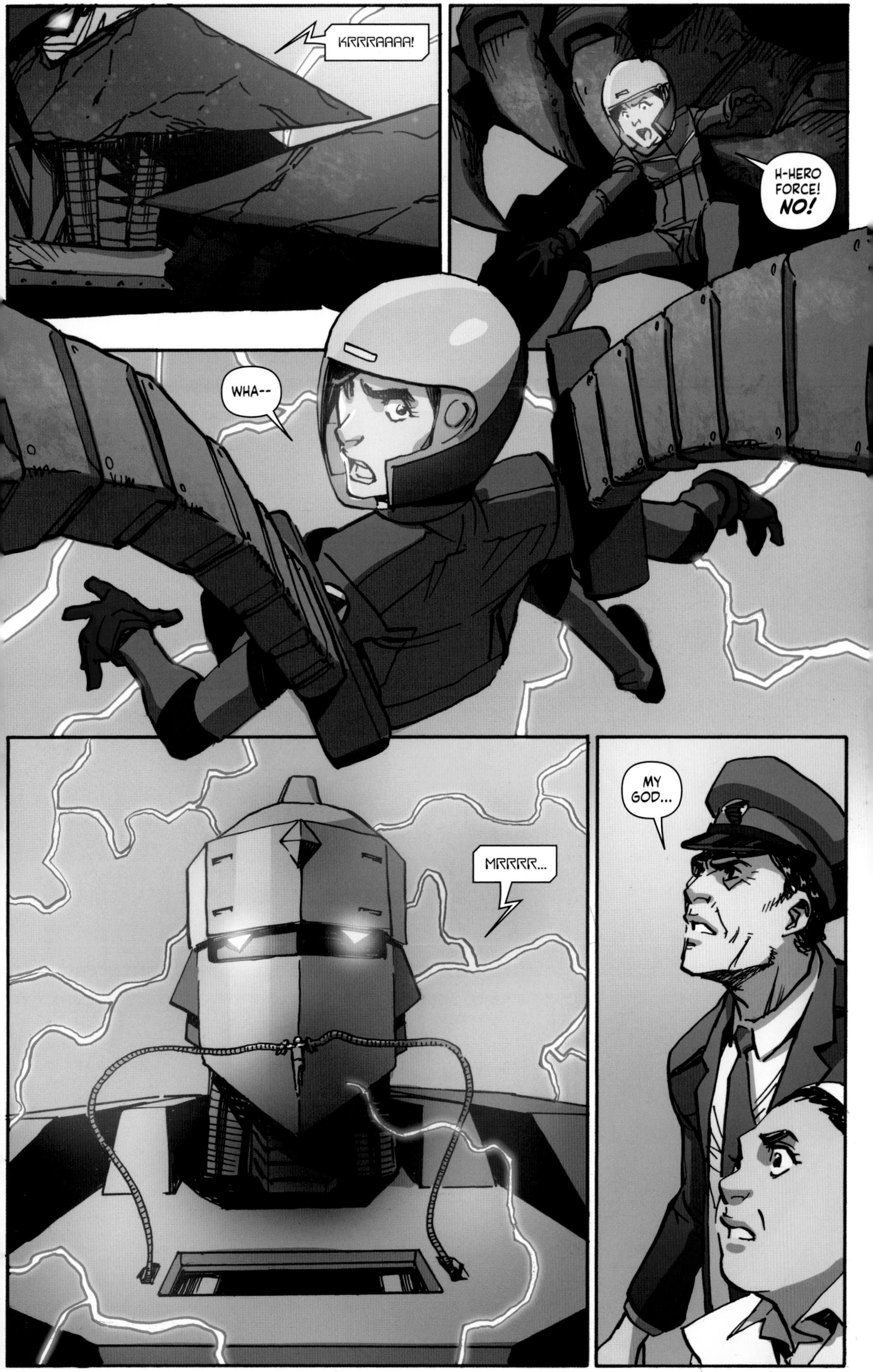
KRRRAAAA!
H-HERO FORCE! NO!
WHA--
MRRRR...
MY GOD...

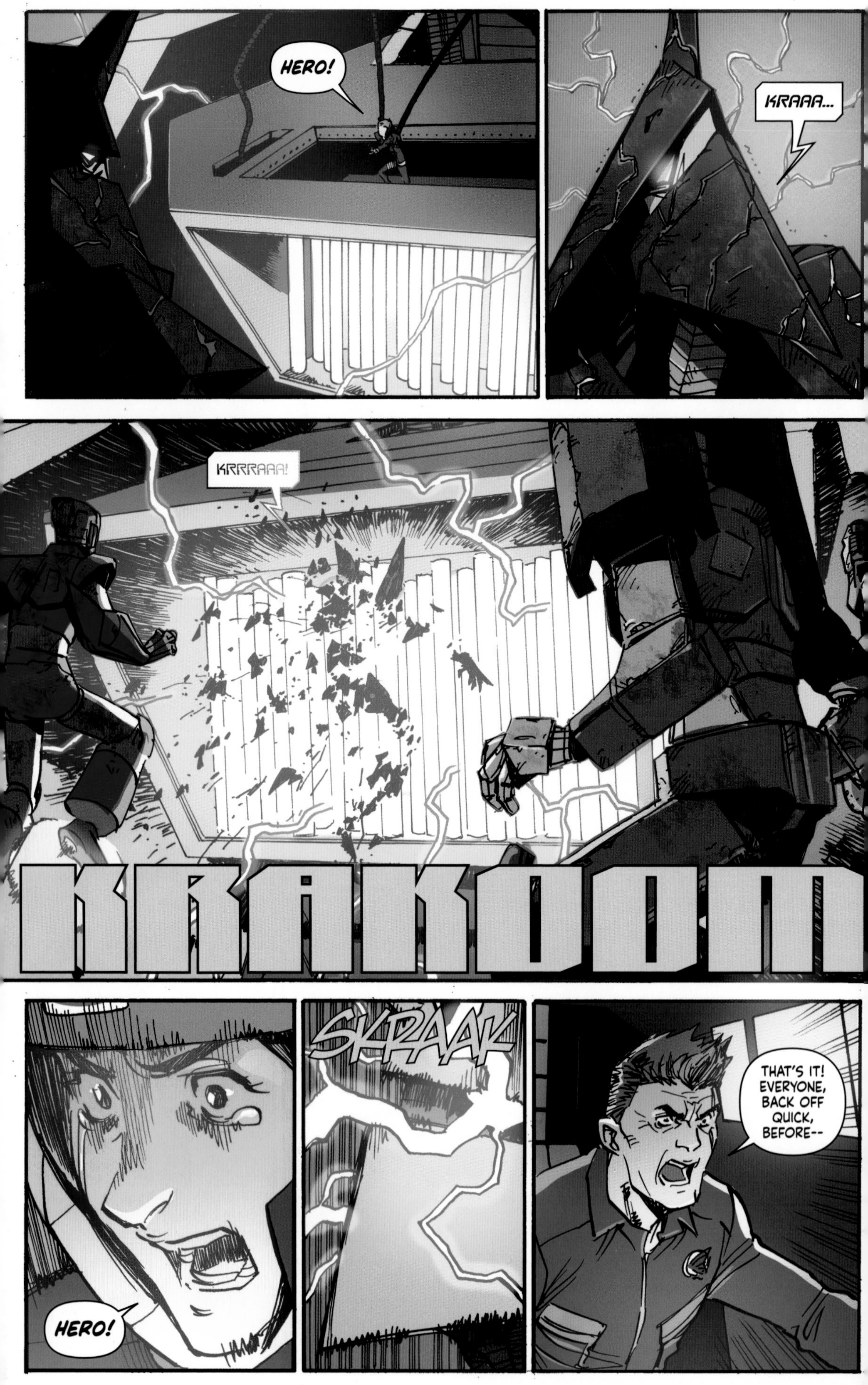
HERO!
KRAAA...
KRRRAAA!
KRAKOOM
HERO!
SKRAAK
THAT'S IT! EVERYONE, BACK OFF QUICK, BEFORE--

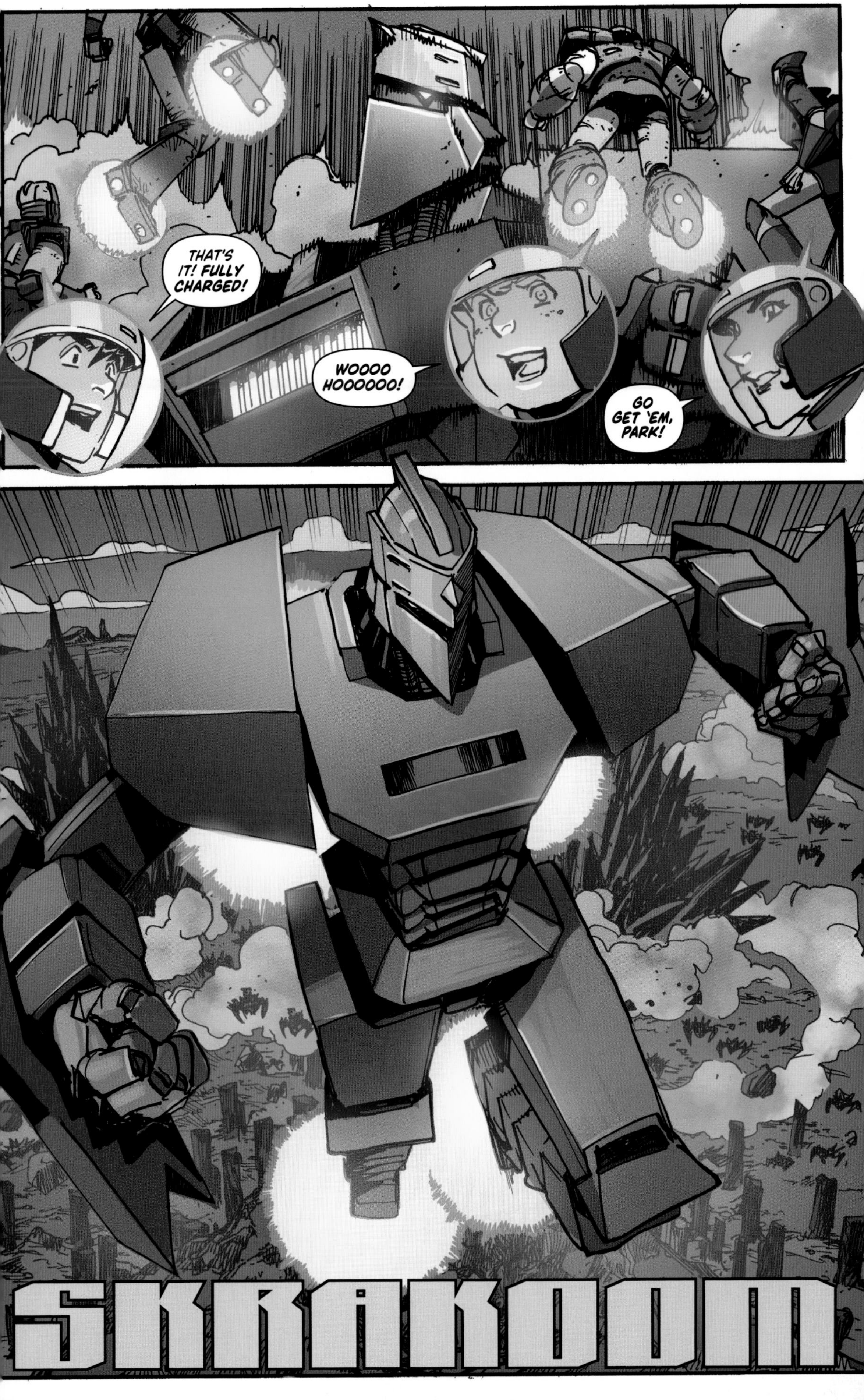
THAT'S IT! FULLY CHARGED!
WOOOO HOOOOOO!
GO GET 'EM, PARK!
SKRAKOOM

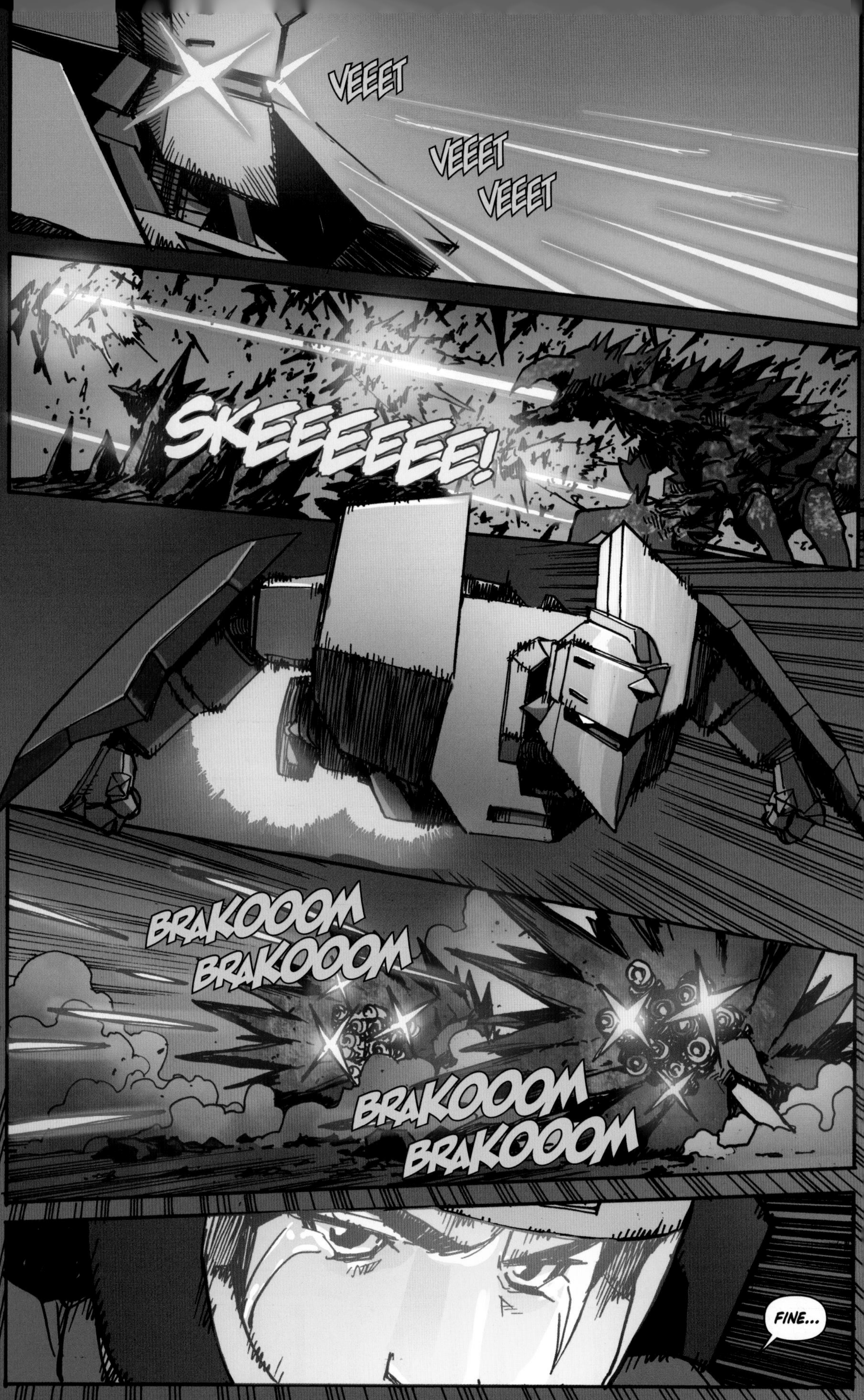
VEEET
VEEET
VEEET
SKEEEEEEE!
BRAKOOOM
BRAKOOOM
BRAKOOOM
BRAKOOOM
FINE...

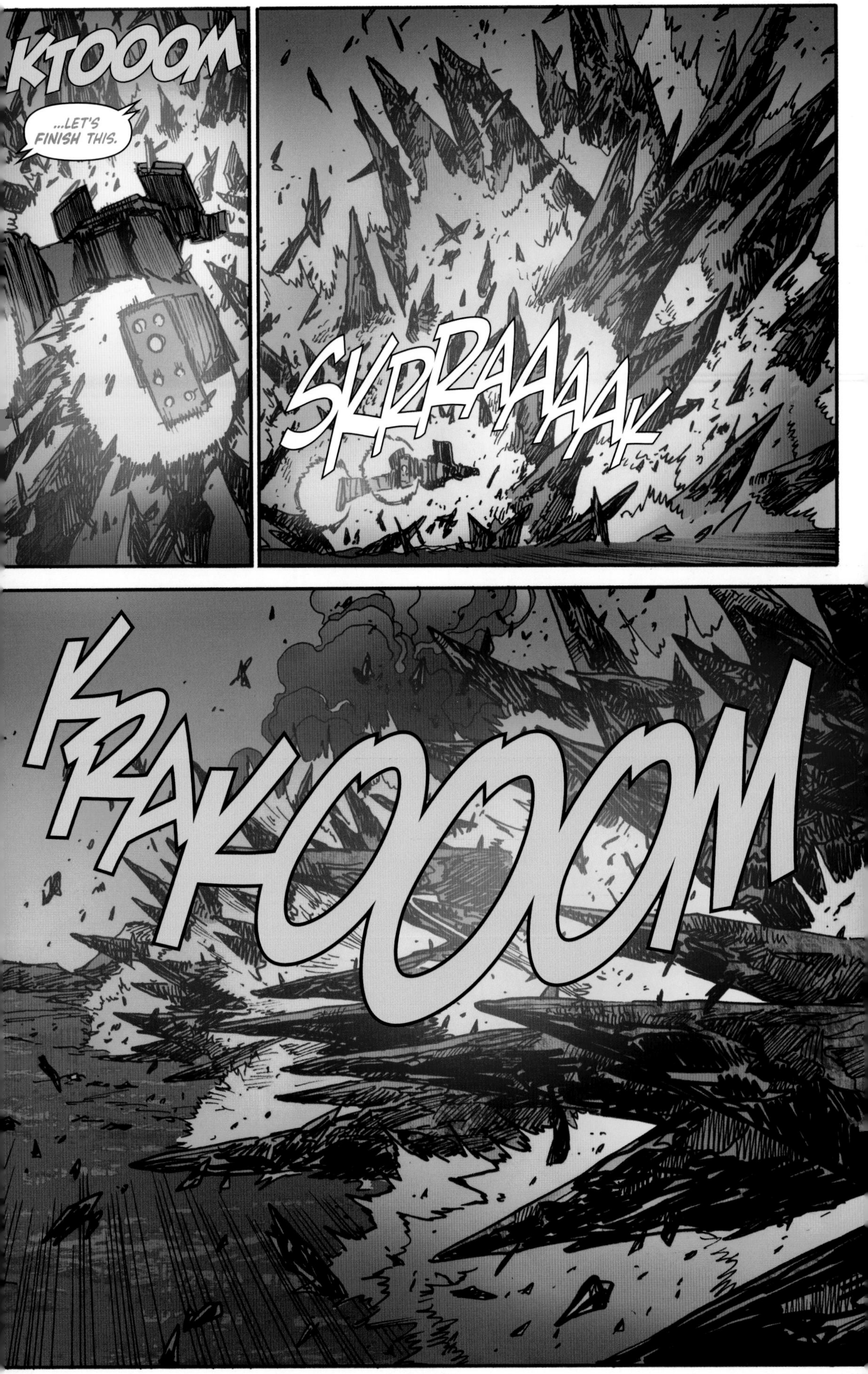
KTOOOM
...LET'S FINISH THIS.
SKRRAAAAK
KRAKOOOOM

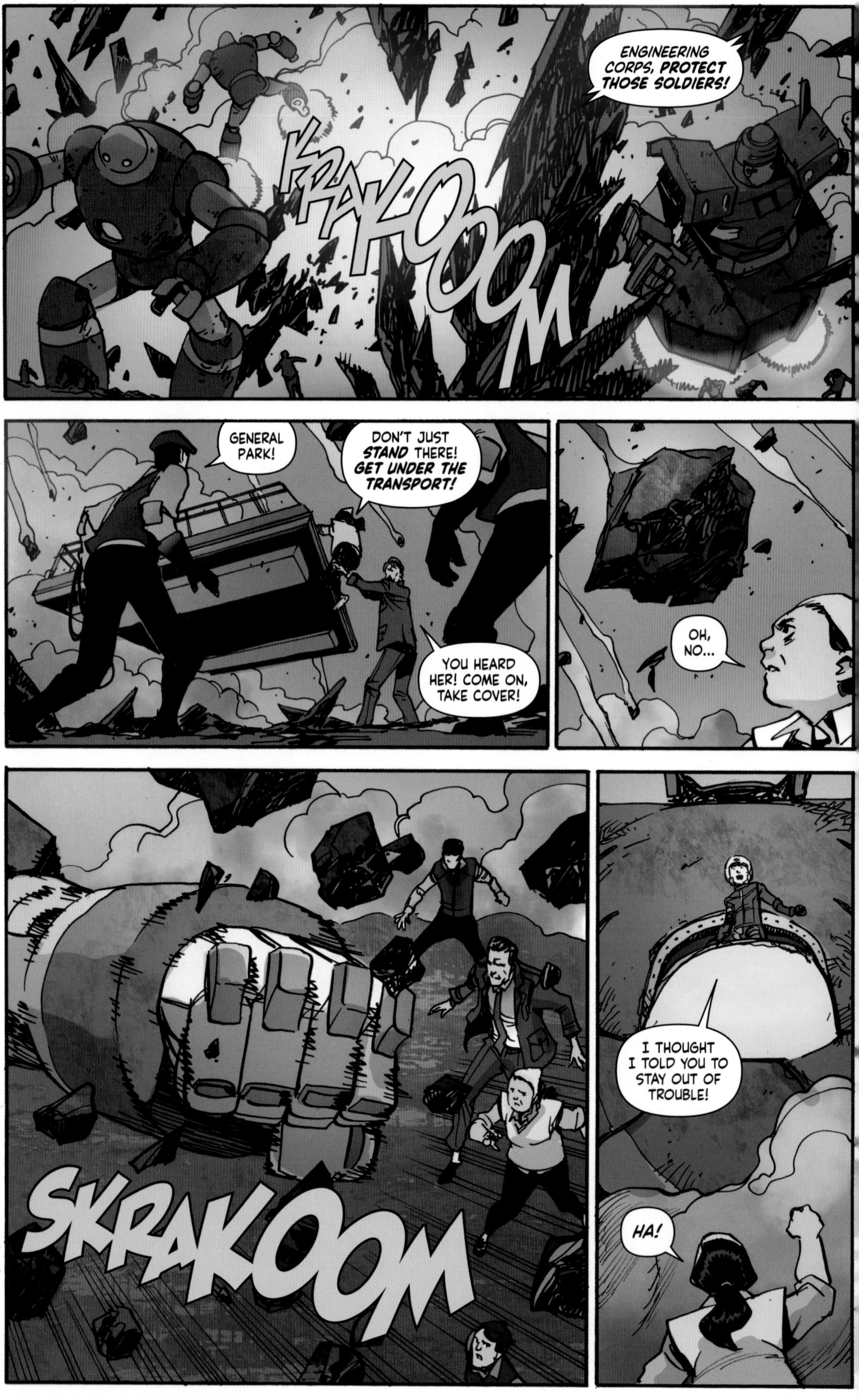
ENGINEERING CORPS, PROTECT THOSE SOLDIERS!
KRAKOOOM
GENERAL PARK!
DON'T JUST STAND THERE! GET UNDER THE TRANSPORT!
YOU HEARD HER! COME ON, TAKE COVER!
OH, NO...
SKRAKOOM
I THOUGHT I TOLD YOU TO STAY OUT OF TROUBLE!
HA!

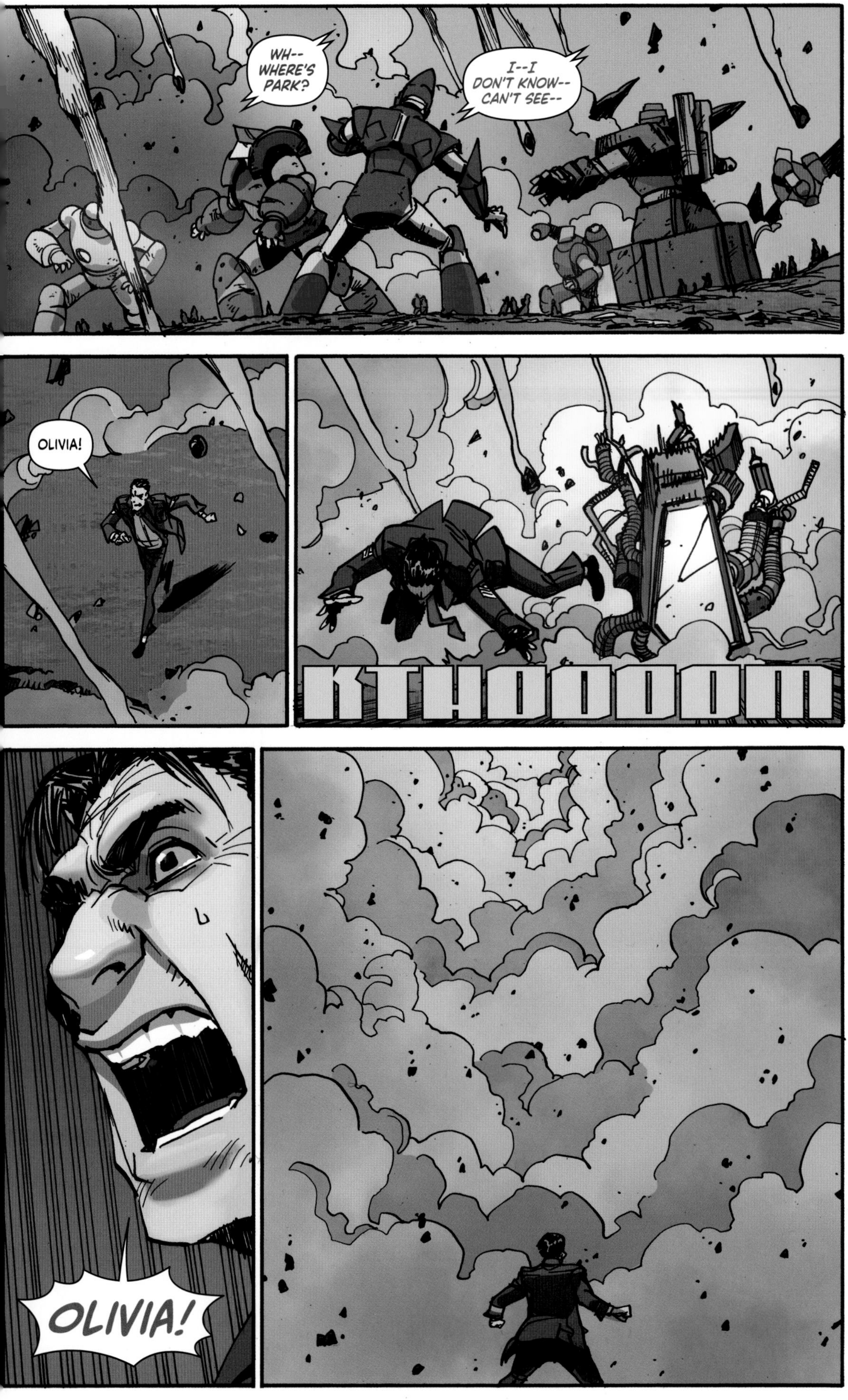
WH-- WHERE'S PARK?
I--I DON'T KNOW-- CAN'T SEE--
OLIVIA!
KTHOOOOM
OLIVIA!

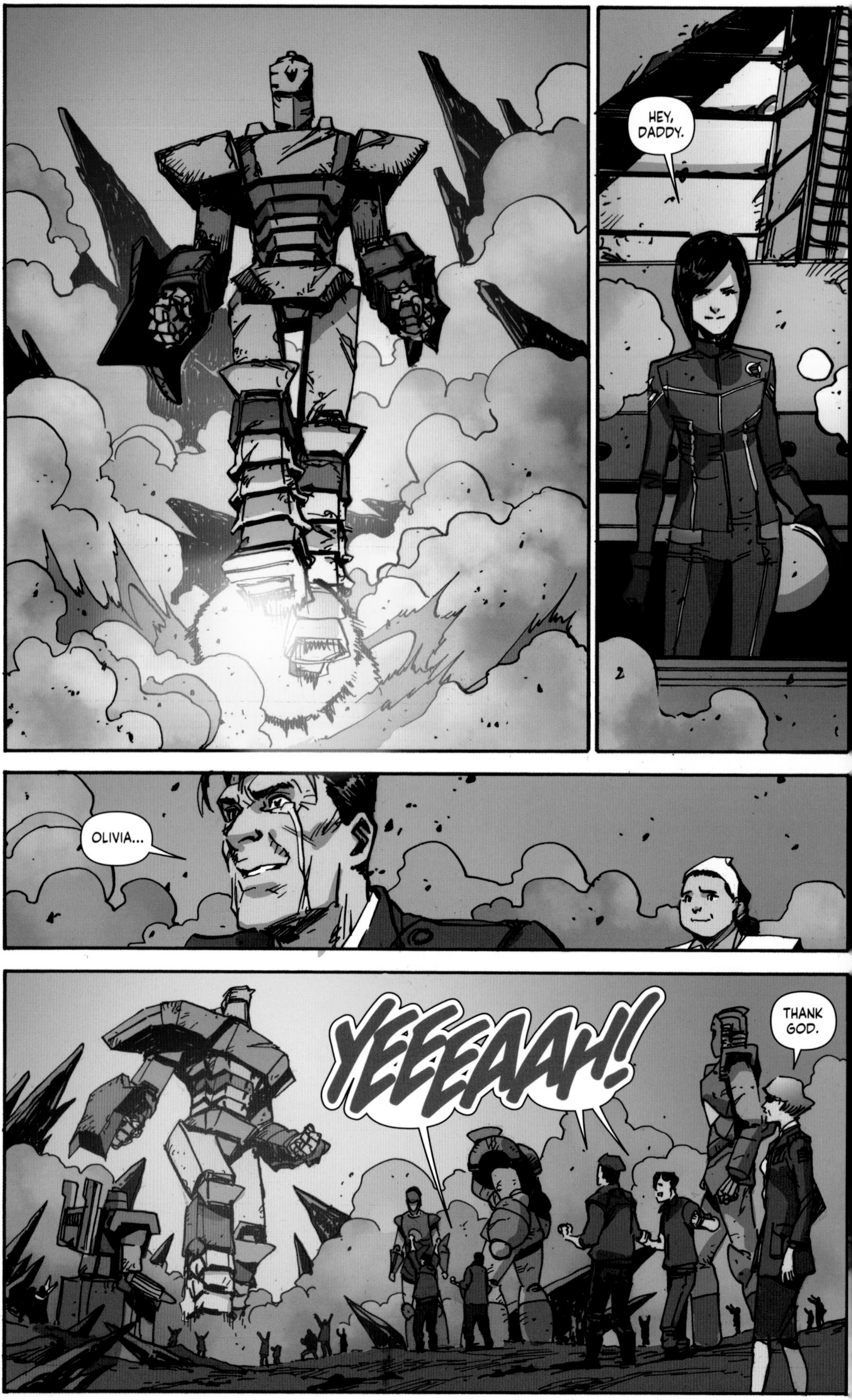
HEY, DADDY.
OLIVIA...
YEEEAAAH!
THANK GOD.

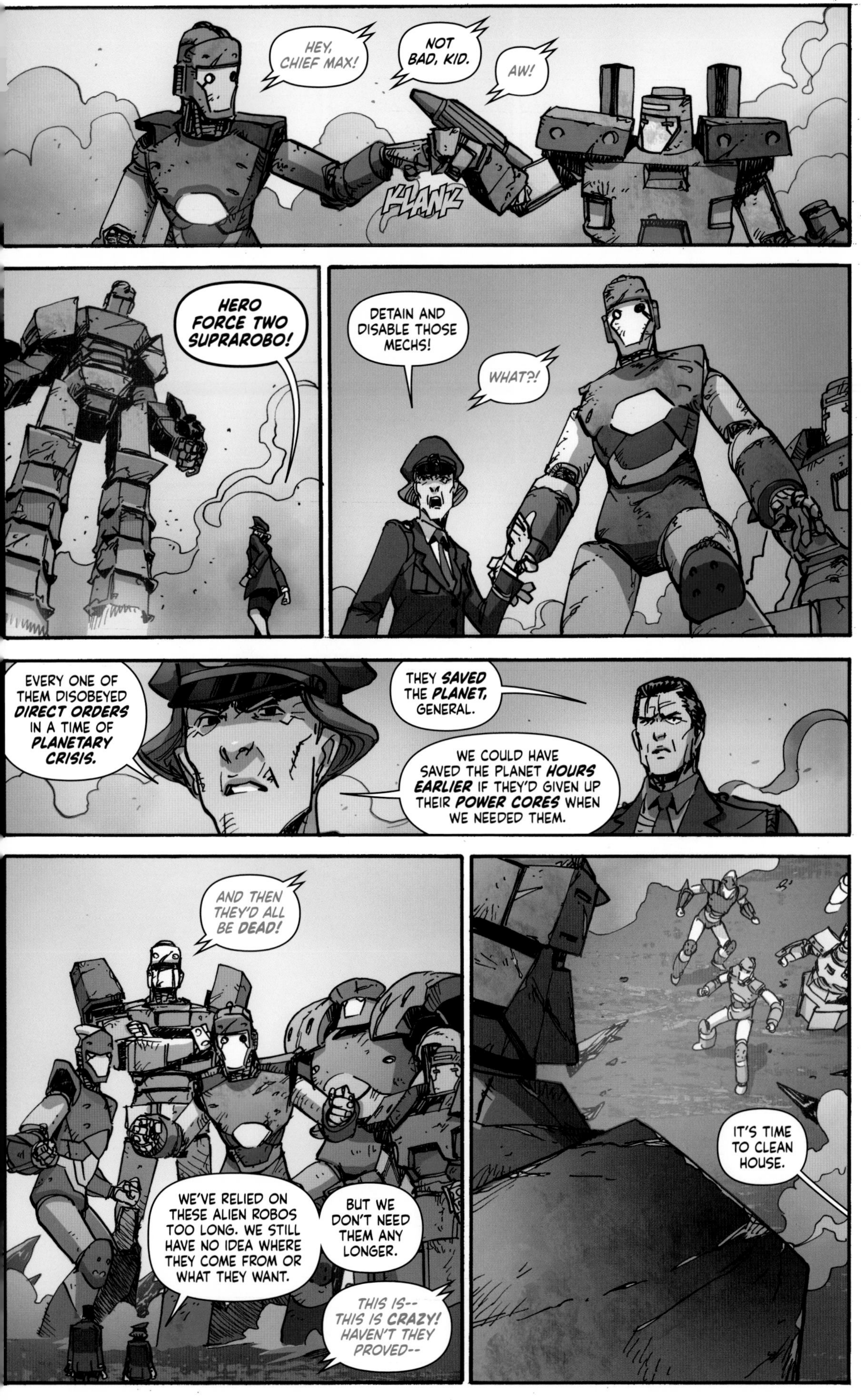
HEY, CHIEF MAX!
NOT BAD, KID.
AW!
KLANK
HERO FORCE TWO SUPRAROBO!
DETAIN AND DISABLE THOSE MECHS!
WHAT?!
EVERY ONE OF THEM DISOBEYED DIRECT ORDERS IN A TIME OF PLANETARY CRISIS.
THEY SAVED THE PLANET, GENERAL.
WE COULD HAVE SAVED THE PLANET HOURS EARLIER IF THEY'D GIVEN UP THEIR POWER CORES WHEN WE NEEDED THEM.
AND THEN THEY'D ALL BE DEAD!
WE'VE RELIED ON THESE ALIEN ROBOS TOO LONG. WE STILL HAVE NO IDEA WHERE THEY COME FROM OR WHAT THEY WANT.
BUT WE DON'T NEED THEM ANY LONGER.
THIS IS-- THIS IS CRAZY! HAVEN'T THEY PROVED--
IT'S TIME TO CLEAN HOUSE.

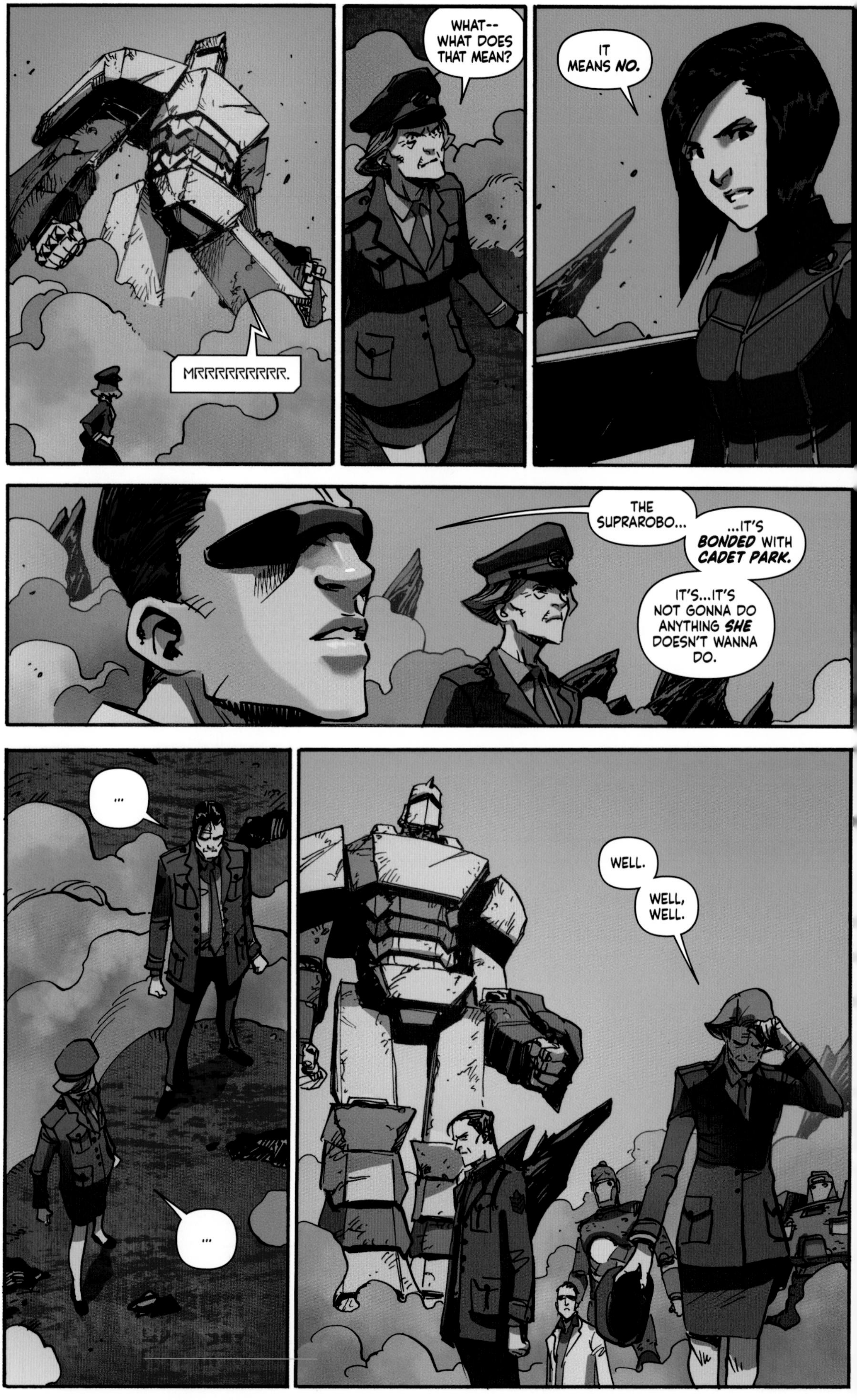
MRRRRRRRRRR.
WHAT-- WHAT DOES THAT MEAN?
IT MEANS NO.
THE SUPRAROBO...
...IT'S BONDED WITH CADET PARK.
IT'S...IT'S NOT GONNA DO ANYTHING SHE DOESN'T WANNA DO.
...
...
WELL.
WELL, WELL.

THREE MONTHS LATER.

SKY CORPS ACADEMY, LOS ROBOS, ARIZONA.

MEMORIAL DAY.

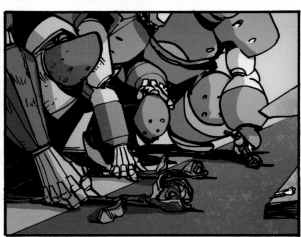

Huh...I THOUGHT IT WAS RIGHT HERE...

IT'S OKAY, MA. I'LL RUN BACK TO THE OFFICE AND GET A MAP...

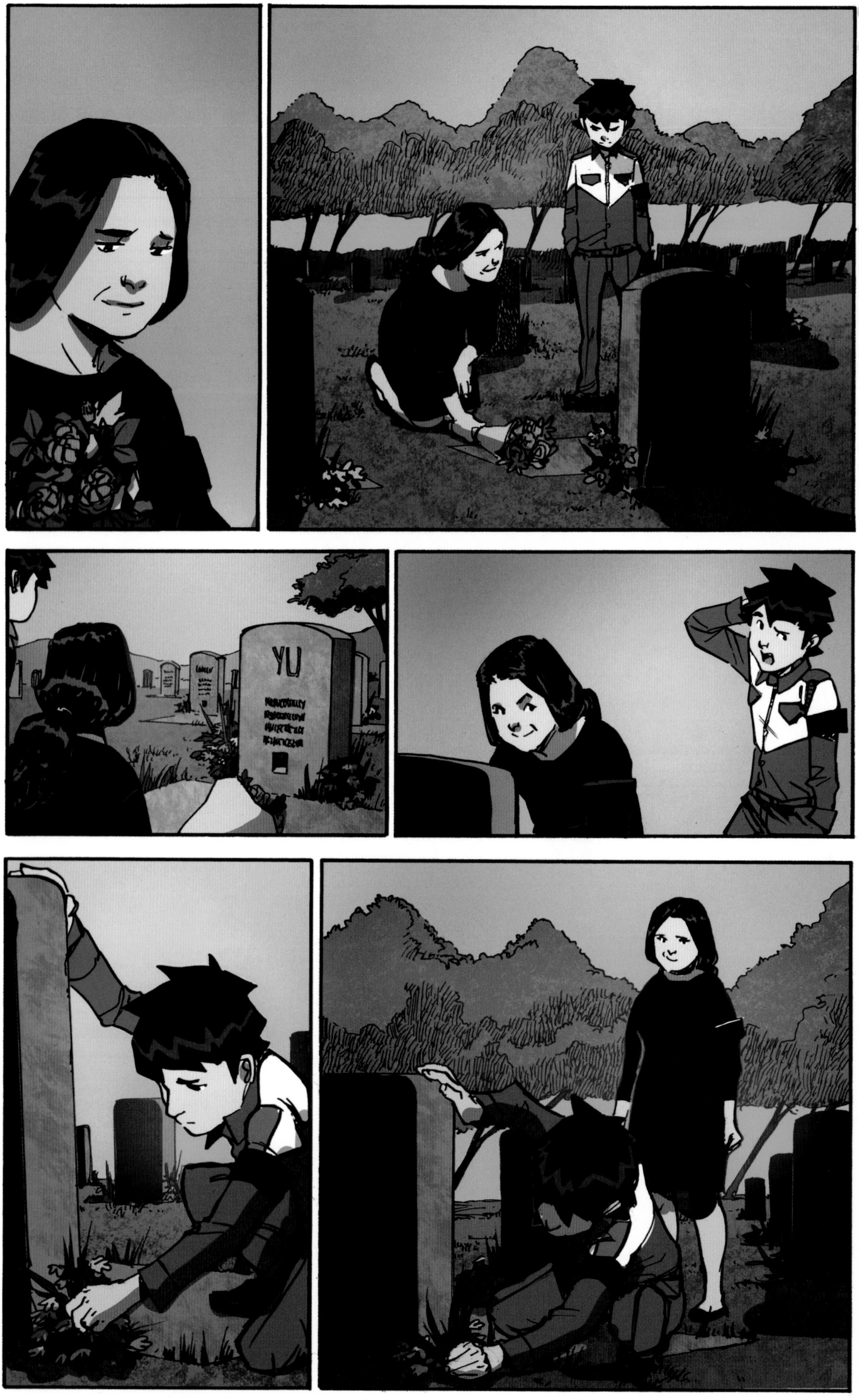
YU

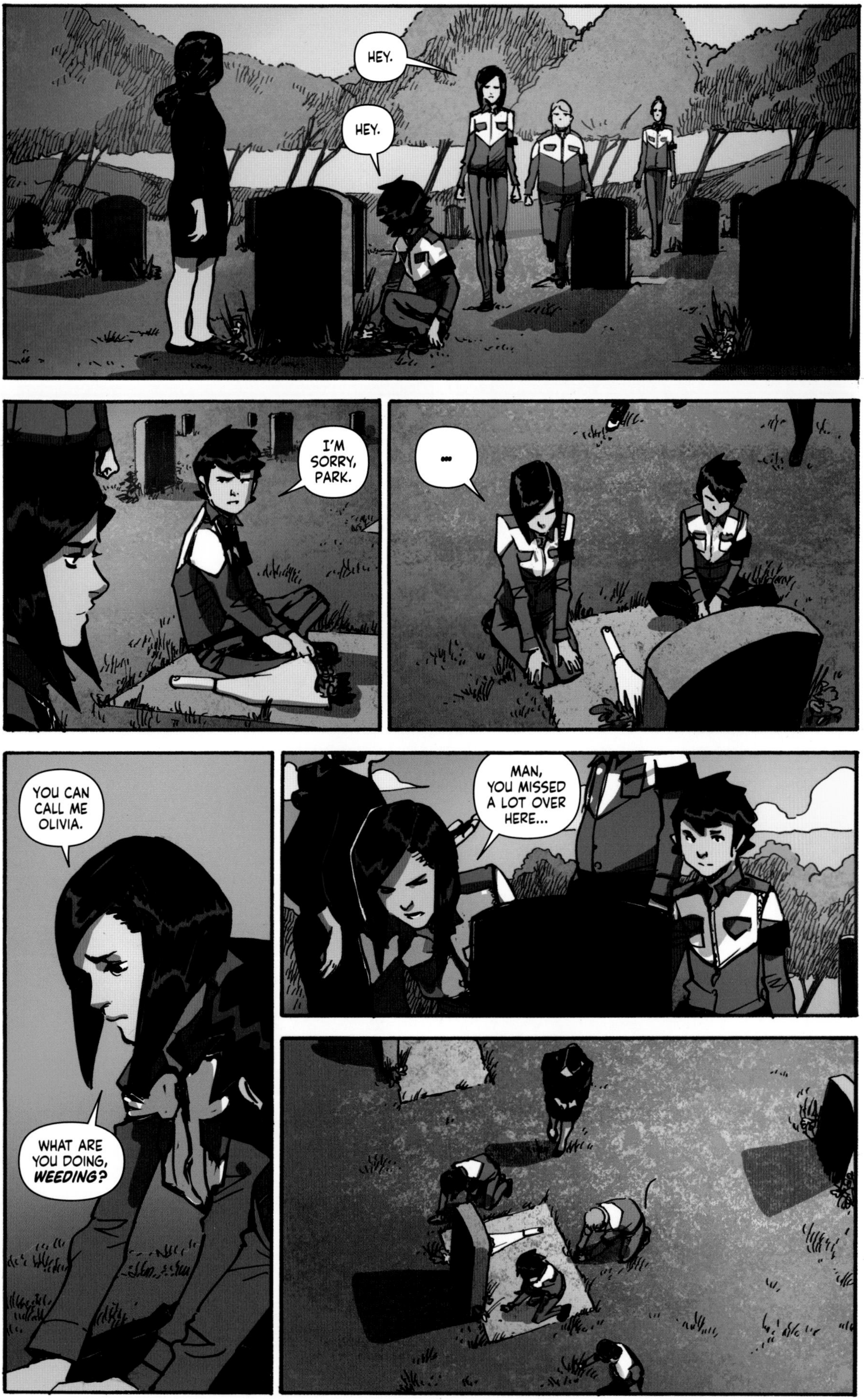
HEY.
HEY.
I'M SORRY, PARK.
...
YOU CAN CALL ME OLIVIA.
WHAT ARE YOU DOING, *WEEDING?*
MAN, YOU MISSED A LOT OVER HERE...

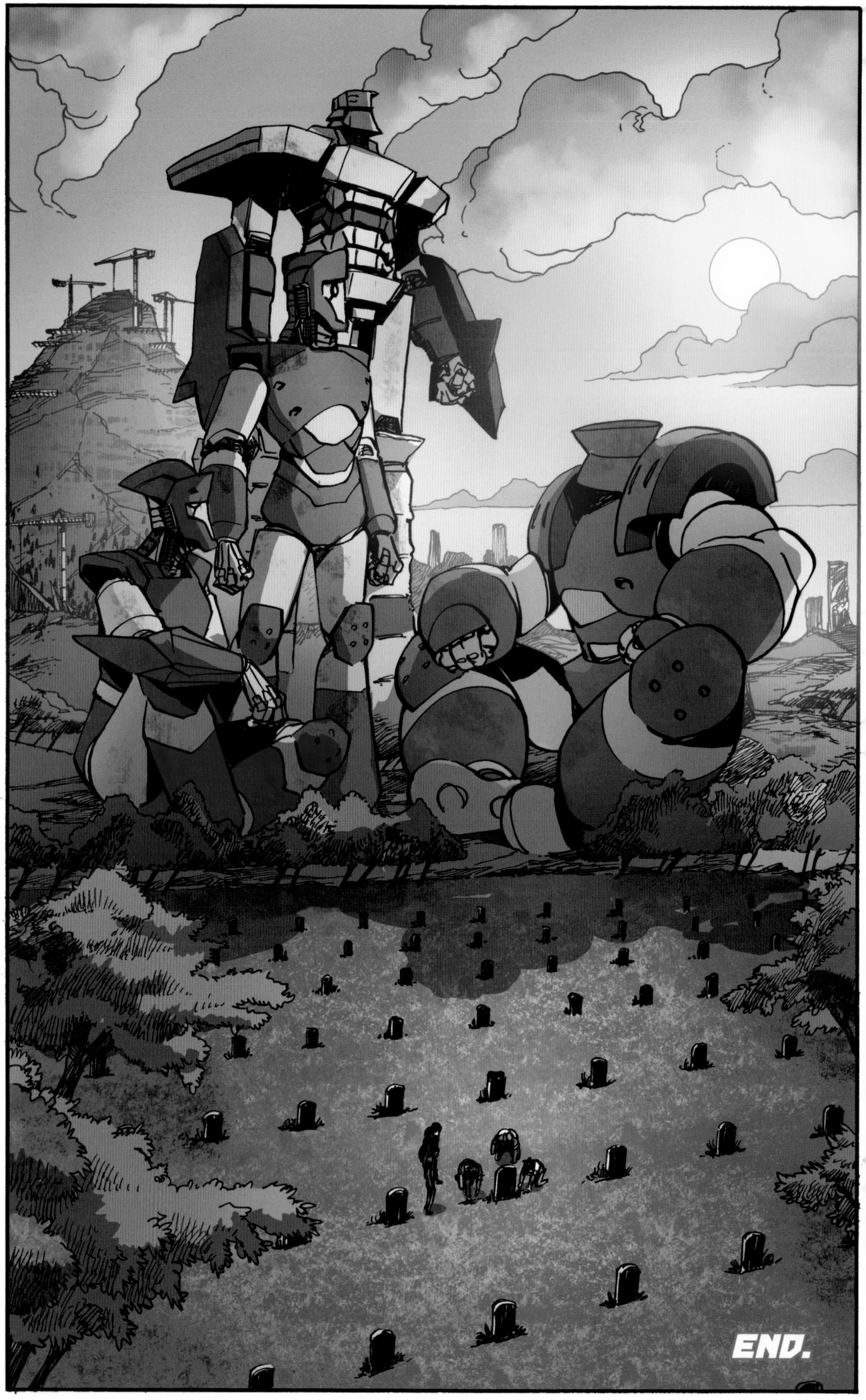
END.

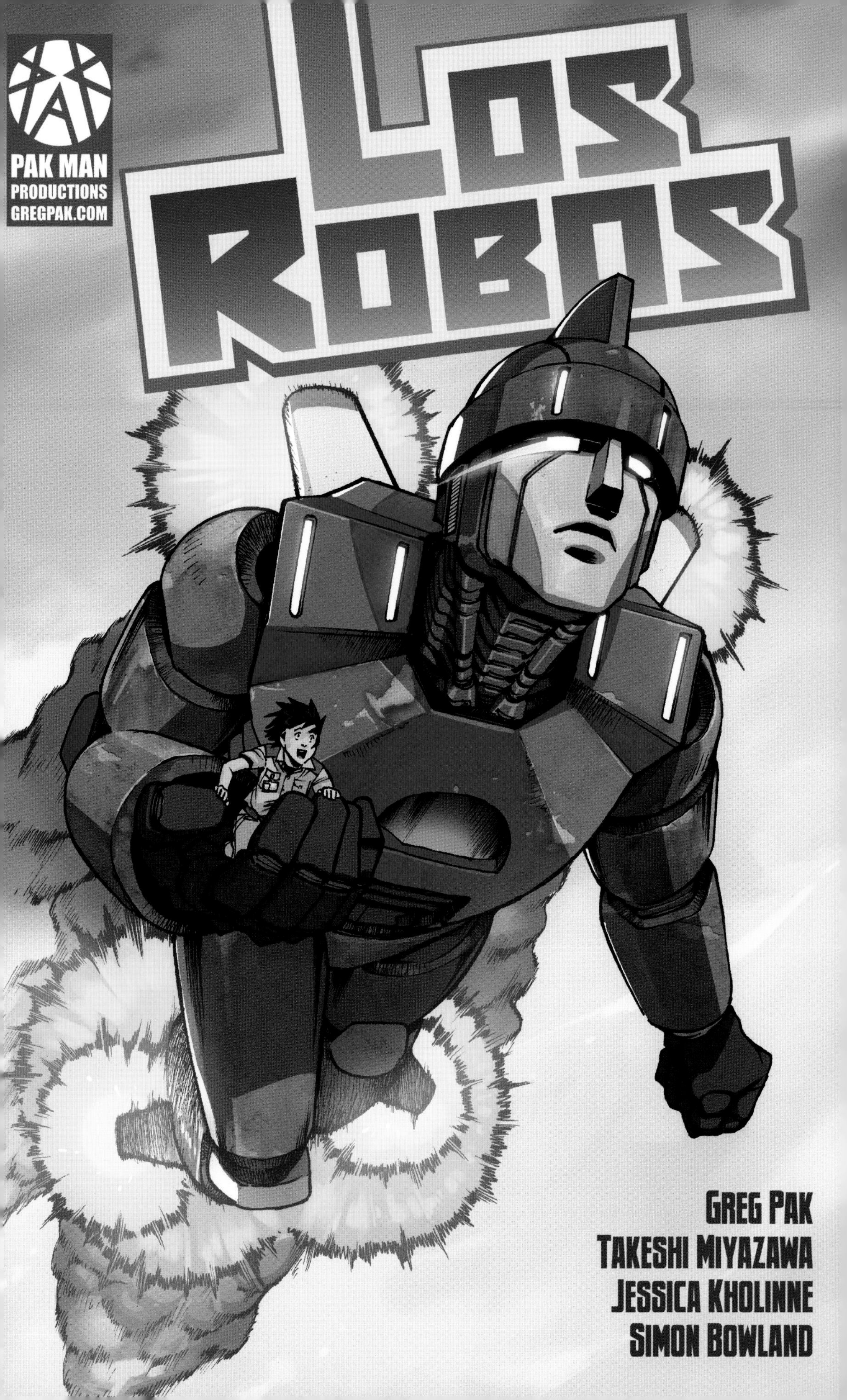
PAK MAN
PRODUCTIONS
GREGPAK.COM
LOS
ROBOS
GREG PAK
TAKESHI MIYAZAWA
JESSICA KHOLINNE
SIMON BOWLAND

LOS ROBOS
THE UNTOLD ORIGIN OF STANFORD YU

Written by
GREG PAK

Illustrated by
TAKESHI MIYAZAWA

Colored by
JESSICA KHOLINNE

Lettered by
SIMON BOWLAND

Logo and Cover Designed by
BRANDON J. CARR

Originally Published in
Shattered: The Asian American Comics Anthology

Before there was *Mech Cadet Yu*, there was *Los Robos*, a ten page story first published as part of *Shattered: The Asian American Comics Anthology* in 2012. The original ten-pager was written by yours truly with art by Takeshi Miyazawa and letters by Simon Bowland. I later self-published it as a one-shot comic with colors by the great Jessica Kholinne and a logo design by Brandon J. Carr, and I'm thrilled we're able to showcase it here so you can see how the story initially came together.

The scenario and characters of *Los Robos* should be instantly recognizable to *Mech Cadet Yu* readers. The story features the same set up, with an underdog janitor's kid unexpectedly bonding with a giant robot and joining the elite Sky Corps Academy. But there are some fun differences, including slightly different robo designs and terminology, and a gender switch for Stanford's main antagonist.

As the cliffhanger at the end of the ten page story shows, Tak and I always dreamed of making *Los Robos* an ongoing series. So huge thanks to the editors of *Shattered*, who gave the story its first place to spread its wings; to our editors and friends at BOOM!, who have loved and supported *Mech Cadet Yu* every step of the way; and to all the readers who have actually bought the thing and made it real. You're all our favorite.

GREG PAK
November, 2017

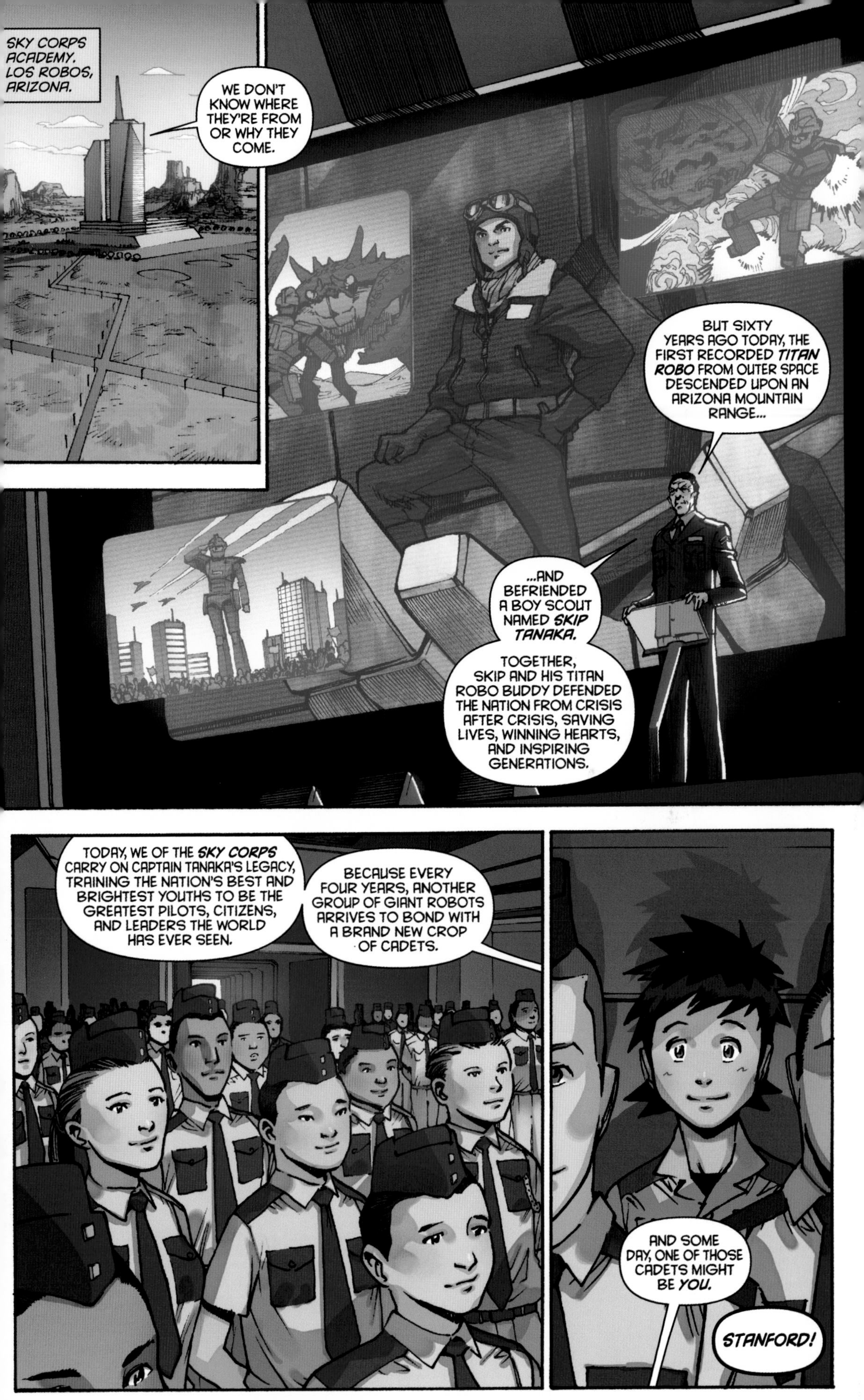
SKY CORPS ACADEMY. LOS ROBOS, ARIZONA.
WE DON'T KNOW WHERE THEY'RE FROM OR WHY THEY COME.
BUT SIXTY YEARS AGO TODAY, THE FIRST RECORDED *TITAN ROBO* FROM OUTER SPACE DESCENDED UPON AN ARIZONA MOUNTAIN RANGE...
...AND BEFRIENDED A BOY SCOUT NAMED *SKIP TANAKA.*
TOGETHER, SKIP AND HIS TITAN ROBO BUDDY DEFENDED THE NATION FROM CRISIS AFTER CRISIS, SAVING LIVES, WINNING HEARTS, AND INSPIRING GENERATIONS.
TODAY, WE OF THE *SKY CORPS* CARRY ON CAPTAIN TANAKA'S LEGACY, TRAINING THE NATION'S BEST AND BRIGHTEST YOUTHS TO BE THE GREATEST PILOTS, CITIZENS, AND LEADERS THE WORLD HAS EVER SEEN.
BECAUSE EVERY FOUR YEARS, ANOTHER GROUP OF GIANT ROBOTS ARRIVES TO BOND WITH A BRAND NEW CROP OF CADETS.
AND SOME DAY, ONE OF THOSE CADETS MIGHT BE *YOU.*
STANFORD!

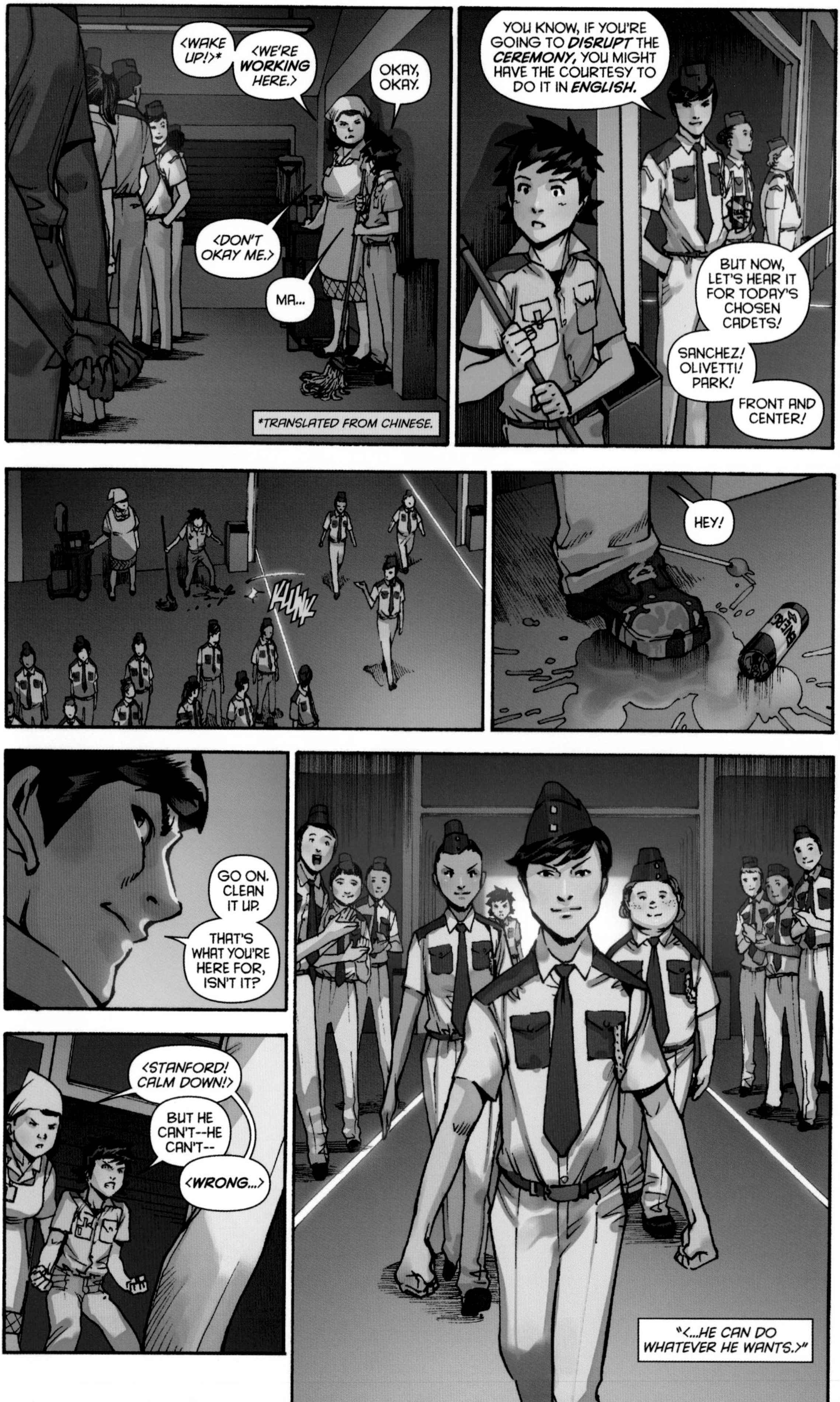
<WAKE UP!>*
<WE'RE WORKING HERE.>
OKAY, OKAY.
<DON'T OKAY ME.>
MA...
*TRANSLATED FROM CHINESE.
YOU KNOW, IF YOU'RE GOING TO DISRUPT THE CEREMONY, YOU MIGHT HAVE THE COURTESY TO DO IT IN ENGLISH.
BUT NOW, LET'S HEAR IT FOR TODAY'S CHOSEN CADETS!
SANCHEZ! OLIVETTI! PARK!
FRONT AND CENTER!
KLUNK
HEY!
GO ON. CLEAN IT UP.
THAT'S WHAT YOU'RE HERE FOR, ISN'T IT?
<STANFORD! CALM DOWN!>
BUT HE CAN'T--HE CAN'T--
<WRONG...>
"<...HE CAN DO WHATEVER HE WANTS.>"

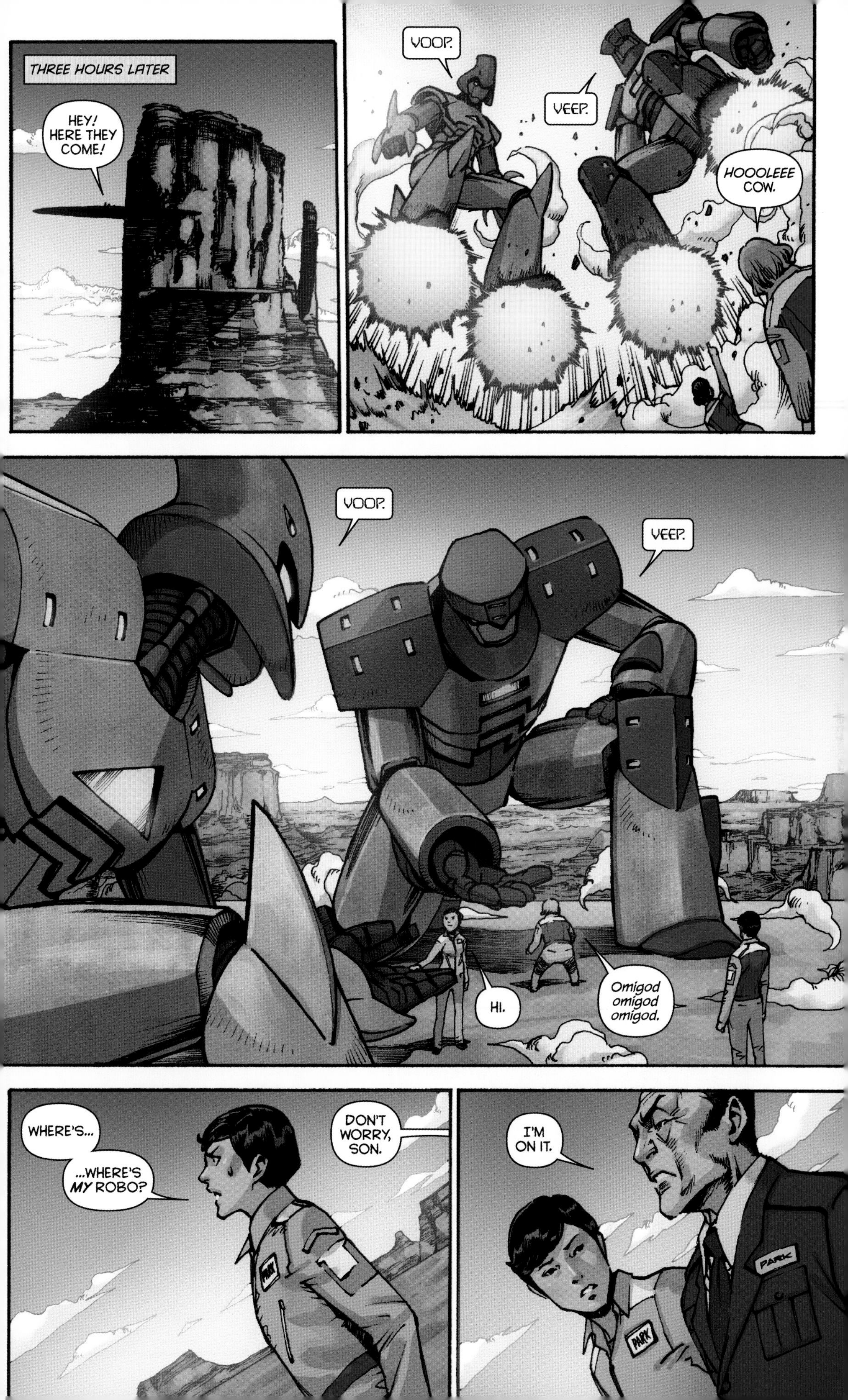
THREE HOURS LATER
HEY! HERE THEY COME!
VOOP.
VEEP.
HOOOLEEE COW.
VOOP.
VEEP.
HI.
Omigod omigod omigod.
WHERE'S...
...WHERE'S *MY* ROBO?
DON'T WORRY, SON.
I'M ON IT.
PARK
PARK
PARK

THREE MILES AWAY

Tch.

CLEAN IT UP.

IT'S WHAT YOU'RE HERE FOR, HUH?

?

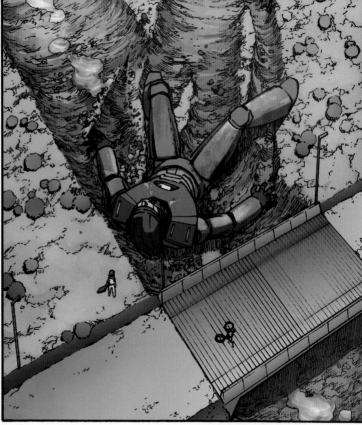

VEEEE?

HOOO BOY.

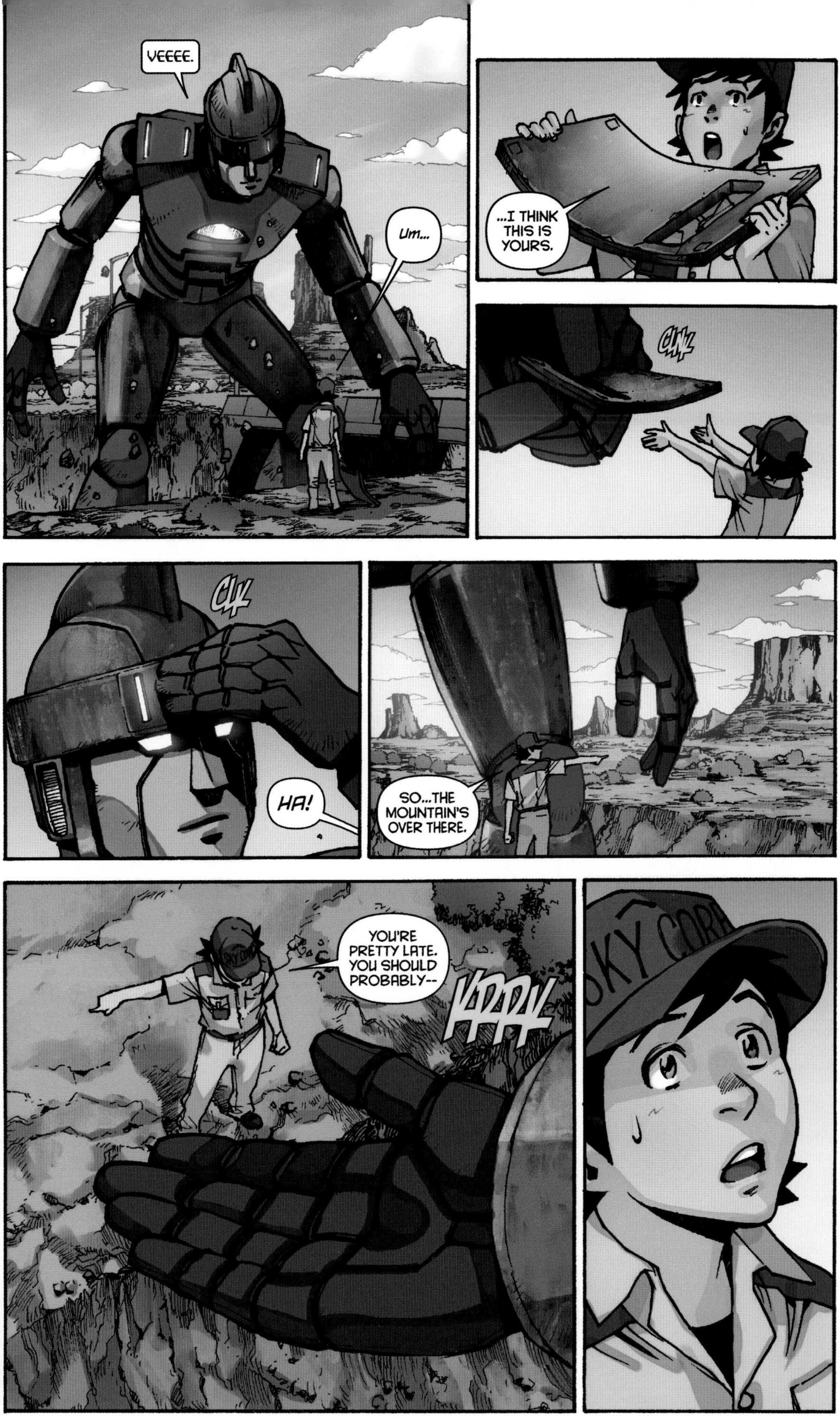
VEEEE.
Um...
...I THINK THIS IS YOURS.
HA!
SO...THE MOUNTAIN'S OVER THERE.
YOU'RE PRETTY LATE. YOU SHOULD PROBABLY--
SKY CORP

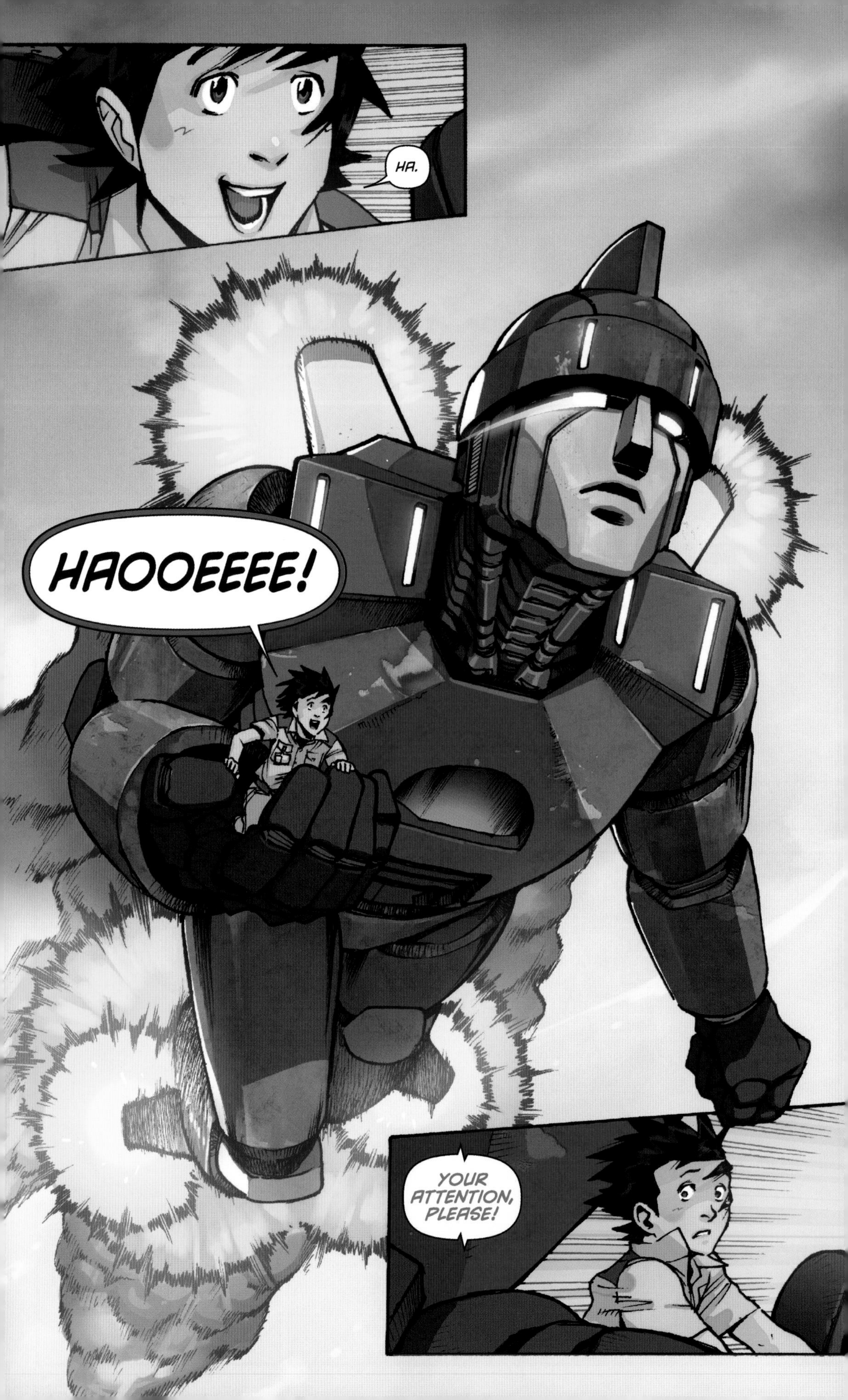
HA.
HAOOEEEE!
YOUR ATTENTION, PLEASE!

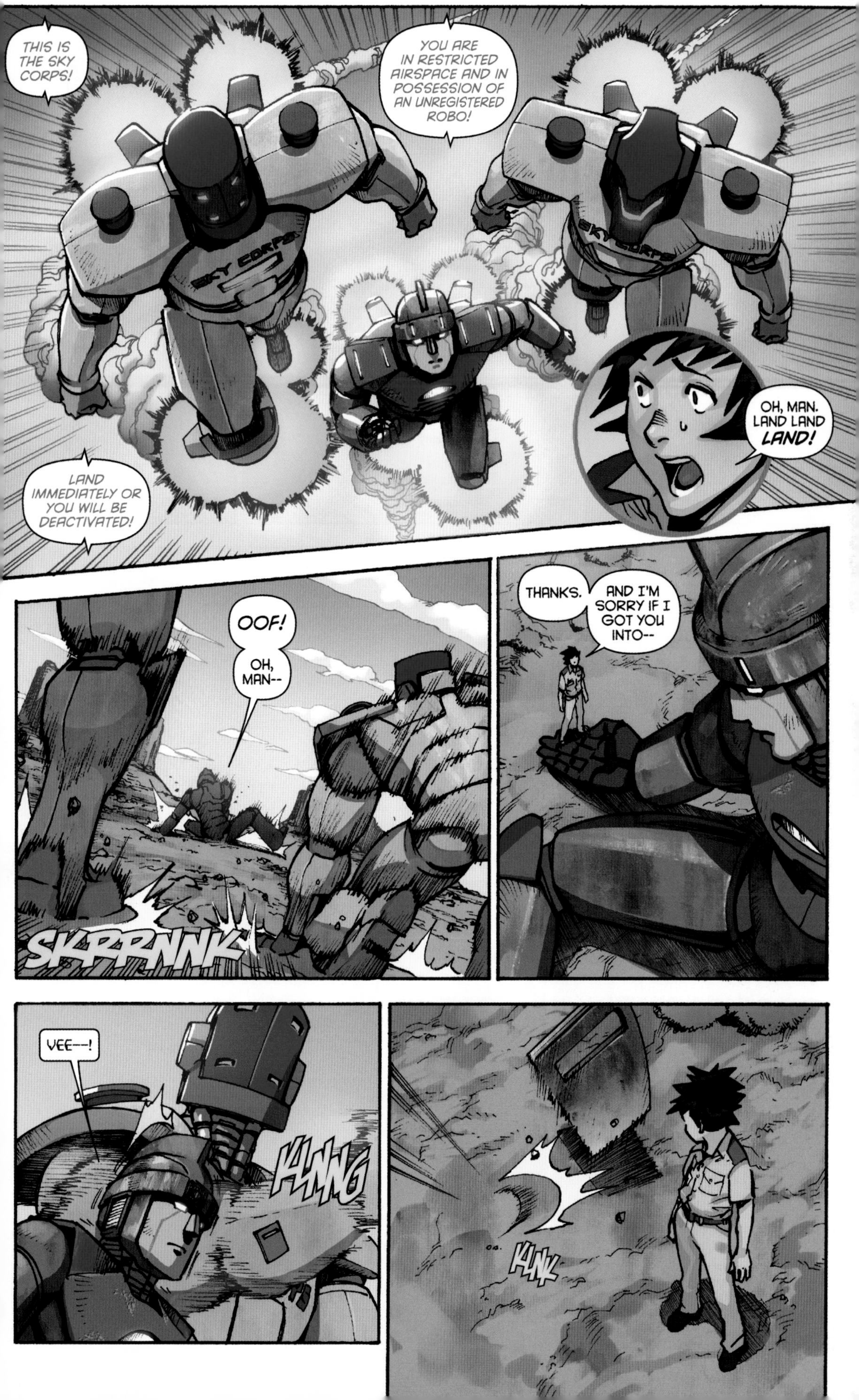
THIS IS THE SKY CORPS!
YOU ARE IN RESTRICTED AIRSPACE AND IN POSSESSION OF AN UNREGISTERED ROBO!
SKY CORPS
SKY CORPS
LAND IMMEDIATELY OR YOU WILL BE DEACTIVATED!
OH, MAN. LAND LAND LAND!
OOF!
OH, MAN--
SKRRRNNK
THANKS.
AND I'M SORRY IF I GOT YOU INTO--
VEE--!
KLNNG
KLNK

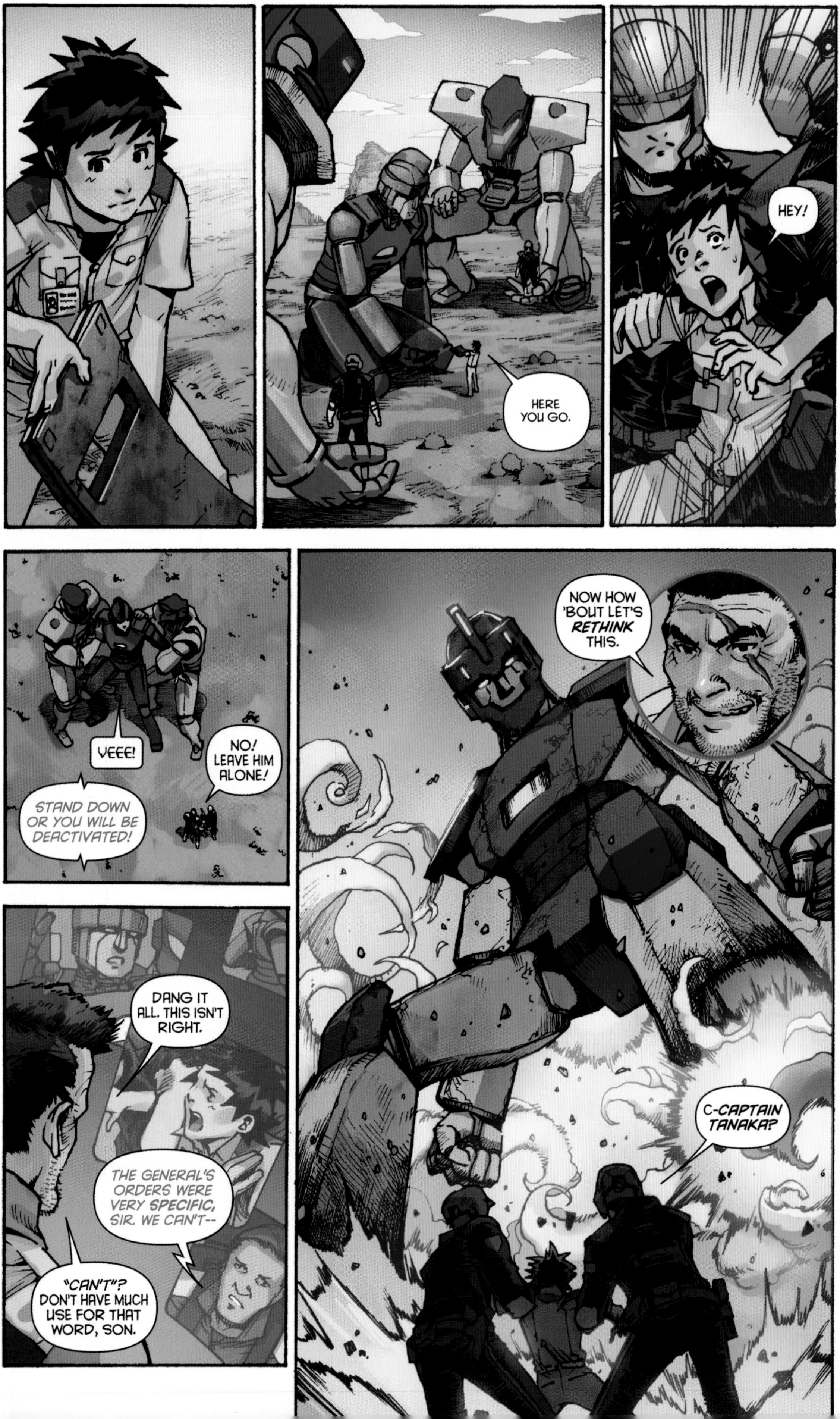
HERE YOU GO.
HEY!
VEEE!
NO! LEAVE HIM ALONE!
STAND DOWN OR YOU WILL BE DEACTIVATED!
NOW HOW 'BOUT LET'S RETHINK THIS.
C-CAPTAIN TANAKA?
DANG IT ALL. THIS ISN'T RIGHT.
THE GENERAL'S ORDERS WERE VERY SPECIFIC, SIR. WE CAN'T--
"CAN'T"? DON'T HAVE MUCH USE FOR THAT WORD, SON.

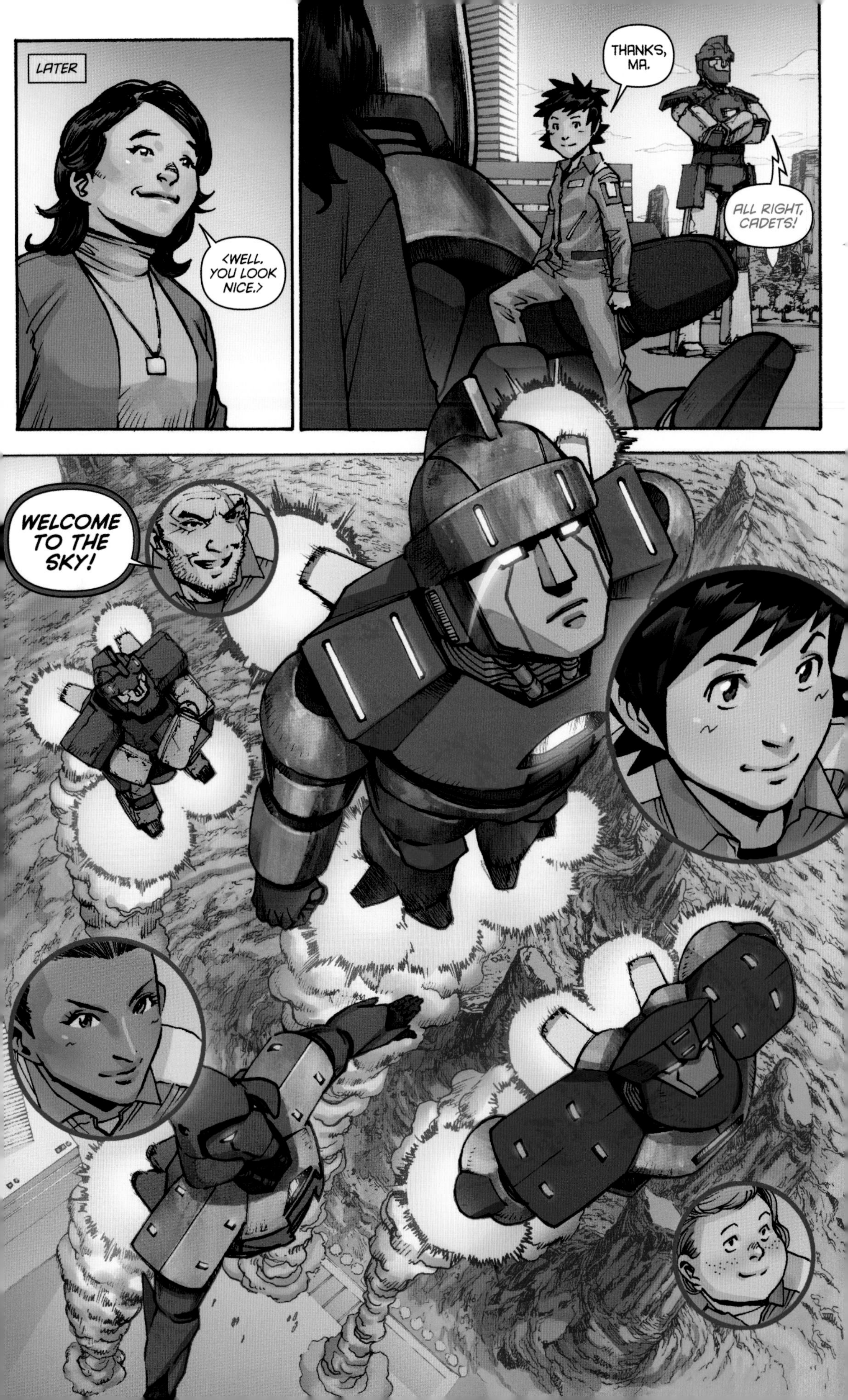
LATER
<WELL. YOU LOOK NICE.>
THANKS, MA.
ALL RIGHT, CADETS!
WELCOME TO THE SKY!

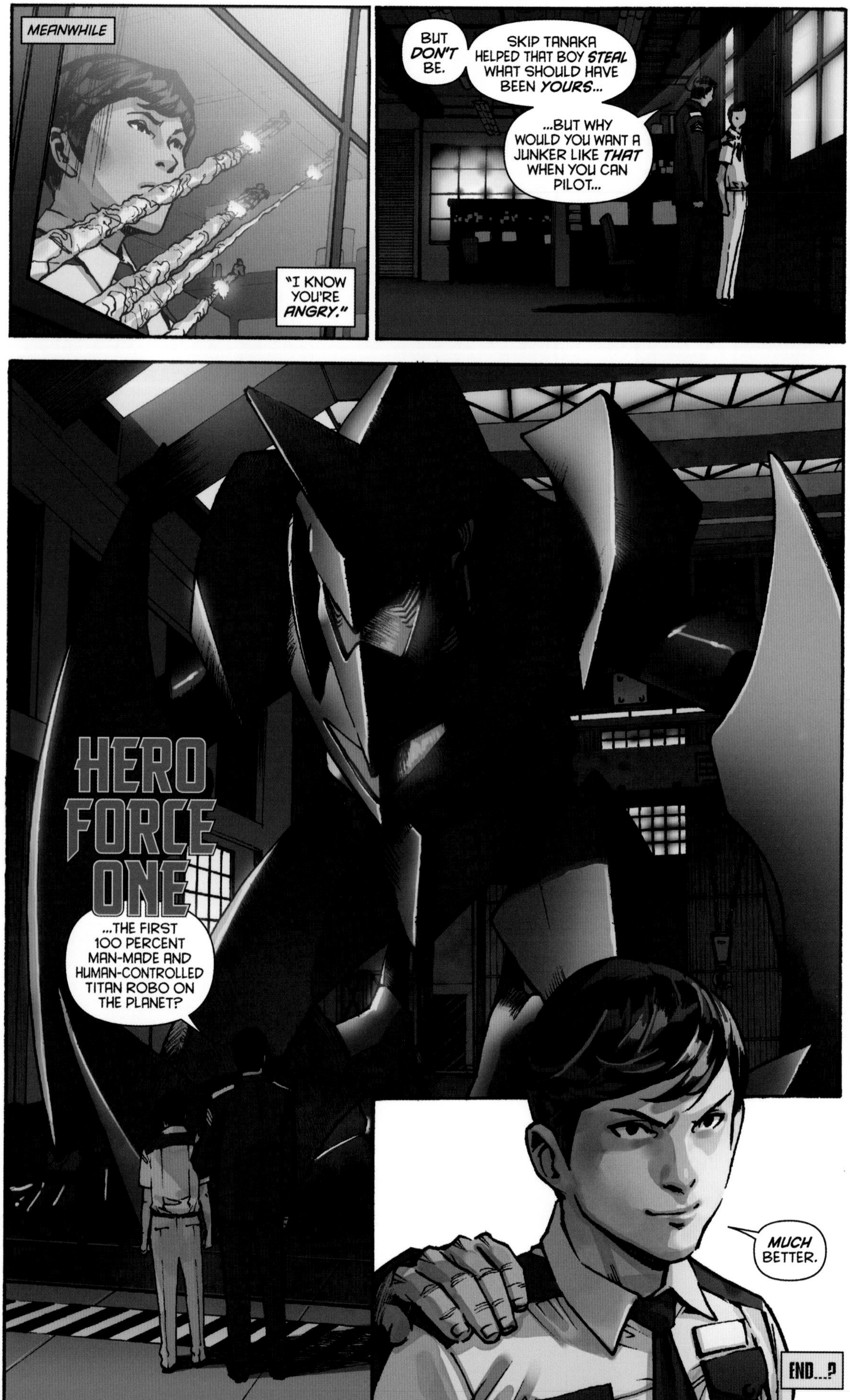
MEANWHILE
"I KNOW YOU'RE ANGRY."
BUT DON'T BE.
SKIP TANAKA HELPED THAT BOY STEAL WHAT SHOULD HAVE BEEN YOURS...
...BUT WHY WOULD YOU WANT A JUNKER LIKE THAT WHEN YOU CAN PILOT...
HERO FORCE ONE
...THE FIRST 100 PERCENT MAN-MADE AND HUMAN-CONTROLLED TITAN ROBO ON THE PLANET?
MUCH BETTER.
END...?

Mech Cadet Yu SKETCHBOOK
Concept Art Illustrations by TAKESHI MIYAZAWA

STANFORD AND DOLLY YU
CHARACTER DESIGNS

SKY CORPS ACADEMY UNIFORM DESIGNS

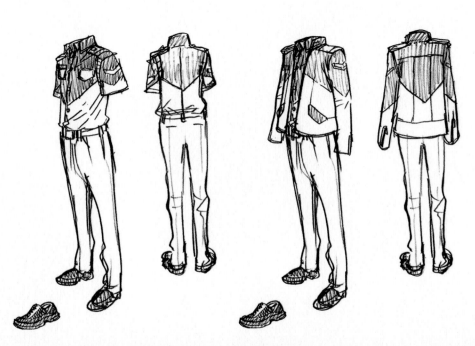

CADET STANFORD YU
ROBO MECH PILOT, FIRST YEAR
SKY CORPS ACADEMY

VERSION 2.0

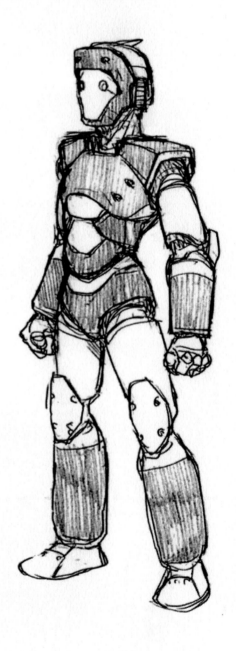

ORIGINAL BUDDY DESIGN
FROM LOS ROBOS

Mech Cadet Yu SKETCHBOOK

Concept Art Illustrations by **TAKESHI MIYAZAWA**

CADET FRANK OLIVETTI
ROBO MECH PILOT,
FIRST YEAR
SKY CORPS ACADEMY

ORIGINAL THUNDER
WRECKER DESIGN
FROM LOS ROBOS

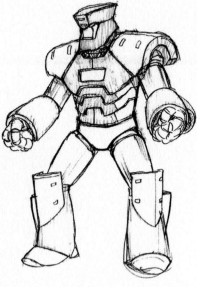

VERSION 2.0

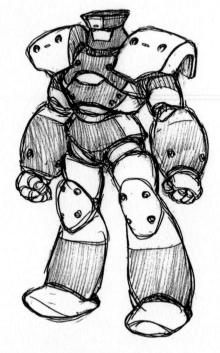

CADET MAYA SANCHEZ
ROBO MECH PILOT,
FIRST YEAR
SKY CORPS ACADEMY

ORIGINAL BIG RED DESIGN
FROM LOS ROBOS

VERSION 2.0

Mech Cadet Yu **SKETCHBOOK**

Concept Art Illustrations by **TAKESHI MIYAZAWA**

HERO FORCE MARK I

CADET OLIVIA PARK
ROBO MECH PILOT, FIRST YEAR
SKY CORPS ACADEMY

HERO FORCE MARK II SUPRAROBO 1.0

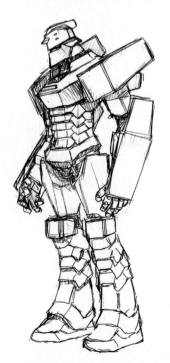

VERSION 2.0

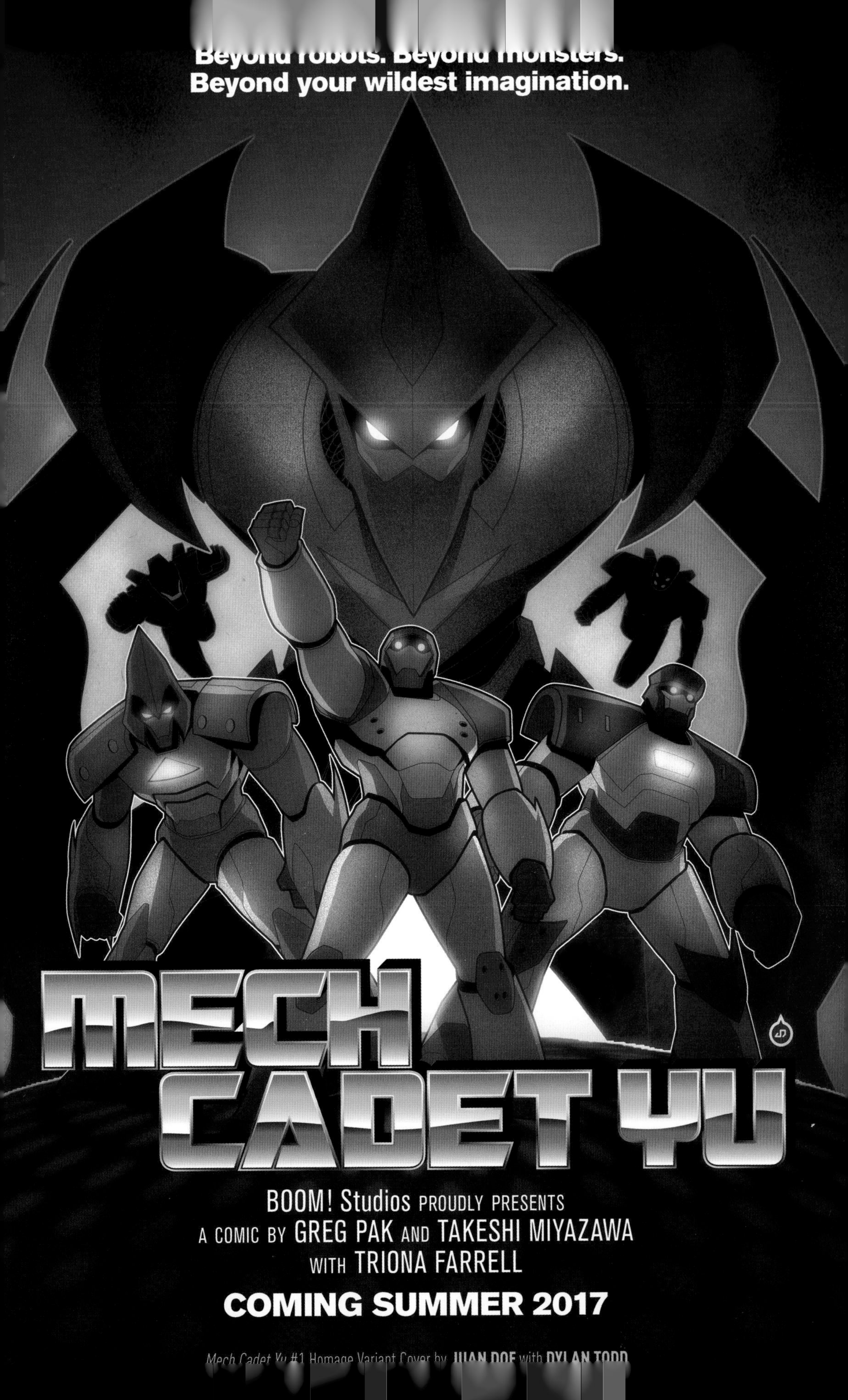

Beyond robots. Beyond monsters.
Beyond your wildest imagination.
MECH CADET YU
BOOM! Studios PROUDLY PRESENTS
A COMIC BY GREG PAK AND TAKESHI MIYAZAWA
WITH TRIONA FARRELL
COMING SUMMER 2017
Mech Cadet Yu #1 Homage Variant Cover by JUAN DOE with DYLAN TODD

Mech Cadet Yu #1 Unlocked Retail Variant Cover by **SONNY LIEW**

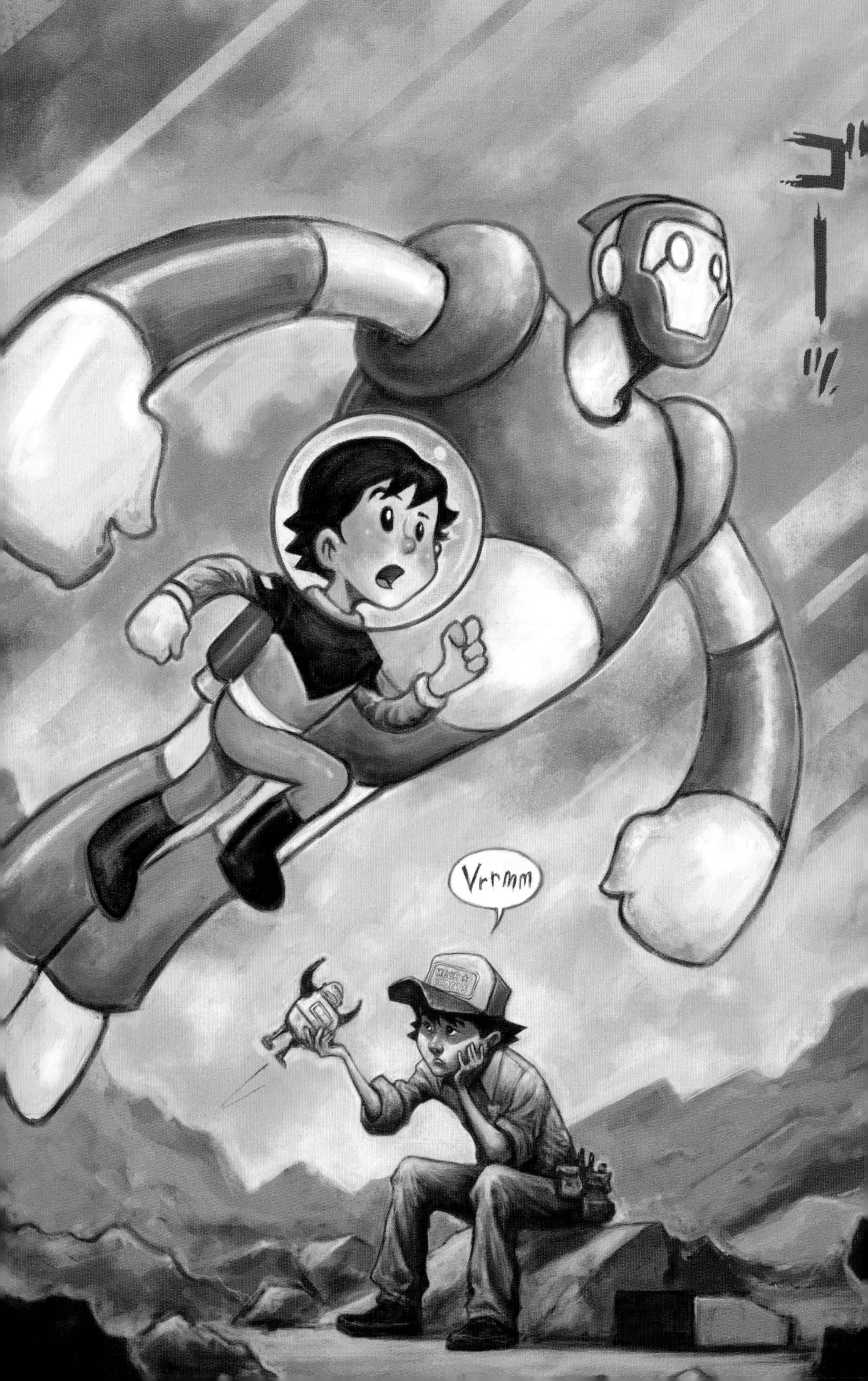

ゴーッ
Vrrmm
MECH ★ CADETS

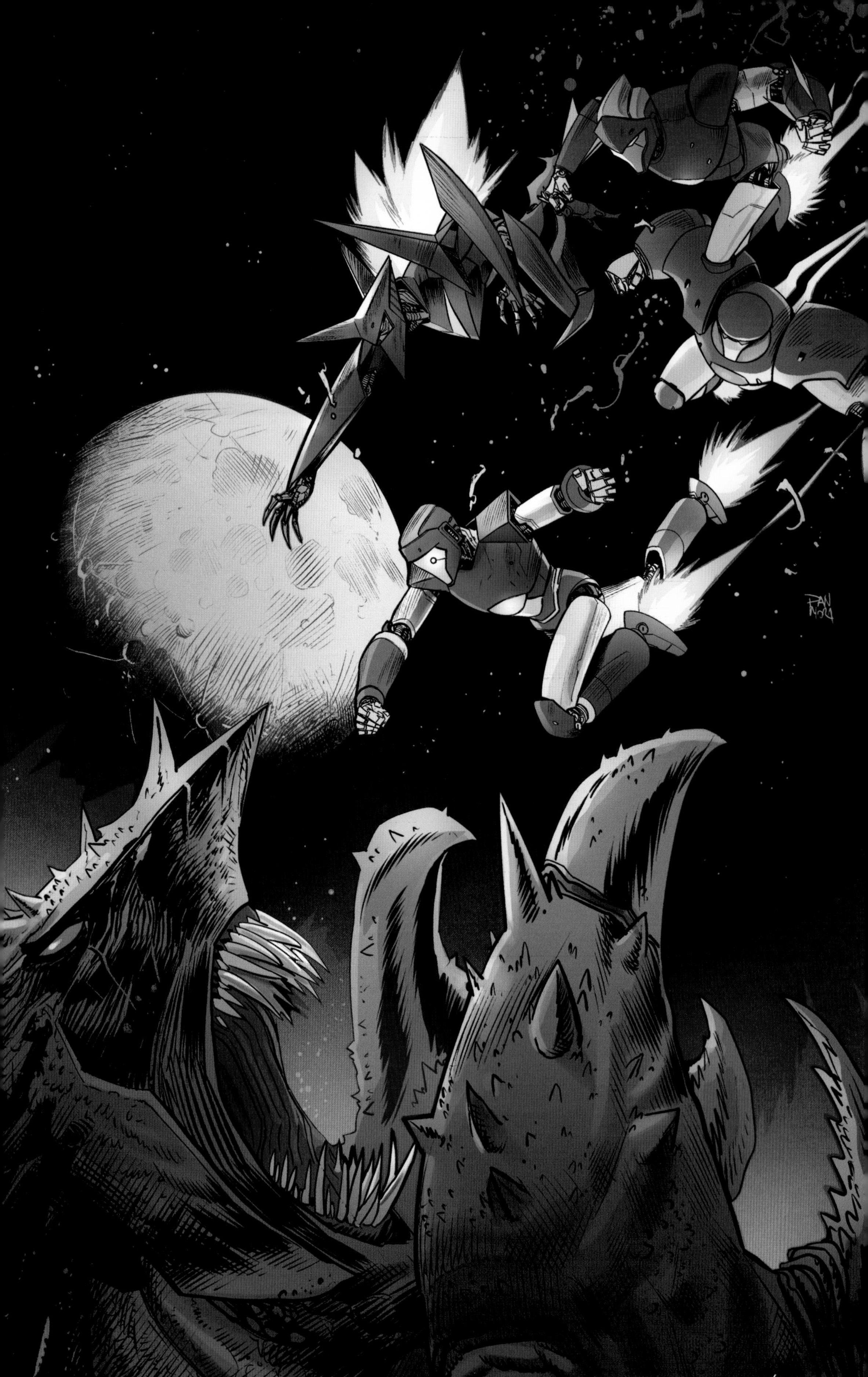

Mech Cadet Yu #5 Unlocked Retail Variant Cover by **DAN MORA** with colors by **RAÚL ANGULO**

Mech Cadet Yu #1-#4 Connecting Covers by **MARCUS TO** with colors by **ADAM METCALFE**

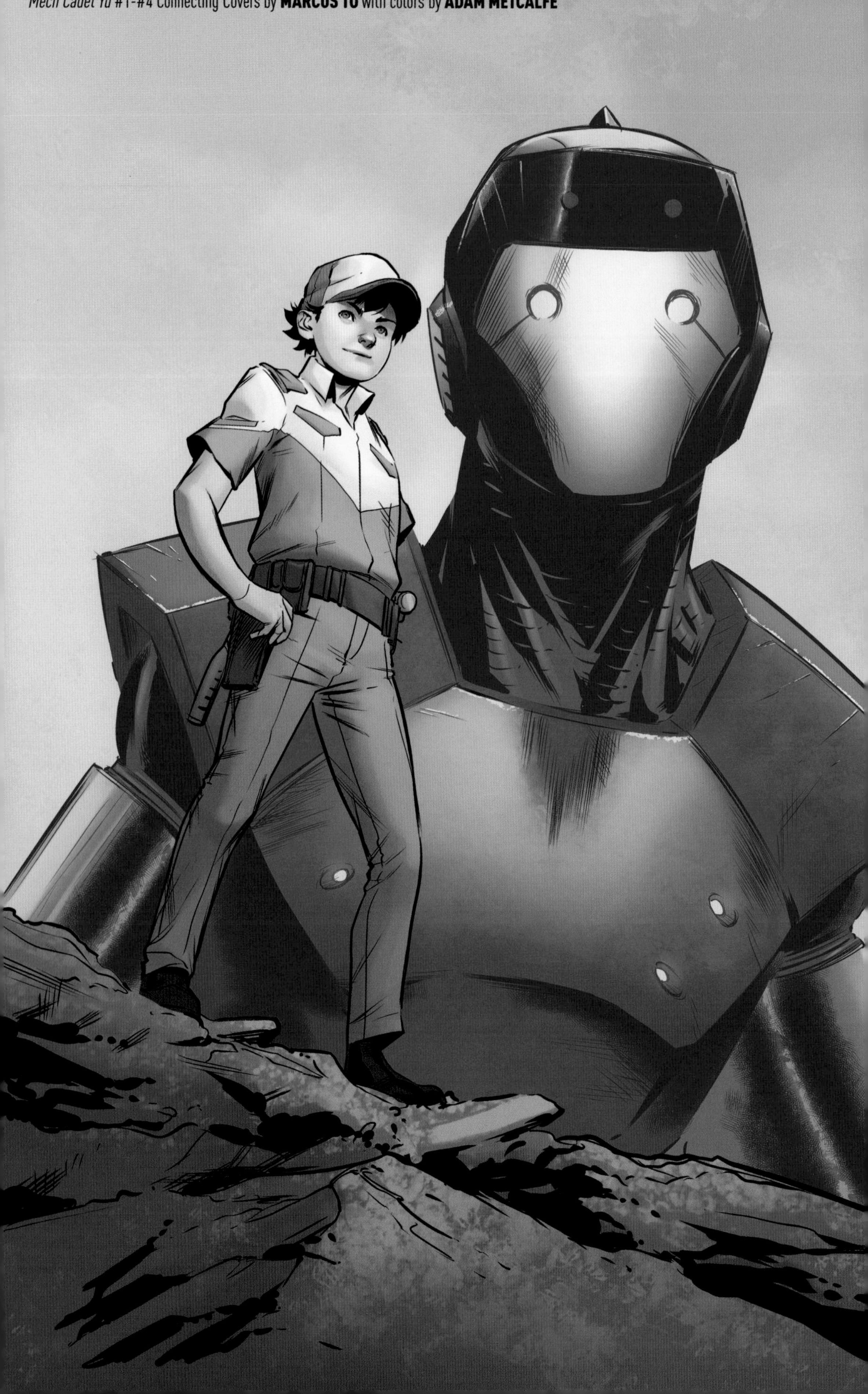

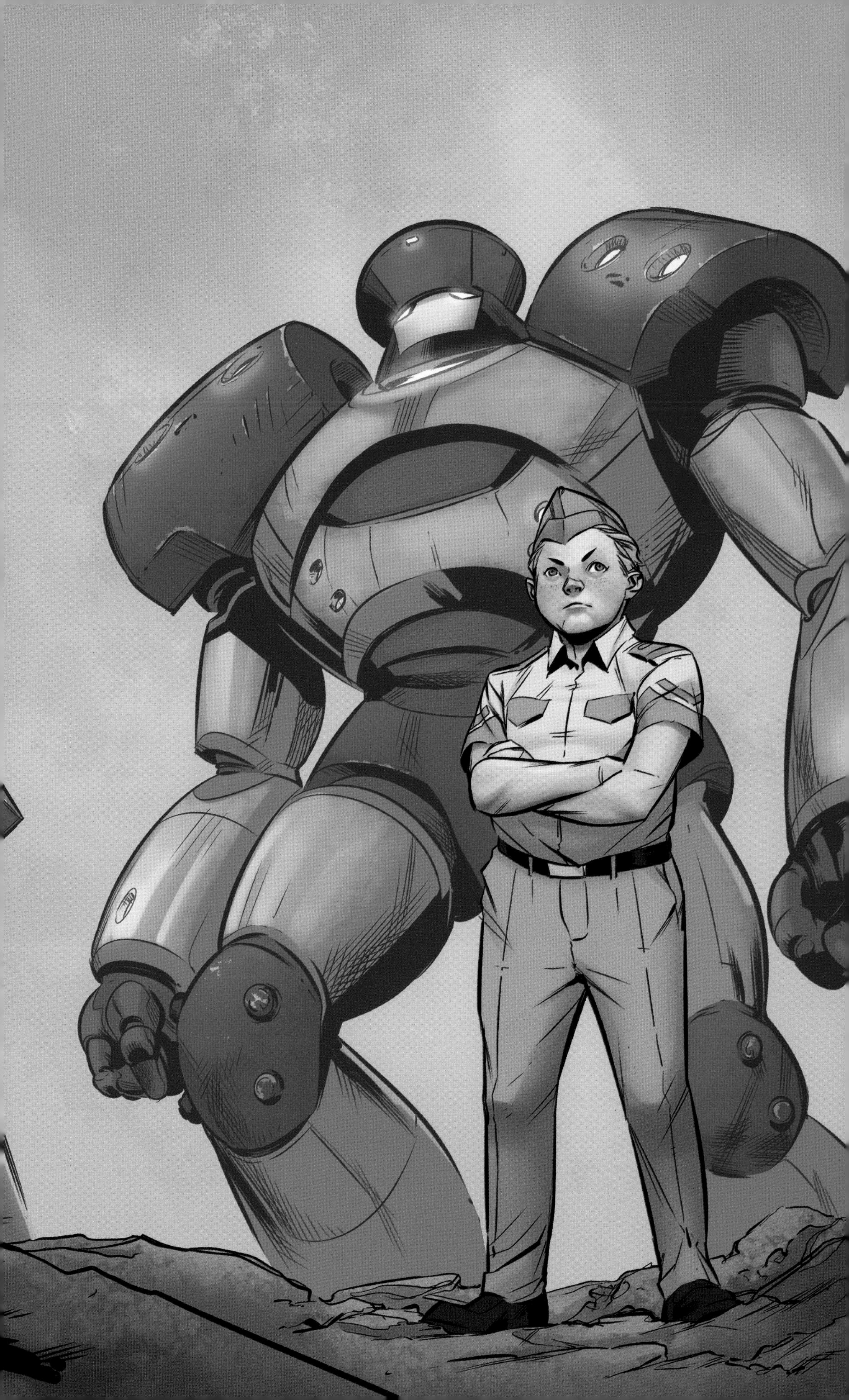

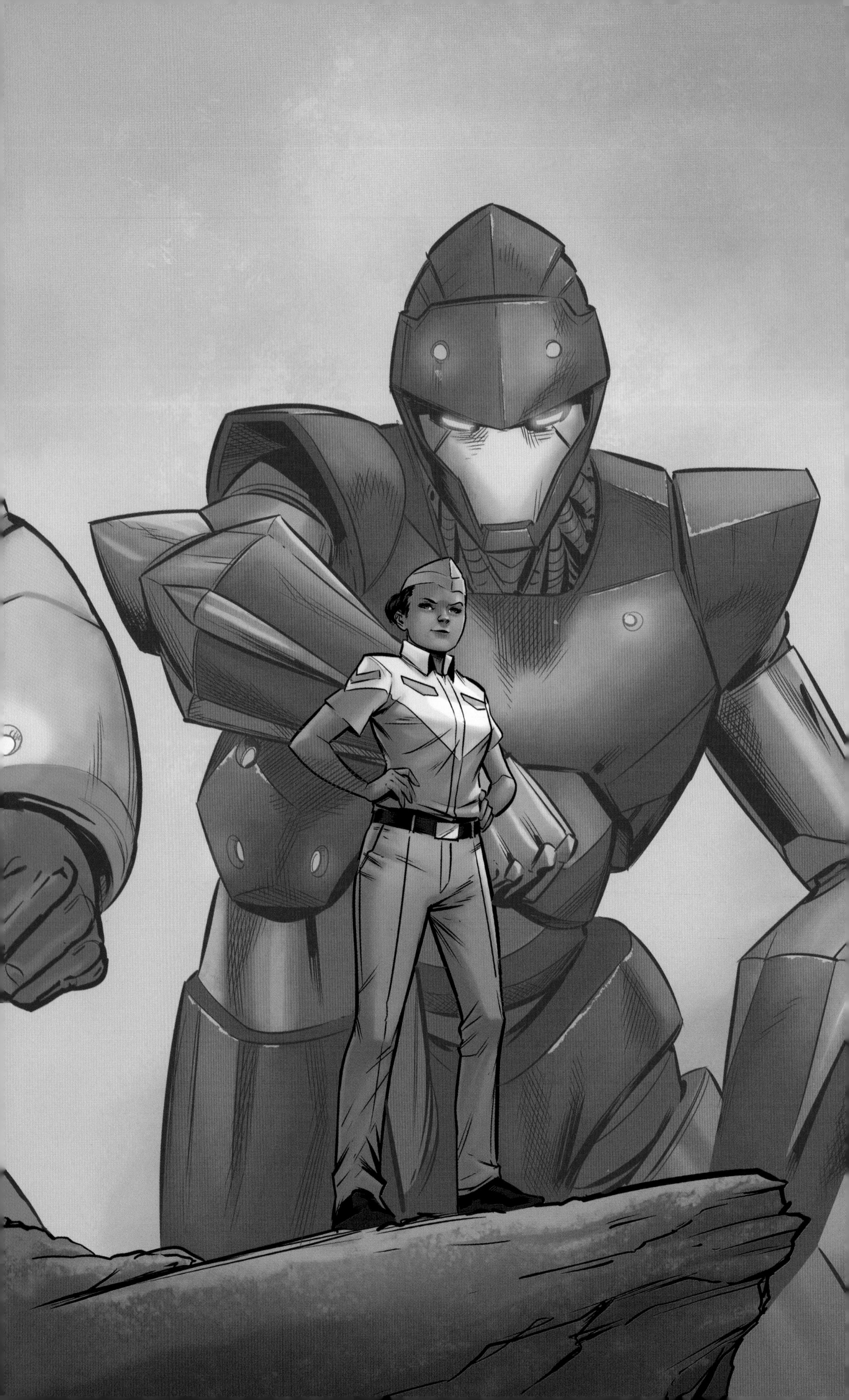

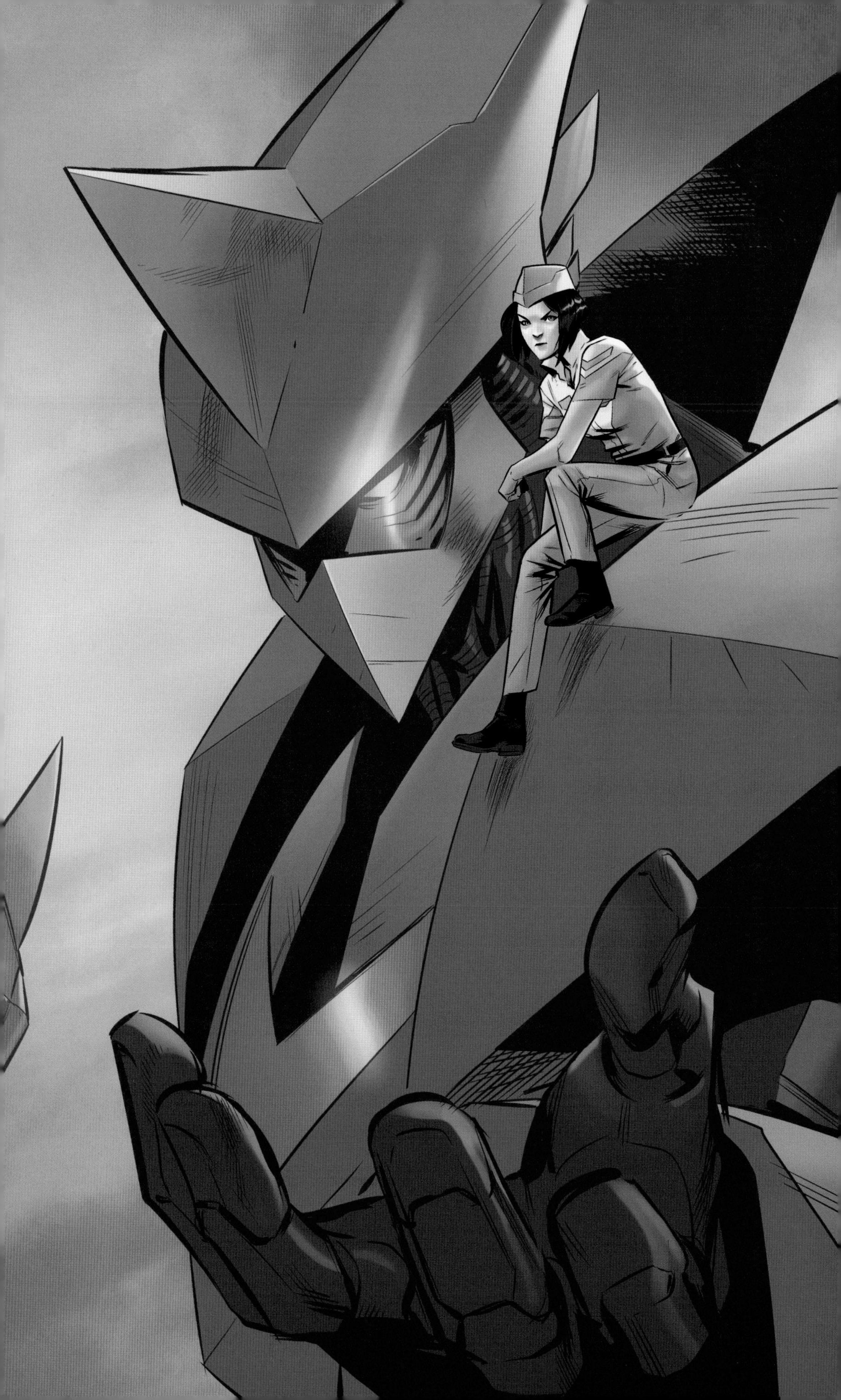

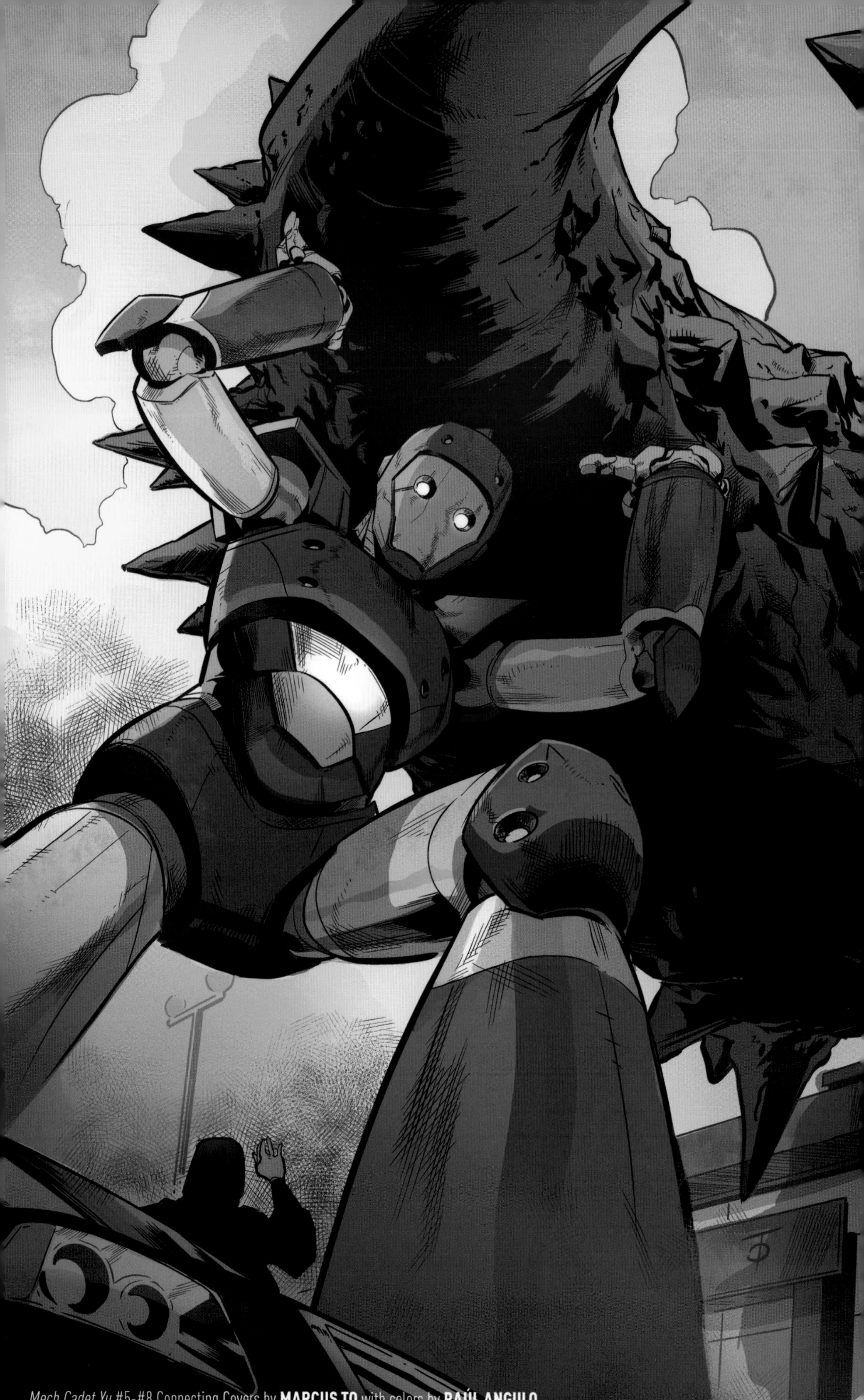

Mech Cadet Yu #5-#8 Connecting Covers by **MARCUS TO** with colors by **RAÚL ANGULO**

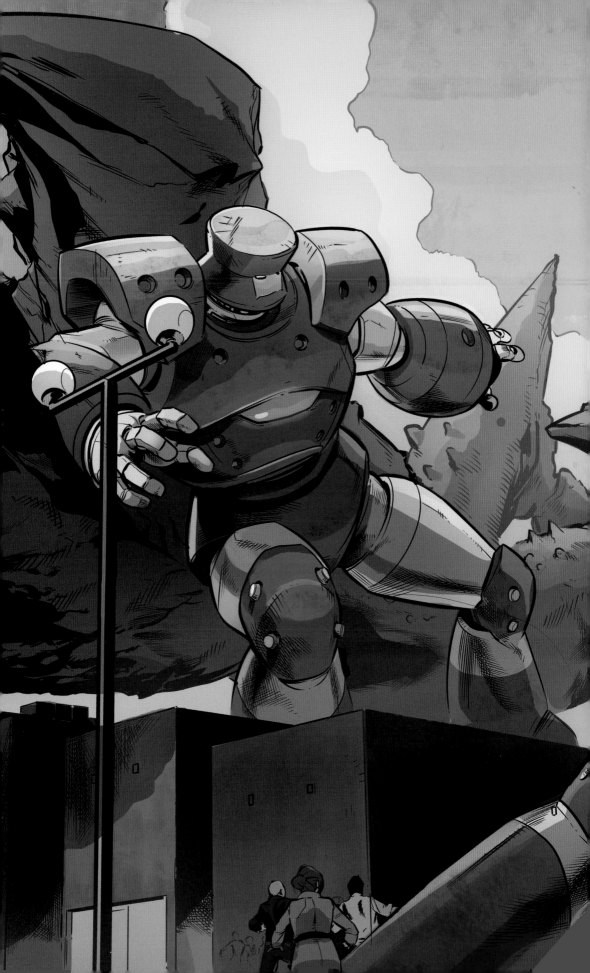

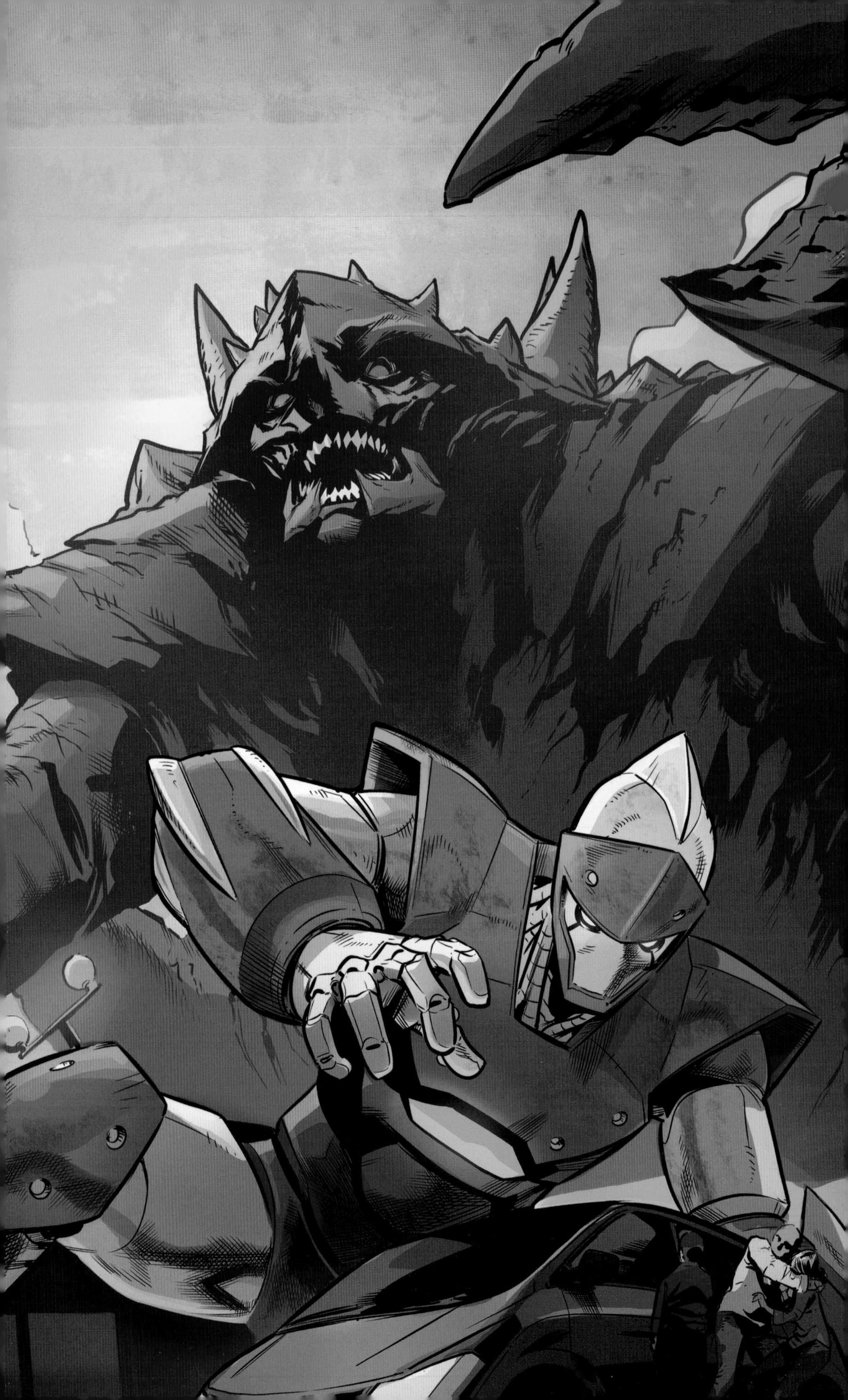

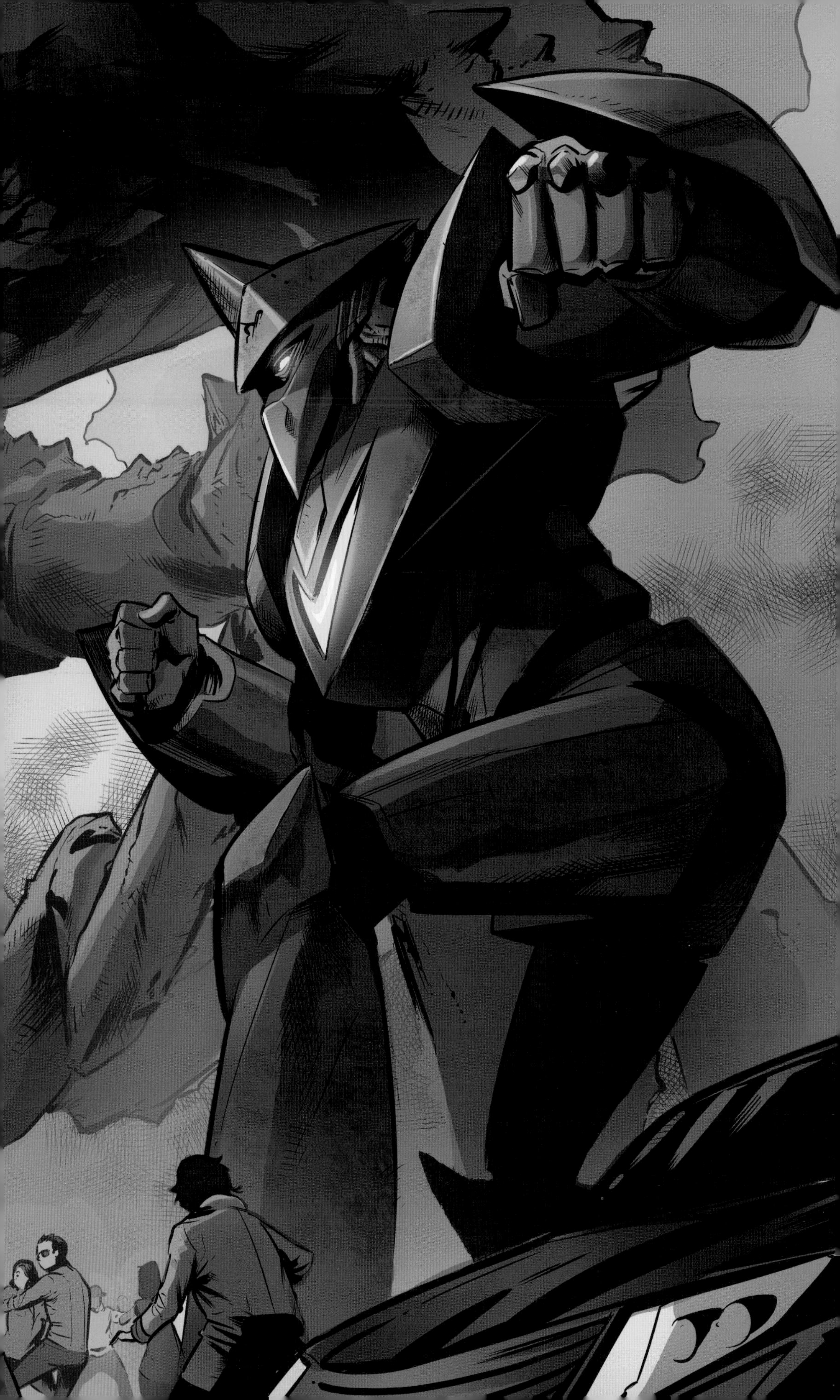

GREG PAK & TAKESHI MIYAZAWA'S
MECH CADETS RETURNS FALL 2023!

Olivia Park is now the pilot of the Hero Force Two SupraRobo—the most powerful robo on the planet. She's achieved everything her father ever dreamed for her. But now, as Earth's greatest protector, she has to figure out for herself what her true responsibilities are. What happens when a sixteen year old kid becomes the most powerful person on the planet?

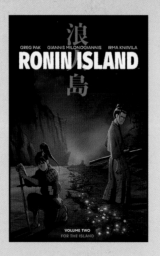

Ronin Island
Greg Pak, Giannis Milonogiannis, Irma Kniivila

Hana, the orphaned daughter of Korean peasants, and Kenichi, son of a great samurai leader, have little in common except for a mutual disdain for each other. But these young warriors will have to work together when an army invades the island with shocking news: there is a new Shogun and the Island is expected to pay fealty in exchange for protection from a new enemy …a mutated horde that threatens to wipe out all humanity.

Volume 1: Together in Strength
ISBN: 978-1-68415-459-3 | $14.99 US
Volume 2: For the Island
ISBN: 978-1-68415-557-6 | $14.99 US
Volume 3: A New Wind
ISBN: 978-1-68415-623-8 | $14.99 US

The Princess Who Saved Herself
Greg Pak, Takeshi Miyazawa

Based on the song by Jonathan Coulton, The Princess Who Saved Herself reinvents the princess myth for a new generation, telling the story of an awesome kid who lives with her pet snake and plays rock 'n' roll all day to the huge annoyance of the classical guitarist witch who lives down the road. Hijinks, conflicts, and a fun reconciliation ensues!

ISBN: 978-1-68415-710-5 | $16.99 US

The Princess Who Saved Her Friends
Greg Pak, Takeshi Miyazawa

Princess Gloria Cheng Epstein Takahara de la Garza Champio continues to explore the good, and sometimes bad, sides of friendship and its effects. Gloria has always used determination, bravery, and understanding to build relationships and overcome strife in her friendships with monsters and witches, but how will she handle the discovery that the witch she befriended might not be such a great friend after all?

ISBN: 978-1-68415-810-2 | $16.99 US

 AVAILABLE AT YOUR LOCAL COMICS SHOP AND BOOKSTORE
To find a comics shop in your area, visit www.comicshoplocator.com
WWW.BOOM-STUDIOS.COM